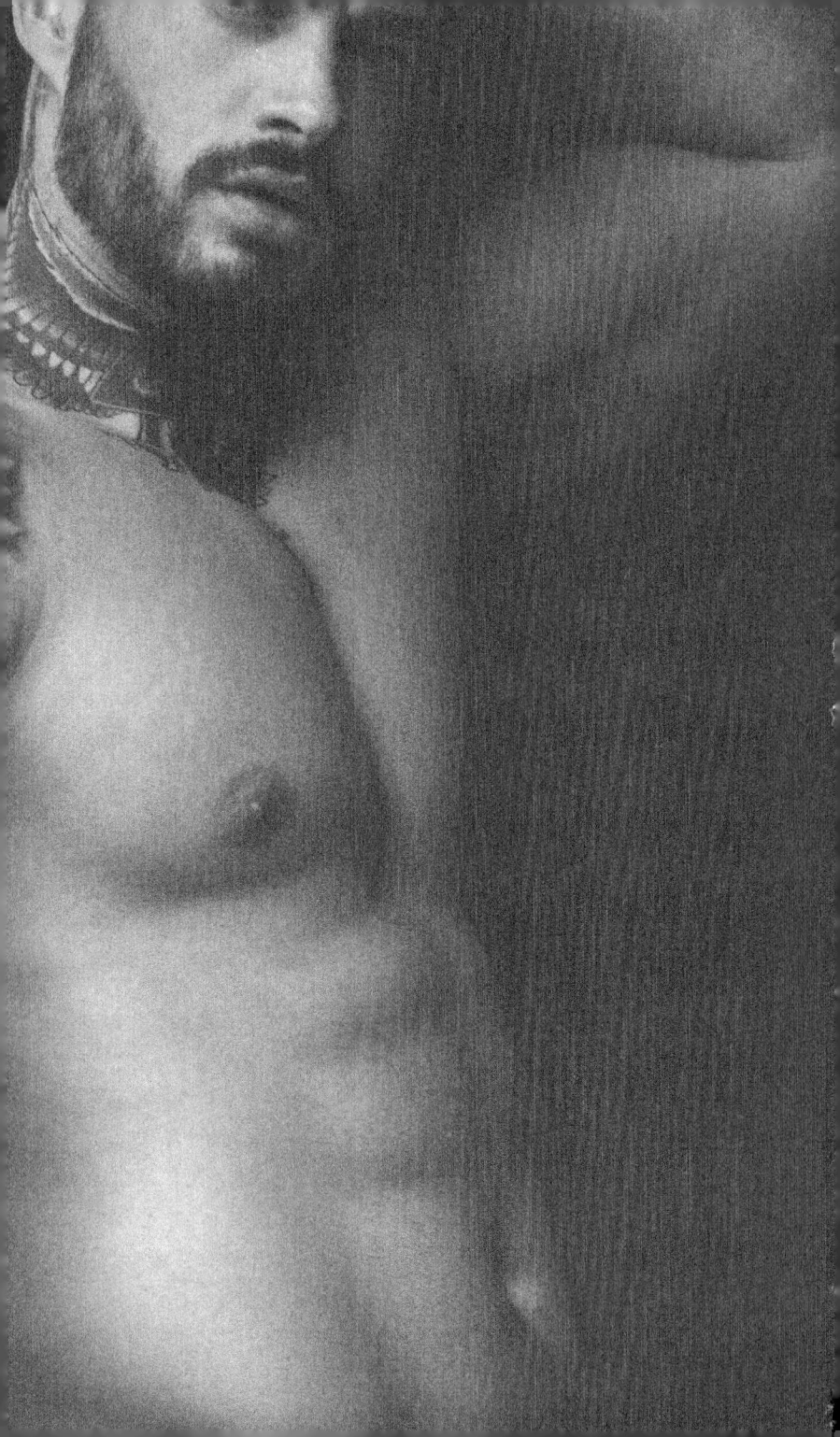

COERCED

ABIGAIL DAVIES YOLANDA OLSON DANA ISALY ISABEL LUCERO

A.D. MCCAMMON C.A. RENE S. RENA & BL MUTE JM WALKER

PERSEPHONE AUTUMN ALLY VANCE NICHOLE GREENE

LP LOVELL & STEVIE J. COLE

Coerced:
Copyright © 2022
Abigail Davies, Yolanda Olson,
Dana Isaly, Isabel Lucero, A.D. McCammon, C.A. Rene, S. Rena, BL Mute, J.M. Walker, Persephone Autumn, Ally Vance, LP Lovell, Stevie J. Cole
All rights reserved.

No parts of this book may be reproduced in any form without written consent from the author. Except in the use of brief quotations in a book review.
This book is a piece of fiction. Any names, characters, businesses, places or events are a product of the author's imagination or are used fictitiously. Any resemblance to persons living or dead, events or locations is purely coincidental.
This book is licensed for your personal enjoyment only. This book may not be resold or given away to other people. If you are reading this book and have not purchased it for your use only, then you should return it to your favorite book retailer and purchase your own copy.
Thank you for respecting the author's work.

Cover Design: Pretty In Ink Creations
Formatting: Pink Elephant Designs

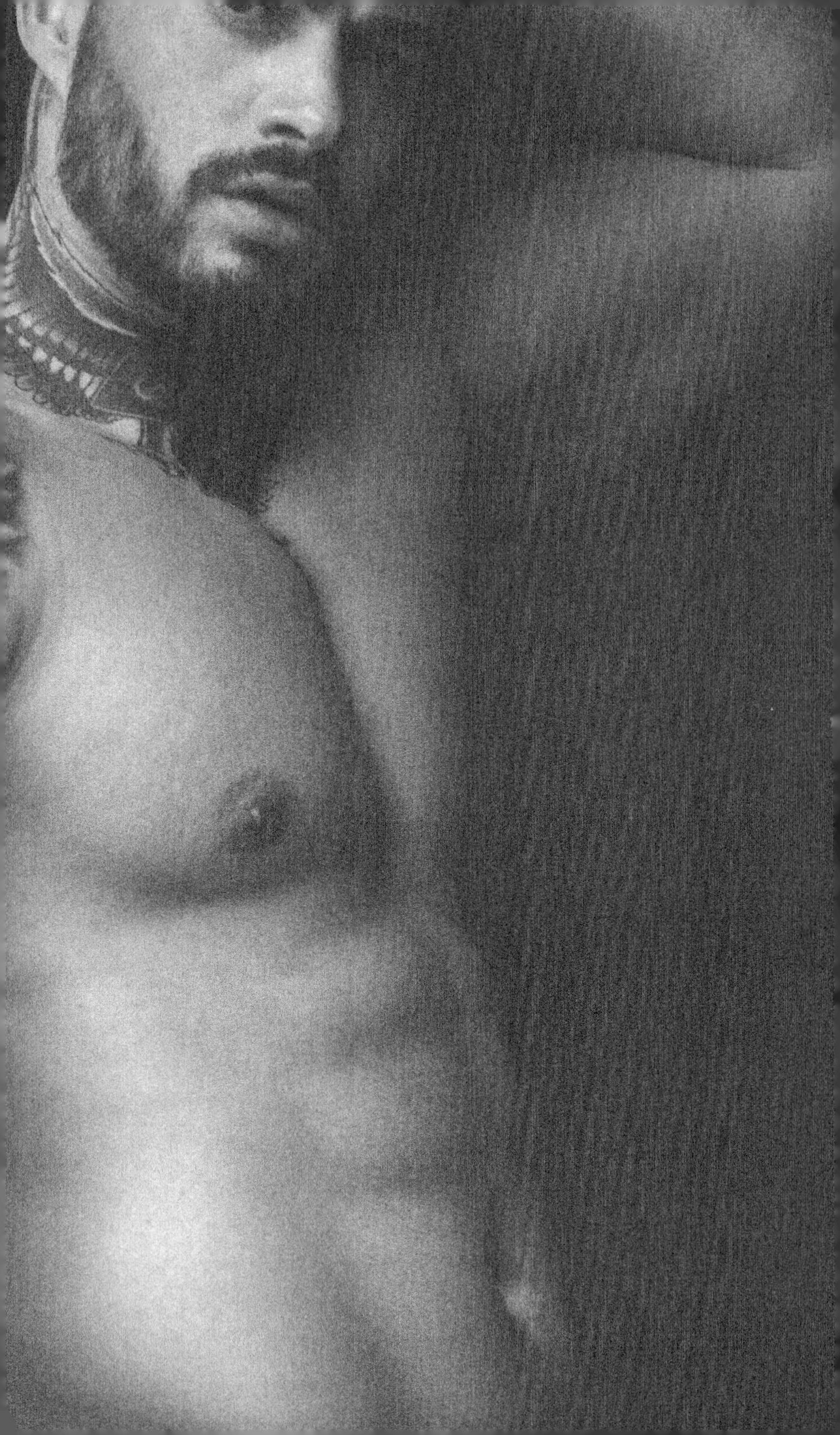

LUCA BERETTA

AN UNSEEN UNDERGROUND PREQUEL

BY ABIGAIL DAVIES

CHAPTER ONE
LUCA

I kept my head down as I slowly lifted my fork to my mouth, doing my best to blend in with the other patrons in the restaurant. The mediocre food wasn't the reason I'd been to this exact building every second day for two weeks in a row. No, it was the people, mainly the person who owned this place: Eduardo Bianco, boss of the Bianco crime family. Although, from the scouting that I'd done, it didn't seem like much of a family to me, more like a dictatorship.

One of the things I'd learned from my father back in Italy was that people always let their guards down when they were comfortable. And that was exactly what I needed—for the man whose territory I was going to steal to let his guard down.

He had no idea what was coming—*who* was coming for him.

I glanced at the man in question, taking in his fedora that was too small for his head and the large nose that seemed to grow bigger with each passing day. He was Italian, but he was third generation, which meant he was Americanized. He'd lost his way; the traditions not being passed down.

There was nothing wrong with moving here to start a better life, hell, I'd landed three months ago to do just that. But it wasn't my only plan. My rightful place was meant to be at my father's side, running the family business with him back home in Italy.

I didn't want to stay there though. The opportunities were scant. But in America, they were everywhere. The possibilities here were endless, which was how I'd convinced my father to let me come here and expand. All we needed now was to get a foothold and some territory.

The Bianco's had originated in Italy, Eduardo's great, great grandfather had run a small crime family where his territory backed onto the Beretta's. Our families had years of getting along and then not. Finally, when they'd lost too many men trying to take some of our territory, they'd escaped here. That was the story that was always told to us. We'd been at war with them and at peace, but it had been generations since the two families had met.

I'd be changing that.

"Tell Joe the shipment is coming tonight," I heard coming from his table. He was always too loud when it came to talking about business. Like I said, he was comfortable here, thinking that anyone listening wouldn't cross him. "Eleven sharp," he tacked on the end.

It was what I'd been waiting for, my opportunity to hit them where it hurt. The problem was, I was only one person. I'd come to this country alone. No back up. None of my father's men. Deep down I knew my father didn't think I'd be able to get territory here, but I was determined to prove him wrong. I'd set up an entire new venture here and hand it down through the generations, just like all the men in my family had before me.

I was making my mark, something that my father wished he could do, but he had no choice other than to take over from his own father. I did have a choice. I could try something new with being the youngest brother. I could spread my wings. I could take what I wanted.

A chill ran over me as the restaurant door opened, whooshing in cold air. Grunting, I muttered under my breath in Italian. I hated sitting near the door, but it was non-negotiable in case I needed to make a quick exit. Always keep your wits about you, that was another thing my father had taught me. And it hadn't failed me yet.

My plate was nearly empty, my time almost up, but it didn't matter because I'd found what I'd come for: a time for the next drop. Adding that to finding out the location last week, it meant that I could finally make my move, I just needed a plan of action now.

"Dad?" a soft voice asked. I snapped my head up at the melodic tone, blinking as I tracked my gaze over the woman who was now standing next to the man who I intended to take everything from.

He didn't turn to acknowledge her; didn't even look away from the men around his table.

"Dad? I need a ride home." She placed her hand on her hip, her frustration evident, but her tone was neutral, almost bored, as if she knew not to talk to him in any other way.

"Alonzo will take you," he said, waving her away.

"Alonzo?" She turned her head, her gaze roving over the people in the restaurant. "Who's Alonzo?"

"That would be me," another voice said.

I leaned back in my chair, watching the exchange, knowing that I was being obvious, but there was something about her wavy black hair and voice that called to me.

"I..." She turned, but still not enough for me to see her face. "Erm..."

The man—Alonzo—didn't make a single move, he just waited, his arms behind his back just like a soldier. And that was what he was: a soldier.

The woman's shoulders slumped. "Fine. I just need to get home to do my homework."

Homework...was she still in school? I tilted my head and narrowed my eyes, willing for her to turn around so I could get a good look at her face.

Alonzo didn't say another word to her as he nodded then moved toward the door—toward me. His gaze met mine briefly, but it was just in passing. He hadn't seen the threat right in front of him.

I picked up my napkin, wiping my mouth as the woman's face came into view—

Fuck.

My stomach dropped at the sight of her. Beautiful brown eyes framed with long lashes, plump lips and a straight nose. Her tan skin was lighter than mine, but her Italian heritage was obvious for everyone to see. A simple thin chain laced around her neck, forming to the contours of her skin. She was at least a foot shorter than Alonzo. Small, tiny, like a mouse.

She stumbled over something. She tried to catch herself, her arms flailing as she tried to grab onto the nearest thing, but there was nothing there. When she realized that all she was grasping was air, her eyes widened. She was going to go down. And Alonzo hadn't notice because he was too busy opening the door.

I had no choice. I shot forward, grabbing her arm to keep her upright.

I shouldn't have done that. I shouldn't have touched her skin. I shouldn't have shown mercy to her.

Because now...now I wanted her.

ABIGAIL DAVIES

And what I wanted, I always got, no matter the cost.

ROSA

I hated coming here. I hated the men who ate here. I hated the conversations that happened within the walls. The only thing I liked about this place was the food. Too bad for me that I rarely got to eat here even though it was my dad who owned the place.

It was his office, the place where he did most of his business. He always sat at the same table, his chair different from all of the other's in the restaurant—larger, grander—just to show *who* he was, as if people didn't already know when they looked at his face.

Inhaling a deep breath, I pushed open the door and made a beeline for him. I didn't want to come here and ask for a ride, but I'd missed the bus and I had my final project to work on. The restaurant was only a couple of blocks from the sanctuary I called school. I was three weeks away from graduating high school, then after that...I had no idea what I'd do. My father said I'd marry a man of his choosing and give him a male heir to take over the business, but I didn't want that. I...I wanted to go to college.

I hadn't been brave enough to broach that subject, probably because I already knew what the answer would be. But I was determined to ask him about it, I'd even filled in paperwork and applied to the local college. I'd been accepted, all I needed now was his permission to go there.

"Dad?" I asked, my stomach dipping with nerves. I only spoke when I had to around him because in his eyes, children should be seen and not heard. It had always been the same, ever since I was little. It wouldn't have been so bad if I would have had a brother or sister that I could talk to and play with. But as an only child, the seen and not heard thing made it so that I had no one to talk to at home.

I shivered when I thought about the place I'd grown up in. It had always been cold and lackluster, but it was all I knew. Ma had tried to give me a sibling time and time again, but she hadn't been able to carry another baby to full term like she did with me. Part of me wondered if that was why she always looked like a zombie, her pain taking over her and morphing her into someone she didn't used to be.

"Dad?" I asked again, hating how he completely ignored me. "I need a ride home." I was careful in my tone, trying not to let my frustration slip through. I'd learned my lesson in the way I should talk to my father when I was six years old. A backhand across the face and a cut to my cheek from his diamond ring scared me enough to know how I should address him.

He huffed, his gaze not moving off someone from across the table. "Alonzo will take you."

I frowned. "Alonzo?" I'd never met anyone called Alonzo. "Who's Alonzo?"

"That would be me," a deep voice announced from right next to me. Where in the heck did he come from?

Swallowing, I turned to look at him. His black hair was as dark as ink, his features screwed up into a pissed off expression. "I...erm..." I'd never met this man before and now I'd have to sit in a car with him for twenty minutes while he drove me home? I didn't like it one bit, but... he was my only option. So I caved. "Fine. I just need to get home to do my homework."

He spun around without another word and sauntered toward the door. My nerves were taking me over, my fight of flight instinct trying to kick in. I'd heard of the dangers surrounding my father, and now he was simply passing me off to someone I didn't even know. He could have just given me money for a taxi, that probably would have been safer than this.

I followed after Alonzo, barely able to keep up with his long strides. "Crap," I murmured as my foot caught on a chair leg that was sticking out. My arms windmilled, trying to keep my balance. I tried to grab for the chair, the table, *anything*, but all I managed to grasp was air. Dammit, I was going down and there was nothing—

A hand grasped my arm, fingers wrapping all the way around. He held me up with one hand, and when I looked up, I realized how he'd stopped me so easily. The man was over six foot, his broad shoulders tapering down to a thinner waist—the build of a swimmer. My gaze hit his cut jawline, his dark eyes, and ridiculously handsome face.

I opened my mouth, trying to say thank you, but all that came out was a squeak.

He pulled me up fully, keeping hold of me as I steadied my feet. Outwardly I knew that I needed to check to see if anyone saw what had just happened, but inwardly, I was swooning—did people still swoon? His almost black eyes bore into me, and I felt like he was seeing right down into my soul with a single look. His lines were hard, his edges unforgiving, but...he'd helped me from falling.

Who was this man?

"Thank you," I managed to croak out, smoothing my hand down my side and straightening my top.

"You're welcome, Mia Topolina." *My little mouse.* He was Italian, his accent so strong it was as if he'd just stepped off a plane.

I blinked, not sure what to say while he was still staring at me. He towered over me, at least a foot taller, and for once, I didn't feel intimidated by it. I was always trying to make myself seem taller than I was so that people didn't look down at me, but with him, I felt...comfortable.

"Let's go," Alonzo demanded. I'd forgotten about him.

The man moved his hand off my arm and I hated that I instantly missed his touch. Who was this guy? Was he one of my father's men? No, he wouldn't have been sitting all the way over here if he was.

I swallowed, taking one last look at him, committing his face to memory in case I never saw him again, then followed Alonzo out of the door and into the car parked right outside the restaurant.

I was going home to do homework, but I somehow knew that my brain would be too occupied with the handsome, dark-haired stranger.

CHAPTER TWO

LUCA

I rolled my shoulders back, trying to stay as calm and as silent as I could from where I was hiding behind a large trash can. It was one of the industrials ones, perfect to hide a body. It was the only thing separating me from the two trucks in front of me, loading things from one to the other. They were pulled up, so the trunks were a foot apart, clearly trying to take as little time as possible.

This was the shipment. It was either guns or drugs, but either way, it would be the start of everything to come. Eduardo needed whatever was in those boxes to sustain his failing business. I'd looked up the numbers, done the intel, and he was living far beyond his means. That was what happened when men got too greedy. They stopped doing it for anything other than the money and to feed whatever addiction they had.

Eduardo's addiction was drugs and women. At the same time preferably. It would be his downfall. I'd make sure of it. But first, I had to bide my time. I had to break him down piece by piece. I had to hit him where it hurt the most and take everything from him.

This was the first step in that plan, but it was the second step that I was looking forward to the most. My own father doted on his two daughters, and if anyone ever touched them, they wouldn't live to see another moment, let alone another day. Daughters were the knife to a father's heart. Which meant the beautiful little mouse that I'd met earlier today would be another step in my plan to take Eduardo's territory away from him.

She had no idea what was coming to her. No idea what I'd take or what she'd give. She'd soon find out though.

"This the last box?"

"Yeah."

I stood upright, keeping my back to the rusting metal surface of the trash can as I dipped my head around to see what they were doing. The guy whose truck was now empty got into the cab and drove off, leaving just the one guy. I was presuming this was Joe.

He stood at the back of the truck, staring at the loaded boxes in awe. This was my chance, my one move to take him out and get the shipment.

I closed my eyes, centering myself, then opened them and shifted forward. He didn't notice me, not until I was only a few feet away, but by then, he was too late. I fired off a single bullet from my pistol, right between the eyes, not hesitating for a single second. Jumping back, I let him fall where he was, careful not to touch him. The last thing I wanted was for DNA or evidence to get left behind.

Twenty boxes sat neatly stacked high in the back of the truck. I stepped over the dead body and pulled the flap of one of them open. Inside were cereal boxes. I yanked one out, ripped the top off then poured it out all over Joe. A thump sounded out and I grinned as I spotted the brick of carefully wrapped white stuff.

Exactly what I was hoping for. Step one was almost complete, all I needed to do now was load it all into my own truck then drive away. I slammed the trunk closed then rushed to the driver's door, intent on taking it to where I was parked a couple of blocks away. But as I opened the door, a figure moved.

"Freeze," the deep voice demanded, and a second later the metal of a gun was being pressed against my forehead.

The figure shifted forward and into part of the light from the streetlamp. "Alonzo," I greeted, acting as if having the gun to my head wasn't a big deal. To some, it may have been, but to me, it was just another day in my life. It wasn't the first time it had happened, and I could guarantee it wouldn't be the last.

His eye twitched, probably wondering how I knew his name. "Who are you and what the fuck do you think you're doing?"

I was right, he was new. If he wasn't then he would have shot me and not asked any questions.

Tilting my head to the side, my lips lifting into a half smile. "I'm taking the shipment," I explained simply. "Isn't that obvious?"

He pushed the gun harder into my skin. "You know whose shipment this is?" He sounded bored, almost as if he was talking off of a script.

"Yeah." I paused, staring at him. "Eduardo Bianco." This was the same guy who had taken little mouse home earlier and he hadn't seemed pleased about it. Men didn't get into this life to babysit the daughter of their boss. "Are we gonna stand here all day?" I asked, slowly putting the pieces together in my head. He'd been sat here the whole time, which meant he'd watched me shoot and kill Joe and hadn't made a move to help him. He could have slid over to the driver's seat and peeled out of here.

But he hadn't

He'd stayed.

"You don't talk much, huh?" When he didn't respond, I leaned on the car door, crossing my arms over my chest. "You work for him yet you don't stop me killing one of his men." I raised a brow. "Explain that."

"I don't have to explain shit to you," he ground out, the gun shaking in his hand. He'd held his arm in the same position for too long and now he was starting to waver.

"Do you like who you work for?" I asked, genuinely curious. There was something about this guy that told me he could be loyal to a fault, that he had more skills than driving someone around. It was clear he wasn't being utilized to his full potential.

His nostrils flared. "It's a means to an end."

I tutted, shaking my head as I feigned disappointment. "Where I come from, the people who work for you are family." I let that sink in and slowly reached up. He saw what I was doing, yet he didn't make a move to stop me. "Family has each other's backs, always. Do you have family, Alonzo?"

He growled, letting his arm drop. "Fuck!" He slammed his hand on the dash in front of him, over and over again. "I don't even know who the fuck you are."

"Luca Beretta," I said slowly. His head snapped around, his eyes widening. We may not have a foothold in the states yet, but that didn't mean the Italian families here hadn't heard of one of the original organizations from Italy.

"Holy shit," he murmured. His gaze snapped left and right, his brain working overtime. "You're trying to take him down." I didn't respond with words or actions. There was no point in admitting to something he obviously already knew. "I want in," he told me jerking forward. "If you're taking that motherfucker down, I want in."

"He crossed you?" I asked, standing upright. I could see it written all over his face, if that didn't tell me, then the fact that he hadn't shot me did.

"My family," he started, clearing his throat. "They were murdered because of him." I didn't say anything as he turned to face the windshield, his gun on his lap, loosely gripped in his palm. "We were a stash house; had been since before I could remember. Then one day," he heaved a breath, "it was burned to the ground. I was the only one who made it out."

"So, you want revenge," I said, my smirk coming back into place. Revenge was easy.

The time ticked by, the sounds of machinery in the background mixing in with motors on the main highway nearby.

"I want revenge," he ground out, turning to face me. "It's the only thing I want."

I nodded, jumping into the cab of the truck and closing the door behind me. "Then revenge is what you'll get." I reached my hand toward him. "Welcome to my family, Alonzo."

ROSA

"What the fuck do you mean the shipment is gone?" Dad roared from his seat at the dinner table. His overly round race turned bright red, his anger on display for everyone to see. He thought I wasn't listening, but how could I not when he was only a few feet away from me?

Men lined up on one side of the room, men who all worked for him, meanwhile, me and Ma were eating our dinner, acting oblivious. It wasn't the first time Dad had his men come into the dining room to talk business. I knew more than I should have, but I wasn't sure if that was a good or bad thing.

"It's gone," one of the men said, shuffling on the spot. "And Joe was killed."

I winced. I liked Joe. He was rough around the edges, but he was always nice to me. He was married to the organization, forgoing having a wife and kids. I asked him once why and he said it was safer that way. I hadn't known what he meant back then, but now, I understood.

"Who went with him?" Dad asked, slamming his fist down onto the table. All of the glasses shook, teetering on the edge of falling and breaking.

"I did," a new voice said, one that I recognized. I flicked my gaze up, staring at the man who had driven me home: Alonzo. "They knocked me out then took off with everything." His black eye and cut on his head were proof of what he was saying.

Dad didn't talk for so long that even I got uncomfortable with what would happen next. I knew he was a bad man, not only because of what I overheard from him, or the blood he always seemed to have on his clothes, but also because everyone was scared of him. I didn't have a single friend at school because of my last name.

"Find out who the fuck took the shipment. There's no way they can take that much powder without being noticed." He turned his attention down to his overflowing plate of food. "Now get the fuck out of here."

They all filed out, walking past me as they exited. One of them touched my shoulder, and I spun my head around to see who it was, but all that greeted me was the back of Alonzo. I frowned. Did I imagine that?

Shaking my head, I started to look down, but at the last second, I saw him turn his head and look me straight in the eyes.

I wasn't sure why he was trying to get my attention, but the darkness swirling in his eyes scared me. I may have been raised by evil, but that didn't mean I liked it. In fact, I hated it. I hated this life; I hated the blood that surrounded me. I may not have been pulling the trigger, but I always heard when other people did.

Alonzo's eyes narrowed. I frowned. Then he left, leaving me wondering why he was looking at me like that.

CHAPTER THREE

LUCA

"If he finds out I lied, he'll kill me on the spot," Alonzo said, fidgeting in his seat.

"He won't find out," I murmured, keeping my eyes glued to the front of the school. Step one of my plan was complete, now it was time to put step two into motion. Although, I knew it wouldn't be as easy as the first step. It'd take time, and some damn good acting on my part.

Alonzo huffed. "How do you know that?"

"Because there are only two people who know what happened last week: me and you. And I won't say a word to anyone." The doors to the school swung open and teenagers filed out in a rush, all wanting to make it home for the day. "You need to not worry so much," I told Alonzo, still not taking my attention off the school. I was waiting to see her face. For five days I'd been watching her every move, making mental notes on what she did on which days. It was all pretty much the same: go to school, go home. She hadn't been to the restaurant since that day that I had been there.

"I worry because I don't know the plan," he ground out, his frustration evident. I understood it because if I was honest, I didn't know the plan fully yet either. All I knew was that the little mouse would be the key to everything, I just didn't know how yet. "And what does Rosa have to do with all of this?"

Rosa. The name suited her.

"You don't need to worry about her," I told him. "Just stick with what I told you to say and we'll be fine. Everything is in motion." I was acting like I had it all figured out, when in reality, I didn't. But Alonzo didn't need to know that, the last thing I needed was for him to doubt me.

He let out a deep breath but didn't say another word. There was no point in him keep asking me because the parts of my plan that I *had* figured out, he wasn't going to know about, not unless I needed his help with it.

Neither of us said anything as we waited for Rosa to come out. She was one of the last. She held a stack of books to her chest, and I had no doubt that her bag was full of books too. In the time that I'd been following her, I'd learned that she loved school. According to Alonzo she only had a few weeks left and then she'd be done with it.

Part of me wondered if she wanted to go to college, but I knew her dad would never allow it, just like my dad wouldn't allow it for my two sisters, Lucia and Vivianna. They were only sixteen and thirteen, but they knew when they were of age that they would have to be good Italian girls and find husbands. I knew something my father didn't though. As soon as I was set up out here, they'd be on the first plane out. This was my opportunity to break away from my father—to help my sisters start a new life—I just had to get there first.

Rosa didn't look around as she walked toward the bus that was parked right outside the school. She was oblivious to her surroundings, something that came in useful for me. She hadn't noticed me once since I'd been following her.

We tailed the bus as it made its stops, all the way to the house where she lived with her mother and father. I'd never seen her mother come out of there, but I'd watched countless men go in and out as Eduardo conducted business. He was only ever at two places: here or the restaurant. And as we pulled up, I didn't see his car, so I knew he was at the restaurant today.

I pulled into an open space between two others and idled the engine as Rosa jumped off the bus and slowly walked up the small incline to her house.

"What happens next?" Alonzo asked.

"Next..." I kept my eyes on Rosa, waiting until she'd entered the house. "I get into that house."

Alonzo's head whipped around. "How the hell are you going to do that?"

My lips slowly spread into a grin. "Maybe it's time my father called Eduardo and I made a 'visit' to the states."

"You're already in the states," Alonzo said, clearly confused.

I lifted my hand, pointing at the house. "He doesn't know that.

Keep your friends close and your enemies closer, that's the saying, right?" I paused, breaking my stare from the house to look at Alonzo. "The closer I get to him, the better prepared we'll be."

Alonzo's eyes widened a little as he figured out what I was saying. "You're gonna be right under his nose when you take him out?" He grinned, leaning back in his seat. "Damn." He whistled. "He'll never suspect you."

"Always expect the unexpected," I told him, taking the handbrake off and driving away from the house that I would soon be in.

ROSA

A gentle knock rang out from my bedroom door. I didn't look up as I called, "Come in," already knowing it would be Ma. I only had a couple of sentences left to write on my project, and I knew if I didn't get them down now, I'd forget them. So I kept on scribbling the words onto the paper, hearing the door squeak open and her footsteps echo.

"Rosa?" Her voice was practically a whisper. She hadn't always talked like that. I remembered a time when I was little that she spoke with confidence, but now, she was just making it through each day with the least amount of words spoken as possible.

Part of me wanted to ask her why she couldn't go back to how she was, but the other part of me left it unsaid, too afraid that I would say something I wasn't meant to. The last thing I needed was to upset Ma, and in the process, piss my dad off.

"You're late for dinner," Ma said when I didn't answer her.

"I'm just finishing this," I rushed out, needing to get the last couple of words down.

I heard her let out a breath. "He's not happy, Rosa. He has a visitor over from Italy."

I scrawled the last word onto the paper and slammed my notebook closed. "I've finished." I wasn't sure whether I was talking to her or myself, but either way, a smile lifted onto my lips. I'd been doing this last project for what felt like forever, and now I was officially done. Apart from a few last tests.

Then it would all be over.

My smile dropped, my stomach flipping.

I'd have to become...I glanced up at Ma. I'd have to become like her. I winced, hating the thought, but knowing that I didn't have a choice in the matter. I did what I was told, that was how it worked in this world. The women didn't get a say—we never got a say.

"Rosa." She shuffled on the spot, grasping her hands in front of her and wringing them. "He's going to be mad."

I closed my eyes, letting my head drop back. She was right, he would be mad that I was late to the dinner table. It wasn't like he'd understand that I was so close to finishing that I thought a few minutes wouldn't matter. To him, there was nothing more important than to do as you were told and follow the rules that he set.

"I'm coming," I said, opening my eyes and standing from my chair. "It'll be fine, Ma," I told her as I walked toward her. I took her hand in mine, not stopping as I pulled her out of my room with me.

"He has company," she repeated. "From Italy."

"You already said that." I smiled over at her and let her hand go as we got to the top of the stairs.

Her face screwed up, her footsteps getting a little quicker now that we were closer to the dining room. I could hear my dad's booming voice from here, and it wasn't until then that the nerves really kicked in.

I shouldn't have been late. It was the number one rule in this house: don't keep Eduardo Bianco waiting.

Ma stopped just outside of the door, her head swiveling so she could look over her shoulder at me. Her eyes were wide, her apprehension clear for me to see. She waited until I was only a couple of feet behind her then pushed the door open.

"Where the hell is she?" Dad asked, his voice carrying.

"She's here," Ma replied, her voice the complete opposite to his loud one.

I stepped inside, my gaze focusing on my dad. "Sorry, Dad. I had some homework to finish off and I thought I'd be done in time." I slumped my shoulders, trying to make myself look smaller than I already was.

"I'm more important than homework," he gritted out. "Sit down and don't speak a word." I raised my brows as I pulled my chair out. Was that all he was going to say? He never let things like that go. What the heck was going on— "We have a visitor from Italy."

"Hello," a deep voice said, and I snapped my head around to the other side of the table.

It was him from the restaurant.

"Hi," I squeaked out, hating that in the two times I'd spoken to him, I hadn't been able to do anything but make a high-pitched sound.

"Luca will be staying with us," Dad announced from his spot at the head of the table.

Luca. His name was Luca. I couldn't stop staring at him. The man who had stopped me from falling was sitting feet away from me, in my home. I'd tried to get his face out of my mind since that day in the restaurant, but it was almost impossible. My hand moved to my arm where he'd grabbed me to stop me from falling, and I swore I could still feel him there.

"He only landed this morning, so he'll have some jet lag," Dad continued, and I finally turned away from Luca. "Make sure you keep the noise down." He directed that at me.

I opened my mouth, about to say that he was the only one in the house who ever made any noise, but I decided better of it and pressed my lips together. Back chatting would only get me a backhand.

"How are you finding the States so far?" Ma asked.

"Did you not hear me, woman?" Dad snapped back. "He landed today. He hasn't had time to make a decision about America." Dad rolled his eyes, shaking his head. "You never listen."

I stared down at the plate in front of me, having no idea what the food was. I never really ate it anyway, only when I was so hungry that I couldn't help but eat. Ma always cooked Dad's favorite foods, which were always fatty, fried things. I was a pasta girl myself, and Ma's homemade pasta was divine. But he rarely let her make it.

"It's okay," Luca said. My stomach dipped even more at the sound of his voice. He was a foreboding man, tall, handsome, and—I glanced up through my lashes—an Adonis. He was just so…Italian. I wondered how old he was; he didn't look much older than twenty-five. Maybe I'd ask him, or maybe if I listened carefully enough, I'd figure it out. I was always good at picking up the small cues—

Wait…

"You landed this morning?" I blurted out, not able to stop the words coming from my mouth.

His gaze met mine, his dark orbs pulling me in and threatening not to let go.

"Are all the women in this damn house deaf?" Dad grunted, but I didn't turn to acknowledge him. I was caught up in Luca's stare, feeling like he was reading every single part of my brain and I was hopeless to stop him.

"Yes," he said slowly, his accent strong. God, there was something about his accent and the roughness of his voice that made me squirm. "I landed in America this morning."

He was lying. I knew he was lying. I'd seen him a week ago in the restaurant. I frowned, tilting my head to the side. He knew that I knew he was lying, yet he just sat there, silent, staring at me.

Was he testing me? Was my dad testing me?

Dammit, my head hurt.

I opened my mouth, not sure whether I was going to vocalize my thoughts, but Luca beat me to it. "So, Eduardo, my father tells me you own the most territory in this state." He was still looking at me, daring me to say something with his raised brow.

Dad laughed. "Yeah. My men have got it on lockdown. No one crosses me."

I broke Luca's stare, not able to hold it for a second longer. I played with the food on my plate, listening intently to their conversation while calling bullshit on it all in my head. It was only a few days ago that Dad had his men in here to tell him that someone had stolen his shipment. That was the definition of someone crossing him.

I turned my head just a little to look back at Luca. If Dad was lying to him, then maybe this guy was important. I had no idea who he was, but I'd never met anyone from Italy before.

Luca's gaze met mine again, and instead of keeping it connected to me, he winked, then looked away.

Holy shit. He just winked at me.

My stomach rolled with nerves again, my palms sweating. I had no idea who this guy was, but I was determined to find out, even if it meant putting the detective skills I'd learned off of the TV to use.

CHAPTER FOUR

LUCA

"You landed this morning?" Rosa blurted out.

I snapped my attention to her, suddenly realizing that there was a huge fuckin' hole in my plan. Shit. I hadn't even thought about the fact that I'd seen Rosa that day in the restaurant. If I'd have let her fall flat on her ass then she wouldn't have ever seen me.

My fists clenched on my lap beneath the table. All she had to say was that she'd seen me in his restaurant days ago and it would alert Eduardo that I'd been here longer than he was told. It had only taken one simple call from my father back home to get me an invite to this house. He'd used the old family connection as well as his status.

My father was well-respected not only in Italy, but here too. Product came from him to the states, funneling down. He wasn't their boss, but he was a higher up member in the entire organization. All of these men thought they had their own pieces of land, but the fact was, all it would take was a handful of words from my father, and it would all be gone in an instant.

They knew this deep down, whether they wanted to admit it or not. So me staying in this house would be a message to all of the other families. It gave Eduardo standing...for now.

"Are all the women in this damn house deaf?" Eduardo grunted.

I didn't turn to look at Eduardo, too transfixed on Rosa. She had a pull about her, one that made me want to dive deep inside her mind. "Yes," I answered her. "I landed in America this morning."

She frowned, her action telling me that she knew I was lying. I waited, seeing what she'd do with the information. A good Italian girl would tell her dad what she'd seen. She'd dote on her father and want nothing more than to please him. But as she opened her mouth, I decided I didn't want to see what her choice would be. "So, Eduardo, my father tells me you own the most territory in this state." I didn't look away from her.

Eduardo laughed, finally gaining my attention. "Yeah. My men have got it on lockdown. No one crosses me."

Everything in me wanted to call him out. To tell him that people *did* cross him, myself included. He was trying to make himself look bigger and better than he was. He was simply a figurehead, one who had lost touch a long damn time ago. He had no idea what was happening around him, and I wanted to keep it that way.

I felt her eyes burning into the side of my head, so I turned, just enough to quickly look at her, winked, then slipped my attention back to Eduardo.

"Good. Good. It's always good to have loyal men." I was saying what I had to, biding my time until I knew how I was going to end all of this. I tried not to think back to the conversation I had with my father only yesterday, but I couldn't stop his voice from entering my head.

"You have no plan, Luca." He made a noise in the back of his throat. "You left this country not knowing how you would tackle this situation. And now you have come to me to help. That was not the deal we had, son."

"I know, Father." I hated that what he was saying was the truth. "I have men at my side. That is the first step." I was lying, I only had one man, but he didn't need to know that. One man was better than none, right?

He was silent for so long I thought the call had dropped. "And the next step, Luca?"

"I need to get into his house." I paused, wincing as I sat on the edge of the hotel bed. "I need you to call him and say I'm coming to visit. Once I'm in the house, I can work him from the inside and destroy his entire operation."

His breath sounded over the line, and I could just imagine him sitting at his desk in his office at home, staring at the wall while holding a glass of red wine. It was his drink of choice. Mine was whisky. "Fine. But this is the last thing I do, Luca. If you don't have his territory by the end of the month, you are to come back home."

. . .

Twenty days. I had twenty days to gain control over everything Eduardo had. And I knew, the only way to do that, was to end him. But to end him, I had to take out the people around him.

My gaze veered to Rosa.

I'd have to destroy her to eradicate her father.

I didn't want to do it. But I didn't have a choice. I never had a choice.

ROSA

Nobody was ever up when I headed out for school. I was always left to my own devices, had been since I was eleven years old. Ma didn't have the energy to be the mother that she always so desperately wanted to be, and Dad...he had better things to do. His words, not mine.

So as I exited the house and saw Luca standing there, I couldn't hide my shock.

My eyes widened, my feet skidding to a halt on the stoop of the front porch. "You're awake." I blinked, the morning sun hitting him right in the face.

He lifted his hand to shield his eyes from it, his lips lifting into a smirk that was both terrifying and inviting. "A man who sleeps the morning away wastes his best opportunities."

I had no idea what he meant by that, but I didn't care because he looked even more enticing in the daylight than he did last night.

He's a liar.

My eyes narrowed. "You lied." I couldn't hold it back anymore. I'd been thinking about it all night until I'd fallen asleep, and then when I woke up an hour ago, it was the first thing on my mind.

"Want a ride to school?" he asked, pushing up off the shiny black sports car that he was leaning against.

"I..." I frowned. He hadn't even acknowledged what I'd said. "I take the bus."

I stood there, not moving a single inch, and I had no idea why. When he looked at me—really looked at me—it was like he'd frozen me to the spot. My muscles wouldn't work. My brain wouldn't co-operate.

"That bus?" he asked, and at his words, I snapped my head around to see where he was pointing, seeing the bus rolling around the corner.

"Dammit," I cursed under my breath. I never missed the bus to school. I hadn't since I was eleven and my dad had made me walk all the way there. It had taken me two hours and I swore I'd never miss the bus to school again.

"So...do you need a ride?"

I glanced back at the still open front door. I could go inside and ask Ma if she'd drive me to school, but that would mean waking her, and she'd still probably say no. Biting down on my bottom lip, I moved my attention back to Luca. He was still there, waiting for my answer.

Could I trust him? I had no idea, but Dad had said he was staying here for a while. And if Dad had welcomed him into the home, that meant he was safe. Right?

"I..." My shoulders sagged and I turned to close the door. "Sure."

He grinned, completely changing the way his face looked, then opened up the door he'd been leaning against. "Your chariot awaits." He waved at the open door, standing to the side.

I had no idea what I was doing or whether this was a good idea, but I still closed the front door to the house then slowly walked toward his car. This was my only way to get to school, so it wasn't like I had any choice in the matter.

Luca closed the car door once I'd slipped inside, then sauntered around the hood of the car. I clicked my belt in place and gripped my hands in my lap as he turned the engine on and reversed off of the small driveway.

"You like school?" he asked when he stopped at the end of the street.

I blinked. Dad's men never conversed with me. But then, he wasn't one of Dad's men, was he? "Yeah, I do." I worried my bottom lip, trying to decide whether to offer any more information. Usually I kept everything short and to the point, but there was something about Luca that made me want to tell him more. "I'd love to go to college."

"My sisters want to do that too." I turned to look at him, my gaze settling on where his large hand rested on the top of the steering wheel. He took the right turn, quickly glancing over at me. "Lucia and Vivianna." A soft smile lifted at his lips. "They're sixteen and thirteen."

"You have two sisters?" I asked, settling back in his seat.

"Yeah." He slowed down because of the traffic lights ahead. "And a big brother, Paolo." His voice changed when he said his big brother's name, his body going taut and his hand gripping the steering wheel tighter, causing his knuckles to turn white.

"I'm an only child," I said, trying to change the conversation. I didn't like it when he was tense, it made me...uncomfortable. "I wish I had siblings."

Luca didn't say anything as he continued down the main road. We were only a few minutes away from my school now. The time had whizzed by, and I wasn't afraid to admit to myself that I wished it would slow down. I wanted to be in this small space with him for longer. To get to know him more. To find out— "Why did you lie?"

He didn't look at me, didn't say a single word as he pulled into the parking lot of the school. If he thought not answering would get me to stop asking, then he was so very wrong.

"I can tell you why," he said slowly, shifting in his seat so that he was facing me fully. "But it won't be the truth, Mia Topolina." He tilted his head to the side, his hand lifting. I held my breath, soaking in the way he stared at me like I was the only woman in the world. "You don't want to know why I lied." He smoothed the pad of his finger down my cheek, stopping at the corner of my lips. "You only *think* you want to know."

My tongue slipped out, wetting my bottom lip. I couldn't help it. He was making me lose all of my senses, drawing me in and not letting me go.

"I want to know," I whispered.

"You don't," he said, tracing my bottom lip with his fingertip. "But you'll find out soon enough." He slid forward, pushing his face closer to mine, then kissed me on the cheek. His lips connected with my skin, causing goosebumps to break out over my entire body. "Be a good girl, Mia Topolina."

Be a good girl. Was he telling me to not say anything? I'd already missed my opportunity to tell my dad that I'd already seen Luca. There was no going back now, I knew that, and so did Luca.

He pulled back, just enough to look into my eyes. He waited, I wasn't sure what for, but when I nodded, he smiled, winking at me again. *God, that wink.*

"You'll be late," he said, laughing. "Want a ride home too?"

"Yes, please," I managed to whisper instead of shout. I wouldn't turn down more time stuck in a small space with him

I opened the door, not looking back at him as I grabbed my bag off the floor then pushed out of the car. I could feel his gaze burning on my back as I took the steps to the main doors of the school two at a time, the smile on my face growing bigger by the second.

He'd touched me.

He'd kissed my cheek.

I placed my hand on my cheek, wishing I could bottle the feeling he'd caused in me from that simple touch.

Luca was taking over my brain, and I wasn't sure I could stop it.

I could still feel his attention on me when I got to the top of the stairs, so I turned, waving at him. He drove away and I watched as his car pulled back out onto the road. Once he was out of sight, my senses came back tenfold and my body jerked forward as I realized...I hadn't given him directions this entire time.

He knew where I went to school.

He knew how to get there.

What did that mean?

CHAPTER FIVE

LUCA

"How much longer do you have?" Alonzo asked from his spot next to me in my car. We were out on patrol again, getting the lay of the land on the outskirts of Eduardo's territory. I was right in thinking he had the most territory in the state, but that didn't mean it had to stay that way. I'd already heard rumblings of a breakdown in the family that had the territory next to his.

"Sixteen days," I murmured, feeling like I was a ticking time bomb waiting to go off. Each day was slipping by faster than the one before it.

"And have you come up with a final plan yet?"

"Not yet," I growled out, slamming my hand down on the steering wheel. Alonzo had been by my side every opportunity that he got. He was proving his loyalty with his actions, unlike the people we were watching. Eduardo spoke of having loyal men, but everything that I had witnessed was anything but that. "You know him?" I asked, keeping my gaze pointed to the two men on the other side of the street. They were sitting in a diner at a booth, opposite two other men.

"Yeah, that's Eduardo's underboss." I raised my brows at that. Huh. Hadn't seen that coming.

"Jesus Christ." I scrubbed my hand down my face. "I thought this would be a simple cut the head off and take over job, but I'm seeing now that the bad seeds run deep." I let out a breath. "I'm gonna have to get rid of them all."

The silence stretched between us, the air shifting in the car. It was the first time I'd spoken about getting rid of anyone. It was unsaid between us, but we both knew the only way to fully take over was death.

I turned, seeing Alonzo squirming in his seat. "Well, you may not have to get rid of everyone."

I waited for him to expand on it, but when he didn't, I demanded, "Explain."

He cleared his throat, placing the notebook on his lap that we'd been jotting everything down in. We'd kept detailed records, not just of Eduardo's men, but the people he dealt with, the ones who he owed money to. There was no doubt they'd switch loyalty once I was in charge. "I was talking to some of the newer soldiers. The ones the same age as me."

I nodded. I forgot that Alonzo was only eighteen—the same age as Rosa—because he was so much wiser than his years. At twenty-four, I may have only been six years older, but I'd lived this life longer than everyone around me.

"And they want out from Eduardo. The way he runs things means that it's not even worth being in the organization." He cracked his neck to the side. "The people at the top get the most. Nothing is funneled down." He paused, his eyes narrowing. "I got two hundred dollars split this month. That won't even pay my damn rent."

"I figured that was the way he'd been doing things," I commented, leaning back in the seat and thinking it through. Loyalty didn't just come from nowhere. You had to look after the people you brought into the family. Which was why I reached over into the compartment underneath my dash and pulled out a wad of money. "Here." I threw it down onto his lap. "That's our first split from the shipment."

"What?" He slowly picked it up, handling it carefully like it was a bomb about to explode. "I didn't say that to—"

"I know." I waved him off. "This is how things *should* be run." I stared back at the men in the booth, wishing I could hear what they were saying. All of Eduardo's men were turning on him, that was if they hadn't already. And if Alonzo was right about the soldiers he'd spoken to, then this could work out better than I'd hoped.

If I have soldiers that Alonzo trusted, ones who hadn't been with Eduardo long enough to give him their loyalty willingly, then it would mean I'd have more of a fighting chance. But still, I had to get rid of the Captains and this Underboss who was working for both sides. He should have been more secretive about meeting up with the obvious agents. I'd spotted them a mile away and I'd only been in this country for three months.

"Can you get the men together?" I asked, thinking out loud.

"Yeah," Alonzo said, sitting up straighter, coming out of his trance. "What are you thinking?"

"I'm thinking," I started the engine, "that we just found the start of the *new* organization."

LUCA

Thirteen days.

I had thirteen more days to take everything away from Eduardo otherwise I'd be back on a plane and flying home. My plans would be ruined, but not just mine, my sisters too. They were relying on me to get them out of Italy, to start a new life of their own without my father ruling everything with an iron fist.

I couldn't let them down.

I couldn't let myself down.

I had to take everyone out. Kill them all.

But...fuck. What about Rosa? The thought of taking her out with the rest of them didn't sit right. It made my stomach churn and my hands shake. But it was the only option, right?

I paced the bedroom I was staying in, my gaze fixated to the door. I was only ten feet away from her bedroom. So close, yet so far away.

If it was my father's choice, he'd kill her no questions asked. She was a means to an end, an object standing in the way of desires. But to me, she was a woman who wanted everything she couldn't have. She wanted more than what her father would ever allow her. She was trapped, just like I had been.

Grasping my hair in my hand, I pulled at it, feeling the burn in my scalp. Killing her wasn't my only option. I had one more, but the question was, did I risk everything just to save her from myself?

I didn't know what to do...I didn't—

I rushed toward the door, not able to stop my forward momentum. My body had made the choice before my mind had even considered every option open to me.

I'd take her, just not in the way I'd originally planned. I'd let her make the final decision, give her some control, but first, I'd take what I wanted. I'd show her what kind of man I was. I'd prove to her that the grass wouldn't be greener on the other side.

I turned my head left then right, making sure the coast was clear.

Eduardo's snoring rang from the other side of the house, drowning out all of the other noise. Placing my back against the wall, I slithered down the hallway, stopping when I got to her door.

The moment I went in there, everything would change, more than I ever thought possible. Yet, I didn't hesitate. I grasped the door handle, turned it, then let myself inside and closed it behind me. A lock sat halfway up her door, so I slid that over so no one could disturb us.

It was just me and her now.

My breaths sawed in and out of me as I stood in front of her door, staring at her bed. Her long hair was spread out over her pillow, haloing her beautiful face. She lay on her back, the comforter only covering half of her body. One leg was kicked out—a naked leg—and the large T-shirt she was wearing was rolled up to her hip. I could see part of her black panties, and the sight of it had my mouth salivating.

Slowly, I pulled my T-shirt over my head, dropping it onto the floor. My bare feet sunk into the plush carpet as I stepped forward, undoing the top button of my jeans then my zip. I let those fall right next to her bed, leaving me naked, standing beside her.

My palm wrapped around my hard cock and I slowly moved it up and down, relishing in the feel of it. But it wasn't the same, not as when someone else was touching me. I glanced at her hand, imagining it was her small one around my velvety smooth hardness. Then without me thinking twice, I slowly lifted her hand and placed it on my cock, wrapping my fingers around hers to guide her.

She made a noise, but her eyes remained fully closed as I jerked myself off in her hand. Her body shuffled on the bed, her leg drawing up and exposing her panties fully to me. In the midst of it, they'd moved slightly, showing me one of her pussy lips.

"Fuck," I whispered.

I had to touch her. I had to know what she felt like.

Leaning forward, I kept her hand gripped onto my cock as I slowly trailed my finger up her pussy lips. She groaned but didn't say a word. She probably thought she was dreaming, especially when she opened her legs fully, giving me even more access.

Her wetness spilled out between her pussy lips, lubricating her, and I didn't wait another second to flick her clit. The lump of nerves hardened, getting bigger the more that I touched them.

"Goddamn," I murmured, moving her hand faster on my cock. I was so close to her opening. I tempted myself with it, stroking around it, but never penetrating it.

"Luca?" her sleepy voice ricocheted around the room. If I was anyone else, I would have let her go and run. But I wasn't anyone else. I was Luca fuckin' Beretta, and I took what I wanted, no matter the consequences.

I swirled my finger between her pussy lips, drawing out a moan from her, then glanced up, piercing her gaze with mine.

"Luca?" she asked again, this time more alert. She slapped her legs together, trying to block me, but all she managed to do was trap my hand there. "Wh-what are you doing?"

She tried to crawl away from me, and for a second, I let her. I let her move her hand off my cock, I let her pull her knees up to her chest, but I didn't make a move to leave. I'd touched her, so now she was mine, she just didn't know it yet.

"Rosa," I countered, using her name for the first time. Her hair was wild around her, the moonlight bathing her in just the right amount of light so that I could see her face clearly. "I'm taking what's mine."

She blinked, wiped her eyes, then blinked again. "What? I...I'm not yours." She shook her head, trying to deny it.

"You are," I told her, taking a step forward and placing my knee on the edge of her bed. Her eyes nearly popped out of her head when she looked down at my naked body.

"No." She held her hands in the air, trying to ward me off, but she didn't make a single move to get off the bed.

"You can deny it all you want." I grabbed her, relishing in the moan she was helpless to release. "But you want me to touch you, don't you, Mia Topolina." My fingers wrapped around her ankle then I pulled her down so her back was on the mattress. Her small body was no match for my strength.

"Luca, no," she breathed out. She was saying no, but did she really mean it? I wasn't sure, not when I trailed my hand up her leg and she didn't make a move to stop me.

"You're so wet." My fingers met her pussy again, this time even wetter than before.

"Oh, God," she moaned out.

"Not God...Luca." I grinned at my words then flicked at her clit. "You like that?"

Her stare met mine, her chest heaving as she tried to catch her breath. "Yes. No." She slammed her hands over her face. "I don't know."

I circled her opening again, but this time I pushed one digit inside, feeling her wetness coat me instantly. She wanted this—wanted me.

Her brain was at war, but her body have given in the moment I'd touched her.

"You want it," I told her, stating the facts as I pulled my finger out then added a second as I thrust it back inside of her.

I crawled over her, my body on top of hers, our faces as close as they could get without touching. "Kiss me," I demanded.

She gasped, her back arching. "Luca."

"Kiss me. Now."

She jerked her head forward, her lips grazing against mine in the softest of kisses. She wasn't sure what to do, how to act, and if the tightness of her pussy was anything to go by, she was a virgin. I'd be the one to break her hymen, to make her bleed. I was the first one there, and if I had it my way, I'd be the only one.

"More," I demanded, opening my mouth and stroking her tongue with mine. I wanted my fill of her, I wanted to take everything she had, over and over again, then come back for more.

The sounds of her wetness permeated the room, her hips coming up to meet my fingers, and I knew then, she was ready for me. Ready to take what I was going to give.

I slipped my fingers out of her, strumming her clit like a goddamn pro. "Something is happening," she gasped out, pulling her lips from mine.

Grinning down at her, I moved my fingers faster, right up to the point where her entire body went taut. Only then did I shuffle over a little and pummel my cock into her. She was tight—so goddamn tight.

She screamed but I managed to slam my hand over her face just in time.

"Shhh," I ground out, keeping deathly still inside her. "It'll only hurt for a little while."

Her orgasm was still washing through her, taking her over, and I used that to get her as comfortable as I could, because there was no way I was going to walk out of this room without fucking her.

The problem was, now that I'd had her once, I wanted her again. And again. And again.

I'd come in here to fuck her, but in the process, I'd fucked myself over.

CHAPTER SIX

ROSA

I couldn't move.

Not when the birds started chirping outside of my window.

Not when the sun rose.

And not when my alarm rang out, obnoxiously loud.

He'd taken my virginity.

He'd sneaked into my room and...touched me.

I placed my hand on my lower stomach. I swore I could still feel him in there.

Why? Why did he do that? And why did I like it so much?

I shouldn't have liked the fact that he came in here uninvited and touched me in my sleep, right? I shouldn't have not wanted him to leave in the early hours of the morning. I shouldn't have wished he'd have stayed with me.

So why was I lying here, confused as hell about whether what happened was right or wrong?

I rolled over, feeling the soreness between my legs.

No, it *was* wrong. He'd taken something that I hadn't given him permission to take.

Or had he? Did I give him permission by not stopping him? Did I let him take it?

I growled, frustration burning through me like lava from an erupting volcano.

The blinking numbers on my alarm clock told me that I was already running late, and if I didn't get up as soon as possible, I'd miss the bus. And missing the bus meant Luca would offer to take me to school again.

I couldn't be in a confined space with him right then. I couldn't even look at him.

So I jumped out of bed, putting the soreness between my legs to the back of my mind as I quickly showered and got ready. I was running down the stairs ten minutes later, but as soon as I exited the front door, he was there, waiting in his usual spot.

"Good morning, Mia Topolina." I screwed up my face at the nickname he'd given me and strolled right on by him. If I ignored him then I'd stand a chance with getting away. "Where are you going?" he asked, a playful lilt to his voice.

"School," I snapped back, walking down the driveway. I didn't turn as I made it onto the sidewalk, even though every fiber in me wanted to see if he was watching me. I didn't need to look to know that though because I could feel the burn of his stare on me.

It was wrong. It was wrong. I chanted over and over in my mind.

I inhaled a deep breath, pushed my shoulders back, and decided that I'd pretend last night never happened. He wouldn't tell anyone, and I definitely wouldn't. So it'd be a secret, mine and his. Never to be spoken about again.

LUCA

I stared at all of the men in the abandoned warehouse, my gaze taking each one of them in. There were at least twenty of them, more than enough to do what I wanted to. My plan was fully formed now. It was only a matter of time until everything would come to fruition.

"You're all here because Alonzo trusts you," I started, gaining all of their attention. Alonzo had already told me that he explained to them who I was and what we were doing, but I knew it had to come from me too. They needed to hear it first-hand. "I'm Luca Beretta." I waited for that to sink in. "Some of you may know of my family." A roomful of nods greeted me. "I come from Italy, but I intend to make a home here. Not just for me, but for all of us."

Whispered words of agreement flung around the cold, derelict building.

"Before I start, know that if you're not willing to put your life on the line, you can leave now without retribution." I waited, my expression carefully neutral, but not a single one of them walked out. In fact, they all seemed more eager than when they first walked in.

It was time to tell them.

"The plan is simple: we kill them all." I was matter of fact and to the point. "It's the only way to get rid of the corruptness that runs deep in the organization." I paced in front of them, keeping my shoulders back. "Six days ago, Alonzo and I observed your Underboss talking with authorities." I spoke slowly, making sure that they could understand me. All of these men were American, although they all had Italian heritage. "He's turning on Eduardo, and in turn, that means he's turning on you too."

Rage filled voices rang out and my lips quirked on one side. Good. I wanted them angry. I wanted them to see that what was happening with Eduardo would only bring them down.

"This is your way out." I moved closer to the storage box that Alonzo was holding. "If you're not with me, you're with them." I halted next to Alonzo. "My organization will be a family. *We* will be a family." I clicked the lid off the box. "And family looks after each other." I picked up one of the wads of money. "Each of you collect one of these before you leave. This is your payment from the shipment that I stole from Eduardo." I paused, seeing some of the eyes widen in the crowd. Alonzo clearly hadn't told them that part of it. But there wouldn't be any secrets, not with me. "Family looks after each other. You have a problem then you come to me, or," I turned to face Alonzo, "your new underboss: Alonzo."

His eyes widened, just enough for me to see the shock on his face. He'd been loyal in the time I'd known him, and even I wasn't stupid enough to admit that we wouldn't be where we were now without him. He was valuable, and I needed him to know that.

I let the wad of money drop back into the box and turned toward the new men of the organization. "We move in a week's time. Until then, study the plan Alonzo gives you and keep your mouths shut." I took a step forward, readying to leave the building. I didn't want to be here for any longer than I had to be. "I only have one final thing to say." I raised my arms wide, grinning. "Welcome to the family."

CHAPTER SEVEN

ROSA

I hated that the first thing I noticed when I walked into the dining room was that Luca was missing. I'd avoided him at all costs over the last five days. Outwardly, I was portraying like I wasn't bothered about what had happened. In fact, I was flat out ignoring it. But inwardly, I couldn't stop thinking about how good I felt when he touched me. How my lips still burned from his bruising kiss. How I was still sore between my legs.

And now, he was nowhere to be seen.

Every morning he had been waiting outside the front door for me. And every evening he'd been sitting at the dining table, waiting to catch my gaze at any opportunity.

But now he was gone.

"He's eating at the restaurant tonight," Ma said as I pulled out my chair and sat down.

I snapped my attention to her, frowning. Had she seen me looking? "Huh?"

"Luca. He's eating at the restaurant tonight, isn't that right Eduardo?"

Dad grunted, too busy eating his fried food to look up and acknowledge Ma with real words.

We all sat there in silence, something that hadn't happened since Luca had arrived in the house. The dining table had been a hub of conversations, but now it was like someone had hit the mute button on the clicker.

"Is school finished yet?" Dad asked, finally looking up at me.

"Friday is my last day." I shuffled on my seat, feeling my nerves flowing through me. I hated having his attention focused solely on me. I was hyperaware that in two days, it would be my last at the school I'd attended for four years. It had become my sanctuary, the one place where I didn't have to think about the people who surrounded me.

But it also meant time was running out. I had to ask him about college, even if I had to beg.

"Good." He wiped his face with the back of his hand, sauce smearing all over it. "I have some prospects lined up for you. We'll have you married within a week and then you can be out of here."

My heart raced. I was too late. "What?" I placed my hands on the table, trying to steady myself as his words sunk in. "What do you mean 'prospects'?"

He leaned back in his seat, his gut nearly touching the edge of the table. All of the fried food he was eating wasn't doing him any good. The buttons on his shirt were begging to pop, but they held on for dear life, just like I did.

"A husband, Rosa. I've chosen some of my men, but I will let you have the final say on which one of them you marry." He stood, his chair scraping against the hardwood floor. There were two dented lines ground into it where he did the same thing every day, ruining the wood. "Be grateful that I'm giving you that."

I stared at him, trying to process the words coming out of his mouth, but they refused to sink in. Everything was happening too fast. Everything I knew was turning upside down and back to front.

I'd known this was coming, but I hadn't realized it'd be as soon as I finished my last day of school. While everyone else in my class year would be getting ready to celebrate the summer then moving onto college, I'd be stuck here, about to marry someone that I had no desire to marry.

"But..." He started to turn toward the dining room door but halted at my voice. "I..." He turned, his stare piercing mine. "I want to go to college."

"No."

It was his final word, but that didn't mean I had to accept it. I had to fight for what I wanted.

"I already applied." His face started to turn that shade of red that signaled he was getting angry. Normally I'd back down, stop talking, walk away, but this wasn't something I was going to let go. I needed to go to college. I needed to give myself the best start I could and do it on my own. I wanted independence, not to be a dependent.

"You did what?" he ground out, stepping toward me. I stood, feeling like I was at a disadvantage if I stayed seated.

"I applied for college." I pushed my shoulders back, trying to make myself as tall as I could but it was no match to him. "And I got accepted. I can start in the fall."

He stared at me, unblinking. The air became stifling, making it hard to breath. "You disobeyed me," he whipped out a second before his hand impacted my face, his stupid diamond ring hitting my eye and knocking me forward. My chest slammed into the table and on my plate, all of the food smearing into my white T-shirt. "I am the boss in this family. I have the final say." He grabbed the back of my neck, lifting my head so he could look directly at my face. "And I say you'll marry one of my men so he can fuck you and give me a rightful heir."

His hand tightened around my neck, his fingers sure to leave bruises behind.

"You'll do what your mother couldn't." With those parting words, he pushed my head down as he let me go, then stormed out of the room, leaving me alone with my mother, the one person who was meant to protect me.

"You'll be okay," she whispered.

Tears streamed down my face, my sadness mixing with frustration and the pain thumping away in my face. My gaze slid to Ma where she sat in her usual seat, her knife and fork still on the table unused.

"I didn't get to choose," she whispered, slowly bringing her face up so that she could look at me. "My father chose *him*." She slowly stood, using her hands on the table to push her up. She looked so weak lately, like she'd given up on life completely. "Just do as he says, Rosa. It'll be easier for you that way."

I didn't move from the spot he'd left me in as my mouth opened and closed, no words able to come out, but by the time I said, "I don't want the easy way," she was gone.

LUCA

"Not now," I told Alonzo, shaking my head as I spotted Eduardo coming into the restaurant. I was surrounded by the young guys in the organization, all of who didn't want to be under Eduardo. They'd seen the way he treated people, seen the way he kept everything at the top, refusing to give the poorest families in the neighborhood even an ounce of his wealth.

I mean, damn, he didn't even live in the kind of house that I knew he could afford. Instead, it all went on drugs and women, wasting it away like it was him that did the work to earn it.

He didn't. He just gave the orders, not willing to get his hands dirty.

When I took over his territory, everything would change. The neighborhood would be looked after, the families helped, but most of all, the soldiers wouldn't be skimming just to survive.

"He doesn't look happy," Alonzo murmured, only low enough for me to hear.

He was right, he looked murderous.

"Friday," Eduardo announced to his usual table as he sat down and slapped his hand on the wooden surface. "You'll come to my house and she'll choose one of you."

I frowned at his words, trying to figure out what he was saying, but it didn't take long for one of the Captains to comment, "It's a damn shame I've got a wife at home otherwise I'd be putting my hat in the ring to claim that daughter of yours."

I blinked. My fists clenching on my lap.

"What the fuck did he just say?" I asked, but we were far enough away that the main table couldn't hear us.

"He's giving Rosa to one of his men," Alonzo informed me. "As soon as she finishes her last day of school, he's marrying her off." He paused, his gaze turning to me. "Didn't you know?"

"No." I clenched my teeth so hard that I heard a crack. "I didn't fuckin' know." My attention moved over the men sitting at the table, all of them at least forty years old.

I tried to listen to what else Eduardo was saying, but the hammering heartbeat in my chest was all I could hear.

"We're bringing the plan forward," I ground out, standing from my seat. "Get everyone together. We have two days to plan our attack."

Alonzo's eyes widened, his shock evident. He was confused, but I wouldn't explain why we had to do this before Rosa was carted off to the highest bidder. I didn't want to admit it to myself. But I knew...I knew it was because the moment someone else touched her, she'd no longer be mine, and I refused to not to have her.

I'd kill every last one of them just to have her. I just didn't know it until that moment.

CHAPTER EIGHT

ROSA

I stood with my back against the wall in the dining room, the stupid dress I had on making my skin itch. Ma had gotten me it, but it was a size too small which meant my chest was practically bursting out of the top of the bright-red material. I hated how it looked on me, hated what it meant.

This wasn't just any dress. This was the dress that showed the best parts of me to entice the men who were on their way.

Shuffling on the spot, I grabbed my hands in front of me, wringing them in the same way Ma did. I understood it more now than ever. I wanted out of here, away from what everyone called my home. To me, it had never been that. It was just a place where I went to sleep at night.

I wanted a home, a real home. But I'd never get it. Not if my father had anything to do with it. All I was to him was a baby making machine.

Footsteps echoed from somewhere in the house, getting closer and closer, and by the time the door swung open, I was a nervous wreck. The room spun, my head pounding.

"Ma," I whispered, hoping that she'd do something to save me from this. I'd finished school three hours ago, and already I was being thrust into the lion's den with my father's prospects.

"Come," Dad's voice boomed out. "We have a feast for you all."

One by one, men came through the door, each older than the last. These weren't prospects, I realized as they all sat down, these were Captains in my dad's organization.

More men filed in, seven in total, but I knew at least half of them were married, in fact, I even went to school with some of their kids.

"Sit," Dad told them, waving his hands at the chairs. "Tonight is a celebration." His beady eyes turned to me. "You all know Rosa," Dad said, waving his arm in my direction.

I didn't look at anyone but my father as the burn of their eyes washed over my body. I felt even more uncomfortable with my dress now.

I swayed, leaning my back on the wall as conversations started around me. I blocked them all out, not wanting to hear a single word, that was until my dad ordered me to get the food. The thought of serving all of the men while they ogled me had my stomach rolling, the little food I'd eaten at lunch threatening to come back up.

But he'd given an order, and I was helpless to deny it. I knew my place, especially after dinner the other night. I lifted my hand to my face, wincing as it touched the purple bruise that I hadn't bothered to cover up. I wasn't going to hide myself, not from these men.

My hands shook as I exited the dining room then crossed the hallway into the kitchen. It was an old galley type one with two doors at the end, one for a cold room pantry, and the other leading to a set of stairs that we never used. Food was ready on platters, so all I had to do was place them in the middle of the table so that they could help themselves. Then maybe I could escape for a little while.

I halted at the edge of the counter, needing to take a breath. It was too much, all of it was too much. I couldn't marry one of them. I couldn't give myself freely to them.

The sound of the door creaking opened sounded out, but I didn't look up, knowing it was probably Ma coming to help me.

Hands gripped my hips then I was jerked back, my back slamming against someone's front. I was ready to freak out, thinking one of the men must have come in from the dining room, but as soon as I took a breath, I knew who it was.

"Luca," I murmured, my shoulders slumping. I didn't know him, not really, but my soul...my soul spoke to his on a level that neither of us would ever understand.

"Mia Topolina," he whispered back, right into my ear. "Did you miss my touch?" His touch was bad. Wrong. Forbidden. But I was done denying how damn good it felt.

"Yes." I let my head drop back onto his chest then turned to look him in the eye.

His lips quirked on one side. "I knew it would only be a matter of time." His arms banded around me then one hand slipped down to cup between my legs. "Has your pussy missed me too?" I nodded, not able to get the words out as he backed us up and opened one of the doors. It led to the stairs, so he closed it then opened the second one. "Perfect," he murmured, dragging me into the small space.

He pulled on the tie at the front of my dress, exposing my chest to him. "Luca!" I quickly covered myself with my arms. "We can't do this here, not with," I looked behind him at the closed door "not with them out there." They were waiting for their food. It would only be a matter of minutes until my dad noticed I hadn't come back.

"Them?" he asked, advancing toward me until my back hit the wall. "You mean the men that your father thinks he can give you to?" His face was like thunder. "You won't be going to any of them, Rosa." He pressed his front against mine, maneuvering my arms so that they were at my side, and I couldn't deny that relief washed through me. "You know why you won't be with any of them?"

I shook my head, too enthralled with the way his hand slid under the skirt of my dress and found my pussy right away. He knew exactly how and where to touch me for maximum effect.

"Because you're mine, Mia Topolina." He trailed his nose up the side of my face, breathing me in as he pushed my panties aside. "Want me to show you how much you're mine?"

I closed my eyes, words evading me. I wanted to escape to a world where it was just me and him. One where I didn't have to worry about the men in the other room and what my life will be like. It was a momentary reprieve, and I intended to relish in it then lock up the memory tight, only accessing it when I needed it the most.

"Show me," I murmured, opening my eyes and catching his stare right away. "Show me how much I'm yours."

He growled, the sound deep and guttural. "Fuck, you make me lose my damn mind." His hands ripped at my panties then traveled up to my waist to pick me up. "Wrap your legs around me." I did as he said, feeling his hardness against my inner thigh and within seconds he was penetrating me, pushing his cock all the way in.

"You feel so good," I moaned out, letting my head drop back against the wall.

He buried his face in my chest, his mouth finding my nipple at the same time as he thrust in and out of me.

"I'm." *Thrust.* "Never." *Thrust.* "Letting." *Kiss.* "Anyone." *Thrust.* "Else." *Groan.* "Touch." *Thrust.* "You."

I nodded, agreeing with him. Logically, I knew it would never be the truth, but living the fantasy in that moment was all I'd ever need.

"You are mine, Rosa." He pressed his thumb on my clit, thrumming three times. "All mine." Fireworks burst behind my eyelids as my orgasm slammed through me so suddenly that it threw me off balance. But Luca was there to hold me up. He was there to make sure I wouldn't fall.

"Never gonna let you go," he whispered as he thrust two more times then emptied himself into me. The warmth of his seed mixed with my wetness, and for a second, I was sated, happy, on top of the world. But it all came crashing down as several loud bangs on the front door boomed through the house.

Luca's body straightened, his peaceful expression disappearing.

"Go to your room," Luca demanded, letting me down. My feet hit the floor, my equilibrium off balance.

"What?" I was trying to get my focus back, but I was finding it really hard after everything he'd just done to me.

"Go to your room," he repeated. "And don't come out. Lock the door. Only open it to me." His face turned to stone, his demeanor completely changing right in front of my eyes. "Got it?" I relished in his accent and it took me several seconds to register what he'd said.

"Luca? I—"

Another bang reverberated through to the kitchen and the small pantry we were hidden away in, followed by loud shouts.

"Now, Rosa!" He jerked open the door and pushed me through it then guided me to the back stairs. "Remember what I said, Mia Topolina, don't open your door to anyone."

I nodded, my eyes widening as gunfire rang out.

"Go!"

I didn't think, I just did as he said, spun around, and ran straight to my bedroom, slamming the door and locking it behind me. I backed into the corner, covering myself as more shots and shouts vibrated through the house. Slamming my hands over my ears, I squeezed my eyes closed, trying to block it all out.

It was okay. Luca was here. He'd get me out unscathed.

Right?

LUCA

"Go!" I waited as she scrambled up the stairs, falling up several steps as she tried to move as fast as she could. As soon as she hit the top, I slammed the door closed, moved a chair in front of it, then spun around.

It was the start of the end. My plan coming into motion.

Eduardo was about to offer his daughter up to one of the devil's in his organization, and he didn't care who it was, so long as they gave him a fee.

He was selling her. Her father, a pimp.

Jesus Christ. The man had no morals. No code.

I rolled my shoulders back, hearing the shouts coming from the dining room, then slowly pulled my gun from my waistband. It was time to put on a show, to show Eduardo how a real boss acted.

My palm met the wooden door of the kitchen and I crossed the hallway then entered the dining room. Each one of my men were standing behind the men sitting at the table, pointing a gun at their heads to keep them in place. My gaze hit one corner of the room where guns and knives were piled. They'd done what I'd told them to: took their weapons away.

"Luca?" Eduardo's tone was shocked, his face morphing from angry to confused.

"Eduardo," I greeted, sauntering around the table and taking stock of the men surrounding it. "How are you this evening?" I loosely held my gun in my hand as I brought it up to scratch the side of my face, showing him who's side I was on. He had no idea that I was running this show, not yet.

"What the fuck is going on?" He tried to get up, but a second gun on the back of his head stopped him.

"What's going on?" I repeated, taunting him. "Isn't it obvious?" I smirked over at him, relishing in the way his face turned a deep shade of red. He was slowly putting it together. "I'm taking over."

"Taking over what?"

"Your organization." I halted in one of the back corners, making sure I could see everyone without my back being exposed. There were enough men in here to stop anything happening, but the lessons my father had taught me were ingrained deep. "You don't run it very well. What with the money you waste fucking whores and snorting drugs." I tilted my head to the side, staring at him like I was a dog and he was my favorite chew toy. "Your men skim money and drugs to feed their families because you don't pay them. And then there's the fact that your underboss is a mole for the feds."

His head snapped around to his underboss. "Is this true?" When he didn't answer, he slammed his fist on the table. "I'll kill you. I'll chop your fucking head off and—"

"Now," I interrupted him, giving my men the order. One by one they shot each person around the table, leaving only Eduardo and the wife he'd clearly abused over the years. I didn't want to kill her, not really, but she was a means to an end. Keeping her around would only sully what I was trying to build.

Eduardo shot back in the chair, trying to escape, but the three men surrounding him pushed him back in place, keeping him there.

"Get the fuck off me," he roared, trying to save himself. But it was no use, there was nowhere he could escape to. He was trapped, just like his wife and daughter had been all of these years.

"You've taken everything from these men," I said, pushing out of the corner and sauntering toward him. Each step was slow and methodical, biding my time. "You use everyone for your own gain. This isn't a family you have here."

"A family?" He laughed, the sound manic. "I'm a fuckin' Mafia boss, I don't need a goddamn family."

I stopped beside his wife, lifting my gun and pointing it to her temple. She glanced up at me, her eyes glazed over, acceptance washing through her. "That's where you're wrong." I fired off the shot, not moving a single muscle as blood and brain matter flew all over me. She slumped over, her head smashing against the table, her body going limp. "Family is *everything*." I took one more step, now only two feet away from him. "And I just took all of yours." I grinned, placing my finger on the trigger. "And now all that's left is to take your daughter too."

"Kill her," he sneered. "I don't give a fuck."

I tutted, shaking my head. "I'm not gonna kill her, I'm gonna fuck her, over and over again, until she gives me the heir that you always so desperately wanted." I winked as he opened his mouth, but he didn't get the chance to reply because I fired off two more shots, one in his head, and one in his chest for good measure.

Dead bodies lay everywhere, blood spurted up the walls and over the wooden floor, reminiscence of a horror movie. The room was ruined, but it didn't matter because Alonzo had his own little plan.

"Burn it down to the ground, Alonzo," I told him, not bothering to see where he was. I knew he was in here. I knew he was just waiting on the chance to get his own revenge.

"You got it, Boss."

Boss, I liked the sound of that.

I stared around the room, taking in each of the dead bodies, knowing that this wouldn't be the last time I took a life. Darkness was engrained in me, and I had no intention of keeping a lid on it, not now that I was the boss.

I'd taken what I came here for, but now there was just one thing left.

Rosa.

I heaved a breath, trying to figure out how I'd explain all of this to her, but the door swung open, making the decision for me. All of my men swiveled, training their guns on the figure as she stepped into what could only be described as a blood bath.

"Luca?" Her voice was small, unsure, but her eyes took everything in. "What...what have you done?" Her gaze landed on her dad then her ma, but she didn't step forward. She stayed in the doorway, her black eye marring her beautiful face.

I'd told her to stay in her room, but she hadn't listened, and I was beginning to think it would become a pattern. But I somehow liked it on her.

"You have a choice to make," I told her, not bothering to wipe the blood off my face. "You can join them." I pointed at the dead bodies around the table with the barrel of my gun. "Or you can join me." I paused, strolling toward her. "You can be mine, Mia Topolina. Say the word, and I'll give you everything you've ever wanted."

She blinked rapidly, her hand moving to her face where the bruise was. "You...you killed them all?"

"Yes."

"And..." She glanced around the room at all of the men who still had their guns trained on her. "And now you're the boss?"

"Yes."

Her stare met mine. I wasn't sure what I thought I would find in her beautiful eyes, but it definitely wasn't the relief that was shining there. "I have a choice?"

I nodded, not saying a word. Her choice wasn't really a choice. She either died or became mine. But I was giving her the illusion of it, more than her father ever did.

"You." She said, her tone full of confidence. "I choose you."

Two steps was all it took to close the distance between us, and as soon as my body was against hers, I placed my hand on the side of her face. "Then you're mine, Mia Topolina. Forever mine."

She licked her bottom lip, lifting up onto her tiptoes to place a soft kiss on my bloodied lips. "Forever yours."

Luca Beretta is a prequel to the Unseen Underground Mafia Series. Read about their son: Lorenzo Beretta here

ABOUT ABIGAIL DAVIES

Abigail is the author of over twenty novels; her favorite to write being anything full of angst and drama. Her writing space is her safe haven where she can get lost—and tortured—in the world of her characters. When not writing, Abi is mother to two beautiful daughters, a black cat, a chocolate labrador, and three guinea pigs.

View all of Abigail's books here

Connect with Abigail here

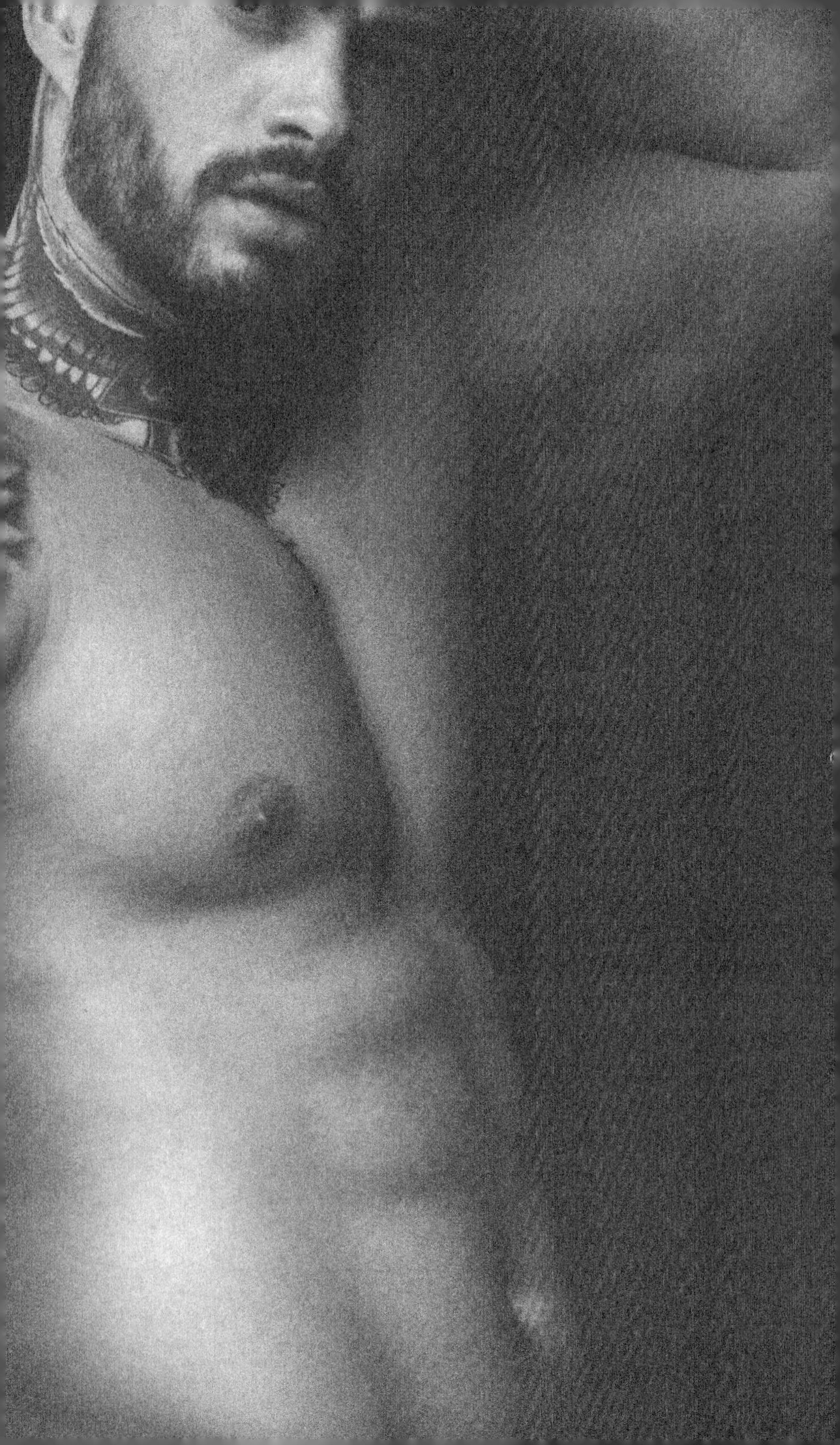

THE DEVIL'S MELANCHOLY

BY YOLANDA OLSON

BLURB

The strangest obsessions start with an idea.
One that's festered for longer than it should have.
The kind that sat quietly and grew inside of me waiting for this very moment.
I never realized how badly I had wanted this to happen until she walked through the door of my establishment.
The woman that used to torment me daily after school, and even got me locked up for a summer.
And it seems she's brought the perfect piece to use against her.
To finally glean the obsessive revenge of the teenage boy that never had the opportunity to do so.
I shouldn't feel as good about this as I do, but it seems that the payback I used to dream about is finally mine for the taking.

CHAPTER ONE

CELESTE

I hold the door open for my niece as we enter *Bay City Body Arts*, still trying to figure out how she talked me into agreeing with her decision to get a tattoo.

When she begged me for permission, she promised me that it wouldn't be too big, too gaudy, or anywhere anyone would be able to see it.

"Hi! I have an appointment!" Ava tells a beautiful young woman with the wildest, emerald-green hair that I've ever seen. She smiles up at us brightly, holding up a finger, then pointing to the phone receiver in her hand.

Ava nods in embarrassment as she takes a place in front of the woman's desk and signals for me to stand next to her. While we wait for the young woman to finish her conversation, I open my purse and begin to fish around for the notarized document required for Ava to get her first tattoo at sixteen years old.

Once I locate the folded piece of paper, I hold it against my leg and attempt to smooth it out as best as I can before I zip my purse back up.

"Hey there!" The young woman finally greets us after a few more moments. "What's your name, sweetheart?"

"Ava Beckett."

The young woman nods as she turns her attention back to the computer in front of her and punches a few keys before she glances back up at us again. "You're booked in with Finley, right?"

Ava nods and I shrug, assuming that the information is correct.

"Great, my name is Rya. If you can fill out this form and ..." her voice trails off as she glances down at the screen again, "show me your identification and notarized parental permission, I can go grab him."

Rya looks up at us expectantly with eyes that match her hair color. I glance over at Ava who's pulling her ID out of her pocket and I hand her the document she needs to get this done.

"Thanks! You can have a seat anywhere. I'll be right back," she tells us with a big smile as she takes the paperwork and Ava's card, setting them down on her desk before she gets up and disappears down a long hallway.

"It's not too late to leave," I tell Ava quietly as I take a seat next to her on the opulent, black leather couch in the reception area. She scoffs as she leans back against the cushions and begins to fill out the form.

I do my best not to sigh.

She doesn't need someone to tell her what to do at her age; she needs someone who will understand and guide her as best as they can.

"Aunt Celeste, you have to sign here," she tells me after a few more moments of abject silence.

I lean over and sign my name with a flourish before I turn my attention toward the front desk.

Rya has reappeared and she's busy with the paperwork, making copies of Ava's ID, and tapping away at the keys of her computer.

"He'll be right out," she offers when she finally realizes that I'm staring at her.

I nod as I turn my attention back to my niece.

She's so damn excited that I have to fight the urge to grab her by the arm and run.

The body is a temple.

It's not meant to be marked with anything; it's an affront to God, but try as I might, I haven't been able to get her to understand that.

"Hey, Rya?"

The voice that calls out to her is smooth and silky. It piques my interest enough to turn my attention toward the source, but there's no one there.

I arch an eyebrow at Rya, and she rolls her eyes at the ceiling briefly.

Letting out a long-suffering sigh as she gets to her feet, she gives us an apologetic smile before disappearing down the hall again.

"You okay, Aunt Celeste? You look like you're about to pass out," Ava teases, and I give her a stern look.

"I would feel better if I could walk out of here without you being all marked up."

Ava rolls her eyes, almost the same way that Rya just did as she crosses her arms loosely over her chest and leans back against the cushions again.

"Aunt Celeste, I told you that I wouldn't get anything sacrilegious. I'm not going to embarrass you either if that's what you're worried about. I just really want to get a tattoo."

"But, why?" I ask her louder than I mean to.

"Because."

The reply is simple and final enough that I *should* let it go, but just as I'm about to open my mouth and tell her that she needs to come up with a better reason in the next five seconds or I'll haul her out the front door, we're interrupted.

"Unless you consider an anchor and a couple of small flying birds sacrilegious, I'm pretty sure we'll be okay here," comes the same voice that called Rya earlier.

I turn sharply to look at the young man when he comes over and perches himself on the arm of the couch, right next to me.

He gives me a warm smile, and I scoot a little further away from the end of the couch, bumping into Ava, who hasn't budged.

But as his light amber eyes settle on me, as I take in the tattoos on his body, I find myself becoming slightly uneasy for some reason.

It's not until the warm smile on his face falters slightly and he tilts his head, peering a little closer at me, that I have the feeling I know him from somewhere.

I just can't put my finger on it yet.

CHAPTER TWO

FINLEY

"Is everything good?" I ask Rya, glancing over my shoulder at her. She gives me a quick thumbs up before she picks up the ringing phone.

"So, where are we placing these, Ava?" I ask the young blonde girl with the hazel-green eyes. I do my best to keep my focus on her and not on the woman she brought with her, because I'm hoping that she isn't who I think she is.

"I was thinking maybe here," Ava says as she stands up and begins to roll up her cut-off jean shorts, and points to her inner thigh. Why she couldn't have just done that to begin with is beyond me, but I'm not going to lecture this little girl. I'm here to do a job and then send her on her way.

"Cool. And you're aware that I freehand everything, right?" I ask as I stand up and steal a glance at the woman again. *There's no way...*

"Yes."

"Alright, well follow me, I'm all set up," I instruct her as I turn and head down the hallway.

I glance at Rya who catches the expression on my face, and I cut my eyes to the side quickly before I disappear down the hallway with Ava and the possibility of it being *her* in tow.

"Isn't there a more appropriate place you can put those, Ava?"

I sit down on my stool as I snap my gloves on, and glance up at the woman. She's giving Ava a pleading look, but the young girl seems to have her heart set on the spot.

"Is this going to hurt?" Ava asks, ignoring her guardian.

"Nope. There's a lot of meat in that area, so unless you're a pussy, you should be fine," I tell her with a grin as I turn my floor light on and scoot closer to the recliner she's lying on. "You're not a pussy, are you, Ava?"

Her face turns crimson, and when she giggles, I have to bite back a sigh. My personality is, and always has been, the exact same way.

I like to joke with people.

I like to smile and laugh at the corniest jokes in the world.

I'm flirtatious even when I don't mean to be, however, I find that sometimes it can ease tension and help clients relax instead of being wound as tightly as this little girl's guardian is.

"You know," I say as I lean over and rest a hand on Ava's leg. "I can't help but feel like I've seen you before."

"Me?" she asks, curiously.

"No," I reply, shaking my head. "Remember to breathe, I'm going to start," I say as I power on the machine and press it against her skin. Ava inhales a deep, sharp breath and I glance up at her briefly. "Are you okay?"

"Fine," she states through gritted teeth, and I smile. After a few tense moments of wondering if she's forgotten how to breathe, she finally lets out a deep breath. "Anyway, who do you mean?"

"Huh?" *Oh. I forgot already.* "Her," I say, not turning my attention to the woman standing on the other side of Ava.

"Aunt Celeste?" she asks doubtfully.

Celeste? Maybe it's not her after all.

With a quick shrug, I go back to outlining the anchor, then the birds. About half an hour later, I give the outline a wipe down as I look up at the woman.

"Did you ever go by a different name?" I ask her curiously.

Her mouth becomes a tight line, but she doesn't answer me.

Ava does.

"Aunt Celeste is her real name. Well, you know what I mean," she says with a girlish giggle. "But she—"

"Ava, that's enough," Celeste tells her sharply.

"Sorry," she mumbles as she folds her arms behind her neck.

"Fin!"

I roll my eyes when Rya shouts for me and get to my feet. I set the gun down on the tray before I pull my gloves off, then apologize to my client before I walk quickly out of the room.

"What's up, Ry?"

When I reach the front of the studio she looks up at me with a nervous expression, chews the inside of her mouth, then waves me over.

I put a hand on the desk as I lean down to peer over her shoulder, then let out a laugh when I see what she has on the computer screen.

"Well, I'll be damned," I say quietly.

"Maybe get Oakley to finish the tattoo and take a walk?" she suggests gently as she reaches over and puts a hand on my wrist.

I stand up straight for a moment; years of being subjected to in-school abuse at the hands of *Aunt Celeste*, and her long, wooden ruler come flooding back to me. I shake my head.

"No, I think I'm going to have some fun."

"Fin—"

"It's all good, Ry. I'm not going to return the favor if that's what you're worried about," I tell her with a grin. "Take that shit off the computer and wipe the history. I'm almost done with this tattoo, as it is. They'll be out of here in no time, so I need to go play."

I give my older sister a pat on the head before I click my tongue against my teeth, and head back to Ava and *Aunt Celeste*.

And to think when I woke up this morning, I thought tattooing a sixteen year old was going to be a pain in the ass.

CHAPTER THREE
CELESTE

I watch as Finley wraps up Ava's leg. He stole so many glances at me while he worked on her tattoo. He spoke to her, made polite conversation, and even asked her how school was going, but I felt his eyes on me even when mine weren't on him.

"Here," he says as he gets up and reaches into one of his rolling, stacked containers. "These are the aftercare instructions. Everything I just told you is on here, but sometimes being able to see something helps too."

"Thanks," Ava replies enthusiastically, as she takes the paper from him. "Do we pay you or at the desk up front?"

He rocks on his heels for a second, his arms now crossed over his chest as he looks at me. I look at the floor.

"Tell you what," he begins slowly. "If you aren't busy this Friday night, it'll be free."

"What?" I bark at him. Clearing my throat loudly, I grab my purse and pull out my wallet, before looking at him expectantly.

"Come on, Aunt Celeste. He's nice, who knows, I might have some fun for once that doesn't include staying at home and watching old black and white movies," Ava begs me excitedly.

I roll my eyes.

She knows good and well that I won't allow her to date anyone at her age.

"If you'll just tell me what I owe you, please," I counter in a clipped tone.

"Do you live with her?"

"Huh?"

I look up at him to see he's looking at Ava, who's nodding with a huge grin on her face.

"So, what you're telling me is that I already have your address," he begins slowly, as he turns his eyes back toward me. "I could just show up on Friday night and take you out for dinner."

The way he punctuates his statement with a shrug, like it's something he does on a regular basis turns my stomach.

"And I could call the police," I reply tightly.

"And I could tell them that he's my friend and I invited him over," Ava intercedes with a shrug.

Finley laughs as he and Ava exchange a glance, and I sigh loudly.

"I won't let her go to dinner with you," I relent hopelessly, "but if you want to come by and have dinner with us, then I guess that will be okay."

He gives me a triumphant grin before he does a grand, sweeping gesture with his arm, letting us know that we're free to leave, and as we do, I notice that Rya is watching us.

Her look isn't so friendly anymore.

The brightness that she greeted us with a couple of hours ago has dimmed, now there's a darkness that sends a slight shiver through me.

We're never coming back here again, I think evenly as I put an arm protectively around Ava and escort her out the front door.

"That was completely uncalled for, Ava," I scold her as we pull into the driveway of our modest home. "Not to mention, it's illegal. He's too old to date someone so young."

"Aunt Celeste," Ava begins patiently as she tucks her hair behind her ears, "I'm not going on a date with him. He's coming over here, remember? Besides, I just wanted a free tattoo."

I grip the steering wheel tightly for a moment before I turn the key in the ignition and slip it out.

Ava leans over and rests a hand gently on my arm. "I know we can use the money. I know you couldn't afford to pay for this, so I agreed so the money could be used for bills instead."

I give her a sidelong glance.

Poverty is a rule that I'm supposed to live by, but considering I'm the sole guardian of my niece, I've been given more leeway than anyone else has in my vocation.

I can't let her live at the convent and she can't live alone.

Concessions were made and I feel like I've already started my slippery downward slope into hell just by allowing her to get those marks on her body.

"Thank you," I say quietly.

Ava gives me a quick peck on the cheek before she pushes the passenger door open and practically bounces across the lawn to the front door of our home.

I stare at the ceiling, unable to sleep.

Anytime I've closed my eyes, I've started to toss and turn. I even managed to slip into a nightmare for longer than I cared to and have now forced myself to stay awake, instead of trying to sleep.

Friday night, I'm playing host to some hooligan that makes a living out of committing sin by permanently marking the body and has a penchant for little girls.

I should alert the proper authorities. Maybe if he spends the weekend in jail instead of at my dinner table, he'll understand the consequences of his potential actions.

I sit up and rub my face irritably.

Ava did what she felt was best at the moment because she knows we're having financial trouble, however, I'd saved up for her to get that damn tattoo.

Granted, I had to skip paying a bill to have the money, but I can always catch up on it next month.

As I turn my face to glance out the window, I start to think of anything and everything I can do to keep my niece safe; to keep her away from that man.

Tomorrow, I'll fix this before he has a chance to set foot on my doorstep.

CHAPTER FOUR

FINLEY

"There you are," I say quietly as I dig my high school yearbook out of the box in my closet. I blow the dust off the hardcover, then go back to sit on the floor in front of my bed.

Saint Sebastian's School for Boys.

I scoff at the way the gold foil catches the moonlight as it shines through my bedroom window. I never liked that place for one reason, and one reason only.

Sucking my teeth, I open the book and begin to flip quickly through the pages until I find myself somewhere in the middle.

I run the tip of my finger over the color photo until it stops on someone in the front row, standing just to the left of me.

The young, teenage boy ready to graduate and get the fuck away from that place. A scowl where a smile should be and inching as far away from the authority figure that made those years miserable as possible.

My eyes travel down to the list of names, each in order of how we were seated and how *she* was standing.

Sister Emma Agnes Tremaine.

I feel a quick surge of rage go through me as I flick the book shut and toss it across the bedroom floor.

I bend my knees, rest my elbows against them, and drop my face into my hands.

Ava called her Celeste. Why? What are you hiding from, bitch?

I drop my hands and take a deep breath as I interlace my fingers and stare at the book. It's lying open on the last page and I can see all of the scrawled messages that my friends left for me that year.

And even that wasn't enough to make me happy.

Theology.

That's what she taught all four years.

Trying to ingrain our heads about *her* religious beliefs, how they came about, and why they're so important, but it never interested me.

I wasn't the nuisance she treated me as.

I was a bored, teenage boy with better shit to think about, and it made her angry.

Sister Emma Agnes must have felt less than decent at her job, because when I finally severed her last nerve, she would keep me after school and cane my bare ass with her long, wooden ruler.

And now I finally have the chance to pay her back in the best way I know how.

She clearly loves her niece; it was obvious in the way she barked at me when I invited her out for dinner.

She doesn't want to embarrass her by wearing her holy getup out in public.

The thing is, I'm not interested in little kids. Never have been, but this is an opportunity that I can't give up.

Her Holiness seems to have forgotten all about how she treated me, but I'm going to make damn sure that she knows exactly what she's turned me into.

"Hey."

I glance up from my client's back and look at Rya who's standing uncomfortably in the doorway.

"What's up, Ry?" I ask her curiously.

"You've got someone out front that wants to talk to you."

"Who?"

She looks down for a moment before she mouths *her*, and I roll my eyes.

"I think now would be a good time to take a break," I tell my client as I set my tattoo gun down and get to my feet. Peeling off my latex gloves, I roll my shoulders and smile at the middle-aged man that's clearly going through a mid-life crisis based on the design he's getting. "Take as long as you need; I don't have anyone after you."

He nods in thanks as he reaches for his jacket and fishes out a pack of smokes and his cell phone.

"Send her in," I tell Ry as soon as my client leaves the room. I take a few steps toward the black massage bed that sits along the wall, directly across from the door, and wait.

It only takes a minute or so before she's standing in the doorway, giving me a look that I grew far too familiar with in high school.

"Shame you don't have your ruler," I remark evenly.

"Excuse me?" she barks as she closes the door behind her.

"Nothing," I say with a smile. "What can I do for you today, *Aunt Celeste*?"

Her body stiffens at the way I say her name, but she takes a deep breath to relax herself then puts her hands on her hips.

I remember that look far too well.

It was the same one she gave me the first time I got detention, and the same one she gave me when I hobbled out of school with angry tears in my eyes.

"You're not allowed on my property," she says sternly. "If you come to my home, I *will* call the police."

I shrug. "Okay."

She falters slightly at how quickly I adhere to her request, but then she narrows her eyes at me.

"I mean it," she warns, holding up a finger.

"I know," I reply in a bored tone. "Anyway, if that's all, I have to get back to work."

"If that's what you can call this," she remarks haughtily as she drops her hands and turns on her heel.

Something somewhere deep inside of me, snaps.

I rush *Aunt Celeste,* pin her body against the door with mine and chuckle into her ear.

"You don't remember me, do you?" I ask quietly into her ear.

"Let me go or I'll scream!" she threatens, her tone rising slightly.

"I was just wondering what that sounds like," I say as I turn her around, wrap a hand around her throat, and reach for the waistband of her pants. Moving quickly, I pull them down to her thighs, then drop to my knees and run my tongue up her slit.

She closes her eyes tightly as her body begins to tremble.

In fear?

In lust?

Who the fuck knows or cares, but I'm going to give her something to think about.

I wrap my arms around her legs and pry them apart as much as I can before I gently trail her slit again.

She gasps as I press the tip of my tongue against her clit and give it a gentle lick.

When she attempts to push me away, I bury my face between her legs, flicking my tongue against her clit, nibbling it, and making her pussy so fucking wet that I can feel her juices starting to pool on my chin. The way her coarse hairs tickle my cheeks makes me hungrier for her.

I assume that I'm playing with a still unpopped cherry and I'm so tempted to make this bitch bleed for me.

Aunt Celeste places her hands on the door with her palms flat, and more than likely praying for the will to get me to stop, but I'm not done yet.

Not until she comes on my tongue.

Then, and *only* then, will I let her walk out.

And it's not as hard as I thought it would be.

One more gentle nibble of her clit as I slip a finger into her ass, and I can feel her pussy starting to convulse.

Getting to my feet, I use the back of my hand to wipe my mouth, then reach down to pull her up her pants.

"Get out of my place of business, lady. And if you come back, perhaps *I'll* call the cops myself," I tell her with a grin.

Her face is flushed.

Her legs are trembling.

But try as she might, she can't hide the look in her eyes that I see from time to time with most of my female clients.

"Not interested," I say with a smirk as I shake my head. "Maybe you can go home and pray this one away."

CHAPTER FIVE

CELESTE

"Are you okay?"

Ava's hand is resting on my shoulder as gently as her voice.

I've been home for at least thirty-five minutes, but I haven't gone inside.

I don't know what just happened or why I felt like I needed it as much as I did. I haven't been able to go inside and face her, because if she knew where I had been all afternoon, she'd be rife with questions that I'm not in the right mind frame to answer.

Shame you don't have your ruler, he said, and I can't help but think that was supposed to jog my memory.

When was the last time I held a ruler? Ten years ago? Fifteen? I can't remember because it was never a big deal to me.

I sit up instantly and drop my face from my hands.

"I'm fine, Ava. Go inside and get dinner started," I say in a rush as I walk past her and head down into the basement.

There are boxes upon boxes piled up along the wall from when I used to teach. I had to stop when Ava's parents died, so I could stay home with her full-time and raise her to the best of my ability.

"Aunt Celeste—"

"Ava, I said to start dinner, please!" I bellow over my shoulder.

I can hear the shuffle of her footsteps as she moves away from the basement door and then listen as they move across the floor until she's in the room I told her to be in.

I glance around until my eyes land on a box cutter. I grab it then dutifully start to open all of the boxes that contain mementos from years long past, flipping through yearbooks, letters from parents, commendations, and even a few reprimands.

I blow out my breath twenty minutes later when I feel like I'm never going to solve the mystery, until I notice one box that I'd missed.

Reaching for it with trembling hands, I set it on the floor, open the tape with the box cutter, then sit on my heels.

I have to do some digging before I find the yearbooks for that school, and I have to flip through at least five of them until I find the one I'm looking for.

Theology I.

My eyes begin to search the faces of the boys in the picture, wracking my brain for some kind of memory of any of them, and then I see him.

Shoulders hunched, leaning away from me in the front row of the photo. So much anger and disdain in eyes so goddamn unique that I'm kicking myself for not placing him the moment I saw him.

I look down at the rows of names and my chin drops to my chest.

Finley Bradshaw.

"Fuck," I mutter quietly as I toss the yearbook back into the box and go back to putting all of them in their rightful places.

———

My breath comes out in small shudders as I wait for the phone to be answered. I've been locked in my room for the past ten minutes debating making this call, and when I decided that I had to, I felt myself dreading the conversation.

"*Bay City Body Arts,* this is Rya speaking," comes the cheerful tone.

I close my eyes tightly.

I never would have placed Rya because Finley attended an all-boys high school, so the likelihood of seeing her outside of school would have been slim to no chance.

"Hello?" she asks, cheerfully.

I clear my throat nervously as my finger begins to spin around the phone cord, until I finally let out a breath and speak.

"Yes, hello," I begin, my voice cracking slightly. Rolling my eyes, I try again, "Hello Rya, this is Celeste, Ava's aunt. She left her aftercare paperwork at the shop I think, and I was wondering if I could speak to Finley and take some notes?"

Rya sighs. "I'll ask him. Please hold."

The drumming of my fingers along the nightstand is the only sound I hear besides that of my heart beating loudly in my ears.

A few tense moments later and the phone is picked up again. "I'm sorry, Celeste. Finley said you can Google it."

I let out a heavy sigh.

"Thank you," I tell her softly as I disconnect the call.

I want to apologize to him for being the person I had been so many years ago, but I think his little display in his room was more than enough for him.

Perhaps he thinks it's some kind of revenge and that now I'll treat people better, but I changed after Ava's parents died.

I was new to the Church when I took the job as a teacher, and he frustrated me beyond belief.

Since he was something of a problem at home too, his parents gave me permission to use corporal punishment on him.

Maybe I went too far, maybe I didn't go far enough, but he has no right ...

The thought trails off as I get to my feet and place the phone on the nightstand. I tuck my hair behind my ears as I start toward my bedroom door, then into the hallway.

I'm not entirely sure what Ava cooked up for dinner tonight, but it smells divine.

Divinity; something I just lost today, I think miserably as I make my way down the stairs.

"Hey, Aunt Celeste," Ava greets me in a cautious, cheerful tone. "I was just about to come up and get you."

I give her a small smile as I continue toward the dining room, so damn sure that she can see the shame I'm wearing like some kind of invisible giant scarlet letter.

"Did you have a nice day out?" she asks me a few minutes later once she's set the roast on the table. I look down at my hands in my lap as Ava purses her lips, then goes about fixing me a plate.

I don't want her to be angry with me, and I don't want her to admonish me for what happened, either.

"I watched TV for the most part," she offers as she sets a plate down in front of me then makes one for herself. "There was a great rom-com on earlier. I'll have to see if I can find it streaming and we can watch it tonight if you want."

"That would be nice," I say as I reach for my fork.

"Aunt Celeste?"

The piece of roast is hovering an inch from my open mouth as I glance over at her.

"Aren't we going to say grace?"

Grace. The one thing I don't deserve.

My mouth becomes dry as I set the fork down and nod. I fold my hands in front of my face, fingers intertwined so tightly that I'm afraid I'll break them if I don't ease up some, then ask Ava to say the prayer to bless our dinner

I'm not worthy of speaking to God tonight.

CHAPTER SIX

FINLEY

I yawn and then cover my face with a hand as I lean my head back against the headrest. I was supposed to come over tomorrow for dinner before we got into a pissing contest, and if Rya knew where I was right now, she'd have a fucking fit.

I made sure to park a few spaces down so that Her Holiness and Ava wouldn't be able to see me if they looked out their windows for any reason.

I haven't been able to get the taste of her out of my damn mouth. I ended up shooting whiskey after I closed the shop, and it still lingers.

I can't tell if it's punishment or intoxication, but here I am. Parked on *her* street, watching *her* house, wondering what the fuck is wrong with me all of a sudden.

Raking a hand back through my hair, I sit up and put one hand on the steering wheel and the other on the key hanging from the ignition.

This isn't like me at all.

I've hated her for as long as I could fucking remember, and seeing her again only served to drudge up all of those memories again.

I can't believe I mentioned the ruler, I think with a groan.

If she still had the damn thing, I'd more than likely try to break it on her ass the way she did mine.

"I gotta get out of here," I mumble as I turn the key and start my car.

Turning to glance over my shoulder, I begin to ease my car back a bit so I can pull out and drive away, when something catches my attention out of the corner of my eye.

Putting the vehicle in park, I press the button to lower my window and let out a low whistle.

When Ava glances around the street with confusion on her face, I chuckle. "Hey!"

She raises an eyebrow when she sees me waving at her, then holds up a finger. I watch patiently as she disappears around the side of the house with a garbage bag, then reappears, wiping her palms on her jeans.

"What are you doing here?" she asks curiously as she leans down slightly and peers in through the window.

"I got lost. Thought I would stop and see if I could get the GPS going," I lie with a shrug and friendly smile.

She grins as she folds her arms on the window frame, and I chuckle.

"Wanna go for a ride?"

The words are out of my mouth before I have a chance to second guess the idea, and the way her eyes light up tells me that she's not going to turn me down.

"Yeah," she replies enthusiastically, "just let me lock up quick."

I run a hand over my face and internalize a groan as Ava runs back toward her house. I have no idea what the hell possessed me to ask her to get into my car, and I'm not sure what I'm going to do with her.

She's not the prize in this.

She's the pawn, and I have to figure out how to use her accordingly.

After a few tense moments of me trying to think of a way to talk myself out of this, Ava is pulling the passenger door open and slipping into the seat.

"Buckle up," I tell her softly with a quick glance. 'I have a feeling we're going to be in for a hell of a night."

We find ourselves at a small park in the middle of town. I figured it would be the safest place to take her and I've been pushing her on the swing she jumped on the moment we got out of the car.

Ava seems to be in good spirits, happy enough to talk about anything, and I decide now is as good a time as any to find out about the bitch that made my teenage years a walking nightmare.

"Hey, so how come your aunt goes by Celeste now?" I ask nonchalantly as I give her back another gentle push.

Ava straightens her legs, then tucks them on the way back, and I give her another dutiful shove.

"Ava?" I ask after the third push, still not having received an answer.

"Because that's her name," she calls back as her body swings up into the air.

I catch the chains when she comes back toward me and bring her to a halt.

"What? I thought she was a nun?" I ask, peering around at her.

"She is, but only sometimes."

I let go of the chains as I move to take the swing next to Ava and give her an incredulous look. "How?"

"She used to teach at a bunch of boys' schools when she first decided that was what she wanted to do with her life. Be a nun, I mean." Ava tucks her hair behind her ears before she continues. "Anyway, after Momma and Daddy left, the state asked her if she'd be willing to take me in. She agreed, and after some haggling with the Archdiocese, they basically released her from the 'draft' to take care of me. They've been good to us about it so far."

I turn my eyes away and stare at the seesaw in the middle of the park. In a weird way, I feel that basically what she's telling me in layman's terms is that her aunt got stuck with her, so she took it out on me?

It only makes me angrier for some reason.

"Oh."

"Hey, how did you know that Aunt Celeste was a nun?" she asks me suddenly.

I force a smile onto my face and shrug. "She has that look, I guess."

Getting to my feet, I hold a hand out toward Ava and lead her over to the seesaw. "Come on, let's have some fun."

CHAPTER SEVEN

CELESTE

I turn over on my side and pull my pillow over my head. It's damn near impossible for me to fall asleep—again—and I'm going to end up taking it out on Ava if I don't get some rest.

I had to grow up quickly when she became my responsibility. I was barely able to care for myself, but when the state awarded her to me, I knew that the last thing in the world I would allow myself to do would be to let her down.

It took some doing before I was brave enough to request a meeting with the Archbishop, and when I finally found the nerve, I knew that he would have to see things my way.

At least that was my hope.

And when he did, I almost fell out of my chair. Granted, he stripped me of my privileges in the Church, however, every day that I wake up and see Ava blossoming into the young woman that I know her parents would have been proud to call theirs, I become less bothered by it.

Outside, a car door opens and closes, followed by the sound of tires slowly moving down the street.

I roll the other way and hold the pillow tighter against my ears.

It's not unusual for people to be out at all hours; it's just grating on my nerves tonight, a little more than usual.

Probably because I never had the chance to be a wild, free spirit myself, I think glumly.

My parents raised very good children.

We weren't allowed to swear under their roof, drinking and

smoking were absolutely out of the question, and we attended Mass every Sunday as instructed.

I fell so in love with the concept of Heaven at such a young age, that I knew the only thing I ever wanted to be when I grew up was a nun.

And now I can't even be that anymore.

I sigh heavily as I toss the pillow to the floor and brush my hair out of my eyes. A single tear rolls down my cheek as I think about everything I gave up to achieve my dream, only to have it snatched away.

But I refuse to blame Ava.

She needed a home, family to take care of her, and I happened to be the only one around.

And I know it's not having to give up my life for Ava that's bothering me.

It's what he did to me in that room.

I haven't been able to stop thinking about any of it.

The way he held me against the door with his body.

The way he turned to force me to face him.

The way he gripped my throat like he wanted to snap it.

Then the way he lowered himself to his knees and ...

Stop thinking about it, I admonish myself when I feel my core start to become warm.

I get up from my chair, letting it slam against the wall behind my desk. I'm so frustrated with him at this point, that I hope the sudden movement stuns him into behaving for the rest of the period.

Finley Bradshaw and his ragtag, misfit friends glance up at me. They seem to be taken aback by my sudden outburst, while he seems to find it amusing.

"Sorry, Your Holiness," he begins with a smirk dancing across his lips. "I didn't realize that having a quiet chat would get your panties in a bunch."

I make my way down the rows of desks straight to the back of the room, and I wedge myself between his and the student's in front of him.

"Do you like spending your afternoons in detention, Mr. Bradshaw?" I grind out as calmly as I can.

"Not really," he responds breezily. "But at least I know that's the only time one of us will get some wood."

My mouth becomes a tight line of anger as I remind myself that he's just a child, and prone to ridiculous outbursts like this.

Do I enjoy punishing him after school? No, and that's only because it still doesn't seem to get anything through his thick skull.

If it did, then we wouldn't have to go through the archaic procedure almost every single afternoon during the week.

"Unless you'd like to join us for an afternoon session, I suggest you regain control of yourselves," I snap at his friends.

"Yeah, guys. I don't know if a gangbang is in the Bible," Finley chimes in with an eye roll.

"Get out of my classroom!" I boom at him as my hands become tight fists by my sides. "Go to the principal's office and stay there for the remainder of the day!"

———

I let out a heavy sigh and wonder if that was the exact day when everything went so wrong.

CHAPTER EIGHT

FINLEY

A laugh escapes meat Ava's obvious joy each and every time the seesaw tips and she ends up on top. She uses her feet to push off the ground as hard as she can, and I've almost fallen off my end a time or two.

And while I study her happiness, I can't help but wonder how much of it has to do with her aunt.

Did this lady finally change and learn how to treat children, or is she still the dragon lady I remember, and Ava's merely masking the bullshit she's been going through?

I never had the chance to put on a façade.

I had always been an angry child and I even spent one summer in juvie because of Her Holiness.

She didn't like the fact that I followed her back to the convent one afternoon after *detention*, and threatened to shove her ruler up her ass if she ever hit me with it again.

She had the head nun call the police and then lied to them when they arrived. She said that I had been stalking and threatening her, so instead of having summer school to catch up on my grades, I had a mini-vacation in the local detention center for unruly youths.

"So," I begin as I push against the ground and send her back down to the bottom. "You were saying that your parents left. Where did they go?"

Ava shrugs. "I'm not entirely sure. I think they died, but I was so out of it when they were telling me, that I never got the entire story."

"And it doesn't bother you? Not knowing for sure, I mean?" I ask as

I dig my heels into the grass and bring our juvenile playtime to an abrupt halt.

I'm starting to get bored with this, and I didn't bring her out here to have a little *feelings* chat.

"Nope."

She shakes her head, her blonde hair swaying from side to side. I arch an eyebrow at her as I smile, then clear my throat.

"Well, then if it doesn't bother you, it doesn't bother me," I conclude as I run a hand back through my hair.

"I should probably be getting back home soon," she remarks as she motions for me to settle the seesaw down on her end.

"Why?"

"Because Aunt Celeste is going to notice that I'm gone soon... if she hasn't already," she answers, dryly.

"You could," I begin slowly. "Or we can stay a little longer, then I can drop you off."

Ava purses her lips as she gets to her feet, and puts a hand on her hip. I can tell she's weighing her options, so I'm going to have to sweeten the deal.

I climb off my end and walk the few steps toward her, standing a mere few inches away from her, I smirk when her body starts to visibly tense.

"Got a crush, little girl?" I tease her in a soft tone.

I brush some loose strands of hair out of her eyes, and lean my face closer to hers, my smirk turning into a grin when she begins to tremble.

"Yup; you've got a crush all right," I confirm with a low chuckle. I trail a finger down the side of her face, before I let it rest on her chin. "What are we going to do about that?"

"Um ... what?"

Ava stutters and stammers as her chin begins to quiver, and I find myself becoming amused by the entire situation.

I'm not going to fuck her, although I'm pretty sure that's what she's expecting, but I'm not going to let her just walk away from tonight without a little something special, either.

"Follow me," I instruct her as I jerk my head to the left then start to lead the way back toward the pair of small bouncy horses we passed on the way in.

Without pausing to see if she's following me, I swing a leg over one and take a seat. Ava's visibly distressed, but it's clear she doesn't know why, and if she does, she doesn't understand.

She will shortly, I muse to myself as I chuckle and nod at the horse next to me.

"Have a seat, little girl. And watch the ink; I wouldn't want to have to touch it up so soon," I finish with a wry grin.

Ava's eyes never leave mine once they reconnect as she lifts a shaky leg over the side of her horse, then sits down. Her knuckles turn white as she grips the handles tightly, then licks her lips nervously.

"So, here's what I want you to do for me," I begin conversationally as I lean forward and rest my arms over the head of my horse. "I want you to start rocking."

She looks confused, but nods anyway and pushes her feet off the ground to get the horse moving.

I let out a laugh as I stand up and walk over to settle behind her.

"Not like that," I chide her as I place my hands on her sides. "Like this."

Ava looks up at me as I begin to guide her into grinding her hips against the playground toy; a smirk spreading across my lips.

"Think you can manage?" I ask softly into her ear, sending a chill down her body.

She closes her eyes for a moment, then begins to grind down against the horse. I keep my hands where they are, still guiding her in the way that I like to be fucked, because she's obviously new at this.

"Don't you look pretty, little girl? Does that feel good?" I whisper as I use my fingertips to trail her arms. When my hands reach her wrists, I use a knee to give the horse a push. "I know you can go faster than that, Ava."

She lets out a whimper as she moves her hips a little faster, grinds down a little harder, and her knuckles start turning whiter.

"Just like that," I tell her, as I grip her wrists and hold them in place.

Each time her body rocks back into mine, I find myself thinking of Her Holiness and how angry she'd be if she could see me now.

Definitely worth a ruler across the ass, I think wryly as Ava's whimpers start to get louder.

"I ... can't ..."

"Yes you can," I assure her as I knee the tail end of the horse, causing her body to jump again. "And you're doing such a good job, too."

"I am?" she gasps out as she grinds down even harder.

I smile. "You're almost there, aren't you, Ava?"

I dig my nails into the flesh of her wrists as she continues to rock, her movements becoming a little more restricted with each buck.

"What's ... happening ... to ... me ..." she stammers uncertainly before another strangled sound escapes her.

"You're showing me what you've got," I say, my lips an inch from her ear. "And it's definitely what I like."

Ava inhales sharply as I let go of her wrists and run my fingertips lightly up her arm. Her skin instantly becomes covered in goosebumps and she attempts to lean back against me, but I move away, walk toward the front of the horse and look into her eyes.

"Be a good girl, Ava," I tell her in a stern tone as I push her hair out of her face. "Come for me."

It takes a few more rocks and ragged breaths, but when she *finally* finishes, I stand up and grin.

"See? I knew you had it in you."

Reaching into the pocket of my jeans, I jingle my keys in my hand before I give her a nod and wave.

"Go home before Celeste realizes you're missing."

Sending her home smelling like pussy and playground dust is going to get a hell of a reaction from Her Holiness, and I kinda wish I could be there to witness it.

"What?" she sputters as she clumsily tries to dismount the horse.

I walk quickly toward the curb where my car is parked, hop in, turn on the engine, then pull out onto the vacant street.

In the rearview I can see Ava standing in the middle of the dimly lit street, arms wrapped around her shaking body, looking alone and afraid.

Now she knows how her fucking aunt used to make me feel, I think as I reach the corner and take a left turn.

"Out of sight, out of mind, Ava," I mutter to myself as I continue on the way home.

CHAPTER NINE

CELESTE

The front door opens slowly, then closes quietly.

I've been sitting in the dark living room for the past hour wondering where in the world Ava's been, and now that she's trying to sneak back in unnoticed, I know that she was probably up to no good.

At first, I was worried, then as I sat and listened to the hands on the clock mounted on the wall continue to tick seconds, minutes, and hours away, I became angry.

And now that she's finally home, I feel numb.

She's still alive and that's what should matter, but I can't let this go unpunished.

I take a deep breath as I get to my feet and walk toward the doorway. She'll have to pass the living room to get to her bedroom and I'm going to make sure that she knows she's been caught in the act.

I listen silently as her footsteps shuffle along the floor, then when I know she's mere inches away from where I'm standing, I reach for the light switch on the wall next to me and flip it.

Ava gasps as the living room becomes flush with light. I cross my arms over my chest as I struggle to find the words.

I have to make her understand how disappointed I am in her actions, but I also have to be careful how I say it.

I don't know if I said something earlier that caused her to sneak out, and it's the only thing staying my hand at the moment.

"Aunt Celeste—"

I raise a hand to cut her off as she begins to wring her hands nervously, her face turning crimson.

In shame?

In embarrassment?

Or maybe her actions are a reflection of the defeat she's probably feeling now that she's been caught?

"You're grounded for a month," I finally manage to say in a steady tone.

I don't want my voice to reflect the absolute rage that I'm starting to feel again at her deception, because then she'll become just as angry, and we'll wake up the entire neighborhood screaming at each other until the other one gives.

"Go to your room. We'll talk about this in the morning, which if you haven't noticed, is in a few hours."

I finish the conversation in an even enough tone to let her know that I won't be entertaining any excuses she may be trying to fabricate.

And it also warns her that I won't be accepting lies at the breakfast table either.

"But –"

"Go to sleep, Ava!" I shout at her in frustration.

Her face crumples and tears immediately begin to roll down her cheeks. She puts her hands to her face and runs to her room, slamming the door shut behind her.

Turning the light off, I shake my head as I leave the living room and decide that maybe it won't be so hard to sleep now that she's home.

Ava quietly sets a plate of scrambled eggs, hash browns, pancakes, and bacon down in front of me before she sits down at the other end of the table.

Normally, she doesn't cook this big of a breakfast because she doesn't usually finish her meals, however, I think the reason she may have done this is to give us time to talk about her little disappearing act last night.

I reach for the cloth napkin and give it a quick whip, before laying it on my lap and smoothing it in place.

Without a word, I reach for my knife and fork and cut a small section off one of the pancakes, then place it in my mouth and raise my eyes toward Little Miss Defiance.

When she steals a glance up at me, she can tell that I'm still plenty angry from the night before, and she slumps down a little in her chair.

I clear my throat as I cut away another piece and pop it into my mouth, enjoying the silence between us for the time being.

What Ava doesn't seem to understand though, is that I'm giving her the opportunity to explain herself without me having to ask any questions.

I reach for my cup of coffee, raise it to my lips, then take a sip. I keep my eyes trained on her as I set the cup back down on the table, then reach for my fork again.

This girl is acting much more dense than she really is, and it's starting to make me angry all over again.

"Um," she finally says tentatively as she tucks her hair behind her ear. "I guess I owe you an explanation."

I set my fork down and give her my undivided attention. I won't speak until I absolutely have to, because I don't want to upset her and stop her from telling me where she was for almost the entire night.

I clear my throat as I fold one arm over the other on the table, and lean slightly forward.

Do you ever, I think evenly.

"I was taking out the trash last night and ..." she looks down, biting her lower lip so damn hard, I'm surprised she hasn't drawn blood yet.

"And?" I press in a stern tone.

Ava takes a deep breath as she looks up at me. "You have to promise me that you won't overreact."

I roll my eyes and nod once in agreement.

"And Finley was outside."

I sit up so quickly that when I inadvertently bump the table, the utensils clatter slightly.

"Wait, let me finish," she pleads, her eyes becoming dangerously watery.

I grind my teeth together and lean back in my seat. I gesture with my hand for her to continue and do my best to hold onto my end of the bargain of not *overreacting* to anything else she may divulge.

Or leave out.

"Okay, so he got my attention, and I went over to talk to him for a little bit." Ava pauses long enough to look up at me before she diverts her eyes toward the wall, then continues, "And he said he was lost, so I was going to give him directions... but then I got in his car."

"That's enough, Ava. Go to your room and stay there," I tell her as I get to my feet.

"No, I'm not done yet, Aunt Celeste. You have to let me finish."

I place the tips of my fingers firmly against the table, close my eyes tightly, and against my better judgment, nod again.

As Ava tells me all about their sordid little escapade the night before, I wonder why I'm losing all of the anger I felt when she snuck in.

And why it with was her instead of me.

CHAPTER TEN

FINLEY

"What the fuck did you do now?" Ry's voice barks at me through the phone.

"Good morning to you too, big sister," I reply groggily through a laugh.

"It's afternoon, and I'm serious, Finley; what did you do? That crazy lady has called the shop five times in a row demanding to talk to you."

I sit up in bed as I rub my face tiredly with a hand. "Which one, Ry?"

I didn't mean for the question to come out as cocky as it did, but I'm used to clients taking my personality for more than it's worth and assuming I want to move in with them or some shit.

Rya laughs despite herself, then lets out a heavy sigh. "Celeste."

I stifle a yawn as I lie back down and close my eyes.

"To her? Nothing."

"Fin—"

"Relax, Ry. I didn't do anything with her sweet, little thing either. She's still innocent. Sort of," I finish wryly.

"You need to tell me what you did so I know how to handle this if she comes in," she says as patiently as she can.

"Call the cops if she shows up. There's no discussion to be had," I answer simply as I turn on my side.

"Hold on."

Ry covers the receiver with her hand as she greets a client, then sets the phone down on the desk. I yawn again as I can feel myself starting to get sleepy. *Afternoon? What time is it?*

I pull the phone away from my ear, then chuckle when I see that it's ten past two and wonder when the last time was that I slept so damn well.

A few moments later, my sister picks up the phone. "I'm coming over. Starla is going to watch the desk for me, since I feel like we can't have this conversation over the phone."

"Ry—"

"See you in twenty," she cuts me off before disconnecting the call.

I groan as I toss my cell phone onto the nightstand then turn onto my back.

I'm not in the mood for lectures.

Especially not since I woke up feeling like today was going to be a good one, but I guess I *did* cross a line I shouldn't have.

Oh well, fuck it.

Rolling my shoulder, I try my best to get comfortable again, but the impending "talking to" that's headed my way is inhibiting my ability to fall back to sleep.

With a grunt, I reach over for my phone and tap out a quick message to my sister to tell her that I'll take care of things and to stay at the shop.

I place the phone on my chest as I rub my eyes with the palms of my hands. It takes Ry a few minutes, probably spent deciding what to do, but she finally agrees to stay put if I promise to make things right.

With a grin on my lips and a new plan formulating in my brain, I say what I need to in order to put her mind at ease.

I promise, Ry.

My hands slide down the slick, bathroom tiles as I stand under the hot torrent of water.

Ava is a casualty in a war that she doesn't even know she has become part of, but those are the breaks, and I'm sure she'll get over it eventually.

Besides, it's not like I fucked her.

I didn't place a finger on her, or *in* her, so I think I actually made my move against Her Holiness in the suavest way possible.

Can't go to the pen for watching a girl practically fucking a toy horse until she comes, I muse with a chuckle as I turn around and finally begin to wash the shampoo out of my hair.

I'm actually kind of proud of myself for thinking of that on the spot. When I took Ava to the park, I had no fucking clue as to what the night would entail, and it was better than just letting her get away scot-free.

As I turn the water off and step out of the bathtub, I shrug and repeat, *she'll get over it,* to myself more times than I want to.

Maybe she will.

Maybe she won't.

Either way, the blame should go squarely where it belongs; on Her Holiness.

I clasp my hands over my head as I stretch, then blow out a heavy breath.

Sometimes, wars are won when the enemy has no idea that a move is being made, and I'm going to make one hell of a power move before the day is over.

CHAPTER ELEVEN
CELESTE

"Ava!"

Her bedroom door creaks open slowly, and I watch from the end of the hallway as she peeks her head out and barely has the courage to look me in the eyes.

"I have something I want you to do for me," I advise her as calmly as I can.

She steps out into the hallway and makes her way tediously slowly toward where I'm standing, then takes a deep breath. "Yes, Aunt Celeste?"

I give her a once over before I beckon for her to follow me into the kitchen. Grabbing my purse from the counter, I pull out some money and hold it out to her. "Do the groceries for me, please."

She takes the money without a word, then heads for the living room. I wait patiently while I hear the closet door open then close, followed by the jingling of her set of car keys, then the front door closing firmly behind her.

I run a hand over my face as I lean against the kitchen counter and think.

He stole her innocence from her by somehow managing to talk her into that little performance, and I'm not going to stand for it.

Rolling my eyes, I make my way toward the front door and crack it open to make sure that the driveway is empty.

I don't know what it is that this boy thinks he's accomplishing by pulling this damn stunt, but I'm not going to let him bully me any longer.

Ava's mental health is on the line now and I have to stand up for her.

I arch an eyebrow when I get to Finley's neighborhood. I stop at the end of the long, dirty alleyway before digging my phone out of my purse and bringing up the email again.

Stepping back slightly, I glance at the street sign a few feet away, then shake my head.

This is the exact address that Rya sent to me, but what kind of place does he live in that I would have to walk down a desolate alley to reach his front door?

Squaring my shoulders, I tell myself that I've had more than enough time to talk my way out of this, and if I've made it this far, I should at least knock on his damn door.

Tossing the phone back into my purse, I pull the zipper closed, then start down the alleyway.

Nothing about this should surprise me anymore. This entire situation is completely fucked all the way around, and I have to be the adult in this situation.

Just like always.

I never got the chance to be a child myself, and it was no one's doing but my own.

I was raised by good parents, in a Godly household, and early on during childhood decided that I wanted to take the path I had finally been able to.

Only it was cruelly swiped away a few years later.

I blink rapidly when I find myself standing in front of a side door, not realizing that I had been so lost in thought on the short walk down the alley that I've already reached it.

Stepping back slightly, I glance up the decaying brick building, take in the dusty industrial windows, then grind my teeth together.

Finley Bradshaw may have gotten his outward appearance together, but this place that he calls home shows that he's still exactly the same on the inside as he was so many years ago.

Rotten, unkempt, and miserable.

Here goes nothing, I think as I raise my fist and bang it against the rusting, industrial door.

When no one answers immediately, I knock again, then kick the fucking door in anger a few seconds later.

"Rya, I told you not—"

I glance up sharply at the sound of his voice. When his eyes lock on mine, he lets out a laugh and crosses his arms on the windowsill, giving me an amused glance.

"Well, well, well. Are you stalking me, *Aunt Celeste?* That's a crime, you know," he finishes pointedly with a smirk.

"I'm not leaving until you open this door," I bark up Finley, who shakes his head and disappears from sight.

After what feels like an eternity later, he pulls the door open, places one hand against the door frame, then leans out. I take an inadvertent step back, not wanting this hooligan so close to me, but it only makes his smirk shift into a grin.

"What can I do for you?" he asks before he sucks his teeth.

"Stay away from Ava. She told me all about last night and I've had it with your bullshit, Finley Bradshaw—"

"Yeah, I know. You've had enough of my 'bullshit' for years, but I never did get a chance to pay you back for how you treated me and made me feel, did I?" he cuts me off evenly.

The smile drops from his lips, his eyes harden, and his jaw becomes square and prominent.

"And you think that abusing a minor makes you some kind of big shot, tough guy?" I snarl at him.

"I didn't touch her."

I don't know what comes over me, but all I see is red. I reach forward and slap him across the face.

If he's playing a game with me—

"Oh, that was definitely the wrong move, Your Holiness," he snarls as he reaches for my wrist and grips in his hand like a fist. "You've hit me one too many fucking times in my life."

Before I have a chance to fight him off, to get my arm out of his grip, Finley Bradshaw gives me a violent jerk into his home and slams the door closed behind us.

CHAPTER TWELVE

FINLEY

I have to drag her up the fucking stairs for the most part, but when she finally composes herself and gets to her feet, I keep a firm grip on her arm as I push the door open to my home.

"Sister Emma Agnes Tremaine," I begin slowly as I finally let her arm go and kick the door closed behind us. "I never thought I'd have to see you again, but when you walked into my shop, I knew that I wouldn't be able to pass up the opportunity to teach *you* a fucking lesson for once."

She turns quickly to give me a deadly stare, but I can see her lower lip trembling, and I know that she's afraid of me. With a smirk and a shrug, I turn around and slide the bolts across the door to lock it, then give her my undivided attention.

"The thing is, I didn't know that you'd bring me something to use. How does it feel, *Aunt Celeste?* To be beaten into submission my fucking way, and me not even having to lay a finger on you to get it done?"

"If you think there's some score to settle with me, that's fine, but you leave my niece out of this," she warns in a trembling tone.

"Or else, what? You'll paddle me with a ruler?" I ask, shaking my head. "Tell you what, let's try it and see how it ends this time."

I walk by her, my shoulder bumping her on the way, and head to my bedroom. In the closet, I have the exact same ruler that she used on me when she felt that I was "misbehaving."

It was the one thing I stole on prank day in senior year. Most of my friends did the usual; hiding frogs in the teachers' lounge, putting hard liquor in a batch of punch to be served at lunchtime, and some even put stink bombs in the vent.

But this ...

I run a hand down my face as I reach into the closet and pull out the two-foot long, six-inch wide, heavy wooden ruler and close my eyes.

I have to force myself not to feel every indignity crash against me like a monsoon trying to knock me off my feet. I have to take deep, steadying breaths to try and not remember how painful it had been to sit after the first, second, and third time she had done it to me.

With this exact same fucking ruler.

It was my prize when I finally graduated because I reasoned she could never use it on another student again, though no one else ever told me if she had.

She had it in for me and I never knew why.

And now, she's going to tell me what it was about me that she hated so much once and for fucking all.

Stalking back to where I left the bitch, her favorite instrument of punishment firmly in hand, I do everything I can to maintain my temper when I see her again.

She's standing in the open space that I use as a living room, arms crossed over her chest, and watching the cars drive by on the highway in the distance.

Maybe if I paddle her hard enough with this fucking thing, she'll end up in the middle of those racing vehicles, and all of the problems she caused me—all of the fucking mental scars I still carry, will end with her.

"Look familiar?" I snarl at her, slapping the ruler swiftly against my leg to get her undivided attention.

Her Holiness glances at me with a stoic look on her face, and I feel my anger falter slightly.

"Is that what all of this is about, Finley?" she asks me tiredly.

"Do you have any idea what kind of impact this fucking had on me as a child?" I all but shout at her.

"And as an adult as well, I see," she responds softly as she lets out a sigh and shakes her head. *Aunt Celeste* turns her eyes back toward the window again. "You were an unruly child. The only one in my classroom that would always give me grief. I was young at the time too, you know. Not as young as you were, but I was in the middle of losing everything I wanted in life to help Ava."

"I'm sorry, but when did this become about you?" I snap at her.

THE DEVIL'S MELANCHOLY

"You raised welts on my body. You made it so that I hated going to school, hated seeing my friends every day, hated my fucking *self* because I felt like I wasn't good enough to be in your precious classroom."

She turns around to face me and shakes her head as she raises her hands in the air, then drops them to her sides.

"I'm sorry. Is that what you want, Finley? Because I am. Had I known what this was going to do to you in the long run, I wouldn't have done it."

I give her a level stare.

This is all bullshit.

I can smell it in the air like low-hanging clouds of smog on the Los Angeles freeway.

"Great, so you're sorry, but you know what? I'm not. Not for what I had Ava do, and not for what I'm going to do to you."

Aunt Celeste scoffs as she tucks her hair behind her ears.

"Then get it over with already."

CHAPTER THIRTEEN
CELESTE

With the slightest idea gently floating in my mind of what he's planning on doing, I cross the room and stand a few feet away from him.

"Well?" I ask him softly. "What is it that needs to be done to get you out of our lives once and for all?"

A malicious twinkle shines in those eyes that I once found to be so unique and beautiful, and I have to fight the urge to take a step away from him.

"Go to the couch and bend over, obviously," he instructs with a nod and a grin.

I grind my teeth together as I remind myself that this is for Ava, then do as I'm told.

Dutifully, I lay my body across the arm of the couch and brace myself for the impact that doesn't come right away.

"No, I'm pretty sure that my ass was bare, *Aunty*. Drop 'em; this will bring back fond memories if we do it the right way."

A flush of red goes through my body as I realize that he wants to embarrass me as well as punish me for what he's held onto for all of these years.

With shaky hands, I reach back for my jeans, pushing them down, then my panties next.

Finley lets out a low whistle as he takes his place behind me on the couch, then reaches for my ass, giving one of my cheeks a firm squeeze.

"Who knew you were packing this?" he muses with a laugh. "Shame I'm gonna have to fuck it up now."

"Get your goddamn hands off me and get it over with," I bark at him over my shoulder before I bury my face into the cushion and try to brace myself.

"Ever the control freak," he grumbles.

Finley clears his throat as he gently taps the ruler against his leg a few times, then I feel the inevitable sting of pain as the wooden object is cracked against my ass.

"Ow!"

It comes out as a strangled sob as tears immediately begin to roll down my face. One strike and I'm already reduced to tears, and something tells me that he didn't swing it as hard as he could.

"Steady, steady, steady," he whispers as the air splits with the sound of the ruler being swung again.

It's the exact same thing I would yell at him whenever he buckled and his knees gave way.

"Steady on your feet, Mr. Bradshaw. If you're such a tough guy, then act like it."

Another *crack* against my flesh and I end up biting the cushion to keep from crying out again. "How's it feel, *Aunty?* Not as good as you probably hoped, huh?"

Another crack, followed by another, then one more, before he finally drops the ruler. It clatters against the hard, industrial floor, but I can barely hear it.

The sound of my heart pounding in my ears, and my uncontrollable sobs are more prominent than anything else in the room.

It's hard to breathe.

It's hard to see.

I never knew that something like this could cause so much damage to the psyche— more than it could repair it—and I feel ashamed of what I put him through.

Though, I wonder if it'll be gone when the pain is; these feelings of shame and remorse.

Finley leaves me half-lying on my stomach for a few moments, before he gently runs his hand across my ass.

"That's definitely gonna leave a few marks," he states with a chuckle.

But it's what he does next that I know will cause me enough shame to last me the rest of my life.

"Maybe I can make it all better, *Aunty?* What do you think?"

I shake my head vigorously, face still buried in the cushion, but if he sees me desperately rejecting his *idea*, he ignores it.

THE DEVIL'S MELANCHOLY

Or perhaps, he knows that I want him to disregard it.

Because he does.

The tip of his finger is gently running down my crack, the same way he ran it down my pussy a few days before.

I hear him clear his throat briefly, followed by the sound of his belt being undone, and the zipper on his jeans being pulled down.

"Steady," he says again, and I close my eyes tightly. My fingers dig into the cushions, and I pray to God that I won't rip holes into the damned things.

Finley spreads my cheeks apart roughly, then gently begins to tease my pucker hole with the tip of his tongue.

My lower lip begins to tremble harder.

He's taking everything from me, and I'm not entirely sure that I want him to stop.

He buries his face between my cheeks as he begins to lick, then spit on my hole. I bite down on my tongue to keep from moaning like a whore, especially since the pain is still stinging my flesh as a reminder that this is all my fault.

Finley lets out a soft moan as he uses the tip of his tongue to tease my hole open, then pulls his face away.

He slips the tips of his thumbs into my opening, and slides one in further as he quickly bites my ass, then begins to fuck my hole.

It's violent and painful, even with just his thumb.

"Steady, steady," he teases in a thick tone when he sees me struggling on the couch.

"Does Aunt Celeste like having her tight, little hole fucked?" he continues with a low, chuckle. "Because if you think this feels good ..."

Finley's voice trails off as he pulls his thumb out, then pushes me forward onto the couch. I don't even turn to look at him because I swear he would be able to see every shameful thing I've done in my entire life—and not just to him—written all over my face.

But I think that's what he wants, because he leans down and flips me onto my back with ease.

"Open your eyes, *Aunty*," he instructs quietly.

I shake my head as I place my hands on my face.

"Suit yourself," he replies in an amused tone.

The sound of his clothes making a gentle pile on the floor causes my legs to shake.

The way he lowers his body over mine, using his knee to pry my legs open, his breath gentle on my neck as he reaches his hands under my shirt and pushes it up over my face ... *So much shame.*

"Nice!" he remarks in appreciation as he pulls my breasts out of the bra and squeezes them roughly. "You really are a hottie, aren't you? I always had a bit of a crush on you, you know."

He ...what?

"I guess that's why I was such a bad boy. I wanted you to spank me," he continues mischievously. "I learned to enjoy it after a while, but you know how teenage rebellion is. I didn't want you to know it, so I always acted like I hated it. And you."

Before I have a chance to move my hands from my face and ask Finley why any of this has to happen then, I feel the head of his cock as he lines it up at my entrance.

"So, that's how I know you want me right now. Because you're acting the same way I used to."

He finishes with a grunt as he pushes himself roughly inside of me.

Another sob escapes me as the sensations of pain wrack my body again. Finley grinds out a groan as he pushes into me again. "I had a feeling this pussy hadn't been used yet. Who knew that I was actually right about something for once when it comes to you?"

The young boy that spent a lifetime feigning hate for me, begins to move his body against mine, his cock pushing in and out of me.

The intense feeling of pressure and pain; it causes the shame to slowly start to melt away into something else.

He runs a hand down my body as he begins to move a little faster. The sounds of his heavy breathing, his balls slapping against my ass, and the occasional chuckle greets my ears.

My hands move from my face to his forearms, fingernails digging into his flesh, as Finley fucks me a little harder.

He leans down and runs his tongue across my lips, then uses it to part them, lying his body down against mine.

His hips are still moving at a rapid pace, and Finley grabs a fistful of my hair as his tongue searches my mouth with a seduction and intensity that I've never experienced before.

He pushes his body off mine and pulls his cock out of me, I look up at him as the shame starts to wash over me again.

And I think he sees it, because he gives me a grin, raises a finger in the air, and makes a motion for me to turn around.

I shake my head and he laughs as he pulls me off the couch, then roughly spins me and pushes me against the couch again.

His hands grip my hips as he shoves his cock into me again, and continues fucking me.

My tits are bouncing so hard and fast. My pussy is warm, wet, and aching for each and every thrust.

Finley reaches forward, grabs a fistful of my hair, and bends me back toward him.

And then it happens.

I let out the moan I've been struggling so desperately to hold onto. To let him think that I wanted this was something that I hadn't planned on doing.

"Good girl," he whispers into my ear with a soft chuckle. "That's exactly what I wanted since I first laid eyes on you. For you to moan like the whore I knew I could turn you into."

Pushing me roughly away from him, he raises a foot on the couch to *steady* himself, then fucks me harder, rougher, and faster until I feel a warm rush spill out of his cock and deep into me.

"Good, God," he breathes as he lets my hips go and pulls out of me.

Finley drops onto the couch next to where I'm still prostrated and reaches over to give my ass a firm slap.

He glances down at his dick and nudges me gently with his elbow. "Look. I finally got baptized," he mocks as he shakes his slightly bloodstained, fluid covered cock at me.

I turn my face away from him, hoping that he isn't able to catch onto the feelings of confusion that are flowing through me.

I've always wanted to hate Finley Bradshaw for being such a disobedient, little son of a bitch, but ... now, I don't know what I feel.

"Hey, so make sure that Ava is taking care of that tattoo. And send her back in, in a couple of weeks, I wanna take a pic of it for my portfolio."

He gets to his feet as I finally manage to get to mine, looks me up and down for a moment, then smirks.

Leaning over, he kisses me deeply and hungrily, almost causing me to lose my footing, then shakes his head.

"You know where the door is, *Aunty*. See you around sometime."

EPILOGUE
FINLEY

"Good afternoon wonderful body modification artists," I ring out cheerfully as I walk into the shop a few weeks later.

Rya shakes her head as I stop by the front desk and grin at her. "What?"

"I still can't believe you. You're impossible, little brother," she remarks as she chuckles.

"Always have been," I confirm as I ruffle her hair with a grin. "What's on the roster for today?"

"I'm not your personal secretary; check your appointment book yourself," Rya replies breezily as she jerks her head toward down the hall.

"You really need to get laid," I say, shaking my head at her attitude.

"Oh? Know of any priests that are looking for a good time?" she asks me pointedly.

A sheepish grin forms on my lips as I slide my hands into my pockets. "No, but I can ask around if you really want me to."

Rya gives me a playful shove off her desk, and I laugh as I shake my head and start to make my way down toward my room, but suddenly stop in my tracks and head back toward the reception area.

"Hey," I say, leaning around the side of the wall. Rya glances up at me and waits.

"You never did tell me why you gave her my address."

My sister grins at me before she shrugs, "Best way to teach you a lesson. You have to learn to clean up your own messes when you make, them Fin."

I shake my head and roll my eyes.

I should have figured it was something as simple as that.

Raking a hand back through my hair, I turn around and finally make my way toward my room.

Once I step into my station, I stop short and raise an eyebrow curiously.

"How long have you been waiting?'

"Half an hour. I got here early," Ava replies quietly.

"Oh, so .... What's up, kid?" I ask as I close the door softly behind me.

"You told Aunt ... You said you wanted to take a picture of my tattoo."

Duh, I think with an eye roll as I nod and walk over to the small bookcase. I reach up for the camera and then turn back toward Ava, "Okay, so if you can shimmy out of those, that would make this a lot easier," I tell her as I nod at her jean shorts.

She gives me an even look before letting out a sigh and undoing the buttons holding them up, then pushes her shorts down to her knees.

"I mean, this is gonna be pretty awkward but if you can open your legs for me, Ava, that would be great," I tell her with an amused look.

"What?"

"I can't take a good pic of the tattoo if your legs are still kind of together," I explain with a laugh.

She juts out her chin as she pushes her jeans down the rest of the way, and steps out of them, then lifts a leg and places her foot on the recliner.

"Good enough?" she barks irritably, and I lick my lips as I shake my head.

She's starting to sound a hell of a lot like her aunt used to when I was in school.

"Yeah, just hold still," I instruct as I bend down and angle the camera. I snap a few shots before I look at the screen and scroll through them. "Cool, I got it. Thanks."

Ava quickly gets dressed as I turn to set the camera back on top of the bookcase.

I wait patiently for her to leave, but when she puts her hand on the doorknob, she hesitates for a moment.

"What's up, Ava?" I ask her gently.

"Um, that night at the park ..."

"What about it?" I press.

"Did it ... did you ...?"

I smile patiently as I walk over to my chair and take a seat. This should be interesting, and I've been curious about her thoughts on what she did.

"Did I what?"

"Did you do it to get back Aunt Celeste? Did you use me for some kind of sick amusement, Finley?" she finally asks in a quiet, subdued tone.

I lean back in my chair as I give her a carefully blank look. She's still too young to understand the rules of war, and what I say next could have repercussions on how she sees life from now on.

"Honestly? Kind of," I say, thoughtfully. "I mean, at first I wanted you to go home and have to explain to her where you were and why you smelled the way you did."

"But then?" she presses as her shoulders slump a little. Her eyes bore into mine as she waits for some kind of hope in what my next words could possibly be.

"But then, I went home and rubbed one out. It's why I left so fast, Ava. I didn't want you to see that you rocking on a busted, old toy got me hard," I finish with a shrug.

The smallest of smiles starts to curve up the edge of her lips, and I grin as I get to my feet and walk over to where she's standing.

"Let's keep that between us, though," I tease her with a grin. "Anyway, look me up in a few years if you're still interested. I'll be around."

Ava lunges forward and wraps her arms around my neck, and I can't help but laugh as I return her hug.

"Ease up there, Champ. You're going to render me unconscious with as hard as you're squeezing."

"Sorry," she replies sheepishly as her cheeks turn red, and I shake my head. Ava pulls the door open, then glances at me over her shoulder. "Thanks, Finley."

I smile at her and tilt my head. I should ask her what she's thanking me for.

Is it for how I just lied to her and made her feel like everything was okay, or is it because I managed to fuck the stick out of her aunt's ass?

Either way, I'm willing to leave it a mystery for now as I reach forward and give her arm a reassuring squeeze in response.

Ava finally walks out of my room, and practically skips down the hallway before she exits the shop.

Letting out a sigh, I close the door to my room and go check out my appointment book.

I have better things to do today than worry about some young little girl and her bitch of an aunt that tried to ruin me.

And while I did have a tiny crush on Sister Emma Agnes when I was in school, she beat that out of me before I had the chance to let it grow into something more.

I can only hope that now, she's a reflection of what she's turned me into.

Cold.

Desolate.

Angry.

Stuck in that damn vortex of feeling like I'm not good enough.

Unable to feel love for anyone else in this world, the way I should have been able to one day.

I begin to whistle quietly as I flip my book open to today's date and check out the workload for today. A smile starts to play on my lips, because in the end, I finally managed to get my revenge.

I took something from her that she'll never be able to give to someone else.

Grab your FREE copy of What Lies Beneath here!

"The atmosphere is dark and ominous, and there's seemingly no escape from the monster. But the question is, who is the real monster?" – USA Today Bestselling Author Ellie Midwood

ABOUT YOLANDA OLSON

Yolanda Olson is a USA Today Bestselling and award-winning author. Born and raised in Bridgeport, CT where she currently resides, she usually spends her time watching her favorite channel, Investigation Discovery.

Occasionally, she takes a break to write books and test the limits of her mind. Also an avid horror movie fan, she likes to incorporate dark elements into the majority of her books.

Sign up for Yolanda's newsletter.
Join Yolanda's reader group and become a Creep.
View Yolanda's books here

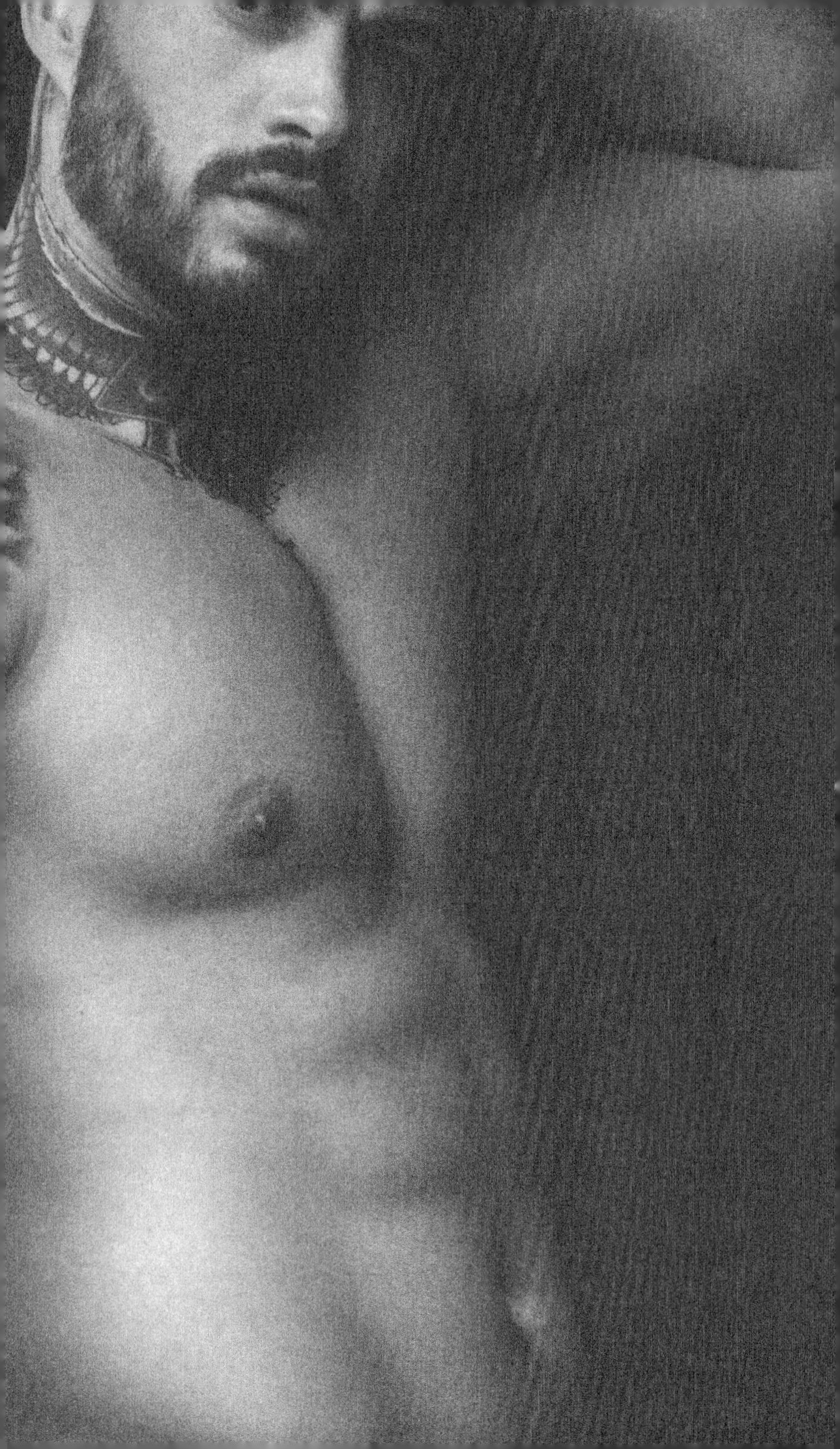

RUNE

BY DANA ISALY

CHAPTER ONE

RUNE

I love putting on my mask. It's my nightly ritual before the carnival opens. I use my fingers, dipping into the black pot of paint to smear it over my face. By the time I'm done, my eye sockets are a solid black, making the normally blue irises look silver. The tip of my nose is also black, along with the outline of my teeth, making my face look like a hollow skull, outlined by my white hair that hangs down into my eyes.

"Opening in five!" I hear the ticket master shout outside my tent.

Something is happening tonight, something big. I can feel it pulse its way through my veins, and Kali slithers around my body with nervous excitement before settling around my neck and collarbones. I trace my fingers over her inky scales, and her tail twitches in anticipation.

"You feel it, too," I tell her before throwing on my clothes. She moves under my skin so that her head is at the base of my throat. She likes to watch the feeding, and I can't blame her. It is brutal and bloody as the humans scream and writhe beneath us.

"Rune," Mara sings as she lets herself into my tent. She's dressed head to toe in tight black leather. She twirls a blade between her fingers as she walks around. For a demon, she looks incredibly angelic with her blonde hair and blue eyes.

"Looking especially tempting tonight, Mara," I tell her as I rinse the black paint from my hands. I walk around the tent, lighting more candles and organizing my divination props, essentially setting the stage for the fortune teller's act.

"Mmm," she says as she plops herself down in the customer's chair and tosses her feet up onto the table. "Nemo said you were jittery."

"Something is coming," I singsong to her, wagging my eyebrows.

"How fitting that you play the part of a fortune teller when you actually have the gifts of one. Yet here I am, stuck swallowing knives every night. Do you know how painful it was to learn how to do that properly?"

"It's not like you can use your actual power," I tell her. "The humans would run screaming if they saw you shapeshift. We'd never get to feed." I push her feet off the table and mess with her too-perfect hair.

She rolls her eyes and leans her head back on the chair.

"What is it you saw, then?" she asks.

"A man," I tell her, walking over to the opening of the tent and peeking out. People are beginning to trickle in, and their scent slowly makes its way over to me. All humans smell different, and their smells have evolved over time. When I first walked this Earth some five hundred years ago, they always seemed to smell more of natural things. It was pleasant. These days? They all smell like synthetic perfumes and MSG.

"A man?" she asks, joining me at the door, looking out at the people filing into the carnival.

"A man," I repeat. "*My* man." A giddy feeling takes over, causing Kali to slither excitedly around my skin.

"Oh," Mara drawls, understanding dawning across her soft features. "You mean your little Fated?"

Her eyes light up at the possibility. Demons don't mate like humans; we don't feel the need or the desire to do so. But we do need to feed off them if we don't want to return to Hell. Their blood masks our scent, keeping us from being hunted by the hounds and dragged back below, kicking and screaming. Just because we were spawned in Hell, doesn't mean we like it there. It is *Hell*, after all.

Every so often, our equivalent of a match comes along, and we feel ourselves inexplicably drawn to them, to their blood, and to their soul. So we keep them with us, keep them on tap. In my hundreds of years of staying up top, I've not had one, and the possibility makes me almost dizzy with excitement. I've been told drawing from your Fated is as close to a spiritual experience as us demons would ever be allowed to experience.

"Possibly," I tell her, my eyes going back to scanning the crowd. He isn't here yet, but he will be any minute now. I can feel him inside of me as if he was already a part of me. Another demon, Egan, walks among the humans, breathing fire in their direction as they gasp and laugh, watching him in awe.

"Show-off," she says. "Good luck with your human." She smiles, her sharpened fangs poking out from behind her lips before she disappears into the crowd.

I stand at the opening of my tent, not wanting to turn any of my lights on to draw any attention my way. I want to see him when he arrives. I don't want to miss a moment. Carnival goers begin to wander my way, and as one makes eye contact with me, I smile, showing my sharpened teeth, and chomp in his direction. He quickly averts his gaze and directs his little friend group in the opposite direction.

That's when I smell him. I breathe deeply and close my eyes, relishing in his scent. He smells like tobacco and chocolate. My mouth waters as I lick my tongue over my teeth. I chew my lip as my eyes scan across everyone walking through the ticket booth, the golden-and-red glow of the carnival light illuminating their features.

"There's my man," I whisper to Kali, and I feel her little head peek out from the collar of my shirt, trying to steal a glance as well.

He is beautiful. My human is dressed head to toe in black: black boots, black denim, and a black T-shirt with rolled sleeves. His arms are covered in tattoos all the way down to his fingertips that light a hand-rolled cigarette in his mouth. That full bottom lip has a ring on either side, and as he draws in on that little stick of cancer, I imagine my dick in its place.

My human is the exact opposite to me in almost every way. He seems to be covered in tattoos where I don't have a single one, except for my snake companion, Kali. He has jet-black hair compared to my stark white. I can't see his eye color from here, but I wonder if they are dark to my light as well.

One of his friends playfully pushes him, and I straighten up, anger instantly flooding my veins. No one touches what is mine, even if he doesn't know it yet. I step out of my tent, making sure the curtain closes behind me before following him into the crowd. He and his friends head directly toward the main tent for the opening show. It will be easy enough to keep eyes on him from there.

My body thrums with the adrenaline of him. My heart begins to beat in time with his, syncing our blood and breaths. From what I've been told, he'll feel drawn to me as well...eventually. But if he doesn't, I have a ritual I can perform to make him stay. The blood tastes so much sweeter when it isn't soured by fear.

He tries, and fails, to *casually* look over his shoulder, but when he scans the crowd, he can't find me. I smile and run my fingers over Kali, trying to calm her excited slithering. She is moving around my entire torso, tickling my sides as I feel her tongue dart out across my skin.

"Settle," I soothe her.

He turns back around, taking a final drag of his cigarette before stomping into the dirt with his heavy boot. A girl he is standing with takes his arm in hers and leads him into the tent. That gives me pause. I never even thought the universe would give me a straight man. Surely he isn't.

I walk around to the back of the tent and make my way through everyone working in here tonight before I find a place on the side where I can see everyone. My eyes find him easily in the crowd now, like they know exactly where to look. He scans the crowd as well, feeling my gaze on him like a physical touch. The lights go down, and I settle in, getting a plan together of how to approach him after.

CHAPTER TWO

CASH

This carnival looks like it's straight out of a horror movie. Everything glows a faint gold and red, casting shadows that seem to move around every corner. It's filled with red-and-white-striped tents, crude dirt paths outlined by candles leading the way. How they stay lit or don't catch the entire place on fire is beyond me.

And the people working here are otherworldly gorgeous, from the man working the ticket booth to the fire breather and acrobats. There's something about them that makes it difficult to look away when they catch your eye, and there's someone watching me—I can feel it. Ever since I stepped foot in this carnival, I've felt eyes on me in the crowd, and I can't find the source, no matter how hard I look through the mass of people.

The lights dim in the ring, and the main event starts. I pull the guitar pick out of my jean pocket and stick it between my teeth. It's been a nervous habit for as long as I can remember. I continue to glance around in the low light, trying to find the source of this feeling.

When I catch the gaze of a man in the wings of the tent, off to my right side, it clicks. It's been him. His face is painted in a rudimentary skull, and his shockingly white hair hangs down into his eyes. He's dressed in dark baggy clothes: an oversized T-shirt and what looks like a skirt paired with boots. His skin is incredibly pale, almost as white as his hair. There isn't a spot of ink on his body that I can see except something that pokes out from his collar. He sits in a chair, his legs spread wide in a cocky gesture.

He lifts his hand and wags his fingers at me, a slow grin spreading across his face. My stomach flips, and my heartbeat picks up. Suddenly I feel light-headed and dizzy. My body can't decide if I'm terrified or interested. I flip the guitar pick over in my mouth and lean forward, tilting my head with my own grin. I narrow my eyes, asking him a question with a look. He smiles wider and refuses to break eye contact. We've entered some type of war with our gazes, and neither of us wants to lose.

Even with him being so far away, I can tell that his eyes are the palest color blue I've ever seen. They almost shine with a silver glow against the black of his face paint. He pushes his hair out of his face, smearing some of the black paint into it, and leans forward as well, matching my posture. His hands clasp in between his knees, and I can see his nails are painted black.

I've never encountered anyone like this in my life. There's something about him that draws me in, makes me want to walk over to him and see him up close. I wonder somewhere in the back of my mind what he smells like. My eyes snag on how wide his legs are spread, and my mind wanders, thinking about how easy it would be to lift that skirt and see what's underneath. I move up his torso, taking in his thin frame, the little black spot of a tattoo on his neck, and his sharp jawline.

When I finally meet his eyes again, he's looking at me like he knows where my mind went, like he can see every dark fantasy that has somehow wormed its way into my imagination. He blows me a kiss, and I rear back like it hit me with a smack in the face.

Something happens in the ring, causing one of my friends I'm with to nudge my attention reluctantly back to the show. When I look back, the guy is gone, and I feel something in my chest deflate. For the rest of the show, I scan all the nooks and crannies where he could be hiding, but I can't find him. I can't feel his gaze on me anymore, and my heart returns to a normal rhythm. I rub my sternum at the dull ache there as I try to forget the weird encounter.

"What's wrong with you?" my friend Alyssa asks.

"I just need a cigarette," I tell her. "I'll be right back."

"You just had one before we came in! And it's almost done," she complains in a whiny voice that sets my nerves on edge.

"That's the definition of an addiction," I tell her and pull my arm from her grasp. She pouts and goes back to talking with our friend on the other side of her.

I exit the tent and look around as I pull out my silver cigarette tin. I only have one left; I'll have to roll more before the night is over. I tap it on the tin before pulling the pick out of my mouth and taking the cigarette between my teeth. Before I can light it, I feel his gaze again. He appears in front of me, lighter in hand, and holds it up in front of my face.

I was right—his eyes are a molten silver, the color in the irises seeming to shift and move in the glow of the firelight. He's almost the exact same height as me, if not the slightest bit shorter. I lean in to light the tip of my cigarette, our faces getting so close all I can see is the fire reflected in his eyes.

We stare at each other again, not speaking. I lean back and take a drag. His eyes follow the hollowing of my cheeks, and I smirk, blowing the smoke out of my nose and mouth. Beyond the overwhelming scent of the tobacco is him, and it permeates the smoke. He smells rich like incense and sweet like apples.

I wonder if he tastes the same.

The little grin spreads across his lips again, and it takes every ounce of strength in me to not reach out and touch them. I take the cigarette out of my mouth and lick my lips before swiping my thumb across my piercings. His eyes follow the movement, and he leans in toward me ever so slightly. I see his nostrils widen as he breathes me in.

The energy between us is palpable. I can feel it between us, pushing and pulling on our bodies. My eyes drop to his neck and see the head of a snake poking out of his collar. I blink when I think I see it move, but it's still there, resting on his collarbone and disappearing beneath his shirt.

I open my mouth to speak, but the tent opens up, and floods of people begin pouring out. I turn toward the light shining on us and squint, knowing my friends will be out and looking for me at any moment. When I turn back toward him, he's slowly backing away, keeping his gaze on me until he gets far enough away to turn around.

My eyes are glued to him. I watch as he moves through the crowd, over the many dirt paths of candles, and then as he disappears into another tent. It's dark on the outside with just a faint yellow glow coming out when he opens and moves inside.

I begin to make my way over to his tent, like a bloodhound on a scent trail. I can't let it go. I take a deep drag of my cigarette, letting my lungs fill with the comforting burn, numbing the strange feeling of loss that fills my chest and throat.

"Cash!" Alyssa yells, dragging my attention back to the group I arrived with. "Where are you going?" I take another drag and then point with the cigarette in my hand.

"That tent over there. I want to know what it is," I tell them.

"Well, let's all go together, silly!" she says, grabbing my arm again and leading me over. As we get closer, it begins to light up on the outside. It's surrounded by tall pillar candles in antique glass jars. They begin to light on their own, casting his entire tent in an eerie glow of reds, oranges, and yellows.

The sign next to the opening reads "Fortune Teller" in exaggerated red ink on a white background. I look around, and no one else is paying this attraction any attention. We're the only ones that have made it over this way.

I stomp my cigarette out in the grass under my boot and disentangle myself from Alyssa's grip. She says something to the others, but I'm too distracted watching him as he opens the curtain. He's surrounded by a hellish glow, like a sinful halo around his entire body.

"Looking to have your fortunes told?" he asks. It's the first time I've heard his voice, and he isn't even looking at me while he speaks. A hot poker of jealousy flares to life in my stomach. His voice is deep and smooth, and yet there is a playful undertone to it that promises something I'm not sure I want to accept.

"Definitely!" Alyssa cheers, stepping past him. As the rest of my group enters, his eyes swing to mine.

"Coming?" he asks me. There's a challenge in his silver gaze, and I accept.

CHAPTER THREE

RUNE

It makes both me and Kali ecstatic that he can feel the pull to me. He isn't sure what it is, but he looks for me in the crowd and follows me when I'm out of sight. His friends are an unforeseen obstacle that I'm very willing to overcome. Once I get him separated and get his blood to complete the binding, he won't even care about them anymore. I will be the only thing in his sight.

His friends are in my tent, laughing and chatting as they make their way around the circle, pointing and looking at all the crystals and herbs I have set up for the act. He and I are still standing outside in the cool air, staring at each other in a silent battle. I know he wants to come in—I can feel it. I can *see* it in his mind. He wants to come inside more than anything. But there's a part of him that's fighting it, a part of him that doesn't want to be the one to give in and lose whatever fight it is we have between us.

That only makes me want to fight harder for him, for us. I want to break that part of him down and mold it into what I need. I want him crying and bleeding at my feet, begging me to take him in as mine. I want him in a puddle, weak and needy for anything I could possibly give to him or take from him. I smile at the thought and see his body respond and react to me.

His brain isn't sure what to make of me yet, but his body is already making decisions for him.

"Cash!" one of his friends yells at him from inside. He drags his eyes off me and through the tent flaps I'm still holding open.

"Cash?" I ask him, the name gliding off my tongue like honey. His skin breaks out in goose bumps. "Like Johnny?"

"Funny," he murmurs. "Never heard that one before." His voice is melted butter, and I want to hear him say my name with it. My cock stirs as he looks up and down my body one last time before walking past me with a little shove of his shoulder. That small touch makes my heart kick up, and I can feel my mouth salivate with anticipation of what he's going to taste like as I take him for the first time.

I moan and follow him inside, watching as he takes a seat on the side, not wanting to go first. That suits me just fine—it will be better if he goes last. It'll be easier to keep him with me. The small, loud one sits down first, and her scent overpowers me. She reeks of synthetic chemicals and sugar that make my fucking teeth hurt.

As I put on a show for each of his friends, he watches me out of the corner of his eye. His body is constantly in alignment with my own, and when it's his turn, his entire body stiffens with anticipation. I can sense every little emotion that flows through his body like a tidal wave. I've never been able to read anyone as easily as I can read him. It's like I'm flipping through the pages of a book.

"Go on, Cash," the little one says in her high-pitched voice, pushing him out of his chair and into the one across from me.

"Yeah," I urge him on in a playful voice. "Come on, Cash." He narrows his eyes at me, then reluctantly gets up, watching me the entire time, and walks the few feet over to my little table. He rests his beautifully tattooed arms on the green velvet cloth and extends his hands out to me, palms up. His smoky scent invades my nostrils, making me almost drool with hunger.

I slowly look over his palms, tracing the lines that move across them with the very tips of my fingers. His hands are calloused and warm. There's an energy moving between us, and with every little movement, his fingers pulse like they want to reach out and touch me back.

"Something big is coming into your life, Johnny," I tell him.

"Cash," he says, staring into my eyes with a warning. I smile at him and then continue dragging my fingers across his palms. I lean my head on my free hand as I move to the heel of his hand with the other and then across the small lines on his wrists that his tattoos try to cover. I move across his horizontal scars, and I hear his breathing pick up as I continue up his arm.

"Don't be afraid of it," I tell him in my smoothest voice. I reach the inside of his elbow and trace the bright green vein and feel the slight raising of his skin there. His skin is dotted with goose bumps. I can feel myself getting hard as his fingers move in circles under my elbow where I'm hovering. I don't think he even knows he's doing it, but his touch is like a lightning bolt straight to my dick.

"Afraid of what?" he asks in a whisper. When I look up, his eyebrows are scrunched together, making a small line of worry form between them. I stare at him for a moment, tilting my head to take him in. I lean forward, the table creaking slightly under my weight.

He leans forward as well, unknowingly drawn in by the connection we share. He's mine, and he's so blind as to not see it yet. I smile, knowing that he can now see how my teeth are sharper than anyone's should be. When his eyes drop to them, he swallows thickly, his Adam's apple bobbing, and I watch sweat break out across his forehead.

"Me!" I say with a wide smile, leaning forward quickly and grabbing his mouth in a kiss. He tastes like the smoothest milk chocolate as his mouth opens to me for a split second before he realizes what's happening.

He pushes me off him, and I fall back on the floor, laughing so hard I feel tears slip from the corners of my eyes. His friends begin to grab onto him as he stands over me with a hard look. Cash shakes them off and squats down next to me. His eyes are so dark in this light, they look like two black holes. I smile up at him.

"You don't get to touch me," he says, taking my throat in his grasp and pushing me into the floor. His knee finds my chest, and he digs into it. He thinks he's holding me down, making it difficult for me to move and breathe. He has no idea of the strength I possess or how I'm going to turn the tables on him tonight, so I let him soak up this small moment of power.

"But you like it when I touch you," I whisper, moving my hand up the inside of his thigh. I grip his rock-hard cock, and he jumps off me and falls to his ass like I've stung him. I grin and roll my neck. "I can't wait to see the monster you're hiding underneath those jeans, Johnny," I tell him. "It felt very...sizable," I say with a wink in his direction.

"Cash, come on," Alyssa says, trying to pick him up off the floor.

"In your fucking dreams, psycho," Cash swears, spitting in my direction.

"Can you please let me know when you're going to do that?" I ask him as I stand up and brush myself off. "I'll open my mouth and move into the line of fire. You're being wasteful." He looks at me like I've lost my mind. He stands and backs up toward the entrance of the tent with his friends. "And you got my new skirt all dusty," I pout.

"Fuck your skirt, asshole," he says before pushing his way out of the tent. I smile as I watch him go, knowing I'm going to break in that bratty little mouth later.

"You shouldn't touch people without their consent," the little one huffs in my direction. I bite in her direction, my teeth clacking together. Her eyes widen, and she rushes out of the tent with the rest of them.

"Oh, this is going to be fun, Johnny," I say aloud to myself before blowing out all the candles in the tent and following my prey through the festivities.

CHAPTER FOUR

CASH

I swear that fucking tattoo around his neck was moving as I pushed him to the floor and grabbed his neck. I could almost feel it under the palm of my hand, slithering and struggling under my grip. He had looked completely unfazed at my assault; if anything, he almost looked amused by it. Not many people would react that way to my anger. I've been told I'm one intimidating fucker when I'm angry, but that's what happens when you grow up on the streets without a home or a family.

But him? He didn't give a shit. He loved every second of it. Even now I can feel his fucking hands on my arms and his eyes on my face. Leaving his tent did nothing to cool the anger I felt toward him.

"Cash!" I heard Alyssa shout from behind me. The others we had come with were giving me a wide berth, knowing that my anger wasn't something to fuck with. But Alyssa always thought she was an exception to the rule, the only one who could handle my moods. She always thought she was special, that I cared for her. Tonight was no exception. "Cash!" she shouts again, closer this time as she takes my arm for the third time tonight.

"Alyssa!" I say in a crude imitation of her voice as I rip my arm from her grasp. Her hands drop to her sides like she touched a live flame. Her eyes instantly show hurt and fear as she takes a step back. "Stop fucking touching me like it's your right to do so," I tell her in a low voice as I advance on her.

She's over five feet tall on a good day, and I tower over her. There are already tears threatening to fall over her lashes, but I'm too far gone in the darkness to care. He's pushed me to become the thing I hate being.

"Do not touch me right now."

"Alright, Cash," one of the other guys says. "Enough. You're scaring the shit out of her."

I back up and leave them, hoping they won't follow. I need some time alone. I need to figure out what the fuck happened back in that tent. I make my way through the carnival, stopping at a picnic table that's off to the side. I pull out my supplies with shaking hands and lay them out of the table.

I place the guitar pick between my teeth to distract myself as I get to work. Taking the tobacco out of the tin, I place it on a flattened wrapper and then carefully roll it almost all the way before bringing it to my mouth to lick the seam. I do this over and over again, until the worn silver tin is full again and my brain has stopped humming with anger.

There are people all around me, but they've become background noise, like a sound machine playing white noise. All I can see replaying in my mind is how his silver eyes raked over my skin like a fucking caress. Even now, as I pick everything up off the table and shove them back in my pockets, I can feel his fucking eyes on me.

I try to look around my surroundings without coming off as paranoid, but I can't see him, and it makes my chest feel like it's caving in. I don't know what the fuck has come over me. This isn't normal behavior. A normal person doesn't see someone and become obsessed like this. But I can't talk myself out of it. Every time I try, my brain somehow pivots right back to him. I can't shake his incense-and-apple scent from my brain, and I can feel his eyes on me around every corner.

And I know he's out there somewhere—he's in my blood. My outburst has only spurred him on, intrigued him. I've laid down a challenge, like a fucking alpha fighting for territory, and he's answering the call.

"Hi there," a woman says, sitting down next to me at the picnic table. She has golden-blonde hair and bright teal eyes. She looks like an actual angel sitting next to me. Her voice is musical and light, completely at odds with how she is dressed and the blade she's twirling in her hands. "Name's Mara," she announces, sticking her hand out in my direction to shake.

I hesitate but take it.

"Cash," I tell her, moving the pick out of my teeth and in between my fingers. I fiddle with it like she fiddles with her knife. She looks me up and down, a calm smile on her face as she takes me in. What is it with the people here and them staring at me like I'm their fucking dessert?

"Can I help you?" I ask her after the silence has stretched on too long. I can feel his eyes on my back, and it's making me feel on edge. It's like a hundred spiders making their way up my spine and into my hair. I can feel him creep over me like a dark cloud.

"I'm a friend of Rune's," she says with an easy smile, like she can't feel the tension surrounding us.

"And Rune is?" I ask her, looking around, knowing I'm going to find him lurking somewhere in the shadows like a creep.

"He hasn't even introduced himself? How rude." She waves her hand and rolls her eyes. "The little white-haired boy with the skirt," she says, nodding her head to the left. I follow, and I see him there, leaning against one of the food trucks, his legs crossed at the ankle and that same smirk gracing his mouth.

"Little isn't a word I would use to describe him," I blurt before I can stop myself. But it's true—he isn't little. I'm easily six two, and he's a bit taller. And I'd be lying if I said I didn't feel how ripped he was when I shoved him. It was like pressing against a chest made of rock.

"Mhm," she hums, winking in Rune's direction. Keeping eye contact with him, she leans in and runs her nose along the outside of my neck, inhaling all the way up to my temple. I sit frozen, wondering what the fuck she's doing, before a low growl carries itself over my skin. I swear it shakes the ground at my feet and the bench under me. I look over at Rune, but his gaze is trained on Mara this time.

She just laughs and gives me a kiss on the cheek before standing up and walking away, making a show to the passersby with the knives she seems to keep in every part of her outfit. People stop and stare, and she soaks it up like a sponge, smiling and laughing, throwing them into the air and catching them in her mouth. She lowers one slowly into her throat and waits for people to ooh and ahh before pulling it out and skipping down one of the paths. Their claps echo through the open space until they filter into different spaces.

I look back to where Rune was standing, and he's no longer there. I can't feel him anymore, either. I pull a cigarette out of my tin and walk away from the other carnival goers to smoke. After I finish this, I think to myself, I'll go find the group. I'll have to apologize to Alyssa to get back on everyone's good side.

I groan and crack my neck as I take the last couple of drags before putting it out. I lean my head back on the same truck Rune had been leaning on moments ago. I roll my head to the side, looking off into the forest that surrounds the carnival. It's quiet and incredibly dark past the reach of the lights. It's a new moon tonight, so the sky is lacking that extra bit of light.

Just as I'm about to walk away, something in the brush catches my eye. I push off the truck and squint, trying to see what it is. I stumble back as two glowing eyes catch my attention and blink. My arms flail and catch the brunt of the fall as I careen back onto my ass. My wrists scream from the jolt, and the red eyes blink one more time before they disappear. My heart is racing as I sit on the damp grass and try to catch my breath.

That didn't feel like Rune, and it certainly didn't feel human. What the fuck is this place? I take a few deep breaths and stand, looking around as I brush the wet blades of grass from my jeans. I walk away to find my friends, glancing back at the forest until it's completely out of sight.

CHAPTER FIVE

RUNE

I'm taking a fucking walk.

The sight of Mara smelling and touching what's mine nearly sent me into a blind rage that would have destroyed the entire camp. I know she did it to force my hand, to make me realize if I didn't make a move, any of the other demons could try. Cash wouldn't smell the same to them as he did to me, but he was still a vulnerable human in a sea of hungry demons. And I wasn't about to let one of them take him from me.

I can still feel him. He's still here, walking around the carnival, looking for his friends. If I want to keep him, I need to make sure he doesn't find them. They need to think he went home on his own so that they don't go looking for him or try to convince him to leave with them instead of staying with me.

He has no choice. He's staying here.

I can't wait to sink my teeth into him and feel the wet heat of his blood pour over my tongue. I've never tasted someone that was born to be mine. He must taste like Eve's apple in Eden, the perfect temptation for the perfect sinner.

"There you are," I say to myself as I see him walking aimlessly around the pathways. He really does look like the perfect prey. He looks lost and confused; his guard isn't up at all. I can feel every fleeting emotion that passes through him.

I step into his path, and he halts, staring at me from a few feet away. He didn't even see or sense me coming.

"Leave me alone," he says, stalking toward me and then pushing me out of the way to get past. A flush of heat spreads through my entire body at the contact, and I groan and bite my lip. I catch his arm, pulling him around and backing him up against the wall of the mirror maze. I push myself into his body so that we are nose to nose. His arm flexes against my grip, but I just squeeze tighter.

My free hand moves up his hard stomach and across his chest. He breathes in, and I can feel his dick starting to swell against my hip. I blow my hair out of my face and finally grip his jaw, making his eyes lock with mine.

"What's got you so excited, Johnny?" I ask him. I run my nose up the same path as Mara's, my mouth watering at the scent there. He smells the strongest at his pulse point, and I take the opportunity of him being frozen to dart my tongue out and lick across that little spot. His sweat coats my tongue, and I suck his skin into my mouth.

His hips involuntarily rise to seek mine, pressing against my own swelling cock. His groan lights my blood on fire, and my mouth salivates as I continue my assault on his throat. I refuse to feed from him until I'm inside of him, but I can't help but lick and suck at his sensitive skin. I pull the blood to the surface, leaving red bruises up and down his neck. I pull away, my mouth wet with the effort, and appreciate the marks I've left on his skin.

Marks that make him mine.

"Stop," he says, barely able to push me away. His brain may still be against this, but his body knows the drill. I run a hand down his torso and cup him roughly in my palm. His head falls back against the wall, and I watch the delicious jerk of his Adam's apple. I lean forward and take the soft skin there between my teeth as I rub against him with my hand.

His hands stay pressed against my chest, pushing against me with hardly any strength.

"Please, stop," he pleads again, his hips rolling against my palm. My thumb moves up and grazes the band of his boxers. He pushes me with a little more force, and I step away, annoyed that he won't give in. I need to feed, and his protests are getting in the way of that.

"You want this," I tell him, taking his throat with both hands and pushing my face into his. His hands slide from my chest to my hips, and I lick the seam of his lips, tasting the rich tobacco that lingers. They part just enough for me to take his bottom lip into mine, biting it gently between my teeth. I can't have him bleed yet. I need to hold off. It will be so much better with my dick sheathed deep inside him.

"I don't," he murmurs against my mouth as I play with one of his piercings. Our hips move together, and a deep growl makes its way out of my chest. The stiff, rough fabric of his jeans pushes against the soft linen of my skirt in the best fucking way. I grab one of his hands and plant it directly over my dick.

"Do you feel what you do to me, Johnny?" I ask him, moving my lips harsher against his, forcing him to open up to me. His hand grips my dick, and he groans before opening his mouth fully to mine, swallowing me whole with one kiss.

He flips us, pinning me against the wall, and I let him lead since I like where it's going at the moment. The hand on my groin stays there, moving in slow, methodical strokes while his other grabs my throat and pins me against the wall.

"I told you to stop," he says, biting my lip hard enough that the iron taste of it floods into my mouth.

"You don't seem like you want to," I tell him, grinning as he continues to rub me. All the blood in my body pours into my dick, making me hard as a rock. Electricity shoots down my spine, causing my hips to buck against his hand. I refuse to come in my fucking skirt the first time we're together. How fucking embarrassing. So I'm going to have to take control back of the situation before it gets out of hand.

"I said I wanted you to stop touching me," he says, smirking as I fight to control my thrusts. "I didn't say anything about *me* touching *you*. I kind of like how pitiful and weak you look underneath me right now."

I laugh and take a deep breath, getting my dick under control. I use just enough force in my shove to get him off my body, but not to send him flying backward onto his ass.

"Johnny, Johnny, Johnny," I say as I stalk toward him, tucking my cock into the waist of my skirt. He follows the movement with his eyes, and they flare with heat before he gets himself under control. "You are so fucking adorable. But you aren't in charge here, I'm afraid."

Kali decides to make an appearance, slithering up and around my neck to where she can see him and he can see her. His eyes bulge as she moves through my skin and sticks her tongue out at him. At least, that's what I tell myself she's doing. I can feel the little tickle of it, and I like to think she's on my side here.

"What the fuck are you?" he asks, fear lacing his words.

I clasp my hands behind my back and walk around him while he stands frozen with fear. He has a very nice ass that I take a moment to admire as I round on him. He's making my heart race with his adrenaline, and it's making me a little dizzy with the need to have his blood.

His thoughts are going a mile a minute as he stands there, fixed with indecision. His body is telling him one thing while his brain tells him another.

"It doesn't really matter what I am," I tell him. "I want you, and therefore, I'm going to take you, whether you want it or not. But—" I pause as I face him again. "I think we both know you're lying to yourself when you say you don't want it. I can see and feel the way your body responds to me, Johnny."

Before I can see it coming, he takes off, running past me and into the maze of mirrors. I let my head fall back as a small laugh escapes me. He is fucking perfect for me. He has no idea that the chase is the best part to a demon.

I walk slowly over toward the maze and take the steps one at a time. I can smell his fear, sour and sharp. We're going to have to fix that before I feed. I don't want his inability to be open-minded to ruin my first ever feeding with him.

"Come out, come out, wherever you are," I sing as I step inside the darkened maze.

CHAPTER SIX

CASH

I instantly realize I've made a huge fucking mistake. I wasn't paying attention when I ran from him; I just knew I needed to get away. The shit he's capable of making me feel...it's dangerous. And that tattoo around his neck? I swear that fucker moved as he stalked around me. What in the hell is he?

But as I make my way inside this building, I'm blinded by the flashing neon lights that bounce around the mirrors. As I look for a place to run, I'm confronted with a hundred different angles of myself. There's a smoke machine somewhere that floods the floor, making it impossible to see anything below my knees.

This place is a fucking death trap, and I've walked in willingly.

I can't hesitate, so I run in, knowing getting out of here is my only fucking chance to get away from him. All I can do is hope that he gets lost and I can find my friends so that we can leave this place.

My arms are outstretched as I feel my way through the maze, trying not to face-plant into a mirror or trip and fall, but I can't be slow. I know he's going to follow me in here, and even though I want him to struggle to make it through this fucking maze, he works here. Hell, he probably helped set it up.

There's creepy music playing, and I can barely hear it over my panicked breaths, but it does nothing to settle my nerves. It's tinny and sounds like it's coming from a haunted music box. How could anyone ever think this was a fun carnival attraction? It's something straight out of a fucking horror movie.

"Want to play a game of hide-and-seek, Johnny?" His voice surrounds me from all angles, but I can't tell where it's coming from.

"Fuck," I whisper to myself, continuing to push myself through the maze. I come face-to-face with my reflection at a dead end and feel my throat constrict. His maniacal laughter fills the space.

"Try again!" he sings into the void.

I feel like a wild animal backed into a corner, and it makes me wild with determination to get the fuck out.

"Fuck off, Rune!" I shout into the air, taking off back down the way I came. When I make it back to the fork, I steer left. My eyes are almost fully accustomed to the strange mixture of darkness and glow of the neon. Every time I catch my own reflection, I see my eyes wide and wild, and I look absolutely terrified.

"I'd rather fuck you, sweetness." His voice has taken on a whole new tone, and as I make another turn, I swear I see the white flash of his hair reflected in the mirrors. When I look around though, I don't see him.

I feel him in the maze with me. I can feel him staring at me, watching me fail as I take wrong turn after wrong turn. His anticipation leaks into me like a dripping faucet, slowly filling me up until I'm mad with it. It feels like the maze stretches on forever, constantly changing and morphing, growing beyond the walls that contain it.

"Johnny," he sings, elongating his little nickname for me until I think there won't be an end. The hairs on the back of my neck stand up, and goose bumps break out across every inch of my skin. I can barely catch my breath, and my chest feels heavy and tight.

"My precious boy," he says, his voice an octave lower than his playful tone. It skirts across my flesh like velvet, planting a seed of doubt in my brain.

Do I really want to escape him?

"Johnny!" I hear him whisper like he's right behind me. I whip my body around. He's not there. I run down another aisle, turn left, then right, then right again. I don't know what's real anymore. The panic and fear have my vision blurry. I shut my eyes, trying to get my vision to focus, but the whole world tilts on its axis, and I stumble into my own reflection.

I glance to the left, and he's there.

When my head turns fully, he's gone.

He's playing with his fucking food.

I growl and push off the mirror, taking off through the maze again, determined to get the fuck out of this place. I take turn after turn, never hitting a dead end no matter how far I run. I'm out of breath, my chest is on fire, and the mirrors keep stretching and warping around me.

I stop in my tracks and scream.

"Fine!" I shout at all my reflections. "You win!"

It goes silent. The music stops, and all I can hear are my own ragged breaths. There's sweat dripping down my body, soaking my shirt and making it cling uncomfortably to my skin. I try to control it, listening to the silence for any sign that he's here, that I didn't make it all up in my head.

My body is frozen—it can't decide if it's safe to move or if it should prepare for a fight. My feet are planted to the floor with frozen muscles. I take a few deep breaths and try to look at all of my reflections out of the corners of my eyes, looking for any signs of movement or flashes of white. I don't see anything, and my heart rate slows.

I flex my fingers and toes, trying to loosen the tension and work up the nerve to start walking again. I can't stand here forever. I have to get out of here and get to my friends. I need to get home. I need to fucking move.

I turn around and come face-to-face with him. My heart picks back up, trying to force its way out of my throat. He looks at ease, his hands clasped behind his back, a grin on his skull-painted face, and his white hair falling across his eyes in a way that makes me want to reach out and push it out of his face.

He tilts his head, and I take a slow step backward. His eyes fall to my feet, watching me step away from him. When his eyes meet mine again, his grin grows into a wide smile, displaying his sharp white teeth.

"Gotcha."

CHAPTER SEVEN

RUNE

I pounce. He turns to run, but I'm faster. I slam his body against the nearest mirror, and he grunts as his face makes contact with the glass. Blood runs out of his nose and drips down his lips. He struggles and tries to fight me, but he has no idea just how strong I am. I've let him think this entire time it's a fair fight, but it's not.

Humans are so pathetically weak.

I inhale and smell the sweet scent of his need and want underneath all that fear. I know he wants this, whether he admits it to me or not. It doesn't matter. I'm going to be taking what I need from him.

I roll my hips into the soft curve of his ass and groan into his ear. He drops his forehead onto the mirror in front of him and whimpers. I have his hands held behind his back, and his fingertips graze over the head of my dick as I roll into him again. I can feel myself dripping for him.

"You are going to taste so sweet," I tell him, taking his ear between my teeth. He pulls away from me and starts to fight all over again. I roll my eyes and let him get it all out, fighting against my grip until he's tired himself out. "Finished?" I ask him as he pants against the glass, fogging up the reflection of his face.

"What do you want from me?"

I push up against his body again and use my free hand to move around his waist and palm his dick. It grows and hardens under my grip as I move my own against his ass.

"I want this," I tell him, unbuttoning his jeans and pushing them down over his hips. They fall to the floor, exposing his legs, covered in the same black-and-grey tattoos that cover the rest of his body. His thighs are thick with muscles, and if he wasn't fighting me every step of the way, I would drop to my knees and bite my way across them.

"I am not a fucking bottom," he growls.

I just smile and run my hand up the front of his thigh and over his tight grey boxer briefs, the only thing on him that isn't black. In the reflection of his body, I can see the dark spot where his precum has collected. My hand cups his balls, and he squeezes his eyes shut and bares his teeth.

I move my hand further up, using my fingertips to run along the band from one hip to another. His hips move slightly before he catches himself, begging me to go lower, to go below the fabric and touch him skin on skin. His arousal begins to overpower the scent of his fear, and I know his blood is going to taste like the fucking nectar of the gods once I finally sink my teeth into him.

"Stop," he whispers as I slip my fingers inside his boxers. I finally touch the head of him, where I play with the slit, collecting the ample amount of precum that has collected there. I smear it around his sensitive head, listening to the beautiful way he gasps under my touch. I give him a few firm strokes and relish in how his knees almost give out underneath him.

I release his hands from behind his back, and he plants them on the mirror to help hold himself up as I continue to pull and tug at him, making more precum collect at his tip. While he's distracted, I use my free hand to slip his boxers down over his ass, just far enough to let me slip inside him.

"Rune," he whispers. I love hearing my name on his lips. It makes my dick swell with the need to be inside him. "You can't. Stop."

My fingers dip into his crease, and he squeezes, freezing up with panic all over again. The sweet smell of his sex is gone, and in its place is fear. I groan and realize this is going to have to be done a different way.

"Fuck off, Rune!" he warns me. "I do not want your fucking dick inside of me!" Lies, lies, lies. I can smell them on him.

"I love the fight of topping a top," I tell him as he begins to struggle all over again. "But let's make you a bit more pliant, okay? We don't have all fucking night." I grip the back of his hair and force his eyes to meet mine in the mirror. His widen as mine turn jet-black, eclipsing the irises until there's nothing left but darkness.

"Cash," I say in a smooth voice, letting my energy seep into him. "I need you to stop fighting me now. It's time."

I can still see the hint of fear in his eyes, but his body complies with my words, relaxing and stopping the fight. I pull my skirt up, take the hem of it under my chin, and pull my own dick out. I smear my precum around the head and then spit down onto it, knowing it's not near enough lube, but it's all I have in the moment.

I spread him wide and push the tip of my dick against him, forcing my way past the tight ring. He is so hot and so fucking tight I have to bite my lip until I taste blood to make sure I don't blow my load in one swift push. Putting some force behind it, I'm balls-deep within seconds, basking in the feel of his ass pulsing and gripping my shaft.

"You feel so fucking good, baby," I tell him as I begin to move.

"Fuck you," he says, fighting past my mind control. My strong man, so brave and willful.

"I think you'll find it's the opposite," I say as I pull myself almost all the way out of him before thrusting back in. His face smashes into the mirror, and he grunts. I dig my fingertips into his hips as I do it again and again, pulling out almost completely before ramming home.

Pleasure overtakes my body. Goose bumps break out across my flesh, and white heat floods down my spine and into my balls. He's so fucking tight there's no way I'm going to last much longer. I look up, and he's watching me but not my face. His eyes are glued to the way my hips are moving against him in a wild rhythm. I tuck my skirt into my shirt to keep it out of the way.

"You like watching yourself get fucked, Johnny?" I ask him, picking up speed. His mouth drops open, and a low moan makes its way out of his chest. "You like the way we look together?" I grip and squeeze his throat as he swears at me again. What a little firecracker my Johnny is.

I grab the back of his scalp again, pulling his head to the side and exposing his neck as I feel the orgasm creep up. My toes try to curl, and electricity shoots through my stomach as I bite the tender flesh of his throat.

His blood pours over my tongue as my cum paints the inside of him. With each pulse of my orgasm, I suck on his neck, drawing more and more from him as I prolong the high. His blood is like nothing I've ever tasted, and I know what people mean now when they talk about their Fated *mate*.

It is spiritual, it is orgasmic, it is fucking sinful.

I pull away from his neck at the same time I slip my cock free from his ass. He falls to the floor, weak from the blood loss and exhausted from pleasure. He didn't come, but he still enjoyed it, and I'll make up for it next time. I look down at him, his ass leaking my cum, mixed with the red of his blood. His face is pale, and his eyes are dull.

"You just need some rest," I tell him, squatting down to get a better look. "The feeding always takes it out of you. Rest up, buttercup." I lean over and give him a quick kiss on the forehead before standing to get myself together.

I feel positively giddy with the feed. My head is light, and my body feels refreshed. This is a high I have never experienced with any other feed. I'm so happy I get to keep him.

When I look down to adjust my clothing and see my dick painted red from where I forced myself inside of him, butterflies flutter through my stomach. I have his blood on me now. He's marked me just as I have marked him.

"I like seeing your blood on my cock, Johnny," I tell him, meeting his eyes and seeing the defiance begin to creep back in. His anger is red-hot and almost uncontrollable, a challenge I happily rise to. "I think I'll keep it there as a reminder of our first time together."

I adjust myself in my boxers and pull my skirt back into place. I smile down at him. His cock is swollen and hard. The feeding has a sexual effect on the humans as well, and I know he's feeling the need to touch himself. But he won't while I'm still around. So I twirl and bow in his direction before leaving him alone. He'll come find me if I don't find him first.

"See you soon!" I sing.

CHAPTER EIGHT

CASH

My mind is cloudy, and my dick is fucking throbbing. I can barely register the pain in my ass for all the blood rushing to my cock. I sit up and lean back on the mirror, feeling his cum leak out of me as I move. I hesitantly grab my dick with my hand, feeling an almost instant relief at the contact.

"Fuck," I moan, gripping the base and squeezing up to the head as I run my fingers over the sticky precum that's collected at my slit. The pain in my neck from where he bit me is thrumming and burning, sending waves of pleasure through my body. There's a haze over my mind, making the world around me sway.

Did he do something to me? I try to think back to when I stopped fighting, when he had called me by my real name and made me calm. Something in my brain had told me to relax, and so I had. Did he do that? What the fuck kind of monster was he to be able to control my mind?

My body jolts with fear as I remember the way his eyes had gone black, darker than black. They were soulless and haunting, soaking up everything in the room. I was drawn into them, lost and searching for a way out.

But the way he made me feel after that...

When he first pushed into me, practically ripping me open as he forced himself into me, I'd never felt so full as he stretched me open and filled me up. It was the first time I had ever received, and the burn had been brutal, but it turned to white-hot pleasure as he continued, his cock swiping against my prostate with every fucking thrust.

I hadn't wanted it, had I?

I groan and fist myself harder, stroking myself violently to the memories of how he felt inside of me. Watching him in the mirror, seeing the way his body had moved as he rutted against me, was unlike anything I had ever experienced.

Everything about him terrified me, but underneath all of that fear was a desire I couldn't deny. I had wanted him to catch me as I ran from him in the maze. I wanted him to take me, mark me, claim me against the mirrors just like he had done.

And when he had bitten my neck, sucking and feeding off my blood, fireworks exploded through every fiber of my being, ripping me apart and laying me bare for him. It clicked into place, and I knew I wasn't ever getting away from him.

Heat spreads through my body as I use one hand to palm my balls and the other to continue my vicious strokes. I can see him behind my closed eyes, like he is watching me do this, and that makes my pleasure skyrocket.

My muscles tense, and his name falls out of my mouth without my permission. I make a mess of my shirt, my cum standing out on the black fabric. I quickly try to wipe it away, but it just makes a bigger mess.

I try to clean the rest of myself up by stepping out of my jeans and boxers and using the latter to wipe away the evidence of both his and my own pleasure. I grunt and wince in pain when I try to clean up the blood from where he tore me open and decide that that can wait until later. For now, I pull up my jeans and discard the soiled underwear on the floor.

My legs and steps are wobbly, struggling to hold my body weight upright as I wander through the maze again. I can still feel him here, but it doesn't feel like a threat anymore. He's here, and he's watching, but only out of curiosity. Like he's waiting to see what I'll do next.

There's a tightness in my chest that I can't get rid of, pulling me in different directions as I make my way out of the maze. All I can think about is getting out to get to him. I want him. I need him. I fucking *crave* him.

"What the fuck have you done to me?" I ask him out loud because I know he's fucking here, and I know he can hear me. I see the exit sign lit above a blacked-out door and hobble over to it. Just pushing open the door takes a lot of energy. He has completely drained me to the point I can barely walk.

As I stumble out of the maze, I fall into the metal railing, causing it to clang and creak and bring every eye within a fifteen-foot radius on me. I pull myself up straight and run my fingers through my hair before making my way down the steps and back into the crowd. No one seems to notice me once I pull myself together.

Except for the performers...they do.

I pass Mara as she throws her knives at someone spinning on a large wooden target, and she pauses and turns, sniffing the air in my direction. When her eyes find me, her mouth forms into a sinister smile, setting my teeth on edge. She winks and turns her attention back toward the spinning human dartboard.

I dig frantically in my pockets for my cigarette tin, nearly dropping it on the ground as I pull one out and light it. The familiar burn down my throat and into my lungs helps settle my mind. Once that one is gone, I pull out another one, taking my time and soaking every bit of comfort the nicotine can give me.

"I spy with my little eye," someone sings from behind me. I turn around and see an older man with a top hat walking toward me. He has a bushy grey beard, and he swings his cane with a flourish and smiles. "A scared little human."

I don't respond, so he leans in and smells me, getting a good whiff in before I take a few steps back and throw my cigarette butt on the ground. He looks from me to it and then back again.

"Litterbug," he tsks. "I'd prefer you not dirty up my carnival. I'll have to have a talk with Rune about you before we move on to the next location." He eyes me up, and it takes me a moment to register what he said.

"What do you know about Rune?" I ask him, taking another step back. I'm ready to bolt at any moment, although if I ran on my wobbly legs now, I'd probably look like Bambi trying to learn how to walk.

"I can smell him all over you, sweet boy," he says with a grin, taking a step closer to me. "Such a shame he got to you first," he pouts. "Something that smells as sweet as you must be heaven on the tongue." He clicks his tongue, and I stumble away back toward the front of the carnival.

My mind is still spinning and trying to put the pieces together for the last couple of hours. It's like trying to fit the wrong pieces into the wrong puzzle. Square peg, round hole. Something is missing, and all I know for sure is that I need to get back to Rune. There's something in me, begging and pleading for me to get back to him.

"All of these tents look the same," I groan as I look around at all the red-and-white-striped tents surrounding me. I suddenly can't remember which one is his or even what his act was, what part he played.

I swing open one tent, opening my mouth to yell his name, when I'm met with two sets of black-as-night eyes with mouths soaked in blood and a naked girl hanging from a beam by her wrists. I cover my mouth, and they hiss in my direction as I fall back on my ass and crab crawl away before I can get back on my feet.

"What the fuck, what the fuck," I whisper in panic before taking off down another path. I vaguely remember him being at the front of everything, near the main event tent. If I can just make it back to the front, surely I can recognize something and get back to him.

Every carnival performer looks at me with narrowed eyes as I pass them. I don't remember there being this many of them when I first got here. It almost looks like there are more performers than people. They all sniff me with interest before watching me walk away.

Ahead on the left is the last tent before the gate, and there's a fortune teller sign out front. My entire body sags with relief. I know he's in there—I can feel it. I limp over to the tent and throw back the tarp. He's sitting in the same chair as he was when he read my palms.

"Is my little pet lost?" he asks, smiling up at me like he expected me to come crawling back all along. His face paint is smeared by his sweat, making his face look melted and morphed. A bolt of desire crashes through me, and I stalk toward him with purpose.

I pull his painted face toward me and kiss him, forcing his lips open as I fuck his mouth the way he fucked me earlier, brutally and with abandon. He kisses me back and pulls me to straddle his lap in the chair. I'm already hard again, grinding against him like I need him to survive.

I pull free and grip his jaw, forcing his eyes to meet mine.

"What the fuck have you done to me?"

CHAPTER NINE

RUNE

"Do you really want to talk about that right now?" I ask him, pushing away his hand and claiming his mouth with mine again. I can smell my scent all over him, and it makes my cock swell. He's mine.

"What are you?" he asks as my mouth strays lower, grazing across his jaw and down his neck.

"Your demon," I tell him, finding the bite mark from where I fed from him earlier. I suck the tender skin into my mouth, and he moans, grinding his hips against my own.

"What do you mean?" he asks breathlessly as his hands rake and tug at my hair. The way he touches me sets my black blood on fire and causes my gums to ache with the need for him.

"God, Johnny," I groan, standing up and taking him with me. He wraps his legs around my waist, and I carry him to the back, where I sleep. "Just shut up," I tell him as I throw him down onto the bed. I crawl over him, and he flips us to straddle my waist.

"Just fucking tell me," he growls as he leans down over me before taking my lip between his teeth and biting. He kisses the sting and then moves down my throat.

"I'm a demon," I tell him, out of breath from the way his hands are moving across my body. "I need to feed on humans." I swallow a groan as his hands push my shirt up and his mouth latches onto my nipple. "It disguises my scent to the hellhounds, keeping me from going back to Hell."

"Where's your tattoo?" he suddenly asks, his mouth leaving my skin.

"Giving us privacy," I tell him, pushing his mouth back to my heated flesh. "Continue."

"Hmm," he murmurs, leaving a trail of hot openmouthed kisses down my sternum and over my stomach. He takes the soft flesh beneath my belly button in between his teeth before dipping even lower. "So, why me?" he asks, pausing his fingers at the waistband of my skirt. "Why call yourself *my* demon?"

"Because!" I groan, grabbing ahold of his hair and forcing him to look at me. "You were made for me, making me as much yours as you are mine. Now, if you don't fucking stop yammering on and put that sweet mouth on my cock, I will use my goddamn mind control and *make* you do it."

He smiles and kisses his way across the vee of my hips before tugging at my skirt. I lift my hips, and he pulls it completely off me. He wastes no time and immediately wraps his lips around my head. I hiss through my teeth and tug tighter on his black hair, pushing him further down. His cheeks hollow as he moves back up my shaft before he descends, taking me completely in his throat. It constricts as he gags, and it only makes me push deeper.

"Fuck, baby," I moan as he comes up for air, drool coating his lips. He wipes his chin and then licks me from base to tip, his tongue circling the underside of my head and making my abs jump. My head falls back, and I pull my own hair. "You're going to make me come already."

"Is that what you used in the maze?" he asks, continuing to lick me up and down, his hand rolling my balls in his palm at the same time. Heat spreads through my spine until I can't fucking think straight.

"Yes," I tell him, squeezing my eyes shut and trying not to come yet. "You were being annoying, kind of like now." He laughs, and it vibrates through me.

His hands move under my knees, and he pushes them to my chest, leaving me completely open for him. He sucks one of my balls into his hot mouth before kissing his way down, his tongue pressing and circling around my hole. My hips move of their own will, trying to get him closer and deeper inside of me.

"Yes," I breathe through gritted teeth. I move to stroke myself as his tongue breaks through, pushing and licking inside of me. He smacks my hand away from my dick before standing up and away from me. I watch him as he unbuttons his jeans and shoves them off his hips. He pulls his shirt off as well, and he's absolutely covered in ink. Every inch of skin is blackened with ink.

"I didn't notice that before," I tell him, eyeing the piercing under the tip of his cock. It's silver and glints in the low light of the candles. I wag my eyebrows at him, and he just rolls his eyes.

"My turn," he states before squaring himself between my legs. He spits on himself and then on me, working his finger inside. "I'll do you the nicety of getting you ready first."

"You *really* don't have to, babe," I tell him, reaching down and urging him on by pulling his hips with my fingertips. "I like the pain."

With one hand, he pushes one of my knees back to my chest, opening me up for him. His finger leaves my ass and is replaced by the head of his dick. He pushes it in slowly, making my hips move and roll, trying to get him to push into me further. I want every single inch of him inside of me.

He spits again down onto where we are joined together and works it around my tight hole with his finger. Pushing the rest of the way inside me, I can feel the chill of the metal piercing the entire way. Once he's inside of me, he leans over me, and I wrap my legs around his waist.

"Fuck me, Cash," I tell him, grabbing his jaw and pulling him to me. Our kiss is violent. It's a war neither one of us wants to lose…or win. He begins to move inside of me as he assaults my mouth with his tongue. The burn is the most exquisite pain.

"God, you're so fucking tight for me, Rune," he says as he grabs my cock and pumps it in time with each thrust. "Do you like the way I feel inside of you? Do you like being claimed just as you claimed me?" His whole body lunges forward with each thrust, pushing me down into the mattress.

"Yes," I tell him, kissing my way across his collarbone until I find the red and bruised spot from earlier. I suck it into my mouth again, licking and teasing the sensitive skin.

"Go ahead," he tells me, his rhythm becoming more erratic as he chases his orgasm. "Bite me, please," he begs. Warmth spreads through my body, flushing my skin with a sheen of sweat as he pounds into me. I can feel my own orgasm building.

I bite down, my teeth slicing into his skin with ease. He cries out as his hips stutter, and I moan as his blood flows over my tongue again, ripping my own orgasm from my body. I explode between us, coating his stomach and my chest with cum. I feel him empty his hot seed inside me, marking me as his.

I pull my teeth free of his skin and lick the bite, cleaning the mess I made. He breathes heavily as he stills, catching his breath and coming back down to Earth. He kisses me and pulls out slowly, letting his cum drip down onto the sheets below us.

Before I can move to clean up, he wanders down to my chest and stomach, licking my cum off my skin and cleaning me up. He sits back and uses his fingers to scoop it off his own skin before sucking each finger clean.

"I would take the lord's name in vain right now if it wouldn't summon him," I tell him, watching as he moans around his fingers. It's enough to get a demon going again, fuck.

He smiles down at me before situating himself between my legs once more. His lips surround my sensitive head and suck it hard into his mouth. I see stars and buck my hips off the bed. I push his face away from me, but he just pushes on, going lower and licking up his own cum that has spilled from me.

"We taste so good together," he says, kissing me to show me just how good we taste. The salty and musky combination of both of our releases mixes with his blood and makes me dizzy.

"God, I've been missing out," I tell him as he collapses down on my chest. "I've never had a Fated," I confess to him. "You're my first."

"Tell me more about that," he says.

"Let's at least get cleaned up first," I tell him, not particularly wanting to lie on soiled sheets as I explain the inner workings of a demon to him. My face paint is also getting incredibly dry and itchy at this point.

"And then you explain this shit to me," he says again.

"Yes, Johnny," I tell him, kissing his pouty lips. "Then I explain everything."

CHAPTER TEN

CASH

Whatever it is that Rune has done to me, I don't want to fight it anymore. He's the best sex I've ever had, and I have no desire to give that up. He walks back into the room, his usual careless swagger still there, but his face paint is gone. It shocks me to see his bare face. I had never thought about what he might look like without it, but it isn't disappointing.

Rune has ghostly white eyebrows to match his hair, and without the black around his eyes, they look a bit more blue. His cheekbones and jaw are sharp, giving a natural hollow look to his cheeks. His lips are pale pink and full as he chews on them with those sharpened teeth.

I take the last drag from my cigarette before snuffing it out in the little bowl Rune gave me for an ashtray.

"How is no one else absolutely terrified of your freaky demon teeth?" I ask him from where I'm lying propped up on the few pillows he has. It's one giant tent but sectioned off by jewel-toned drapes and seventies-style beaded curtains. There's a washroom, as Rune calls it, but it isn't hooked up to any type of plumbing, so everything has to be brought in with buckets and heated with fire if you want it hot. It's like stepping back into the fucking sixteenth century.

"I can control what people see," he says, waving his hand in front of his face, making his teeth disappear before they pop back out. He crawls onto the bed next to me and lies on his back, his head in his hands. His white hair is wet from washing the paint out of it, making it almost translucent.

His abs jump and flex as he gets comfortable. His inky snake moves around the skin of his torso, like she's trying to get comfortable as well. It's bizarre to watch.

"Her name is Kali," he tells me when he finds me looking. I glance up at him and then back to her as she settles in place across his stomach, her tail flicking every so often across his ribs.

"So, you just travel the country as a touring carnival, collecting humans to feed off of so that you don't get dragged back to Hell. You're a demon—isn't Hell your home?"

"Hell may be my home, but it isn't homey," he answers. "And we don't *collect* humans. We feed off of them and then let them go. They don't even remember it." He waves his hand in dismissal. "We only keep the ones that are ours," he says as he rolls over on top of me, running his nose up my throat as he inhales.

"And how do you know who is yours? How do you know who is a Fated?"

"You smell different," he murmurs, his breath hot against my skin. "And you certainly taste different." He licks from the base of my shoulder to my jaw, biting at my ear before his hands begin to wander across my chest.

"My turn," he says, trailing his fingertip down my arm. "What is this?" he asks as he grabs my wrist and pulls it in front of his face. His thumb traces the scars there that the tattoos fail to hide completely.

"Past trauma," I tell him, pulling my wrist free of his grasp as he flops over on his back. "I saw some other...demons, I guess? Are you all demons?"

He nods.

"On my way back here, when I was trying to find you after the maze. I couldn't get my head on straight, and I couldn't remember where your tent was or even what you were here. So I stumbled into the first tent I saw, and there were two demons with black eyes like yours and blood covering their mouths. They were feeding on a girl that was strung up like a cow at slaughter. Is that what's going to happen to me? Is that what you do?"

He shrugs noncommittally.

"Have I done it before? Yes. I'm thousands of years old, and I'm a demon. I'm not some romanticized version. I've killed people, and will probably kill many in the future. I've tortured, and will torture." He pauses and tickles Kali, who moves under his touch. "Your taste is like nothing I've ever experienced," he says, meeting my eyes. "Who's to say I won't tie you up and keep you as my enslaved pet if you ever decide you want to leave me?"

My stomach begins to churn with anxiety at the thought of being tied up like an animal, carted around from one city to the next, never being allowed to walk around freely again. All because he's claiming I'm some sort of mate for him.

"But for now?" He shakes his head. "I know you want to stay with me. You're drawn to me just as much as I'm drawn to you. So it won't be an issue."

"Does anyone else have a Fated human?" I ask him, swiftly changing the subject because I'm afraid if I think about that for too long, I'll try to run. And I don't think that's the best course of action. I also want to stay right now. I don't want to give up the great sex or the orgasmic blood-sucking thing he does.

Christ, that shit is good.

"Nemo does," he answers. "He's the ringleader, the one that was leading the main show when you first got here. He has a woman he keeps tucked away in his tent. I think they've been together for about fifty years or so now."

"Rune." I sit up, my stomach in knots all over again. "Does feeding off of me make me live forever? Have I just signed on for thousands of years of this?"

"Stop being so dramatic, Johnny," he says with a smile. "It can if you want it to." He wags his eyebrows at me before he pulls me back onto the bed. I land on top of him, Kali scurrying off of his stomach and hiding somewhere on his back. "I didn't think the universe would send me such a worrywart. Shut the fuck up and make out with me," he pouts. "My dick is hard again."

He grabs my hand and rubs it against his dick, which is, in fact, already hard again. He leans up and takes one of my lip rings in between his teeth, making me groan and roll into him. His lips are so soft, and he tastes too fucking good. I can't say no to him.

"What about my friends?" I ask between kisses.

"Taken care of," he says as he sucks the tender flesh of my throat into his mouth.

"As in dead?" I ask him. I should be more worried, but we aren't even that close. I keep them out of necessity to not become a full-fledged hermit. And with the way his dick keeps rubbing against mine, I'd probably let him kill them if he just lets me come again.

"As in they won't remember you," he says nonchalantly, flipping us over so that he's on top, and then his mouth is back on mine, hot and all-consuming. I can barely breathe when he's on top of me, sucking my damn soul out of my body through my lips.

He reaches between us, freeing both of our dicks and gripping them together as he continues to abuse my mouth. He rubs over our heads, collecting the precum and using it to lubricate our cocks as they move together. They slip and move against each other as he pumps them in his fist.

"I'm going to come," I tell him, the sight of us together like that pushing me to a quick release.

"Come, baby," he tells me, stroking his hand harder and faster. "I'm right behind you." His eyes go black as he watches me fall over the edge.

"Fuck," I growl, throwing my head back onto the pillow as I empty my load onto my stomach. He follows soon after, mixing my release with his on my abs. He runs his finger through the sticky liquid and brings it to his mouth. I watch him through heavy-lidded eyes, exhausted from the night.

"You were right," he hums, the black in his eyes slowly fading back to his normal silver. "We do taste fucking delicious."

CHAPTER ELEVEN

RUNE – THE NEXT CITY

I use my finger to fill in the space around his eyes with black paint. He looks more demon than any of us like this with his dark brown eyes. I move on to paint his nose and then the outline of his teeth over his white cheeks. We slick back his hair out of his face, accentuating his cheekbones even more.

"I can't wait to come all over this pretty face later," I tell him as I finish. He rolls his eyes and pushes me away to get a look at himself in the mirror. He's been with me for over a week now, and every night I have to perform, he lets me paint his face as another way for me to stake my claim on him.

Then, after everyone leaves, we ignore everyone else and fuck like rabbits as I feed from him. We've discovered my little Fated likes me to bite him near his groin, drinking from him as I stroke him to climax. The noises he makes as I pull and pull from the wound could probably wake the dead.

"Opening in five!" the ticket master shouts from outside our tent.

"Come on, you two!" Mara sings from the front of the tent. "Stop fucking and come join the show!" Kali skims along my skin, settling in her usual spot on my collarbones as I pull my shirt over my head. Her tongue pokes out a few times, making me twitch and smile.

"That tickles," I tell her, stroking her head.

Cash walks up behind me and wraps his arms around my waist.

"Let's go before Mara decides to drag me out by my ear again," he says, a look of real fear in his eyes. A few nights ago, he had screamed like a little girl as she ripped him out of bed by his ear, still naked as the day he was born, to join whatever party she was throwing that night.

"Come join the revelry!" she shouts again.

"Coming!" he shouts back, kissing my neck before and pulling out a cigarette as he moves through the curtain to join her. Once he's gone, I'm struck sick, bending over and vomiting into the water basin in front of me. It's all blood, seeing as the only thing I've eaten today is Cash.

I watch as it swirls and morphs with the water, forming the shape of what looks like a dog. My stomach turns again, and I fight against the urge to empty the rest of the contents into the bowl. Dread sweeps through my body, causing me to break out in a cold sweat.

If this means what I think it does, we've been found, and Hell is coming for us.

"Rune!" Mara's shrill voice pierces through to my skull.

"Fucking coming!" I shout back, wiping my mouth and fixing the bit of paint around my mouth before following them out into the oncoming crowd.

ABOUT DANA ISALY

Dana Isaly is a writer of dark romance, fantasy romance, and has also been known to dabble in poetry (it was a phase in college, leave her alone).

She was born in the midwest and has been all over but now resides (begrudgingly) in Alabama. She is a lover of books, coffee, and rainy days. Dana is probably the only person in the writing community that is actually a morning person.

She swears too much, is way too comfortable on her TikTok (@authordanaisaly and @auth.danaisaly), and believes that love is love is love.

You can find her on Instagram (@danaisalyauthorpage) or on Facebook with the same name, but she won't lie, Facebook is not her forte.

www.danaisaly.com
Scars
Games We Play

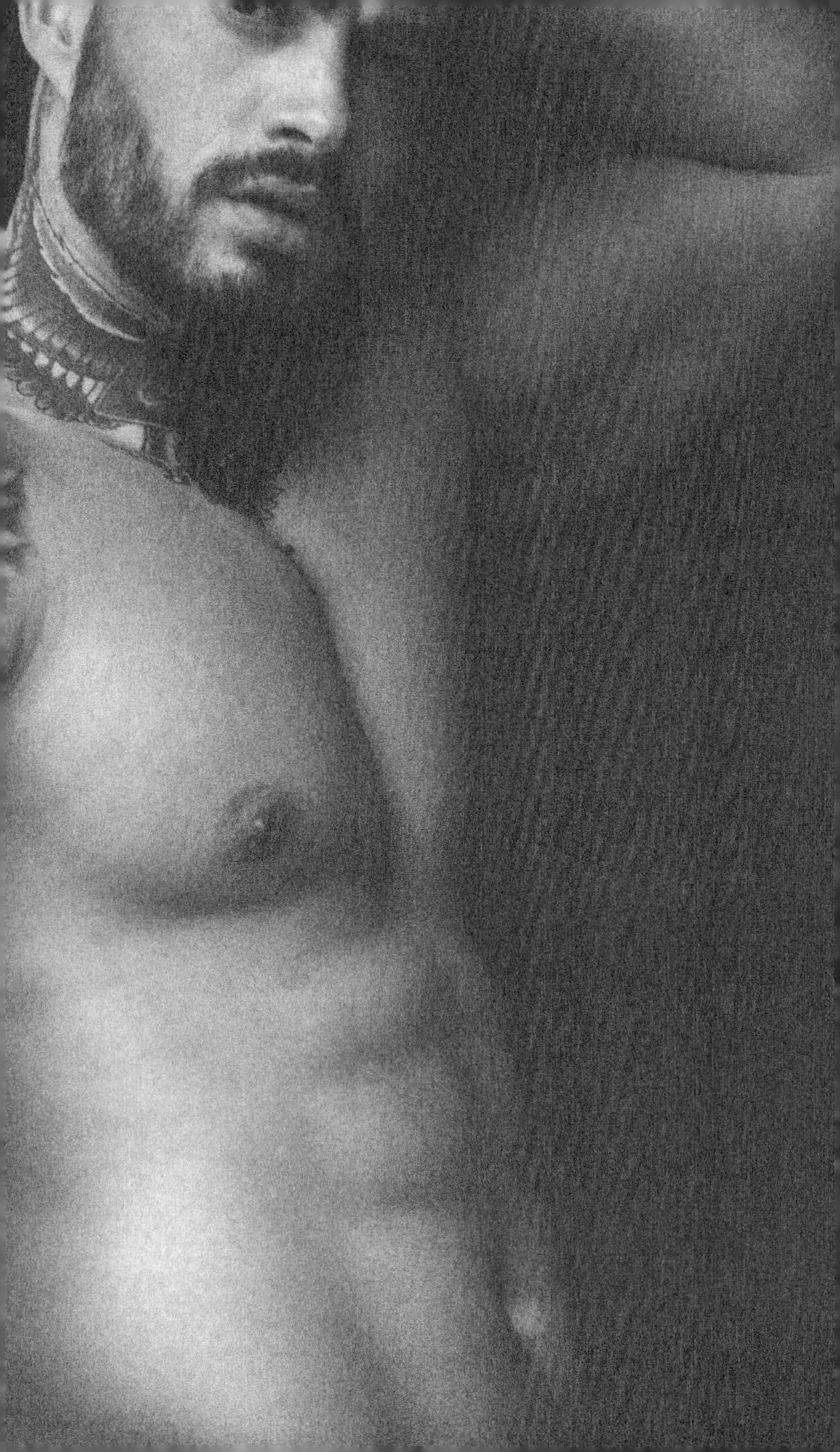

DANCING WITH THE DEVIL

BY ISABEL LUCERO

Copyright © 2021 by Isabel Lucero
All rights reserved.
No part of this book may be reproduced in any form or by any electronic or mechanical means, including information storage and retrieval systems, without written permission from the author, except for the use of brief quotations in a book review.
This is a work of fiction. Names, characters, places, brands, media and incidents are either the product of the author's imagination or are used fictitiously. The author acknowledges the trademarked status and trademark owners of various products referenced in this work of fiction, which have been used without permission. The publication and use of these trademarks are not authorized, associated with, or sponsored by the trademark owners. Any resemblance to actual events, locales, or persons, living or dead, is entirely coincidental.

PROLOGUE

There are times in your life when you look back at specific moments and wonder if you should've done something differently. Sometimes the decisions you make can affect what happens, but oftentimes, you're going to get the hand fate dealt to you, regardless of what you do.

When I was sixteen, if I had taken my usual route from my friend's house to mine, instead of going the long way just in the hope of seeing the cute boy I liked, maybe I would've made it home before my father left for the last time. Would him seeing me have made him stay? Probably not, but I would've been able to say goodbye, even if I thought he would be returning.

On my eighteenth birthday, I drank way too much. I slept with a guy I normally wouldn't have. I can't remember half the night because of all the shots of tequila my friends kept passing to me. If I hadn't gotten that drunk, I wouldn't have slept with Johnny, who was five years older than me and kind of disgusting. I wouldn't have been hungover the following day, therefore missing out on breakfast with my mom—the last morning that was normal before we found out she had cancer.

Days after turning twenty-one, I had no idea who I was about to encounter. I didn't even want to go out. My friends all but kidnapped me and forced me to have fun, knowing I'd spent the last few years working my ass off just so me and my mom could continue to live in the house we shared with my dad. They said it was time for a break. I was numb. Mom had passed and I was alone, using work as a way to keep my mind off of everything that was happening around me.

They called him El Diablo, and I stumbled into his lair. Looking back, even after everything, I'm not sure I would do anything differently. Maybe this was fate. Maybe this is what I needed.

CHAPTER ONE

"Come on, chica. I'm not taking no for an answer," Angelique says, rifling through my closet. "Where are all your clothes?"

"Dirty, probably," I say, sitting cross legged in the center of my full-sized bed.

She scoffs, moving to my dresser. "You gotta have something that's not," she glances at me, eyeing my pajamas, "that."

"I haven't been out a lot lately. Maybe you forgot."

She gives me a pitiful look before standing up straight, her hands on her hips. "Audri, you know I love you. You're my best friend, *mi hermana*. Yeah?" She nods. "I admire the shit out of you. You're strong, you're capable, and probably the bravest person I know. You've done nothing but work and struggle for the last three years. I know you're still grieving for your mom. It's only been a few months. I get it. But you need to get out of this house. You need air. You need food. You need some fun."

"I have to finish packing, Angie. I have to move out of here soon. They're foreclosing on this place, and my apartment is going to be ready for me in two weeks. I have to have the house cleaned out." I run my hands through my hair, realizing I haven't brushed it in two days. "I have a lot to do."

"Go out with us and I'll come back here tomorrow and help you, okay? I'll bring my yellow latex gloves and a gallon sized bottle of Fabuloso. We'll have this place smelling like lavender and shit, okay? Come on. It's just one night. Nothing life changing. Let's just get drunk. We haven't celebrated your birthday yet."

"I didn't feel like celebrating anything," I murmur, falling to my back.

She sighs before laying next to me on the bed, her arm wrapping around my stomach. "I know. Let's drown our sorrows. For one night, let's pretend we're other people. Who do you want to be?"

I snort. "Someone rich."

After a few seconds, she clears her throat. "Your name is Tinsley Livingston. You're married to a sixty-year old millionaire who you hate, but he gives you money and leaves you alone most of the time. You're mainly eye-candy for his old, liver-spotted friends that attend his fancy schmance parties. I'm Cressida Lowell, a stuck-up bitch who thinks I'm better than everyone even though I've never worked a day in my life and I'm only rich because my Grandpa is the founder of some manufacturing company."

I laugh, turning to look at her. "You're crazy."

She grins. "Come on. We'll go raid my step-mom's closet. She's got some high-end shit."

"Are you for real?"

Her dark eyes light up. "Yes! It'll be fun." She stands and yanks me to my feet. "Get in the shower, Tinsley. I'll call Leo and Naomi and tell them our plans."

I groan but her excitement starts to grow on me. "Tell them to pick out new names, then."

She squeaks and pulls out her phone, and I quickly get showered and ready.

Almost forty minutes later, we show up to her dad's house.

"Are they here?"

"Nah. They went on vacation. Funny how when he was married to my mom, he never had time for vacations, but now that he's married to this bitch, he has all the time in the world."

"Does she still try to be friends with you?"

"In front of my dad. I know she hates me, but the feeling's mutual."

A year ago, Angelique's dad told her he was divorcing her mom. She later found out her dad had been having an affair with Piper for two years before he decided to leave her mom, and then she found out that Piper was twenty-four, while her dad was fifty. She's been angry ever since.

Turns out, Piper comes from money, and they mostly live off her family's wealth.

"If she knew my dad gave me a key to their house, she'd be livid,"

Angie says with a wicked grin. "But Dad's still trying to make nice with me."

She opens the door, turns off the alarm, and we head up to Piper's closet. After going through half her stuff, I find a pair of Louboutins that scream my name. Black heeled sandals that'll add an extra five inches to my five foot four frame. The red lacquer on the soles is flawless, making me wonder if she's ever worn these. I find a white dress with a halter neckline and a slightly ruffled hem. It hugs my body and then flares a little right above my knees.

"I feel like an uppity bitch already."

Angie snorts, then pulls out a beautiful sequined dress. "Maybe this will be my uppity bitch dress." She strips down and steps into it.

It's nude-colored with navy-blue lace embellished with sequins. The lace layer extends past the nude slip, falling below her knees, and the plunging V-neck exposes some of her cleavage.

"It's stunning," I tell her.

"I can already feel myself changing," she whispers before busting out into a loud laugh. "I saw some YSL heels somewhere that would go great with this."

After a few more minutes, we spritz some perfume on our wrists and necks, then cackle into the wind as we make our way back to her car.

It's nearly ten o'clock when we reach the bar.

"The Devil's Lair?" I question.

"Sounds creepy, right? I heard good things about this place, though." She checks her lipstick, fluffs her hair, and then grabs her phone. "Naomi and Leo are here. Let's go."

We walk as fast as we can across the street, hop onto the sidewalk, and round the corner. "Why are we here anyway? El Paso has plenty of bars downtown. Why are we on the outskirts?"

"Why not?" Angie says with a shrug. "Always good to try something new."

We spot Leo and Naomi lingering on the sidewalk several feet ahead. Naomi and Angie have been dating for the last nine months and are still head over heels in love with each other. Leo's been a friend of mine and Angie's since we were all ten. I love Leo to death. He's been there through every heartbreak, illness, broken bone, and fractured friendship. He's the brother I never had.

They obviously got Angie's message, because Leo's dressed in a pair of black slacks and teal colored button up, when usually he's in jeans and a hoodie, regardless of the temperature. Naomi, who's more comfortable in big T-shirts and ripped jeans, is absolutely jaw dropping in a burgundy blazer and pants set, with a black lace undershirt, showing hints of skin.

"Baby!" Angie squeals, throwing herself at Naomi. "Holy fuck, you're so hot."

"No, you are. Where'd you get this dress?"

"My evil stepmother."

Naomi shakes her head, grinning at her before holding her chin between her fingers and planting a soft kiss. "I love your thieving ass."

Angie giggles. "I'm just borrowing."

Leo elbows me. "You don't look too bad yourself. Are those red bottoms?"

I lift my foot. "Yep. Hopefully I don't fuck them up too bad." I push him back gently, looking him up and down. "What's your name, sir? Don't look like a Leo to me."

He straightens his back and adjusts his expression. "I'm Preston Vandenberg."

I laugh. "I love it. Naomi, what about you?" I ask, turning to face the lovebirds.

"Margaux Carmichael," she says with a bow. "Margaux ends in an aux not just an o. So, it's fancy."

"Literally nobody's gonna ask you to spell your name," Angie says with a laugh.

"Well, okay. Let's go mingle with the peasants," I say, holding my head up high and interlocking my arm with Leo's.

Inside, the bar is immediately to the left, and the room stretches out in front of us. It's narrow but still spacious. We order a round of shots and down them immediately before taking our drinks and walking down the center of the room. The walls are lined with high-backed leather booths, leaving you unable to see anyone sitting behind you. Past the last booths, the room opens up a little wider and has an almost living room type setup with deep red velvet couches and a rug. Around the corner is a doorway where music filters in.

"Wow, this place is unique," Angie says.

We follow the bass and find a small dance floor, but it's packed with people. After finishing our drinks, we all head in and start dancing. Thirty minutes later, Leo and I head back to the bar to get more drinks. When a guy approaches me, I turn on my Tinsley attitude and tell him all about my aging husband who I hope dies soon so I can inherit his money, while Leo, or Preston, chimes in about his rich family and how they own and operate container ships and ports.

Once we've annoyed people enough to leave us alone, we crack up and make our way back to Naomi and Angie, drink and dance some more, and then finally find a booth to rest in once our feet have had enough. After another round of shots, a few people hang around our table, and it's the lovebirds turn to spin tales about their lives. We laugh and have so much fun that I almost forget about the turmoil my life is in.

"I gotta pee," I announce, getting up from the booth. "Does anyone know where the bathroom is?"

"Maybe in the dance room?" Angie offers.

"No, I thought they were in the other corner," Leo says, pointing behind us. "Like, in that corner."

"I'll find it. Be right back."

"Be careful," Angie says.

"I'm a big girl." I stumble as soon as the words leave my mouth. With a laugh, I say, "That's just because of the shoes."

I finish my drink before I walk off, looking for a bathroom sign. My vision is a little blurry, taking a bit more effort to see where I'm going. I bump into a few people, apologizing and blaming the heels, but I know it's the alcohol. I had one too many shots and not enough food. I don't even remember when I ate last.

There's no bathroom in the dance room. I clumsily text Angie and tell her just that, but probably with a lot of misspellings. I head back to the main room and cross it, finding a door that has no telltale signs of a bathroom, but attempt it anyway. Inside is a small hallway with doors on either side. I barely make out the figure of a person on a sign next to a door before I hurry through.

"Yes!" I exclaim out loud, rushing to the stall and texting Angie that I found it.

Me: *Foun bathrom. Feeels goodto peeee.*

Angie: *You're dumb.*

She sends three crying laugh emojis, and after what feels like releasing a gallon of pee, the door opens and I hear a man's voice.

Me: *Shit. Think 'm in thr mens roon*

Me: *Guy jus vame in*

Angie: *He hot?*

I stop texting, waiting for the guy to leave, but he stays on the phone for way too long. Luckily, I'm on the end and he hasn't noticed my heels but it's really hard not to move or make any noise.

Eventually, I hear the lock of another stall sliding in place and I peek between the gap in my own door and don't see him. I quickly flush and run out of the room, my heels click-clacking loudly across the floor. It's not that I think he'll try anything, though you never really know, but it's embarrassing to be in the wrong bathroom.

I go straight across the small hall and into what I believe is the women's restroom so I can wash my hands and inspect my appearance. However, as soon as the door closes, I realize it's not at all like the men's room. While there is a small entryway, there's also three steps, a platform, and three more steps.

Why would they put fucking stairs in a women's bathroom? They obviously hate women and want us to break our ankles.

When I get to the bottom, the sound of an angry male voice stops me in my tracks. Luckily, the stairs are carpeted, so my footsteps seem to have gone unnoticed.

He isn't yelling, but you can tell he's pissed off. He's speaking Spanish, and though I'm half Mexican, I never learned the language well enough to understand. Another voice chimes in, and they suddenly switch to English.

"I don't know why they didn't fucking show up. Esteban and Julio had scoped it out already. We were in the clear. These *pinche pendejos.*" He scoffs and the other man speaks again.

"We have a new date? Time?"

"*Si. Dos semanas.* Midnight."

"*¡Mierda!*"

"Sorry, boss."

I don't know what the hell they're talking about, but my gut tells me it's dangerous and I probably don't want to know. I turn, ready to quietly make my way back up the stairs, but when I hit the platform, a voice stops me.

"Hey! Who the fuck are you?"

I panic and flee up the last remaining three stairs, before I can open the door, I'm hit in the head and the lights go out.

CHAPTER TWO

When I wake up, I'm shrouded in complete darkness, hardly able to see anything around me. My head throbs with a viscous headache, and when I run my hand across the back of my skull, there's a tender spot that has me hissing while I snatch my hand away.

I've also been stripped of my borrowed dress and heels and left in my underwear on what feels like the thinnest mattress to exist. I get to my knees and blindly reach around me, finding a scratchy blanket before my fingers touch something cold. I use my knuckles to knock on it a little and determine my little bed must be directly on concrete.

I'm not chained or tied up, which is good news. Well, if there can be good news when you've been hit over the head, abducted, and thrown into a dark room.

After getting up and making my way around the room while pressing my palms against the walls, I never come across any windows or a doorknob. But there has to be a door here somewhere. How else did I get in?

Before I reach my mattress again, I kick something over, the sound making me jump. My heart races and sweat forms under my arms instantly. Someone may have heard and could be on their way in here. I freeze in place for several minutes before dropping down and searching for the item I knocked over.

It's a bucket. They must mean for me to use this as a toilet.

I crawl over to my bed and my shock begins to lift, penetrated by panic and engulfed by fear. I don't know how long I've been here or how long I'll be kept. I don't know what they plan to do with me, or why. Sure, I heard some of their conversation, but I have no clue what they were talking about.

Time drags, minutes feeling like hours. I don't know whether it's daytime or night. I think about my friends and how concerned they must be. Have they called the police yet? Will they be able to find me?

Eventually, my stomach rumbles with hunger and my bladder threatens to burst whether I sit over a bucket or not. So once I've found my way back to the makeshift toilet and relieve myself, I begin pacing the room. I find that I can take ten steps one way, with the heel of one foot touching the toes of my other, and nine steps the other way. This information helps me absolutely zero, but it's something to do.

Hours later, when I'm back in bed, rousing from sleep once more, I spot a light shining down from above.

If I was religious, I'd think it was God coming for me, but I'm not stupid. I know I can't rely on anyone but myself to get me out of here. I've always been the responsible one, finding a way to get out of any problems that come my way. I'm determined. I've always found a way to make things work, even when it was looking bleak. I didn't rely on prayer and miracles. I just did any and everything to get what I needed. So, the light I see, the one that's quickly disappearing, isn't any sort of savior. It's my captor. It's who I need to get to know in order to find my way out of here.

"Wait!" I yell, sitting up.

The light widens and I squint at it, wondering how the hell the door is in the ceiling. Maybe I'm hallucinating.

A voice says something in Spanish.

"What? I don't understand."

I scurry forward, trying to get a look at the man, but I can't see him.

"Who are you?"

I don't know why I say it, maybe fear. "Tinsley. Tinsley Livingston."

The door closes without a word.

"No, wait!"

It's too late, they're gone.

I'm unsure how much time has gone by before that light appears again.

"Who are you?" the accented voice asks.

"Why am I here? What are you going to do with me?"

Silence.

"Hello? Please. I'm hungry."

The door begins to close again.

"Okay. Stop! My name's Audriana Bernal."

The light disappears as he traps me in darkness once again. Tears of frustration burn the backs of my eyes as I sit on the bed and wait.

When the door opens again, this time it's followed by the dropping of a ladder and then the descending figure of a large man.

I scoot up, pushing my back against the wall, my heart battering my ribs with every rapid beat.

He throws a mini water bottle to my bed and a sealed sandwich bag that you can get from almost any convenience store. I lunge forward and grab them before scurrying back to the wall.

The man stands to the right of the light beaming down, mostly cloaked in shadows. Part of his face is highlighted, letting me know little more than he has a short beard, dark hair, and menacing eyes.

¿No hablas español?"

I shake my head and the brow I can see lifts slightly. "I know enough that you asked if I can speak spanish. I can't."

He grunts. "You say your name is Audriana Bernal."

"It is."

"Where are you from?"

"Here. El Paso."

"Where do you work?"

"I have two jobs. I work at a casino and I babysit for a family."

"There are no casinos in El Paso."

"The one in New Mexico. It's fifteen minutes away."

I finally tear into the sandwich, unable to wait any longer. It's just ham and cheese, but I'm not complaining.

"What did you hear in my club?"

"Nothing," I say around a mouthful of food.

"I don't believe you."

I question what I should tell him. Should I admit to some of it or deny hearing anything? I was so close that it's obvious I would've heard something.

"Nothing I understand," I offer, uncapping the water and taking a drink.

"You work two shitty jobs and yet you were wearing designer clothes. You tell me your name is Tinsley and now it's Audriana. You didn't hear anything, but now it's nothing you understood. You're a liar," he snarls, stepping forward.

I hunch my back and turn to the side, afraid he'll hit me, but instead he takes the food and water bottle back. "Wait."

"No," he bites. "Liars don't get rewarded."

"I'm not fucking lying!" I yell, crawling to the end of the mattress and peering up at him. "I don't know what the hell you were talking about. I don't even care. I was drunk and looking for a bathroom. The clothes aren't mine. Me and my friend took them from—"

"So you're a thief?"

"No, we borrowed them."

"I'm tired of listening to you," he says, making his way to the ladder. "You'll be staying down here for a little while. Get comfortable."

"Can I get some clothes? Use an actual bathroom? Maybe get a light."

"No."

"My friends are gonna call the cops. They'll be looking for me."

"And they won't find you."

It's the last thing he says before he disappears through the hole in the ceiling. I run to the ladder but he pulls it up before I can get a grip.

"You're a fucking asshole!" I yell. "You think starving girls in a dank room makes you tough? You're a piece of shit!"

The door closes but I keep yelling and cussing. He doesn't return again for a while.

CHAPTER THREE

I feel like a whole twenty-four hours goes by before I see that light again. I'm starving and my mouth is dry. I don't even want to talk about how gross and dirty I feel. I need a shower and to be able to brush my teeth. I want to run a comb through my hair that already feels matted. I want to feel like a human again. Not even an animal should be treated like this.

When he gets to the bottom of the ladder, he once again steps out of the light so I can't get a good look at him. "Are you going to be a good girl this time?"

I bite my lip, wanting to have a smart remark, but I'm not really in the position to be feisty. I'm weak and in need of things only he can give me. I have to play nice, plus I don't know how dangerous this guy is. He obviously has no qualms about abducting women. Who knows what else he's capable of?

I nod.

"Use your words."

"I'll be good."

"We'll see." He appears to lean against the wall opposite me. "What did you hear in my club?"

"Two men's names. I can't even remember what they were. And something about a new date."

"That's it?"

"Some stuff in Spanish."

"Which you say you don't understand."

"I don't."

He huffs. *"Me pregunto cómo sentiría estar dentro de esa panocha mojada."*

I stare back at him, confused. He must've said something that he thought would garner a reaction if I understood.

"Do you know who I am?" he asks in English.

"No."

Several long seconds tick by as we watch each other. He produces another mini water bottle and tosses it at me. I snatch it up and down half of it in one gulp.

"Do you have any food?" I question softly.

"You don't work for Gomez?" he asks.

"Who?"

"Don't play stupid."

"I'm not. I told you, I work at a casino. The family I babysit for are Elizabeth and Abel Perales. I don't know anybody named Gomez."

He stares at me silently, the seconds ticking by without any action. My stomach growls so loud I feel like it echoes in this small room. He pulls something from his coat pocket and throws it at my feet. It's a Snickers.

Not what I was hoping for, but something is better than nothing. "Thanks," I murmur before ripping it open.

"I don't trust people," he states, and I lift my head to gaze in his direction. "I don't trust people I've known for years, because everyone is always out for themselves, you understand? And I definitely don't trust young women who are caught eavesdropping on information meant for very few ears. I don't know what you were doing down there. Maybe you're telling the truth, but I don't know that for certain. So, you're going to stay here with me until a specific date, so I know for sure that you won't be releasing any information to anyone else before then."

My jaw drops. "How long is that?"

"You don't need much more than that."

I choke out a humorless laugh. "Do you think I'm going to dig myself out of here? I don't know where I am." I shake my head. "I'm not sure who you think I could be, but I can assure you, I'm absolutely nobody of importance. I'm not into any crazy criminal activities. All I do is work."

"Criminal activities?" he repeats.

"I—" I close my mouth, wondering if I shouldn't have said anything. "I mean, you abducted me. That's criminal. I assume it's not the only illegal thing you've done."

He takes a slow, deliberate step closer to me, his lips drawing up into a wicked smirk. He crouches down to meet my gaze, and I get the first good look at him since being here. A gasp leaves my throat before I can control myself.

He's striking. More attractive than I could've imagined, but also terrifying to look at. I find it hard to keep eye contact.

Dark, cold, menacing eyes meet mine. He watches me from beneath a lowered brow, his gaze unabashedly moving down my body, lingering on my breasts before traveling all the way to my ankles. He has a sharp jaw covered by a five o'clock shadow, a strong chin, and beautiful slicked back hair. It mimics the ocean at night—dark and wavy. A scar cuts across his cheekbone, but doesn't marr his frightening beauty.

"You'd be right," he says in a husky tone, his tattooed hand coming up as his knuckles rub across the hair on his jaw. "I've done awful things, and worse yet, I don't regret them. I don't feel bad because it was what needed to be done. So remember this," he offers, reaching out and grabbing my face in his hand, "I'll do terrible things to you if you prove that it's what needs to be done. I'm not one to fuck with."

I attempt to nod frantically, but his grip on my face makes it difficult.

"Don't let me find out you've lied to me."

His hand moves down, grazing the side of neck before he wraps his fingers around my throat, his eyes meeting mine.

"I'm n-not lying. I swear. I'm nobody. I'm just a girl struggling to find a reason to live."

"And yet you want to, don't you?" he questions.

"Want to what?"

He squeezes my throat. "Live."

I reach up and grab his hand with mine. "Yes," I squeak out.

"Why?"

"I don't—I don't know," I say, trying to pull his hand from my throat. "Please."

His top lip pulls up on one side, sneering at me. "You might be interested to know that begging has never helped anyone when it's me who controls whether they live or die." His gaze moves to my mouth. "But I do enjoy hearing pretty girls beg. It's just usually for something else."

I try to relax and not fight. I can still breathe, but it's difficult. Fighting and panicking will only make it harder, and he just gave me a thought. A plan.

My tongue slowly wets my bottom lip as I force myself to stare back at him, relaxing my eyebrows and allowing my gaze to become hooded.

He pulls away, standing up and moving back toward the ladder.

"Sir." I pause for a second, reaching for my neck with my hand, running my fingers across the hollow of my throat. "I was wondering if, at some point, I could use a bathroom? Or maybe get some clothes? I'd even take one of your shirts."

His nostrils flare slightly when he looks at me. "We'll see."

For the first time since arriving here, a tiny smile graces my lips. I think I know what I have to do to ensure my freedom.

Men. No matter their background, job, morality, or lack thereof, you can always be sure of one thing: they are ruled by their cocks.

CHAPTER FOUR

My confidence wanes when he doesn't show up after several hours, or at least what I assume is several hours. I use my bucket, the smell of urine getting stronger and requiring me to move it farther from my bed, and then I crawl under my ratty blanket.

Luckily, and probably from the minimal food I've consumed, I haven't had to do anything but pee, but I need to convince this man to let me use a bathroom, and soon.

I'm not sure how long I'm asleep for, but when I do wake up, it's due to the sound of the ladder being lowered into my room.

"Get up," he orders. Once I'm on my feet next to the mattress, he says, "Come here."

My steps are slow and careful, and when I finally stop in front of him, he brings a dark cloth bag up and attempts to put it over my head.

"What're you doing?" I ask, stumbling back.

"Don't question me. I'm putting this on your head, now get the fuck back up here."

I only take one step before he reaches out and yanks the bag over my head, tightening it around my neck. Before I can protest, he scoops me into his arms and throws me over his broad shoulder.

"What? Oh my god," I screech.

His arm wraps around my legs, his hand hot against my cool thigh as I dangle upside down, my hands holding onto his waist.

He carries me up the ladder, and in any other circumstance, I'd be impressed by his strength.

When we get to the top, he grabs hold of my hips, flipping me back over and depositing me on my ass on something cold before pushing me back.

Clunking and clattering around me has me jolting, and then he clasps his hand around my wrist and yanks me to my feet. He's quiet the entire time, but my feet can tell when we move to different rooms based on the flooring, and the stairs we climb.

When he brings me to a stop, I hear a door close and then he's loosening the bag and removing it from my head. I squint, bringing my hand up to shield my eyes as the bright fluorescent lights nearly blind me.

My head swivels, inspecting my surroundings. I whimper as I realize I'm in a bathroom. My eyes find his and tears threaten to fall down my cheeks in overwhelming gratitude. "Thank you."

He barely nods, but doesn't make a move to leave. If he thinks I'm about to use the bathroom in front of him, he'd be wrong. I take a minute to study the room and can't help but notice the opulence.

The walls are the color of desert sand and appear to be stucco textured. Teal tiles with the hue of a shimmering exotic sea, cover the entirety of the shower enclosure and the back wall where a clawfoot tub sits in an alcove beyond a rounded archway. The toilet is just past the white washstands and countertop basins, separated by a false wall. A colorful rug sits in the center, and plants and potted cacti are placed around the spacious bathroom, giving it more of a spa-like atmosphere than your usual restroom.

"Can I get some privacy?" I ask with a bit of annoyance, but quickly add, "Please."

"You don't have anything I haven't seen before."

I flatten my lips and stare at him. "It's not about that."

"No?"

I spread my arms. "I'm basically naked now. Can I use the toilet in peace?"

He looks annoyed by me, but I don't care. Don't kidnap women if you don't want to deal with them.

"I'll be right outside this door. You have ten minutes."

I think to argue, but I don't. "Thanks."

He leaves, closing the door louder than necessary, but I don't waste any time. I use the bathroom as quickly as I can before heading to the sink to wash my hands. It's there that I get the first glimpse of myself in nearly a week in the round mirror hanging on the wall. My hair is a rat's nest, my makeup mostly smeared off, the black liner and mascara I had on is smudged around my eyes. I look awful.

I run my tongue across my teeth and hate how dirty they feel. I do a quick search on the shelves nearby and find a toothbrush and toothpaste. I don't even care if it's his or not.

Once my mouth feels clean again, I eye the pristine white tub, surrounded by plants and bamboo stools, wanting nothing more than to take a relaxing bubble bath. However, the water would probably be filthy, and I doubt he'd give me time to actually enjoy myself. My feet pad across the gray tiled floor, getting me to the shower where I turn the water on. The doors are glass. Clear, not frosted.

Before I can step inside, the bathroom door opens and he walks in. I pause, hating that this is the time he decided to join me. He doesn't say anything, choosing to sit in a chair that gives him the perfect view of the shower.

I stare at him for several seconds and he simply arches a brow. He's even more attractive than I thought when we were surrounded by darkness and shadows. Now that I've adjusted to the lights of this bathroom and actually take the time to study him, he's beautiful in the most intimidating way.

Turning the hot water up, I hope it'll steam up the glass enough to obstruct his view. When I can't wait any longer, I turn my back to him and remove my panties and bra before stepping into the shower stall and closing the door.

The hot water feels amazing as it cascades down my body, washing away the dirt and grime. I reach for a sponge in a hanging basket in the corner and squeeze the soap in it. After scrubbing my skin, I turn around and allow the water to soak my hair. When I open my eyes, his dark gaze staring in my direction is the first thing I see.

His hair is long on top, mussed up like he's been running his hands through it all day. He's wearing a long sleeve black shirt, his tattoos peaking out at the wrist, under a gold watch, and down his hand, all the way to his fingers. His thumb runs back and forth across his bottom lip as he watches me, and my stomach does a little flip.

I remember I have to play nice. I have to pretend to be more docile than I am. He needs to think I'm soft and vulnerable. He needs to think I'm afraid, but also interested.

Forcing myself to stay facing him, I wash my hair and let the water pour over me, ridding my body of bubbles.

When the water begins to cool, I know I can't drag this out any longer, but I'm not exactly in a rush to go back into the dark dungeon.

Realizing I didn't bring a towel with me, I steel myself and open the shower door, presenting my fully nude and wet body to him. I've never been too modest or insecure. I like my body. I'm curvy—my hips rounded and my thighs thick. My stomach is a little soft, but it doesn't bother me. My tits have always garnered me attention, even when I was teenager. I was a D cup when I was sixteen, and while I hated it then, I've learned to embrace what I have no control over.

"Towel?" I ask.

He lazily gestures to the sinks, his eyes never leaving my body, and I notice the folded towels at the bottom of the washstands.

Sauntering over, I'm aware his eyes are likely watching my ass jiggle, but I still bend down and grab a towel and do my best to cover myself while also absorbing the water from my skin.

"Do you have anything for me to put on?" I question, securing the towel around my body. "And maybe a comb?"

"You're beginning to ask for a little too much."

"I'm sorry," I reply, making my voice soft. I start walking toward him, but keep my eyes down. "I-I was hoping to be able to eat something. I can do without a comb, but I need food."

He sighs, actually frustrated with my need to eat. I could roll my eyes and say something snarky, but I believed him when he said he's done awful things. I just need him to like me enough to be willing to free me.

I slowly kneel between his parted legs and drop my head forward, letting my hair curtain my face. "Please."

His hand fists a chunk of my wet locks at the base of my skull, yanking my head up. My eyes widen as I rise up higher on my knees to keep the pull from hurting too much. My hands go to his thighs for balance and he stares at me with a snarl etched on his face.

"Stop playing games with me, little girl."

"What do you mean?" I cry.

He pulls me closer, bringing my face within six inches of his. "As much as I enjoyed your little show in the shower, I know it was exactly that. A show. And now you fall to your knees in front of me. For what? The only time you should be on your knees in front of a man is when you're ready to take his cock in your mouth. Is that what you want? You want me to bruise your throat?"

I shake my head frantically.

"Then why are you trying to seduce me? You think I haven't seen tits before? You think I'm that easy?"

"No, no. That's not...I wasn't trying—"

He brings his lips closer to mine. "You're nothing but a filthy liar."

"I'm not," I whimper.

The man shifts, reaching into his pocket. When he brings his hand up again, he's holding a knife. With a flick of his wrist, the blade pops out and my pulse spikes. I underestimated him.

Bringing the tip of the blade to my cheek, he says, "Tell me something true."

I lick my lips, my chest heaving as I look from the knife to his eyes. "I'm scared."

He grins. "Were you putting on a show for me?"

I hesitate and he grips my hair harder, tugging my head back as he begins to drag the blade down my cheek. A burning sensation streaks down my face before he situates the point at the hollow of my throat.

"Yes," I whisper.

"Why?"

"I want to live. I want you to free me."

"Tsk, tsk, tsk," he murmurs, shaking his head. "*Pobre niña*. So naive. So young. I can call three women over here right now. I don't need you."

"Then why haven't you killed me?" I ask, tears in my eyes.

"You want me to?" he asks, cocking his head slightly.

"No, but why am I here?"

"Because I don't think you are who you say you are."

"I'm not lying."

"We'll see. Until then, you'll be here." He sits back, releasing me and running his finger along the blade. "You wanna suck my cock?"

"What?" I question, eyes widening.

He smirks. "You're still on your knees with your hands on my thighs. I just assumed." I snatch my hands back so quick, I fall onto my ass. He flies out of the chair and gets on one knee, his hand reaching under the towel, fingers grazing me. "Wasn't a no."

I push myself back, towel coming open as my body shakes with fear. "Stop. Please."

"Expose yourself to me again," he says, ripping the towel all the way open, eyes dancing over inch of my body, "And I'm going to assume it's permission to do whatever the fuck I want." His fingers squeeze my breast before he slaps his palm on my thigh. "Come. We'll eat and you'll answer more questions."

He doesn't wait for me, leaving me to scramble to my feet and readjust my towel as I follow him into a massive bedroom, my heart lodged in my throat.

When we reach the bed, he turns around and grabs my wrist, swinging me to the mattress and forcing me to sit near the headboard.

He reaches into the bottom drawer of his nightstand and brings up a piece of rope. My jaw drops, ready to protest, but when he cocks his head, I pin my lips together.

"You're having a hard time biting your tongue, aren't you?" he asks, amusement in his tone as he secures my wrist to the headboard.

"I'm not really in a position to say anything."

"What position do you want to be in?"

My stomach clenches but I keep my mouth shut. His lips pull up again. "You know what I think?"

I raise my brows. "Hm?"

"I think you hate that you find me attractive, even though I've stolen you and brought you to my lair. I'm a bad man, and you should loathe everything about my existence, but you like what you see when you look at me."

With a scoff, I roll my eyes and look at the wall. "You're full of yourself."

"I can smell your arousal from here."

Heat flames my cheeks as he takes my other hand and rubs the pad of his thumb across the tattoo that stretches from my wrist to the middle of my forearm. While he studies it, I do the same to him. I catalogue every inch of his face, from his nearly black eyes, to his dark lashes, and fully proportionate lips. Lips that appear to be too soft to belong to a man like him. My eyes skate down his throat where he has a thick scar on the side of his neck.

"What's this?" he asks, tapping the tattoo.

"Just something dumb I got when I was young."

"Interesting."

"What?" I ask.

He straightens up, sliding his hands in his pockets. "That you'd have a tattoo of me on your arm."

My brows furrow. "What're you talking about?"

"El Diablo."

"You're calling yourself the devil?"

He grins in a way that reveals no joy. "Other people do."

I study my ink, the image of the devil and a woman dancing the tango, her leg hitched over his hip. "Oh."

"The devil, known as the personification of evil, and yet, you dance with him."

I turn my arm over. "I was a stupid kid."

"Because of the tattoo? Or because of your actions?"

My eyes fly to his. "What do you mean by *my actions*?"

DANCING WITH THE DEVIL

"You tell me."

Several seconds tick by before I say, "I thought we were going to eat."

His penetrating glare stays focused on me for a while before he walks out.

The truth of the matter is, I've also done bad things. Maybe not in the same way he has, but definitely more than the average person.

While he's gone, I stand and test how much I can move and how far I can go while being tied to the headboard. It's not much, but I'm able to open the drawer of the nightstand. I freeze when I see what's inside. Guns. Several of them. Mostly black, but the one that catches my eye has a gold plated grip and trigger. Written in script across the top is *el diablo*.

Once my heart starts beating normal again, I reach inside and gently push them to the back, grabbing for the papers underneath. I need a name or address. I need to know who he is and where I am. Maybe I'll be able to get to a phone or be able to escape. I need to know where to send people.

As my eyes scan over a paper that I can't even read because it's in Spanish, the sound of heavy-footed steps has my heart jumping into my throat. I put the papers back and shove the guns back on top, but before I can close the drawer, the door to the room opens.

"Tsk, tsk," he says, like he's not at all surprised to find me snooping. "*Niña mala.*"

I'm too afraid to ask what he said. I swiftly sit on the edge of the bed while he places the food on a table in the corner of the room. I may have just ruined my chances at eating.

"Find anything interesting?" he asks, slowly making his way toward me.

I don't reply, not even bothering to shake my head. I watch as he pulls the drawer open even more, removing the gold plated gun.

"You like this?" he asks.

I shake my head and then realize that's probably not the best answer.

"No?" He sits next to me, his leg touching mine. "It's my favorite gun. You see what's written here?" he questions, bringing the weapon closer to my face. "You like dancing with the devil, right?" He yanks my arm, flipping it over so we can see the ink. Pressing the tip of the gun to my skin, he drags it down the length of my forearm. "That's what this says."

I move my head frantically from side to side, my heart threatening

231

to explode, fear climbing up my spine as my eyes flicker from the weapon to his face. "Please."

"Please what? Were you going to try to take one? And hide it where?" He uses the gun to rip the towel apart, leaving me naked.

"I wasn't going to take one." My voice quivers with panic.

He drags it between my breasts, moving lower.

"Maybe I can get you to like it." My breath hitches as the gun travels past my belly button. "You clearly like to flirt with danger. After all, I've told you I've done terrible things, I'm holding you prisoner, and yet you're still going through my things like you have the right to."

"I'm sorry. P-please," I say, pushing myself back.

He pounces, shoving me all the way down, his hand clasping around my free wrist while he guides his gun to my pussy.

"I told you about begging."

I can't explain the strange reaction I'm having. I'm absolutely terrified for my life. I believe he's capable of killing me without a second thought, and I know he'd never experience a single ounce of regret. However, as he leans over my naked, trembling body, his favorite gun making its way to the spot between my legs, I know he'll find it wet and inviting.

Thrill-seekers are always thought of as the people who jump from planes, cliffs, and dive with sharks. I've never done any of those things, but I'd still consider myself a thrill-seeker. I get my adrenaline rush through other means, and maybe this is a new discovery. It's like the times I've stolen money from my job, ran out on a bar tab, and tricked a man out of his belongings. It's scary as shit. It gets your heart racing, blood pressure rising, and gives you a boost of energy that gets you so emotionally charged you feel like you're invincible. The high is incredible.

The only difference between this and the other things is that I'm not in control here. I *had* to steal. I needed money to survive. My mom needed me, and I was willing to do anything I had to for her. For us. Maybe it's not right, but you can't judge someone until you've been in their shoes when they're at their most desperate.

Right now, the fear of getting killed and the desire to get off are warring with each other, but if he decides to shoot me, hopefully it's after he makes me come.

He places the muzzle directly over my clit, pushing hard, and my chest heaves as I suck in deep breaths. His eyes study me, curiosity flashing in the dark irises. The gun moves once again, this time sliding inside me.

My gasp quickly dissolves into a moan and his eyes shine with a burning deviance that lets me know he's also getting off on this.

"You want me to stop?" he asks as he pushes it in further.

I nod, but it comes after a brief hesitation. He smirks, sliding it out and then shoving it back in.

"Ah!" I exclaim.

"Tell me you want me to stop. Use your words like a good girl."

Another pleasure-filled noise escapes my throat, but I manage to say, "Please."

His speed picks up, but the insertable length of the gun isn't that long.

"*Please* isn't *stop*."

"Stop," I say through panting breaths.

"I don't believe you."

I'm not sure I believe myself, but the sane part of my brain, however small that might be, is telling me I shouldn't want this. "Then why make me say anything?" I bite. "Of course I don't want this!"

He pushes the gun inside me with a forceful thrust. "I want the truth. Do you work for Gomez?"

"No! I said that."

The steady pace is a tease. It feels good, but not good enough to get me off.

"You weren't in my club looking for information to tell my enemies?"

"I was looking for a bathroom."

"And found the devil." He removes the gun and holds it up. "Do you like it now?"

"Not big enough."

He grins, then brings it to my mouth. "Lick it clean, *niña traviesa*."

I jolt back. "Is it loaded?"

"Clean. It."

The barrel is pushed between my lips before I can say another word. The taste of my arousal hits my tongue in a reminder of how turned on I was by being fucked by a gun. And my pussy throbs and drips, needy for more.

CHAPTER FIVE

"Good girl," he says before tossing the gun to the nightstand while also releasing his grip on my wrist. "Though I'm tempted to believe you're just an innocent girl who ended up at the wrong place at the wrong time, I don't believe you're that innocent."

"Maybe not, but I'm not some sort of spy. I don't even know what you do."

I attempt to sit up straighter, though my pussy still begs for attention.

"How about you tell me something illegal you've done? That way I have dirt on you just in case you decide you want to run your mouth once you're out of here."

"You're gonna let me go?"

"Do you want to stay here?"

When I don't reply with an immediate no, he cocks his head.

"Do you have a wife?"

His brows furrow. "No. You applying for that position? I'll tell you now, it's a dangerous job."

"I don't want to be owned."

"What do you want?"

"It's what I don't want. I don't want to have to worry about anything."

He's quiet for a little while. "Hmm. So, tell me the worst thing you've done. Something nobody else knows."

"I've stolen money."

His brow arches. "Oh yeah? From who?"

"My job. A guy. Wherever I can get it."

"A thief."

"It was for survival."

"Lots of people need money to survive and don't steal."

I shrug. "My mom depended on me. She's dead now."

He doesn't seem surprised, and doesn't offer condolences or pity. "And your dad?"

"I haven't seen him in years."

"Nobody will miss you then."

Fear rears up slightly. "I have friends."

"And I have your phone. They don't have reason to fear for your safety."

My nostrils flare. "What did you tell them?"

"What does it matter?"

I inhale deeply through my nose, my spine stiffening. "Where am I? Who are you? Why do you get to know all this stuff about me but I don't get anything from you?"

"Because I'm the one in charge. I hold all the power. You stumbled into *my* world, and I don't owe you anything."

"Yeah, exactly! I didn't infiltrate your business or anything. I'm not a spy or whatever you think I am. I literally drunkenly stumbled into the wrong room, and yet you take me and throw me in a dungeon. You deprive me of food. You threaten me with a gun."

"Threaten? Is that what we're calling it now? You nearly came all over my gun. Nobody will find you if I don't want them to. You claim innocence, but you're rifling through my drawers. For what?"

I yank on the rope as I lean forward. "I wanted to know your name or an address. I'm not gonna apologize for acting like any normal person would if they were given a chance to find out more about their captor."

"What were you gonna do with my name or address?"

My bravado dies down. "In case I was able to get to a phone."

He laughs a humorless laugh, finding it funny that I'd think that a possibility. "You have nobody to run to, *princesa*. No Mommy, no Daddy. You're better off here anyway."

Standing, he makes his way to the table that holds the food I had forgotten about.

"Where is *here*?"

"My home. Well, one of them."

"In El Paso?"

"No. We're in Mexico, *mami*. Now, be good, and I won't leave you here when it's time for me to return to Texas."

"When do you go?" I ask.

"Do you want to eat?" he questions, ignoring my own.

"Yes, please."

A moan rumbles in his throat. "Mm. I like that."

I roll my eyes, and he catches me when he spins around. Instead of being pissed, he seems mildly amused.

"Can I trust you to feed yourself or will you attempt to steal one of the utensils and stab me?"

"You're safe," I say. "Don't know how you got me into Mexico without a passport, so I don't know how I'd get out."

He grins and my stomach does a somersault.

Not much longer after he gave me some food, he disappeared into the hall and I overheard him on the phone. Nothing I could understand, but nearly thirty minutes goes by before he returns, this time throwing clothes at me.

"Get dressed."

I point to my tied up arm and he quickly unties the rope and takes two guns from the drawer, sticking them in the back of his pants.

"What's going on?"

"Don't ask questions. Get dressed. We're leaving soon."

I have at least five more questions to ask, but I don't. Not yet. I pull on the pair of jeans he gave me, and though they are a little snug, they fasten, so I can't complain. The shirt is a plain black, V-neck tee, and a small part of me wonders who these clothes belonged to, and what happened to her.

"Sorry, *mamacita*, but it has to happen this way."

I don't get a second to figure out what he's talking about before he secures a bag over my head and throws me over his shoulder.

"What the fuck?"

He spanks me on the ass. "*Cállate*. Don't make me gag you. Or are you into that kinda thing?"

I roll my eyes though he can't see me, and then the voices of other men surround us. They converse in Spanish, the cadence quick and the tone serious. I don't know why I thought we were alone in the house, but that's clearly not the case.

Before I know it, the familiar sound of the ladder dropping into my dungeon room hits my ears.

"No. Please don't leave me here."

He doesn't reply, but soon he drops me to my feet, and my hands fly quickly to the tie around my neck, trying to figure out how to get this damn bag off.

Scraping noises and loud bangs fill the room, and as soon as I pull the cloth from my head, I'm met with the sight of a hole in the room I've been kept in. Cinder blocks lay on the ground to his right.

"What the hell is that?"

"A tunnel," he answers. "Let's go."

He brings out a flashlight and extends his hand to me. When I hesitate, he gets up with a huff and yanks me to the opening.

"What're you doing with me?"

"This has nothing to do with you, but unless you want to stay here while I'm gone, I suggest bringing your ass on."

"I don't have shoes."

"Oh, poor *princesa*," he mocks. "You'll be fine."

From what I can see, the tunnel is fairly well built, considering we're underground. It's not just a small hole surrounded by dirt. We're able to stand and walk with ease, wooden planks lining the floor.

"Is that a train track?"

He snorts. "It's for electric rail carts."

"Smuggling?" I muse, mostly to myself, but he hears me.

"And now you know something bad about me."

"Considering you kidnapped me, I had no false ideas about you being Prince Charming."

"Kidnapped? You're no kid. Not with that body."

My cheeks turn warm. "Younger than you," I say. "How old are you anyway? Forty-five?"

He moves swiftly, never looking over his shoulder at me. "Not quite."

"Are you gonna tell me?"

"Why do you care?"

"Just curious."

"Thirty-eight."

"I'm twenty-one." He doesn't say anything. "What's your name?"

"Why? You want to know what to scream later?"

My eyes widen as my jaw drops. "Uh."

"You can call out for God."

"I don't believe in a god."

"The devil is tattooed on your arm. To believe in evil, you'd have to believe in good."

"I believe in neither. Dancing with the devil is a phrase. It just means to engage in immoral or risky behavior. I'm not a devil worshiper."

He stops suddenly, spinning around and charging forward, making me run into him. He backs me into the wall, his hard body flush against mine.

"I bet I could make you worship me." His mouth moves to my neck, brushing over my goosebump-covered flesh before reaching my ear. "By being with me, you're already engaged in risky behavior. Shall I bring my gun out again?" he asks, his hand cupping my ass.

I half-heartedly push him away but he barely budges. "Stop."

"It's funny," he whispers, his hand curving around my thigh before sliding to my pussy. "When you say *stop*, it sounds a lot like *keep going*."

He bites my earlobe, his palm rubbing hard against my clit. With a gasp, a squeak escapes my lips and my hips rock.

"Funny, when you touch me, I have to think about somebody el—"

"Don't lie to me, Audriana," he growls, cutting me off. He drops the flashlight to the ground, his hand going to my throat while his other one keeps rubbing against my clit. "I can feel the wetness of your cunt on my hand. If I slid a finger inside of you right now, you'd be dripping."

The sound of my name leaving his mouth sends a thrill up my spine, desire flowing through my veins, but the impulse to fight him and be stubborn burns through me.

"Awfully confident for someone who has to steal women in order to get their attention."

The light shines in our direction, giving me just enough illumination to see his sinful smirk. My heart rate spikes, and I start to feel that adrenaline rush I love so much.

"You want my attention," he says, unsnapping the button to my jeans and dragging the zipper down. "Don't you?"

I pin my lips together, trying to control my breathing as he tugs the material down my hips. I never got my underwear back, so I'm exposed to him instantly, the denim bunched around my knees.

"Answer me, Audriana."

His fingers splay across my upper, inner thigh.

"N-no."

"You don't?" he questions, cocking his head, his fingers inching closer to my pussy.

I bite down on my lip, trying to keep from writhing in order to find his hand. I shake my head, not trusting my voice to not sound breathy.

He doesn't even penetrate me. All it takes is him barely grazing his finger over my lips, and he smears my arousal up toward my clit.

Tsking me again, he says, "Liar."

Rubbing circles, he swiftly brings me to the point of breathlessness. To my own ears, I sound desperate. I don't even try to push him off me, but I should. He's a fucking smuggler, a kidnapper, and possibly a murderer. I don't know anything but bad things about him, and yet, I still want him to make me come.

When his fingers travel lower, the tips pushing into my soaking wet entrance, I'm almost embarrassed. I can't remember ever being this turned on before, but then his chest rumbles with an appreciative moan.

"Fucking heaven," he murmurs, pushing his fingers deeper inside me. My arousal is so heavy you can hear the wet sounds as he penetrates me. "And I'm about to be your God."

I whimper, unable to form words.

"I knew you were a *puta sucia*," he says, mouth moving to my neck where he bites a small chunk of flesh. "You know what that is?" he asks. I shake my head, my arm reaching around his back. "Dirty slut."

He stops touching me long enough to undo his pants and pull his cock out. It's too dark to get a glimpse at what's coming, but it doesn't take long before I feel it. He hitches my leg over his hip, mimicking the image inked on my arm.

In one viscous thrust, he's inside me, filling me up and stretching me out with his impressive size. I let out a yelp and he grunts before releasing a moan.

"I knew you wanted me," he growls.

"I don't want you," I manage between breaths.

"Your cunt is so fucking wet you might drown my cock. You can't lie to me."

"I can't control my body." I suppress a moan when his cock travels deep. "I-I don't want this."

His large hands keep a tight grip on my hips as he slams into me over and over again. There's no way to stay silent through this type of defilement. I know he'll leave bruises on my skin, and my back will carry scrapes from the rough thrusts sending me up and down against the side of this tunnel. The cries escaping my throat echo around us.

As he continues to fuck me, his grunts animalistic in nature, I wrap both of my arms around him, holding on for dear life. I keep myself from chanting anything encouraging like *yes, oh god, fuck me, I love it*, because while I might be thinking those things, I'm not about to praise this man. He can think he needs to step his game up even if he's already mastered it. That's why I've never understood faking orgasms. Why let them think they've done enough to get you off? They'll keep giving you mediocre dick and never realize they have a lot of work to do.

He comes with a roar, his fingers digging into my skin as he burrows his face into my neck, panting and grunting while he releases inside me.

Before he can catch his breath, I pull a gun from the back of his pants and bring it to his head.

CHAPTER SIX

"What're you gonna do with that?" he asks, not at all concerned that I hold his life in the palm of my hand.

"I'm halfway to the states now. I can shoot you and find my way back home."

He grins, pulling away slightly, allowing my leg to drop. "You don't know what you'll find at the other end of this tunnel, *princesa*."

"With this gun, I'm sure I'll be able to figure it out."

"Okay, but first..." he lets the statement hang there as he lowers himself to his knees.

Surprised, I keep the gun trained to his head while our gazes stay connected. "What—"

"I'm not a man to leave a woman unsatisfied."

Before I can say anything else, his tongue slips between his lips and lands on my clit.

"Oh god." The words fly out before I can think twice about them.

"Wrong one, *mamacita*," he murmurs against my cunt.

My body sags against the wall as he devours me. His cum drips down my inner thigh, but he doesn't seem bothered by it. He penetrates me with his tongue, and I can't stop myself from fucking his face, my free hand grabbing his hair to make sure he doesn't stop.

His tongue travels up, flickering over my clit as he shoves two fingers inside me, curling them up. Fuck, his mouth is intoxicating, diminishing any sort of control or logic I have. I'm unable to keep any sort of composure. I need him to keep tasting me. I need to come all over his tongue.

He pulls away briefly. "Still want to kill me?" he questions with amusement in his tone.

"I will if you don't keep going."

His chuckle is low and deep. "Beg me."

"I'm the one with the gun," I say, pushing it into his forehead.

With speed I wasn't suspecting, he stands up and whips out the second gun. The gun I forgot about. While pressing it to my temple, he smothers my body with his own, sandwiching me between him and the wall.

"Now we both have guns. The question is, who's less afraid to use it?"

"I'm not afraid."

"No?" he asks. "Shoot me then."

He's a fucking psychopath.

I pause, unsure what to say to him. I don't know why I haven't shot him yet. I should. It would be self defense, right? I wouldn't go to prison. He fucking kidnapped me and smuggled me to Mexico. But something keeps me from pulling the trigger. Not only have I never fired a weapon, I actually find this man intriguing.

With a shove to his chest, he stumbles back a little, and I reach down to grab my pants. "Well, if we're done here."

He grabs me by the arms and throws me to the ground, the gun flying out of my hand and landing out of reach. "Oh no, baby. We're not done. Not yet." After ripping my jeans completely off, he pushes my knees apart and settles between them. "Enrique," he says. "You yell that out when I make you come."

Before I can process that he's given me his name, his mouth is on my cunt, ripping every conscious thought from my brain, sending me reeling into cloud nine.

The steady pace of his flattened tongue running over my engorged clit has me reaching down and pulling on his hair while I moan like a porn star.

"Oh god," I cry, my back arching as my legs squeeze against the sides of his face.

He eases away, and then his hand comes down in a sharp smack against my pussy. "That's not my name."

"Ah!"

"What's my name?" he questions, his fingers teasingly dipping into my entrance.

I moan again, lifting my hips and hoping his fingers slide in deeper.

I'm punished with another slap against my cunt. His finger hitting my clit.

"Oh!" I screech. Maybe it's not punishment after all.

"Say my name, Audriana."

"Oh god." My name coming from his lips in a sexy, gravelly tone while he teases me with gentle touches has me going crazy. "Please," I beg. "Please, please, please."

He moves, getting to his knees and once again releasing his cock through his pants, and then he's thrusting into me with brute force. He's so fucking deep and he's not holding back. My goddamn cervix is gonna be bruised for days, but I don't care. My self-control slips and I'm nothing but a submissive slut, begging for more, imploring him to never stop, telling him how good it feels and admitting to how big he is.

Enrique is loving every second of it, too. He leans over me, his mouth on my neck, and then his teeth sink into my flesh. He's an animal. His tongue dances over my skin, soothing the bite, and then he's up on his knees, his hand wrapped around my throat as he nearly rips me open with his massive cock.

"You're such a fucking slut, aren't you?"

I nod, even though he's the first guy I've had sex with in quite a while.

"Words, baby. Use them. Tell me you're a slut."

"I'm a slut," I cry. "Ah, god. Yes."

"Whose slut?"

"Oh fuck. Yours! Please. Don't stop."

"So fucking needy."

"Yes. I need it," I say on a moan, feeling an orgasm building.

"Take it, then. Take. Every. Fucking. Inch," he says, punctuating the words with violent thrusts.

"Yes, yes, yes. Oh god, yes. Fuck me. Oh god."

His hand releases my throat and he gives me a smack across my cheek, nothing too painful, but it's jarring before I realize I hardly felt any pain at all. "Oh yeah," I moan.

"You like that?" he growls. "You like being treated like a whore?"

I bite my lip, grabbing onto his arms. "Yes!"

"If you say God's name one more time, my palm will meet your cheek again. You know who I am, and I'm far from a savior."

I release a wanton moan, and after three more thrusts, I scream when my body starts convulsing with my climax.

"Oh, oh, Enrique," I cry. "Oh fuck yes."

An appreciative moan rumbles in his throat. "That's a good girl."

After several more brutalizing thrusts, he comes again, this time pulling out and keeping his tip between my lips, releasing his cum on my pussy and smearing it over my clit. Like he's marking me.

CHAPTER SEVEN

There's no cuddling, kissing, or gentle touches once we're done. He gets up and buttons his pants, finding the guns and tucking them back in place. I get up with aches and pains all over my body, wiping his cum from my pussy, only to rub it on my jeans.

The rest of the walk to the end of the tunnel is relatively quiet. The high from sex has worn off and now I feel like a stupid little girl who allowed herself to be used just to get some pleasure. He got what he wanted, but then again, so did I.

I wonder if he regrets giving me his name.

"Enrique."

"Yes, Audriana?" he replies.

"Where are we going?" I ask once I realize he's not mad to be called by his name.

"I have business to take care of."

"Smuggling business?" I question.

"It's related."

"You don't care that I'm starting to learn all of this about you?"

"All of what?"

"Uh, that you kidnap women, smuggle them and who knows what else through these tunnels, have guns that I'm assuming you use, and I don't know, appear to be a criminal with the nickname El Diablo. I know too much."

He looks over his shoulder, the flashlight illuminating half his face. "You're right. You do know too much."

"But you said you'd let me go back home," I add quickly, knowing what typically happens to people who know too much.

Enrique turns back around. "Did I?"

"You said you wanted to know something about me. I told you about the stuff I've done. So if I go to the cops, you can tell them what I've done, too."

He chuckles. "The federales are going to be more concerned with international drug trafficking than a girl who took a few bucks from her cash register. I don't think I'd get much time off with that information. Do you?"

His admission stops me in my tracks, but he keeps moving. After a while, he spins around and shines the light on my face.

"*Qué?*"

"What?"

"Don't act surprised, *princesa*."

"Are you," I pause, wondering if I should even say it out loud, "in a cartel?"

"No," he answers simply. "I work for one though."

"Is that not the same thing?"

"No."

We start moving again, and I'm left with all these questions that I may not want the answers to.

"You have every reason to kill me."

"That's true."

"Are you going to?"

"I don't know. Maybe I'll just keep you with me, then I'll know you'll never run your mouth to anyone." He comes to a stop and turns to face me. "Would you like that?" His grin is full of wicked promises. Almost threatening. However, I'm not completely opposed, which just might make me certifiable.

I never get the chance to answer, because he pivots and starts climbing up a makeshift ladder on the wall, pushing open the top before turning and reaching for my arm.

When we emerge, we're still in the dark, but city lights flicker farther away, and the moon shines down on us. A car with two armed and terrifying men standing near it watch us get out.

"*¿Dónde está?*" Enrique says.

The men continue to speak in Spanish before Enrique ushers me into the back of the SUV. I can hear them speaking through the closed doors, but nothing registers anyway. Fear climbs up my spine, making me stiff and tense. Are we in danger? Is there about to be a gunfight between different cartels?

Doors open and the men climb in, Enrique sitting in the back with me as he types into his phone. "Can't trust these fucking *gringos*," he says, sitting back and running a hand through his hair.

"What's going on?" I ask quietly, my eyes flickering to the men in the front.

He regards me. "You really want me to tell you? The more you know the less likely you are to get your freedom."

I stare into his dark eyes for several seconds. "Tell me."

"My money launderer has gone missing."

"Missing?"

"Sí. Gone."

"You think he ran?"

He sighs. "He'll be dealt with later. They're already looking for him, but in the meantime, I have a lot of money that needs to be cleaned."

I sit back and let the cogs in my head spin. I may have found a way to ensure I stay alive.

"I might be able to help."

He cocks a brow. "How so?"

"I work at a casino." He lifts his chin, waiting for me to continue. "We could go there."

"Buying chips and cashing out," he says. "I know, but I have a lot, and even if all four of us went in and exchanged the money for chips, there's no way we'd be able to do that with all the cash. They'd be suspicious immediately."

I chew on my bottom lip for a while. "Give me the rest. You and your...co-workers can go in and gamble a little, but if you give me the rest of it, I'll take care of it."

His brows furrow. "You want me to hand you my money?"

"Do you want it cleaned or not?"

He rubs his palm over the scruff on his jaw, weighing his options. "If you try to fuck me over, I'll kill you, but not before I kill your friends."

I swallow. "If I don't?"

His lips pull up on one side. "I'll reward you."

My cheeks heat up, but I turn and look out the window. "I'll need to get my uniform from my house."

An hour and a half later, I'm wearing my long-sleeved red button up shirt with black vest and a pair of black slacks, and we're walking into the casino.

Enrique has a suitcase and will be checking into the hotel as a guest, only to pass me the money later. We've gone over the logistics and hopefully this will work as I imagined. I've missed one day of work since I was kidnapped, having taken a few days off to coincide with my already scheduled days off, so I could focus on packing, but hopefully that won't cause any issues. Turns out I've only been in Mexico five days.

I clock in and spot Suzie and Pilar right away.

"Where you been?" Pilar asks. "I thought you were supposed to be here yesterday."

Suzie looks me up and down with an air of superiority simply because she's thirty years older than me. "She was."

"I thought I was off," I say, playing dumb. "I asked for four days off."

"Three," Suzie corrects.

I slam my hand on my forehead. "Shit. I thought it was four. Ever since my mom died, time's been a little off."

Pilar gives me a look full of pity, but the dead mom card doesn't work as well on Suzie. "Make sure you pick up an extra shift. Lionel wasn't too happy about your absence, and you didn't answer any of his calls."

"Okay."

I work for three hours before I'm due for break, and I send a text to the only number in this burner phone, letting Enrique know it's time to meet.

We go to a spot where I know there's a blind spot from the cameras and he hands me a backpack, playfully pulling out a water bottle and tapping me on the nose with the cap.

"In case anyone's watching, I'm just a loving boyfriend here to bring you lunch. Now smile."

I grin and take the bag from his hand. "Thank you."

"Don't disappoint me," he warns, before leaning in and barely brushing his lips against my cheek. "See you soon."

A shiver runs down my spine as I watch him walk away.

"Damn girl. Who is that fine specimen?" Pilar asks, her presence making me jolt.

"Oh. New boyfriend," I say with a shrug.

"Good job landing that one. He got any brothers?" she jokes.

"Not sure. Where's Suzie?"

"Bathroom, but I gotta run over and talk to Lucio. I'll be right back."

Now's the best time to do it. The other cashiers are up front behind the cages, and with Suzie and Pilar gone, I have some alone time to take this bag of cash and replace it with money we keep back here.

My heart hammers in my chest as I rush into the back section of the cashier cage, open the safe, and exchange the dirty money for clean money. I head to the bathroom when Suzie is back and give him the bag before heading back to work.

Hours later, after his two friends have already been to my register to exchange their chips for cash, in which I gave them extra, it's time for another break, so I meet up with Enrique again, this time in the women's bathroom closest to me. He gives me the bag, and I do it again, my adrenaline pumping the entire time. Sweat beads across my hairline and under my arms, terrified someone will walk back here and catch me. Suzie already went home, but Gigi is here now and she's the cage manager. However, her break isn't for another hour.

After another exchange with Enrique, he tells me he's about to cash his chips in and we'll be good to go. He's already worried that I'm bringing too much attention to myself by being seen with a backpack that I've never brought to work before. However, knowing I likely won't be coming back to work after this, I decide on a last minute decision that I hope won't come back to bite me in the ass.

When I clock out, I sling my purse over my shoulder and walk straight to the bathroom, locking myself in a stall and securing the stacks of cash to my body by stuffing half of them in the waistband of my pants, and the other half under the band of my bra. Once I'm redressed, I check myself out in the mirror to make sure nothing looks off. Thank god we don't have to wear tight clothing.

I tell Enrique via text that I'm exiting out the back, because that's what I normally do. However, once the door is closed behind me, a man shoves me against the brick wall.

"There you are. I want my fucking money back."

CHAPTER EIGHT

When I get my bearings, I lift my head and come face to face with the man I stole from a few weeks back, and he's not happy.

"I know you took everything I had in my wallet, you stupid bitch. I want it back."

"What are you talking about?" I ask, my eyes trying to look past him, hoping Enrique shows up soon.

He shoves me again, my head banging against the wall. "You got me drunk while we were playing at the tables. I don't know how many chips you swiped from me, but I know that once I got you up in the hotel room, you took everything in my wallet and left."

"I didn't get you drunk," I say. "You were buying drink after drink, hoping I'd get inebriated enough to fuck you, but I'm not so stupid to actually consume multiple drinks from random pushy men."

"Oh, fuck off, you dumb whore. I had two thousand dollars in there and I want it back."

He crowds me, trapping me between his arms as he looks down from the nearly eight inch height difference.

When he approached me as I was leaving almost three weeks ago, I thought he was moderately good-looking, but after sitting with him at some slot machines for about fifteen minutes, his attitude made any attractive qualities disappear. He kept talking about how much money he made, flaunted the recent purchase of a new car, talked about the business he was in with dear old daddy, and acted as if he was put on Earth for women to flock to. So cocky it made me sick, but I figured I could get some cash out of him.

Though my mom was cremated, it was still an expense I didn't have money for. It put me behind on bills, and I'm still struggling to catch up. The money I got from this guy helped quite a bit, so I don't regret it.

"I don't have two thousand dollars," I say, pushing his arm away and moving around him. "Leave me alone."

"Listen, bitch," he snarls, gripping my forearm and yanking me into him. His hold on me is so tight I know I'll have bruises later. "I'm out over 2K, and you were nothing but a cock tease who didn't put out. We're gonna go inside and you're gonna do whatever you have to do to get me the money I'm owed, and then I'm getting some pussy for my troubles."

"Stop it!" I yell, snatching my arm back and stumbling out of his grip.

He reaches forward and grabs my shirt, the buttons flying open and revealing the money I have strapped to my body.

His lips twist into a greedy smile and his eyes flicker to mine. "Fucking lying cunt." He pounces, his fingers dipping into my bra.

"Stop it! No!" I try fighting him off but he shoves me against the wall, his forearm across my throat as he grabs the money with his other hand. I dig my nails into his arm as I attempt to pull his arm away. "I thought you were rich. All you did that night was talk about it." He doesn't answer. "Or is that just what you say to get girls to sleep with you?"

He releases his hold on my throat just long enough to backhand me. "Shut up, bitch."

"Problem here?"

Enrique's voice is a welcome intrusion. The man who's name I don't even remember turns and eyes him. "Get lost. This doesn't concern you."

"I'm afraid it does. This woman you've laid your hands on is technically my property. That money you're trying to steal is also mine. The pussy you said you were gonna take was just filled with my cum. So, you see, I'm very concerned."

The man's face twists in disbelief and his head swivels to survey me before turning back to Enrique. "This whore stole money from me. I want it back."

Enrique takes two calm steps forward and smiles at the man in a way that shows not a fraction of amusement. I watch as I hold my palm to my stinging cheek, and notice the moment the man starts to become afraid.

"Look, man. Let me take what I'm owed and you can have the rest. She's not worth either of our time. Just a stupid slut who thinks she's better than everyone."

"She's definitely better than you," Enrique says. "And you don't get to call her a slut." His hand comes from around his back, the black and gold plated gun in hand, the words *El Diablo* staring at me when he pulls the trigger and puts a bullet in the man's head.

His body drops with a thud, and a screech leaves my throat before Enrique's in front of me with his hand over my mouth.

"Shh. *Vamos.*"

With his hand on my back, he ushers me around the dumpsters where his two guys almost collide with us, guns in hand.

"*Estas bien, jefe?*"

Enrique nods. "All good. Let's get out of here."

In the car, he eyes my open shirt and gestures for me to close it. It's then that I realize I have blood on me, and I start freaking out.

He says something in Spanish to the men in front, and soon, we're pulling over on a dark dirt road where he guides me outside.

"There's blood on me," I say.

"Yes."

"There's blood on me," I repeat. "You killed him."

"Did you think I was a good guy? I know you're smarter than that."

"Why?" I ask, voice monotone, the shock stealing any and all emotion.

"Why not? He touched you. He hurt you. He threatened to steal my money and fuck what I've just claimed."

My eyes finally focus on his. "I don't know what's happening."

He starts removing my shirt, his eyes tracking the stacks of cash. "You took this for me?"

"For you. For me. Us, I guess," I say with a shrug. "I don't have a lot of money. Just a lot of bills. It's why I stole from that guy in the first place."

"Hmm," he murmurs, removing each stack of money before throwing them and my bloodied shirt in the back of the SUV.

I watch as he unbuttons his white shirt, leaving him in only a wife-beater, revealing the ink on his arms and chest. He's lean but cut with muscles, the veins in his arms protruding through his brown skin.

He guides my arms in the sleeves of his shirt, buttoning it up for me.

"Thank you."

"You will," he says with a smirk.

CHAPTER NINE

Enrique instructs his men to take us to a hotel, and though he doesn't give me a reason, I'd like to think it's for my benefit. I'm still in shock, and we'd have to travel through the tunnel again to get back to his house. Honestly, I'm not up for that trip right now, so I'm grateful for the hotel.

"Did you check into the casino hotel with your real name?" I ask once we're inside our room.

"Of course not."

I nod. "I can't go back to work now. They'll suspect it was me."

"Do they have cameras back there?"

"Yes. They aren't watched live, but someone will check when they realize the extra money is missing."

"I can have someone hack into them and clear it up."

My lips part in surprise. "Really?"

"I know a lot of people," he replies.

"I still don't think they'll let me back. They'd have to know it was me."

"Why couldn't it be anyone else? You're not the only person who steals from their job."

"Well, I don't know when you'd let me go, and when I don't show up tomorrow night, they'll suspect me. And with a dead guy out back..." I let the sentence trail off.

"Shower," he commands. "We'll figure it out later."

I nod, willfully following his orders. I need to get the blood off of me, but I also need the alone time to think.

Maybe he was joking about keeping me with him, but I'm starting to wonder if it's not the worst idea. Yeah, he's a criminal but so am I, just on a different level. At least with him, I'd have a home in Mexico. I wouldn't have to work my ass off and steal just to get by. I don't have any parents or siblings I'd be leaving behind, but I do have a few friends. I'd have to let them know I was okay. I'd need to tell them something so they don't call the cops, but other than that, it seems like a relatively easy decision. Plus, maybe they'll connect the dead guy out back with the missing money since we didn't take what he stole from me after he hit the ground.

Enrique is scary, but if I'm with him, I don't think I have anything to worry about. I'm not an enemy. He's also sexy as fuck. That helps. It's probably what's making this decision easier. A hot man kidnaps you, fucks you like you've never been fucked, kills a man for touching and threatening you, and you're supposed to want to get away from that? No thanks. This is my kind of fairytale.

When I exit the shower, I dry off and use the hotel lotion to moisturize my body while also putting their stiff ass toothbrush to work. Running my fingers through my wet and wavy locks, I study myself in the mirror before strutting to the door.

When I pull it open and step under the doorframe, I recognize my mistake. While I expected Enrique to be sitting on the bed or one of the chairs waiting for me, I didn't anticipate his men to be in the room as well.

Three sets of eyes turn to my naked body.

"Get out. Now," Enrique commands, his eyes never leaving my body. The men scurry through the door, not risking taking a glance at me again.

"What are you doing?" he growls, standing and marching toward me.

"I didn't know they'd be here."

He smacks my ass, pulling me into his frame. "You're gonna make me kill men I've known for years."

My breath catches in my throat. "Why would you need to kill them?"

"For having seen you naked," he says, his lustful gaze inspecting my body.

"I hate to break it to you, but you're not the only one who's seen me naked," I tease.

"Give me their names."

DANCING WITH THE DEVIL

I laugh but he doesn't. Instead, he walks me to the bed, the backs of my thighs hitting the mattress. "You putting on another show?"

I shake my head. "I want you to fuck me again."

One brow arches slightly, his fingers traveling down my chest until he reaches my left nipple. "I think you're right. You've seen too much."

"I have?" I ask breathlessly.

He nods once. "I can't let you go now."

My heart races, but not out of fear. "You can't?"

He shakes his head. "I'm afraid you're stuck with me for a while." His fingers twist my nipple, making me gasp.

"Oh." It comes out like a moan. "Okay."

"That easy?" he asks, his hand journeying down my stomach.

With my eyes on his, I say, "I have to give my friends a story. I have to be able to talk to them."

His jaw tightens slightly. "I'll allow it but I'll be with you when you make the call."

"You still don't trust that I won't snitch on you?"

"I told you I don't trust people."

"Hm," I murmur, dropping to my knees. "Do you trust me to take your cock into my mouth? I could bite it off, or I could blow your mind."

"Maybe I'll keep a gun to your head, and the second I feel the scratch of your teeth I'll end it before I can register any pain."

My lips pull up into a smirk. "A little pain isn't so bad."

After undoing his pants, I let them fall to his ankles and then push his boxer-briefs down, freeing his cock.

My fingers wrap around his thick shaft, stroking the hot flesh before I open my mouth and run his tip across my tongue.

His hand instantly grips my hair as he hisses, and I go to work, taking him as deep as my throat will allow.

Enrique lets me be in control for about five minutes before he takes over, his other hand coming to grab a chunk of hair before he begins fucking my mouth. I gag and slobber all over his cock, pushing back against his thighs to take a breath before he's touching the back of my throat with his crown again.

"Take it," he grits. "You know you like it."

Garbled noises is all I can manage as he treats me like a sex toy, but he's not wrong. My pussy is already dripping wet. I fucking love it.

He pulls away from me, reaching down and lifting me up, tossing me onto the bed. "I wasn't lying when I told that *pendejo* that you were my property. Just because you may have a little more leniency when we're back home, doesn't mean you're not mine."

I nod eagerly.

"You have a lot to learn about this life, about me, and what'll be expected of you, but you'll never want for anything."

My teeth sink into my bottom lip and I spread my legs. "I want something right now."

His lips stretch into a mischievous grin and he whips out the gun he used to kill my harasser. "This?" He grips his cock in his other hand. "Or this?"

"Maybe both," I say in a husky tone, my tongue sliding across my lips.

"Dirty, dirty girl." I smile, and he tosses the gun next to me before stripping his clothes off and climbing onto the bed. "Get on your hands and knees. I'm gonna fuck you like the little whore that you are."

I have to fight off a smile. This is what I've always wanted. I don't want someone telling me I'm beautiful while they make love to me. I want them to degrade me while they annihilate me. And maybe, just maybe, I want a little praise for being such a good slut.

Enrique smacks my ass cheek before pushing my face into the pillow and grabbing a hold of my hips. He buries himself to the hilt in one quick thrust, eliciting a scream from my throat.

"Fuck, your cunt is so—" He drives into me, moaning as he stills deep inside. "You get this wet for everyone? Are you always so desperate for cock?"

I shake my head and he wraps my hair around his fist in a makeshift ponytail, yanking me back. "Speak. You're not an animal, even if you're on all fours and panting like a dog."

"No. I've never been this wet." He yanks my hair again. "Or desperate. Only for you."

A murmur of approval rumbles in his chest. "Good." His hand comes down hard on my ass cheek. "Such a good girl when you want to be."

I nearly start preening, but with another tug on my hair and his free hand digging into my hip, he fucks me like an animal, grunting and panting behind me while I yell and moan, my fists gripping the covers.

"It's a shame you don't believe in heaven, because I swear it's right here between your legs. This is where I'll worship every fucking day. This is where I'll see angels."

I cry out, my pussy weeping around his cock. "I'm so close."

He lets go of my hair and my head drops, then I feel his fingers reaching around and rubbing my clit as he moves in and out of me.

"Come for me," he breathes. "I want to feel every fucking drop."

"Ah, ah, oh shit," I moan. "I'm coming!"

My legs shake and my back bows when the orgasm hits. The screech coming from my mouth scratches my throat, and I wouldn't be surprised if someone complained to the front desk.

"That's it, baby," he says. "Yes, that's what I fucking want."

His thrusts quicken and deepen, and my body collapses flat on the mattress, but he keeps going. He grabs my hips with his hands, lifting me up enough to slide in deep. His hand slaps my outer thigh, making me yelp, and then he spanks me again.

"Fuck!" he grunts, slamming his cock into me before pulling out completely.

Warm spurts of his cum land on my ass and back as he lets out a roar, and I release a satisfied moan, only upset that I didn't get to watch the cum land on my skin.

His hand rubs it into my flesh like it's lotion.

"Mine."

CHAPTER TEN

The next day, I wake up and find Enrique emerging from the shower, a towel wrapped around his waist as he talks into his phone.

He has no right being this attractive. His muscles flex with every movement he makes, and my eyes trace the cuts in his torso, leading to the monster that rests under the white towel. His ink is a variety of script and images I haven't had enough time to decipher yet, but there's no doubt I won't mind studying them a little closer.

Enrique's head swivels over his shoulder, catching me staring at him. I bite down on my bottom lip and he says something in Spanish before ending his call and dropping the phone on the table.

"See something you like?"

I nod, grinning like a schoolgirl.

He steps to the bed and yanks the covers off of me, revealing my naked body. "Me too."

"Do we have time?"

His hand squeezes my thigh, fingers torturously close to my pussy. "Unfortunately, no."

"What's the plan?" I ask, sitting up.

"Well, you need to call your friends, grab whatever you need from your place, and then I have business to tend to."

The idea of talking to Angie has me nervous. What sort of story can I come up with that she'll believe? I don't have much time to figure it out, because apparently Enrique has a schedule, so once I'm dressed in an outfit he had sent up, he hands me my phone.

"You kept it."

"I went through it too."

I twist my lips up and narrow my eyes. "Find anything interesting?"

"Not really. Your friend Leo seems to be in love with you, though."

"What? No way."

He shrugs. "Doesn't matter now."

When I look through my texts, I find several from my friends before Enrique responded for me, giving the excuse that I needed to get away. A few back and forths make it obvious that he read enough of my previous texts to know my mom died and that I was moving out soon. The excuse is believable enough. I needed to get away from the house my mom died in. I needed to grieve alone. But before then, Leo had sent a text telling me how beautiful I looked the night we went out, and then he asked if I wanted to go out to dinner with him.

I look up and find Enrique watching me.

"He's probably better for you than I am. Most people will be, but if anybody tries taking you from me, they'll never see another sunrise again. *Comprendes?*"

I nod, wondering why him threatening the lives of others makes me feel so good.

When I call Angie, she picks up on the third ring. "Oh my god, you *are* alive!"

I snort. "I am."

"Where the hell you been?" Her voice softens. "You doing okay?"

"I'm fine. Just...processing, I guess."

"You never really allowed yourself proper time to mourn. You were back at work so soon."

"I didn't have a choice."

"I know. But damn, you didn't have to run away while we were at the club. We thought you were kidnapped at first."

I eye Enrique. "Kidnapped?" His gaze sharpens as he watches me. "Nah. A kidnapper would send me back. I'm too much to deal with."

She laughs and Enrique shakes his head.

"Oh stop. So, where did you go? I didn't think you had any family nearby, and I know you ain't got no money. No offense."

"I actually have a cousin," I lie. "She called me while I was in the bathroom. She heard about my mom and invited me to stay with her. It was probably all the alcohol, but I was emotional and impulsive. I told her I'd meet her. She lives in Mexico."

"I didn't know you had a passport. Or a cousin."

"Yeah." I don't elaborate, because I have neither.

"Well, that's nice."

"I'll probably stick around here for a while. It's not like I'm in a rush to move into that tiny ass apartment."

She's quiet. "Well, damn. I'll miss you."

"I'll be in touch, don't worry."

Angie cusses. "Fuck. I gotta get back to work. Manager's staring at me. Call me later. Love you!"

The call goes dead before I can say anything else.

"Well, that's solved."

He nods and pulls me to my feet. "Good girl."

My cheeks blush with his praise and he runs his knuckles over the heated skin. "Not sure what you like more, being degraded or being praised."

"Both, please."

He grasps my chin between his fingers. "So fucking needy."

I nod, a grin on my lips. "Can you handle me?"

A growl rumbles in his throat. "I think I'm the only one who can, so no, this kidnapper won't be sending you back."

"Prove it," I say, goading him. "Prove you can handle me."

His hand wraps around my throat, forcing me into the door. "I think you forgot who makes the demands around here." With his other hand, he unsnaps my pants and yanks them to my knees. "Tell me who's boss."

Horny and already breathing heavy, I drag my teeth across my bottom lip. "You are."

"Mm. That's right." His fingers slip inside my wet cunt, and I gasp, feeling the soreness from last night. "And who are you?"

I moan as he fucks me with his fingers, his grasp on my throat tightening. "Nobody," I say, holding onto his wrist.

"Wrong." He smacks my pussy before pushing his fingers back inside. "You're my little slut."

A whimper leaves my lips. "Yeah."

"Say it."

"I'm your little slut."

"Do you want to come?"

I nod frantically.

He removes his fingers and lets go of my throat, pushing the wet digits between my lips so I can taste myself. I hold his hand between mine, sucking my arousal from his fingers.

When he pulls them from my mouth, he grins. "Too bad. We have things to do. You'll have to wait."

Sadly, it doesn't take long to gather the belongings I want to keep from my house. I pack a few things that belonged to my mother, pictures, clothes, and my hygiene and beauty products. Before we set out for the next place of business, Enrique has one of his guys go to the car and bring in the dress and shoes I was wearing the night I was taken. The officially stolen dress is now hanging in a dry cleaner's bag.

"You should put this on."

I study him as I take the garment. "We going to a party?"

"Just put it on. No panties."

Figuring I have little choice, I change in the bathroom and take some extra time to fix my hair and makeup. The dress stops a little above my knee, the top part snug against my torso, while the bottom half flares out a little.

When I come back into my living room, Enrique's got a fresh pair of black slacks and a white button up on. He drinks me in with his eyes, obscene thoughts almost visible in his dark irises, and a salacious smirk on his lips.

The ride in the car is thick with sexual tension. My eyes keep skating over his powerful thighs, tattooed hands, and sinful mouth. He angles his body against the door and watches me, his eyes traveling up my bare legs and over my cleavage.

"What're you thinking about?" I ask softly.

"How I want you riding my dick with your tits bouncing in my face."

My eyes shift to the front seat as my warmth blooms in my cheeks. "Oh."

"Mm."

"Maybe later?"

"Definitely."

We come to a stop outside the back of a building, and once we get out of the vehicle, we enter through a black door and find ourselves in a nice sized office while his men stay outside.

"Is this where you work?"

"Sometimes," he says, sitting behind the large desk.

I wander around the office, but there's nothing in here that gives anything away. No pictures or decorations, just a desk, two chairs, and a mini bar in the corner.

When I get to a doorway, I look up, and it hits me. This is the club we came to. The Devil's Lair.

"This is where you knocked me out."

"I wasn't the one who did that. An associate of mine did."

"If what you were discussing was so private then why was the door unlocked?"

"It wasn't supposed to be. Someone didn't lock it, and that person has been dealt with accordingly."

"So, murdered?"

He looks up at me but doesn't answer. Which is an answer in itself.

"Where is the woman's bathroom anyway? I thought it would've been across from the men's."

"It was next to it. You must've passed it."

"Hmm." I decide it's not important to dwell on. "Do smugglers have paperwork to do?" I ask, walking around his desk. "What do you smuggle? Drugs? Weapons? Oh god. It's not women, is it?"

He laughs. "Smuggling women is your limit? Not trafficking drugs or guns, not murdering people, but smuggling women?"

"Well, I know you smuggled me."

"Only you," he says, grabbing my thigh and pulling it up by his hip while his other hand presses against my lower back.

"Good," I moan. "No more women allowed in your dungeon."

"Just you?" he asks, his mouth getting closer to mine. "What about in my bed?"

"I know where you keep your guns in your room. Not a good idea."

He rocks into me, the length of his hardening dick pressing against my pussy. "Mm. Good point."

"Is that a gun in your pocket or—"

"They both like you," he answers before I can finish the cliché line.

He sits me down on his desk, spreading my legs apart before reaching under my dress.

"No panties," I tell him just as his fingers graze my pussy. "As requested."

Sitting in the chair in front of me, he removes the gun from the back of his pants and places it on the desk next to me.

"We're gonna have company soon."

I start to close my legs, but a hand on my knee prevents me from doing so. "Not yet. Soon."

"Okay," I say, forming it like a question.

He takes the gun in his hand and touches the muzzle to my inner thigh, slowly dragging it up while his eyes never leave mine. When I feel the tip pressing against my entrance, I arch my back and spread my legs even wider.

"Starting to think this might be your favorite gun as well."

"It is," I say with a moan as he pushes it inside me.

Enrique teasingly fucks me with the gold and black weapon, using slow and gentle thrusts. I lift my hips, trying to take it deeper, needing more even though it's nothing compared to his cock.

"Patience," he says, easing it out of me. "You have to bounce on my dick later, remember?"

A knock on the back door startles me, so I push my legs together and sit up, but Enrique keeps the gun right at my entrance, hidden under my dress.

His two men bring in another guy, his hair greasy and stomach hanging over his pants. "What's going on?" he questions right away, yanking his arm away from one of Enrique's guys. "Who the fuck is this bitch?" he asks with venom, eyes flashing from me to Enrique.

A slow smile stretches across Enrique's face and his eyes meet mine. Something passes between us. Something I can't quite pin down, but it looks like he's relieved. Then he pulls the gun from under my dress and aims it at the angry man. His guys have just enough time to take a step to the side before the gun goes off, a bullet flying through his mouth.

I jump at the noise, my heart battering my ribcage like it wants to escape and run away from my body. Enrique puts the gun on his desk and dismisses his men.

"You can go. I'll call you when I'm ready."

They say nothing before leaving through the back door, abandoning the body that laid at their feet.

"Who is that?"

"Gomez," he replies easily. "And now I know for sure he doesn't know you."

My jaw drops. "You still didn't believe me?" He doesn't reply, just stares at me. "And if he had shown any sign that he recognized me, then what? You would have shot me too?"

He shrugs. "I believe you now. That's what matters. I even offered him a taste of heaven before he died."

I furrow my brows as I try to understand what he's talking about, and then he slides his hand under my dress and presses his thumb against my clit.

"Heaven."

"Oh," I reply in an airy tone. "What did he do to you?"

"Stole from me."

"Oh," I say again. "Don't you think someone heard the shot?"

"We're closed." He takes my chin between his fingers. "Listen, you can lie, but not to me. You can steal, but not from me. As long as you know where your loyalty lies, you'll never have anything to worry about. You understand?"

I nod. "Yes."

Enrique stands and undoes his pants, pushing them and his boxer-briefs down before sitting in his chair again. "Come on, *princesa*."

I straddle him in the leather chair, thankful it doesn't have arm rests. "Oh god," I moan, loving the way his cock fills me up.

He grabs my face in his hand. "Try again."

"Enrique," I moan.

"Good girl."

And then his lips are on mine. Our first kiss. It's rough and passionate, his tongue dancing with mine before I bite on his bottom lip.

He snarls, his hand gripping a chunk of my hair and tugging back, exposing my throat. He licks, sucks, and then bites my flesh, once again marking me, this time with his teeth. I pull away and bring his face to mine, plunging my tongue into his mouth while I rock back and forth in his lap.

His hands move to my hips, lifting me up and slamming me back down. He rips my dress in the front, my breasts falling through the torn material and bouncing in his face. He sucks a nipple into his mouth before biting down on it, yanking a yelp from my throat.

We're so caught up in each other that we seem to forget there's a dead body a few feet away. I don't even look in that direction, instead getting lost in the eyes of a man who kidnapped me, a man who I hope never gets sick of me and sends me away.

I want this. I want excitement and thrill. I want danger and passion.

EPILOGUE

The front door opens as I'm in the kitchen checking on the stew in the slow cooker. Angling my head over my shoulder I watch Enrique strut toward me, his shirt wet with sweat and his skin glistening.

"Fucking hotter than hell out there," he says, grabbing my hip and kissing my temple before walking to the fridge for a bottle of water.

"How's things at the farm?"

"Ruined," he says, gulping down half the bottle before removing his shirt.

"I'll take that. I have a fresh shirt hanging up in the laundry room." Enrique sits on one of the stools while I toss his dirty shirt in the basket and bring him a new one. "The fire took it all out?"

"Mostly. Whatever wasn't burnt was too close to the fire. Everything's fucked. The smell and taste will be off, and the soil is compromised so we'll have to replace it."

"Fuck."

He finishes his water and pulls on the fresh black T-shirt. "Exactly."

"Well, your guest is waiting for you."

"Have you heard anything from him?"

I pull open the cabinet door on the side of the island and then unlatch the lock on the trapdoor that lies inside. "Not much. I've had music on." After reaching into one of the other cabinets, I grab a lantern, and then pull a sharp knife from the butcher's block and place them on the counter. "I'm sure you'll get him to make some noise."

Enrique walks forward, wrapping an arm around my waist and yanking me into him. "I fucking love you, you know that?"

I grin. "I think so."

He presses his lips to mine in a fiery kiss that gets me hot and bothered instantly. When we pull away, I'm breathless. "I guess I love you, too."

He grips my jaw in his hand. "I'm gonna fuck you until you're sure. Until it's all you know how to say."

I squeeze my thighs together as I whimper. "Might take some convincing then," I tease, biting down on my lip.

A rumble in his chest and the flash of a promise in his eyes has me anxious for when he's done with the guy currently in the dungeon.

"Gotta see what this guy knows about who burnt my marijuana, but I'll be back." He grabs the lantern and knife, pressing the blade flat against my mouth. "Give it a good luck kiss." I purse my lips and peck the steel. "Good girl."

He disappears down the stairs and into what was my first room in this house, and I go back to cooking. I've been here with him for almost eight months, and we're still obsessed with each other.

Occasionally, I go back to Texas to see my friends, but I'm happier here. Enrique was true to his word about getting the cameras at the casino wiped, so nobody was able to prove I did anything with the money. I don't know what ended up happening, all I care about is that I wasn't charged. They can suspect me all they want, but they'll never be able to prove I did anything, and Enrique will burn the whole town to the ground before allowing me to be taken in.

After nearly twenty minutes of hearing their muffled voices, followed by a few screams, he emerges from the trap door. I take the lantern as he slips the lock in place and closes the cabinet, hiding the secret room below our kitchen.

He drops the bloodied knife in the sink and washes his hands.

"How'd it go?" I ask.

"I got a name."

"So my good luck kiss must've worked."

He grins that sinful grin I love so much. "Let's go to the room and see what else that mouth of yours can do."

"What do you say?" I ask, provoking the animal that lives right under the surface of his skin.

He stalks toward me, eyes piercing me in place while his murderous hands hang at his sides. When his body clashes into mine, the fingers of his right hand come up and wrap around my throat.

"Now."

A breathy moan leaves my mouth as I experience a full body shiver. "Okay."

Leaning in, his lips brush over the shell of my ear. "Remember I love you, because I'm about to fuck you like I'm trying to kill you."

ABOUT ISABEL LUCERO

Isabel Lucero is a bestselling author, finding joy in giving readers books for every mood. She loves connecting with her readers and fans of books in general. You can find her on Facebook, Twitter, Instagram, and TikTok.
https://msha.ke/isabel__lucero#books
https://msha.ke/isabel__lucero#links
https://msha.ke/isabel__lucero#about-1

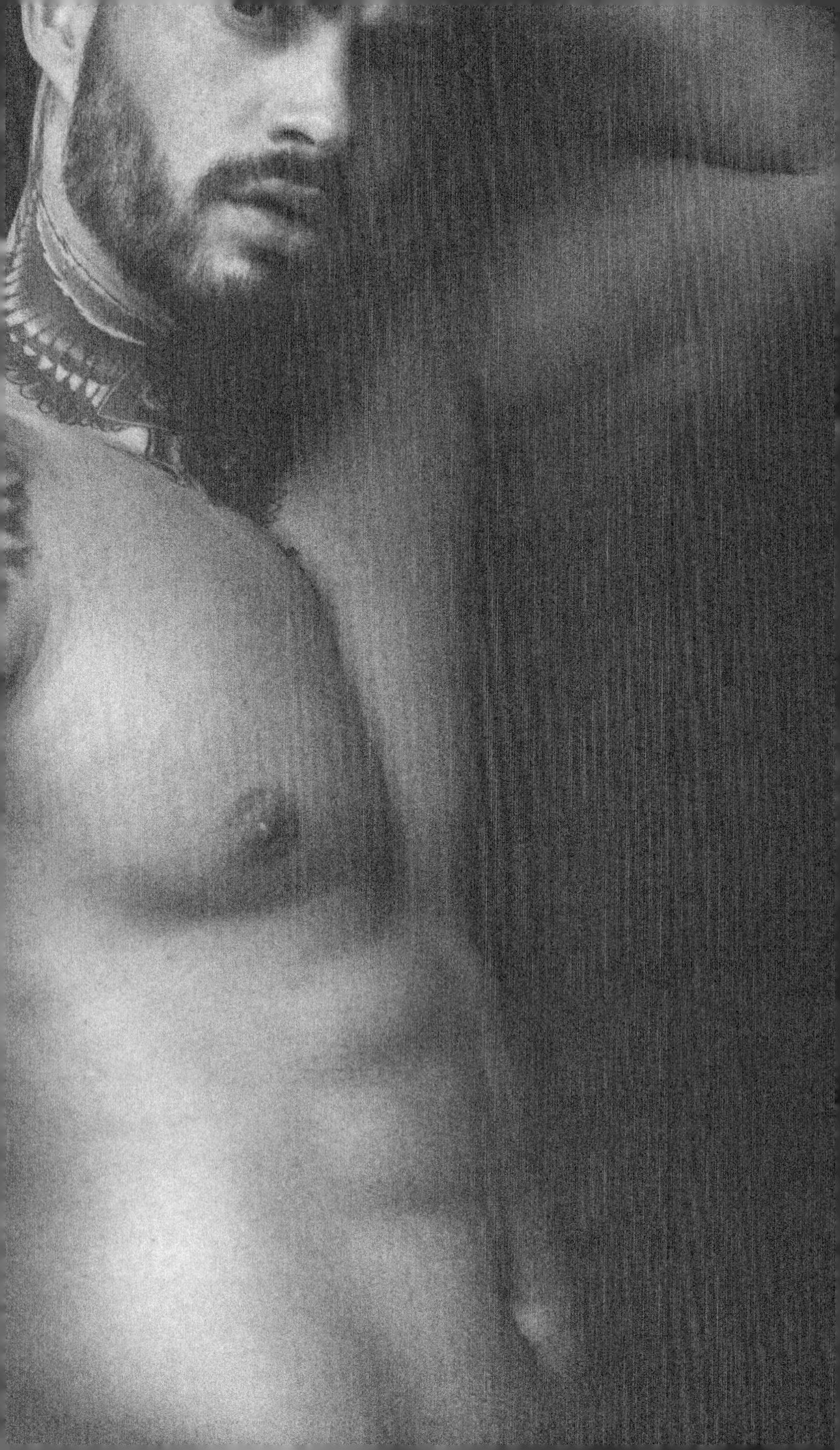

INTO THE FOX'S DEN

BY A.D. MCCAMMON

CHAPTER ONE

RAINA

The moment my eyes meet his, I feel a shift. Like my entire life is about to alter course, and there's nothing I can do about it. Dread and excitement course through my veins as he approaches. My skin hot, my heart racing. The familiarity in the stranger's gaze making it impossible to look away.

He's handsome. The kind of handsome that screams danger. His ashy-blond hair is perfectly in place, his salt-and-pepper beard sculpted, his suit fitting him like a damn glove.

He's the only person in this club not wearing a mask, yet the only one truly hiding behind one. There's darkness lurking in him. And every instinct in my body is telling me to run in the other direction. But it's too late. My fate is already sealed.

He comes to a stop in front of me, his green eyes trailing down my body with leisure before locking on mine again. "Hello there..." His voice is deep and smooth, equally as inviting and dangerous as his pretty face. "Are you lost, Rabbit?"

My stomach twists. It's so obvious I don't belong at a kink club. This place is way out of my element. Everything about it makes me feel uncomfortable, the glow of the purple lights uninviting, the copious amount of bare skin overwhelming. They even forced me to leave all my belongings behind at the door and sign an NDA.

But there isn't anything I wouldn't do for my twin brother. He's my best friend, and I think he's in danger.

Which is how I ended up standing here, feeling like prey. I waltzed into The Fox's Den wearing the skimpiest dress I own and my lacy bunny mask from last year's Halloween costume, determined to speak to the club's owner. Gaining his attention by sticking out like a sore thumb, however, was not part of the plan.

"No..." I breathe.

His reputation precedes him—he's every bit as intimidating as I imagined. Cillian Fox: mogul, philanthropist, and criminal. Of course, the latter is merely a rumor. Nothing more than whispers on the street. It's suspected that the wealthy club owner is the head of a very successful criminal empire. No one's ever been able to prove anything though, despite their efforts.

I heard the DA's office has been trying to build a case against him for years. But every time they get a lead, the trail suddenly goes cold. Possible witnesses go missing or turn up dead, and new evidence magically appears that clears Cillian.

The air grows thicker as he inches closer, his lips curving. "Is this your first time?"

"No," I stutter, my face heating at the innuendo behind his question. "I mean, yes."

His features dance with amusement. "Why are you here?"

"To see you."

"Is that so?" He chuckles, the sound more ominous than humorous. "And you are?"

I fidget with the thin gold chain around my neck, his eyes watching the movement a little too intently. "I'm Raina."

"Raina." My name passes through his lips like a promise. Of what, I'm not sure. "What can I do for you?"

"I'm looking for my brother." It isn't all that uncommon for Noah to go missing for a day or two. My twin was impulsive and irresponsible before our parents died. But after...keeping him out of trouble became a full-time job. Something is wrong this time though. I feel it in my bones. "I believe you know him. Noah Walker."

Recognition filters through Cillian's gaze before he has a chance to hide it. "And what makes you think that?"

"I know he's been working for you." The lie comes out of my mouth with so much conviction I almost believe it myself.

After forty-eight hours of complete radio silence, I headed to Noah's apartment to check on him. There was nothing out of place. No sign anything was wrong. But Cillian's business card was sitting on his kitchen counter, like a clue that had been purposely left behind. It's hard to believe my brother would resort to peddling dope on the streets, no matter how strapped for cash he was. But I can't think of any other reason he would be involved with someone like Cillian.

"And what is it you think your brother does for me?" His voice is cold now, menacing.

"All I know is that he's missing." I pause to take a deep breath, the tightness in my chest making it hard to speak. "And I'm hoping you can help me find him."

"I see. Perhaps we should discuss this further in my office." The dark tone behind his words suggests I don't have much of a choice, his hand landing on the small of my back before he ushers me away from the crowd. "Did you come here alone?"

"Yes," I answer, anxiety evident in my voice.

Two large men step in behind us as we head down a hallway, and icy panic starts to pump through my veins. No one even knows I'm here. If everything I've heard about Cillian is true, this could end very badly for me.

It's not like anyone would notice if I went missing either. Noah is my only family, and I've got no real friends.

His bodyguards stay outside when we enter his office, one perched on each side of the door. My heart beats angrily in my chest as Cillian closes us inside, my breaths shallow.

"Why did you come here?" He stands far too close for comfort, his arms crossed. "Why not go to the police?"

It's obvious that most of the cops in this city are corrupt. My guess is that they're all on Cillian's payroll. Going to them would've done more damage than anything.

"The police wouldn't help me. Besides, I don't want to cause trouble for anyone. Whatever my brother was or wasn't doing for you is none of my business. I just want to know he's okay."

His head tilts, his eyes studying me like I'm a puzzle he's trying to figure out. My attention is drawn to the tattoo on his neck, the black ink peeking out from the collar of his shirt.

"Still...you understand why I need to check you for a wire."

Heat floods my veins, my eyes flying back to his. "What?"

A devious smirk spreads across his face. "All it will take is a quick glimpse at what's under your dress. Or if you'd feel more comfortable, I'd be more than happy to pat you down."

The thought of his hands on me causes my stomach to flip, and I quickly shake my head. Taking my clothes off for Cillian wasn't on the agenda, but it's not like I've never gotten naked with a stranger before.

I'll do whatever it takes to get some answers about my brother. This seems like a small price to pay.

I reach behind my back to unzip my dress, my defiant stare staying locked on him, my shaky hands fumbling. I allow the dress to fall and pool at my feet, my bare nipples hardening. His eyes roam over my body, even though it's clear there's nowhere for me to hide a wire.

"Satisfied?"

"On the contrary, Raina." My abdomen tightens as he kneels in front of me and slides my dress back up, his breath leaving goose bumps on my skin, his stare holding mine. "I've never felt less satiated in my life."

His words leave me speechless as warmth pools between my legs. My arms hook through the dress, and he slides it over my shoulders before turning me around. The air stills in my lungs when he sweeps my hair off my back, his hand searing my skin as he zips up the dress.

"It's a shame." His whispered words send a shiver up my spine, his lips finding the shell of my ear. "Under different circumstances, we could've had a lot of fun."

My stomach dips, an unwelcome need building in my core. Someone needs to examine my head. This man is dangerous, immoral. I should be terrified, not turned on.

He snickers as he steps back, the sound like having a bucket of cold water dumped over my head. Embarrassment floods me, my fists balling at my sides as I slowly turn to face him.

My eyes narrow at the smug smirk on his face. "Where's my brother?"

Cillian walks over to the bookshelf and pulls it away from the wall, revealing a secret passageway. "Right this way."

My feet reluctantly move toward him. I could be heading to my death, but if Cillian killed my brother, he might as well kill me too.

I pause at the doorway, my limbs shaky. "Where are we going?"

"To Noah," he answers as my stare finds him, a hint of humor in his tone. "Are you scared, Rabbit?"

"Fuck you." I rip off my mask and toss it on the floor before stepping into the creepy hallway.

Cillian follows in behind me, huffing out a laugh as he secures the bookshelf back in place. My vision is still adjusting to the dim light when his hands grip my waist, his body pressing into mine. "Be careful what you wish for." My traitorous body trembles under his touch, that same mixture of fear and anticipation swirling in my gut. He urges me forward, his hands squeezing before he releases me.

My footsteps are slow and unsure, my anxiety growing with each one. "What is this anyway?"

"Just keep walking," he answers dismissively.

I keep my mouth shut as we make our way toward the light, my mind racing with different possibilities of what awaits me, each horrifying scenario more gruesome than the last.

The large room at the end of the hall looks like a small warehouse, crates and boxes stacked all along the walls. My heart sinks into the pit of my stomach when I spot my brother tied to a chair, a gargantuan man standing next to him. Noah is bloody and bruised, his head hanging, his body almost lifeless.

"Oh my god, you bastard!" Tears spring to my eyes, my stomach churning. "What did you do to him?"

"Your brother brought this on himself," Cillian answers, his voice icy.

"Noah!" I run for him, but a strong arm wraps around my waist, stopping me.

"Raina?" He coughs, lifting his head, his tired eyes struggling to stay open. "What are you doing here?" His frightened gaze turns angry as it swings to the man restraining me. "Fox? What's going on? She has nothing to do with this."

"I didn't bring her into your mess, Walker," Cillian hisses, his hold on me tightening as I squirm. "She came here, *to me*, looking for you."

Panic flashes on Noah's face, his limbs thrashing against his restraints. "Let her go! Please! She doesn't know anything, I swear."

"Oh...I know. But I think she might be the motivation you need. Tell me what I want to know, and I promise no harm will come to her."

"I already told you, it wasn't me," Noah spits. "I'm not dumb enough to steal from you. If I knew who it was, I'd tell you. Kill me if you want, but please...just let my sister go."

"You're in no position to make demands. I think I'd quite like keeping her around." Cillian tucks my hair behind my ears, brushing the backs of his knuckles down my cheek. "As for you..."

My head swims, my entire body going limp with fear as Cillian's henchman points a gun at Noah's head.

His frightened eyes meet mine, the sorrow behind them meant for me. "I'm so sorry, Rae."

"Wait," I plead. "Take me! My life in exchange for his."

The words are out of my mouth before I've even fully processed them. But even if there was time for careful consideration, it wouldn't change a thing. I'd do anything to save my brother.

Including selling my soul to the devil.

"What? Raina, no!" Noah shouts, trying in vain to get free.

The man holding the gun looks at Cillian before slowly lowering it, and I release a ragged breath of relief.

His lips find the shell of my ear again. "What exactly are you offering?"

Noah shakes his head, silently begging me not to do this. But I can't just stand by and watch them kill him. I won't.

"He owes you money, right? I could work for you. Help pay off his debt."

"Work for me?" His laugh brushes my cheek. "Doing what exactly?"

"Whatever you want, for as long as it takes."

"That's an interesting proposition..." Cillian muses, his head lifting as he addresses Noah. "What do you think, Walker?"

"No, no fucking way," Noah protests. "You want your money, I'll get it. Raina has nothing to do with this."

"Yes, you should be the one to get my money." His agreeable tone causes my stomach to spasm with worry. "But Raina here...she gets to be my collateral."

"What?" Noah and I both call out in unison.

"I'll spare your brother's life. *For now.* And he'll be given time to right his wrong." There's malice in his answer, his beard scratching my jaw as he nuzzles into me again. "But only if you give yourself to me. Completely. You'll be mine. Do what I say, when I say it."

"You motherfucker!" Noah barks. "She's a person, not a piece of property!"

I scream as the man with the gun pistol-whips him, the shock of it keeping me frozen in Cillian's arms.

"This offer is nonnegotiable, I'm afraid." Cillian's tone is clipped, impatient. "Ticktock, Rabbit. What will it be?"

My chest aches as fresh blood spills down Noah's face, and I nod. "I'll do it."

CHAPTER TWO

CILLIAN

Liam's head shakes with disapproval as he puts his gun away, his eyes saying what he won't. He thinks I've lost my mind. Hell, maybe I have. Making a deal like this is reckless. Walker clearly can't be trusted, and letting him go is a huge risk. I'm not one for gambling on these types of things, but *she* was too sweet of a temptation to pass up.

"Wise choice," I tell her, delighting in the way her body trembles in my arms.

I noticed her the second she walked through the door—dark curls, curvy body, and bunny ears. She looked like a scared rabbit, lost and alone in the dark depths of the forest. It was obvious she hadn't walked into The Fox's Den ready to explore her sexual fantasies. We see it all the time, looky-loos who come here to judge or satisfy their curiosities. But she didn't seem remotely interested in her surroundings.

"Go to hell." She bucks against my hold. "Just let my brother go."

This little minx caught me by surprise when she told me Walker is her brother. She was so brazen, even as she lied to my face. Her fear was outweighed by her determination to find him. It was hard not to admire that. Despite her presence being a threat.

Thousands of dollars' worth of product went missing this week. Product that had been in Noah's possession. After hours of *grilling* him, he continued to maintain his innocence. But it doesn't matter. Even if he's telling the truth, the debt is still his responsibility. Losing that much money made him a liability. Giving him a pass would send the wrong message.

With a curt nod from me, Liam grabs a knife from his boot. He cuts through the zip ties around Walker's wrists and ankles, but he's too weak to stand. This time when Raina tries to free herself from my hold, I let her go. She rushes to her brother's side, helping him to his feet. He winces when she wraps her arms around him, a whimpered sob rushing out of her.

"You shouldn't have come here." His voice is surprisingly stern as he pulls out of her embrace. "Cillian is my problem. I can't let you do this. You can't fix this, not this time."

Walker was thoroughly vetted before he was brought into my organization. All my *employees* are. I know everything about his past, how the death of their parents led to them bouncing from one foster home to the next. It didn't take long for him to start getting into trouble. Mostly petty stuff that earned him short stays in juvie as a kid and a few nights in a holding cell as an adult. He always seemed to land on his feet though. I'm guessing she had something to do with that.

Raina. I knew I'd heard that name before. She came up during our search, but there wasn't much there. Noah's sister must've been too busy taking care of him to get into any trouble of her own. There wasn't anything that stood out about her at all. She seems to have lived a very quiet and mundane life.

That is about to change. Nothing about her time with me will be dull.

I clear my throat. "We already have an agreement. You aren't the type of person who goes back on their word, are you, Raina?"

Walker's eyes find me as I inch closer, his brow knit with anger. "You're going to have to kill me, Fox. I'm not going to let you take her."

"No, stop," she pleads, taking his face in her hands. "I can do this. It's not that big of a deal. Whatever he has planned for me will be a lot easier to bear than losing you."

My jaw tics, her love for him making me uneasy. "Time to go, Rabbit."

She releases him without hesitation and comes to stand at my side. *So obedient.* I don't even try to hide my smile, the absolute agony in Noah's eyes like icing on the cake. He thinks I'm going to corrupt her. She's so young, only twenty-five, and fifteen years my junior. But Raina isn't as naïve and innocent as he believes. She stripped in front of me without even batting an eyelash, her body coming to life under my stare—her nipples pebbled, practically begging me to take her perky tits in my mouth.

Noah tries to charge toward me, but Liam quickly subdues him, locking him in a chokehold. Raina gasps next to me, her hand covering her mouth as a tear rolls down her pretty face, but she doesn't move.

Such a good girl. I can't wait to play—to see how well-behaved she can be.

"You have ninety days to get me my money," I grit out.

It's an arbitrary timeline. Regardless of how much time he's given, there's a very slim chance he'll be able to make that much money. This is merely a ploy to spend time with her. He knows it too. Raina is the only one clinging to the notion that they can escape this unscathed.

But there's no way out of this. I just may decide to keep her forever.

Her stare is focused out the window as my driver takes us through the city, the silence in the back seat of the Range Rover deafening. It was much easier to get her to leave with me than expected. We walked out of the club together, her arm wrapped around mine. *So cooperative.*

"Where are you taking me?" Her timid voice barely cuts through the quiet, her head still turned away from me.

It's a little late for questions. She hadn't asked a single one before taking my offer. Not very smart on her part, but it certainly worked in my favor. I'm not so sure she would've liked my answers.

"I will not talk to the back of your head."

She takes a deep breath before facing me, shifting her entire body in my direction with a huff. "Happy?"

That isn't an emotion I'm very familiar with, but I *am* very pleased by tonight's turn of events. As soon as she walked into The Fox's Den, I felt drawn to her. It was like this intense need to know her—to taste her, fuck her, *possess* her.

I smirk. "No, mask off."

She was told to put it back on before we left my office. Best not to bring more attention to ourselves than necessary. But now, I want to see her beautiful face.

She takes the mask off teasingly slow. There's a hint of defiance in her gaze as it meets mine, red glowing under the freckles sprinkled across her cheeks.

"We're going to my house. It's about thirty minutes outside of the city."

Her eyes widen but not with panic. They're twinkling with curiosity. "What about my things?"

I collected her coat and purse as we left the club, pocketing her phone before giving her the rest. But I'm not letting her go to her apartment to pack a bag. We can't take the chance of someone figuring out where she is and coming to look for her.

"I'll buy you whatever you need."

She scoffs. "And what about my apartment? My job?"

Her shitty bartending job won't exactly be a great loss. As for her apartment, it might be smart to send someone to clear it out. It probably won't be very hard to pay off her landlord and keep him quiet.

"They'll be dealt with."

She shakes her head. "You can't just completely cut me off from my life."

"Actually, I can," I growl.

"Don't you think people will notice if I suddenly disappear?"

Worry crawls up my spine. She isn't the only one who didn't think to ask questions before setting this whole thing into motion. I honestly have no idea if there are people in her life who will miss her. Friends. *Lovers*.

The thought causes my veins to heat, my muscles tensing.

"Let's take care of that right now, shall we?" Panic dances across her features as I retrieve her phone from my jacket pocket, quickly holding it up to her face to unlock it. I click on the green square at the bottom of the screen. There are four threads, and I work my way down. Noah obviously won't be an issue, and Jodi seems to only contact Raina to ask if she'll cover her shift at the bar. The next conversation consists of nothing more than work schedules and shit. "Mike, he's your boss?" I ask, typing as she nods. "You just quit." Her eyebrows lift, her plump lips parting as if she's going to argue, but she doesn't say a word. It's the last contact that truly piques my interest. No name, just *asshole*. There are hundreds of messages, all with no reply from Raina. Apparently, this guy doesn't know how to take a hint. Maybe that's why she's decided to keep them all. Documentation. Smart girl. I'll do some digging to find out who this creep is later.

"You can have this back once I'm sure you can be trusted with it," I inform her, slipping the phone back in my pocket.

"That's it?" There's a hint of trepidation in her tone. "I'm just your prisoner now?"

"The idea of you in a cage is rather appealing," I quip, my lips curling as she sucks in a breath. "But I suppose that depends on you. Is that how you want this to go?"

She bites her lip, her gaze falling. "No."

"Eyes on me, Rabbit." Her jaw tightens, fury in her stare as it lifts.

"Our time together can be very..." My hand cups her face, my thumb brushing across her pink lips. "*Pleasurable*. For both of us." I slide my hand into her hairline, tugging on her curls, my dick twitching when she grunts. "But make no mistake. I own you. Every part of you. You. Are. Mine. This is the deal *you* made to save your brother, and I expect you to hold up your end of it. I can have him killed with one phone call. Are we clear?"

She swallows, her bottom lip quivering. "Yes."

CHAPTER THREE

RAINA

Cillian's threat is still hanging in the air between us as the car turns into a driveway. I've literally signed my life away. And he's made it very clear how things will go if I don't play along. But my brother is safe. For now, anyway. That's all that matters.

My breath catches when we pull up to the house, all lit up with a warm amber glow. It's stunning, unlike anything I've ever seen before, yet somehow very understated at the same time. This is nothing like I was expecting—lavish, gaudy. The kind of place you'd equate with the head of a criminal empire. This looks like a family home, right down to the two-car garage and basketball hoop.

"I've got a place in the city too," Cillian explains, as if he could hear my thoughts. "This is where I come when I want to be alone."

I'd say that's easy to achieve. The house is very secluded, surrounded by acres of big, beautiful trees. His nearest neighbor was at least five miles back.

Dread weighs heavy on my chest. That's probably why he decided to bring me here.

Cillian gets out once we're parked, coming over to open my door. He offers me his hand, and I take it, allowing him to help me to my feet. My stomach flips when our eyes meet, the seductive smile on his handsome face almost enough to make me forget who he is—what *this* is. I'm not in a fairy tale, and he's certainly no Prince Charming.

He places his hand on the small of my back, leading me to the front door. I take a mental note as he enters the code to unlock it, though I'm not entirely sure why. Getting in isn't the issue; it's getting back out I'm worried about.

He stands in the doorway, gesturing for me to go inside. "After you, Rabbit."

My back straightens, my stare avoiding his as I walk into the foyer. The interior of the home is even more impressive, the tall ceilings and walls of windows bringing in the natural beauty from outside.

"Come on, I'll show you to your room."

My pulse races as I silently follow behind him. He leads me up the stairs and down the hallway to a massive bedroom. It's nearly as big as my studio apartment, certainly nicer. There's a king-size bed, a balcony, and a private bath.

This is nothing like the cage he threatened me with, yet it feels just the same.

He stands by the door as I roam around the room, his watchful glare heating my skin. "The room is stocked for my...*guests*. You'll find comfortable clothes in the dresser and toiletries in the bathroom."

My stomach twists with an unwarranted pang of jealousy, my mouth opening without thought. "Do you entertain *guests* here often?"

He stalks toward me, an arrogant smirk on his face. "If I said yes, would that upset you?"

I shake my head in protest, my cheeks flaming as he stops in front of me. "No."

He grabs my chin, his grip punishing. "That's your one and only free pass. The next time you lie to me, I'll bend you over my knee."

I swallow, wetting my dry mouth. "What?"

He chuckles, his hand sliding around my neck. "Don't be alarmed, Rabbit. I think you'd quite enjoy a good spanking." His husky voice causes my skin to tingle, my heart fluttering as he leans in. "One where I make your ass pink and tender." His words brush across my lips, and I press my thighs together as my center throbs. "Leaving you wet and aching for me."

I blink at him, my head swimming. "I—"

A moan escapes me as his mouth crashes into mine, my parted lips allowing his demanding tongue access. The kiss is brash and all-consuming, and I melt into him as his arm snakes around my waist. I get lost in the taste of whisky and the smell of sandalwood, his soft lips easing the scratch of his beard. He presses his body into mine, his erection pushing into my thigh, making me dizzy with need.

This is wrong and so screwed up. Cillian is a ruthless criminal. He wants to kill my brother and *own* me. My brain keeps trying to remind me I'm in danger, but my body doesn't seem to care.

I'm panting by the time he breaks the kiss, terrified to open my eyes. I shouldn't want this. Or him. He shouldn't be able to make me feel this way.

"Eyes on me, Rabbit." I look up at him through hooded eyes, my face hot. He brushes his thumb over my swollen lips. "So damn sweet. I can't wait to devour every single inch of you." He sighs, releasing me. "Tomorrow."

Panic floods my veins as he backs away, moving toward the door. "Wait…you're leaving me here? Alone?"

I don't do so well with being alone. I'm a twin; I didn't even come into this world solo. And even though I technically live by myself now, there are hundreds of strangers right down the hall. We're currently in the middle of nowhere. In a house I'm not familiar with. In the dead of the night. The idea of being left here completely isolated is terrifying.

He stops, his brow knitting as he studies me. "Does that scare you?"

"Yes," I admit.

He gives me a crooked smile, looking both pleased and disappointed by my honesty. "There's nothing to be afraid of. You're perfectly safe here. The alarm will be on. If anyone so much as sets foot on this property, I'll know."

His reassurance does nothing to bring me comfort, the memory of being locked in a cold, dark room haunting me.

"Why can't you stay?" I whine, hating the desperation in my voice.

His features darken with anger, and I instinctively take a step back. "You belong to me, not the other way around. I don't answer to you."

Fucking bastard.

I grind my teeth, my fists balling at my sides. He waits, watching me. Almost as if he's hoping I'll say something. But I keep my mouth shut.

His lips twitch, a smile fighting to break free. "There's plenty of food in the kitchen. Someone will be here in the morning to bring you clothes and other supplies."

He looks at me expectantly, turning and walking out the door once I nod. It feels like I'm being strangled as I listen to him head back down the stairs, my eyes wet and breathing shallow. I remain frozen while he turns on the alarm and locks me inside, the weight on my chest growing heavier when I hear the roar of the SUV.

The full gravity of the situation hits me moments later, and I fall to my knees, tears streaming down my face. I may not make it out of this. My only hope for survival is to make myself more valuable alive than dead.

CHAPTER FOUR

CILLIAN

Liam is waiting for me when I get back to my office at the club, a worried scowl etched into his features. "What the hell are you thinking? You know we can't let Walker go. It's too dangerous."

Liam has been my right-hand man since the beginning, my one constant. He's like family to me, one of the few people I truly trust. His concern is valid, but he can't change my mind. Not about this.

"If I want your opinion, I'll ask for it," I clip out, hanging my jacket on the coat rack. "A deal was made, and I'm going to keep my word."

He scoffs, crossing his massive arms. "You're seriously going to put our entire organization at risk for some pussy?"

I cut my eyes to him in warning, rolling up my sleeves. "What the fuck did you just say to me?"

He may be family, but I'm still his boss. This is *my* organization. I won't tolerate disrespect.

He shakes his head, running a hand through his hair. "I don't get it. You've got a club full of women dying to fuck you. What's so special about Walker's sister?"

That's something I don't fully understand yet myself. There's just something so intriguing about her.

I hadn't planned on kissing her tonight. It seemed only right to give her some time to adjust and accept her fate. But her eyes darkened with lust when I threatened to take her over my knee, her labored breathing giving her away. She was already wet and needy for me, and it took everything in me not to bend her over the bed right then and there—to get her bare and spread open for me.

The thought makes my cock swell, and I take a seat at my desk. "Since when do I need to explain myself to you?"

It's not like Liam hasn't questioned my choices before, but he's never pushed back on anything like this. I think he feels personally responsible since he was supposed to be keeping an eye on Noah for me. He's the one who told me we couldn't trust him.

"You know I'm right," he grits out. "That little fucker has always been a loose cannon. What's to stop him from going off and running his mouth now?"

It's true. Noah never struck me as someone who feared death. That's part of why I considered him an asset. Threatening his life wouldn't be enough to keep him in line. But Raina's life. That's a different situation entirely. There was genuine terror in his eyes when he saw her in my arms. His love for her is his weak spot.

"She gives me leverage over him. As long as I have her, he won't do anything stupid."

My words sound more confident than I'm feeling. Noah knows there's only one way out of this for him. But he might do whatever it takes to get Raina away from me.

He huffs. "You can't be sure of that. Besides, the bastard stole from you."

That still doesn't make sense to me. Noah is my newest recruit, but he's been loyal. He isn't an addict, so he didn't take the drugs for himself. And I would've heard about it he sold them. Something isn't adding up.

"I'm not so sure he did. You beat the shit out of him for hours and his story never changed. If it was someone else, keeping him alive might smoke them out. In the meantime, he'll be working his ass off to get my money back and save his sister. It's a win-win situation."

"Whatever you say, boss."

I raise an eyebrow at his tone, relaxing back into my chair. "Where is he now?"

"Connor followed him to his apartment after we let him go. There hasn't been any movement since."

"Good. I'll give him some time to lick his wounds and come up with a plan before we talk. Until then, make sure we've got someone trailing him at all times. I want to know every single move he makes."

Liam lets out an agitated breath, giving me nothing more than a nod. He's clearly still not happy with me, but I don't give a fuck.

"All right, get the hell out of my office." I dismiss him with a wave of my hand, opening my laptop. "I've got shit to do."

INTO THE FOX'S DEN

Once I'm alone, I log in to the security cameras at the house. It's kind of pathetic how desperate I am to see Raina. She certainly hadn't made it easy to leave her there, the panic in her eyes nearly enough to be my undoing.

Unease prickles on my skin when she isn't in her room, my eyes frantically searching each camera for her. I find her in the kitchen, eating ice cream straight from the carton. She looks freshly showered, her hair wet, the dress she'd been wearing replaced with a basic white T-shirt. My dick strains against my pants at the sight of her bent over the counter, her perfectly round ass up in the air.

Fuck. I can't wait to bury myself balls-deep inside of her.

I lean back in my chair and unbuckle my pants, taking my throbbing cock in my hand. Liam is right—I could easily find someone in The Fox's Den willing to take care of this for me. But I want *her*.

My eyes stay trained on her, my grip tightening as I stroke myself, thinking about the sweet taste of her mouth and the way her body became completely pliable in my hands.

I picture myself there with her, slowly pulling her panties down her thighs, just enough to give me access. Her soft moan echoes in my memory as I imagine gliding my dick over her slick entrance, her pussy clenching around me when I slide into her, pushing her forward and tugging her hair until her back is nice and arched for me, allowing me to drive deep inside of her.

As if she knows I'm watching, she looks over her shoulder, her dark eyes locking on the camera, *on me*. I fist myself harder, faster, my muscles tightening. Red splashes across her cheeks as she bites into her bottom lip, sending me over the edge.

My body shudders, my other hand catching the white rope that shoots out of me. She turns to face the camera as my orgasm subsides, cum covering my palm. Her stare stays focused on the camera, her head tilted as she shovels another bite of ice cream into her mouth, tauntingly licking the spoon.

Is she toying with me?

I groan, my dick already getting hard again. "Silly Rabbit. You have no idea the kind of wicked things I have planned for you."

CHAPTER FIVE

RAINA

My heart jumps in my throat when I hear the front door open, my bloodshot eyes unblinking as I listen to them disarm the alarm. I'm still frozen in place when a woman walks into the kitchen, her arms full. She spots me and startles, things falling to the floor as she comes to an abrupt halt.

"Oh, shit," she chuckles, placing the rest of the bags on the counter. "You must be Raina. I'm sorry, I wasn't expecting you to be awake already."

Her Southern accent is thick and oddly endearing, her blonde hair and blue eyes making her the perfect Georgia Peach.

I let out a breath, my pulse slowing. "Yeah, well…I couldn't really sleep."

I was on edge all night, tossing and turning. The house was eerily quiet, every noise from outside making me jump. By the time the sun started to rise, I decided to give up and came downstairs.

"I heard you had an *interesting* night." She gives me an apologetic smile before quickly changing the subject. "I'm Everly, by the way. Cillian's…*assistant*. He sent me out to pick up some things and bring them here for you."

I fight the urge to roll my eyes. It's not like he's doing me a favor.

"Thank you." I sigh, looking over my shoulder at the camera.

After Cillian left last night, I took a long, flesh-burning, hot shower. It took me a minute to pull myself back together, the water running cold before my eyes dried up. But I eventually recognized that tears wouldn't do me any good. They couldn't save me.

Once I was done, I decided to explore the house. I'll be staying here a while—figured I might as well get acquainted with the place. It's so much bigger than I realized. Far too big for one man. There are three bedrooms upstairs, including Cillian's master suite. The kitchen, dining room, living room, and his office are all on the main floor. The basement has two more bedrooms, an informal living space, a fully equipped gym, and a home theater. Which is totally absurd, but at least there are ways for me to entertain myself.

When my search was complete, I started to feel a little more comfortable—and thankful I hadn't found some kind of *sex room*. But that was before I discovered the cameras. I hadn't noticed them at first, all of them hidden high up on the walls.

I could feel him watching me though, goose bumps forming on my skin. Turns out I'd never truly been alone here. And I'm not sure if that makes me feel less afraid or more.

"Here," Everly says, gesturing to the kitchen table as my gaze lands on her again. "Why don't you sit down. I'll make you some coffee and a bite to eat."

I nod and make my way over to the table, my tired body plopping down on the chair. She flurries around the kitchen, seeming to know exactly where everything is, and I find myself wondering if she's ever been one of Cillian's *guests*. The thought makes my stomach twist.

"How long have you worked for Cillian?"

"Uh...a while," Everly answers, keeping her back to me. "How do you take your coffee?"

I roll my eyes at her vague answer. "Black is fine."

She walks over with a fresh cup, that pageant-ready smile on her pretty face as she places it in front of me. "How does an omelet sound?"

My stomach rumbles in response. "Great. Thank you."

"You got it." She turns to walk away but quickly spins back around. "Oh...before I forget." She takes a phone out of her back pocket and sets it on the table. "Cillian wanted you to have that."

My eyebrows shoot up in surprise. "He's giving me a phone?"

It isn't my phone, but at least I could call my brother. If I could just talk to him and make sure he's still okay...

The forlorn expression on her face makes my stomach sink. "Don't get too excited. There's only one number it can call and accept calls from. Cillian's."

My throat clogs with emotion, my face tingling. "Oh..."

She pulls out a chair, taking a seat across from me. "He's not as bad as you think."

"No?" I huff out a laugh, swiping away a rogue tear. "Do you have any idea why I'm here?" She gives me a reluctant nod, having enough decency to look ashamed. "Then how can you seriously sit here and defend him?"

She presses her lips, her shoulders rising and falling as she takes a deep breath. "I don't expect you to understand, but there's a lot you don't know about Cillian. If it wasn't for him, I would be dead right now. He literally saved my life."

The sorrow behind her confession leaves me speechless as she gets up from the table, my eyes seeing the cracks in her flawless exterior now. She goes back to preparing my breakfast, softly singing a Taylor Swift song to fill the silence while she cooks, like she hadn't just shared this deeply personal thing with a complete stranger.

I want to believe what she's saying—that Cillian isn't the heartless beast he appears to be. It would mean there's a chance of surviving this. For me and my brother. But hope can be dangerous a thing.

"Oh my god," Everly coos as I step out of the bathroom. "That looks amazing on you."

After breakfast, we came upstairs to put away my new clothes, and Everly insisted I try some of the outfits on to be sure they worked. None of them feel like me. I've never seen so many soft tones and frilly dresses in my life. But I had to give it to her, everything fit me perfectly. And they're a huge improvement from the T-shirts and sweats I'd found in the dresser last night.

My nose wrinkles as I step in front of the full-length mirror, my hand running over the silky, nude material. The dress is kind of cute, short and simple with an A-line skirt and billowed sleeves, but it isn't something I ever would've picked out for myself.

I miss my clothes, my apartment, my life. It may not have been much, but it was mine. And it beat the hell out of being Cillian's prisoner. Most of all though, I miss my brother.

I don't even realize tears are streaming down my face until Everly steps up behind me, her kind eyes meeting mine in the mirror. "It's going to be okay."

I turn to face her, drying my cheeks with the back of my hand. "You can't promise me that."

She sighs. "You're right...I can't even pretend to understand what Cillian is thinking, but I've never known him to be unnecessarily cruel."

Unnecessarily. That doesn't bring me any solace. Cillian believes my brother stole from him, which is all the justification he needs.

"Have you met my brother?"

A warm smile spreads across her face as she nods. "Yeah. Noah is a sweetheart. He talks about you so much, it kind of feels like I know you."

My chest aches, another fat tear rolling down my face. "Do you think he did it? That he really stole from Cillian?"

Her blue eyes fill with pity. "I don't know, but it doesn't look good."

The image of Noah, bloody and bruised, pops into my head, and I take a seat on the end of the bed. "I didn't even know he was working for Cillian," I admit. "He's my best friend. How could I not know?"

I knew he was struggling to make ends meet a few months ago, even offered to let him move in with me. But he got that new carrier job... My mind starts to put the pieces together, the long hours and good pay making a lot more sense now. I can't believe I didn't see it before.

"If you didn't know, why did you go to the club last night?"

My stomach twists with unease when I think about how stupid I'd been, walking into The Fox's Den without a clue. All because I'd seen Cillian's business card on Noah's kitchen counter. My decision to go there was impulsive and dangerous, but I wouldn't take it back, despite it landing me here. I'm the only reason Noah isn't dead right now.

"I don't know." I shrug. "Twin intuition, I guess. My gut told me he was there, but I never imagined I'd find him like...*that*."

She sits next to me, taking my hand. "I'm sorry you had to see that. This may be hard for you to believe right now, but Cillian takes good care of everyone who works for him—watches out for them like family. I think he likes Noah and really wants to give him the chance to prove his innocence. You wouldn't be here otherwise."

She's trying to plant another seed of hope, but I'm still too afraid to let it blossom, only to have it wilt away.

"How is he?" My voice wavers as I meet her stare. "My brother. Have you seen him?"

She shakes her head. "I heard Liam did a number on him, and he was in pretty rough shape. I haven't seen him though. Cillian told me Noah was back at his apartment this morning."

My throat swells with emotion, more tears rolling down my face. "Do you think he'll let me talk to him?"

Her gaze falls, her lips pressing thoughtfully before her eyes meet mine again. "You could always ask. He's coming back here this evening to check on you."

My heart flutters at the thought of him seeing him again, my lips tingling with the memory of his kiss.

I can't wait to devour every single inch of you.

If it's my body he wants, I'll give it to him. Whatever it takes to get my brother back.

CHAPTER SIX

CILLIAN

Everly is coming down the stairs as I walk through the front door, her eyebrows raised with suspicion. "I thought you weren't coming until later."

This definitely isn't where I'm supposed to be right now, but I was eager to get back to Raina. If it wasn't for my meeting this morning, I would've been here sooner. The second it was over, I had Nick drive me out.

"I had some free time," I lie with a shrug, my stare flickering behind her as she steps on the landing. "Where's Raina?"

She gives me a knowing look, her lips pursed. "She's taking a nap. Poor thing didn't sleep well last night."

There's nothing subtle about the hint of disapproval in her tone. "Go ahead, Ly. Say whatever's on your mind."

When I told Everly about Raina last night, she made her displeasure about the situation very well known. Not that I was surprised. After everything she's been through, her heart is still so kind—too trusting. She doesn't have the stomach for the types of things I have to deal with. But she's the only one I trust to be around Raina.

I met Everly twenty years ago, back when we were just kids—both of us so desperate to make it out of our neighborhood. There wasn't anything we wouldn't do, and one night that desperation nearly got her killed. I just so happened to be in the right place at the right time and heard her cries. The first life I took was to save hers, and I'd do it all over again. Without hesitation.

She's been blindly loyal to me ever since then.

"What's your plan here?" she asks, a hand on her hip. "How do you see this playing out?"

"I don't know," I answer honestly, heading toward my office.

There's no point in lying to her. Everly always sees right through me. Even if that weren't the case, I don't know what I'd tell her. There's nothing I could say that would make her be okay with all this.

Especially after the two of them spent most of the day together. It wouldn't shock me if Everly was already growing attached to her. She sent me updates throughout the morning, letting me know they were eating breakfast together and that Raina was putting on a little fashion show for her.

She stays right at my heels, clearly unwilling to let this go. "Is this about her or punishing Noah?"

Her. Definitely her. At least in the beginning. Even if she hadn't offered herself up to save Noah, I would've found a way to know her. She just made it easy.

I sit on the edge of my desk, crossing my arms. "If that asshole stole from me, he deserves to suffer."

"If?" Her eyebrows shoot up, hope lighting up her eyes. "You don't really think it was him, do you?"

Everly has a soft spot for Noah. She's the one who made me question his involvement in the first place. She seemed so sure it couldn't have been him, but I didn't want to hear it. He had the product—that made him responsible. The same way I'd have to answer for the missing money to my supplier.

"I'm not sure anymore. When Liam first told me, I was too pissed to think straight. But the more time I've had to reflect on everything, the less it all makes sense. It's possible Noah was set up. If that's the case, someone in my organization might be trying to take me down. Having her here gives me some time to figure this shit out and the reassurance that Noah won't turn on me."

"Have you talked to him today? Do you know what he's planning to do?"

I shake my head. "I'm going to have Connor bring him in tomorrow night."

I wanted to give Noah some time to calm down and clear his head. He needs to play this smart. His only hope of getting out of this alive is to give me my money or help me figure out who took the product so I can get it back myself.

"You know..." she sighs, her eyes sad as they lock on mine, "if he's innocent, he's not going to forgive you for Raina. And...if he's not, she won't be able to forgive you for killing him."

It's not like this hadn't occurred to me already. But what's done is done. I can't let myself care. Caring too much in my line of business can get you killed. It's not just Noah's life that could be on the line here. If my supplier finds out someone has been stealing from me, he'll find another distributor.

"What makes you think I give a shit about their forgiveness?"

She walks over, leaning in to place a soft kiss on my cheek. "Just be careful."

I groan when Liam's name flashes across my screen. The fucking prick hasn't stopped blowing up my phone since I got here. Apparently ignoring him isn't an option. I might as well answer the damn phone.

I slide the potato slices off the cutting board into the pot of water, drying off my hands before picking up the phone. "What?"

"It's about fucking time," Liam hisses. "I've been trying to reach you for hours."

"I've been busy. What's so fucking important?"

The truth is, I've been sitting around, waiting very impatiently for Raina to come out of her room. I considered going up there and breaking her door down a couple of times, before deciding dinner is probably a more productive way to lure her out.

"You didn't tell me how the meeting with Lorenzo went. As far as I knew, you could've been lying somewhere with a hole in your head, motherfucker."

There's a pang of guilt in my chest. It was shitty of me not to tell him how things went. My supplier isn't known for having patience or grace. But once the meeting was over, my only thought was getting back to Raina.

"Everything is fine," I reassure him. "I paid him in full. Took the money out of my savings. He doesn't even know that the product went missing."

I took a big hit paying Lorenzo back with my own money. Money that's supposed to get me out of this life one day. But telling him I didn't have his money wasn't an option. He would not have shown me the same mercy I'd shown Noah.

"Do you think that was smart? What are you going to do if this isn't an isolated incident?"

"I've got it under control," I snap.

That couldn't be further from the truth. This is a fucking mess. One that's only going to grow if I don't clean it up soon.

"Do you? Because last I checked, you were letting Noah roam free, and you aren't doing shit to set this right. Where the fuck are you anyway?"

I hesitate, knowing he's not going to like my answer. Guess it's a good thing I don't answer to him. "I'm at the house. I'll be in later."

"Are you fucking kidding me right now?" he bellows. "This is not the time for you to be distracted."

I hate that he's right. I'm preoccupied, and it's dangerous.

Before I can respond, Raina walks into the kitchen, her dark eyes full of curiosity. She looks fucking incredible, the sight of her long legs in that dress already making my dick hard.

"We can talk about this tonight. I've got to go." I hang up the phone, turning it off before slipping it into my pocket. I don't want anyone interrupting us.

"It smells amazing in here." Her gaze travels down my body, pink tinting her cheeks as it meets mine again. "Are you cooking?"

I nod, inching closer to her. "Thought we could have dinner together before I head into the club tonight."

"You want to have dinner with me?" Her eyes fall as she scoots around the kitchen island, slowly creating more distance between us.

Doesn't she know the chase is part of the fun?

"Are you trying to get away from me, Rabbit?" I taunt, my feet moving faster. She freezes, her breath hitching as I step up behind her, planting both hands on the counter to cage her in. "Before you open that pretty little mouth of yours..." I bury my nose into her curly hair and inhale, my cock growing painfully hard. "Remember what will happen if you lie to me."

"I, uh..." She sucks in a shaky breath, turning around to face me, her eyes hooded as they find mine. "You make me nervous."

"Good." A soft whimper passes through her lips as I press my body into hers. "I like you being a little afraid." Her throat bobs as I sweep the hair away from her neck, my thumb brushing over her racing pulse. "And I think you do too."

I lean in, my lips caressing the same spot my thumb had before they work their way up. My hands grip her waist as I suck and nibble the sensitive skin below her ear. She rocks into me as my mouth fuses with hers, her needy moan swallowed up by my kiss.

Raina's lips part without prodding, her tongue timidly seeking mine out. She tastes even sweeter than she had the night before, the kiss gentle yet hungry. My hands slide down her hips to her ass, and she wraps her legs around me as I lift her onto the counter.

She plants her hands on my chest when I slip under the short skirt, prying her lips away from mine. Raina's eyelashes flutter open, her dilatated eyes struggling to focus on me. "Cillian?" she pants, those plump lips pink and swollen. "Will you please let me call Noah? I need to talk to him."

My jaw tics, anger burning in my chest. All that shit just now was for show. She was just trying to manipulate me—playing me to get what she wants.

Her eyes widen as I wrap my hand around her delicate little throat, squeezing just enough to show I'm not fucking around. "What makes you think I give a fuck what you *need*?"

"Everly," she wheezes. "She thought if I asked..."

Goddamnit. I should've known. No doubt Everly tried to convince her I'm a decent guy, simply misunderstood.

"She was wrong." I release her, taking a step back. "*If* I let you talk to Noah, it will be on my terms. Not yours."

A tear rolls down her face. "I just want to know he's okay."

"Well, you'll just have to take my word for it." I walk back over to the stove, hating the way her sorrow makes my chest ache. "Right now, your brother's only concern needs to be how he's going to get my money back." She scurries past me, out of the kitchen. "Dinner will be ready in an hour," I call after her. "Make sure that sweet ass of yours is planted in a dining room chair by then."

CHAPTER SEVEN

RAINA

I clumsily make my way through the dark house, purposely leaving the lights off in hopes Cillian won't be able to see me through the cameras. His car left about twenty minutes ago—two hours after I was supposed to come down for dinner. My stomach growls angrily as I slowly descend the stairs, the smell of garlic and steak still lingering in the air. Refusing to eat with him probably wasn't very smart. A part of me expected him to bust down my bedroom door—to make good on his threats. But the strong-willed, stubborn side of me hoped he would give in and let me talk to my brother.

Neither happened.

A mixture of relief and disappointment washed over me as I watched the taillights of his SUV fade into the distance. He left me here all alone again, and I still have no clue if Noah is okay.

My heart stops as I enter the kitchen, the sound of ice clinking against a glass making me freeze. I wait and listen, too afraid to even breathe, telling myself it was just my imagination.

"Come here, Rabbit."

The dark tone in Cillian's voice sends a shiver through me, all the air rushing out of me. I turn my head toward the dining room, my eyes slowly adjusting to the darkness. He's sitting at the table in a halo of moonlight, a tumbler of liquor in his hand and an angry scowl on his face.

"Don't make me repeat myself," he warns.

His cold eyes watch me over the rim of his glass as my feet pad slowly in his direction, my body trembling with trepidation and a little bit of anticipation. There's something about seeing him in a T-shirt and jeans, the tattoos on his muscular arms on full display, that makes him seem more dangerous. And in a very fucked-up way, it only makes him more appealing.

When I reach the end of the table, he places the empty crystal down and scoots away from the table, sitting back lazily in his chair. "Take your panties off."

My body burns hot at his command, my thighs pressing together. "What?"

He can't be serious. There's no way in hell I'm doing that.

Do what I say, when I say it.

My stomach drops as his words echo in my head, the image of Noah's beaten face flashing through my mind. I already disobeyed Cillian once tonight; defying him again could be dangerous. For me and my brother.

"This is not the time to push me," he hisses. "My patience is very thin."

I grit my teeth, my hands shaking as they slip under the skirt of my dress, quickly pulling my panties down my legs and off my body. I'm not sure where this is going, but I don't want to make it worse for myself.

"Good girl. Now, bring them to me."

My heart hammers in my chest as I move around the table, my breathing shallow by the time I'm standing next to him. I place the panties in his palm when he holds out his hand, my mouth dropping open as he sniffs them—inhaling as if my scent is his life source, his eyes rolling back with pleasure.

He tucks the lacy material in his pocket once he's done, a fire blazing behind his green eyes. "Get on the table."

I scoot between him and the table on wobbly legs, trying to ignore the way his stare caresses my skin. I've never felt more degraded than I do right now, following his orders liked an obedient child. But it's not like there's another choice. Fighting him will only get my brother killed.

His arms hook under my knees once I'm perched on the edge of the table, my ass sliding back as he lifts them. He places my feet on the armrests of his chair, his hands gliding up my thighs. They move back down and up again, and my body revels in his touch, my tense muscles becoming more lax with each stroke.

"What are you doing?" I ask, my voice cracking.

"Since you chose not to join me for dinner, I've decided to have you for dessert."

I gasp, the thrill that shoots through me making me feel ashamed. This is my punishment—a power play. A reminder that he owns me and can do what he wants with my body. The only things I should be feeling are anger and disgust.

"Lie back and spread your legs," he demands.

My nipples harden as I lean back and prop myself up on my elbows, but fear keeps my knees locked in place. That familiar ache builds when he pries my thighs apart, opening my legs wide for him.

He sucks in a hissing breath, the release brushing against my bare pussy. "So fucking perfect." Desire pools at my center as his stare finds mine. "Don't resist this, Rabbit," he cautions, placing a kiss on the inside of my knee. "This doesn't end until you come." His lips move to my other leg, higher this time. "I want to hear you scream as you come undone." My clit throbs as his mouth travels closer to the apex of my thighs, his hands gripping my hips. "To see your body limp and lifeless after it completely succumbs to me." He stops just before reaching my core, his eyes hooded as they meet mine once more. "Do you understand?"

I nod, catching a glimpse of his grin before he dives between my legs. A moan escapes me with the first swipe of his warm tongue against my aching slit. My head falls back as he sucks my clit into his mouth, my hips moving into him.

His beard tickles my sensitive flesh, his tongue dipping low, then back up again, circling the bundle of nerves there. My abdomen tightens as he repeats the pattern, my panted breaths growing louder. I close my eyes, my nails clawing into the wooden table.

"Don't hold out on me," he growls.

I cry out as his tongue plunges into me, teasing my entrance. His attention returns to my clit, flicking and sucking until it feels like every nerve in my body is about to explode. He slips a finger inside of me, slowly working it in and out before adding another. My walls clench around him, my body becoming desperate for a release.

"Please, Cillian." My plea is breathy, needy.

"Give me what I want."

He curls his fingers, and the pressure sends me over the edge. My loud cries echo around us as my orgasm crashes through me, his tongue lapping up the evidence. He removes his fingers from me as the waves subside, my chest still heaving as I work to calm my breathing.

"Look at me." My eyes pop open at his order, shame flooding me when my gaze finds him, a pleased smirk on his face. I enjoyed that way more than I should have, and he knows it. My skin tingles when he puts his fingers into his mouth, a hunger in his eyes as he licks them clean. "You taste so damn good."

I sit up as my eyes narrow at him, despising the way his praise makes my swollen clit pulse.

My legs fall when Cillian stands, positioning himself between them as he takes my face in his hands. His mouth slams into mine, his tongue forcing its way inside. He tastes like me, his beard wet with my arousal, and it's intoxicating.

His possessive kiss leaves my lips tender, my eyelashes fluttering open as he pulls away.

"You're mine, Rabbit. Every part of your body and every minute of your day belongs to me. The sooner you accept that, the better. Next time you refuse to share a meal with me, you won't eat. Temper tantrums will only get you in trouble. Got it?"

I grind my teeth, the rage I'm feeling making my eyes water. I want to scream—to tell him to go to hell. But I submissively nod, my stomach queasy with self-loathing.

"Good." He pats my head like I'm a fucking dog. "I'm going to go clean up. I've got to get to the club," he tells me, walking away. "*Someone* already made me late."

It should be a relief that he's leaving, but panic quickly takes ahold of me, melting away any anger or frustration I'd been feeling. The idea of quiet isolation is much worse than Cillian.

I hop off the table, following behind him. "Please don't leave me here alone again."

My desperate plea stops him in his tracks, his jaw clenched as he turns back around to face me. "That's funny. You didn't seem too concerned with being lonely during dinner."

"I'm sorry. I was upset, but I..." My voice wavers from his hard glare, my steps slow and timid. "I want you to stay."

"Be careful what you wish for, Rabbit." His words sound menacing, a wicked grin curling his lips as he stalks toward me. I don't even realize I'm backing away until I'm trapped, my back pressed against the wall as he crowds me. He grabs my hand and places it on his hard crotch, his dick twitching under my touch. "I can think of about a hundred different ways I'd like to fuck you right now." My eyes widen, my core tightening as he leans in, his lips finding the shell of my ear. "Hard and fast. Slow and deep. I want to take you in every room of this house, to fuck you until your body is completely spent." My breathing is erratic by the time he meets my stare again, a knowing twinkle in his green eyes. "You think you can handle that?"

His *threat* leaves me dizzy, my body and mind fighting for dominance. There's a big part of me that just wants to lean into the madness. I've already sold my soul to the devil; there's no need to worry about my sins.

"I..." My tongue sticks in my dry mouth, words failing me.

"Yes, I believe you could," he chuckles, backing away from me. "But I'm afraid it's just going to have to wait."

CHAPTER EIGHT

CILLIAN

My dick twitches as Raina walks down the stairs, her delicious curves framed, those long legs on full display. She's practically glowing, the slate-blue dress complementing her brown skin beautifully. Everly did her job well. Maybe a little too well. I'm not sure how I feel knowing she'll be turning a lot of heads tonight.

I've felt oddly possessive of her since that first night, but now…I've tasted her pleasure—I've heard her screams of ecstasy. And I want them all. The thought of anyone else touching her makes me want to break shit.

"God, you're so fucking beautiful."

She takes my hand, blushing as I help her down the last step. "Are you going to tell me what this is about?"

She wasn't very happy with me when I busted into her room earlier, telling her to get ready and meet me downstairs in an hour. I half expected another repeat of last night, that she'd force me to drag her out of that room.

I'm pleased to see she learned her lesson, yet slightly disappointed. *Disciplining* her was so much fun, the way her body responds to me intoxicating. It was hard as hell to walk away from her last night, knowing she was ready to let me fuck her. Despite her hatred for me. But her willingness isn't enough, I want her aching and needy for me. I might even make her beg for it.

"Here, you'll need this." Her eyes light up as I hand her the rabbit mask. "You're going with me to the club tonight."

This is a bad idea. I seem to be making a lot of questionable choices lately. All of them involving her. Liam's entire head might explode when she walks into The Fox's Den on my arm tonight. But there's no way I'm leaving her again, and I've got too much shit to deal with. I can't hide away from the world here with her.

"What?" she breathes, her brow knit with confusion. "Really? But why?"

Because I'm an idiot. Because she's getting under my skin. Because leaving her last night was even harder than the night before. Because I can't keep putting my entire life on hold to be with her. Because I can't spend another night watching her walk aimlessly around this house, seeming as if she might break at any moment.

My eyebrows lift as I cross my arms. "I thought you hated being here alone."

It's obvious there's some type of trauma behind her fear, and I'm tempted to make her tell me. They were moved around to a lot of different foster homes as kids; there's no telling the kind of shit they had to deal with.

"I do," she scoffs. "I just didn't realize you cared."

I shouldn't. It's only going to bring me trouble. Everly was right—I need to be vigilant. If I let her get the upper hand, this whole thing could blow up in my face.

"I don't." Her eyes narrow at my flippant tone. "But your purpose will be better served by my side tonight."

Noah is coming to the club later. It might be good for him to get a reminder of what's at stake here—that's there's more than one life on the line. Her presence will help ensure his cooperation, and it will give her the reassurance she's been looking for.

———

Raina is nervously pacing around my office when I get a text from Connor telling me Noah has arrived. She was quiet all the way here, her leg nervously bouncing the entire time. She's not dumb—she knows I brought her here for a reason.

"Come here, Rabbit."

She freezes, faltering only a moment before making her way over to my desk. "No..." I push my chair away from the desk, patting my leg. "Come here."

Her freckles shine brighter as her cheeks turn pink, her wild curls falling over them like a curtain when she looks down. "I thought you had a meeting."

"I do," I clip out. "Do you want them to see what happens when you don't do as you're told?"

Her eyes are wide as they lift to find mine, her feet quickly carrying her over to me. A smile tugs at my lips as she squeezes around me and the desk, timidly positioning herself between my legs.

My arm wraps around her waist, my dick swelling as I pull her down onto my lap. I tuck her curls behind her ear and grab her chin, turning her head toward me. "I want you to sit here and be quiet. No matter what you see or hear. Understand?"

She nods, her breath hitching as I bring her mouth to mine. There's no resistance, no hesitation, her tongue eagerly colliding with mine. I take my time with her, keeping the kiss soft and sensual. This isn't like the ones we've shared before. It's chaste, designed to leave her wanting more. I pull away as soon as her body begins to melt into me. Her eyelids stay closed, her needy breaths filling the silence as she licks her lips, pressing them together as if she's savoring the kiss.

Her eyes pop open when I place my hand on her knee, my fingertips softly caressing her skin. "Are you wet for me right now, Rabbit? If I were to slide my hand between your thighs, would I find your panties drenched?"

The color on her cheeks darkens, her eyelids briefly falling again. She doesn't want to tell me the truth, but she's too afraid to lie. "Yes."

Her confession makes my cock rock hard, and I'm considering locking the door when there's a knock on it. "Come in," I grit out.

Raina gasps when Noah walks into my office, her body going stiff in my arms. I bite back a smile as panic and confusion washes over her gorgeous face. She's not very good at hiding her emotions.

Noah's bruised face twists with pain when he sees her perched on my knee. "Oh god, Raina...I'm so sorry."

She tries to get up, but I hold her in place, my fingers digging into her soft skin. "Be a good girl, or I'll have to punish you," I whisper in her ear.

She silently nods, and his glare turns angry as it focuses on me. "What the fuck is this, Fox?"

I gesture at the empty chair across from my desk. "Sit down, Noah. We need to talk."

He does as he's told before returning his attention to Raina. "Are you okay? Has he hurt you?"

I chuckle as she shakes her head, her body shifting uncomfortably. "Don't worry. I've been very kind and *giving* to your sister. But that could just as well change if you don't get my money back. What's your plan?"

"I don't know," he admits, a hand running over his buzzed head. "But I swear, I didn't do this."

There's honesty in his stare as it locks on mine, the desperation behind it making it hard to doubt him. It would be easier for me if he were lying. Less complicated. At least it would've been before Raina came into the picture. Now, I find myself hoping he's telling the truth.

"Let's say I believe you. Who was it, then? The bricks were in your possession. Who could've taken them from you?"

"That's the thing, boss...I'm not sure they were ever in my bag."

I take a deep breath, my irritation growing. "Are you telling me you didn't count your stash before you left?"

He sighs, his shoulders sagging with shame. "It was stupid. I royally fucked up. I've been doing this for months and have counted it every single time. I was distracted that day, in a rush..."

Fuck. If he was never even in custody of it, then the problem is definitely within my organization. It would have to be someone higher up. Someone I trust. Which could mean it's someone looking to take my place. They're trying to take me down from the inside.

"When did you notice you were short?"

His jaw tics as my hand glides higher up Raina's leg. "When I got to my last delivery."

"Can you say for certain no one else could've taken it? Did anyone have access to you or the product between locations?"

"No." There's certainty in his answer, his head shaking. "It was careless of me not to check my load before I left the warehouse, but I was always very careful. There's not a chance in hell someone got the drop on me."

"Why didn't you tell someone, then?" Raina flinches as I raise my voice, my tone growling. "Why run if you were innocent?"

Innocent men don't run; guilty men do. Noah hadn't even called to tell us, he just ran. We had to hunt him down, caught him trying to hide out two days later.

"Because I panicked. I knew it would fall back on me. It's like you said, I'm responsible even if I'm not. And I fucked up, but I didn't steal from you."

He gets credit for admitting and accepting his screwup, but it won't save him from this. We all know the risks of doing what we do. There's no avoiding the consequences when we fuck up.

"Did you tell Liam all of this? That you think someone shorted you?"

Liam hadn't told me much about what Noah had to say for himself, though I hadn't really asked either. I wasn't ready to accept the possibility of his innocence. But it seems like this is information he should've shared with me.

"No..." His eyes fall. "I wasn't sure who I could trust."

If Liam can't be trusted, I'm even more screwed than I realized. He plays a big part in running my organization, knows all the ins and outs of my *business* dealings. If there's anyone who could potentially take over, it's him.

"Are you saying that you think he could be involved?" I push.

His stare finds me again as he answers, his expression guarded. "I don't know."

Unease settles over me. There's something he's not telling me, a reason why he suspects Liam. He just doesn't trust I'll believe him. To be fair, I'm not entirely sure I would. Not without some kind of hard evidence. I'll need more than simple suspicion before I go after a man who's been like family to me.

"That's bullshit, but I'll let it slide for now. Here's what we're going to do... You're going to get back to running for me, taking on more locations to help recoup my loss."

I'm not entirely sure that letting him get back to work is the smartest move, but he seems to be telling the truth. Even if he's not, he won't do anything to jeopardize Raina's life.

"Yes, sir." He nods. "And Raina? Will you let her go now?"

"Don't test my kindness, Walker. Nothing changes with our arrangement. She stays with me until your debt is settled."

His eyes narrow. "You and I both know that's never going to happen."

"There is one other option..." I tell him.

Raina shivers with anticipation as my fingers crawl higher up her leg, her breathing growing heavier with each soft caress. I smirk as Noah watches my hand, looking as if he wants to chop it off.

"And that would be?" he asks through gritted teeth.

"You could prove your innocence by helping me identify the real thief. If you do that, your debt will be wiped clean."

Raina sucks in a breath, her eyes hopeful as Noah meets her gaze. She thinks I've just given them both an out, but I was very careful with my words. His life will be spared, but she's mine now. I'm never letting her go.

CHAPTER NINE

RAINA

The bartender places a shot of tequila in front of me, his lips curved with amusement. "On the house. You look like you could use it."

He's not wrong. This has been one hell of a night. My emotions are all over the place. Cillian brought me here tonight to fuck with Noah, but he'd also given me what I wanted—what I *needed*.

My brother is okay. Or at least he seems to be, the cuts and bruises on his face starting to heal. I just wish Cillian had let me talk to him—hold him. My chest ached as I watched Noah walk out of his office, wishing I could tell him how much I missed him, wanting to reassure him that Cillian hadn't done anything to harm me.

Their meeting did give me hope though. I think Cillian is starting to believe Noah didn't steal from him. He's even giving him the chance to prove it.

"Thanks." I give him a weak smile, picking up the glass with a quick salute before knocking it back. It's much smoother than anything I've ever had, the liquor warming my body as it washes down. He's still watching me as I set the glass back on the bar, curiosity dancing behind his eyes. "Do you think I could get one more?"

He chuckles, already pouring me another one as he answers. "Just don't tell the boss."

I throw back the second shot, thankful there's a mask covering my flaming cheeks. There's no telling what this guy must think of me. Cillian left me here about thirty minutes ago, telling me to stay put while he handled some business. And here I sit, like a well-trained pet.

I'm already starting to feel the tequila by the time I set the small tumbler down again, liquid courage filling my head with bad ideas.

"Our little secret," I tell him before walking away from the bar.

The last time I came into The Fox's Den, there was only one thing on my mind—finding my brother. I felt overwhelmed by my surroundings, my stare purposely trying to avoid the things that were happening around me.

But now, I find myself intrigued by the dark allure of it all, gravitating toward the sounds of carnal desires. My heart begins to beat a little faster as I make my way to the back of the club, my tingling skin growing hot. There are women dancing in cages to my left, people fucking on velvet couches to my right, and I know this is only the tip of the iceberg.

I climb the stairs, my head dizzy with the mixture of booze and excitement. A woman's scream lures me down the dark hallway at the end of the landing, my feet quickly carrying me toward an open door. I gasp when I peek through the doorway, completely unprepared for what's inside.

I step into the empty room, cautiously inching closer to the glass wall, my wide eyes mesmerized by the couple on the other side of it. The woman is blindfolded, leather cuffs around her hands, her naked body suspended from the ceiling. The man circles her, the riding crop in his hand trailing over her skin. My stomach flutters when his stare moves in my direction, but it's as if he's looking through me, like he can't see me.

Of course. This room is designed for *watching*. He's looking at his own reflection.

The woman cries out when the man flicks the crop, smacking her ass. She squirms, pulling against her restraints as he continues moving around her, the crop licking her skin. My own nipples harden when the second flick lands on her breast, my thighs pressing together as it switches to the other one. The next tap hits her clit, and a moan escapes me, my center pulsing as if the man had struck me.

Goose bumps erupt on my skin as soon as Cillian walks into the room, the familiar scent of sandalwood surrounding me as he approaches. My body shivers with anticipation, desperate for his touch.

His strong arms snake around me, his hold tight as he hisses in my ear. "You're not where you're supposed to be, Rabbit."

"I'm sorry," I pant as his erection presses into my back.

INTO THE FOX'S DEN

"Do you have any idea what I would've done if someone else had walked in here? If they had tried to touch what's mine?"

His possessive tone causes my insides to quake, the idea of him hurting someone because of me both frightening and thrilling at the same time. "I just wanted to look around."

He cups my breast, his thumb rubbing my pebbled nipple. "Oh yeah? And do you like what you see?"

I'm too turned on to hide it. There's no point in even trying to deny it.

The next time you lie to me, I'll bend you over my knee.

For just a moment, I consider testing him. A part of me wants him to make good on his threat from that first night. But I'm already aching with need.

"Yes," I answer honestly.

The scene playing out in the other room stirred something inside of me. But the truth is, I forgot about the couple the second Cillian walked in. His presence is consuming, my attraction to him disturbing.

His other hand slides down my stomach, dipping under my dress. "I'm not sure how I feel about that." It floats up to the apex of my thighs, then slips into my panties. "You belong to me." I whimper as his fingers glide through my drenched folds. "*This* belongs to me." His finger circles over my swollen nub. "You only get wet *for me*, only come *for me*." My head swims as he increases the pressure, my release already teetering on the edge. "Tell me you understand."

I nod, crying out when he bites into my shoulder.

"I want to hear you say it," he growls. His finger dips low, diving into the puddle at my entrance before returning to my clit, the movement torturous in the most glorious way. My hips buck, trying to create more friction, and he chuckles. "Tell me what I want to hear."

I should put a stop to this, refuse to give him what he wants. But I signed over my free will days ago. And I'm too far gone, too lost in my desire to care right now.

"I belong to you," I pant.

"Good girl." His finger plunges into me again, thrusting in and out before he adds another. "Do you want me to make you come?"

"Yes," I moan.

He tweaks my nipple through my dress, his lips making a path across my shoulder to the base of my neck. "Ask me nicely."

I groan, my jaw clenching with frustration. I'm so close it's painful, and the wicked bastard knows it.

"Please make me come, Cillian."

He nibbles at my ear, his beard brushing my cheek. "I like it when you beg."

His soaked fingers move back up my slit to the sensitive bundle of nerves, rubbing it with a perfect rhythm. My muscles tense, my entire body becoming rigid as I chase my pleasure. I throw my head back onto his shoulder, reaching behind me to grab his head, my fingers running through his soft hair.

He lets out a primal sound, the vibration in his chest radiating through me. "Come for me, baby."

I fall apart on his command, gasping as my orgasm violently rips through me. My body goes limp in his arms seconds later, my heart still racing and legs weak. He doesn't even give me a chance to catch my breath before he's shoving me forward, forcing me to brace myself with my hands against the wall.

"It's my turn now, Rabbit," he tells me, pushing my dress up. "I'm going to fuck you right here, hard and fast." His words have my center tugging with need again as he hooks his fingers into my panties and pulls them down my thighs. "Then we're going back to my condo, and I'm going to take my time with you."

My body trembles as he unbuckles his belt, my skin buzzing at the sound of his zipper falling. His dick slides against my wet heat, teasing my opening. He grabs my hips, jerking them back as he slams into me. I cry out as he stretches and fills me, the feeling almost overwhelming. His hips rock slowly at first, his grip on me tightening as he slowly picks up speed.

"You feel so fucking good," he murmurs, his breathing more erratic.

He drives deeper, his thrust becoming merciless, his rhythm unrelenting. I arch my back, my own climax building with each pump. He groans as my walls clench around him, the sound of his pleasure enough to send me over the edge a second time.

"Oh, god..." I scream, my orgasm crashing into me like a wave.

He fists my hair, yanking my head back, his movements slowing as they become more rigid. With one last hard thrust, he stills, his cum spilling inside of me.

"You feel that, Rabbit?" he asks, his heavy breaths fanning my face. "I just left my mark on you. There's no escaping me now."

It hits me then, the reality of what we just did—what *I* just let him do. Things are getting out of control. It feels like I'm losing myself to the chaos that is Cillian Fox a little more with each minute that passes. And I'm not sure it's possible to survive him.

CHAPTER TEN

CILLIAN

TWO MONTHS LATER

"If you could live anywhere in the world, where would it be?"

I sigh and close my book, my lips curling as my gaze finds Raina. She looks so beautiful sitting there in the glow of the fire, all snuggled up on the other end of the couch, nothing but my T-shirt covering her naked body. The softness in her eyes makes my chest ache. Something has shifted between us since the night I took her to the Gala. She seems happy and content. Almost as if she enjoys being here—being with me.

I want to believe this is real, but I'm not fully ready to trust it—to trust her. I can't. Not when she still thinks her brother's life is on the line. Things have been quiet with that situation. Noah is keeping his head down and working hard to pay off his debt, but I'm no closer to finding out the truth. Liam is adamant that Noah received all his product that day, says I'm letting Raina blind me to the truth. But he's been acting cagey lately too. I'm not sure if it's because he has something to hide or if it's just the seed of doubt Noah planted taking root.

I shake my head as she gives me an expectant look. "No. We aren't doing this again."

My busy life never bothered me before Raina, but I hate having to run around all the time now. Even when she comes to stay with me in the city, I'm always on the go, dealing with the club and the dozen other businesses I use as cover for my real *business*. It never stops.

Sunday is *ours* though. We spend the day fucking and talking. We watch movies or go for a walk. But the moment it gets quiet, she starts trying to play twenty questions with me. It's like she can't stand the silence.

She sticks her bottom lip out, crossing her arms. "Fine, I'll answer first." Excitement lights up her face as she tucks her legs under her, rubbing her bare thighs. "I wouldn't live in one place. I'd just keep moving to different places all over the world, experiencing new things and new people all the time." She tilts her head, one eyebrow quirked. "Your turn."

I chuckle, beckoning her with a crook of my finger. "Come here, Rabbit."

She gives me a coy smile, crawling across the couch to get to me. I place the book on the side table as she straddles my lap, my dick instantly getting hard. My hunger for her is insatiable.

Her arms lift without hesitation as I pull the shirt up and over her head, her nipples tightening the moment they're free. I toss the shirt to the floor and cup her breasts, my thumbs brushing over her pebbles. She sucks in a breath, her eyelids falling as she grinds her hips, rubbing her warm center against my hard-on. Her eyes are dark with lust by the time they lock on mine again. She grasps my face, her fingers running through my beard as they work their way to my hairline.

"You're trying to distract me," she pants.

I smirk, one hand skimming down to her hips, then between her thighs, my fingers skating over her slick folds. "Always so ready for me."

She brings her mouth to mine as my thumb circles her clit, her kiss ravenous. I love when she loses herself and takes control. "Please," she whimpers against my lips. "I need you inside of me."

I pull my hand away, relaxing back. "If you want it, you're going to have to take it."

Her brown eyes twinkle with mischief from my challenge, excited by the chance to take charge. She quickly reaches for my sweatpants, and I raise my hips, allowing her to tug them down. My dick springs free, and she wraps her hand around it, pumping up and down the shaft. A pleased expression dances through her features as a throaty moan escapes me, precum leaking into her palm. She likes knowing how much she turns me on.

She positions herself over the head of my cock, sinking down on it with one swift movement. She's wet and warm, her tight pussy squeezing my cock. It feels so damn good, too good.

"Fuck," I hiss, grabbing her ass.

Her teeth scrape over her bottom lip, red already blotching her skin as she begins moving. She goes slowly at first, giving her body time to adjust to the fullness. Her hands grip my shoulders as she picks up speed, her nails digging into my back.

Thick curls float around her face as she bounces, her stare glossy with ecstasy. She's so damn sexy. There's nothing better than seeing the pleasure on her face when I'm inside of her like this, raw and deep.

Her walls clench around me as I tilt my hips, her movements growing needier. She's already so close.

"Cillian," she moans, throwing her head back.

My name on her lips is nearly enough to unman me, my balls tight as I draw her nipple into my mouth. Her cries grow louder as I lick and suck, her body convulsing on top of me. My grip on her ass tightens with the final rock of her hips as we come together, my cum shooting inside of her.

The first time I fucked her bareback wasn't intentional. At least not completely. I was just so wrapped up in her and the moment—so desperate to bury myself inside of her. But I also liked the idea of there being nothing between us, of claiming her that way, of possibly planting my seed in her belly. Maybe one day I'll get her off birth control and do exactly that. Then I'll always have a claim to her.

She rests her forehead on mine, a smile tugging at her lips as she pants.

So damn perfect.

"You still want to ask me questions?" I tease.

"Just one." Worry creeps through me as she sits back, her expression falling somber. "What happens if Noah can't figure out who stole from you? What if he can't pay you back?"

There it is. The one question I've been dreading the most, knowing the answer could drive her away.

"What happens if he does?" I tuck her hair behind her ears, taking her face in my hands. "Are you going to run from me, Rabbit?"

"I don't know." She shrugs, her eyebrows shadowing the moment. "Are you going to chase me?"

Her playful response doesn't do much to help ease the tension in my muscles.

"No..." I breathe. "I want you to *want* to stay."

Her breath hitches, her lashes flutter. "I—I, uh..."

"If I said you could leave right now and Noah wouldn't be harmed, would you choose to stay?" I press.

This hypothetical is never going to happen. She's mine. There's no way I'm ever letting her go. But I meant what I said. I need to know where her head is. That this isn't just about saving her brother anymore.

"I don't know," she sighs, her stare avoiding mine until she speaks again. "But... I know I have feelings for you. As fucked-up and confusing as they may be. And I know I'm happy here. Before I met you, my life was dull. You brought color into my black-and-white existence. I'm not sure it's possible to go back to living that way. Or that I'd even want to."

There's so much sincerity in her words, the warmth in her stare melting the icy exterior around my heart. Maybe is good enough. For now.

I pull her mouth to mine, the kiss delicate yet greedy, letting my tongue tell her how I'm feeling without words. She's my addiction, one that very well could get me killed, but at least I'd die a happy man.

She pries her lips from mine as my phone buzzes on the table next to us, giving me a quick peck on the forehead before climbing off my lap. "You should probably get that."

My jaw tics as I pull up my pants and pick up the phone, Connor's name flashing on the screen. They all know to leave me the hell alone on Sundays unless there's an emergency. This better be fucking good.

"What," I clip out.

"Boss, we have a problem." He pauses, his apprehensive tone leaving a bad feeling in my gut.

"Spit it out, Connor."

"Noah is missing."

Well, fuck.

ABOUT A.D. MCCAMMON

Amber McCammon lives in Tennessee, where she was born and raised, which means she often gets caught with the south in her mouth. She loves to travel, though, and dreams of being a nomad one day. When she isn't writing, you'll find her reading, spending money she doesn't have in Target, or hanging with her hubby and two kiddos. Amber McCammon decided to take her passion for writing to the self-publishing world in 2017. She's since published several novels with many more to come.
To contact Amber, please email her at: a.d.mccammon@outlook.com
Represented by Two Daisy Media. Email: info@twodaisy.com

https://linktr.ee/authorad_books
https://books2read.com/admwtsf
https://admccammon.com

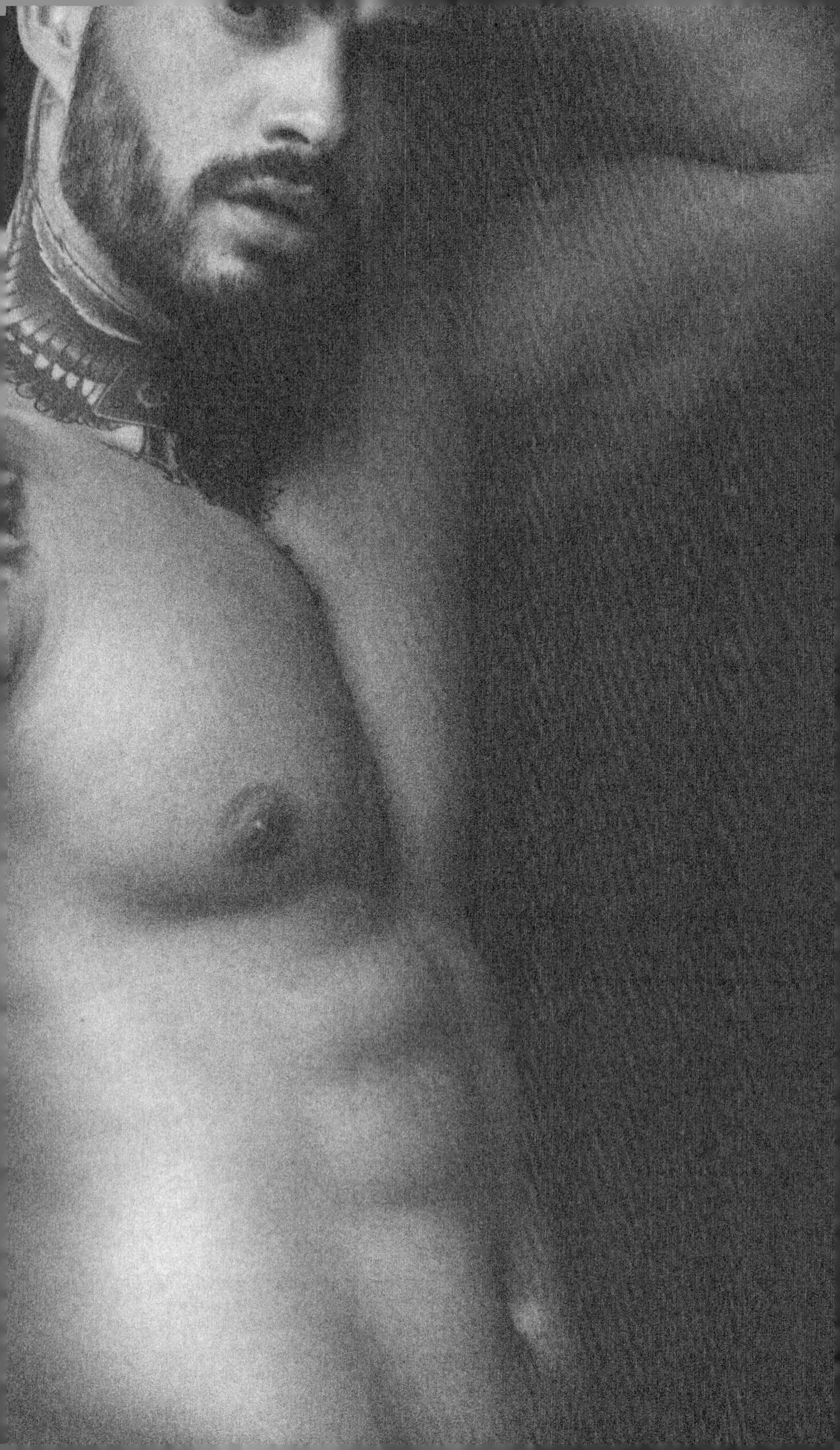

BAD

BLOOD

BY C.A. RENE

Copyright © 2021 C.A. Rene
All rights reserved. This book, or any portion thereof, may not be reproduced or used in any manner whatsoever without the express written permission of the publisher, except for the use of brief quotations in a book review.
This book is a work of fiction and any resemblance to any person, living or dead, is purely coincidental, the characters and story lines are created by the author's imagination and are used fictitiously.
No copyright infringement intended.
No claims have been made over songs and/or lyrics written. All credit goes to the original owner.

BLURB

In a thick, towering forest sits a ramshackle cabin. Inside is a small family on the verge of starvation. Times are tough, food is scarce, and self-preservation is most important. How many choices does this family have?

Only one that they can see.

The father takes his children on a journey far away from the cabin, his plans filled with death and regret. But when he can't fulfill his end of the bargain, he abandons them to the harsh elements instead.

Soft music lures them to a large mansion surrounded by an orchard. They gorge on apples and meet their savior in the form of a beautiful woman. Inside the mansion, strange things happen, symbols written in blood, rituals performed, and feasts prepared with spells and chants. Strange things happen to people inside the mansion too, little sisters grow into young ladies, and the familial ties blur for big brothers.

The only way to be free is to kill their captor and try to make it back to their family. But it's not easy to kill a woman who hunts young human flesh, bathes in the essence of children, and worships at an altar made of human skulls.

The need for revenge becomes a heady drug for the siblings, their carnal sins shape their dark descent, and survival is a dark road lined with the bodies of those who wronged them.

PART 1

The trees are sparse, the ground is dry, and the birds and insects have all disappeared. In the center of this desolation stands a derelict cabin, home to a small family. A father, a mother, a brother, and a little sister. All starving, teetering on the edge of survival.

Drought plagues the land, heat scorches all day, and nothing bears fruit. There's no sign of life; everything is sucked dry of vitality. How can you feed four rumbling stomachs in such conditions?

The seasoned hunter father knows he cannot. He can no longer find animals to hunt, not a rat nor a squirrel for miles, and their stores of dried meat are nearly depleted.

Nearly.

There's barely any jam left, the grain is practically gone, and the water is going fast. Four people could never survive on such small rations. They wouldn't make it through winter.

But maybe two could.

The father knows this decision is not to be made lightly, but if he rids the cabin of the two children, in a few years, the wife could have more. This is the plan, and his wife is adamant it's to be done soon, so as not to waste any more food on the dead.

"Tomorrow, Henry. You must do it in the morning, before first light." His wife clutches his arm with her hand, its bones no longer cushioned with flesh.

"Yes, Caroline. We will leave tomorrow."

Her body relaxes, and as sleep slowly overtakes her, a smile forms on her thin, chapped lips, something which has become so foreign to Henry. His wife no longer smiled; but this? Surely must be a sign from God.

Henry and his wife were not God-fearing people, but he truly believes taking a person's life could only result in the worst karma. Something he would have to live with for the rest of his days, and that he could do, as long as his wife remained happy with a smile upon her face.

Time rushes by and early morning finds Henry still wide awake. His troubled mind won't let him rest, and his broken heart lays heavy in his withering body. Caroline stirs, flinging her arms over her head, and stretching the length of her rail thin form. Jealousy like a hot poker slices through Henry's chest as he envies her contentment. Then guilt pools in his stomach as he swallows down bile, this is all his fault. He should've hunted more, stored more, and paid attention to the signs of catastrophe.

"Take them to the edge of the wood," Caroline whispers in his ear, "take them to her territory, and when they are found slain, she will be to blame."

"That is a two-day hike," Henry exclaims, "how will I have the energy to make it back?"

"Take the last of the jam," Caroline's hand lands on his gaunt cheek.

"Papa?" Little Pearl calls from her cot in the corner of the room. Her eighth birthday is tomorrow, and Henry's heart sinks with the realization his daughter won't live much beyond that.

"You will be taking a hike with Papa today!" Caroline hops out of bed, shocking her daughter with an energy she hasn't had in many months.

"A hike to where?" John sits up, rubbing his fists into his eyes.

John watches his mother warily, her chipper voice, and strange demeanor making him sense something is amiss. With no food to eat, and barely any water to drink, everyone in the cabin is listless. This energy she exudes would only come from consuming food.

"Did you eat without us?" John's eyes narrow on his mother, and when her palm meets his boney cheek, he doesn't even flinch.

"How dare you question me, boy!" She shrills. "Now, both of you get up and prepare for your hike. I expect you to bring me home a venison."

John, being the big brother at ten years old, has become accustomed to taking care of his little sister, and doing most chores around the cabin. He's quiet and thoughtful, very wise beyond his years. He likes to observe; watching his parents and their interactions has become his pastime. Seeing his mother hum as she packs them a meager lunch of bread scraps casts an uneasiness over him, and the way his father shuffles around the cabin, his head to his chest, gives him cause to be skeptical.

"Where are we going?" John asks, his head cocked to the side, and his too long white-blond hair falls over his forehead.

"To the meadow," Henry replies.

"That's a two-day journey," John retorts.

"No," Pearl whines, "I will not go. I hate hiking, it's too hot." Her hair, the same color as John's, billows around her face as she shakes her head vehemently.

Henry sees the mistrust in his son's icy blue eyes, and guilt once again threatens to consume him. He grabs his rifle off the hook on the wall, fills his tote bag with ammunition, and while avoiding his children's identical set of eyes, he heads outside.

Henry unlocks the exterior doors to the cellar, and slowly descends the stairs. The room is practically empty save for a few deer hide, and a short row of dried meat. On the shelf sits two small jars of raspberry jam, the last of their spring harvest. Henry wraps both in strips of cloth and puts them in his tote, then he palms three strips of meat, tucking them in as well. What Caroline doesn't know won't hurt her. His children should experience something good before they perish.

Swallowing down the emotion clogging his throat, Henry fills three canteens from the last barrel of water, then closes the tote. Not for the first time, he worries about how he will find the strength to finish the task given to him, and he squeezes his eyes shut when moisture hits his lashes. There's no other way, he reminds himself.

After wiping the tears from his eyes, Henry heads back up the cellar stairs, and back out into the blistering sun. Standing there in a solemn line are his two children and Caroline. Pearl is sniffling, and her cheeks are red and swollen from crying, maybe there's something instinctively telling her of the danger that lurks ahead. Her two platinum pigtail braids lay over her shoulders, and her pale white skin looks sickly against the bright yellow of her threadbare sundress.

John's demeanor is drastically opposite. Standing straight, with his arms folded over his chest, he stares at Henry with accusation in his eyes, and Henry can't stop the thick swallow as he forces his heart back down into his chest.

John knows.

Caroline clears her throat just as another wail erupts from Pearl's throat, "please Papa, you always said girls shouldn't go hunting with the boys."

"You little bit-" Caroline starts and John cuts her off with a hand to her arm.

"Carol." He chastises, then he looks to his devastated daughter, her beautiful face so red and soaked in tears, "Pearl, I need my little berry finder with me. While your brother and I hunt the meat, I will need your expertise to find berries."

She runs her frail arm under her nose, dragging her snot along her skin, "there are no more berries, Papa." She whispers as she shakes her head.

"No meat, either." John snarks and his mother's hand claps the back of his head. He's gotten so accustomed to his mother's abuse he's practically unfazed with her attack. He straightens back his hair and tosses her a glare. Henry studies him closely, noticing his boy is beginning to grow into a young man, his shoulders widening, and his legs lengthening, making him tall for his age. His knobby knees are on display in his shorts, and his skinny arms open in his sleeveless shirt. Both children's toes hang over the front of their sandals, long having outgrown them.

"Let's get going," Henry says dejectedly as he kisses Caroline on her cheek, "take care, honey."

Each child carries a pack on their back; blankets, molding bread, and Pearl's homemade doll are folded neatly inside. Then off they go with Henry in the lead, and both children shuffling slowly behind. John takes up the rear, and looks over his shoulder at his beaming mother, his gut telling him once again something is wrong.

After the day of hiking, John rolls out his blanket in the spot they chose to make camp, and Pearl spreads hers out next to him. She's always needed to be near her brother, especially in times of distress. John watches as Henry unrolls his blanket and feels a wash of anger at the sight of him, why does he have them out here with him? As if sensing his son's stare, Henry looks up and their eyes clash, one set cold and the other sad.

"I brought us some meat, but you must conserve it." Henry reaches into his tote and hands each of his children the small strips of meat. "We still have one more day of traveling."

John observes his father closely and takes note of the extreme changes in his appearance. His once thick, dark hair is now limp and grey, he used to have large, bulging muscles used to carry home large deer, now he's shrunken down to bones, and his eyes are cavernous pits with somber orbs drowning in dark bags.

"Why are we going near the witch?" John demands as he ferociously bites into the jerky, smacking his lips exaggeratedly, "she will curse us if we get too close to her land."

Pearl curls up tighter to John's side and a scared whimper escapes her. Henry tuts loudly, the sound reverberating around the still forest, "there is no such thing as a witch or her curse."

"I've heard you and Mother talk," John sneers, "you blame this drought on the curse of the witch."

"The witch cursed us, Papa?" Pearl looks at Henry with large, scared eyes, making his heart lurch in his chest. Soon, that fear will be turned onto him.

"No," Henry gives her a sad smile, "there is no witch, only an old lady who lives alone. She's mean and cruel but does not possess magic."

"You spoke of her having apple trees whose fruit looks like rich red candies, beautiful gardens with flowers the colors of taffy, and soil so fertile and dark, it could be mistaken for fudge." John recites as he takes another bite of his jerky, his stomach grumbling.

"She has fertile land," Henry mumbles, not wanting to talk of the witch who lives at the edge of the forest. "Now sleep, we have another long day."

"Papa?" Pearl's little voice sends a stabbing sadness through his core, "will the witch let us take some of her candy fruit?"

"Maybe we'll ask her," Henry says through a yawn, then turns his back on the children.

His words ring through the night into John's mind repeatedly, if he wasn't already suspicious, he would be now. Nobody ever ventures onto the witch's property; the risks are too great.

So, why did Henry lie to his children?

Their feet crunch over dry grass and foliage as they continue their trek. The heat is stifling, and it steals every bit of energy from the children's bodies, making this trip even more tedious for Henry. Pearl whines every few minutes, John stays watchful, and Henry questions his decision every hour, but all he must do is picture Caroline's smile, the tiny dimple winking in her right cheek.

"There are no berries," Pearl stops and sits at the base of a tree, "there are no deer, Papa, there is nothing nowhere."

"We are nearly there," Henry pants, "and then I have a surprise for your birthday."

John wondered if his father had forgotten as they walked all day without speaking, so hearing about a surprise both worried and soothed him. Maybe his gut was wrong this whole time, maybe Henry really wanted to take his children on a hike, no nefarious motives at all. Or Henry's surprise will not be one the children will enjoy.

John's tumultuous thoughts are only amplified when his father begins to pace, the worn soles of his shoes surely made worse by the dry ground beneath them. This erratic behavior is an unsettling sight.

"Johnny," Pearl whispers, her large blue eyes focused intently on their father. "What is wrong with Papa? Does he have sun fever?"

"We need to continue," Henry says aloud, his fist to his temple. "It's only a little further ahead." John doesn't miss the shake in his father's tenor or the tremble in his chin.

No, this is not a simple hike to find food. An ominous feeling descends on John, and he links his fingers through his sister's small hand, something is amiss.

"Let's go, Pearl." John helps her to stand, "if Father says it's just a little further ahead, then we should not doubt him. He would never lie to us."

Henry feels his insides burn at his son's words. Flaming, scorching insides, and for the hundredth time today, he questions his plan. It's getting more and more difficult to conjure his wife's smile, and all he sees is the blood of his children seeping into the dry earth, soaking it with much needed moisture.

Finally, they make it to the forest's edge, and as they stand in a single line behind the last row of trees, they see more desolation. The meadow is no longer green with life, there are no flowers peppering the grass, and everything hangs limp without a breeze.

"There are no berries," Pearl's words crash into her father's heart, and he crumples to his knees. "Papa?" Her small hand lands on his shoulder.

"Let's stay here for now," Henry says, defeat heavy in his words, "let's enjoy your surprise."

The children both sit next to each other against a large oak tree, the tree's scarce canopy providing some relief from the sun's heat. Their father reaches into his tote and withdraws a jar of jam, handing it to Pearl.

"It's all we have," he whispers, "I want you to eat it all. Of course, share with your brother."

John's mouth salivates at the sight of the dark red, sticky preserve. He watches as Pearl's little hand struggles to open the cap, and he reaches over, popping the lid easily. Just as Pearl's little fingers reach inside the glass jar, scooping a glob of sugary jam, a troubling thought invades John's mind. Would his father poison this surprise?

As worried as he is, he doesn't want to ruin his sister's delight. They're already on the brink of death anyways. Who could survive this dry, grey world much longer? John could feel his hunger gradually becoming a constant pain, one he knows will not ease, his exhaustion is no longer assuaged with sleep, and his mental awareness is fogged and murky. He can feel their ends are near.

"Johnny," Pearl's excited voice pulls him from his dark thoughts, "have some!"

"I think we should save it for-"

"Eat the damn jam, John." Henry's sharp words cut through his, and Pearl gasps around her sticky fingers.

Pearl stares at her brother with wide scared eyes, never having heard Papa say that word before, knowing it's not a nice one. Were they in trouble? John's fingers dip into the sticky berry goo, and Pearl watches as he lifts them to his mouth, his eyes still watching their father, and sucks them clean. He loses the battle with his poise and his eyes roll back, a slight moan escaping his mouth.

The last of the jam is licked clean from the jar, and both children feel a heaviness settle over them, something they haven't felt in a long while. Full bellies.

Henry watches as his children doze off, their faces serene, and their heads pressed together as they lean against the tree. Complete contentment radiating from their small forms, and just the sight of them, washes him in crippling sadness. A soul crushing guilt consuming his insides and impaling him with an emptiness worse than his shrunken stomach.

Swinging the rifle off his back, he stands on shaking legs, and walks slowly to the children. It's better if they go while in a satisfied sleep, dreaming of rich berries and venison stew. It would be an injustice to force them to live this life of deprivation any longer.

Henry's slick palms slip along the polished wood of his rifle's handle as he lifts it up, bringing it level with his daughter's head. The barrel shakes with his stifled sobs, and he shuts one eye, making sure his aim is true. His finger curls around the metal trigger, its slightly cool temperature soothing his heated skin, and when he begins to apply pressure, a pale hand shoots out, fisting the barrel in its fierce grip.

"Don't do this, Father," John's quiet, sleepy voice slips through the sound of his pounding heart in his ears, "just leave us here. I will make sure we don't come back home."

Henry relaxes his grip and the smooth handle slips from his hands, hitting the ground with a thud. He stares down at the rifle, nestled into the dead brown grass, and feels a tidal wave of despair sweep him up, drowning him. He drops to his knees, the weight of his remorse dragging him down, and covers his face with his hands, unable to meet the disappointed look in his son's eyes.

"Leave us, Father." John's hard voice breaks through, "leave now, or I will shoot you instead."

Henry looks up to find his own rifle now turned on him, his son's small hands holding it steady with expertise.

"Johnny."

"We are no longer your children, Pearl is mine now, and I will take care of her forever. Go back to our mother, and I wish you both the most terrible deaths." John's pale blue eyes burn with a hatred so intense and each word he spits out, is another shot to Henry's heart.

John throws the gun to his father's feet and waits for him to pick it up, but his movements are so slow. John can't remember any other time he's felt anger this intense, hatred this consuming. Not even when Father killed their dog Benji so they could eat, not even when Mother beat his back raw with her hide belt, and especially not when Pearl was punished with hot wax for sneaking meat. The growing ball of resentment exploded inside him when he woke up and found his father with his gun to Pearl's head.

Henry picks up the rifle and slowly stands to his feet, finally accepting he cannot kill his children. He swings the gun over his shoulder and grabs his tote, reaching inside. His fingers meet the cool glass jar, and he brings it out, setting it down beside John. "I hope you survive." He says as the words collect like ash in his mouth, "I hope you live and forget this moment."

"It would be better for you if we die," John says, his words full of guile, "I will never forget the day our parents planned the deaths of their children."

Henry solemnly nods, knowing forgiveness was never in the cards, and turns his back on the two children, slowly walking into the darkening forest. Back home to his wife, to live in starvation, and hoping with all hope, she doesn't turn her sights on him.

John watches as the form of his cowardly father disappears into the forest, back the way in which they came, and then he looks down to his peaceful looking sister, smiling in her sleep. His dirty fingers, still sticky from jam, skim across her forehead, and John sighs, long and hard. Pearl is his now, and he makes a promise to her sleeping form, never to put another above her.

A few hours later, John feels Pearl stir, and when her eyes open, they're filled with love and contentment. She sits up straight as she looks around them, her eyes landing on the untouched jar of jam.

"John," her voice is small, "where's Papa?"

"Father has left us, Pearl." John settles on telling her the truth, believing she'll be able to handle it. "We have been abandoned by Mother and Father, and now we must become our own family, just you and I."

Pearl begins to cry, the sound is filled with anguish, and her small hands grip the front of John's thin shirt.

"We will die without our parents." She moans once her sobs have subsided.

"We would've died with them, that's for sure, sweet sister." John says as his sticky hand runs over her hair. "We will find our own place, and we will live."

"How?" She sniffs, her eyes skating back to the jam every so often.

"Because fate is on our side, dear sister. And I will never abandon you." John kisses her forehead. "Now sleep some more, soon we cross the meadow, and see what's on the other side."

The sun shines down, its intensity never waning as the children wade through tall, brown grass, and pass the glass jar between them, enjoying the last of their sweet gooey treat.

"I'm still hungry, John." Pearl moans as she clutches her stomach.

"I'll find us something." John says, the lie feeling like ash in his mouth.

"It's so hot out here, there's no trees to protect us."

"Just a little further," John feels his patience thinning, but steels his spine, and continues. There must be something out here.

The end of the meadow is a steep drop to a valley below and nestled in the center is an orchard of apple trees surrounding a large house.

"The witch." Pearl whispers. "Do you hear that?"

John looks down at his sister, worried the heat has damaged her senses, when he too hears a musical noise. A slight tinkering, chimes or bells, and the strangest part of all is when a melodic voice begins to sing. There are no words, just a harmonious humming, sending a fog of relaxation over the children, and they begin their descent into the valley, lulled by the gentle song.

Their feet burn with the strenuous downhill decline and their bodies feel overcome with exhaustion as the heat continues to drain them, but they carry on toward the sound, unable to ignore its pulsing allure. Soon after they reach the valley's floor, the brittle sound of dead grass subsides and in its place is the plush feeling of soft earth covered in healthy pasture. There's a breeze grazing their flushed and sweaty skin, providing immediate relief from the searing heat.

Pearl moans, tipping her face up to feel the cool gust, and John mimics her, looking up to the sky, the clouds looking dense and fluffy. Like cotton candy.

"John," Pearl gasps, "look." John reluctantly drops his gaze and follows Pearl's finger, finding a tree with large red apples, glistening in the sun's light.

Pearl begins to run, already energized by the drastic change in environment, and the prospect of eating fruit. John trails behind her, a little more wary of their situation, even though hunger is ripping his stomach to shreds.

"Pearl," he calls out, "the music stopped."

But she doesn't acknowledge him as she starts picking up the apples from underneath the tree. She bites into one, the sound of her teeth breaking the skin's surface loud in the wide-open area, and John's heart begins to slam against his ribcage. Something is wrong.

"Pearl!" He calls, his voice more frantic, but she's too absorbed inhaling apple after apple. He tries to run to her, but his feet feel heavy, and his body isn't responding fast enough.

After her fourth apple, Pearl falls onto her back, her arms and legs spread wide, and grins to the darkening sky. Maybe they could make it on their own, John and her, they didn't need Papa or Mother, and they could live right here, under the apple trees.

"Well, hello there."

The voice is low and raspy, smooth like velvet, and Pearl pops her head up to find a beautiful woman smiling down at her. Her hair is so black, it hangs like ink around her shoulders, her skin gleams like porcelain, and her eyes are startling, one dark brown and the other ice blue.

"Hi." Pearl squeaks, just as John approaches, his skin looking sallow, and panting heavily.

"My name is Hyldah." She holds her hand to her ample chest, and Pearl notices her long sharp nails, painted in black.

John collapses on the ground beside Pearl, still breathing heavily, "Pearl, we need to leave."

"Leave?" Hyldah looks at him in amusement, "you just got here. Do you not like my apples?"

"Oh!" Pearl exclaims, "I do like them! I like them very much!"

"You poor sweet souls, you look near starved to death," she purrs, "won't you come inside for some sweet tea and mushroom stew?"

John's stomach rumbles violently at the mention of food, and the sharp pains that follow are hard to ignore.

"I can hear your belly from here," Hyldah bends over, her face parallel to John's. "Come inside and eat, and if you still want to leave, I will not stop you." The red of her lips are hypnotizing and John can't seem to draw his eyes away. "But, if you would like to stay, that would make me immensely happy. I haven't had children here in a long, long time."

"Because you are the witch." John says. His eyes are still on her plump, red mouth.

"Witch?" Her face falls, and her bright white teeth bite into the flesh of her juicy bottom lip, "I'm no witch, just a woman who is victim to vicious tales and rumors. Do I look like a witch?" She asks Pearl.

"No," Pearl shakes her head slowly, "you're too pretty to be a witch."

"There you have it," Hyldah claps her hands, the long nails on the tips of her fingers clicking together. "Come on inside to eat and rest."

John watches as Pearl jumps to her feet and chases behind the beautiful woman who looks like a dark angel. He picks up an apple, taking a large bite, and moaning around the juicy flesh. He won't deny his sister some food and rest, but they will be leaving first thing in the morning.

Because John knows, even the most beautiful angels became demons.

Both children sit at Hyldah's table, their stomachs swollen with food, and their eyes heavy with exhaustion. It's been months since they ate anything this decadent and even then, it wasn't like this.

"Dessert." Hyldah sings as she brings a pie tray to the table, "apple, just because you enjoyed them so much." She coos to Pearl, bopping her nose with a long nail.

No matter how full the children are, they know how quick that could change back to starving, and so they dig into the pie, foregoing the slices and eating straight from the tray.

It wouldn't be until much later when John admits he was coerced by a witch.

———

5 years later...

"Make sure you straighten her sheets; you know how much she hates those wrinkles." John reminds Pearl as she brushes by him in the hall, her hair swiping his face, and the scent of apples invading his nose.

"Yes, brother." She tsks.

Pearl has developed an attitude that makes John grit his teeth often, and yet, she's becoming more and more beautiful by the day. Her long white hair gleams, her porcelain skin glows with health, and her blue eyes shine with love for him. To her, he saved them by leading them here to Hyldah's house, but to John, he condemned them to Hell.

Luckily, for now, Hyldah's attention has revolved around him, and she pretty much ignores Pearl, except when she's driving her point home to John. He's learned not to fight her anymore and just do as she asks.

He would've attempted escape by now if it wasn't for the drought's continuation. He could never provide for Pearl out there, they need this place, and they need Hyldah's magic.

"Johnny." Hyldah's low rasp finds them all the way from downstairs, "come here."

"Go," Pearl waves her brother off, "I'll finish cleaning up here." She takes the broom from his hands.

Instead of relinquishing the wooden handle, John yanks it in, bringing his sister with it. She gasps as she hits his chest, and her light blue eyes look up into his. Large circular orbs, looking at him in confusion, and he feels it too, this confusing electricity between them. With their hands still on the broom handle, John's other hand slips to her waist, and he pulls her in a fraction more, just to feel her everywhere.

"Johnny," she breathes, her brows crashing together, but despite the wariness of her tone, he can see her chest heaving in reaction. Her chest which has grown this past year, tempting him in ways no sister should.

Her hand lands on his chest and the heat of her palm burns through his shirt, hitting his skin. His hand tightens around her hip and his fingers slip up beneath the hem of her shirt, touching her smooth skin. With her head tipped back, her pink lips parted, John begins to lower his, he just wants a small sample, just to find out if she tastes of apples as well.

"Well, well," Hyldah's voice sends them scrambling apart, and John curses his weakness. "What have we got here?"

"Nothing, Hyldah," John retorts and passes the broom to a startled Pearl. "Let's go." He turns his back on his sister and brushes by Hyldah who grabs his arm, her long, pointed black nails digging into his skin.

"Maybe she could begin to join us," her sensual voice masks her evil intentions.

"No." John grits through his teeth as he steps into Hyldah's body, "you will keep to our agreement."

"Okay." She laughs, a high tinkling sound, and turns her back on his sister, once again ignoring her existence.

Hyldah begins to hum as she leads him down the stairs, and into the back room, the same sound the children heard five years earlier on the edge of the meadow. Alluring, sensual, and primal. The sound slips beneath his skin and awakens a hunger he can't contain, not when she's forcing it from deep within him. It bubbles up, chasing the sound emitting from her throat, and rips its way out of him, transforming him into something like her.

She opens the door to the one room she keeps locked in the house. The room no one can enter without her permission, and the children obey because it feels wrong; it radiates evil. Luckily for Pearl, John will make sure she never has to come in here, he does it for them both.

The room is shrouded in darkness, candles flicker sporadically around the room, and the walls pulse in time with Hyldah's humming; John pulses in time with Hyldah's humming. He knows what comes next, he's been through this, many times before. He walks to the stone altar in the center of the room, blackened with the blood of many before him, and adorned with the skulls of her victims. Some large fully developed, others small, varying from infant to child.

Hyldah needs life's essence to keep herself young, and her land fertile. It's rare for someone to stumble upon her grounds since more and more people are perishing from the prolonged drought. So, John gives her the essence she needs, and in turn, he and his sister survive.

He climbs up on the altar, the stone pulsing with the walls, and its surface warm to the touch, almost as if it's breathing, living. Laying his back to the stone sends a jolt of energy through him and his most instinctual urges come forth. His body begins to thrum with a slow-moving vibration, starting from the tips of his toes, rolling up his legs, and when it reaches the apex, the sensation has him bucking off the altar, searching for something he's never had.

At nearly sixteen years old, John has never been with a woman in the carnal sense, but each time he's here on the altar, his yearning amplifies, and he craves more. The vibration moves through his stomach, leaving his engorged member throbbing in its wake, and slipping down his arms, concentrating on his fingertips. He waits for Hyldah's touch, usually around his wrists or neck, points where his essence can run freely, but today is different.

"You have grown nicely, Johnny." She purrs, "so big, and so strong." The sound of her voice has his stomach clenching, and his hips pumping, looking for relief. With each brush of his pants fabric against his most private place, jolts of lightning race to his toes, and they curl in anticipation of what, he's not sure. "I think you're ready to become a man."

Become a man.

His head can't completely comprehend what that means but his body tenses, coiling with a pressure that's threatening to snap. His body knows what it needs, and when her hands begin to pull his pants down, he moans so deep. She continues to hum, the sound making him jerk his hips, needing her to do more, needing a touch to his electrified skin.

His pants are completely removed, and as he stares up into the blackened, pulsing ceiling, he feels her begin to crawl over his feet, up his legs to straddle his thighs. Her nails scrape along his skin, lightly at first, and then harder, enough to draw blood to the surface. He hisses through the pain, and yet, it's not enough, he needs something more.

Then he feels something sharp press into the base of his hardened genitals, the painful touch making his thighs clench, and his privates to pulse, all in time with the humming.

"Such a majestic cock." Hyldah murmurs, her voice sounding like thick, sweet honey, "It's time you became a man, Johnny. Today, I will take your most potent essence." John leans up on his elbows to see what she means by his most potent essence, surely, she can't mean to cut his cock off. The thought sends his heart into overdrive, and as if sensing it, Hyldah's mismatched eyes meet his. "Shh, my Johnny boy, I just want a taste."

Her hand wraps around him, the feel of their skin melding together has the tight coil in his lower stomach pulsing and threatening to snap. But then she moves, her hand glides from his base, all the way to the tip, and John watches as a pearl of moisture appears at the top. He knows what this is, he's woken up many mornings with the excretion in his underwear. His member—his *cock*—pulses with her ministrations, and he swells even larger to Hyldah's delight.

"Such a big, big boy." She says, her voice hoarse. She leans over him, and John watches in shock as her long, pointed tongue swipes along the head of his cock, the white secretion stark against the bright red flesh. "This is the essence I require today; we no longer need to take your blood." John is transfixed on her face as her features tighten, the very aura around her sparkling, and with just one drop.

Such a drastic difference from when she takes his blood, there's no pain, only pleasure. Her thick, blood red lips part once again, and her bright white teeth gleam in the dark room. Then she lowers her mouth over his cock, the soft, wet, warmth like Heaven over his hardened flesh. Her cheeks hollow, and then she begins to bob, the movements sending shards of pleasure straight to his sack underneath, making them tighten. He can feel it, the coil beginning to convulse, on the verge of something he can't describe, and just as he's expecting an implosion, her mouth releases him with a pop.

No.

No, that can't be it.

His fingers tighten into fists to stop himself from grabbing her and forcing her face back to his groin. She chuckles when she sees the look of frustration on his face, and she leans up with a tut.

"Don't worry, Johnny," her husky voice feels attached to his cock, yanking on him with each word, "I'm not done with you, yet." She lifts her skirts high up around her waist, and John stares down to the apex of her thighs. Thick, coarse, black hair stands out against the milky skin of her thighs, and when she lowers it down to press against his cock, he can feel the moisture, similar to her mouth. She adulates her hips, slipping her mound up and down his length, panting and moaning, and just as he begins to feel the pressure snapping, she lifts up.

"Stop toying with me!" He growls up at her, his voice filled with gruff need. One hand grabs his chin, hauling him into her, the look of pure rage in her features has him teetering between lust and terror, and then she reaches between them, grabbing his length.

"I will play with you how I see fit," she grinds out as she holds his cock to the apex of her thighs and begins to sit down over it. The raven hair between her thighs meets John's pale blond ones, and the difference is startling. John is up inside Hyldah, in a place he knows nothing of, and when she circles her hips, he can feel wet, velvet walls, cushioning his cock. Her muscles inside clench around him, and when she lifts herself up to the very tip, John can see her glistening moisture thick on his cock.

She slams back down, and grinds into him rapidly, making noises of pleasure. Noises come from between her legs as well, wet sounds, like rubber boots in sludge, and then her insides tighten, gripping him like a vice as she tips her head back with a scream. The feeling of her wet walls pulsing around him, ignites the pressure inside him, and he explodes, his cock jerking deep in her.

Hyldah continues to grind down onto him in little movements, making sure she gets every last drop, and John lies back on the stone, his heart nearly racing from his chest. A bright light suddenly illuminates the room, seeping in through his thin eyelids. When he opens his eyes, he sees it's Hyldah, looking the most youthful he's seen her, and glowing with purity. Only John knows the truth, her exterior is just a trap, meant to cover her depraved insides.

"You may go now, John." She dismisses him with a wave of her hand, and even though she just made him feel elated, he wants out of her presence immediately.

John realizes night has descended while he was in there, what felt like minutes, must've been hours, and he decides to check in on Pearl. Their rooms are across from each other, and even though they're forced to stay in this evil house because of the extreme climate, they have everything they need. He opens her door slowly, so as not to make too much noise, and finds her tangled in her blankets.

John moves to her bed, yanking softly on the material, and pulling it from between her legs. Her nightgown has become too small for her, making it tight around her chest, and too short on her legs. She's a restless sleeper, and most nights, John fixes her blankets, recovering her. But tonight, after what just happened, he has a new curiosity for a woman's body, and his sister is spread out on her bed, with her gown around her waist.

He can see perfectly between her legs, her mound's hair a snowy blonde like his own, and her insides pink and vibrant. He can feel his cock swelling again and he wants to feel the way he did downstairs, only not with Hyldah.

John wants to press his cock inside Pearl.

Would she scream out in pleasure like Hyldah did? Would her insides be warm and wet? Would her fair skin warm with a blush as John moved inside her? John knows it's wrong to have these desires for his sister, but their situation is different, and it doesn't feel wrong. He gently sits at the end of her bed and trails his fingertips up the inside of her thigh, barely a whisper of a touch. Her skin breaks out in goosebumps and her air leaves her in a breathy moan.

"Johnny."

He halts his fingers and peers up into her face, seeing her still asleep, and smiles. She said his name while unconsciously enjoying his touch. Pearl feels it too, this forbidden temptation between them, and while they're here inside Hyldah's house, there's really no one to judge them. He reaches her pubic hair, brushing over the softness of it, the strands looking like spun gold, and then his finger descends downward, skimming her pink folds. She gasps and her legs spread further apart, revealing a small, hardened bundle. He flicks his finger over it, and she lifts her hips, seeking more of his touch. He presses the pad of his finger against the nub and rubs it softly, listening to her breath hitch. This is their pleasure spot. John's mouth waters with the need to taste it, the forbidden thought makes his cock strain uncomfortably against his pants.

He sees her pink flesh begin to glisten with her arousal, throwing a musky scent into the room, and he inhales deeply. He moves his finger down to the moisture and slowly pushes inside, this is where his cock goes. Pearl clenches around his finger, her channel so much tighter than Hyldah's, and it's John's turn to moan. He wants to be inside her so bad.

"Johnny?"

He looks up into her sleepy confused eyes, but the blush on her cheeks intensifies as he pulls his finger out, and pushes it back in.

"Does it feel good?" He whispers, and her hair sways as she nods.

He pulls out again and begins to rub his wet finger against her little ball of hardness, making her cry out. "Johnny, what is this?" She asks, moving her hips, seeking more friction. "This is wrong."

"We love each other," he soothes her worried words.

"No," she leans up and grabs his wrist, "Johnny stop."

Instead of heeding her request, Johnny slips two fingers inside of her, pumping in and out, desperately wanting to make her scream. Her mouth falls open, and her head falls back, "that's it," he says to her, "let me make you feel good." His thumb presses to the nub at the same time he fingers her, and then he feels it, that similar pulsing. Moments later, she's screaming as she falls back to the bed, and her cheeks are coated with tears.

He pulls his fingers out from inside her and stares at the wet digits, slipping them into his mouth. They taste earthy and addictive as he sucks them dry.

"Get out." John looks down into Pearl's angry eyes. "Get out, John." John?

"Did you not enjoy that?" John looks at her, confused with her anger.

"You are my brother, not my husband. Don't ever touch me like that again!" She exclaims.

John stands quickly from the bed, the force of her anger like a knife stabbing into his chest, over and over. She glares at him as he backs away and out of her room, her eyes never wavering as he closes her door.

How could something so wrong feel so right?

Pearl ignores John for a whole week, seven days of silence even when he personally addresses her. She's made everything feel bad and dirty, and it makes him feel like his feelings aren't warranted. Is it wrong to love a sister more than the average brother does? John didn't think so.

And that's how he finds himself, standing in the shadows at the edge of the house, watching as Pearl immerses herself in one of Hyldah's novels. There's a naked man on the front, bulked with muscle, and gripping a woman around the waist. Fury and jealousy surge through him, and he barely holds himself back from ripping it out of her hands. Is this where she's learning about husbands and wives?

Pearl lets out an exaggerated sigh, and John grits his teeth, wondering what she's reading. He knows these romance novels have sex, and if that's what his sister wants, then why did she hold onto this anger? He could give her all of what she reads and more. John feels himself harden and hangs his head, cursing his forbidden feelings. If only Hyldah was even, then John could pull himself together, and leave his sister be.

He steps out of the shadows and his sister turns, as if sensing his presence. Her cold blue eyes narrow on him and then she turns back around, her head back in her book. The pain he feels from the utter disregard she pays him is devastating, and John envisions yanking on her hair, pulling her face into his cock. Her spine is ramrod straight, knowing he's standing behind her, and yet, not knowing how detailed his fantasy of her is in that moment.

Having her on her knees, her head tipped back, and her long hair hanging in a white sheet over her back. Those plush pink lips would open, and her red tongue would slip out as she waited for his cock.

"Go away," Pearl snaps, "I can hear you breathing and it's disgusting."

Instead of doing as she asks, John crouches down behind her, and picks up some of her hair, bringing it to his nose. Apples. Fresh, crisp, tart, and sweet. All of them are his lovely Pearl.

"Stop it, John!" She swipes her hair out of his hand. *Tart* especially.

"One day I'll have you, Pearl." John watches as the breath from his words brush against a few strands of her hair, making them lift. "You won't be able to fight it forever, I'm the only man here with a *cock*."

Her body shudders from disgust or desire, and John grins knowing he could work with either one.

---

3 years later...

"I see the way you watch your sister," Hyldah murmurs as she strokes John's cock, it's firm length twitching in her hand. "You want to be inside her, too. Don't you?"

"Stop talking, Witch." He growls, "suck my cock."

She does as she's told, like the sadistic bitch she is, and John can't help but like it. He likes the feel of her ungodly spirit as she sucks or fucks him. He likes slamming her dark head down onto the altar, spreading her wide, and fucking every hole. It's addictive, nearly as addictive as pretending it's his sister. The black hair morphs into white, and her body shrinks, becoming thinner, more youthful. John knows he's obsessed with his sibling, and it's becoming more and more dangerous each day.

Pearl doesn't understand her own appeal. Her breasts so full, her waist slight, and her ass, like a fucking peach. Her skin smooth as alabaster, her hair like snow, and those eyes, cold as ice. She doesn't know how close she pushes John to the edge every time she bites her pink bottom lip, or scrunches her pert nose in thought, she can't even comprehend how precariously he walks along the edge. If he loses even an iota of will, he'll make her his.

With that thought, John grabs the witch's raven tresses, and slams up into her throat, coming so hard, he nearly blacks out. She swallows every drop, needing it to survive and thrive. He yanks her head off his lap and shoves her aside, pushing off from the altar. Her glow radiates around the room as he does up his pants, and her hands land on his back.

"When are you going to tell her, Johnny?" The soft purr of her voice no longer has the same effect it did a few years ago. She just sounds like an old hag now.

"Tell her what?" He growls.

"That the drought is over, and you can leave this place." She sounds smug, already knowing his answer.

"Shut the fuck up, Hyldah." John strides for the door, his long legs eating up the distance in no time. Standing at six foot five, John is a mountain of a man, and just as thick as one too. He grew his hair out and likes it down around his shoulders in white waves, and his beard hangs low, nearly touching his chest.

John knows the drought is over, the land once again green and thriving, the trees full, and the animals once again in abundance. But he would rather he and Pearl stay here where he can slowly possess her without the watchful eyes of others. It's selfish, completely deranged, but he can't pull back from it now, not until she's his. Which isn't going so well since she barely speaks to him, and it's been three years of this madness.

John walks outside to the lush garden in the back, every color of the rainbow found on the petals of the exotic flowers and sitting smack dab in the center is Pearl. She's sitting with her legs crossed, and reading another one of Hyldah's romance novels, sighing every now and then. Her white-blonde hair is free from her usual braid, and hanging down her back in messy waves, the ends flirting with the green grass. He watches her with the familiar consuming hunger, the need coating him from head to toe, and his cock once again hard, even though he just fucked the witch's face.

He pulls off his shirt, tossing it to the bench beside him, and walks toward the large water fountain. He can feel the heat of her stare, and it makes him growl in frustration, he wants her to give in, to leave behind this absurd notion of decency. They haven't been in the real world for so long, so why should they abide by its rules? Here in the witch's lair, there are no such restrictions, and it's time she realizes it.

"Pearl." His voice is sharp, cruel.

"Yes, John?" She replies, sounding bored and perfunctory.

"Tell me what happens in your stories." He dips his head under the cool water, letting his hair soak up the moisture, and knowing the water is coursing down his chest in thick rivulets. All part of his plan.

John turns at her silence and beams savagely when he finds her cheeks heated. Her eyes tracing the water running over his muscular chest, and between his defined abs, noticeably swallowing.

"Well?" He taunts her further.

"Read them yourself and find out." She retorts.

"Why don't you read it to me," John points to the open book in her lap, "read those pages." His words come out clipped, laced in anger as a result of her attitude.

Her eyes widen as John stalks to her, but she doesn't cower, and that alone has him rock hard. His fingers slip into her silky strands, and he curls them into a fist, making her whimper with pain.

"Read. It." The edge is slipping away from under his feet as he watches her eyes tear up, her bottom lip begins to tremble. But she does as he demands and begins to read the scene on the pages in her lap. And wouldn't you know it, it's about a woman who is in love with a man, letting him fuck her tight throat. Of course, that's not verbatim, no, the words are sweet, filled with love and longing, but all John hears is the man shoving a cock into the woman's throat, and the edge is gone, completely disappears as Pearl continues bringing to life one of his fantasies.

He undoes his pants with the hand not ensnared in her hair, and she stops reading, her mouth dropping in surprise.

"What are you doing, John?" No matter how hard she tries, she can't hide the heat in her voice. John knows she wants this, too.

"Giving you something you're too afraid to take for yourself." John's cock springs free, and Pearl stares at it in wonder.

She's read about many cocks in Hyldah's books, and about the women who suck them, take them inside of their bodies. She's read about the intense pleasure you can get from large cocks, and about the pain they can inflict as well. Right now, she's eye to eye with her brother's cock, and instead of being disgusted, she feels the telltale gathering of moisture between her legs. She's aroused by her brother and shame courses through her as she remembers what he did to her three years ago, a memory she repeats constantly. The same one she's pleasured herself to many nights after.

His large hand wraps around his equally large cock, and she takes note of its angry dark red head, the drop of precum on the tip. She's read about this many times but when John growls at her to open her mouth, fear of the unknown clouds her. When she doesn't react quick enough, he takes his large dick, and slaps her in the face with it.

"Open your fucking mouth, Pearl." She can hear his patience has run out, and if she doesn't give in, this will be rough and painful. So why does that arouse her even more? Another slap to her cheek with his heavy cock, and then John grabs her chin, squeezing it in his fist.

"I will break this fucking jaw, don't even doubt it for a second." John threatens, and Pearl whimpers as she opens her mouth.

John taps his cock's tip against her bottom lip, and Pearl dips her tongue out to flick the smooth skin without much thought. But when she sees her brother's lips pull back taut against his teeth, she knows he's completely lost it, and she's ready. If she's being forced to do this, then she might as well enjoy it. He entangles both hands into her hair, hauls her up to her knees, and slams himself into her mouth, his thick cock straining her jaws. He forces himself down her throat, groaning when she gags, and then stays there, reveling in her struggle to breathe.

"I've wanted this for three years," he grunts out as he continues to fuck her throat raw, "I've wanted you every time you turned me away, every time you ignored my presence. But no more Pearl, you now belong to me. Your mouth and your cunt are mine."

Possession, that's what this is, he wants to own Pearl, and she knows she's done trying to deny it. What's the point? It's not like they could ever leave this place, and who else is here to see them? Who else is here for her to enact her urges on? Her own fingers can only do so much, she wants more. With those final thoughts, she stops resisting, letting her brother fuck her throat relentlessly until his hot cum fills her mouth.

"Get on your back." He snarls, and she does as he says, letting her hair fan out over the grass. "Spread your legs."

He rips her skirt up the center, the veins in his neck and forehead prominent, and his still damp chest dripping onto her legs. He growls loudly when he finds her without underwear, and dives down into her pussy. He spreads her open with his fingers and his mouth attacks her clit, sucking and biting it. Nothing has ever felt this good, and when she looks down to find his light blue eyes on her, she moans his name.

John takes that as the final straw and slips his hands under her ass lifting her to a better angle, fucking her pussy with his tongue. His nose is rubbing into her clit, his wide, thick tongue in her cunt, and his fingers digging into her ass, there's never existed another brother who loves his sister this much, surely.

Then Pearl feels it, the burning in her lower belly, only this is more intense than she's ever felt it, and when she clenches, John pulls his face away.

"No," she grabs his hair, trying to force him back when he chuckles. He slides two fingers inside of her, the stretch burning until he curls them upward, stroking a sensitive spot inside her.

"You're too tight for me to fuck yet," he tells her as his fingers rub that spot, "I have patience though, and this will be enough for now."

His words are a trigger which sets off the grenade nestled deep inside of her, the explosion works its way outward, and Pearl's legs begin to tremble, stars appearing behind her eyelids. She opens her eyes as the waves of pleasure subside, John reaches up to palm her breast, and she's left with a troubling thought. Is this happening because they had terrible parents? Did their mother and father spread to them some kind of tainted blood? Because that's what it feels like.

Bad blood.

John stares down at his sister, her face relaxed and looking to the sky in awe. She's beautiful lying here in the lush grass, her dress ripped open, and her heavy breasts on display. He can't help but fondle them, tracing the blue veins that stand out from the milky tone of her skin.

That's when he feels it, the ominous aura that follows Hyldah, it's dark tendrils slink around you, and try to pull you in. He looks up and finds her watching them from the second-floor window, a sly, evil smirk on her face.

PART 2

6 months later...

John watches Pearl as she gathers apples for her delicious pies and swallows the saliva gathering in his mouth. Nothing compares to his sister's apple pie, *nothing*, except the one between her legs. Which he's been feasting on frequently. It takes some coercing, but eventually she opens those milky thighs, giving in to her most primal desires.

"She's so naive, isn't she?" Hyldah appears behind John, her taunting voice triggering a deep snarl. "Has she let you inside of her yet?"

No.

But soon.

"Go away." John flicks his wrist, "I could hold back my essence from you, and watch you wither."

Hyldah's hand is quick to wrap around his throat, the grip unnaturally strong, and the tip of her nail nicking his skin.

"Watch me wither, you say?" Her hot breath fans his ear. "I would make you watch me take *her* essence instead."

It is not an idle threat, John knows better than anyone what Hyldah is capable of, and he doesn't want his sister exposed to it. Pearl is too pure, and too innocent.

The witch releases his throat and chuckles when he sucks in a large breath, "you make her so much more tempting when you refuse to share. Maybe *I* can convince her to partake in our sessions."

"Stop, Hyldah," John sighs, "you know I won't hold back my essence, but you must leave her be."

Hyldah begins to hum, the sound like a slow vibration, working its way around John and Pearl, engulfing them in serenity, and coating them in warmth. John's toes curl as he feels the beginnings of desire seep into his body, making his cock hard, and his vision stays trained on his sister. Her chest begins to heave, the heady perfume of yearning dropping over her, and she drops the basket of apples as she turns her head to John.

He knows this melody is only amplifying what's already there beneath the surface, but if Hyldah keeps up her song, he and Pearl will liquify, quickly giving in to all their desires. All under the watchful eye of Hyldah. He shakes his head clear and turns abruptly on the witch, licking his lips as he watches her chest vibrate with the noise.

He rips open the front of her dress, spilling her ample breasts from the fabric, and she laughs making the humming stop. John hears Pearl gasp behind him, but it's too late. He's hard and pulsing, needing to spill his essence, and if it's not on the witch, it'll be Pearl he forces. John will be damned if he gives the witch a front row seat to that.

He forces Hyldah to her knees, using both hands to push her tits together, "spit," he growls, and the witch does just that, the fluid pooling on her chest. John hauls down the front of his pants, and his cock springs free, hard, and aching for Pearl. "On my cock, too." He demands and Hyldah does as he asks.

Pearl runs by just as he pulls Hyldah's tits apart, pushing his cock between them, and pushing them back together, cushioning his hardness on all sides. Then he fucks her chest, making sure his cock jabs her in the throat with each thrust, the soft feel of it rushing him toward his release.

"Open your fucking mouth," he growls, and when the witch smirks instead, he jams his cock up under her chin, making her whimper. "Do it, Witch."

And she does, her eyes rolling back into her head, the white prominent as her eyelids flutter. John slams his cock into her mouth, the tip hitting her soft throat, just as he spills his cum down it, fantasizing about white-blonde hair. Then releases her with a shove, forcing her to fall back onto her elbows, and she lets loose a cackle making his insides crawl. He pulls up his pants and tosses Hyldah a glare as he turns and picks up Pearl's basket.

John finds his sister in the kitchen, her hands flat on the wooden tabletop, and her breathing erratic.

"I brought the apples." He says as he places the basket on the table beside her.

"Do you enjoy being with her?" Pearl whips her hair to the side to glare at him, but it falls short when he smells the apple scent.

"Yes," he crowds her space, making her press her back into the edge of the table, and his hands landing on either side of her, "I do."

"Then why do you pursue me?" Her hands land on his chest as she tries to push him away. Her shoving doesn't budge him, and his large hands engulf her waist as he lifts her onto the table, forcing his way between her legs.

"Because, sweet sister, I made a promise to our father a long time ago," he brushes his nose along the length of hers, "I told him you were mine and I would take care of you forever."

"Our father was a coward." She snarls and the sound has John's cock straining to get to her, "no promise to him needs to be carried out."

He gathers her skirt in his hands, pulling them over her waist, and groaning when he finds her bare, the soft white of her pubic hair nestled between her legs.

"Why do you refuse to wear underwear, Pearl?"

"It's restricting." Her cheeks blaze red.

"Restricting from what?" His fingers glide up her thighs and Pearl leans back onto her hands with a small moan.

"From the fresh air, from..." John's fingers find her core, "from... the... oh my."

John finds her wet and dripping, her clit hard and begging for his touch.

"Restricting from my touch, little sister?"

"Yes, John. Please," she whimpers as John inserts a single finger, her walls clamping around it. "Why do I want this so badly?" She tosses her head and John can feel her internal struggle.

That just won't do.

His other hand grips her chin and forces her eyes to meet his as he begins to pump his finger in and out of her, "because you know this feeling between us trumps our blood."

"Our bad blood." She whispers as she adulates her hips, finding the friction she needs to reach her peak.

"Filthy blood," John concurs, dragging her face into his. She hasn't let him kiss her yet, and he's dying to find out if she indeed tastes as good as the spot between her legs.

"It's Mama's and Papa's fault," she nods, needing someone to blame for her illicit thirst.

John's mouth opens around her bottom lip, sucking it into his mouth, and biting down on the plush flesh. Just as he's about to push his tongue inside, she whips her face away, and tosses her head back, screaming through her release. He pulls his fingers out of her wet cunt, holding them up between them, and grinning when Pearl gasps at the sight. Proof of her disgusting need for her brother.

He sucks the fingers into his mouth, moaning around their musky taste, and sucky them clean. Pearl watches, her eyes a mixture of horror and fascination, something John has grown used to in the aftermath of their shared weakness. One the brother finds thrilling while the sister feels ashamed.

Pearl looks to the front of John's trousers and sees the large bulge, instantly making her feel sick for what they've yet again succumbed to.

"I see it, sister." John's large hand grasps her face, the fingers sinking into her cheeks. "You want to run in fear again, my cock may be large, but it will fit."

Bile rushes up her throat at his words, and she shoves him away, taking deep breaths to hold in the vomit. "Stop, John." She holds up her hand. He sees her as being fearful of his large privates, when in actuality, she's disgusted.

"Fine," he grins, "Hyldah took care of me anyway."

He strides away with a small smile on his face and running those fingers under his nose, making Pearl feel ready to dispel the contents of her stomach once again.

"I would say he looks like he's in love but that would make you feel even worse, hmm?" Hyldah says as she comes into the room. She changed out of her destroyed dress and into a black lace that covers her from neck to toe but leaves nothing to the imagination of what's underneath.

No wonder her brother is always so eager to be inside of her, Hyldah is gorgeous and sexy. Pearl watches Hyldah with a bit of envy, not because she has her brother in the palm of her hand, but because she's beautiful and *powerful*. She can feel the strength of it, the absolute dominion flowing off her in waves, hitting everything in its large radius.

"Yes," Pearl finally answers her and scoots off the table, she can feel her cheeks become inflamed, this is the most Hyldah has ever spoken to her. "It would make me feel worse."

"I blame it on you two being cooped up here like caged rabbits. You leave a brother and sister rabbit together alone in a cage, and well, they'll go at it like bunnies." She giggles.

"So, it's my Mama and Papa's fault." Pearl nods, she already knew this.

"In the beginning, yes." Hyldah nods, "but now, only you two are to blame."

"But you said... the bunnies..." Pearl becomes consumed with guilt at her words, and her tears begin to pool on her eyelids.

"Sweet girl," Hyldah coos as she holds Pearl's face in her hands, "the drought is long over."

The words sink into Pearl's head, but she doesn't quite understand their meaning. "Over?"

"The land is now thriving with food and water." Hyldah nods, a slight smile on her face.

"But..." Pearl looks around, "why are we still here?"

"John thought it best."

"John thought..." Pearl trails off as her body swims with betrayal, John wanted to keep her here so he could continue to have her. To own her body in ways she abhorred but also craved. To throw her beliefs into limbo and nurture her own self-loathing.

"You look unwell, dear." Hyldah snickers, "go on upstairs and lie down, I'll make the pie."

"Thank you, Hyldah." Pearl whispers as she rushes from the room.

When she reaches her bedroom, she quickly shuts herself in, and lets her emotions explode. Sobs wrack her body and hot tears splash onto her cheeks, their salty trails coating her skin. John is no different from Papa, he led her into a false sense of protection, only to force her into a dangerous situation. Maybe Mama, Papa, and John have bad blood, but she could be different, as long as she continues to fight him off, and one days escapes him.

Once her sobs subside and her energy is depleted, Pearl crawls up into her bed, hauling the covers up around her neck. She needs to sleep, but once she wakes, there will be a plan of escape.

It's wet and warm, sliding along her core, and flicking against her most sensitive bud. Pearl's core clenches, wanting to be filled, a craving she so desperately needs. Her thighs are pushed open wider, the thick, wet object pushes into her, and she grinds downward, searching for friction, forcing the object in deeper.

Her body is slowly climbing a crest she knows all too well, and she moves her hips faster, chasing it, ready to fall into the dark abyss of pleasure. Just as she reaches the top, her body coiling for that first drop, it stops, and rushes away from her.

"No," she comes to consciousness, her hips still moving, searching for relief. Her hand reaches between her legs, ready to continue what her dream so savagely didn't finish. It's slapped away and she sits up quickly, coming face to face with a set of cold blue eyes, and a sinister smile.

"There you are," John smirks, looking up at her through his lashes, "glad you could join us." He grabs his cock through his pants.

Pearl feels the rage come over her and before she could think it through, her palm cracks against John's cheek, the pain flaring through her hand. His face whip to the side and Pearl watches with bated breath as his jaw flexes, anger evident in the tightening of his body.

"You hit me." He says as he slowly comes to face her again, "you put your hand on me, just like Mother used to do."

She chokes on a sob, her hand quickly covering her mouth in shock, and guilt overriding her anger quickly. She really is no better than Mama. Her hand drops, ready to profess her guilt and apologies sitting on her tongue, but she doesn't get the chance. John grips her face in a firm hand, and his angry eyes bore into her as he removes the tie from his trousers.

She tries to speak around his hold but she's unable to form words, and then he moves, grabbing both hands in his one. The tie is secured around her wrists quickly and then tied to her bedpost before she even thinks to struggle.

"No, John. Wait," she pleads, "I'm sorry, I've just been so angry with you."

He doesn't care to hear her and even if he did, he doesn't react, too focused on making sure her bindings are tight. He settles back up onto his knees, his trousers slipping down dangerously low, showing the trail of hair from under his belly button, and leading to his pubic hair. The deep V at his hips is prominent as he tries to catch his breath, and all the bumps of his defined abs flex with anger.

"The drought is over, John." Pearl yanks on the cord around her wrists, only to gasp when it cuts into her flesh, "you've kept me a prisoner here."

His brows cut a straight line over his eyes as he listens to her words, "Hyldah." He growls.

"Why?" Pearl screams at him, "why are you doing this?"

"Because you are mine!" He bellows into her small room, the

sound crashing into the walls around her. "I've been patient long enough; you will be mine in every sense."

Her skirts are thrown up and over her chest, and John's trousers lose their fight with gravity, slipping down to pool around his knees. He fists his cock in his hand, squeezing it, making the red head swell.

"I was going to wait, give you the time to come around, but you keep fighting me." John growls as he falls over Pearl's body. "I wanted you to love me as I love you, beyond blood, beyond reason."

Pearl feels the blunt tip of his flesh line up with her most intimate part, and she bucks wildly, but it only serves in having him slightly sink inside her, eliciting a long groan from John.

"Keep doing all the work," he grins.

Pearl lies still, feeling her pussy adjust to having the tip of her brother's cock inside of her. The stretch burns but what she doesn't expect is the need for more climbing up from her core and settling in her chest. Her soul must be black, completely depraved.

"Are you giving in to me, sister?" He knows she is, but she refuses to voice it. What other choice does she have when her brother and her body are against her? How can she change anything when she's bound and open for him?

He flexes his hips, slipping in another few inches and the burn intensifies. He's large and her small opening is no match, she feels like she's ripping in two.

"I can't be gentle," he begins to pant, and Pearl is clenching her hands and eyes to stave off the pain. "I'm sorry." He groans just before he slams inside of her.

The world tilts on its axis, the insides of her eyelids are coated in red, and a blood curdling scream rips from her throat, echoing throughout the forest. Surely this pain means death is on her doorstep, its claws sinking deep inside of her. But it doesn't end there, no, her brother is a sadist, and he doesn't let up. He pulls all the way out, only to slam back in again, the pain intensifying.

"Fuck, I don't know why I waited so long. You're so tight," he grunts through his pleasure as Pearl trembles beneath him, silently begging for death to just take her.

John grabs her leg, hooking his arm under the knee, and forcing it up higher, opening her further. She's so wet, her greedy pussy sucking him in and coating him in arousal. He's never felt this way with Hyldah, never. He leans up, staring down into her face, her pained expression, and clenched eyelids making him grin. Soon the pain will ebb, and she'll want him inside of her all the time.

He looks down to where they're joined, and the bright red of her pain is startling at first, especially with how much of it is there. But then he can feel something dark inside of him, spurring him on, making him thrust harder, marking her virginal blood as his own. She begins to cry, large fat tears dripping from her eyes, and skating to her temples.

John falls forward, continuing to fuck her hard, and licks a line from her temple to her eye. Those tears belong to him as well.

"It hurts just this once, little sister, but next time, you will be begging for more."

"No," she sobs, keeping her eyes shut, "I never want this again. I want to die."

Die? John stalls his movements and looks down into her face, waiting for her to look at him. When her eyes do open, pure pain is reflected in their cool depths, and John's cock pulses at the sight. She whimpers through the pain and shakes her head.

"I will have to keep you tied up then and fuck you as many times as it'll take for you to start to enjoy it."

"No, please." She sobs again, "Johnny..."

She called him *Johnny*. It's been a while and it only serves to remind him how long Pearl has been fighting him, fighting *them*. With his anger anew, he begins to pound into her at a punishing pace, his large hands gripping her waist, and bruises blooming on her too pale skin.

John's balls tighten and a liquid pool of pleasure slips up his cock, trying to push its way through. He tries to hold on, just a little bit longer, but he loses the battle, and slams into his sister one final time, his cum spurting deep inside of her. When he pulls out of her, his cock is bright red, and the bed beneath her is saturated with blood.

He makes his way to the washroom, gathering rags and cold water, then sits back between her legs. She's still crying, her face a swollen, red mess, and averted away from him. He begins to clean her, paying attention to the areas which look red and inflamed. He presses the cool water against it, hoping it soothes her flesh because he wants her again soon.

"Untie me," she demands when he's finished, "I need to change my bedsheets and use the washroom."

"You will not harm yourself?"

"Untie me!" She screeches, and John smiles. He likes her fire and does indeed untie her. She gets up out of bed and sways on her feet, her hand pressed against her lower belly.

"The pain will lessen..." John begins.

"Get out." Pearl growls and stalks to the washroom, her steps sloppy and uneven.

Instead of feeling guilty or ashamed, John feels sated and accomplished. He took what he's wanted for so long, and that in itself is an achievement. Sure, his sister is mad, it was painful as most first times are, but what she doesn't know is the extent of the pleasure that awaits her, and he can't wait to show her.

John looks down to his lap to find his pants and lower belly coated in her drying virginal blood, almost as if he went to war. In a way he did, and he came out victorious. After losing many battles with his sister's virtue, he finally won the war.

Pearl stares at herself in the cloudy mirror of her small washroom. Her cheeks are flushed bright red with anger, and if she's being honest, also with reverence for what just transpired. Her innocence was taken in the most primal way, and by her brother, but she can't help the warming in her lower belly at the thought of him inside of her.

Next time, you will be begging for more.

Is it true? Pearl's fingers drop lower, and she touches the blood stains on her skirts. After this, will she really be begging for more? With a sigh, she begins to fill up the bath with hot water, letting the steam coat her sticky skin. In all the books she's read, never has there been a brother who lusted for his sister, who tied her to a bed only to force his way inside of her. It's unnatural, immoral, and debased. But she did read about virginal girls losing the most precious part of them, the last remnants linking them to a child's innocence, and the detailed pain.

Will she really be begging for more?

Pearl can't imagine wanting more of what just happened, but as she lowers herself down into the hot water, she immediately begins to feel better, and the pain throbbing between her legs begins to fade.

A sharp knock sounds on the washroom door and just as she's about to curse her brother, Hyldah's head pops in.

"I came to bring you a few elixirs." Her face looks sympathetic, "I remember when I lost my-"

"Was it your brother also?" Pearl retorts, her stomach twisting with the words.

"No, it was my father." She steps in with a pot of ointment and a steaming cup. Pearl looks at her, shock saturating her features. *Did she say her father?* Surely, that's worse than her brother. "This is for your..." she points to the ointment, "sensitive area," she throws her a grin with a shrug, "and I made this tea. It will soothe you and help you sleep."

A sob hiccups from Pearl's mouth as she holds her hand over her pounding heart. Why must men be so consumed with lust, the need to spill their seed? Why is it the most forefront thought they possess?

"Men have only one true purpose on this Earth, child." Hyldah says as she kneels down by the edge of the tub, grabbing the sponge from Pearl's clenched hand. "We women need them to reproduce and then nothing more. We are the strongest entity on this spinning orb and nothing else compares. We nurture, grow life, birth it, raise it, feed it, make a home, and we do it all with love and compassion. *We* are the Earth's fruit and men are put here to assist *us*."

"I do not want to bear children," Pearl looks at Hyldah aghast, "that would be an abomination."

"Would it?" Her head tips as she looks at Pearl in question, "the Bible tells stories of brother and sister, son and mother, and good Christians parrot its phrases for anyone who will listen. Children are a *blessing*, isn't that so?"

"Do you have children, Hyldah?"

"No," she gives Pearl a sad smile, "I was not blessed with such miracles in this life. Maybe the next."

"I will not take my brother back into my bed." she shakes her head, clearing her mind of him moving inside of her. Ignoring how her sore pussy begins to hum in approval.

"He is a big man," Hyldah hums, "you may not have a choice. But may I give you some advice?"

"Yes."

"Enjoy it. Make him believe you want him, and then when his mind is consumed with his vile intentions, you can make your escape." She grins conspiratorially.

Pearl feels a niggling of mistrust, working its way deep inside of her, "then you would be here with him."

"Oh, don't worry about me," she snickers as she runs the sponge over Pearl's back. "I can handle myself."

Something sickening begins to twist in Pearl's stomach, it feels slick and unnerving.

Jealousy.

Hyldah wants John to herself, to suck his cock, to fuck him as often as she wants, and the thought has Pearl filling with guile.

"That sounds like a great plan." She grins at the witch while on the inside she's fuming with rage.

John is her brother, and Hyldah will never have him.

The next morning, Pearl awakes to crippling pain in her lower abdomen, this is not her menses, but something stronger and unnatural. She sinks into a depression; fearful she's now carrying her brother's child. She spends the day in bed, recouping, and sleeping. But the ugly thoughts never stop bombarding her mind, was Hyldah sinking her claws even further into John? Did she somehow poison her so she could have her way with him again?

The gardens are beautiful. John sits on one of the hard stone benches and looks out among the sea of rainbow colors. Everything is in technicolor today, and he can only attribute it to finally pushing past the last barrier with Pearl, claiming her completely. The sun shines brighter, the trees exude majestic beauty, and the flowers shine brilliantly under the cascading sunlight. Everything is different this morning, including John himself. She will come around and when she does, they can live in peace.

John will make plans to leave the witch's lair, build him and Pearl their very own home, and they can raise a family. Everything will come together, and they will live happily ever after, just like those novels she reads.

"Such a lovely day, hmmm?" Hyldah's voice breaks through his reverie, and not even she can put a damper on his mood.

"The best day."

"But she still fights you," Hyldah murmurs as she sits beside him on the bench. "I can help you."

"Help me?" John turns to look at the witch with skepticism.

"I am a witch," she holds out her hands and chuckles, "I can make you a potion which will force her to love you."

"She already loves me." John's brow creases in the center.

"As a brother only."

Yes, that's true.

"I can make a strong love potion, one to affect her forever, but it needs to be done on the full moon." Hyldah glances behind her, then leans in closer, "it would mean you two could be together, in the marital sense, without feeling ashamed or dirty."

"I do not feel ashamed nor dirty." John retorts.

"But she does."

Yes, Pearl cannot fully accept them until she lets go of her humiliation.

"When is the next full moon?" He asks Hyldah.

"Three days." She grabs his hand and squeezes, "I will need to be at my strongest, you understand?"

"Yes," John waves his hand, "take from me what you need."

"I will also need hers."

"No!" He's quick to dispute, shaking the witch's claws from his hand.

"Yes," she nods emphatically, "it is a powerful spell."

"I will think about it." He finally gives in.

"Yes," Hyldah purrs, "think quickly for there isn't much time." Then she rises from the bench and saunters inside.

There isn't much time, and it all boils down to how Pearl is feeling in the aftermath. How did she wake up this morning? Is she feeling complete like John, or does she wallow in the darkest pits of mortification?

If Hyldah can make Pearl live the rest of her days in bliss with John as her husband, then what would be the harm in that?

He makes his way to her room, tapping lightly on the door, and when he doesn't get an answer, his heart sinks with despair. Is she hiding from him? He opens the door and looks around the wooden slab, finding Pearl's small body wrapped tight in her blanket. She's fast asleep, her face looking serene, and her shoulders moving with deep slow breaths. Maybe she's still recovering after last night.

"You will need to take her again," Hyldah appears behind him, "you will have to see how she feels about you. Does she love you in the carnal sense? Or just a big brother?" Her hot breath hits the back of his neck, and he clenches a fist. "There's no other way to know for sure."

"She is still in pain from the first time."

"Use your mouth," her black claw drags across his bottom lip, "prepare her down there, give her pleasure before the pain."

John closes the door and grabs Hyldah by the throat, his cock pulsing. "Maybe if I use you first, I will not be so rough with her."

"Yes," she drags out the last syllable like an evil snake, "use me."

John pushes her against the wall, the side of her head smashing into the blue painted surface. Hyldah cackles as he gathers her dress in his hands, throwing it up and over her waist, baring her wet, dripping pussy. He undoes his trousers and fists his large cock, lining himself up with her greedy cunt.

Moving his grip to her hips, his fingers digging in, and her gasp of pain hardening him further. He slams inside of the witch, her eager pussy taking all of him in a single thrust, nothing like his sister's tight cunt. Still, once he's sated from the witch, he can concentrate on his sister's pleasure instead of his own.

Pearl wakes up to the sound of a consistent pounding just outside her door, the feeling she woke up with earlier has passed, and now all that remains is a slight throbbing in her head. To which the pounding is not helping. She slowly gets out of bed, testing her legs, and the area between. Still sore but feeling much better, thanks to Hyldah's ointment.

She makes her way to the door and quietly opens it, peering out into the hallway. What she sees has her covering her mouth in case her gasp gives her away. Her brother is fucking the witch against the wall, his long, thick cock repeatedly sliding in and out of her, and her juices glistening along his length. Hyldah moans loudly and Pearl's eyes snap up to her face, only to find the witch's mismatched eyes already focused on her, a cruel smile lining her mouth.

She slips back inside her room while anger burns like an inferno inside of her. How dare he fuck the witch right after defiling his own sister?

A few hours later and her door opens slowly, her brother's long white-blond spilling over his face. When he sees her sitting up in bed, his eyes shine with pure happiness, making Pearl's stomach sour. How can he look at her like that after what he's done?

"There's my sweet sister." He says as he comes inside, looking freshly showered. No matter how hard he scrubbed his filthy cock, the sight of him thrusting into Hyldah will never leave her. "Lie back and spread your legs, I am here for my feast."

Her head snaps to him in shock, "I saw what you were doing with Hyldah, you animal." She seethes, "now you think you can slip that filthy thing back between my legs?"

"I used her first so that I may be gentle with you."

"Bullshit!"

John's eyes widen in disbelief as he stares at his livid little sister. "I will have you, Pearl. One way or another." Then he leaves her room.

He storms down the hall and into the west wing, straight for Hyldah's bedroom. When he bursts into her room, startling her, he thunders loudly, "we will do the ceremony."

Much to Hyldah's delight.

———

The full moon shines bright in the starless sky, its eerie yellow glow casts a minacious feeling of foreboding around John. There's something about the large orb tonight, it feels omnipotent and benevolent. John questions his decision for this ritual, one he made in the clutches of extreme anger, making him feel like he had no other option.

"I have prepared the altar, we must do it now, while the moon is high." John can hear the excitement in the witch's tenor and once again, he questions if there's not something more Hyldah is hiding.

"I will get her." He decides the love he has for his sister trumps all, and in the end, everything will be worth her being pliant in his arms.

"No need," Hyldah purrs, "I have her there and strapped to the stone."

"What?" He turns on her, fire coating his insides, muscles tightening and preparing to pounce.

"I did not want her to blame you in the end, better she hates me." Her words give him pause, the anger ebbing as he understands their meaning.

"You did that for me?"

"Yes." She nods, running her nails down his shirtless chest. "You are important to me."

When he doesn't return the sentiment, he sees vexation flare in her eyes. He brushes by her stiff body, feeling it thrum with displeasure, and hurries to his sister's side. John remembers his first time inside those blackened walls, and he doesn't want her to be fearful. He will always protect his baby sister.

He finds her naked body strapped onto the hard, unforgiving stone, and when she hears him, her head slowly turns in his direction. What he sees in her eyes has him stalling.

Emptiness.

A cold blue void.

Her head slowly turns back to gaze at the ceiling, and John clutches at his chest. It feels hollow. He brings himself to stand beside her, touching her cheek, and gasps at the cold skin.

"Pearl," his voice shakes, "I needed to make you love me."

Nothing.

There's an abyss in her eyes, a never-ending pit of desolation.

"Let's start." Hyldah claps behind him.

And they must, there's no turning back. Her eyes are windows into her soul, and all John sees is a black chasm. He needs to refill it with his love for her.

He gives Hyldah a nod, turning to her for further instruction.

"Undress." The witch demands. He drops his trousers and steps closer to Pearl. "You will spill your essence inside of her."

John grows hard with the thought of being inside his sister once more, and he grasps his hard cock in his hand. He gazes between Pearl's bound and spread legs just as Hyldah begins to hum. The sound sends a haze over John's vision, and his cock begins to pulse. Soon, Pearl's hips begin to thrust upward, searching for something, and her juices begin to slip out of her folds.

But her eyes remain dull on the ceiling overhead.

John climbs onto the stone, crawls up his sister's body, and nestles himself between her legs. She blinks, a small reaction to the feel of his cock as he rubs it through her wet folds, and when she whimpers, he damn near spills himself all over her.

"Do not untie her," Hyldah speaks around the humming, "not until the ritual is over."

Pearl begins to grind herself along John's length, searching, seeking for him, and he doesn't want to keep her waiting. He lines himself up and slowly sinks into her wet, warmth. She's heavenly as she clenches around, her whimpering quickly turning into moans of pleasure.

"I love you, Pearl." John kisses her chin, and she turns her head away, still not wanting the intimacy of his kiss. That's fine, he'll slowly love her with his cock, forcing pleasure from her.

John leans up onto his knees, grasps Pearl's hips in his large hands, and begins to drill into her. The humming intensifies and the fluid leaking from between Pearl's thighs is astounding, as are her screams of pleasure.

Hyldah moves above Pearl's head, leaning down, and whispering something into ear. Then her long pointed tongue snakes inside, slowly licking its way along her lobe. Pearl's body begins to tremble, sweat slicks along her skin, and John can feel her tight channel begin to squeeze him harder. Then, much to his surprise, Hyldah grabs Pearl's chin, tilting her head back, and devouring her mouth in a soul searing kiss.

Envy, pure and undiluted rushes through John as Pearl opens her mouth, her tongue tangling with Hyldah's. So, he fucks her harder, his skin slapping against her delicate folds, her swollen pussy blooms red, and when his grip tightens on her hips, he knows she'll be left with his branding. Her pussy clamps around him hard and her release is gathering between them, liquid rushing around his cock. Her screams are swallowed by Hyldah's mouth, and John comes in an explosion of pleasure, his skin tingling all over with fire, and his insides pulsing with the humming.

Then Hyldah is pushing him off the stone and crawling between Pearl's legs. Her mouth lands on his sister's trembling pussy, so wet with her release, and then she sucks. The sound is loud in the room, making Pearl look down at the witch between her legs. Hyldah devours both of their essences and shines brighter than she ever has before.

Pearl can still hear the words the witch whispered in her ear, even though her voice feels stolen, words unable to form. She can still hear what she said, playing on repeat in her mind. She watches as the witch sucks her dry, her brilliant aura brightening the room, and Pearl knows there's only one way to escape her. It'll all be up to her because her brother's cock makes him weak.

I will own the baby which grows in your womb.

―――

6 Months later...

Life went back to normal after the night in Hyldah's dark room, and also everything changed. John's loving gaze lands on Pearl and she returns it, a small smile coating her full lips. Pearl loves John now, and every night is spent in bliss as he owns her body. Still though, she doesn't let him kiss her mouth. She says she doesn't like it and the night she kissed the witch; she must've been compelled. Regardless, John can feel the love pouring off of her, and now her heart is his as well. Hyldah has not required his essence since that night, and yet, she remains youthful, her estate brimming with fertility. Maybe the ritual gave her everlasting life.

The biggest change?

The swell of Pearl's stomach beneath her dresses. She carries their child, a rambunctious bundle who loves to kick John's hand, and rolls with energy all day. It's a boy, he can feel it, and even though Pearl laughs at his excitement, she knows it is as well.

He's been making plans to get them out of the witch's lair before their child is born, but Pearl disagrees. She's worried about childbirth, and feels the witch knows ways to prevent her death. The thought of her dying is scary enough, but he feels like Pearl is strong, so resilient, and their child would never kill its mother. I stay for her though, to help ease her fear, and to make sure she stays happy.

Pearl smiles at her brother, content in making him at ease, and keeping her fears deep inside. Hyldah watches her growing belly with a hunger that grows with each passing day. Her eyes flare with desire, and once a week, she leads Pearl into the dark room. She lies on the stone and lets Hyldah draw from her pleasure, whether it's her release or blood. John doesn't realize and Pearl intends to keep it that way, until the day comes to enact her revenge.

The witch is strong, her power great, and Pearl knows she cannot beat her with strength, she can only accomplish it with cunning. John leaves the kitchen, giving Pearl a sweet lingering kiss to her cheek, and she goes back to peeling the apples.

"Another apple pie?" Hyldah sings as she comes into the kitchen.

"The baby craves them," Pearl snickers, working hard to keep her tone level.

Hyldah has never brought up what she said to Pearl the night she and John used her on that stone altar. Either she believes Pearl wasn't lucid or she forgot, either way, it works in Pearl's favor for deception.

"Hyldah," her voice is sweet as honeysuckle, "I was wondering, when is the next full moon?"

She already knows it's tonight.

"Tonight." Hyldah confirms.

"Would we be able to do... you know... the same as before?" Pearl purposely stumbles over her words.

"With your brother?" She turns, her strange eyes narrowing and looking for any signs of conspiracy. "Why?"

She places her hands over her stomach, lightly brushing her fingers along the taut skin, "I want a protection spell. One born from the strength of the three of us." Then she looks up at the witch from under her lashes, hoping she's portraying a coy girl, "and the pleasure that comes with it."

"You've been insatiable." Hyldah chuckles. "Anything you want," her dark, inky nails glide along Pearl's jaw, "you both want." Her hand rests over Pearl's on her stomach.

She grabs an apple on her way out of the kitchen, biting into its juicy flesh, and humming quietly. The sound sends shockwaves to Pearl's core, and she steels herself against it. She's been working up her resistance to the lure of Hyldah's song, and as long as she's not caught off guard, she won't lose her senses.

After convincing her big brother the need for a strong protection spell, he caves to his little sister's request, and even though she can feel his suspicions, he trusts her. Which she's sure will change after tonight, as long as she doesn't fail in her plan.

This time when her bare skin settles atop the stone, she's not bound, and when Hyldah's humming begins, she's not affected. The candlesticks situated around her body burn with intensity, the flames dancing to the beat of the witch's humming. Of course, John is naked and between Pearl's legs in record time, never having gained control over his urges. As he moves inside of her, she puts on a show. Her moans are loud and drawn out, her hips adulate in time with the pulsing of the room, and when Hyldah stands above her, she yanks her down for a fire igniting kiss.

John manages to pull a release from Pearl, and then he's emptying himself deep inside of her. Hyldah makes her way around the altar, readying to crawl between her legs, when Pearl grabs her hand.

"Could you lie down, and I sit on your face?" She doesn't even need to pretend to be embarrassed, she truly is. She's never even sat on John's face, and the thunderous look he throws her is proof of that.

Hyldah's eyes blaze with heat as she gives one stiff nod, unable to hide her desire. Pearl slides to the bottom of the altar, and Hyldah lies in her place, her black hair fanning out in all directions. She's beautiful and enticing, as all evil things are. Pearl angles herself over Hyldah's face, feeling hers and John's release beginning to drip, and the witch opens her mouth, so she doesn't miss a single drop.

Pearl drops down over the witch's face, gyrating her hips, and wincing when Hyldah's talons sink into the globes of her ass. Her mismatched eyes stay trayed on Pearl's face, unaware of her hand as she reaches out to grab a candlestick. It needs to be quick, just before she devours too much, and so, Pearl yanks hard, then slams the iron down on top of Hyldah's head. The crunch is loud throughout the room, but Pearl doesn't stop moving over the witch's face, as her core tightens, and then she's staring down into an unconscious face as she comes undone.

"Pearl!" John exclaims, as he watches her toss the candlestick aside and hop down from the altar.

"Yes, idiot brother?" She snaps, finally losing her composure. "What is it?"

"You killed her." He's standing there, completely naked with a hard cock, and a fearful look.

"Not yet," she chuckles as she begins to tie Hyldah to the altar, "but I will."

When she's secure, Pearl grabs the knife she knows is kept under the stone top and grips the handle tight as she digs it across the witch's throat. Then she leans forward and begins to gulp her gushing blood in large swallows, taking in her bitter essence, and feeling her body hum with power. A potent strength makes her tremble as Hyldah flinches in death.

"Pearl," a choked sound comes from behind her, and when she turns, her big brother is staring at her in awe. "You're glowing."

"Burn her." Pearl's voice vibrates throughout the room, "and bring me her skull."

It's a few hours later when John finds her still bloodied and sitting in the middle of the garden. Her hair is saturated with blood, and her swollen stomach has large, dried splatters all over it. But what gives him pause are her nails. Long, black, and pointed, the tips of her fingers looking nearly black as the thick blood dries.

"Well?" She turns and looks at him from over her shoulder, making John recoil. Her eyes are now one black and one blue, eerily the same as Hyldah's were. "Where is it?" Her voice was always soft and musical, but now it rasps with unyielding power.

John holds out the blackened skull in his hands, the open sockets still dripping with flesh and matter. Pearl stands and walks to stand in front of him, grabbing it into her filthy hands.

"Not so strong anymore, huh witch?" She cackles then, the sound so similar to Hyldah's, and when those freakish eyes land back on him, they burn with an intensity. "Take off your pants."

He's hard instantly because this is still his sweet sister, and his love for her is unconditional. "Here?"

"I require your *essence*." She hisses.

John does as she asks and sits on the stone bench, grabbing her hips as she straddles him, his thumbs stroking along her pregnant stomach. She sinks down onto him, moving in powerful strokes, and then she grabs his chin, forcing his eyes on her as she hums. The sound is more striking than Hyldah's ever was.

She never releases the skull, the sticky black object stays rooted in her hands, and she leans forward, pressing her mouth to his ear. "We are going back tonight."

His release rushes through him, and he slams up into her, his eyes widening as her aura strengthens. "Go where?"

"Why, home big brother."

Trees are full, the ground is green, and the birds and insects are thriving. In the center of this fruitful forest stands a dilapidated cabin, home to a small family. A father, a mother, a brother, and a little sister. All healthy, happily living their lives.

As Pearl and John approach the cabin, the children stop to stare. A big brother whose white-blond hair hangs over his eyes, and a little sister, her twin braids hang over her shoulders. Pearl holds her finger to her lips, telling the children to remain quiet while still grasping the skull in her other hand. Both children nod, and continue to stay put, even when John kicks the door down.

The abandoned brother and sister stand in the familiar cabin's small interior, staring down at their overweight parents. Their once sunken faces are ruddy and fat, their bodies swollen with an abundance of food.

"Hello Mama," Pearl grins, "Papa, we see you've replaced us."

"Pearl?" Henry falls to his knees, "Johnny?"

"In the flesh," John sneers and then looks at his mother. She's standing there, trembling on the spot, but her eyes still hold a glint of hatred.

"Her first." Pearl rasps and John nods in agreement.

"First for what?" The old woman spits as her eyes widen on the skull in her daughter's hands, then to the swell of her stomach. "You're pregnant."

"Oh yes," Pearl's smile widens, "you would've been grandparents."

The father looks between them, a question in his gaze.

"Yes," Pearl purrs, "your son is the father of your daughter's child." Her laugh is loud and cackling.

"You are the Devil's spawn," Caroline shrieks, "I always knew it."

"Now, John." Pearl demands and begins to hum, "but first, show her exactly what it is her Devil spawn children do."

The hum, such a powerful coaxing sound. Soon after killing the witch, Pearl could feel her power of coercion, and the humming is a tool to enact her every intention.

Pearl continues to hum, keeping her father locked to the floor, and their mother begins to pant, desire coating her body. It's her eyes which stand out, and it makes John laugh as he rips open her dress, she's disgusted. It's about to get a heck of a lot worse.

John throws her over the small table, kicking her legs apart, and dropping his trousers. Caroline is dripping with arousal and their father stares, shocked at the reaction coming from his wife as her hips seek her son's large cock. Henry's no longer struggling against his invisible bonds, and instead stares riveted on his son shoving that cock into his own mother.

Pearl's hums grow louder, and their mother's moans rival the sound as John pounds her into the table with his brutal strength. The sound of her hips smashing against the wood is resounding throughout the room, and when their mother finds her release, she screams to the ceiling, a mixture of moans and sobs. John pulls out, not having spilled his essence, knowing that's for Pearl only.

She approaches her mother and yanks her up by her hair, "*you* are the Devil." She spits in her face, then slams it back to the table. Using her strength, she repeats the motion until Caroline's head is cracked open and spilling with blood and brain matter.

Pearl smiles knowing her mother's last feeling must've been of utter mortification as she came all over her own son's cock.

Then she turns to her father, but already finds him with his own gun to his head. "I deserve to die at your feet for what I did all those years ago. There's nothing I can say to make this better, but please, don't harm your younger brother and sister."

"Do it then." John growls and they both watch as he presses the trigger, his head exploding in a magnificent cloud of brains and skull.

Pearl begins to pull up her skirts, her strength waning, and her lust amplifying. "John, I need you." She pants and her obedient brother falls to his knees behind her, gently pushing her forward. She looks over her shoulder to find his glistening cock still wet from their mother as he shoves it inside of her, one hard, swift motion.

The stretch is delicious, making her fingers curl into her father's blood and gore on the floor. His body lays next to her as her brother fucks her with relish. She begins to feel the tightening, and their child in her belly moves just as she crests, forcing John into coming as well. The relief is immediate as her aura glows, and as always, her brother is struck stupid, watching her.

He doesn't notice when she pushes up to her knees, her fingers wrapping around the wooden handle, and when she presses the barrel of their father's gun to his head, he's not surprised. John knew. He could sense Pearl's lack of love for him, and it began that very same night he gave into his dark, carnal desires for the flesh of his sister.

"I understand," he mutters, as his eyes drift shut, "I know I deserve this for what I made you do."

"I've hated you." She grits out, "mostly because I didn't hate you at all." Then she surprises him as she presses her mouth to his. *She tastes like apples* is his final thought right before his world goes black forever.

Pearl stands, Hyldah's black skull firmly in her grasp, as she looks around the cabin. Blood and gore line the walls and floor, and her heart lifts at the sight. Everyone who's wronged her is now dead at her feet, including Hyldah whose eye sockets serve as finger holds when she's carried around. Finally feeling overcome with peace, Pearl's eyes slip to the door, finding her younger siblings staring in at the massacre, and not showing an ounce of emotion on their little faces.

"I'm your new Mama." Pearl coos and steps closer to them, "do you like apples?"

Both little faces nod emphatically, and Pearl claps her hands as she begins to hum. The children become entranced with the sound and follow her through the woods. More cabins litter the area than ever before, and as she continues on her way, some curious faces peer out from opened doors. The weakest of men step outside, lured by the sound of her gentle humming, and follow close behind her.

The children and the few men make the two-day trek, all coerced by the new witch of the meadow who carries the next generation of bad blood in her belly.

The end

ABOUT C.A. RENE

Lover of all things dark. I love to read it, write it, own it, eat it, whatever it. My addictions include Coffee, books, and WINE, in that order. The computer screen is my canvas and the keyboard my brush, thank you for viewing my masterpieces.

Want to keep up with teasers and new releases?
Here's how:
Website

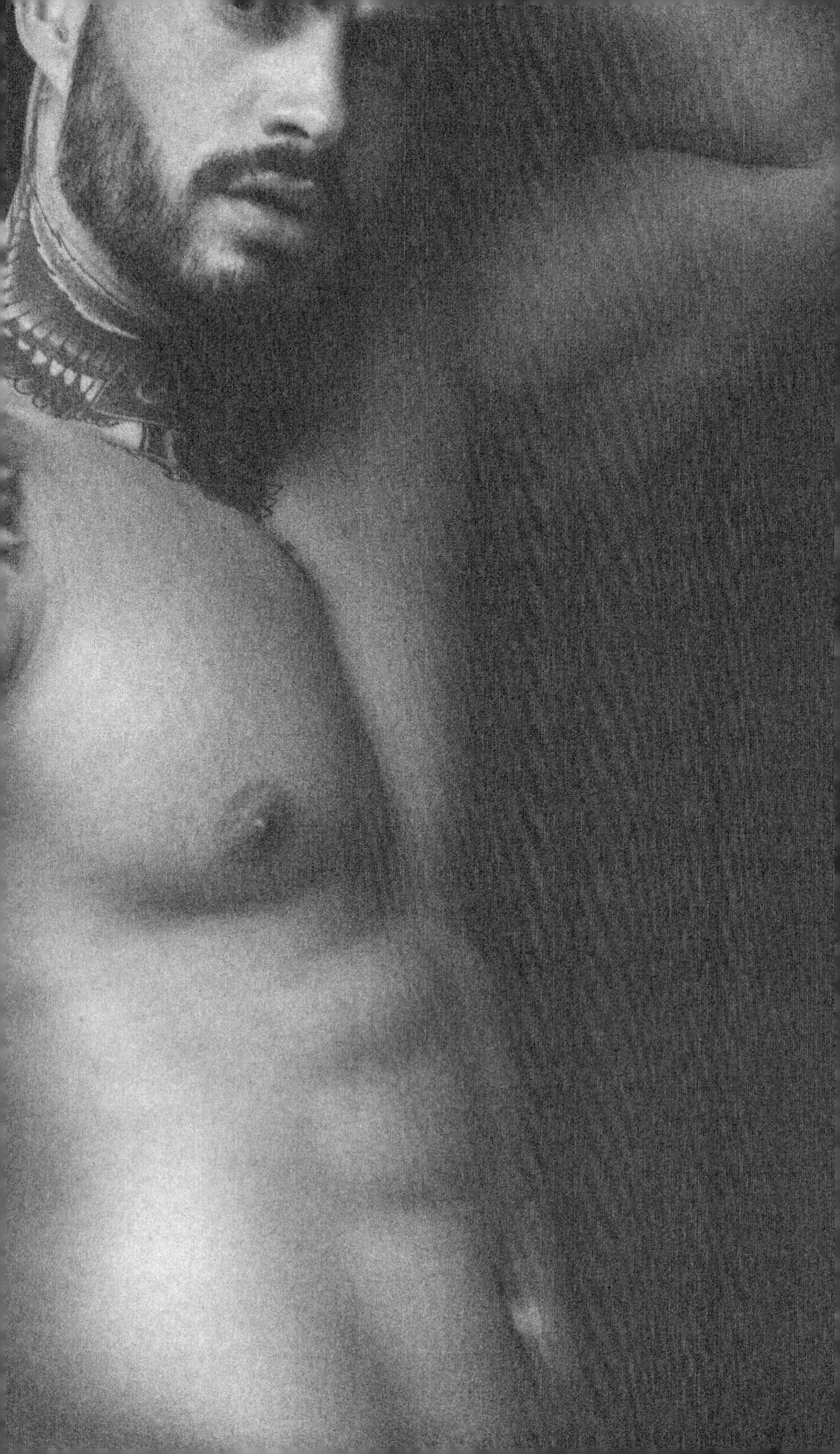

IT STARTS WITH ME

A CICCONE BROTHERS PREQUEL

BY S. RENA & BL MUTE

It Starts With Me
Copyright © 2020 by S. Rena & BL Mute
This novella is a work of fiction. Names, characters, places, and incidents are either the product of the author's imagination or used fictitiously. Any resemblance to actual persons, living or dead, or to actual events or locales is entirely coincidental.
All rights reserved.
No part of this book may be used or reproduced in any form or by any means, electronic or mechanical, including photocopying, recording, or by information storage and retrieval system, without written permission from the publisher or author.
A Novella Written & Published by S. Rena & BL Mute

DISCLAIMER

Warning!
This is a dub-con romance that contains mature content, domestic abuse, cheating, and other content that may be disturbing or triggering to some readers. If such materials offend you, please do not read.

BLURB

Stray.
Reject.
Ward of the state.
That's all I was five years ago. All I thought I would be until Clyde Gallo took me in.
He saw something in me—a hunger for power. No fear.
I would be the perfect soldier in his war for dominance.
But if my time in foster care, group homes, or the streets have taught me anything, it's to trust no one—especially a man like Clyde.
He may have molded me to be the perfect right hand, but I'd be lying if I said I didn't want more.
I play my part, I listen, and I always follow through, but another thing I've learned is to show no mercy, take no pity, and use the stupid fools who trust you as stepping stones.
When Clyde takes something of mine, he'll see just how close I hold those words to my cold, black heart.

CHAPTER ONE

"Eric! Are you listening?" Clyde booms from across me. His fat belly grazes the edge of the table, shaking it with every word.

I nod and fold my arms over my chest, and lean back into my chair. "I'm listening."

In the five years, I've been with him, he's changed. His once full, dark hair is now thinning and more white than anything. His figure isn't as slim as it used to be, and his fingers are fatter—looking a weird shade of red as his gold rings squeeze the life from them.

I used to have so much respect for him. I mean, he practically saved me, but after five long, gruelling years, I realize he's nothing but a stupid pig. He's let his hunger for money and power blind him of what matters— being smart.

In this world— this lifestyle— one wrong move, and you're dead. It's something he instilled in me, and I took it to heart. I make sure to always watch and weigh the options of shit. Something he should do, but he's neglected.

"Do you hear me, Eric?" He says, pulling me back to the conversation I couldn't give a fuck less about. "She owes Raymond more than she's worth and I need you to collect."

The last bit he spills catches my attention. I tip my head and lean over the table. "So you're in bed with Raymond now? Doesn't seem like a good decision, *boss*."

Raymond is *the* supplier of the city. Any kind of drug or weapon you can think of, he can get. Need someone to disappear? He can do that too, which is one of the main reasons we Gallos don't do business with him.

He's sneaky and shady as fuck. One wrong step, and he'll make sure you're the one to disappear. Respect is nothing but a word to him, and Clyde knows this.

"Maybe not, but he has something I want, and in order to get it, I need you to do what I say."

I keep my face impassive. "And what is it you're wanting?" You'd think for a man like Clyde, someone who virtually has everything, wouldn't want more. But that's the thing. There is always more.

"The South side." He grins.

I roll my eyes. "The South side is trash. There is nothing there that could profit you."

"You may not think so, but there is something there that is more profitable than anything else we do."

I jut my chin, telling him to continue.

"South End." He leans back in his chair with the same snarky grin. "An endless supply of boys ready to do anything for a quick buck and a quick fuck. Old enough to decide, but young enough to still be stupid. That's what I need."

I nod slowly when he talks, a new revelation dawning on me.

I was one of those boys years ago. It was in this very restaurant where I met Clyde. When I stole the pizza scraps from his plate and the twenty-dollar bill he left beside it, I was sure he would kill me. It isn't like I knew him, but judging from the gun holstered on his hip and the three kilos of cocaine under his arms when he came from the back with the owner, I knew nothing good could come from him, but I was wrong. Instead of ending my life right then and there, he offered me a job.

He saw something in me. I had always assumed it was my bold manner and don't give a fuck attitude because I never apologized. I stuffed the twenty in my pocket and shoved the pizza crust in my mouth, then spoke between chews, telling him, "*I think I need this more than you.*" But maybe it wasn't that at all. He just thought I was young and stupid—the perfect kind of person to mold into a soldier.

But at this very moment, he's fucked up and doesn't even realize it yet. He's lost sight of what's important, and even more, he's underestimated me. Taking his reign will only be that much easier knowing how he sees me.

"If that's what you want, fine." I say, not even acknowledging the bullshit he spewed at me. "Just tell me who it is and I'll handle it."

IT STARTS WITH ME

"Amy. She's the latest owner of South End Boy's Home. She knows what she owes Raymond, so get it, and get back to me."

I stand from the table and button my suit jacket. "It'll be done."

"Oh, and Eric," He says as I turn to walk away. "Take CJ. Kid has a lot to learn."

I glance out the glass front of the store where CJ stands in the cold, waiting for his next orders, then give Clyde a nod over my shoulder.

I stroll across the cheap white linoleum until I hit the front entrance. Pulling the door open, the tiny bell above it rings and grabs CJ's attention. He turns toward me and squares his shoulders, trying to hide the fact that he's shivering from the bitter wind.

I admire how eager he is to do whatever Clyde may ask, but hearing Clyde's confession makes me almost pity him. He doesn't realize he's nameless and faceless to Clyde. Just another dumb teen, fresh out of whatever group home Clyde has been scoping out, who will eventually die. Either by their hand or Clyde's— because there is no other way out of this life.

"You're making a run to collect with me. Think you can handle that?" I ask him, pushing my thoughts to the back of my mind.

I don't necessarily want him shadowing me because I work better alone, but what Clyde says goes. At least for now.

He nods vigorously. "Yeah. Of course. Whatever you need, Eric."

I raise my brows with a frown. "First, I need you to chill the fuck out. We aren't going to fucking Disneyland."

He nods again, a little less enthusiastically, and looks everywhere but at me. "Yeah. Sure. My bad."

I roll my eyes with a scoff and start down the sidewalk toward the black Tahoe. Before I reach the back door, Alfredo exits the driver's seat and rounds the front. He gives me a curt nod as he opens the door, and I slip inside.

I pull my phone from my pocket and unlock it, ready to busy my mind with anything but what I'm about to do. When the cold air from outside still bites at me, I raise my head and see CJ standing there like a lost puppy.

I suck in a deep breath. Maybe Clyde wasn't so wrong because this kid clearly *is* stupid. "Go the fuck around." I say it as if it's the most obvious thing in the world.

"Right." He replies with another nod, then disappears behind the SUV.

I pull my door closed, then shoot my eyes to Alfredo's in the rearview mirror. He shakes his head with a smile. "You used to be the same way, Eric." He whispers.

"I wasn't an idiot." I deadpan.

He shrugs as CJ opens the door opposite of me. "You were pretty close."

I glance at CJ as he slides inside, then move my eyes back to Alfredo. "Just take us to South End." I wave.

He puts the vehicle in drive and pulls away from the curb, finally letting his eyes focus on something other than me for the short drive.

I've always liked Alfredo. He's been around longer than me, so he knows how shit works, and I know he isn't too happy about Clyde's recent endeavours. He's a wise man— someone who prides himself on using his brain as his biggest weapon— and that's precisely the kind of person I would want beside me. Clyde is too foolish to see Alfredo's worth, though.

The thoughts quickly die inside my mind as we pull up to the front of South End Boy's Home. In the three years I spent here, I went through some of the most brutal shit I've ever had to endure. Rape, beatings, starvation. All the things most places like this promise to be the opposite of, but it seems South End is cursed. Everyone who's ever run it wants the same thing. Money. And a check comes monthly for every child in their care.

It's quite tragic, but also not my problem. If I had the choice, I would never step back inside those doors, but alas, here I am doing Clyde's bidding.

"I'll be waiting." Alfredo says, putting the SUV in park.

I nod and open my door, then slide out, not even bothering to wait on CJ. My shoes tap against the broken concrete as I walk to the door. My heartbeat echoes through my ears as I reach it and feel CJ move behind me.

"Don't fuck this up, understand?" I whisper to CJ as I knock on the door. I'm sure he nods eagerly, ready to please, but I don't look to see.

When a woman opens it, I'm taken aback. She doesn't seem like the type to get tangled up with a man like Clyde. She looks... soft. Pure. With wispy hair, radiant blue eyes, and pale skin.

Immediately, my mind starts to wander to a dark place. A place where she's on her knees with my cock down her throat as I fist her soft hair. I think of all the positions I could put her body in just to destroy her sexually. Her voice, her taste, her touch—I conjure up images and expectations, and that's a dangerous thing. This woman is too sweet for my wrath, but that makes me want her even more, and all it took was a simple glance.

"Can I help you?" Even her voice doesn't fit with the image I've made in my head about what she *should* look and sound like.

"Are you the owner?" I question, trying to silence my thoughts.

She shakes her head. "No. That's my sister, I just help run things."

"I see. I'd like to speak to her, please." I cross my wrists in front of me, widening my stance, and wait.

She tips her head, then looks over my shoulder to CJ. "Sir, I'm sorry, but he seems too old for our care. I can give you information on extended homes and some state assistant programs that may be able to help though."

I glance at CJ, then back to her. "I appreciate that, but that isn't why I'm here."

"Oh." She pauses. "I'm so sorry. We have so many people come by wanting a safe place to leave their children. I just assumed." Her cheeks are stained pink, and she actually sounds apologetic.

"Your sister. Get her. Now." I deadpan. I don't have time to reassure her I don't give a fuck what she thought. I'm here for a job, and that's it.

Her eyes bounce around before she finally looks at me again. I can tell she knows exactly why I'm here. "You can wait in the foyer while I go get her."

I nod and step around her as CJ follows. Once I'm through the threshold and the door is clicked closed behind us, I try to relax, but it's pointless. The same squeaky wooden floors run the entire length of the foyer to the hall. The stairs still have the chipping white paint they did when I left, and the outdated pictures of kids that actually look happy decorate the walls. The only difference is the numerous live plants dotted in every corner and on top of every table, I can see. Colorful flowers overflow the vases as Ivy spills out of ceramic pots.

It's a nice touch to liven the place up and make it seem welcoming if you didn't know the kind of shit that really happened within these walls.

As the blonde starts up the stairs, I move back to the door and flip the lock. "Go down the hall, all the way to the kitchen, and guard the door there. It leads straight into the alley. If she tries to run, shoot her."

CJ's eyes widen slightly with my demand, but he doesn't question me. He starts down the hall I indicated, until he disappears right in time. The woman I met at the door descends the stairs first, taking the first few slowly until finally, another woman appears behind her.

And now it all makes sense.

Her face is riddled with scabs, her hair is matted and unwashed, and her clothes are dirty. *She* definitely looks like the type of person to be involved with Clyde and even Raymond. If I had to guess, it's either meth or heroin.

"Amy?" I question with a smile. It's fake, but she doesn't need to know that.

Her eyes dart around, looking for something, and I guess it's CJ. No doubt the other woman mentioned him, and now it has sweet Amy here on edge.

"That's me." She returns my fake smile, doing her best to keep the twitching of her body under control. "Can I help you?"

I nod. "Clyde sent me."

As soon as his name leaves my mouth, her eyes grow wide, and she tries to run to the kitchen. I grab her knotted hair before she can get away and jerk her back to me, watching as she crumples at my feet. "Now, Amy, you and I both know why running isn't smart, right?"

She nods, looking up at me with tears in her eyes.

"Look, I'll pay whatever debt she has," the blonde interrupts. "Just leave. Please." Her begs are desperate, and as much as I would like to do that because I can't stand even being here, I can't. I need to show Clyde I'm still trustworthy and can finish a job. Even if it means coming back to the very place I hate the most.

I turn, intending to give her a reply, but I don't get the chance. As soon as my eyes meet hers, her hand shoots out, curled into a small fist, and connects with my face. "Run Amy!" she screams, but I can't get them both at once.

I decide to go for the blonde since CJ is at the back. He can deal with the junkie.

As Amy scrambles away, I step closer to the blonde. When my chest brushes her, she immediately moves back, never stopping until her back hits the wall. She looks around for an escape, but there isn't one. I have her pinned.

I grab her throat in one hand and squeeze while bringing my nose to hers. "What's your name?" Instead of an answer, she spits in my face.

Her saliva clings to my lips and runs down my chin, and I'd be lying if I said it didn't make my cock hard. Jutting my tongue out, I lick up every drop I can, then run it over her lips. "That isn't an answer."

Her chest heaves as my grip tightens. "Lily." She finally chokes out, knowing she has no other option. "Lily Ciccone."

"You just made a mistake, *Lily*." I squeeze her neck tighter, using my grip to pull her head from the wall before slamming it back.

The picture frames shake, threatening to fall, as a soft scream bubbles from her throat.

"My issue isn't with you, it's with your sister. Do you understand that?" I ask, leaning close to her ear so I know she hears me.

She shakes her head as much as she can. "She's my blood. My family. Her debt is mine, so let me pay it."

When I click my tongue and give her a head shake of my own, she brings her knee up, ready to ram it into my dick, but I lift my leg, blocking hers.

I smile. "So noble, but so stupid. You want to see what happens to bad girls, Lily?"

Her mouth opens on a silent scream, trying to take more air into her lungs as her face starts to pale. I drop my hold, then grab her bicep and lead her through the hall and to the kitchen.

I'm expecting to see CJ there with Amy, but neither are in sight. The backdoor is wide open, with the harsh air swirling inside. With Lily's stunt, I was angry, but now I'm full-blown pissed.

"Where did she go?" I yell, turning my face to Lily.

She moves her free hand to shield her face and shakes her head. "I don't know!"

"I don't like liars."

"I swear! I don't know!" Her body shakes in my hold. Every ounce of courage she had slipping away.

I reach behind me with the hand that's not holding her and retrieve my gun. I put the barrel to her temple and pull the hammer back. "I'm going to ask again. Where is she?"

Her brows knit together, and she squeezes her eyes shut. "Kill me, but that won't answer your question. I don't know where she went."

I let out a breath and jerk my gun from her head and push her away. I was here to collect, not kill. And I know if I feed into my urges, I'll be no better than Clyde. Clean up is a bitch, and I have no plausible story to cover shit up. I need to be smart.

"I'll be back, and if you're gone, know that I will find you." I snarl before turning on my heel and storming back down the hall and out the front door.

CHAPTER TWO

Pulling up to Clyde's house, I start debating if what I did was right. Leaving Lily seemed like the best option at the moment, but now I'm not so sure. She could run just like Amy, and there would be no link to find either of them.

I should have just killed her— put a bullet between her eyes— and call it a day, deal with whatever shit Clyde had to say about it, and move on, but I hesitated. And I *never* hesitate.

There was something about her, though. I can't put my finger on what, but her attitude excites me. Maybe it's because of her position at South End, and I can finally make that entire place, and the ones who run it, my bitch. Or maybe it's simply her.

I've never had time for women because I've always been so busy running for Clyde, but that is going to change soon. Someone like her by my side could be good. She doesn't take any shit, stands up for herself, and manages to get my dick hard without even trying.

She's the complete opposite of me, but I want to corrupt her. I want to show her exactly why fucking with me is wrong and make her hate to love it.

Before, I always looked at what would be best for Clyde. What would please him and move him further up the totem pole that is the underground network of mobsters— but that ends now. Now it's time to focus on me and build my empire before I dethrone him.

As Alfredo stops the car next to the front of Clyde's house, I bury the thoughts in my head. If I want this shit to work, I need him to think he can still trust me, which means acting as the perfect soldier and admitting my fuck up from last night.

Opening the door, I take a deep breath. "I won't be long." I tell Alfredo. I don't wait for his reply before sliding out and starting up the steps.

About three years after he swept me in from the streets, Clyde moved me to his close circle, which means I have access to his house. I used to pride myself on the fact he had so much trust in me in such a short amount of time, but now I only see it for what it is—making my taking his spot that much easier.

Walking up to the door, I don't even bother to knock. The camera positioned above me will let him know I'm here. Stepping inside, I close the door behind me and cross the foyer, then start down the hall until I make it to the living room in the back of the lowest level.

Clyde is lounging on the couch with his wife tucked under one arm as his twins play on the floor in front of them. "Unc Eric!" Jerry squeals as I stop in the doorway.

He grabs onto my leg and squeezes. I curl my lip and try to shake him off. It's no secret I don't really like kids. They're loud, annoying, and gross. Their tiny hands harbor germs bigger than them, and they're too happy. On top of that, the twins are named Jerry and Bill. If I didn't know their monikers reflected those of late relatives, I would think Clyde hated them.

Looking up, I speak to Clyde. "We have a problem."

He removes his arm from around his wife and leans forward. "What is it?"

"The girl got away and CJ is a ghost." I cross my arms and widen my stance. I tried to warn him about bringing in these kids from the street. Some— like me— turn out great, but more times than not, they're shit and can't get a job done.

He closes his eyes and sucks in a deep breath. Something I've learned he does when he's angry, but he won't do shit about it. He may be above me in many ways, but he knows just how conniving I am. I'm one of the people he wants on his side— not against it.

"Fix it. I don't care how or what you have to do, but I want it resolved in a timely manner, Eric." He spits as he opens his eyes and looks at me.

I give him a nod, then step out of the room and exit the same way I came in. Clyde doesn't care for details. He only wants results, so as my parting gift, I'll do this one last thing.

IT STARTS WITH ME

Walking back to the car, I open the door and slide inside. "Head to South End." I instruct Alfredo.

With a single nod, he puts the SUV in drive and pulls away from Clyde's. Within minutes, we are back at the boy's home and parked across the street. Through the few windows, you can see movement inside. Mainly silhouettes of kids going from one room to another, and occasionally, some of the older ones leave or enter.

We sit for a few hours, just watching and waiting. I was hoping Amy would turn back up, but there hasn't been any sign of her.

With the sun finally disappearing on the horizon, I step out of the car. My issue isn't with the kids, so it's better they aren't around while I try and conduct business. "I'll be back." Alfredo acknowledges my statement by settling further back in his seat.

Crossing the street, I make sure my suit jacket covers the gun at my back. I don't necessarily want to scare Lily. I want her to know I'm watching, and I intend to get what I want. And what I want is her sister. Her too, but it's best I don't act on that.

When I make it to the door, I pause for a moment and listen. It isn't silent, but it isn't as chaotic as I thought it would be either. I grab the knob, surprised when it turns with no resistance.

Bad move, Lily. I think to myself.

I look up the stairs then to the left as I step inside. No kids are running around, but I hear movement in the kitchen. Slowly, I stalk down the hall. When I make it to the end, I stop and watch her move around.

Her back is to me, and she has a small child positioned on her hip. When his head turns and spots me, I raise my hand and place a finger over my lips. Looking at him, I realize he's probably too young to understand, but that isn't the only thing I notice.

His eyes stay locked on me as she pulls a gallon of milk from the fridge then moves to the cabinet above the sink to retrieve a sippy cup. As she pours, I keep my focus on the kid. He's almost an exact copy of the woman holding him. He has the same face structure with a slim nose and high cheekbones, and his eyes... so blue they would make the sky weep— just like Lily. The only difference is his hair. Her's is thin and a pale blonde where his is thick and dark.

When she moves again, it shakes me out of the daze I was in. Grabbing the cup, she secures the lid then turns, finally noticing me. The sippy falls from her grasp and hits the floor, popping the lid and splashing milk all over the cheap linoleum.

She moves back, pressing herself into the counter, and clutches the kid in her arms as I step further into the kitchen. "She isn't here."

"I know."

"Then why are you here?" Her chest heaves quickly, but her voice stays level.

"Because I told you I'd be back. You're the only family Amy has, so she has to come back at some point. I'm making sure I'm here when she does." I answer, telling the half-truth.

I am here for Amy. There is no doubt about that, but at the same time, I'm here for Lily too. She doesn't know it, and I won't admit it, but I want her in every way possible. And as of now, I'll take what I can, which means coming to this fucking hell hole just to see her and watch her get flustered with anger and fear the moment she sees me.

I step even closer, then reach out and grab a lock of the child's hair.

He smiles and grabs my hand. He isn't more than three, so he doesn't realize I'm a bad guy. "Pa—"

Lily clamps her hand over his mouth and jerks him from my grasp. "No, Maxwell." She chastises the baby before looking back at me. "She isn't here." She repeats.

"As I said, I know. I just want to make sure you don't forget I'm always around. When she shows up, I'll be here too." I take a few steps back then turn on my heel.

I wasn't sure what I would do when I made it back here. Clyde probably expected me to kill her, but I won't be doing that. It would be too much of a waste to end a life like hers. So, instead, I'll keep intimidating her—making my presence known in every way I can so that I cross her mind every second of the day.

Soon, Clyde's empire will be mine, and I'll need people on my side in every corner. Whether they help me willingly or from fear is up to them, but I have a feeling sweet Lily will cave soon enough. I need to bide enough time for it to happen as I try and fix the fucked up predicament her sister put me in.

When I make it back to the front door, I turn and see Lily not far behind me, leaning against the wall and watching. "Lock your door, love. I would hate to see someone get in here who isn't invited." I give her a smile and wink as I part ways and head back across the street where Alfredo is waiting.

CHAPTER THREE

"Has it been handled?" Clyde asks, not even giving me a moment to say hello when I answer the phone.

I roll my eyes and cross my ankle over my knee as I unbuckle my seatbelt. "I'm working on it."

I can practically hear the shake of his head and picture the disappointment on his face as there is a brief pause. "Eric, I have you do these jobs because they always end in results— results in a timely manner. I was expecting this to be done by now."

"I understand, but sometimes things take more time than you would think. You taught me that, remember?" I throw his words from years ago back in his face.

"Well, right now I don't have time. Raymond is upset and I told him this would be handled, so handle it." He hangs up before I can reply.

I shove the phone back in my suit jacket and settle further back in my seat. "We're going to be here awhile, Alfredo. Might as well get comfortable."

I never told Clyde how I came back here last night because I knew he would be pissy that I had no new answers to give him, but I have a plan now. Right now, Lily is scared of me, but I don't feel her fear is enough. I need to make sure she sees just how far I'm willing to go to get answers on her sister's whereabouts. So, tonight I'm going to show her.

"You know he's looking for CJ, right?" Alfredo says, dragging me from my thoughts.

"I wouldn't expect anything less. Kid was a coward and ran. Now Clyde will make an example of him."

He shakes his head then twists his body, so he's facing me. "Clyde won't but you will."

"What do you mean?"

"Clyde wants you to be the one to kill him. He was under your watch, so this will serve as a punishment to you, too."

I scoff. "Punishment? He must not know me as well as he thinks."

He shakes his head again. "No, he knows exactly how you are—how you would never turn away the opportunity to shed blood. He has something else planned. Something that ends with your life, as well."

I stay silent with my eyes locked on his, waiting for him to continue.

"He sees his hold on you slipping, Eric. I don't know when, but he plans to use you as an example as well. You need to be careful with how you proceed from here on out."

"Why are you telling me this? I thought your loyalty lies with him."

He sucks in a deep breath. "It did but you're like a son to me. I've watched you grow from a skittish, angry boy into a man with an agenda. I've just come to realize maybe I'm on the wrong side of things lately."

"And what agenda do you think I have?"

He shrugs. "I don't know but I'm hoping you'll let me stick around to find out."

"What makes you think I want you on my side? If you're so easily swayed away from him by me, who's to say you won't do the same to me when someone else comes around?"

He flashes me a smile. "Like I said, you're like a son to me. I feel I've helped mold you in some way and since I don't have kids of my own, I don't want to walk away from that."

He isn't wrong.

Alfredo has been around longer than me, driving me to jobs, helping me make the right decisions. He's the one I always went to when I needed advice, and by that, I mean to bitch about Clyde. It's no secret to anyone in Clyde's close circle that he's changing, and not in a good way. Maybe he just doesn't want to be stuck in the crossfire when someone finally comes unglued and gives Clyde what he deserves.

And that someone will be me.

"So are you asking for a job?"

"No. You'll ask me. Just wanted to let you know where I stand." He turns back around and looks out the windshield.

I turn, letting the conversation die, and glance out the window and see all the lights finally flipped off in the boy's home. Glancing at my watch, I note how late it is. By now, all of the kids and Lily should be snuggled in their beds.

"I'll be back."

Alfredo nods as I step out of the SUV.

Crossing the street, I pull my lock rake from the inside pocket of my jacket and hope Lily took my advice. Regardless, I'll get inside, but I want to gauge how well she follows orders—my orders specifically.

Taking the steps two at a time, I stop when I make it to the door. I jiggle the knob, surprised it's actually locked. I slip the rake inside the hole and shimmy it until I feel it hit the tumbler. I wiggle it again before turning it and disengaging the lock completely.

Once I open the door, I pull the rake from the keyhole and slip it back into my pocket. I make sure I close it softly behind me before starting up the steps. Since I lived here before, I have an advantage by knowing the layout. If someone wakes up, I can sneak around like a shadow— knowing exactly where I can go to remain unseen.

When I make it to the hallway at the top of the stairs, I pause. Everything is silent. No creaking wood, no hushed voices. One by one, I open doors slowly, only giving myself long enough to let my eyes adjust from the dim light in the hallway to the dark rooms before closing them and moving to the next. Opening the last door, I find what I'm looking for.

Her room is small and almost identical to all the others, with dingy-looking walls and ugly green carpet. But one thing that stands out is the old metal crib across from her small twin-sized bed.

I pad over to her bed, thankful for the small lamp on her nightstand because it gives me just enough light to see her features. I already know what she looks like— every curve, freckle— It's burned into my memory, but this is a side I haven't got to see before. She looks peaceful. Completely unbothered and unaware I'm even here.

I could stand here and watch her sleep all night. Count the strands of blonde hair splayed across her pillow, try and decode the words spilling from her lips with no sound, but that isn't why I'm here. I'm here to send a message.

Brushing the few strands of wayward hair from her face, I tuck them behind her ear and tear my gaze from her. Moving to the crib, I do the same thing.

Pause.

Watch.

Think.

You never realize how crazy genetics are until it's right in front of you like now. His resemblance to his mother is uncanny—almost an exact replica, but still so different. I watch as his small body moves with every breath he takes and wonder if my plan will even work, and that's frustrating. I've never been one to care what people think or worry if I hurt them, but for some reason, the thought of causing Lily pain makes me feel something.

Something I've never felt before.

Shaking the thoughts away, I lean over the crib and grab the boy's limp body. As soon as I have him tucked against my shoulder, his head raises. From my peripheral, I see his sleep blue eyes lock on my face. Turning and exiting the room, I raise my finger to my lips, then close the door behind us.

"I'm not going to hurt you, Max. Your mommy just needs a lesson on how far someone is willing to go to get what they want."

Of course, he doesn't even reply. Hell, I don't even know if he's old enough to form sentences. If I had to guess, he's maybe only three, but what do I know? Kids aren't my thing.

When we make it to the bottom of the stairs, I finally turn and look at him. He's still staring at me with curiosity, but he isn't scared. It strikes me as odd because I heard kids know when someone is bad— they can sense it like some sort of animal— but he's completely calm.

"Papa." His quiet voice is high-pitched and soft all at the same time.

I shake my head and cock a brow at him as I slip back out the front door. "No. Eric." I point to myself with my thumb. "Eric. Not papa."

Nuzzling his head back in the crook of my neck, he closes his eyes and repeats himself. "Papa."

Rolling my eyes, I don't even try to argue. What's the point? He wouldn't understand. So, I look both ways before crossing the street and slip back into the SUV with Alfredo.

CHAPTER FOUR

"So, why the baby?" Alfredo asks once we pull away.

"He's not a baby, he's a toddler." I look down at Max's sleeping body in the seat next to me, then change the subject. "She needs to realize just how close I can get when I want."

"So you steal a whole child?" I can hear the concern in his voice.

"Not steal— borrow. We're going to bring him back. I just need to prove something to not only her, but Clyde too."

"What is that supposed to mean?"

"Clyde is starting to lose his trust in me. I knew it the moment he sent me to South End and you only confirmed it earlier. If I can show him I'm still as ruthless, maybe it will earn some of it back and bide me more time."

"More time for what?"

"You sure are asking a lot of questions tonight."

He shakes his head as he continues towards Clyde's place. "I just don't want to see this innocent baby hurt because you're having a dick measuring contest with Clyde."

"Wow. Alfredo has balls tonight." I laugh to myself.

Swerving to the side of the road, he slams on the breaks and throws the car in park. "I'm serious, Eric. A child this small has no business in this life regardless of who his family is."

I tip my head and lean forward in my seat. "Yeah? Are you going to stop me then?"

"If I need to, yes, but you're not stupid. You may think you have everyone fooled into thinking you're a heartless monster, but I see the real side of you."

"Real side?"

He nods. "The side you think you hide. The one where you stare at that woman's silhouette through the window too long. Or how right now, you're making sure your voice stays low so you don't wake him." He shakes his head and turns around. "You can try and play it off all you want, but I see your armor cracking."

I narrow my eyes at the back of his head before pushing back in my seat. "Why do you care so much? The kid isn't even yours."

"Why do you?" He counteracts my question with his own before putting the SUV back in drive and pulling away from the curb.

I let his words hang in the air because I don't know the answer myself. At first, I only looked at Lily as a distraction in the grand scheme of things. It is a way to put some of my focus somewhere else because I get sloppy when my mind isn't clear, and she made it easy with her attitude and stubbornness. Now, I feel it's more than that.

I don't want to hurt her— or even Max— in the slightest way. Maybe in some twisted corner of my mind, I can see myself having a life with her, and I mean more than her standing by my side when I take over Clyde's empire.

I see... happiness? Honestly, I'm not even sure what that word means, but I wouldn't mind figuring it out with her.

"I'm sorry, Eric," Alfredo starts, breaking the long silence that's enveloped us. "I just don't have children of my own and I'm past that time. I tend to take kids' well-being seriously."

I let his words bounce around my mind for a moment. "Don't apologize. Sometimes the best things to say are the words some people don't want to hear. I get it and you don't have to worry. I have no intentions of hurting this kid."

"You don't but not everyone is you."

I shake my head as I rub Max's back. "I don't plan to let anyone else hurt him either."

I can see the slight smile on his lips as we pass under street lights. "I always knew you had some sort of heart under all the tough, don't-give-a-shit exterior."

"Don't let it go to your head, Alfredo. I don't even like kids."

He scoffs. "You say that, but I see you having a ton in the future."

"A ton? And who is going to help raise them? You?"

As he pulls through the gates of Clyde's house, he replies with a shrug. "Maybe. I'm past my prime. No man will want to go through that process with me."

I roll my eyes and gather Max's body into my arms as he comes to a stop. I always knew Alfredo liked men, but he's never voiced it. By him making that one tiny comment, I feel we've reached a new level of trust. Maybe he won't be so bad to keep around when I take Clyde to the ground.

"Give me half an hour. I'll be back." He nods as I exit the car holding the toddler against my chest.

Walking to the door, I already know he'll be awake. He's like a nocturnal animal—conducting most of his business in the night. He's under the impression that cloaked in darkness, he's untouchable, and the rules don't apply to him. Maybe it's more than that, though. Perhaps he thinks it will protect him, but you know what they say.

What's done in the dark will always come to light.

When I step through the threshold, it's a whole new world. Outside everything was quiet. Businesses are closed. Everyone is asleep, but not the Gallo's. The entire inside is lit up with maid's making their rounds, polishing the banister and sweeping the floors as a nanny chases the twins around.

"Watch him." I tell the nanny, passing Max's sleeping body to her. Her eyes grow wide with questions, but she doesn't voice them. She knows better.

Once She has a good hold on him, I turn on my heel and make my way down the hall and to the back living room.

As soon as Clyde's eyes land on me, he speaks. "Hopefully you come with answers."

I shrug. "Not necessarily."

"Then why are you here?"

"Because I have an idea and figured you'd like to be in the know."

He waves his hand, telling me to continue.

"I took her kid. He's with the nanny now, but I need evidence of him being here. I figure if she realizes how serious I am, she'll crack and give up her sister's location."

His eyes widen with surprise. "Kidnapping? That's a new one for you, Eric."

"Anything to get the job done."

His eyes narrow at me as he stands. "You sure that's all this is—a job?"

I pull my brows together. "Of course."

He nods slowly. "Good. Get this settled so you can handle something else for me."

"What do you need?" I cross my wrist in front of me and widen my stance, trying to look unbothered, but the truth is, I'm bothered as fuck.

The thought of being done with taunting Lily—making her squirm and question her morals—makes me feel angry.

Walking to one of the end tables, he pulls out a polaroid camera and tosses it in my direction. "We'll worry about it when the time comes. For now, finish this shit."

I catch the camera with a nod before turning around and walking back to the foyer where I left Max with the nanny.

When he sees me, his sleepy face lights up. He stands on wobbly legs, dropping the applesauce in his hand and tries to walk toward me. "Papa."

I don't even acknowledge his words and snap a photo before he can make it to me. The flash stuns him for all of three seconds before he shakes it away and closes the gap between us. As his chubby arms wrap around my legs, I snag the picture from the camera and wave it around a bit before looking at it.

It isn't the clearest of pictures, but you can most definitely tell the kid is Max. The twins stand behind him, almost shadowed from the angle, but they're visible too. Deciding it's good enough, I hand the camera to the nanny, scoop Max into my arms, and shove the picture into the pocket of my suit jacket.

"Thanks," is the only thing I say to her as I exit Clyde's house.

Slipping back into the SUV, I direct Alfredo to head back to South End.

The short drive is quiet. We've done enough talking for the night, so I'm thankful it's done, but in the silence, my mind screams. Staring down at Max, a thought hits me.

All this time, I've thought Clyde was stupid for bringing in teens from the streets to do his dirty work, but maybe it isn't that stupid after all. Only instead of waiting for them to be grown, why not raise them yourself. It's the perfect way to make sure all of your beliefs and morals are instilled into them without the worry of betrayal. Because what child would betray the one who gives them the world?

As we pull up to South End, I let the thought linger in the back of my mind. That's another worry for another day. Right now, I need to get Max back into bed without Lilly noticing.

When Alfredo parks, I pick Max back up— thankful the car ride seems to lull him to sleep— then cross the street again. Since I left the

IT STARTS WITH ME

door unlocked, it's easy to slip inside and up the stairs. When I make it to Lily's room, I crack the door and see her still peacefully sleeping—none the wiser that I took her most precious belonging.

I pat Max's back as I cross the room then lay him back in his crib. Once I'm confident he won't stir, I turn around and grab the picture from my pocket. Laying it on her nightstand, I give her one last look before leaving again.

CHAPTER FIVE

I guess Clyde thinks I'm too close to the job with Lily because he sent me to collect elsewhere. Normally, I don't do any other collections until the previous one is done. It just makes things run smoother with fewer mistakes. I can't say he's wrong, though, but I don't know how he would know either. It isn't like I voiced my infatuation for Lily, but then again, if Alfredo can see it, am I really doing a good job at hiding it?

I shake the thoughts away as I wipe the blood from my knuckles. Kicking the poor fool who caught my furry below me, I turn to the goon Clyde sent to watch me. "Clean this shit up and make sure you don't leave with any blood on you."

"And where are you going?" He asks as I turn away.

Scoffing, I glance over my shoulder. "That's none of your fucking business."

He holds up his hands in surrender. "Sorry, Eric. I was just told to—"

"Told to watch me?" I finish for him.

He shakes his head. "No. Told to stay with you, Clyde thinks I can learn a thing or two from you."

I shake my head with a smile. Clyde thinks he's smart, but I know exactly why he wants this guy with me. Whoever he is, he's moldable and ready to please Clyde any way he can— even if that means ratting me out for whatever Clyde thinks is going on.

"I'll deal with Clyde. Just do what I said and then find something or someone else to occupy your time." I turn back around and exit the warehouse before he can reply.

I don't particularly appreciate being watched, but knowing Clyde's trust in me is slipping makes this ten times worse. I was hoping the shit last night would curve his uneasiness. That he would see, there is nothing to worry about when it comes to me, but clearly, that isn't the case. Now he has someone keeping tabs on me, which makes figuring out this shit with Amy while keeping Lily safe more difficult.

In this life, it's best you don't keep friends or make a family. They automatically turn into a liability and can be used against you. I know this, and I've lived by it, only ever giving women enough time to suck my dick and swallow my cum before I kick them to the curb. But with Lily, it's different.

Women practically fall at my feet and drool from the mouth when all I do is look their way. Being the type of man I am and knowing I work for Clyde is only a bonus to them. The bad boy allure gets them going, but not Lily.

She's scared of me but tries to hide it, all while masking the clear attraction I can see in her eyes when she stares at me, and that turns me on.

I want to break her— dirty her pure soul and have her screaming my name. I want to fucking own her. But that won't be possible with Clyde in the way.

Once I make it out of the warehouse, I walk across the parking lot and slip back into the SUV with Alfredo. "I need to go back to South End."

"You really think that's a good idea with him watching your every move?" Alfredo asks, motioning to where I left Clyde's goon behind.

"I don't care. He'll be busy cleaning that up for a while and I need to follow up with what I did last night."

He shakes his head but doesn't argue as he puts the vehicle in drive.

I know he can see it— my control slipping— but this doesn't make me lose sight of what needs to happen in the long run. I'm still going to bring Clyde down and take over all that is his. This is simply a detour. A new path I can't see to get off of. Somehow, Lily has infiltrated my mind and won't leave, and I'm not sure I want her to.

When we pull up to South End, I waste no time getting out of the car. I cross the street quickly, watching all the passersby and vehicles just to see if, by some chance, Amy's face pops up, but it doesn't. At this point, it doesn't even matter to me, honestly. It's just an excuse to see Lily anyway.

At first, I did care. I've always wanted to please Clyde and let him know he could count on me, but that changed. I'm not sure when, but it did, and I'm not upset about it. I feel I could run this city better than him. The shit with Amy and CJ were just icing on top of the cake. If Clyde did shit the way he should and stayed out of bed with Raymond, people would fear him more.

He thinks the only way to run things is by loyalty, but that's another thing he has wrong. The only way to keep people in line is with fear.

When I make it to the door, I don't bother knocking. I can hear kids on the other side playing or watching TV, so I know she won't be far. Stepping inside, I cross the foyer and start down the hall before hanging a right under the stairs and into the living room.

Lily's back is to me as I lean against the door jamb. She's passing out snacks and juice boxes to all of the kids sitting on the floor playing with wooden toys and the ones on the furniture with their eyes glued to the television.

When she finally turns around and locks eyes with me, her face goes pale. Quickly, she hurries towards me before pushing past me and heading to the kitchen. Slowly, I follow.

She leans over the sink with both hands braced on the counter. "How could you?" She whisper shouts.

"I take it you got my message?"

Turning around, she pulls the polaroid I left on her nightstand out of her pocket before crumpling it up and throwing it at me. "My son has no part in this!"

Stepping forward, I grab the picture from the ground then press my chest against hers. "This," I start, holding it to eye level with her. "Is to show you just how serious I am."

Her lip curls, and her brows furrow. "He's a child."

"And I don't give a shit."

Her small hand shoots up and swings towards my face. I catch her wrist and dig my nails into her flesh. Her chest heaves— every quick inhale making her tits push against my pectorals— but she stays silent.

I stare into her blue orbs, trying to decipher whatever it is she's thinking. Her nostrils flare, and the vein in her neck throbs.

Anger.

That's what it is, but under all of that, I see the desire. The slight pink tone that paints her cheeks. The way her lips part and her tongue juts out to lick them when I move my eyes to them. I can feel my heartbeat quicken and the mere thought of running my lips over hers, and my palms get sweaty.

I lower my head, so I'm even with her stare, and she doesn't move. Her breaths stop, and her body goes rigid. I'm not sure if she wants me as badly as I want her, but I don't waste time by asking. Leaning down further in one quick swoop, I plant my lips to hers. Immediately, heat settles in my belly, and every muscle in my body relaxes.

She tries to pull away, but I snake my other arm behind her and lock it around the small of her back. With her free hand, she pushes on my chest. I stumble slightly but never let my lips leave hers.

"You want this as much as me. I know it, so stop fighting and give in." I breathe through our sealed lips.

Her head shakes vigorously, so I drop my hold on her and push my hands into her hair.

"I hate you." She whines, limp and helpless in my arms.

"No, you don't."

As if all it took was that one simple statement, she finally gives in. Her small arms wrap around me as her legs spread, and one skates up the outside of my thigh. Moving my hands down, I reach behind and grip her ass before lifting her and placing her on the counter.

"Do you want to fuck me because you hate me or because you want to know what it's like to be claimed?" I ask, moving my lips to the pulsing vein in her neck.

A small moan escapes her, but that's the only reply I get before the phone in my pocket is ringing.

I curse under my breath and pull away. Usually, I ignore anyone who interrupts me, but I can't risk it since I'm already on thin ice with Clyde.

Almost as if she's pulled out of a daze, Lily looks at me with glassy eyes as I jerk the phone from my pocket. She blinks a few times before the same look of anger is back on her face. She slips off the counter and plants her hands on my chest before pushing me away.

"Fuck you."

I scoff as I hold the still ringing phone in my hand. "I almost did and I plan to be back to finish this."

Her jaw tics as she shakes her head and pushes past me roughly, then returns to the living room.

Taking a deep breath, I hit the answer button and bring the phone to my ear. "What?"

"I'm not sure why you think you're able to bark orders at my men, but you need to get back to the warehouse. There is another job waiting for you." I can hear the annoyance in Clyde's voice.

"What is it?" I reply, not bothering to hide my annoyance. He just cock blocked me without even trying.

"CJ." That's all he says before hanging up.

CHAPTER SIX

Pulling back up to the warehouse, my anger is no longer simmering. It's full-blown boiling. I tried to tell Clyde CJ wasn't ready for this shit months ago, but it didn't do any good. Before, Clyde would listen to me —take my thoughts into consideration—but he's gotten to the point where the power he wants is blinding. It's too bad all he's done will be pointless because I plan to take it all.

I just need to bide my time, do my job, and hit him when he doesn't expect it. Which means dealing with CJ. Yes, he ran under my watch, but I'm not a fucking babysitter. Even though I knew he wasn't ready, I didn't think he would pussy out this way. So, if Clyde wants to use him as an example, fine, but I refuse to let him get the upper hand on me.

When Alfredo stops the car, I step out and make my way to the entrance. The same guy from earlier is lingering around the front, smoking a cigarette, and staring at me down the bridge of his nose. He's probably pissed I got him in hot water with Clyde, but I don't give a fuck. Other people's feelings aren't my problem.

He opens his mouth as I walk by, but I disappear inside before he can mumble a word. I look around the bare warehouse, trying to see if anything seems out of place. Since Clyde is questioning me, I wouldn't be surprised if this is some sort of set-up. Everything seems normal enough. The floor is damp from the cleanup of the guy before, and dusty wooden boxes line the walls, leaving the vast center bare other than a single metal chair, with a bloody CJ tied to it.

His head is drooping low with crusty blood clinging to his ashy blonde hair. Clearly, whoever found him already did a number on him. As I step closer and my shoes come into his view, he lifts his head.

I can barely recognize the kid sitting in front of me. His face is swollen in numerous spots, with various shades of purple and blue painting his skin, along with blood still trickling from his nose and mouth. I know I should feel bad— or maybe even sad— but I was never programmed that way. Fear, blood, corruption. All it means to me is power.

This is a consequence of his actions and nothing else. I have no pity for him. And with that thought, I get angry all over again.

Not because of him necessarily, but the fact I can look at him in the state he's in and feel nothing, but when I think of Lily, I feel all the shit I shouldn't. If it weren't for him, I wouldn't be in this position. I wouldn't have to position myself in her life to fix the mistake *he* made.

Without a word, I ball my hand into a fist and send it into his ribs. I can already feel the broken bones, detached from their spots, floating under his skin, and all it does is make me want to do it again, but I refrain.

"Eric... Please..." His pleas are weak and gurgled.

"Please? Please what, CJ?" I seethe.

"Don— don't do this." His once vibrant eyes are hollow and vacant.

I shake my head as I remove my suit jacket and fold it neatly before placing it on the ground a few feet away. "You know why I have to do this."

He shimmies weakly against his restraints. "You don't."

I'm sure I see a tear slip from his swollen eye socket, and again, it makes me feel nothing. "Even if I didn't," I start, pacing in front of him. "That doesn't change the fact that I want to."

His eyes follow me as I pace. A look of horror and realization mixed in his features. "You want to kill me?"

I'm not sure why he asks because he already knows the answer. It has to be noticeable. "I do."

"Why?"

I stop and tip my head as I hike the sleeves of my dress shirt up. "Why does anyone do anything in this world, CJ? Power? Money? Simply because it's an urge?"

He shakes his head. "But you're different— different than Clyde."

I close my eyes and inhale a deep breath as I squat in front of him. The smell of blood floods my nostrils and makes my heart beat faster with excitement. "You're right, kid. I am different, but not in the way you think." I stand back to my full height and roll my neck before cracking my knuckles. "I'm much worse."

His body starts to tremble so hard the metal legs of the chair clank against the concrete floor, and it pulls a smile to my lips. I'm going to make sure he suffers. Not only did he make me look bad with Clyde, but it made him question my motives before I wanted. And to top it off, it's because of him I had to leave Lily tonight. I could have been so deep in her cunt at this very moment, but he ruined it.

"Hey!" CJ jumps at my booming voice as the goon from outside steps in with my call. I don't know his name, and I don't care to. He's nothing to me.

When he stops in front of me, I take a good look at his face before snarling a single command. "Go get my bag from the back of the SUV."

Whoever he is doesn't question me this time. He obeys like the good dog he is and fetches my bag. When he comes back, I take it and order him away, then turn my focus back to CJ. "I'm going to make this brutal. You fucked up a lot by doing what you did."

He shakes his head vigorously and pushes his back harder into the chair. "You don't have to." He whines.

"I told you, I may not have to, but I want to."

Sobs and soft whimpers come from him as I lay my bag on the floor and open it. This isn't my first time doing shit like this, but it's the first time in a while where I want to make it as terrible as possible. Typically, I don't give a fuck about talking or going back and forth, but with CJ, I want him to suffer. I want him to see everything I do to him and remember me when he makes it to hell.

First, I pull out the small baggie of MDMA and lay it on the ground. Then, I grab my pliers and pruning shears. I'm not exactly sure what I have planned just yet, but I know it will come to me.

Scooping the small baggie from the ground, I open it and shake the small pill into my hand. Walking back to CJ, I straddle his lap and grip his cheeks with my pointer and thumb, then squeeze, forcing him to open his mouth. He tries to fight, but he's already so weak that there is no point. He knows I'll win.

Once it hits his tongue, I plug his nose and cover his mouth with my other hand. "This will increase your heart rate and make you feel everything deeper. Normally, people use it for pleasure, but I like to use it for pain."

His eyes grow wide despite the wicked swelling before he starts shaking his head again and jerking his body. Instead of trying to combat his pathetic excuse of fighting, I push my feet on the ground, making the chair teeter back for a split second before letting it crash to the ground.

The impact has him sucking in a deep breath which results in him swallowing the pill. I give him a smile and unclamp my hand from his mouth. "See, that wasn't so bad, was it?" He sucks air into his mouth anxiously, searching for the breath the impact stole from him as I stare down at him, still smiling, trying to think of my next move.

Just when I'm about to move and stand him back up, I feel wet warmth seep into the back of my pants. I stand up, then grip the back of the chair and return it to its original position. Glancing at the crotch of his pants from over his shoulder, I see the wet spot on the denim growing.

"Did you just piss on me?" I ask, stepping back in front of him.

More sobs and cries, but no reply.

I tsk out loud, clicking my teeth to show my disgust, as I walk to where my pliers lay on the floor. "And here I thought you had some fucking dignity. I guess I was wrong."

I uncurl his vice-like grip on the chair's arm and lay his fingers flat against the metal. One by one, I begin plucking the fingernails from his digits. With each one, his screams grow louder, and it does nothing but make me want to keep going.

Once all ten are removed, I take a step back and admire my work. Blood trickles from his fingertips, forming small puddles of blood below them. "You know, even if you didn't want to kill that bitch Amy, you could have stopped her and none of this would be happening."

I reach down and drop the pliers, then grab my sheers. "If you would have just manned up and stuck around for five more minutes —five minutes, CJ—all of this could have been avoided. Now, not only have you pissed off Clyde, but I'm sure Raymond also has it out for you. Even if I was to let you go— which would never happen— you wouldn't last a day. And to top it all off, you fucked up my own plan."

I step back to him and place his left pinky between the shears. "You see, I was going to bring Clyde down— steal everything he had. All I had to do was mind my P's and Q's for a few more weeks. You know, get a really good plan of execution together, but now he's questioning me. And he wouldn't be if it wasn't for you.

"Not only did you leave that night, but you stuck me with the mess, and that pretty, tight bodied blonde is a part of it. She's a fucking distraction I don't need and is making me question shit of my own."

I'm not sure why I'm divulging all this to him, but it feels good in a way. Like a weight I didn't mind carrying is lifted off my shoulders, but it doesn't cloud my anger completely.

I squeeze the sheers together and rejoice in his screams as his pinky falls to the ground. They're music to my ears and make my dick hard coupled with the mere thought of Lily. Blood spews from the wound in a steady beat. With every pump of his heart, more blood pours out.

The sight makes me want more. More blood. More power. More everything. So, I place his ring finger between them next and sever it.

"Eric!" He screams.

It's funny he thinks calling my name will save him. Screaming my name for mercy only makes me feel like the God I know I am.

Next, I slice his middle finger off. His screams grow fainter, but I can still hear them. Just as I'm placing his pointer between the shears, ol' goon I don't give a shit about comes back in. I want to tell him to leave, but if he wants a show, I'll give it to him.

I drop the sheers and unbuckle CJ's pants. With some effort and strategic maneuvering, I get them along with his boxers, down around his ankles.

"What the fuck man?" The guy asks with a disgusted look on his face.

I shrug. "If Clyde wants him to be an example and you're here, you can tell everyone what happens to pussies who run and fuck him over."

Picking the sheers back up, I lean down to whisper in CJ's ear as I place his shriveled limp dick between them. "This is for cock blocking me."

Before I can squeeze them together and see his manhood fall to the floor, his mouth opens, using the last bit of energy he has to speak. "He's conspiring against Clyde. He told me! Him and the blonde from South End!"

I let out a chuckle before clipping his cock from his body, then reach behind me and pull the gun I have tucked in the waist of my pants. Quickly, I press the barrel between his eyes and pull the trigger.

I would have loved to watch him suffer from getting his dick chopped off, but I couldn't risk it. If the prick was willing to scream those words as his last, there is no telling what else he would say.

"Clearly he was saying anything to try and get free." I growl in the guy's direction.

He looks at me with skepticism before finally making his face more somber. "Yeah, for sure." He laughs, and I know it's fake, but what the fuck is he going to do? It's my word against CJ's.

Reaching down, I grab CJ's dick and throw it at him. He fumbles a bit, finally catching it before looking disgusted. "Take that to Clyde. I have other business to handle."

As I walk out, I can hear him dry heaving, but it doesn't stop me. With all of the adrenaline still pumping through my veins, I'm going to go finish what I started with Lily.

CHAPTER SEVEN

Luckily, Alfredo didn't ask any questions when I slipped back into the car. It's almost like he knew I didn't want him to. He just put it in drive and brought me right back where I needed to be. He knew I had shit I needed to finish with Lily, even if he didn't know the specifics.

I leave the car without a word knowing he'll wait— he always waits — and cross the street. When I make it to the door, I'm surprised it's unlocked. It's a silent invitation she didn't even realize she gave me. Maybe she doesn't see it, but I do. She wants me.

Sneaking inside, everything is silent. No kids litter the living room as I pass it, and all the lights are off, minus the kitchen. When I step through the threshold, I see her. It isn't hard considering she's the only one there, but even in a crowded room, I don't think I'd miss her. Her body calls to me without words. The way she moves. The way her eyes stare into my soul when she looks at me. It's silent communication, but I know the language.

Her back is to me as she fills a kettle with water and sets it on the stove. She stares at it a moment before turning around and catching sight of me.

Before I can get a single word out, she shakes her head. "No. You need to leave."

I smirk. Her mouth says one thing, but her body says another, and she doesn't even know it. Her knees press together tightly, and she licks her lips. "You don't want me to leave, Lily."

She swallows hard, almost like she's forcing herself to say the next sentence. "Yes I do. Earlier was a mistake. I'm not sure what came over me but that can't happen again."

I step closer, invading her personal space. I swear I can smell the pheromones rolling off her skin as I watch the vein in her neck throb faster and faster. "Can't or won't?"

She takes a step back, putting a few inches of space between us. "Both. Now leave." She raises a shaky hand and points to the kitchen doorway.

Grabbing her hand lightly, I flip it over and kiss her wrist. "You don't want that, Lily."

"Y—yes I do." I follow her eyes as they land on my hand, stained with blood.

I pull her to me with the hand I'm holding and place it behind my back. Pressing my elbow into my side, I lock her arm around me so she can't move. "Stop denying whatever this is. Just give in." I whisper before flicking my tongue over the shell of her ear.

"I'm not scared of you, Eric. You can't force me to fuck you out of fear."

"There won't be any forcing, baby. You'll fuck me because you want to."

Her body shudders against mine. It's like my words are already getting to her, and she can't stand that. "No."

I walk her backwards until her back hits the fridge, then move so I can look into her eyes. "Tell me you don't want me and I'll leave."

Her brows knit together. "I don't want you."

Smiling, I brush the hair from her face and tuck it behind her ear. "Now tell me you don't want me and mean it."

She pauses, staying silent for a beat before she opens her mouth to speak again, but I don't let her. I swallow her words with my mouth. If she had said them, I wouldn't have left. Fuck that. I'm going to take what's mine. But I didn't want to hear her mumble them.

"You want to fuck me and that pisses you off, doesn't it?" I let out between kisses.

She keeps her lips clamped shut, refusing to kiss me or even answer me, but it's fine. She'll cave.

Sliding my hand down the front of her body, I finger the elastic of her sweatpants, letting my knuckles brush against her skin. Goosebumps break out on her skin. Leaning down, I kiss every single one before opening my mouth wide and scraping my teeth against her flesh. A soft moan escapes her, and all it does is make my dick grow harder.

IT STARTS WITH ME

I drop to my knees in front of her and grab the sides of her pants. Slowly, I pull them down, waiting to see if she'll stop me. She doesn't. Instead, she stares at the wall across from her, refusing to look at me.

"Look at me." I demand.

She shakes her head slightly, keeping her eyes locked on the wall.

"Look at me, Lily. I don't like asking twice."

She unhurriedly drags her eyes to mine. So much contempt. So much anger. But so much passion all at once. "I don't think someone on their knees should be giving orders." She spits.

That gets my blood pumping even more. Standing up, I press my body against hers and grip her wrists in my hands. "Is this better?" I ask, looking over her short frame. "Or would you prefer it rougher? Is that what you want?"

When she doesn't answer, I back up and jerk her body with me. I drag her across the small kitchen before I release her and flip her body around. Bending her over the counter, I rip her panties down, exposing her plump ass. "I murdered a man tonight and all I could think about was you. Does it excite you to know you can get the big bad man's dick hard?" Still no answer.

I skim my fingers over her slit from behind, letting her juices coat my fingers, then pop her ass. "I think it does." I remark, reaching around so she can see her arousal glistening on my fingers.

"Fuck you," is the only thing I get from her.

"Oh, I plan to baby."

Placing her palms on the edge of the counter, she thrusts herself back, pushing me away. When she turns, her blue eyes shine with unshed tears. I'm expecting more insults, more shit-talking, something, but instead, she surprises me.

Launching forward, she grabs my face in her tiny hands and pulls my mouth to hers. It isn't a sweet kiss or even a lust-filled out. This—this kiss is angry.

Her teeth hit mine as her tongue skates across my lips. "I don't even like you." She breathes, never letting her assault slow.

"You don't have to like me to fuck me."

Grabbing her ass, I hoist her up, never breaking our kiss, and plant her ass on the counter. She wraps her legs around me and locks her ankles together. Reaching down, I grab the hem of her shirt and lift it over her head. Pert, pink nipples stare at me and beg to be tasted.

Pushing her body back, I lean my head down and capture one in my mouth. I flick it with my tongue and relish how her body shudders. Moving to the other, I do the same. I want to kiss, lick, and bite every inch of her body. I want to claim her and let the world know she's mine, but it's too dangerous, so I'll settle for this.

At least for now.

Pulling away, I make her legs fall from around me long enough to undo my pants and free my cock. After this, there will be no going back. She'll be mine even if I can't have her by my side.

Pushing myself forward, I nudge her entrance. Her head falls back, and her hands snake around to grip my back. As soon as I slide into her, her nails dig into my skin. I bite the inside of my cheek, urging myself not to come at the mixture of pleasure and pain.

Slowly, I start to thrust, enjoying every fucking inch sliding in and out of her wet cunt. The feeling is more than I'm used to. This isn't a woman who fell at my feet ready to give in to my every command. She's feisty and brutal, and now I've fucking claimed her.

It's part of the allure. The forbidden. She shouldn't want to fuck me— shouldn't enjoy the way my hands send heat gliding across her body— but she does. And that... that will ruin her for anyone else. Once I'm done with her, no other man will be able to bring her body to the heights I have.

I pick up the tempo and listen to the erratic breaths falling from her lips. She's trying to be quiet. "Scream for me, baby."

She shakes her head, pulling me even closer even though our bodies have already eaten up every free inch of space.

"Let me hear you, Lily." I demand again.

When she doesn't comply, I increase my speed again and lock my mouth around her neck. I kiss her lightly before opening my mouth and clamping my teeth onto her delicate skin.

"Ahhh!" It's a mixture of brutal pain and complete euphoria.

"That's it." I praise.

Within seconds, I feel her walls start to close in around my cock. The pressure is too much, so I do the exact thing I asked of her. I let go and shoot my seed inside of her.

CHAPTER EIGHT

"Eric! Are you listening?" Clyde booms, dragging me out of my thoughts and transporting me back to where all of this started. The very first day, he sent me to South End to handle Amy, which resulted in me meeting Lily.

Ever since last night, I haven't been able to get her off my mind. Finally, being inside of her has clouded all of my thoughts. She's completely consumed me, but this isn't' a life for her. It can't be. She's too pure. Hell, she's a fucking mother. It would be a whole new level of dark for me to drag her into this shit, knowing it would put a target on her back. But at the same time, I think I could protect her. Keep her locked away and all to myself, never letting a soul know about her.

I know she wouldn't allow that thought. She's too hard-headed.

"Eric!" He booms again when I don't respond.

I shake my head lightly to clear my thoughts. "Sorry. What?"

His lips press into a hard line. "South End. What's going on with that bitch?"

My blood starts to boil as the word rolls off his tongue. How dare he call my woman out of her name, but I have to keep my cool. Showing even the slightest irritation will only make him suspicious.

Shifting on my feet as I stand in front of him, I cross my wrists over my front and act unbothered. "What about her?"

He tips his head. "Why hasn't there been any news? What the fuck is going on? I've given you plenty of time to handle this shit."

I shrug. "I've done everything I can to get info from her, but either she's tough as fucking rocks or doesn't have anything to give. I think at this point, we need to focus on luring Amy out, but it'll be a lot of work. Are you willing to spend the time and resources on that for someone like Raymond?"

A sick smirk pulls the corner of his lips up. "Killing her would be easier. It'll tie up the loose ends and lure Amy out, but seeing as you can't seem to get the job done, I'll handle it."

My stomach drops to the soles of my feet, and I can feel the sweat start to bead up on my forehead.

Kill her? He can't fucking kill her.

"I can handle it." I try to change his mind, but when Clyde says something, that's it. There is no argument or discussion. What he says goes because he's the boss.

He shakes his head as he stands from the couch. "What's done is done. Go make sure the clean up with CJ is done since you couldn't be bothered to stick around last night. I don't want this shit coming back on us."

My heart beats faster inside my chest, but I keep my stance and face stoic. He can't know I'm upset. It will only fuel his vendetta. "Fine. When do you plan to kill the girl?"

"Tonight. Now go." he waves me off.

I give him a curt nod, then exit his living room, then the front door. Making sure to keep my pace steady, I make it to Alfredo in the SUV and start talking before I can even close the door. "Go. We need to get some things in place."

Without question, he does as I ask as I pull my cell from my pocket. Dialing the landline of South End, I curse to myself when all it does is ring over and over. I'm ready to hang up— say fuck it and drive there and get her now— but I know Clyde is watching. If I had to guess, the fucker who was at the warehouse last night relayed what CJ said, then and it had Clyde on edge.

If I go to South End now, all it will do is confirm whatever he may be thinking, and I don't want that. I need to think. I need a plan.

As the phone rings again, I direct Alfredo back to the warehouse, and her voice pours through the speaker. "This is South End Boy's Home, how can I help you?"

"Lily?"

I swear I can hear her heartbeat pick up speed over the line. "Leave me alone, Eric—"

"Don't hang up on me. It's an emergency." I cut her off, not bothering with any sort of formalities.

After a beat of silence, she speaks again. "What do you mean?"

"Clyde— the man your sister got in trouble with— he's going to be showing up there this evening. I don't want you to panic though. Continue as if everything is okay and I will be there soon for you and Max."

"Wh— no. I can't leave the other children and you're delusional if you think I'll be going anywhere with you." Her voice is raised a few octaves as she shrills.

"This isn't up for debate, Lily. You're not safe. Clyde doesn't give two fucks about the other children— he won't touch them— but he thinks by taking you, it will lure Amy out, so please, let me help."

I may have lied just a bit, but I don't think telling her he has plans to kill her will make her feel any better.

"You're cut from the same cloth as him. How do I know you're not lying to me?" I can hear the uncertainty in her voice.

I suck in a breath, trying to settle my annoyance. Why can't she just listen to me and do as I say? "I have no reason to lie to you."

"Yeah? Well you have no reason to be truthful either, do you?" Before I can reply, she ends the call.

"Fuck!" I yell, gripping the phone too hard in my hand, almost snapping it in two.

I try to call again and again the entire way to the warehouse with no luck.

"Use mine to keep trying her," I start when we pull up to the warehouse and toss him my phone. "And try to get in touch with Gavin Smith. He'll have a safe house nearby. You know him?"

Alfredo nods and pulls his phone from his pocket. "Yeah, I know him. Want me to give him details?"

I shake my head as I step out of the car. "No. He owes me a favor and doesn't need to know." I say before I close the door.

Walking inside, something feels off, but I can't figure out why. Something tells me it's just because I'm on edge because of the shit with Clyde, but I know that isn't the case.

Always trust your gut. Another lesson Clyde taught me.

When I cross the concrete floor to the spot where blood still stains it from CJ, the asshole from last night comes from behind the boxes lining the wall holding a black trash bag with gloves on.

As soon as his stare catches me, he jumps before settling. "Oh fuck, Eric. You scared me." He laughs nervously.

I watch him for a moment. Sweat beads start to form along his brow, as the plastic bag in his hand starts to rattle as his hand shakes slightly. Tipping my head, I step closer to him. "Why so on edge?"

He laughs again, trying to mask his fright. "Edge? Nah, man. You just startled me. I wasn't expecting anyone to show up. I'm only cleaning the blood from the floor then calling it done."

"I don't like liars." I deadpan, knowing damn well he's hiding something.

He drops the bag and holds up his hands in surrender— his demeanor completely changes. "I swear I didn't tell him, Eric."

Squinting my eyes, I take another step closer. "Tell who what?" I let the words slip out low and relaxed. I'm sure he knows better— that I don't give a fuck and will snap his neck without a second thought— but the impression of composure always makes people more comfortable and likely to open up.

"Clyde. I don't know what he told you, but I swear I didn't say a thing." He moves, wanting to put some distance between us, but I take a step forward for everyone he takes back.

"And what is it you think Clyde said you said?" I ask, speaking to him like a child since that's the only way I will get answers.

"The shit CJ popped off with last night— about you and the girl conspiring."

I nod in understanding, pausing to scratch my chin. "I see."

"But I didn't tell him. I mean, I may have said it in joking— how CJ was trying to save his own ass with whatever he could think of— but he knew I wasn't serious and neither was CJ."

I smirk with a scoff. What a poor unfortunate soul. I knew this mother fucker was moldable when I saw him and probably only worked for Clyde because he cracks under the slightest sign of pressure.

But that's another instance where Clyde is so wrong. He thinks that because he runs shit by fear, these punks who will spill their guts at the inkling of something wrong will make sure they stay honest with him. Clearly, that isn't the case, though, because the moment I saw him and the way his body language changed, I knew he was hiding something. I knew he knew something I didn't. And that's bad for Clyde.

Now I know what he's up to, and I won't be playing it safe. I need to get to Lily and save her before he does.

Swiftly, I pull the gun tucked behind me and aim it at his head. Not even a second later, I pull the trigger. Brain matter and blood splatter the wooden crates behind him as his body crumbles and falls to the ground with a loud thud, and I know he won't be getting up.

I turn on my heel and haul ass back out the warehouse, practically screaming at Alfredo as I do. He may not know exactly what's going on because I haven't given him a run down, and in this business, you don't ask questions, but if he wants to stick by my side and work for me when I take shit over, now will be the time to prove himself.

CHAPTER NINE

I don't even give Alfredo time to come to a complete stop before I'm barreling out the SUV. Adrenaline moves my limbs, putting one foot in front of the other, as my mind races with excitement and fear.

Excitement to see Lily again, but fear for what Clyde wants to do to her. It's an obsolete thought, though, because I made it. I'm here to be the knight in raging darkness. Ready to crush anyone and everyone who gets in my way.

Leaping onto the curb in front of the boy's home, all of the thoughts die inside of me. They fizzle out like a light bulb that's run its course and shatter in the pit of my stomach. The door is kicked open, its broken wood swaying in the breeze, and no sound comes from inside. Normally, I can hear faint talking or the buzz of the TV, but none of that is present.

I slow my pace and grab the gun, tucking in the back of my pants. Pulling the hammer back, I raise it in front of me and creep inside slowly, bouncing my eyes over every inch of space I can see. It's all too still— all too quiet. At least, I think so, but the soft wail of a baby rings out.

It's almost drowned out by the soft howling of the wind, but the further I move down the hallway leading to the kitchen, the louder it gets.

As I breach the threshold, I turn quickly, aiming my gun. The small space is empty, but the back door leading to the alley is wide open, and it becomes evident that's where the crying is coming from.

I give the kitchen one last glance, then move to the door. Gripping my pistol tighter, I raise it and step around the corner, ready to shoot whoever stands at the other end. A stray cat leaps out of my gun's path and hops over the old wooden fence out of sight, but there is no other movement.

It takes me what feels like a lifetime to process what the fuck is happening as the rest of the world around me goes silent and black. It's only her. Nothing else. No one else.

First, I see her body— the same body I marked as mine last night. Her stomach is flat on the ground, and her arms are positioned in an awkward position, completely unnatural and littered with bruises.

Then, I see her hair. That perfect, pale blonde hair. It's rustled with wayward strands slightly moving with the wind's help. The pieces that normally frame her face are now matted and stuck, stained red from...

Blood.

I notice the blood pooling all around her body.

And in a second, just as quickly as everything around her faded away, it all comes crashing back to me. The sun is brighter than ever, causing white spots to float behind my eyelids every time I blink. The crying is no longer a soft wail. It's a full-blown scream.

I shift my eyes to the right of Lily's body. Sitting in the puddle of her blood is Max. You can tell he's confused and doesn't understand what's going on. His blue eyes search mine for answers, but I don't have them either.

Standing on wobbly legs, he reaches for me and moves closer. "Papa!" He sobs, opening and closing his tiny hands.

Without hesitation, I pick him up. The blood from his pants seeps onto my skin, running down my frame from my arm as it braces his bottom. "Papa is here." It's the only words I can manage to mumble.

I wipe his tears with my thumb and try to comfort him, but I don't even know how to do that. Pressing his head into my shoulder, I shield his eyes from Lily's body below us, knowing it's already too late. He's seen it all and will be scarred for life.

I suck in a deep breath and close my eyes, and he cries too close to my ear, but I don't care. I bid Lily a silent goodbye, then turn on my heel and leave with the only link I'll ever have to her in my arms.

The hallway seems to be miles long, and the creaking wooden floors seem to scream since every ounce of adrenaline has left my body, and my heart no longer beats in my ears. I try to focus on the obvious. Comforting Max the best I can and making sure one foot goes in front of the other until I make it to the front door.

IT STARTS WITH ME

I step out of the broken door and catch Alfredo's stare from across the street. His lips pull down in a frown, and his brows knit together. Stepping out of the driver's seat, He jogs across the street where I stand. My feet don't move. They're cemented to the ground where I stand.

"Eric?" Alfredo approaches slowly, holding out his hands, ready to take Max.

I jerk him away and open my mouth to speak, but nothing comes out other than a weak puff of air. Clearing my throat, I try again. "I need you to take me to Clyde then get him to safety."

He nods slowly with concerned eyes. "Do you need me to do anything else?"

I shake my head and finally will my feet to move. "No."

I can hear his shoes tap against the road behind me as I make it to the car and open the door. Sliding inside, I press Max into my chest and wrap both arms around him. "Don't worry, Max. I'm going to take care of you."

He nestles into my hold, his small body shaking and convulsing with his almost silent cries, but in some way, I think he understands.

As Alfredo pulls away from the curb, I turn my head and look out the window.

Yeah, I think. *Shit is going to change, and it starts now.*

CHAPTER TEN

By the time we make it to Clyde's place, Max has fallen sound asleep in my arms. When Alfredo stops the car, he exits then enters on the opposite side of me. "Let me take him, Eric."

I'm reluctant to hand him over. I swore to myself I would protect him and his mother, and I failed. What if I let him go now and fail again? I don't even like children, but I feel I owe him the world. It's my fault he was even tangled up in this wicked web in the first place.

"Eric?" Alfredo speaks again, pulling my eyes to him. "Let me take him. You have something to handle." He nods toward the front door.

I know he's right, but that doesn't change my hesitation. I feel I'm holding the whole world in my hands—my whole future—and I don't know if I can let it go. For once, I think I understand a parent's love. I don't think I love this kid, but I know I would kill for him.

I *am* going to kill for him.

"Don't let anything happen to him, Alfredo." I mumble as I pass his limp body over the seat.

He nods and nestles Max into his chest before laying him on the leather seat and patting his back to keep him asleep. "I won't. I promise."

I open the door and step out as he does the same. "That's a promise you don't want to break. Do you understand what I'm saying?" I ask over the roof of the SUV, alluding to the fact I have no qualms of killing him, too, if he hurts Max.

"I understand."

Another nod and I'm off, moving my gun from the back of my

pants to by my hip, so it's easier to grab. When I make it to the door, I don't pause. I walk straight inside like I would any other typical day, so hopefully, he doesn't suspect anything bad.

As I walk down the hall, my shoes tap against the floor, letting him know I'm coming. Entering the living room, I see him positioned on the couch with his wife. His arm is slung over her shoulder like it is every time I see him with her, and their twins are playing on the floor.

He smiles and cocks his head to the side. "Did you get the clean up at the warehouse settled?"

I inhale a long breath through my nose, silently telling myself to keep my cool. "I did."

"And?"

"And what?"

"Anything else to report?"

By the way, his knee bounces and his teeth grind, I know he's waiting to see if I'll bring up Lily.

"I went to South End." I throw it out and wait so I can gauge his reaction.

I'm expecting him to squirm more or stand to his feet. Something to show he knows he fucked up, but instead, he smiles.

He fucking smiles.

"Ah. Got a look at my handy work?" His tongue runs along his teeth.

It hits me that all the things I noticed him doing weren't from nerves. It was him being excited. He *wants* to talk about this shit. He *wants* to see *me* squirm.

"Handy work? Is that what you call it? Didn't seem too original to me." I shrug. "Putting a bullet between a bitches eyes seems kind of cowardice if you ask me."

"Cowardice?" He laughs. "Are you saying that thick, cold, black muscle in your chest actually has feelings now— has remorse?"

See, right at this very second, I have the upper hand. He doesn't think I'll do shit, but he's so wrong. If he paid attention in history class, he would know all good commanders face soldiers turning on them in some fashion. It's how shit works unless you condition them perfectly, which he hasn't.

The only thing he's taught me is to trust no one. An important lesson he should have kept for himself.

"I have nothing to be remorseful for." I deadpan.

He nods. "Well, look at it this way, Eric. With her out of the picture you can go back to doing what you were built for."

"And what is it I was built for, boss?" I ask, letting the venom I've been holding back seep through my lips.

"To be a killer for *me*. I took you in, fed you, clothed you, and taught you all you know. That woman had nothing to give you that I couldn't."

I nod slowly, thinking of my next words carefully. "And what is it you can give me that she couldn't? The basic necessities I need to be a human?"

He stands up swiftly and moves toward me. Grabbing my face in his hands, he stares right into my eyes. "And power. I can give you power, Eric."

"Power?"

He smiles again, and with him so close, I can see the yellow stains on his teeth from all of the coffee and cigars he consumes. "Yes, power. I can make you better than ever. You don't need some pussy to be great."

I grind my teeth in his hold. "Is that really how you feel?"

"Of course. You're like a son to me. I gave you my name and I want to give you the world." The way he speaks makes me want to puke. He's so sure of himself.

Keeping my eyes locked on him, I move my hand slightly to grab the gun from my side. Raising it, I aim at his wife on the couch and fire. Immediately, the twins scream, and her body goes limp. Clyde's eyes go wide, and he tries to move, but I snake my hand up and wrap it around his neck.

"You don't need some pussy to be great, boss. Remember?" Now it's my turn to smile. His body shakes in my hold as I squeeze his fat neck tighter. "A new era starts with me. Fuck your name, from this moment forward I'll go by Ciccone." I spit in his face before moving the gun to his head.

A moment of pride fills me. He took everything from me tonight, but the one thing that means anything in this world. Lily may be gone, but *her* name will live on with Max and with me.

As he stares at me, face turning blue, body frozen from shock, I pull the trigger. Blood splatters on my face, so I drop him, letting his body fold at my feet, and wipe it with the back of my hand.

The twins scramble around the room, unsure of what's going on, crying for their parent's, but I leave them there to play in the blood. Clyde took what was mine, so I took what was his.

When I make it to the living room threshold, Jerry grabs ahold of my leg. "Unc, Eric!" He screams.

Shaking him off, I squat to his level and use my thumb to brush the single drop of blood from his cheek. "When you get old enough, you'll want revenge. You may not understand now, but you will. Come find me then."

Pushing him away, I exit the house and slip back into the car where Alfredo and Max wait.

EPILOGUE
FOUR YEARS LATER

"Okay, boss. I got the word out. Shouldn't take long for some women to come forward." Alfredo says, stepping into my office.

Raising a finger to my lips, I glance at Max asleep on the chase across from my desk.

He's older now, looking more like his mother than before. It's a painful reminder of what she and I could have been, but he's growing to have a lot of my qualities too. He's stubborn, strong-willed, and so fucking intelligent.

I wanted to be pretty hands-off at first when it came to raising him, and it worked since Alfredo was here. The connection and understanding they have for one another are wild to me, but now that he's at a good age and understands more, I think it's time to finally start showing him the in's and out's of what our family will be about.

"Good," I whisper. "I already have a meeting with a woman who just gave birth. Escort her into the formal living room when she gets here. I'll be down shortly."

He nods. "So we're really doing this?"

I let out a small chuckle. When I told Alfredo my idea, he wasn't on board. He feels children have no place in our world, but ultimately, he gave in. I get what I want— boys who will stand by my side, take over the Ciccone name, and rule the fucking city— and in turn, he gets what he wants too. He'll get to raise children and love them as his own.

"Yes."

He nods again, knowing there is no changing my mind at this point and exits the room.

Standing from my spot, I round my desk and stare down at Max.

The day I murdered Clyde, I not only made a silent promise to Max that I would keep him safe, but I also made one to myself. I would take all the shit Clyde taught me and morph it to fit my own agenda along with being smarter, and that starts today.

Clyde almost had it right snagging kids to be his soldiers the moment they came of age, but the issue with that is they already have their own feelings. You can only teach and mold a young adult so much.

Infants, on the other hand...

Max stirs, sits up and rubs his eyes before looking around the room. "Papa?"

I reach down, push his long, thick hair from his face, and stare into his eyes. "You're fine. Sleep." I demand.

He narrows his blue orbs, the same way his mother did so many times. "Is it time?"

I nod. "It is. You'll have a brother within the hour, so rest. I know last night was a lot for you."

"I liked it though. Kids at school say they aren't allowed to play with guns, so it makes me feel special." He smiles, and all I can hope is his front teeth grow back quickly. He looks so fucking weird.

"It's because other parents are raising pussies, but us Ciccone's," I pat my chest. "We're not pussies, are we?"

He shakes his head quickly. "No. We're fucking kings, right?"

I nod. "That's right."

"Max!" Alfredo calls from the door. "You can't speak that way. It's a bad word."

I roll my eyes and ruffle his hair as he stands and runs to Alfredo. "Papa said it was okay, Alfie."

I cross my arms over my chest. "I did, cause it's true."

Alfredo's mouth forms a hard line as he pushes Max out of the office and starts to follow him. "He's seven." He deadpans. "And the girl is here."

I let the argument die as I exit too, grabbing the papers I need from my desk, and start down the stairs. When I make it to the bottom and stop at the living room threshold, a young girl no more than eighteen stands on the other side. In her arms, she has a fresh baby wrapped in a pink blanket, along with another one who is maybe two clinging to her leg.

"Veronica?" I ask as Max comes to stand beside me.

She nods. "Thank you for letting me meet you. I just want to make sure my baby is taken care of." Her body shakes, and I know it isn't from crying.

Her hair is tangled and messy—her clothes, too small and dirty. And I know the scabs covering her exposed flesh are nothing more than her picking. She's a fucking druggie.

I glance at Alfredo behind me. "Get the child and give her cash after she signs the adoption papers."

He nods, pulling a manilla envelope from the inside of his jacket, then steps around me.

"He looks sad, papa, and hungry." Max whispers, pointing to the kid holding her leg.

"He does."

"He could be my brother." He adds, and although I don't want to agree because I want an infant, I feel Max has softened me a bit because I feel bad for the kid. On top of that, I don't want girls. I need boys who will grow into men and carry my name long after I'm gone.

When Alfredo hands her the cash, she tries to give him the baby, but I stop her. "No. Him," I point to the toddler. "I'll take him."

Her eyes widen as she shakes her head. "Easton? No. You can't take him."

I tip my head. "And why not?"

"Well—" She cuts herself off almost as if she's trying to think of the perfect reason.

"I will take him, and Alfredo will find proper care for the baby. If you don't agree, then you get no money and can leave now."

It takes her less than three seconds to think, which doesn't surprise me. "Fine." Squatting down, she looks at the boy. "You're going to live here now, okay? But he has a lot of money and will take care of you like mommy can't."

She doesn't even kiss him goodbye before standing back to her full height, signing the adoption documents, giving Alfredo the baby, and leaving with her envelope of cash.

Alfredo looks at me. "Well?"

"Well what? Take her to South End and find this child some clothes that actually fit."

Normally, I wouldn't send any child to South End, but once Clyde was gone, that was my first order of business— renovating the whole place and getting actual decent people to run it.

He scoffs. "Fine. Keep them alive until I get back, and don't cuss in front of them. We don't want this sweet boy to pick up bad habits."

"Like fuck I won't." I wave him off and lead Max to the kitchen with the other boy following.

"I'm Max, your brother." Max starts, helping the small one into the chair. "And that—" He points to me. "That's our Papa. He's kind of mad all the time but that's okay. And you're Easton. I heard your momma say it. I don't have a momma because she died, so we'll get along."

"What do you like to eat?" I ask, cutting off the conversation he's trying to have with Easton before any more memories of Lily can surface.

"I'll make it, Papa. I think I'm better at it than you." Max says, standing from the table to take my spot behind the counter.

I sink into the chair next to Easton as Max grabs bread, jelly, and peanut butter.

"Papa?" He says softly, his tiny voice reminding me of Max when I first met him.

Glancing at him, I nod. "Yeah. I'm your Papa now."

The End

ABOUT S. RENA & BL MUTE

S. Rena & BL Mute are two USA Today Bestselling besties who met online from opposite ends of the USA. Now they reside only an hour away from each other and have decided to write darker romance books together—lots of them.

Follow Rena & Mute to learn all about their cowriting adventures.
https://msha.ke/renaandmute/

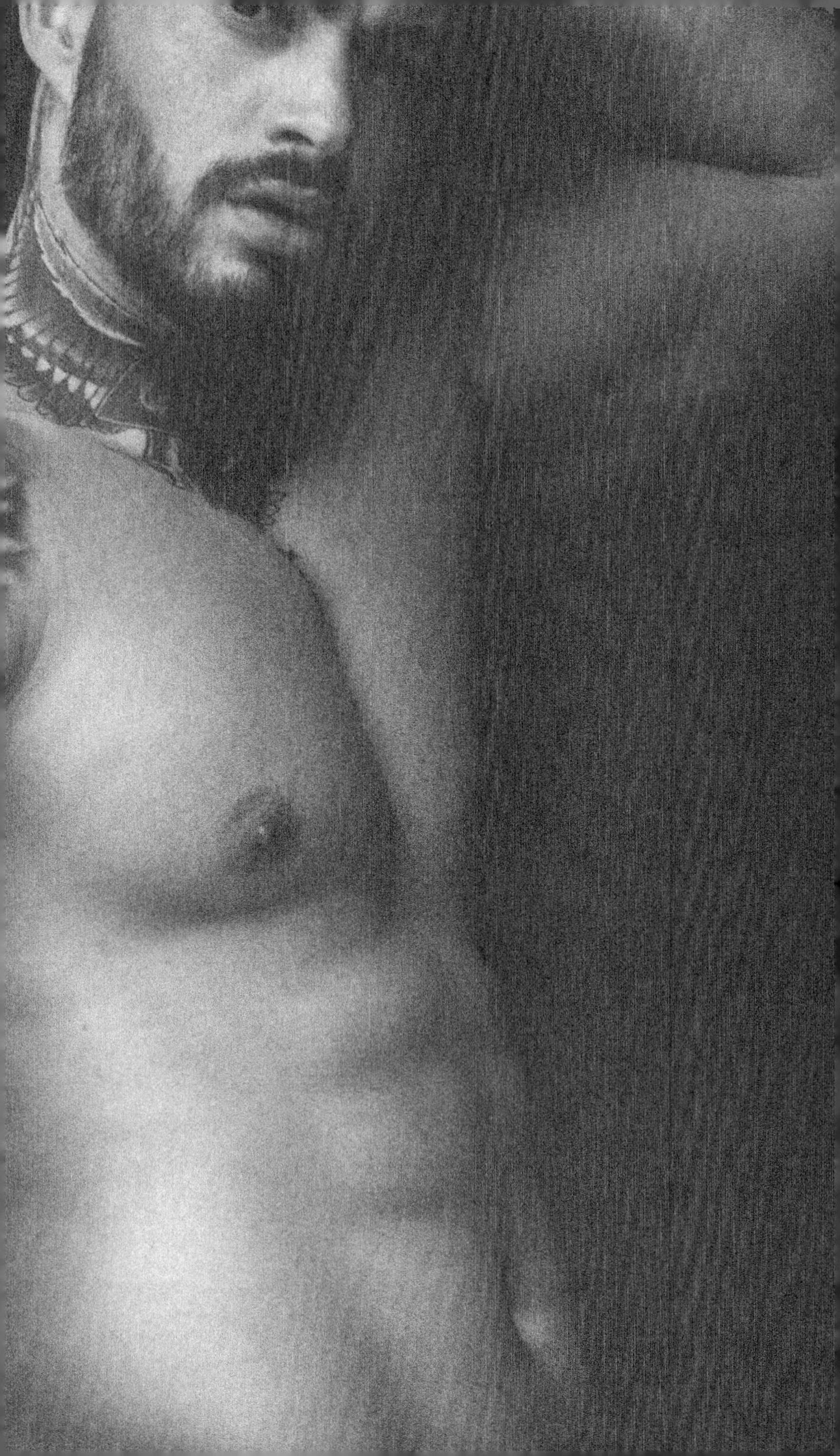

EXPLICIT

VOWS

BY J. M. WALKER

CHAPTER ONE

SASHA

"Did you ever think you would be back here?" Cash Sawyer asked me, brushing his pinky against the side of my hand. His deep blue eyes locked with mine. They held years of experience and things neither of us should have ever gone through.

I noticed then how he had grown. Why didn't I pay attention before? His size never mattered, seeing as I was small, and he and his brothers had always been bigger than me. But it appeared as if Cash had been working out.

Before I could answer him, even though the words were on the tip of my tongue, he pulled away and ran his hand through his light brown hair. It was longer on top and shorter on the sides. A little curly but every now and again, his bangs would fall into his eyes, and he would have to swipe them away. I remembered teasing him once how he needed to get it cut. But he never did, knowing that I liked it just the way it was. And he liked it when I ran my fingers through it.

His gaze seared into me and just when I thought he was going to ask more questions, he linked his fingers in mine, tugging me closer.

My breath hitched but I didn't pull away. Not like I used to. Not like before. Instead, I begged for more. But I just never told him or any of them that. How could I? How could I tell three brothers that I wanted something from each of them? At the same time. Apart. It didn't matter. I just wanted them. Even though it had been a while since I had all three of them together, I still craved things about them. About each of them.

"You good?" Cash ended up asking, releasing my hand and wrapping his arm around my middle instead.

I never answered him and looked out at the old decrepit house standing before us. The Colonial home had white siding with blood red window shutters. The white paint started chipping away when we were kids. Now it was only worse. I remembered back to when I was just a little girl and the four of us had helped with the painting. That had been a warm summer day. It started out nice but like usual, when the sun went down and I was alone in my room, the monsters came out.

"Sasha," Cash said gently, his fingers inching beneath the hem of my t-shirt. When his fingers came into contact with my skin, I almost changed my mind and headed back to his car but I didn't.

"Hey," he whispered, placing a peck on my temple. "We don't have to do this." His hand curled around my side, inching higher and higher. The skin on skin contact was a silent promise that he wasn't leaving me. Most would think our relationship was fucked up, but truth was, it was all we knew and understood.

I stared back at the house I had grown up in.

"Looks like no one kept up on the work," Cash muttered, pointing out the obvious. It had been something he did quite often whenever he was nervous or didn't know how to make small talk. Which seemed to be the norm when it came to having a conversation with me lately. He would tell me random things or talk about the weather because it was safe. I didn't want safe. I wanted danger. I wanted to be scared. It was one reason why I had been attracted to his older brother.

"I haven't been by to make sure the house was being worked on like it should be," I finally said. Some of the shingles were missing. Even the window shutters were barely hanging on. A single gust of wind could blow them off.

"Sasha," Cash said my name gently even though we both knew that to get through to me, he couldn't be gentle. His oldest brother had figured that out rather quickly. "We can go. I can take you home and..."

"And what, Cash? Have sex? Sit there and do nothing?" I stared up at him. "Talk?"

His jaw clenched. "I just want to help you. That's what we all wanted. This whole time."

"I was locked up in a damn hospital for over a year. If they can't help me, no one can." It wasn't overly true. I had acted well enough to let them think that I was fine, so I could get out and move on. But now that I was actually free of that facility, I wasn't sure if my plan had been a good idea or not.

Cash slipped his fingers around to my front, his hand hitting the spot just beneath my right breast. "We should go."

"Not yet." I pulled away from him, the sense of loss that he was no longer touching me hitting me harder than I would have liked. But I shook it off and slowly walked up the gravel driveway leading to the front door. My eyes flicked to an old rocking chair moving ever so slowly on the porch.

Hot breath fanned my ear.

I jumped, spinning around. But when Cash only frowned, I scrubbed a hand down my face.

"You shouldn't be here. Neither of us should be." He sighed, standing up taller and walked past me. "Come on. I'm not letting you in this house alone."

No one lived in this house anymore. But Cash being Cash, always trying to protect me, made a vow to me when we were kids, that once he got me out of this place, I would never have to go back. And yet, here we were.

"Sasha."

My head snapped up, my eyes flicking to where Cash was standing just inside the doorway.

"Let's get this done and over with, Pup."

A shiver rippled down my spine at the nickname he and his brothers had given me when we were kids. Technically, Holden, the oldest of the three, gave me the pet name but it stuck, and the three of them started calling me it. I shouldn't like it. Not when it started out as something derogatory at first. But I couldn't help it. It was something I had shared with them. Something the four of us had.

Forcing my feet to move, I took a step forward and then another. Once I was in the house that should have been my home but was my destruction instead, I felt almost at peace within it.

"I shouldn't be here," I said more to myself.

"No." Cash followed me. "You shouldn't be."

I stepped further into the house, the screen door slamming shut behind me. I jumped, my heart pounding against my ribs.

"You're fine." Cash grabbed my hands, bringing them up to his mouth. His eyes flashed with something I would crave for the rest of my life.

I looked away, taking a deep breath.

"Look at me," he demanded.

I didn't listen and squeezed my eyes shut instead.

"Pup." Cash pinched my chin, forcing my head back.

My eyes opened then, landing on his handsome tanned face. His deep blue eyes hid no emotion but still told me everything I needed to know. He was a survivor. Much like me. He had grown up in the system and was always under the watchful eye of his oldest brother.

I pulled out of Cash's grip and stepped around him.

I needed this.

I needed closure.

Everything that happened in this house, under this damn roof, needed to be laid to rest or else none of us could move on. Even though I had been the only one to experience the things that went on inside this place, a place that should have been my home, the three brothers knew. They knew because I told them everything.

All we could do was take it one day at a time or that was what my psychologist told me at the hospital. Sometimes I didn't think he actually knew what he was talking about. I also caught him staring at me a little longer than seemed appropriate for a doctor/patient relationship.

"I can't believe this place is still standing," Cash muttered. "It should be torn down and the ground should be burned."

"You think tearing this place apart and burning the ground would help get rid of the evil here? You think that would help?" Not all of the memories were bad, but the good ones were so few and far between, that I sometimes forgot what they were.

"I don't know," Cash said, walking to the bookshelf that no longer held any books on it but dust and cobwebs instead. "But it might help."

I doubted that.

As soon as you stepped foot into the house, to the left was the living room. It used to be clean because I was the one who had been forced to make sure it was. But now it was dirty. What I was sure used to be white sheets, covered most of the furniture.

Moving to the couch, I ran my hand along the back of it, watching a few dust particles float into the air. They danced into the sunlight, never to be seen again.

Walking around to the front of the couch, I sat on the floor, bringing my knees up to my chest like I had done as a child.

"This house is haunted."

I glared at my oldest foster brother. "It is not."

He chuckled, moving to the floor beside me. His dark eyes moved back and forth over my face. "It is. The ghosts are going to come feed on your soul," he said, poking me in the ribs.

I squealed, slapping his hands away. "They are not."

He grinned, looking over my head before meeting my gaze once again. "Alright, Sasha. There may not be ghosts like you say but there are definitely monsters lurking within these walls." He winked, pushing to his feet and disappearing down the hall with me staring after him.

If only I knew then how right he was.

I looked down the hall we had walked through so many times, I could navigate the place in my sleep. But so could my foster brothers. No matter how often I hid from the monsters, they always found me.

"Come out, come out, wherever you are."

I jumped to my feet, my eyes frantically looking around me. I could hear Cash off in the distance, rummaging through something in the kitchen. My feet pulled me forward. Down the hall, past the bedrooms and to my ultimate demise.

Once I reached the door that led to the basement, I looked back down the hall. Cash stood at the end of it, his eyes locked with mine. It was one thing I didn't like about him. How he could see into parts of my soul. It was like he was searching for all of my thoughts, my fantasies, and feelings. My wants and needs.

"You should start with something small," Cash suggested, taking a step toward me.

My eyes flicked to the door to my right.

"Maybe smaller." He stopped, crossed his arms under his chest and leaned against the wall.

Ignoring him, I went to the door opposite the one that led to the basement and placed my hand on the doorknob. Before I even entered the room, memories started slamming into me.

"Please stop."

Dark sinister laughter sounded around me. The laugh held no hint of remorse. Because he knew. Even though I told him to stop, he wouldn't listen.

Squeezing my eyes shut, I turned the knob and pushed open the door.

"It hurts," I whimpered.

"It's supposed to."

It wasn't.

But he never cared.

Opening my eyes, my breath caught. The room was exactly the same since the last time I had seen it so many years before. It was dustier of course but everything was still in its rightful place. Just like I had left it.

"What are you doing?" I asked, my voice shaking.

"Come in here and find out." The deep voice traveled over me, bringing me closer and closer to my ultimate demise.

"We have a present for you," my youngest foster brother whispered in my ear.

My eyes widened. Hope filled my body that today would be the day where they would be nice to me. "I like presents," I told them.

"Your birthday is coming up."

"It is." I nodded quickly.

"How old are you going to be, Sasha?"

"Sixteen." I frowned. He knew that. Why would he ask?

"Practically a woman." His eyes roamed down the length of me.

My stomach twisted; all hope gone that they would treat me like a little sister.

I backed up, bumping into a hard body behind me. "I should go," I whispered, not liking the way my foster brother was looking at me.

"Aww. How come?" He slapped the end of a baseball bat against his palm. "We still have to give you your present. I'm sure it'll be one you'll remember for the rest of your life."

He was right. I could still remember it like it had happened yesterday.

The agony. The pain. The depravity and vile things they had done.

Both of them took turns that day, giving me my *present*. And only when our foster father came home later that night, did they actually stop.

I remembered back to a time where I begged our foster father, Earl McGomery, to stay home. It had been the only time when I was left alone. As much as I tried telling Earl what was being done to me, the brothers threatened my life if I said anything, so I never did.

I took a step further into the room, my eyes landing on my bed. It had been my favorite spot in the house. It was the smallest room, but I tried my best to make it as comfortable as I could.

"I promise to get you out of here," Cash whispered in my ear. "If it means fighting, I will, Sasha. I will fight them for you."

Even though I hadn't told him what was going on, he knew. Because I came to him after every time with bruises on my body.

I had been craving attention for so long, once I started getting it, it messed with my head. I wasn't wanted by my parents and thrown into the system when I was a child. I could remember back to the day when I screamed for my parents to take me home and not to leave me at the strange man's house. I tried running after them, but Earl stopped me, grumbling in my ear to behave and that he was my family now.

To this day I didn't know what I had done to make my mom and dad not want me. I blamed them for the sick and evil things that went on in this house. I blamed them for giving up on loving me. I blamed them for how I eventually craved the pain. The anticipation of when my foster brothers would come find me again during the night when they thought no one else noticed. But Earl noticed. He just didn't do anything about it.

I went to one of the other bedrooms at the end of the hall and tried opening the door. When it stuck at the bottom, I remembered when it was kicked in. Now you had to push against it to get it to open completely.

I shoved my shoulder against the door, forcing it open and was met with a musty scent. The dust floated around the room, tickling my nose. Taking a deep breath, I went into the room and pushed open the window. A breeze wafted into the four walls, taking away some of the dust in the air.

Running my hand along the edge of the dresser, I turned toward the bed. "I shouldn't be in here."

"No, you shouldn't."

I could see Cash from the corner of my eye, standing in the doorway.

I ignored him and went to the bed. Sitting on it, I took a breath and laid down.

"Do you think we'll ever leave?" I asked Cash. "Do you think we deserve happiness?" I added, not waiting for an answer to my first question.

He wrapped his arm around my middle, kissing my cheek. "Yes," was all he said.

But I didn't believe him at the time, and I still didn't believe him now.

Closing my eyes, I let myself drift off to how it once was. The way it used to be before it all started. Back to when I was nothing but a girl trying to figure out her purpose in life. To find her place. To be noticed. To be loved. To be something extraordinary.

The bed dipped beside me with added weight.

Opening my eyes, I saw Cash with his head bowed and his shoulders hunched.

"I should have done a better job." He sighed. "I should have done more to save you. We all should have."

His words were so low, they sent a tremor of unease racing through me. "You were just a boy. A kid. All of us were."

Cash looked at me then. So many emotions swam behind the depths of his bright blue eyes. Worry. Sorrow. Fear. And it all had to do with two boys who found it funny at the time, to mess with the weak. But in all honesty, Cash was no better. He was just as evil but in a different way. I just never called him out on it. Not yet. I would. Maybe. In time. One day.

Little did all of them know that I came out stronger in the end.

I rolled onto my side, leaning my temple on the palm of my hand. "Do you remember the teddy bear you bought me after saving up that money that was meant for a bus ticket to get us out of here?" I picked at a fuzz on the blanket. "That teddy bear meant everything to me," I told him, trying to ignore the painful memories of when it was found.

Whenever my foster brothers were finished with me, I always went to Cash. He would console and keep me close, whispering in my ear about how he was going to take me out of there one day.

Even though he was kind and gentle with me, I could sense a darkness in him. He always tried fighting it and keeping it in check. It was like he was scared of that evil lurking within him, so he didn't know how to control it when it finally came out.

"Sasha."

I jumped, Cash's deep voice bringing me back to the present. I sat up, leaning against the wall and brought my knees to my chest. "It's been a while," I said softly.

"It has been." Cash moved back on the bed, leaning against the wall. "I missed you."

My stomach clenched. "I missed you too."

"I wish we could just put an end to this." Cash reached out, brushing his thumb along my ankle. The soft contact sent a shiver down my spine.

It made me want more.

Always more.

"Do you think we can ever find a way to be happy?" Cash linked his fingers in mine.

"If we can get out of here," I answered, watching his hand wrap around mine.

He grunted, pulling me into his arms and wrapped himself around my small body.

It was the only time I ever truly felt safe. From when we were kids to now. When he was inside me, controlling my pleasure, giving me everything I needed. When he touched me, held me and kissed me, I was safe. From the moment I fell in love with him as a mere girl to being with him as an adult, he was what I needed.

Or that was what I told myself anyway, but it had never been enough. I was selfish when it came to him and his brothers. I took from each of them what I had wanted and they did the same with me. While Cash *did* make me feel good, it wasn't enough, but I could never figure out what it was that I wanted.

We were both pawns in a sick game of twisted fate.

He did things for me, to me, without me having to ask and I could never thank him enough for that, but it wasn't the same. Not how it was with Holden. Maybe he conditioned me into wanting what he gave me. Maybe I had Stockholm Syndrome. I wasn't sure. No one could tell me. All I knew was that what Cash and I had as kids was nothing compared to what we had as adults.

CHAPTER TWO

CASH

We met as kids, fell in love as teenagers, and became obsessed as adults. But no matter what sort of feelings we had for the other, we were always together. Even when we weren't.

Sasha was stunning. She kept her hair long for most of her childhood and finally decided to cut it up to her shoulders. The brown locks framed her pale face, making her green eyes appear brighter in a way.

She had been taught to hate. From a young age, she was hurt by those who were supposed to protect her. Including me. It wasn't my fault. It wasn't my brothers' fault either. But there had only been so much we could do.

Somehow, even though I would never deserve it, she forgave me. That was what she had told me. Several times in fact. But there was still something hidden in her dark eyes that longed for more. I tried giving her whatever I could. After being with her for years, I still couldn't reach that certain part of her she had kept hidden. Only one person had ever truly seen it, lived it, breathed it, and choked the fuck out of it.

I was the youngest of three boys. We were thrown into the system at a young age only to be bounced from house to house thanks to Holden not liking anyone who took us in and Landen, who killed any pet he could get his hands on.

Holden ended up liking the last foster family we ended up with, only because they let him get away with whatever the hell he wanted. Even when Sasha slipped into our rooms during the night, nothing was ever done.

Mr. McGomery had been the worst of the foster parents I had ever seen. He didn't put an end to the horror happening to Sasha. He didn't stop the torture, the pain, the agony she endured. He didn't prevent the words leaving her mouth when she pleaded for it to stop.

I remembered laying there at night, staring up at the ceiling and imagining Sasha being beside me. Sometimes she did come visit but not always.

Whenever she did come to me at night, I would hold her as she cried. Before I even knew what was happening, I could sense that something had been going on. All I knew was that as the months wore on, she became skinnier. The bruises faded and were replaced by a hardness in her eyes. That same hardness I saw now. Her feelings were no more. Sasha no longer knew how to show emotion. Not like most people.

Earl should have stopped it, but he didn't. His wife had died not too long before the abuse started up. It was like as soon as she died, she took the happy ever afters and Sasha's life was turned into a nightmare instead.

But to give Earl credit, he made sure there was food in the house. While he drank, Sasha survived. He drank so much, he passed out often. Probably to drown out the noise.

I tried whiskey once, but I didn't like the taste of it and if something worse were to ever happen to Sasha while I was passed out drunk, I would never forgive myself. I refused to have even a sip. I had kept my promise to myself too. Until Holden found out.

"We know you like it." Holden sneered, pouring the liquid into my mouth as Landen held me down.

I coughed and sputtered, the whiskey burning as most of it went into my nose and down the back of my throat.

"I think he wants more, don't you, Cash?" Holden leaned down to my ear. "You think just because you don't drink that it'll keep me away from your little girlfriend?" A sinister laugh left him, the sound evil and depraved.

"Fuck you," I coughed, my stomach rolling.

He chuckled. "You know something. I always wondered why you wouldn't drink with us whenever we stole this shit for ourselves but now it makes sense. You want to protect little Sasha." He tsked. "You should never have let me find out, Cash."

I thought he had done his worst, but little did I know at the time, that my brother's idea of fun, was only just the beginning.

CHAPTER THREE

SASHA

When I was a little girl, I dreamed of puppies, kittens, and rainbows. I thought when it rained, it was God sprinkling glitter on the earth and when it was sunny, it meant he was smiling down on us. But little did I know at the time, that they were only fairy tales. They were hopes and dreams, something for us to latch onto when the world wasn't going the way we had hoped it would.

The day I met the brothers, my world was forever changed. Although I was a couple years younger than Holden, there was something about him that I was drawn to. I just couldn't admit it at the time. Maybe I still couldn't. He was the one who named me Pup or Puppy. Everywhere he turned, I was there, following him around like a lost puppy. I couldn't help it. It wasn't like I had any friends. There were no girls my age who lived in the area. I was constantly bullied at school because I wore the same clothes over and over. They were clean. I was clean. Earl made sure of it. We had just enough where the authorities couldn't be called on him. Not that I was sure he cared or not. But maybe he did because it was what his wife would have wanted.

The brothers were older, so I looked up to each of them.

The first night the brothers came to live with the McGomery's, I was in bed, trying to fall asleep but I wasn't alone for long. My back was facing the door, but I could feel the bed dip behind me. Nothing happened that night, but I still never forgot it.

I kept the blankets up to my chin, holding them tight. My child brain at the time thought the blankets could keep me safe but nothing could keep me from guys like the brothers. I was better off giving into their madness. It hurt less that way. Once I was old enough to understand what they wanted, it was too late. They had already taken my innocence.

"Do you like me?" Holden asked me one afternoon, glancing down at my mouth.

"Yes." I considered lying and saying that I didn't, but I knew that he would see right through it.

"What about Landen?" He inched closer to me.

I stared at him, the boy I had loved for so long, who was now turning into a man. He had just turned seventeen and came to the park after working at the same factory Earl did.

I was only fifteen but had already been through so much at the hands of the boy sitting close.

I fidgeted in my spot on the picnic bench. Any further away from Holden and I would be on the grass. I felt trapped. I could have ran away but Holden would catch me. They would always catch me. So the only place I could go, was right into his arms.

"He's alright," I whispered.

Holden tilted his head. "And Cash?"

"He's nice to me," I confessed.

Holden's brows narrowed. "He wants you. That's the only reason he's being nice to you."

I didn't know what Holden meant by that but nodded anyway.

"What do you like about me?"

I swallowed hard, not liking this game. If I answered wrong, it wouldn't bode well for me. If I answered right, I was sure it still wouldn't go how I expected.

"Tell me." Holden moved closer, towering over me.

My heart started racing at how close he was. How close he always was.

"Pup." His voice lowered. "I'll make you tell me, and I promise that you won't like it." But we both knew I would.

"You protect me," I finally said. He had an odd way of doing it, but he did. It was like he was the only one who could treat me the way he did but if anyone else tried? He would step in, kick their ass or worse. Even when it came to his brothers, Holden never let them do anything to me unless he was there. If he wasn't and he found out, he would go after them.

"I do." He winked.

A boy had pushed me at school one time, and it was almost as if Holden had appeared out of thin air. He shoved the boy to the ground and pummeled his fists into his face and ribs, I was surprised the boy didn't die. I could still hear his bones shattering beneath the impact of Holden's fists.

"What else do you like?" Holden reached out and brushed my hair off my shoulder.

"I like that you give me a part of you no one else sees," I whispered, staring up at him.

His eyes darkened. "No one else deserves that side but you, Pup. Remember that." His head lifted, a dark shadow passing over his face. "What the fuck do you want?" he growled.

"We have a problem," Landen said, coming toward us.

"You can't take care of it yourself?" Holden asked, his eyes sliding back to mine.

"No."

"Until tonight, Pup," Holden murmured, kissing the top of my head.

I hated that I looked forward to nights with him while everyone else was sleeping. He showed me a different part of him when it was just us. I ended up craving these nightly visits. I wanted them. Needed them. He was the monster in the dark corners of my room. Instead of being scared of him, I welcomed him into my arms. But I never understood why. Maybe one day I would but today was not that day. Because as the hours ticked on until I was too tired to stay awake, I slipped beneath my covers and drifted off to sleep.

Sometime during the night, something woke me up. My back was to the door. I tried falling back asleep when the door slowly opened. The light from the hallway cascaded on the wall.

The door shut shortly after, taking all of the light with it, as feet padded across the hardwood floor.

The bed dipped behind me.

When a heavy arm wrapped around my middle, I covered the hand and pulled the body closer. I knew it was Cash just by his scent. He smelled of spice and sugar. I had caught him taking the lotion from my bag one day. When I questioned him, he said it reminded him of me. I wanted to ask more. I wanted to know why his brothers were the way they were. And I wanted to know why the hell I was attracted to Holden.

Cash knew about my feelings for his older brother. He never commented much on it. Just said that he could see the way I looked at him.

"He won't protect you like I will," Cash murmured in my ear.

"Sasha."

Cash's rough voice pulled me from my thoughts and back to the present. I slid off the bed and left the room, heading back down the hall to my own room. I was vaguely aware of Cash following me, but I needed to be alone. Even though it never seemed to stop him at all. He was always there. Whether I wanted him to be or not. It had been the same with Holden and I. But it never pissed him off like it did me. I could never figure out why either. Cash was good to me, and I didn't deserve his friendship. He was patient. Kind. A damn savior compared to what I had been used to.

"Sasha."

"I just need a moment," I told Cash and slipped into the room I had spent most of my childhood in.

It looked like your typical bedroom for a little girl. Even though we didn't have much, Earl made sure to give me a doll for my birthday every year. Even if they were used, I loved them so much. Until the day that one of my foster brothers got jealous and he broke all of them.

The room had pink walls and white furniture. It was deceiving in a way when it looked like it should have held happy memories but instead, the happiness was few and far between inside these four walls. What happened often was anything but happy.

A tremor of unease slid over me, terror over what was done. Confusion over the fact that I had tried getting away but couldn't. Regret because I loved the attention. Holden was supposed to take care of us since he was the oldest.

"Sasha." Cash came up behind me, placing his hands on my shoulders.

My body relaxed beneath his strong hold on me like it always had. Even when we were kids.

Cash took the hint and slid his arm around my shoulders. "I kissed you for the first time in this room." I had snuck out to see him that night. That kiss had been the first gentle touch I had ever felt, and I would never forget it. But with that memory, came a painful one just the same.

My stomach twisted. "Yeah, and I was raped for the first time that night too."

"Sasha." Cash pulled away from me. "Fuck, I wasn't trying to bring that shit up."

"It's fine." I went to the dresser. The mirror was filthy, but I could still clearly see Cash's reflection in it.

"Hey." He came up behind me but never touched me. He didn't

need to. No matter how long we had gone without being with each other, I could still feel him. Everywhere. "Can we go?"

"Not yet." I turned and went to walk past him when he caught my hand. "You know I can't. I need closure, Cash. You know that never happened." I looked up at him then.

He pulled me closer, leaning his forehead against my temple. "Just promise that you won't close up on me. You need something, you tell me. You tell us. I'll call up—"

"No, it's okay. I'll be fine." I tried pulling away from him, but he was too strong.

"They're not here. They won't hurt you again." He placed a soft peck on my cheek. "We need to stop this."

"They don't have to be here to hurt me," I mumbled. "And you know we can't stop this. Not yet." I cleared my throat, shaking my head. "They're doing a damn good job of hurting me and they're not even here." I shoved out of Cash's grip.

Cash sighed, running a hand through his hair. "My brothers..." His voice trailed off. "Listen." He cleared his throat. "Whatever you need, we can give it to you. You know that."

"I do." I went back to him, placing my hands on his chest.

He wrapped his arms around me, holding me tight against him.

Looking up at him, I slowly ran my hand from his chest down to his stomach. Something flashed in his eyes, a slow smirk spreading on his face.

"Careful," was all he said.

I only smiled, turning around in his arms.

He hugged me from behind, placing a soft peck on my neck. "They're waiting for you," he whispered.

"They can wait some more."

"We really should stop. He wouldn't—"

"No, I can't," I said, my voice firm.

"Fine." When he released me completely, a sense of loss washed over me, but I ignored it and went to the door that led to the basement.

I stopped and went to open the door when I saw that my hand shook. The many times I had gone down to the basement, my hands never shook. But now, years later and they did. I was safe. The guys could no longer do the unspeakable things they had done to me as a kid. But if that were the case, then why did I feel like they were about to jump out of the darkest corners of this house and come find me like they always had?

Taking a deep breath, I curled my fingers around the doorknob and pushed the door open. I was hit with a stench that brought me back to my childhood.

It smelled of pain and sadness. Despair and sorrow. Emotions that I spent years popping pills and drinking anything I could get my hands on, just so I could ignore them.

With Cash following behind me, I headed down the steep staircase. I almost laughed as the memories slammed into me now that I was back there. I had ignored them. Fought to keep them at bay and shoved them aside. But now that I was back, it was like they all came rushing into my mind all at once. It was almost suffocating with how many tried taking control.

The basement wasn't completely finished. With most of the flooring being cement, it collected cobwebs and other critters I never wanted to think about.

A memory hit me, forcing bile to my throat.

I was being held down while a dead mouse was almost shoved into my mouth, and I had been terrified of them ever since.

The mouse had never gotten past my lips only because a nearby neighbor heard my screams and cries and put an end to it. That neighbor had died from unknown sources a few years later. I often wondered if one of the guys had killed him. My foster brothers never did like being told what to do and being told that they had to stop playing with their toy? It brought forth a rage in them I had never seen in anyone else. Even when Cash was upset, his rage was nothing compared to them.

Ever since the mouse incident, I tried complying to their ways faster than I would have liked but sometimes I couldn't. And I paid for it.

Always.

CHAPTER FOUR

CASH

The first time I walked in on Holden and Sasha, I was confused because I was jealous. It wasn't a feeling I liked, especially when we were still so young and had the rest of our lives to figure shit out.

She told me at first that it had happened unexpectedly. When I walked in and saw him on top of her and heard her little moans, I wished it would have been me instead of him.

I never voiced those feelings. Not at first. My brother had a wisdom about him that scared the shit out of me.

Even though my fear of him was very real, at the same time, I spent years trying to get him to notice me. He and Landen had a special bond. Or they acted like they did. But I often wondered if Holden had an ulterior motive.

They were closer in age and Landen didn't have a crush on Sasha like I did. He only messed with her because Holden told him to. That was what they led me to believe anyway.

When Sasha headed down into the basement, I couldn't help but think back to the many times all of us spent together. She had told me the stories and how these walls bled with her screams, her tears soaking into the ground beneath our feet.

But what I never understood, and to this day, years later, I still didn't understand, was how she always went back for more.

Then again, she always came back to me just the same. If not more. I hoped it was more, but I could never be sure because she wouldn't tell me. No matter how much I pushed.

"Tell me you love me," I demanded, pulling Sasha into my arms.

Her breath caught, her arms wrapping around my middle. "Cash."

"Say it."

But she never did.

The sound of the door quietly opening sent a flutter of unease racing through me. I knew it was Sasha without even opening my eyes.

The bed dipped beside me, followed by a soft sigh.

I opened my eyes then.

The glow of the moon cast an eerie shadow over Sasha's small form.

"How bad?" *I asked, wanting to touch her but knew I had to wait for her to make the first move.*

When she laid down beside me, she turned her face in the direction of the window.

Even though it was dark in the room, I could still see a faint shadow of a bruise forming on her upper cheek.

"He only hit me this time," *she said, her voice so soft and unsure.*

"I'm sorry for what you've been through." *It had been the same thing I told her every time she came to me for comfort.*

"It's not your fault," *she said which was something she often told me, but it didn't make me feel any better.*

I might not have been the one hurting her, but I didn't stop it either. Not because I didn't want to or never tried but I wasn't even sixteen yet and I was small for my age. Much smaller than my brothers. Last time I tried stopping Holden from doing something stupid, I almost had a dead bird shoved down my throat. I could still remember the maggots tickling my tongue.

My stomach rolled at the memory.

Giving myself a shake, I forced those thoughts to the back of my mind.

"What was the issue tonight?" *I asked Sasha, brushing my pinky along the side of her hand resting between us.*

"Don't know." *She looked at me then.* "Did I do something wrong?"

I hesitated. "What do you mean?"

She looked away and rolled onto her side, facing away from me.

"Sasha." *I wanted to comfort her. I wanted to take away her pain. I had to do something, but I wasn't sure what that could be. Especially with how much smaller I was. But maybe my size didn't matter. Maybe I could figure out a way to save Sasha from this place and the pieces of shit who were supposed to take care of her.*

"Cash."

My eyes flicked to the back of Sasha's head, unsure if I heard her or not.

"Hold me," she whispered, her voice louder that time.

Not even hesitating, I wrapped my arm around her middle and pulled her back against me.

Her breath hitched but I wasn't sure if that was from being in pain or because my pelvis was pressed up against her ass. There was no point in denying the way my body reacted to hers. I also couldn't control it. But I wasn't them. I would never force myself on her.

"Cash." Sasha pulled my arm tighter around her middle. "I'm sorry."

As soon as those words left her mouth, the door slammed open.

Sasha left the bed, a cold draft taking her place.

Holden stood at the door, watching me, waiting for me to do or say something. But I didn't. I wasn't even sure if was Sasha wanted me to.

When she went up to him, that was when his eyes dropped to hers. He reached up, caressing her cheek before leaning down to her ear.

A shudder rippled through her small body at whatever it was he had said to her.

He stepped aside, letting her pass and shut the door behind her.

The sound of another door closing forced me to a sitting position.

"Did it make you hard having her in your bed?" Holden asked, flicking on the light. He leaned against the wall, his cold, calculating eyes searing into the deepest parts of my soul.

While Landen wasn't stable and there was clearly something wrong with him, Holden knew he was fucked up. The only problem with him was that he just didn't care.

"I have no idea what you're talking about," I mumbled.

"No?" He stomped toward me and ripped the blanket off of me and the bed. "What's this then?"

Before I could stop him, Holden had a hold of my dick. He squeezed to the point my stomach rolled. No words came out of my mouth, but my brain screamed for him to stop.

"Feels pretty hard to me," he gritted out through clenched teeth. He towered over me, digging what little nails he had into my cock.

My vision faded in and out at the agony.

"If I ever catch you playing with my toy again, I don't give a fuck if she comes to you herself, I will make it so the next time I use her, I break her fucking soul." Spittle flew out of his mouth, his eyes cold and beyond any type of evil I had ever seen before. "Do you understand me?"

The answer was on the tip of my tongue. To answer him would be admitting defeat and I couldn't do that. Not with someone like him.

"I asked you a question." He squeezed me harder.

"Yes," I cried out.

Holden released me, his eyes searching my face.

A sense of relief flooded through me, and I curled away from him, cupping myself to try and ease some of the pain rushing through me.

He moved to the edge of the bed.

Just when I thought he was going to leave, he looked at me instead. "She needs us. All of us. In very different ways." He looked away, facing forward and pushed to his feet. Leaving the room, he closed the door gently behind him, taking all the air in my lungs along with him.

It was moments like that where I was confused as hell.

Holden was cold, callous, evil. He destroyed the innocent, stomped on the weak, and ripped apart everything in his path. He was a tornado, hurling through everything to get to his final target.

Sasha.

CHAPTER FIVE
SASHA

Cash was following me.

I knew because I could feel him. I also knew because it would have been what I would have done. It didn't make sense for me to go to the basement. Not when I had spent most of my childhood trying to get out of it. But there was something in it that called to me. Even as a girl. I couldn't explain it. Maybe I never would. But as I stepped down those dingy stairs and breathed in the damp air of the run-down basement, I was brought back to a time where I mattered. It wouldn't make sense to most. It didn't even make sense to me half the time. But I felt it anyway. Might as well embrace it.

"Do you miss him?" Cash asked me for the second time that day.

I did, even though I saw him that morning, but I didn't voice that out loud. I missed the young man he once was. The darkness in him that he learned to keep at bay over the years. Even though we were still young and only in our early twenties, what Holden and I had was different than what I shared with his brothers.

Some people would call me a slut, going through three different guys and brothers no less. But I had been with them at different stages of my life. I had needed them in different ways. Together and apart. I just needed...*them*.

Holden took what he wanted from me when I was young and naïve.

Landen was just there when his older brother was not.

And Cash...

As if he could hear my thoughts, Cash stepped up behind me, placing his hands on my shoulders.

My stomach did a flip at being this close to him. I looked around me, expecting Holden to jump out of the dark corners and shove Cash away from me. But when that never happened, I let out a breath of relief.

While Cash and I had been on and off for years and even though it had been quite awhile since I had slept with him, thanks to being in that facility, I couldn't help how my body reacted to him. Holden knew it and while most times, he never did anything about it. Sometimes he didn't overly approve.

"You smell like him." Holden's firm grip on my throat tightened.

"I didn't fuck him," I told him, glaring up at the man I would spend the rest of my life with because I didn't deserve any better.

"Maybe not but he still touched you." Holden pulled me toward him.

"He held me like he did when we were kids." It had become an obsession I would never get over. No matter how much Holden demanded for me not to see his brother unless he was around.

His brows narrowed in the center. With a firm grip on my jaw, he pushed me up against the wall. "Still going through the three of us like a needy little whore." Spinning me around, he pushed his arm against the back of my neck. "Tell me I'm wrong."

I swallowed hard. "You're not wrong."

And he wasn't. No matter how much I tried telling him he was. I *was* needy. For all of them.

My psychiatrist told me I had PTSD.

No shit.

But I wasn't the only woman in Cash's life. Not at first. Not that I had ever seen them, but the evidence of their passion was written all over him whenever I saw him after.

No matter how many other women he had been with, if I said the word, he would stop. A part of me wondered if he was trying to make me jealous. I couldn't give him what they could. Cash needed that emotional connection. He told me he loved me, and I never said it back. Not because I didn't feel something for him. I did. But it wasn't love. Maybe it never was.

There was only one man I loved, and he often used it against me. But it didn't matter. None of it mattered anymore. I had a purpose. And my purpose was to find closure. Of some kind.

"Are you trying to find the courage to leave me? Is that why you're going back to the house?"

I scoffed, turning away from Holden and faced the mirror in my vanity. "You know I could never leave you. That's always been the problem."

"Pup."

I shivered at that nickname he had given me as kids.

"We're meant to be together." He wrapped his long fingers around the base of my throat. "It's always been us."

"And others," I reminded him.

"I was a stupid kid." His hand moved to my throat, tightening around it. "You know I haven't been with another woman. Not since..." He lifted my hand, placing a soft peck on my wedding set. "I'm yours."

My breath caught, my eyes snapping to his in the reflection of the mirror.

"You know I love you." Holden's gaze seared into mine. With a firm grip on my throat, he lifted me to my feet and pushed me up against the mirror. "Tell me you know."

"I know." I sighed, getting lost in his violent touch.

"Such a fucking slut for degradation." He pressed his mouth up against my ear, locking his eyes with mine in the reflection. "If you come home after meeting up with my brother at the house and I find his mark on you, I will hurt you."

I shivered at a promise I shouldn't want.

"Don't test me, Puppy."

That single word snapped me out of the daze. He only referred to me as puppy and not pup, when he was pissed. Sure, it was warranted on my part when I often unknowingly did or said something to make him jealous. Well, he used to do the same to me.

"You're an asshole." I shoved out of his grip and spun around, pushing him back. "Why can't you treat me like a normal person?"

"Because I'm not normal. You are not normal. Nothing about our lives and our fucked-up but delicious relationship is normal. What you have with the three of us. We are who you need. We are who you've always needed." Holden grabbed my hands that were pressed against his chest. His fingers tightened around them, the bones in my wrists creaking under the pressure. My eyes dropped to him touching me, not even realizing I had my hands on him in the first place.

"Holden," I whispered.

He pulled me against him and shoved me back until my ass hit the edge of the vanity table. "Does he know you married me?"

"I'm sorry." Cash's voice pulled me from my thoughts. He had said that he was sorry before. Even though it wasn't his fault. Was it? I wasn't even sure anymore.

"No, you're not." I looked at him then.

His eyes, so dark and vacant of hope while mine were bright and pleaded to hold onto what little hope I had left, searched my face. They begged for me to tell him how I felt. Damn near grovelled at my feet to get me to say those three little words.

Only one man truly had my heart, and it wasn't the one standing in front of me. Even though I sometimes wished it was.

"Babe."

My breath hitched. I wasn't his babe. The other women were. They got from him what they wanted, and he got what he wanted in return. I used to just be a warm body for him to hold at night so he wouldn't be alone. Much like I did, Cash had nightmares of his own. While Holden had kept me as his little toy, his *puppy*, he fucked with Cash's head. But I wasn't any better, knowing whose bed I had left that morning.

One warm afternoon in the middle of summer, I bounded out of the house and ran to the park. When I neared the swing set, I was stopped short by what sounded like grunts and mumbled words.

"Eat it," I heard Holden growl.

I stopped in my tracks, watching the scene play out before me.

Holden was straddling Cash's chest while Landen held his legs down.

"Eat it," Holden demanded, his voice laced with a calmness that sent a hot shiver down my spine. His back was to me so I couldn't make out what it was that he was trying to feed Cash, but I knew that it wasn't anything good.

Cash continued struggling beneath them when I heard a sharp squeak and then silence. The sound forced a gasp from my mouth.

Landen was the first to look my way. He elbowed Holden, who only pulled away from Cash, leaving him on the ground. I took a step forward when Landen moved in front of me.

I tried side stepping around him, but he blocked my path.

"Something you want, Pup?" he asked, tilting his head. He didn't use that nickname often with me but when he did, it always caused the same reaction. A deep seeded longing would swirl around in me, needing more.

"I want to make sure he's okay," I said softly, backing up a step.

"What makes you think he's not?" Landen closed in on me, backing me up into the dark corner beside the big house. *"Cash is a big boy. He can handle himself."*

Who ever said I was referring to him? Before I could mull over that thought, Landen reached out, pushing a strand of hair behind my ear.

"I don't know what they see in you," he murmured.

"Landen."

I jumped as he was pulled away from me.

Holden stepped in front of me, shielding me from his brother.

"What the hell do you think you're doing?" Holden stood close. From this view, I could see that he had gotten bigger. His back muscles rippled beneath his white t-shirt, his thick arms proving just how strong he truly was. He backed up again, his body hitting mine. He reached a hand behind him.

Taking the hint, I slipped my fingers in his, wishing I could take us away from here but both of us were still so damn young, it wasn't possible.

"I wasn't doing anything," Landen bit out. *"I don't know what all the fuss is anyway. She's just a girl."*

Holden looked down at me over his shoulder. His eyes burned into a part of me that only he had ever been able to reach. His eyes promised pain, maybe pleasure if I was lucky. Although, with him, I took what he offered. We were young, pushing late teens, but all of us had experienced more than most adults at the hands of a guy who needed to be in control.

"How old are you now, Pup?" he asked, that muscle beneath his ear ticking.

"Seventeen." And I was counting down the days until I could leave this hell.

His lips twitched. *"Age is just a number, Sasha. Remember that the next time I'm inside—Sasha."*

I jumped, being met with dark eyes. I looked away.

Holden cupped my jaw, digging his fingers into my cheeks. *"I expect you to listen when I'm talking to you."*

"And I expect you to not be a dick but here we are," I threw back at him.

He chuckled. *"There she is."*

Before I could ask what he meant by that, he released me and walked away.

Landen only stared, his eyes moving back and forth, watching the whole exchange between his brother and I.

Holden reached him and clapped his shoulder, muttering something in his ear.

"Pup," Holden barked.

My back stiffened.

A slow grin spread on his face. "I have a job for you."

CHAPTER SIX

CASH

I watched Sasha move around the basement. Most wouldn't think anything of it, but I knew her. Maybe even better than she knew herself. With every touch of her hand as it slid over the dusty furniture, memories hit her. I knew because I could see the pain in her eyes. The confusion. The onslaught of betrayal bestowed on her shoulders by people who were supposed to protect her.

I could see the turmoil, the heartache, the fear. She was the strongest woman I had ever met. Even when we were kids, she had a fire to her that most would kill for. But she thought she was weak only because people made her feel that way. Holden wasn't any better. Hell, none of us were. My oldest brother wanted her submission, even before we understood what that meant.

Most wouldn't expect her to know what love was when she had never received it herself but there had been a time where each of us loved her at some point in her life. I still loved her but not in the way either of us needed.

I loved her but still fucked other women.

She loved me but also loved Holden and Landen. I knew every single thing there was to know about her. Her likes. Her dislikes. Her wants and needs. Things she hated. Things she loved.

Holden was a problem. A big problem. Had been from the moment we met Sasha. I could never quite wrap my head around his obsession with her. Even when she was underage and only a girl. They had a connection that forced the jealousy in me to turn into rage.

"Doesn't it piss you off?" I asked Landen one day, stomping into his room. He was sitting on his bed, reading a comic book.

"What?"

"How she follows him around like a damn puppy." I slammed the door closed and began pacing.

"She is his puppy," Landen reminded me, placing his comic on the bed beside him. "She's his puppy and our puppy. She belongs to us."

"You know what I mean," I huffed, not liking that he wasn't siding with me. We were brothers. We used to be close. Didn't matter that I was the youngest.

"No, I actually don't, Cash." Landen slid off his bed and went to the window. "You know she's ours. She's never been with anyone else but us. Not willingly anyway."

I followed him, glancing out the window that showed the backyard.

Holden was pushing Sasha on the swing. Even though technically, she could be considered too old for it, it was still something they had done quite often. And it left me with this nagging feeling deep in my gut. A feeling I couldn't get rid of.

"You're jealous."

Ignoring Landen, I continued staring out the window without responding.

"I don't know why you would be. She obviously has feelings for him."

"Then why do you mess with her?" I threw at him.

Landen shrugged. "It's fun, I guess. Not like I have a whole lot of friends, Cash." He pushed away from the window and went back to his bed. "And she feels good."

"Holden has too much of a hold on us," I muttered but I couldn't say I disagreed with him. She did feel good, and it was a feeling I had never wanted to be rid of.

Landen chuckled. "He doesn't have shit on me. As soon as I have the money saved, I'm leaving this fucking town."

If only it were that simple.

If only.

I didn't know it at the time, but Landen had meant what he said. I assumed he was just talking out of his ass but after doing an odd job here and there, he was able to save up enough money to get a train ticket out of there. But it had been too late at that point.

"Have you seen him?"

Sasha's question threw me off guard.

Unsure if I heard her correctly, I didn't respond right away. But when she stopped and glanced at me over her shoulder, I realized I had.

"Uh..." I coughed, running my hand through my hair. It was a nervous tic, one I couldn't control but when I was cornered, much like now, it was how I reacted.

Sasha tilted her head, her eyes locking with mine. She was thinking and I wasn't sure why exactly, but I didn't like it.

"You haven't." She turned and walked away. "Because if you did, you would say so."

"Have you?" I demanded of her and followed her deeper into the basement.

"It doesn't matter if I've seen him or not," she responded.

"Yes, it does. He's not good for you. No matter what you think and how you think you feel, Holden is not the one."

She laughed, the sound almost foreign to my ears. "And you are, Cash?"

"That's not what I'm saying. Fuck, Sasha. He's dangerous."

"I can handle him."

I went to argue that she couldn't but if I was being honest with myself, I didn't actually know if she could handle him or not. I didn't know their dynamic as adults and in private. That part I wasn't able to keep tabs on because I didn't actually want to know. The private investigator I had hired, offered to tell me the raw and filthy details but I couldn't bring myself to know.

There was something wrong with Sasha. Maybe there always was. None of us knew where she had come from. Just that she was there at the foster home, when we showed up.

"Were you always in the system?" I heard myself ask.

Sasha stopped, looked at me over her shoulder and frowned. "Feels that way most days. But no, I wasn't. My parents didn't want me. I guess they realized that when I got old enough to talk. I don't know."

"So you know nothing of your real parents and where they are now," I added.

"I don't need to know. I had Earl and Jane. I had you guys. I had...*them*." Sasha shook her head. "But it doesn't matter, Cash. None of it matters."

"Don't you want a better life for yourself? You're almost twenty-two and..." I was going to say that she was still single, to see if I could get an inkling of the lie she had been feeding me for a while now.

"My life is fine. I just need closure. Maybe being here will stop the nightmares." She sighed, coming up to me. "Please don't push me."

"I'm not." I grabbed her hand, pulling her against me. "All the shit we went through as kids because of Holden, as hard as it was, my favorite moments were when you joined me during the night."

"Cash," she whispered, staring up at me with those big, beautiful eyes of hers. Eyes that held so much pain and torment behind them, they took my breath away.

"It's been a long time for us." I wasn't sure what I was getting at. Maybe I wanted to remind her how it felt. How *we* felt.

"It hasn't been that long. Has it?"

"Long enough." I ran a finger down the length of her jaw. "We've kept busy while you were getting the help you needed."

She snorted. "It didn't help much. I'm still..." She chewed her bottom lip. "Me."

"You're perfect." Leaning my forehead against hers, I took a deep breath, knowing we wouldn't be alone for much longer.

"I'm hardly perfect, Cash," she murmured, placing her hands on my hips and pulling me closer.

"You are perfect." I leaned back, staring down into her heated gaze. "Just ask my brothers."

She sighed. "We shouldn't be doing this. Not here." When she went to pull away, I tugged her back. Hard. Maybe too hard by the squeak that left her mouth.

"We can." A part of me hoped that Holden would show up. I wanted him to see that even though she was technically his, any one of us could get her if we really tried.

Besides what her and I had bonded over, Landen and her had something special too.

"Have you gone to visit Landen?" I asked her, pressing my mouth against her ear. "You know that you are the reason he was put in jail in the first place."

"I never wanted that to happen. He wasn't supposed to walk in. None of you were." She whimpered but she didn't pull away. "I couldn't control them. They hurt me, Cash."

"I know, baby." I didn't want it to come out like this but each of us had a part in this fucked up game Sasha needed us to play. And for her, we would continue playing it for however long she asked us to.

"It was a mistake," she continued. "All of it was a mistake. Holden told me...he said...he suggested that I play nice with the guys but after they found out about you three..."

"I know," I repeated, watching her break in my arms. "What do you think Holden would do right now if he saw us here, in the basement where they used to make you cry? Where they used to use you up, spit you out and shove you right into our arms only for it to happen all over again the next day? What do you think, Sasha?" I backed her up until she hit the wall. Gripping her jaw, I forced her head around, pressing my mouth to her ear. "Remember what I walked in on that one night. You were on all fours. It was your eighteenth birthday."

"Cash, stop. I don't want to talk about that night."

"No?" I lifted my head, tilting it to the side. "Are you sure? Because from what I recall, it was a pretty good night for you. You went through all of us. Didn't you?" And Holden made us watch every single second of it.

"I never asked for it." She shoved against me, but my hold only tightened. "I didn't want it to happen."

"See, I think you're lying." Before she could respond, I crushed my mouth to hers.

She gasped, arching her small body against me.

I took the hint and shoved my tongue deep into her mouth, swallowing her moan. The kiss picked up speed as I attacked and ravaged her.

I had no intention of doing this with her. Not here anyway. Not until I could get her home where she belonged. With us.

Sasha owned all of us. Whether we cared to admit it or not. She was ours and we were hers. Just none of us ever dared say it out loud.

CHAPTER SEVEN

SASHA

It had felt like forever since Cash had kissed me. Since I felt his tongue deep between my lips. Since I felt his hands roaming over my body. When really, it hadn't been that long at all.

That tiny little voice inside of my head that I started ignoring years ago, screamed that this wasn't right. That we shouldn't be doing this here. Not in a place that had been my nightmare for years. But at the moment I didn't care. What I had with the brothers, was fucked up at best. They had all gone through other women at one point in time, while I only ever had them. Three brothers. Three men who I thought were very different from each other but as I got older, I realized that they were really not far off from being the same.

Cash nipped at my lips, the slight tinge of pain forcing blood to the surface, and I knew that when Holden saw me later, the evidence would be right on my face. He would know that Cash kissed me and that I never stopped him.

Much to my surprise, Cash released my mouth and lowered to his knees in front of me. Before I could even stop him or tell him that we shouldn't be doing this and that we should wait until it was a more appropriate time, he ripped open my jeans. His teeth sunk into my hip bone as he pulled the fabric along with my panties, over my ass and down my legs to rest at my feet.

With rough hands, he gripped my inner thighs and spread me open before shoving his face between my legs.

I cried out, ripping and scratching at his head. I pulled him closer, needing him in a way I had never experienced before. Not with him.

He growled, digging his fingers into my thighs and spread me open as far as he could with my feet still bound by my jeans.

The happy wet noises coming from him were mixed with an angry bite. His mouth was rough, invading my body in a way I needed. His teeth bit, his tongue licking along the area after to soothe the sting.

With his fingers digging into my thighs, it sent a rush of excitement through me, knowing both Holden and Landen would see the bruises later.

Cash's growl against my pussy pulled me from my thoughts. His mouth moved to my inner thigh, his teeth biting down. Hard.

I cried out, my eyes welling at the sweet onslaught of agony.

He rose to his feet, his mouth glossy. "I hope he fucking sees it."

My eyes widened. "What...what are you talking about?"

A wicked grin spread on his face. It reminded me of Holden. I had never seen Cash look so damn evil before. In a quick move, he spun me around and shoved me up against the wall. "It's been a long time. Too long in fact. I missed you. I fucking missed every inch of you."

"You knew where to find me." But even though that had been the case, it wasn't like I could ever get any alone time with him. The facility I had spent months at had strict rules about visitors. Someone else always had to be around. There had been too many cases where patients got caught doing things they shouldn't have been doing. If my doctors only knew half the shit I had done over the years.

"Do you think it helped? Being in that place?" Cash asked, his hot breath fanning over my ear.

"No," I blurted, without any hesitation at all.

That single word that left my mouth pulled a dark chuckle from him. It had been something I had never heard before. Not in him. Never in him. All of those nights where he consoled me and helped me heal as best he could, he had been nothing but kind. Why now? Why after all of this time, did he let his darkness come out and never before?

"I didn't think so, Puppy. Looks like you're a better actress than we thought. How did you convince your doctors to let you leave?" Cash pressed his waist into the naked flesh of my ass.

"Practice. Lots and lots of practice." I was still broken at best, but I had been better than before. Or that had been what I liked to tell myself anyway. Truth was, the only people who could help me were the brothers I had grown up with. "How come you've never shown me this side of you before?"

"Because I didn't want to scare you away. All three of us are one in the same. You know this. You've always known this. It's why you will never be rid of us. You need us just like we need you."

My heart started racing, my palms became sweaty but as much as I wanted to push him away, I couldn't. Because I needed to know. I had come to this place for closure, and I was sure as hell going to get it, no matter the cost.

"You started out with all of us at different stages in your life, Pup, and now you're with all of us at once. Even when the four of us aren't together, we're all still a team. A unit. We're fucking family." His hand reached between my legs. He shoved a couple fingers into me, pulling a hard moan from the back of my throat.

"Cash, stop." But as I said those words, I couldn't help but arch against him and take him deeper.

"He was right you know." Cash held a firm grip on my head. "You are a fucking slut for it. For all of us."

"No, I'm not," I whined, a hot shiver racing down my spine as his fingers picked up speed.

"No? You're not? So tell me something then, Sasha. Why is your body fucking soaked for me? Why did you let me eat your pussy and why are you now letting me finger you? You are married, aren't you?"

I whimpered, placing my hands against the wall and pushed back against him.

"Say it," he demanded, hooking his fingers inside of me and began rubbing the walls of my center. "Say that you married him. Tell me that you are his wife."

"No," I cried out. "I just wanted closure. I didn't come here for this."

"Yes, you did. Admit it. Admit that you came here because you wanted me again. Admit that you missed me."

"No!" I pushed away from him, his fingers ripping from my body at the movement. I pulled up my jeans, stumbling away from him. "I didn't want this. Not this way. Holden...." I swallowed the bile that threatened to burn my throat.

"Holden, what?"

I jumped at the sound of the new voice, spun around and locked eyes with the man who was my ultimate undoing.

CHAPTER EIGHT

HOLDEN

The look on Sasha's face was laughable at best.

"Surprised to see me?" I stalked toward her, letting my eyes roam down every inch of her. Her jeans were still undone, her lips swollen but not by my mouth and my brother's instead. Her hair was a mess, and her cheeks were flushed but fuck me, she was stunning.

Because of her, I was ruined for other women. She thought I cheated on her, but I never had. Not since we got married anyway. I had spent countless hours trying to convince her otherwise but once she got something in her head, it wouldn't leave. No matter how hard my brothers and I tried, the rampant thoughts never left her.

I thought marrying her was my little way of controlling her. Maybe then she would stop going over to see my brother and stay where she belonged.

At my side and definitely at my feet.

When Cash wasn't surprised to see me, I wondered how long he knew that I was around. I had followed Sasha to the house. Not because I didn't trust her but because we needed to end this once and for all. What her and I had was fucked up to say the least, but she knew where she belonged, and I knew whose bed she would end up in tonight. But the fact that he ate my wife's pussy and fingered the fuck out of her, earned him my rage. Whether we had an agreement or not, my brothers needed to learn their place.

She was no better. Her little pleas for him to stop weren't enough. She could have pushed him away as soon as he kissed her, but she didn't and for that, I would have to take it out on her later. But for now,

I was mulling over what to do next. So playing it cool, I watched them instead.

"What are you doing here?" she asked me.

Instead of answering, I stomped up to her and grabbed the back of her head in a rough move. "Did you like his fingers deep in your cunt, Pup?" I pressed my mouth against her ear. "Did you enjoy having his tongue fucking your pussy?"

"I didn't want..." Her breath caught.

"You didn't want it?" I chuckled, meeting my brother's gaze. "Did she want it?"

He grunted. "She always wants it."

"He has a point." I shoved her toward him.

Cash caught her around the waist, spinning her around to face me.

"Holden." Her eyes were wide, watching me but there was something else there. Something dark, something all of us craved.

I feigned a yawn and leaned against the wall. "Just because I'm here, doesn't mean you have to stop."

Her eyes widened even more. "No, that's not what I wanted."

"What the fuck did you come here for then?" I yelled, charging for her and grabbed her jaw. "If you didn't come here for him to fuck you like he used to, what did you come here for?"

"I wanted you to find me," she whispered.

"Find you how?" I dug my fingers into her cheeks harder when she didn't answer. "It'll be better for you if you tell me."

"I wanted you to find him fucking me." She looked down as soon as she said the words.

"Yeah, you did." I loosened my grip on her jaw and pinched her chin, tilting her head back. "But I had to interrupt your little moment, didn't I?"

Cash stiffened behind her.

I chuckled. "It seems you don't know my wife as much as you think you do. Both you and Landen never knew her as well as I did. As well as I still do."

"I..." Cash released her and took a step back. "I don't know what's going on. This isn't what we discussed."

"Cash." When Sasha turned to go to him, I caught her hand. "This isn't what I wanted. I just...I need closure." She looked at me then. "You promised you would help me."

"I am helping you." I met my brother's gaze. "I know you've been keeping tabs on us. Every time we left the house, even though you were always around too, your boy was always there, watching us.

But it didn't matter really, when I know he went to you and didn't tell you much because we have nothing to hide, brother. You know that."

"You always have a hidden agenda, Holden," Cash bit out. "I needed to know that we...that I could..."

"That you could...trust me?" I chuckled. "Seriously, Cash. We promised each other a long time ago that it was just the four of us against the world." I ran a finger down Sasha's cheek. "There's something that you don't know though. Sasha, my wife," I growled out that last word, "has a problem and since I'm a decent guy, I'm helping her with that said problem."

Cash scoffed then. "You are a lot of things but decent is definitely not one of them."

"No? You have no idea what I would do for Sasha and just how far I would go." I looked down at her, crouching until we were at eye level. "I've never cheated on you. I know you think I have because you can't get it out of your head. I was far from perfect before we married but that stopped as soon as I proposed."

She stared at me. "You're not lying."

"Nope, I'm not."

"Why didn't you try to convince me harder that you weren't cheating on me?"

"Because, Pup." I kissed her softly on the mouth, trailing my lips down to her ear. "I kind of enjoyed keeping you broken."

Her breath hitched. "Why?"

"Ah, now that's the question, isn't it?" I took a step back and moved around the room. It held so many different memories. Some good. Most bad. Some outright filthy. Those were my favorite. Sasha acted like a good girl, but I knew from the moment I heard her beg for more, that she wasn't as much of a good girl as she let on.

"You like that he's watching," I whispered in her ear, low enough for only her to hear.

Her body sucked me in even deeper.

"You like that Cash, the one of us who truly loves you, is seeing you getting violently fucked." I bit her shoulder. *"Isn't that right, Pup?"*

"Yes," she whispered. "It turns me on." Her body convulsed around me, squeezing every inch of my throbbing cock.

"Good." I bit her shoulder one last time. "Then let's give him a show."

A smirk splayed on my face at the memory. Sasha played it off that she didn't like what I had done to her, what we did to her, but she sure as hell loved when she had an audience. It was one of the things I obsessed over when it came to her.

"What's going on?" Cash finally demanded.

"Sasha, my darling wife here, has a certain..." I ran my fingers along my mouth, thinking over the proper word. "...kink," I finally said.

Cash raised an eyebrow.

Sasha did up her jeans, glaring at me.

"Come here," I demanded, using the tone she had come to crave over the years.

Her breath hitched but she did as she was told and moved to the spot in front of me. "Why are you doing this?"

"Because you need me to." I turned toward her and grabbed the waist of her jeans, unbuttoning the button and lowering the zipper. "Because you need me to control you much like you have a control over each of us."

Sasha chewed her bottom lip. "I don't know what you're talking about."

"No?" I chuckled, lowering her jeans down and over her ass. Glancing at Cash, I watched as his eyes roamed down the length of her. If I gave the go ahead, not that it really mattered, he would be on her and fuck her before either of us knew what happened. "What do you think, little brother?"

His eyes flicked to mine. "She's perfect."

Cupping Sasha's cheek, I pushed my thumb under her chin and tilted her head back. "She is, isn't she?"

Something flashed behind her eyes. Something that had only ever been meant for me. As much as my brothers spent years trying to claim it for their own, it was mine.

Slipping my fingers into her panties, I cupped the back of her head with my other hand. "You like being watched, Pup."

Her pupils dilated.

"Don't you?" I asked her, slowly running my fingers back and forth over her soaked center.

She nodded. "God, yes."

Cash came up behind her, pulling a knife from his back pocket.

At that point, I fisted her hair and crushed my mouth to hers.

She arched into me, grabbing on to my shirt and pulling me closer.

I could taste Cash on her tongue. It was minty. It made me wonder if he could taste me on hers when he first kissed her, knowing she had left the house after swallowing my cum.

Slipping my fingers into her, I could feel the fabric of her panties

EXPLICIT VOWS

falling away from her body. Cash must have cut them off of her. Either way, it didn't matter. Because as soon as the fabric disappeared, I shoved my fingers deeper into her body.

She cried out, kissing me harder and faster.

I was vaguely aware of Cash lowering to his knees behind her but as his tongue slipped over my fingers, I knew he was preparing a part of her body she wouldn't want him to fuck.

I swallowed her moans, breathed in her sighs and drank up my wife's ecstasy. I would make sure she would enjoy this and help her heal. That was all I cared about. Her mind was broken. The doctors couldn't help her, so my brothers and I had taken matters into our own hands.

She loved acting, even as a girl. She would sign up for as many plays as she could when we were in school, and she was damn good at it too. So that was what this was. It was all an act. An act to give her the closure she needed that had nothing and everything to do with us at the same time.

Now if only Landen would show up, we could really get this fucking show on the road.

"It seems you've started without me."

Sasha whimpered at the new voice coming from somewhere off in the distance.

Speak of the devil.

CHAPTER NINE

LANDEN

At first, she was just a hole to fill. Three of them in fact.

Her mouth, pussy and ass, were all that I had wanted for years. When I finally got them on her eighteenth birthday, she didn't like me too much after the fact.

Apparently if you cut someone, make them bleed a little, they thought differently of you. Who knew?

But as soon as I showed up, the display in front of me was not something I expected to walk in on. As much as I enjoyed seeing it of course.

Once I announced my arrival, Holden only looked at me over his shoulder, gave me a wink and went back to kissing his wife.

She tried struggling against him, but the filthy little slut liked Cash's face between her legs, that she didn't really want to push either of them away, even though she felt like it was the right thing to do.

For years I had followed Holden around, taking orders from him, tormenting both Cash and Sasha. Most would think it was all for nothing, but it really wasn't. All of us had a goal and that was to make Sasha ours. Once and for all. Her marrying Holden was part of the plan. Since legally, she couldn't marry all of us.

"We need to make Sasha ours," Holden said, pacing in front of Cash and I.

"Why?" Cash asked. He was the youngest and the one who usually had the most questions.

I, on the other hand, usually just did as I was told. Most would think it was a form of submission but really, I just didn't care enough to form an opinion.

"She needs us, that's why." Holden stopped, crouching in front of Cash. "You'll pretend to be nice."

"I am nice," he argued, frowning.

We had just moved down the street from the McGomery's place and met Sasha the day before. Already I knew that Holden had set out to make her ours.

Sure, we were young, and she was even younger, but it wasn't like we had anywhere to go. Living near the McGomery's would be a whole hell of a lot better than where we had come from. Being in the system for most of our lives, you learned to bond with your siblings even more. Even if you didn't want to.

"Yes, you are. You're going to have to be even nicer. Convince Sasha that you are the only one of us she can truly trust. Until we get older that is," Holden explained. "But she needs to be ours."

The three of us had made a pact that day that we wouldn't be with anyone else. Sure, we all fucked women that weren't Sasha, but we had never been truly committed to anyone else but her.

Her whimpers pulled me from my thoughts.

Holden released her, smacked a hard peck on her mouth and stepped out of the way. "Someone missed you."

Sasha's dark eyes locked with mine. She slapped a hand against the wall as Cash continued reining pleasure on her body.

Closing the distance between us, I cupped her cheek.

"When did you get out?" she asked, grabbing my shirt and pulling me closer.

"Yesterday." I brushed my mouth along hers. "Even though it was just a year, it was a long fucking year. Now that I'm out, it's been the hardest fucking twenty-four hours of my life."

"God, I missed you." She shivered.

Cash stood behind her, wiping his mouth. "Holden's kept you warm for us."

"He has." She winked at him.

"Not warm enough it seems." Holden chuckled. "It feels like a lifetime since we've been together."

"I don't know why we had to do it this way." Sasha grabbed hold of my shirt and stepped out of her jeans that were currently curled around her feet. She released me and lifted her top up and over her head.

"Because..." Cash groaned. "Fuck, baby." He shook himself and adjusted his pants. "You asked us to do it this way."

"I know." She pouted. "But I never thought you would go through with it. I just wanted to feel safe. For once in my life, I wanted to forget and move on. I've tried doing it on my own, but it hasn't been enough. Even when I had both of you..." She looked up at me then.

"I'm not jealous." I cupped her cheek. And I wasn't. I knew I would have her once I was released. It had given me something to look forward to.

"I never had her enough because someone was being possessive," Cash threw at Holden.

Holden only shrugged. "I didn't want you moving in with us until Landen was released. That wasn't the plan."

We had agreed that we wouldn't be hers completely until all three of us could be.

"We were also trying to help you heal," Holden continued. "Even though you and I got married as soon as we were legally able to, you still needed help that I couldn't give you. All of us had a part in this sick fucking game but your part was the most important of them all." He went back up to her and pulled her into his arms. "You healing, is all we care about."

"I'm fine," she insisted, even though we knew all along that she wasn't.

"You just got out of the treatment facility a month ago and you're walking around naked in a place you used to be raped and abused constantly, baby girl. You are not fine." Holden lifted her into his arms and carried her out of the basement.

"That treatment facility did shit," Cash mumbled.

"Where are you going?" I asked, grabbing her clothes.

"Out of here," he called out over his shoulder. "We're taking her home. Once and for all."

"Thank fuck," Cash and I said in unison.

CHAPTER TEN

SASHA

I did go to the house I spent my childhood in for closure, but everything else was a lie. The rapes and beatings. The torture. They never came from the three brothers. No. They came from my two foster brothers instead.

Spending every night with Cash had been a figment of my imagination at first but it was a way of coping for me. I got through each night because of him. Because of all of them.

It took me a while to gather up the courage but eventually, I started sneaking over to their house once everyone in my house was asleep. Most nights I would end up in Cash's bed but there had been times where I would end up in Landen's or Holden's.

I had met the three brothers at the playground a block from my house. It had been the furthest I was allowed to go. Mr. McGomery hadn't been as nice as I played him out to be. But he did ignore everything that had gone on. I wasn't even sure how much he had known. Maybe I never would.

Holden and Landen did torment Cash and I, but it was all in good fun. Darryl and Nick Fields were the worst of them all. My two foster brothers ruined the innocence I had tried to save for Holden.

I had every intention of losing my virginity to Holden but both Darryl and Nick took that choice away from me.

"What the fuck happened to you?" Holden demanded as I trembled in his arms. I had snuck over to their place after my foster brothers had gone to bed. I had every intention of slipping into Cash's room but

ended up in Holden's instead. He always left the window unlocked for me even though I usually spent the nights with his brother.

"I...I wanted..." My bottom lip was split but it shook as I tried forcing the words to leave my lips.

"Sasha, tell me," he demanded.

I remembered back to when I told him about the abuse. I thought he was going to tear the damn walls down. It took everything in me to calm him down but I realized now, that he had never been calm.

"You good?" Holden asked, glancing at me over his shoulder before looking back out at the road ahead of us.

"I am now but I can't believe you're leaving me naked," I said, curling into Landen's side.

"The windows are tinted, Pup," Holden pointed out while he drove us to their cottage that was in the middle of nowhere.

"Which means, I can do this." Cash leaned over, bit my shoulder and slipped his fingers between my legs.

I sighed.

"Did you get what you were looking for at the house?" Landen asked, watching his brother thrust his fingers into me.

"I got the three of you, didn't I?" I moaned, spreading my legs even wider.

Cash chuckled, pulling me onto his lap and keeping his fingers inside of me.

"You know what I mean." Landen leaned over and ran his thumb along my nipple. "I just—"

"Landen," Holden barked from the front. "Leave it alone. She'll see her surprise when we get home and then she'll really have the closure she needs."

"What surprise?" I asked, sitting up straight.

"Don't worry about it." Cash pinched my chin, turning my head back around to face him. "Right now, you're going to ride me. I've been fucking throbbing ever since Holden interrupted us."

"I guess I can do that." I had his pants undone and his cock out and in my hand before anyone could take a breath. Slipping my body down the length of him, I sighed, wrapping my arms around his shoulders.

"This'll be fast." He kissed me softly. "But I promise, we'll make up for it later. For the rest of our lives, we'll make up for it."

I didn't get a chance to respond when he started powering into me. Whimpers and cries left me, but I held on, needing him and that delicious release he promised.

"Hold onto me, baby. Fuck hold on." Cash grabbed my ass, lifting me and thrust up and up. "Fuck." His unexpected release shot into me. "You turn me into a two second man, Sasha."

All of us laughed.

"I think she does that to all of us." Landen pulled me out of Cash's arms and onto his lap.

"No kidding," he groaned, righting his pants. "Best fucking pussy ever."

I blew him a kiss.

"Do you want to know your surprise, Pup?" Landen whispered in my ear.

"Yes." I leaned my head against his shoulder, liking the feeling of being in his arms once again. He had gone to jail for assault and battery when he found one of my foster brothers on top of me. I missed him terribly and was glad that he was finally home.

A yawn suddenly trembled through me, earning me a deep chuckle.

"Sleep, Pup," Holden said from the front. "We'll show you your surprise as soon as we're able."

I nodded, closing my eyes.

"How about a quick release first, Sasha?" Landen whispered, adjusting me on his lap.

"You guys fuck, I'm going to sleep." Cash leaned his head against the window and closed his eyes.

"You all are a bunch of fucking teases," Holden grumbled.

"I'll take care of you later," I offered, meeting his gaze in the reflection of the rear-view mirror.

"Fuck," he growled, pressing a foot on the gas.

I laughed and was about to offer to slip into the front seat to give him a little reprieve when Landen turned me in his arms.

"Kiss me, baby," he murmured, running his hands down my back. "I want to fill you with my cum as well."

A shiver trembled down my spine at what he was suggesting.

"Show me how much you missed me."

I smiled, lowering my mouth to his and swallowed his breath. To think that we had come this far. The four of us. Without them, I would have lost myself a long time ago. My foster brothers had been evil, vile human beings.

Darryl and Nick came to the McGomery's after their previous foster parents caught them trying to fuck their eight-year-old daughter. I was happy that she had never gone through what I did but it made me wonder at the time why Mr. McGomery didn't care enough. He had to have known.

"Stop thinking, Sasha." Landen pulled me to my knees, lowering me onto him. "Just feel me."

I shivered, taking him deep into my body.

"That's it, love." He kissed my jaw. "Ride me."

"I missed you," I whispered, circling my hips back and forth. "I missed all of you," I said louder that time.

"We'll make up for it." Landen dug his fingers into the cheeks of my ass and pulled me forward and back. "I promise. Fuck." He groaned. "I definitely promise."

"Jesus," Holden muttered from the driver's seat.

Landen smirked.

I moaned.

It was fucking heaven.

CHAPTER ELEVEN

CASH

Of all the things I had done, getting Sasha to fall in love with me was the hardest. Not even just me, but my brothers too. After what she had been through, we couldn't overly blame her. Even though she came to us willingly, it took a while for her to tell us how she felt.

For most, three brothers sharing the same woman wouldn't make sense but for us, it did. All of us vowed to protect her and in our own ways we did. Sasha brought out a different part in each of us, so it was almost like she had an individual relationship with my brothers as well as myself.

It worked and we wouldn't want it any other way.

While Sasha slept in Landen's arms, I leaned forward. "Pull over, so I can get in the front."

Holden nodded and did as I said.

When he was parked, I slipped into the passenger seat and turned toward him as he pulled away from the edge of the road.

"Do you think she'll like her surprise?" I asked my oldest brother, needing him to reassure me that we had made the right decision.

"I do." His eyes flicked to the rear-view mirror. "I think she'll actually help us finish the job too."

"She's a sick little bitch," I muttered.

Holden chuckled. "Yeah, and she's our sick little bitch."

I smirked, leaning against the door. "She is." But I couldn't help but wonder... "Are we crazy for doing this? For wanting to share the same woman?"

"No." Holden's gaze flicked my way before glancing back out at the road in front of us. "I don't think so. She's been through a lot. If she wouldn't have met you at the playground near our old place, I don't think any of this would have happened. But she did. Because you insisted on going on the swing."

"Swings are freeing in a way," I muttered.

"I thought at first that maybe we just all had a crush on her because she was constantly hanging out with us but as the years went on, she got older, we got wiser, and we learned what her foster brothers were doing..." His hands tightened on the steering wheel. "I'll be happy when they're dead and can no longer torment her mind."

I agreed with him there.

Holden had found Darryl and Nick after they were both released from jail. They didn't get long enough if you asked me. They were let off easy, since there was no proof of what they had done to Sasha.

Because she wouldn't testify, for various reasons, the two brothers didn't spend a long time in jail. Now that they were out, we would take matters into our own hands, and I couldn't wait to watch the life leave them.

CHAPTER TWELVE

SASHA

When we finally arrived at a cottage the brothers owned, Landen helped me get dressed before we left the car. Once I stepped foot outside into the warm night air, I couldn't help but stare at the vast expanse before me. The cottage was your typical looking home away from home, but it was much larger than I expected. I wondered how the brothers could afford such a place but when arms wrapped around my middle and a kiss was placed just beneath my ear, I forced that question to the back of my mind.

"This is our home, Pup." Landen squeezed me tighter. "You won't have to worry about anything ever again. Whatever you want and need, we'll get it for you. No questions asked."

"Really?" I asked, looking up at him.

"Of course." Cash came up beside us. "Holden was able to get this place for cheap and we've been fixing it up for awhile."

"You never told me," I said to Holden, who was still technically my husband.

He closed the distance between us and pinched my chin. Tilting my head back, he lowered his mouth to mine. "I wanted it to be a surprise," he murmured against my lips. He lifted his head, giving me one of his signature smirks I had fallen in love with years ago. "It's probably why you thought I was having affairs, but I wasn't. I spent all of my time away from you, here, helping Cash fix this place up."

"Is this where you lived?" I asked Cash.

"Yeah." He ran a hand through his hair. "When I wasn't at your place, I was here."

"I'm sorry for thinking you had all of those affairs, Holden." I placed my hands on his chest, suddenly needing him. Hard.

He dug his fingers into my jaw, turning my head back to face him. "I meant what I said. I had to keep you broken. It was the only way we could help you heal. You know that. And in a few minutes, you'll understand. You'll understand it all."

"I didn't want it this way," Cash confessed. "But Holden is right. This is better. You'll see in a moment."

"And then Holden will take care of you and the three of us will share you after. Forever, baby," Landen whispered in my ear, running his hand beneath my shirt to cup my breast.

I shivered.

"Let's go," Holden barked. "I want to fuck her in their blood."

My eyes widened. "What?"

Landen chuckled, while Cash only grinned.

Holden took a step toward the house, looking back at me over his shoulder. "Come here. Wife."

I swallowed hard, pulled away from Landen and went up to his brother. My husband. When I stood a mere foot away from him, a grin slowly spread on his face.

"Ready for your surprise, Pup?" he asked, his voice low.

I nodded, all breath leaving me at the intensity in his dark gaze.

"Good, let's go." He grabbed my hand, leading me up to the front of the house with Cash and Landen following behind us.

They were excited. I could feel their energy billowing around us almost like it was a physical thing itself. They were practically bouncing by the time we stepped foot into the cottage. But as soon as I was over the threshold, I didn't even get a chance to take it all in when I saw Darryl and Nick sitting in chairs in the living room.

"Oh my..." I gasped, clasping a hand over my mouth.

"Surprise, baby." Holden moved behind me, cupping my shoulders. "This is for you. They didn't get enough time. So we kind of took matters into our own hands a bit."

"Holden, this isn't...this isn't right." But as those words left my mouth, I couldn't help but wonder what it would be like to watch them die.

"I want to fuck her in their blood."

Holden's words rushed through my mind. My body heated. There was no way. I had been through a lot at the hands of these two monsters, but it still wasn't right. At all. But even though I knew that it wasn't right, why the hell did it turn me on just the same?

Cash took my hand, while Landen took the other. They led me toward my foster brothers who were tied to two chairs. Their faces were already badly bruised, blood coating their shirts and skin.

"What did you do? How did you find them? This...this can't be happening." My body trembled the closer we got to the brothers.

"But it is, Pup." Holden pressed his mouth to my ear. "This is happening because of you and our love for you. You need to heal and the only way for you to do that, is to watch them die."

As soon as those words left his mouth, both Darryl and Nick grunted protests behind the tape covering their mouths.

"But there should be a better way," I said, my voice not coming out as firm as I would have liked.

"This is the best way." Cash brought my hand up to his mouth. "The only way."

"You want me to kill them?" Bile rose to my throat at the thought.

"No." Landen looked at Cash before meeting my gaze. "We're going to do it for you. We don't want anymore darkness on your soul. You've been through enough shit. We'll take care of this for you. Look at it as our little welcome home present." He smirked, giving me a wink.

Holden released my shoulders and gave me a gentle push. "Go on, Pup. Tell the brothers hello."

Hugging my arms around myself, I took a tentative step toward Darryl and Nick. Darryl was the oldest but Nick...I swallowed hard as the memories rushed through me. Even though he was younger, he was meaner. It was almost like he had to make up for things he was lacking in when it came to his brother having the spotlight. I wasn't sure if that was the case, but every time Nick was angry, he had taken it out on me.

Once I stood in front of them, I knelt. "What did I ever do to you?" I asked them, my voice shaking.

Darryl's brown hair was matted to his forehead with dried blood. His one eye was swollen shut but the other, it was wide open and glaring at me. While you could sense the rage rolling off of him, Nick on the other hand, was calm and collected. I wasn't sure what was worse.

I was vaguely aware of Holden, Landen, and Cash moving behind me. One of them touched my head, petting a hand over it and through my hair. That single touch alone, pulled me to my feet.

"I never asked to be your foster sister. I never asked to be put in that home. I never asked for any of it." I took a deep breath, staring at the brothers who had tried their hardest to ruin my life. "Did you ever find out what happened to Mr. McGomery?" I asked no one specific. They never told me while I was in the facility, even though I had constantly asked. Apparently keeping that information from me was part of my healing process.

"He died of a heart attack six months ago," Cash said gently.

"What about your foster parents? They're doing well?" I asked, a breath of relief leaving me that I would never have to see Mr. McGomery again. Even though he had never touched me himself, he never stopped Darryl and Nick from doing so. And for that, I blamed him just as much.

"They're doing well and send their love," Holden added.

I blew out a slow breath, looking between Darryl and Nick. "I should have run away like you said, Holden. I should have listened to you."

"You were just a girl." Holden cupped my shoulders. "You probably would have been found anyway and returned to Mr. McGomery. That could have been worse for you."

"This is better," I added even though I wasn't overly sure it was or not.

"It is." Cash linked his fingers in mine. "We're your safe place, Pup. Always have been. The three of us have gotten you through the worst times of your life."

"He's right." Landen grabbed hold of my other hand. "You are safe with us. Always."

I took a deep breath and then another. "Take off the tape. I want to hear them."

Holden chuckled while Cash and Landen only stared at me.

I loved them all, but it had been Holden who truly knew me the best. He knew that there was a sick, twisted side of me. A side I couldn't control, no matter how much I tried. I had spent years keeping it contained but now, seeing Darryl and Nick sitting across from me, broken and bloody, that part of me wanted loose. It wanted free as I imagined what it would be like to feel the life leave their bodies.

"Do it," Holden instructed, leaning down to my ear. "I've missed that sick part of you, Pup. Think you'll let her come out to play more often?"

I swallowed hard, unable to take my eyes off Darryl and Nick. "Yes," I answered, knowing that there was no point in lying to Holden.

His hand moved to the base of my throat, pulling me back against his chest. "Kill them."

"Fuck you," Darryl yelled first. "We haven't done shit."

EXPLICIT VOWS

"She wanted it all," Nick added.

My blood burned through me. There had always been something off with me, even I knew that, but I never wanted them to rape me. I never wanted them to take it as far as they did. They broke a part of my mind to the point I imagined Cash was with me every night. He was my safe place. Landen, Holden, and Cash were all my safe place. I would have died a long time ago if it hadn't been for them taking care of me. If I wouldn't have gone to the park that one day as a girl, I never would have met the three brothers. The three boys who turned into men that I would spend my life with. It didn't make sense to most, but it made sense for us. They were my life, and I was theirs.

"You wanted it, you little bitch," Nick spat, struggling in his binds.

I pulled away from Holden and went up to Nick. Pressing my mouth up against his ear, I let out a soft chuckle. I held a hand behind my back, waiting for the familiar touch. When Holden placed the item in my open palm, I wrapped my fingers around it, a hot shiver racing down my spine. "I guess you'll never know if I wanted it or not," I whispered in Nick's ear, slowly penetrating the knife into his gut.

He let out a string of curses that made the guys laugh.

I pulled my hand back, thrusting the knife into him harder and harder. I repeated the movement until he stopped talking. Until he stopped breathing. Until he stopped seeing.

While Darryl watched in horror over what I had done to his brother, I couldn't help but watch the thick red liquid coat my hand. There was so much blood that I couldn't focus.

Arms wrapped around my middle.

"Finish him and clean up the mess."

Before I knew what was happening, I was lifted into the air and carried off to another room. I was thrown on a bed, my pants ripped down my body and off my feet. I had no time to process anything when a thick cock thrust into me.

I cried out, my body shaking at the unexpected impact.

A firm hand gripped my hair, turning my head. "Just because I let you fuck my brothers, doesn't mean anything, Sasha," Holden whispered in my ear. "I still own you. I own every single inch of you. I'm the only one who knows that sick part of you. The true part." He covered my hand, the blood from Nick, slipping between us. The crimson sight alone was enough to set me over the edge. A quick release trembled through me, earning me a deep chuckle.

"That's my sick little bitch." Holden released my hair, leaned back and grabbed hold of my hips. He began powering forward and back, fucking me with everything he had.

"Harder," I heard myself beg. I was vaguely aware that we were no longer alone, but I didn't care. It wasn't like Cash and Landen hadn't watched Holden and I anyway. But as much as I wanted the three of them, I knew that Holden and I needed this little moment where it was just us two. "Harder," I screamed, slamming back into him.

He grunted, shoving me face-first into the bed. "Take it. Take it all."

After a few more thrusts, Holden groaned through his release.

I panted, gasping for breath as the tiny hairs on my body tingled.

"Let's get you cleaned up," he said, kissing my temple.

"Everything else is cleaned up too," Cash added, pulling me from Holden and into his arms. He carried me to a room off the bedroom and I realized then that it was a bathroom. A very big bathroom I might add.

"Are we really doing this?" I asked as Cash set me on my feet.

The three brothers looked between each other and then back at me.

"You want out?" Landen asked, raising a dark eyebrow.

"No. Not at all. I want more. I want it all." I was greedy for them. There was no point in denying it.

Holden took a step toward me. "Just remember what I said. You are mine."

"I am yours," I repeated.

He pinched my chin, tilting my head back. "And?"

"You are mine." I took a breath. "Sir."

ABOUT J.M. WALKER

J.M. Walker is an Amazon bestselling author who hit USA Today with Wanted: An Outlaw Anthology. She loves all things books, pigs and lip gloss. She is happily married to the man who inspires all of her Heroes and continues to make her weak in the knees every single day.

"Above all, be the HEROINE of your own life..." ~ Nora Ephron

Find me: https://linktr.ee/authorjmwalker

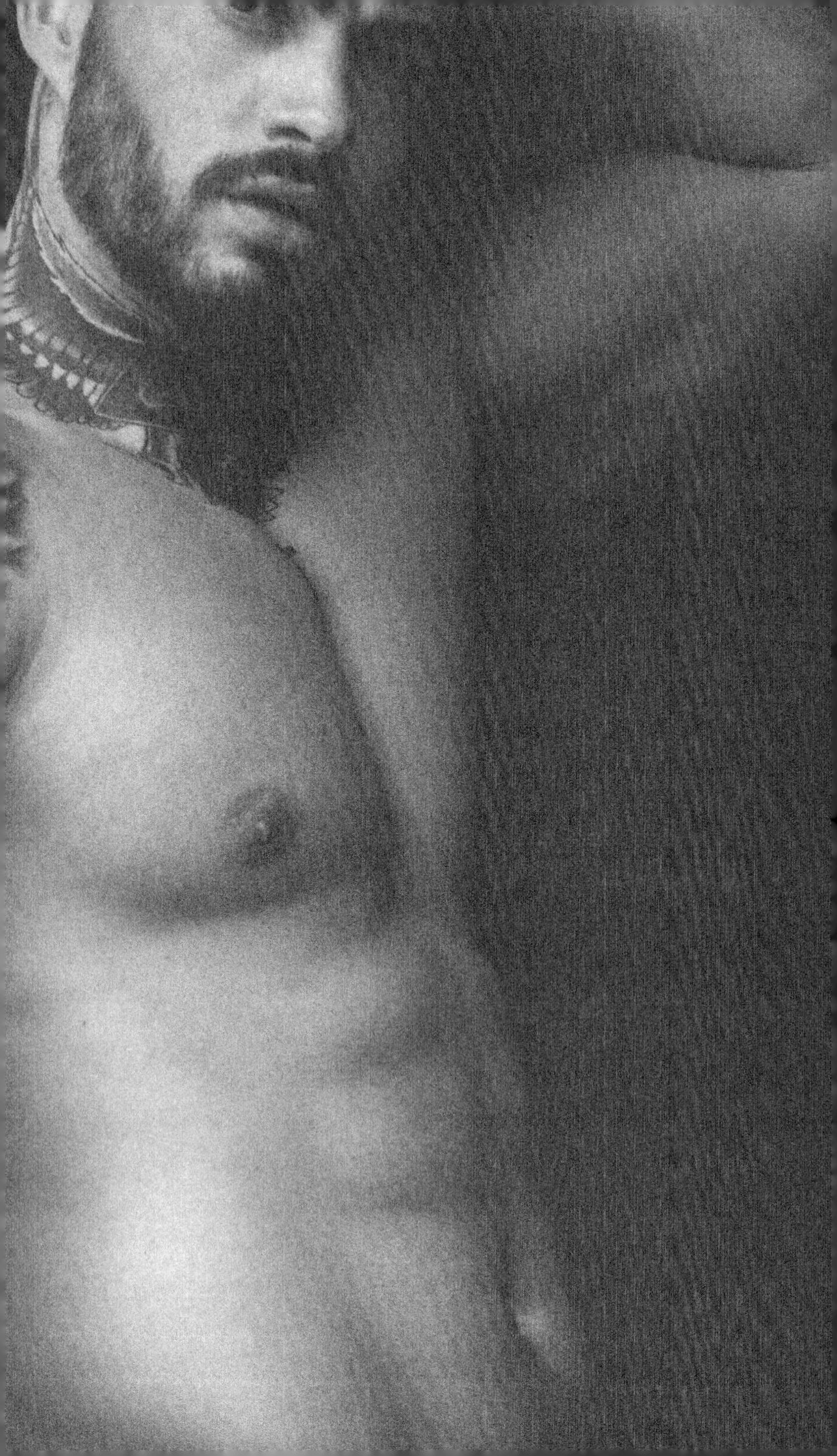

DARKEST DEVOTION

BY PERSEPHONE AUTUMN

CHAPTER ONE
ELLA

What the hell is this place?

"Come out," she said. "It'll be fun," she said.

Naomi. My best friend. The girl who bends anyone to her will. Including me. And although I know her ability to sway decisions, I fall for her pleas every single time. Sales is in her blood, whether it is cars at her father's car dealership or last year's wardrobe to the desperate-to-be-cool freshman class—well, now sophomores.

Somehow, Naomi convinced me to tag along to some mysterious underground club. The kind of "club" that is never in the same location twice. The kind you have to know someone to receive an invite. The kind you only tell trusted people about. Yeah, that is where we are.

Except this underground party is not just loud music, influential substances and gyrating bodies. *"It's like an old-school rave."* Lies. Bald-faced lies.

"What is this, Becky?" Her fake name rolls off my tongue in a hiss.

Naomi and I have been frequenting clubs since before legally allowed. Some guy she dated junior year knew someone who made fake IDs. We never used them to drink, only to get inside. For a year and a half, she has been Becky and I have been Hazel. Additionally, no guy ever gets our actual name. Less worry in the creepsters department.

She spins to face me, trying her damnedest to hide her wicked grin. "I swear." Naomi holds up her right hand. "I had no idea."

I roll my eyes. "Your cheeky smile says otherwise."

"Swear." She dons a more serious expression. "But it is funny."

What the hell is funny about walking into a room that basically looks like a porn studio?

By no means am I a prude. Walking in blind to a secret party thinking it is music and drinks and dancing is one thing. Walking in blind to a secret party and seeing sweaty bodies slapping skin while other people watch is a whole different ball game. More than anything, it just would have been nice to know.

Huffing out a breath, I shake my head and hook my arm in hers. "Fine," I grumble. "But you are stuck with me all night."

She jerks away and meets my eyes. Slams her tight fists on her hips. "No way."

"Afraid so." My lips tilt up in a wicked smirk. A smirk that vanishes seconds later.

"Alright then. You want me at your side all night." Her eyes roam the room until she lands on something that makes my insides twist. "Let's go."

If anyone hears this... save me, please.

When my best friend suggested we party to celebrate graduating high school, an elusive sex free-for-all was not what popped in my head.

One... who visits sex parties with their friend? No one, that is who. I love Naomi, but not on that level.

Two... what does she expect to happen? I easily picture her thinking it would be okay for us to go our separate ways and do our own thing while between these four walls. To spot a hottie and ditch me to hook up with him.

Too fucking bad. She should have given her plan more thought before dragging me into the unknown.

We reach the other side of the warehouse space and Naomi weaves us between a crowd. As they make room for us, two women on blanket-covered pallets come into view. It isn't obscene or grotesque. Actually, watching them pleasure each other has me clamping my thighs tighter. As weirded out as I was when we walked in the door, the sight of these women pleasuring one another has me entranced.

Too entranced.

Sexual preferences have never bothered me. I have always been more attracted to people for who they are, not the genitals between their legs. Naomi, on the other hand, has always given off the vibe that she is straighter than straight.

Looking to my left, I open my mouth to ask Naomi about her sudden interest in women. But... she isn't there.

You have got to be kidding me.

Not only did my best friend covertly lure me to a supersecret sex party. Now, she ditched me.

Super.

Fucking.

Shitty.

I pull my cell from my back pocket to text her, but I already have a message waiting.

Naomi: Sorry, E. A hottie was throwing signals.

Ella: You suck!

I can and can't believe she ditched me. She will grovel for weeks to come, I will make sure of it.

Winding my way through the crowd, I locate a makeshift bar and buy a bottled water. In the corner of the room, several tattered couches sit in a circle around another blanketed pallet bed. Thankfully, one couch remains unoccupied.

Parking myself on the couch, I sip my water and stare at the couple in the middle of the circle. A man, his pants shoved to his knees, sits leaned back, palms on the floor behind him. His erection thick and red and veiny. On her hands and knees, a woman bobs up and down his length. Her skirt too short to cover her bare slit, and her top long since removed.

Much as I don't want to be here alone—hello, unwanted weirdos—I can't seem to make myself walk out the door. Tonight wouldn't be the first time I called a cab because Naomi found someone to hook up with. I shouldn't have expected tonight to be any different.

But this place is not like the other places we partied. Bars with nothing but drunks I can handle. This place is not that. Not by a long shot.

A man sits next to me on the couch and I stop breathing. He doesn't say anything, but I feel his eyes on my profile. The heat of his stare as he waits for me to look his way.

Why did I sit at the end of the couch? Damn it.

Minutes tick by and nothing happens. The guy sits next to me, eventually looks away to watch the woman giving a blow job, and squeezes his own cock through his jeans. Awkward as the situation is, at least he keeps his hands to himself.

A moment later, as if he heard my thoughts, his calloused hand rests on my thigh.

Fuck. My. Life.

CHAPTER TWO

Thomas

When the guys from the firm invited me out to celebrate my birthday, I assumed we would hit up the corner bar, have a few drinks and some greasy food. Talk shit for hours, then go our separate ways. I did not expect to walk into a big orgyfest.

Soon as we passed the threshold, they gave a shoulder slap and wandered off.

Who the hell brings their coworker to a sex party? God, if the firm found out about this, they would probably reprimand us all.

At least they walked away. Don't get me wrong, I am all for bonding with coworkers. Just not like this. I prefer not to share my sexual predilections with business partners.

I wander through the industrial building, hands in my pockets as I avoid eye contact. By no means am I shy or pure, especially when it comes to sex. But I don't know this place, I don't know these people. And although I have tried many nontraditional things in the bedroom, I have yet to perform the act in front of others. So, for now, I keep my hands to myself while I survey the scene.

The space is dark, lit only by the occasional lamp or colored bulb. Sultry music from a portable DJ booth thrums and echoes off the walls like a concert hall. Sweat and sex and marijuana permeate the air. On occasion, an arm or hand brushes against my bicep, shoulder, or abdomen as I move through the crowd. And on every available surface, people are fucking.

Less than a minute after we walked in, my cock was harder than steel. With each step forward, my erection grows achingly painful. My balls thick and heavy and in desperate need of release.

"Fuck," I whisper to myself.

In a dimly lit corner, I sit on a couch facing a couple giving oral. The man faces away from me, but his head is tipped back in ecstasy while a woman sucks him off. Exhibitionism may not be my thing, but voyeurism is a whole different story.

The longer I sit in this place, the longer I hear and see and smell sex, the harder it is to hold back. The harder it is to restrain my hands.

My eyes scan the area. Look for anyone with eyes on me. My surveillance comes up empty and I sag deeper into the couch.

Unable to resist any longer, I unfasten my jeans and fist my cock beneath my briefs. Stroke my erection with a firm hand. Occasionally pinch the tip and moan at the sting it causes. Stroke after stroke, I bring myself closer to release, as the woman does the same for the man feet in front of me.

Then, I stop mid-stroke when my gaze shifts slightly.

Opposite me in the couch circle, a young redhead fidgets next to a man who put his hand on her thigh. I don't know them, don't know if they are together, but her body language screams for someone to rescue her. In this place, there are no heroes, just different levels of perversion.

For her, I may be the lesser of evils.

I fasten my pants, rise from the couch and saunter to where she sits. There isn't much time to come up with a plan of attack. The only option is to say the first thing that comes to mind. And since the man's attention has been solely focused on her and no one else on the couches, I play the easiest hand.

"There you are," I say as I step in front of her. Green-rimmed hazels peek up through a mess of red curls. *Fuck me running.* "Thought I lost you."

For a moment, confusion knits her brow. I extend my hand and widen my eyes a fraction. And then realization clicks in place for her. She slips her hand in mine and rises from the couch. It isn't until this moment that the man snaps out of his sex-induced fog.

"Hey, sugar. We were just about to have some fun," the man says, hand jerking his dick harder. He looks me up and down, then licks his lips. "The more, the merrier."

I tug her into my side and snake my arm around her waist. "Thanks for the offer, but we've already got something lined up. Another time."

The man shrugs off the proposition and eyes the remaining people in the couch circle in search of someone else to satisfy his urges. At least that went easier than expected.

Without hesitation, I lead her away from the couches and near a vacant section of wall. She spins to face me, a soft smile on her lips as she leans against the concrete. My first true visual of her up close.

Damn, she is enchanting.

"Thanks for the rescue," she shouts over the music.

I nod. "No problem. You looked a bit uncomfortable."

She laughs, and I love how it adds a glow to her aura. "Yeah, you could say that. Wasn't my idea to come here." She nibbles at her bottom lip. My eyes follow the action while my dick thickens behind my zipper again. "But I'm not a prude," she says in a rush. "That guy creeped me out, though."

"Same." I lean closer to her. Inhale deeply and detect a hint of peach. "About both." She doesn't shift away from my slight advance, doesn't take her eyes off mine, so I inch closer. "I'm Thomas. Hope I don't creep you out."

"You don't." Her shoulders lift and fall. "Hazel." She licks her lips and swallows.

My lips tug up at the corners. "Does everyone else believe you?"

The lines of her forehead deepen. "Believe me?"

"That your name is Hazel."

She swallows again. "It is."

I eliminate another inch between us. Brush the hair off her neck. Lean close enough to almost taste her skin. "I'll let it go for now." Her chest rises and falls in short bursts, her breath hot on my neck, breasts grazing my chest. "But I will know your name."

Reluctantly, I inch back. Gift her personal space back. Give both of us a moment to breathe.

I may not have come to this place intentionally, but the carnal energy here is off the charts and flooding my bloodstream. Lust fogs my thoughts, but so does she. Moans and whimpers mix with the music, and my cock begs for some form of relief.

Tonight isn't my first exposure to orgies. I dabbled in college. Fucked my share of women and sucked my share of men. But the way she surveys the room, I'd venture to guess this is her first time in such a setting. And fuck me, I want to show her how good it can be. I may not be an exhibitionist, but she makes me want to be.

"You come here with a boyfriend?" My fingers curl into a fist at the thought of her answering yes.

She shakes her head. "A friend."
Thank fuck.
"Are you seeing anyone?"
Another shake of her head. "You?"
"No."

Her frame relaxes as she licks her lips, and my only thought is I want to lick them too. Taste the sweetness of her lips. Feel the softness of her skin. Inhale her peachy scent for hours as I explore her flesh and mark her as mine.

I lean into her again. Press the straining bulge behind my zipper to her belly. She doesn't shift away or gravitate closer. So I cage her in. Invade her space fully. Drop my chin and run my nose along her jaw to her ear. Inhale deeply and groan.

"You'd make a beautiful pet," I say before sucking her lobe. With her curves and alabaster skin... fuck, she would stun me in leather.

She hums and I feel it in my groin. "Not sure if I should be offended" —she exhales against the hollow of my throat and I groan— "or turned on."

"Definitely turned on." My lips and tongue trail down her neck. "Want to get out of here, not-Hazel?"

A soft chuckle vibrates her throat. "Why leave the party?"

I freeze where her neck and shoulder meet. Slowly, I ease back to meet her gaze. For someone who cringed next to a man jerking his cock minutes ago, she seems more open than expected. Or am I reading her all wrong?

"Why indeed."

CHAPTER THREE

ELLA

Stripping bare before dozens of people is uncomfortable as hell and the most liberating thing I have done.

I'd said "why leave the party?" partially as a joke. Thomas asked me to leave with him and I had no clue what to say or do. Not as if I hadn't been abandoned by Naomi in the past and found a ride home. But tonight is different. Hooking up with someone after a sex party wouldn't be the same as leaving the bar and squeezing in a quickie in the back seat.

From the looks of it, Thomas is older. Not much; maybe early to midtwenties. His button-down shirt tucked in his jeans tells me he is not just some schmuck off the street, but not quite big league. He exudes confidence, but watches me as if worried I will run off.

Should I go?

He tosses my shorts next to my shirt, then looks up at me as he kneels at my feet. And it feels so heady... having a man before me like this. Although I still wear a bra and panties, I feel the need to wrap my arms around my middle. To hide myself from passersby. What stops me? Thomas's wanton gaze as he stares up my body from below.

I lean on the wall for support. Let the concrete cool my fevered skin and settle my jittery nerves. Every other second, I remind myself to breathe. Remind myself everything will be fine.

Right?

I don't know this man, yet I let him peel away my clothes without a word, without an ounce of resistance. Yes, he rescued me from some old creepster on the couch. But what if he is some serial killer who preys on innocent—not that I am innocent—women and charms them with his sinful smile and wicked words?

Should I stop him? Should I push him away, put my clothes back on and get the hell out of here? Yes.

Is that what I am going to do? Probably not. Because right now, his tongue is slowly trailing up my thigh and all my rational decisions walk out the door.

"Such a pretty little pet." He licks along the seam of my panties, from the junction of my thighs to the edge of my hip. Fingers hook in the elastic band and slowly tug the thin material down my thighs. "So fucking pretty," he says at the sight of my bare mound.

Since he peeled off my top, I have yet to say a word. Have yet to touch him. Not that I don't want to, it's just... I don't know. Thomas overrides my brain. Short-circuits my thoughts. Makes me question what I am doing and why.

Sex is a good time. I get my jollies and go about life when it ends.

But I have never exposed myself like this. Never made myself so utterly vulnerable. Never let a man take off my clothes in a warehouse full of people. And I have no clue why I am now.

"Thomas, I..." I cover myself with my hands. Everywhere I look, eyes are on me. Watching. Waiting for more. Touching themselves as they watch someone touch me. "I don't think I..."

He rises from the floor and crowds my vision. Steps into me and blankets me in his heat. Grips my chin between his thumb and finger and directs my eyes to his.

"Hey." When my eyes avert to the small crowd, he twists me back to his line of sight. "Ignore them." My brow pinches at the middle. "Me, only look at me."

I open my mouth, objection on the tip of my tongue, but don't get a word out. Thomas crushes my lips with his. For two breaths, I freeze. Question what the hell I am doing. Then I melt into him. Kiss him back. Moan when he licks my bottom lip and parts them with his tongue. Fist his shirt when he deepens the kiss. Haul him flush with my frame and press into his groin.

He breaks the kiss and I smile at how ragged his breathing is. At how much I affected this man. I may be young, I may not have much life experience, but I can bring a man to his knees and make him breathless. If that isn't power, I don't know what is.

Reaching up, I unfasten the buttons of his shirt. Spread the cotton wide and stare down his chest. Slender without definition. A slight smattering a hair that disappears beneath his jeans. *That's a trail I plan to blaze.*

My fingertips trace along his skin and he sucks in a breath when I dip below his navel. Grabs my wrist and halts my touch.

"Keep that up and I'll embarrass myself before I fuck you." Before I complain how unfair it is I can't touch him, he drops to his knees, presses his nose between my thighs and inhales deeply. "So sweet, my pet."

The term "pet" should turn me off. Should make me fiery and argumentative. I am not a cat or dog. Not something you put on a leash and take for a walk. Not at your beck and call or someone you command.

But every time he calls me pet, I purr like a kitten. My pussy aches for him to say it again. To stroke me like the pet he says I am. Reward me like a good girl for being so wet.

As the crowd grows thicker, I keep my gaze fixed on Thomas. Watch as his hands trail up my calves, my thighs, and spreads them farther apart. Watch as he leans in and runs the tip of his nose from my bare mound to my clit. His tongue darts out and licks my slit. The rumble of his moan vibrates my flesh as he tastes me for the first time.

I want to fist his hair, shove him deeper between my thighs and grind against his face. I want to, but I don't.

Him, this place, these people... it is a fantasy existence. What person wants more than sex with someone after being in a place like this?

Thomas is not the swine that sat next to me on the couch earlier, but he may not be much better. He still stripped me bare without asking permission. Still touched and tasted my skin without consent. And because I never said yes, my clenched fists ache to tug his hair and yank him back. Shove him to the floor and make him beg to touch what doesn't belong to him.

But I don't move my hands. Don't fist his hair. Don't push him away.

Because I love the feel of his tongue between my legs. Love the way his fingers bruise my hips and ass as he hauls me closer and fucks my pussy with his mouth. Love the way he groans against my flesh as he devours me whole. Love the way his eyes haven't left mine since his tongue licked my lower lips.

My legs quiver and knees threaten to buckle. Thomas tightens his hold on me. Cocoons my hips with his strong arms. Performs some magical exorcism on my clit with his tongue.

And then I free-fall into oblivion. Get lost in a pool of undiluted lechery.

Thomas doesn't slow his assault. If anything, he takes me harder. Captures my clit between his lips and sucks. Hard. Draws out my orgasm and builds me up for the next.

Then, he releases me from his mouth. I wobble in place as he rises to his full height. Reach for him as he pulls his wallet from his back pocket. Shove his shirt down his arms as he undoes his pants and exposes his thick, swollen cock. Pout when I reach for his cock and he stops me.

My eyes lock on his and ask why. Why can't I touch him like he touched me moments ago?

"Not tonight, my pet." He strokes my cheek with his knuckles. "Tonight, I want to bury my cock in your pretty little cunt and never leave." Corner of the package between his teeth, he rips open the condom wrapper and rolls the latex down his length.

His shirt falls to the floor before he hoists me up. My legs wrap around his waist and arms around his neck. Pants bunched at his ankles, he staggers forward until his weight pins me to the concrete; the tip of his cock grazing my entrance.

Tongue darting out, Thomas licks up my neck to my ear. "You one of those girls that's quiet during sex, pet?"

I rock my head side to side. "Yes and no." He sucks my lobe between his lips. "Don't really spend time getting to know the guys I fuck."

He rears back as if I slapped him. And I swear he growls before responding. "We may have just met. I may have just feasted on your pussy. And we may be seconds from fucking. But that sure as shit doesn't mean tonight is it."

When I first looked at Thomas earlier, I never would have pegged him as the possessive type. The guy who *claims* his woman. If he were any other person, I would tell him to fuck off. Tell him he doesn't *own* me. That no one *owns* me.

The words are right there, on the tip of my tongue, but they refuse to be spoken. Because somewhere deep down, rooted in my bones, I like the way Thomas wants to assert ownership of me. Like the way he wants to command my pleasure.

If Thomas were anyone else, I would have left this place the moment I stood from the couch. But he isn't anyone else. And for some unknown reason, I want him more with each passing beat.

"Okay," I acquiesce, my voice fragile. "Not just tonight."

The tip of his cock teases my entrance. He rocks his hips slightly and the head dips inside. I gasp at the feel of him, at the way he toys with my body. Then he rears back, rocks forward and sinks deeper. My nails bite his skin as my thighs squeeze him tighter.

"So fucking tight." He runs his tongue over my lips. "Ever been with a real man, pet?"

Since the day I lost my virginity, sex has never been anything more than sex. Every guy I hooked up with was the same age as me, give or take a year, but all in high school. So, no, I hadn't technically been with a man.

I shake my head. "Never had the chance."

"Mmm," he hums against my lips. "Guess that makes us both lucky." My brow scrunches as I regard him. "Lucky me, because I get to be your first. Lucky you because you'll never want anyone else."

I open my mouth, ready to call him presumptuous, but the words never come.

Thomas rocks his hips forward and fills me to the hilt. I forget how to think or speak or care about anything but the way he feels inside me. "Oh, god," I moan out as my nails claw his upper back.

"Sweet fucking Christ." His hands on my ass grip tighter, spread my cheeks and guide me as he pistons in and out.

The crowd vanishes and the music fades. All I feel is the bass as it rattles the walls and Thomas's cock as it thrusts deep inside me. His jagged breath heats the skin beneath my ear. His sweat-slicked skin slaps me over and over as he drives us both to orgasm.

It all feels too much and not enough. The exhibitionism and vulnerability. The voyeurism and perversion.

I love sex—not that it has ever been this good—but it was always just an act. A means to an end. A way to get my jollies. But most of it happened in the back of a car, in someone else's bed or a random bathroom. It was fast and meaningless and I usually had to do most of the work if I wanted to get off.

With Thomas, sex is a new experience. The way he speaks and acts and takes. He is both soft and hard, tender and aggressive, light and dark.

A hand snakes up my spine, fingers comb through my hair and curl into a fist, and then he yanks. A sting spreads over my scalp. His arm around my waist grips me harder. Holds me to him. Then his teeth pierce my skin where my neck and shoulder meet.

"Harder," I choke out.

He growls against my flesh as his hips piston faster. "Get there, pet," he commands.

I shut out everything but the unadulterated lust flowing through my veins. Let go of everything except him and me and how good we feel together.

He licks up my neck and sucks the spot beneath my ear. "That's it." Teeth clamp down on my lobe. "Come on my cock like a pretty little pet."

Stars steal my sight. White noise floods my ears. Thomas yanks my hair harder. Pumps his hips faster and hits me deeper as I ride my high. Then his teeth clamp down where my neck and shoulder meet. His hips stop, but his cock jerks.

As he loosens his grip on my hair, the room comes back into view. Countless people masturbate at the sight of us, but I no longer feel the need to hide my body. In fact, I want to watch. Want to join. Want to play.

Thomas kisses up my neck and along my jaw before taking my mouth. "My sweet pet." He strokes my lips with his finger. "Mine. Understood?"

My eyes dart between his, judge the seriousness of his words. Because fucking me in a room of strangers is one thing. Claiming me as yours and no one else's... we will need to have a separate conversation about that. For now, though, I follow his lead.

"Ella." His brows pinch at the middle. "My name. It's Ella."

A wicked grin takes over his expression. "Indeed, it is, pet."

CHAPTER FOUR

Thomas

Ella. Sweet and quiet, yet a firestorm in her own right.

Although she never said no, never pulled away from my advances, I questioned her consent from the moment we reached the wall and I invaded her space. I never asked permission to touch her, to kiss her, to fuck her, yet I took what I wanted anyway. It wasn't until she told me to take her harder that I truly gave over to the beast inside. That one word was all the permission I needed.

With our clothes back in place, I take her hand in mine and weave us through the crowd. An hour ago, I would have stopped and played the voyeur. Watched couples and trios and groups as they gave into their carnal nature. Now, all I want to do is leave this place with her.

Ella shivers as we step onto the sidewalk. At this hour, the warmer temperatures from earlier are nowhere to be found. I drape an arm over her shoulders and hug her to my side.

"Better?" She nods. "We're almost to the car."

"Where are we going?"

Great question.

When I pulled out of Ella and the lust bubble popped, reality crept its way back in. I wasn't embarrassed to fuck her in front of everyone. If anything, claiming her in front of a crowd turned me on more. But now, I wanted her all to myself.

"My place," I say as I unlock the car and open the door for her.

She hesitates getting in. "Uh..."

I step into her and twirl a lock of her brilliant-red hair around my finger. My lips a breath from hers. "Please, Ella." Closing the space between us, I kiss her. Brush my lips gently against hers. Revel in the buzz beneath my sternum as I connect with her in a way so different from before. I rest my forehead on hers. "I'm not ready to let you leave yet."

Her fingers trace down the buttons of my shirt. Fist the fabric and tug me closer. Lips drop back on mine and she controls the kiss. Slow and soft at first. But then her grip on my shirt tightens. Her tongue dives deeper. Explores further. A series of sweet whimpers spill from her lips and I devour each one.

It takes every ounce of willpower to break the kiss. Her groan of irritation makes me chuckle, and I kiss the tip of her nose.

"Please, Ella. Come to my place."

She leans back and holds my gaze. "Don't laugh, okay?"

I furrow my brow, then shrug. "Whatever you need to say, I promise not to laugh."

After a deep inhale, she licks her lips. "I know we just had sex in front of a bunch of people, which I was surprisingly okay with." She huffs out a laugh. "But this feels different."

"Going to my house?" She nods. "Why?"

Mentally, I prepare myself for some outlandish answer. Like I might be some serial killer who preys on young women, has sex with them in public, then lures them back to my place to off them. Or that I am some extremist with twisted fetishes I only perform in my own home.

I do like kink, but nothing involving blades or body fluids.

What I don't prepare myself for is her actual answer.

"I've hooked up with a lot of guys." I grind my molars and growl. Her lips kick up at the corners. "Mostly in public places, but not in the open." She pauses a beat. "On rare occasions, I'd hook up at someone's house. Parties or the random hangout that turned into more." I close my eyes and take a deep breath. Work to tamper down the heat in my veins. She flattens her palm over my heart. "What I'm trying to say is, there was never anything beyond the sex. No connection afterward. No desire for more." Her eyes momentarily drop to her hand, then lift to pin me in place. "With you... going to your place... it scares me."

"I scare you?" I ask in a weak voice.

She shakes her head. "No, not you." Her fingers toy with the button at the hollow of my throat. "More than sex with another person scares me. Meaning more to someone scares me."

DARKEST DEVOTION

My arms wrap around her protectively and hug her close. "It's okay to be scared. I am too."

"You are?" she mumbles into my chest. I nod. "Why?"

"Because I've never wanted anyone the way I want you." And I mean it.

Since losing my virginity the summer before high school, I've had a lot of sex. College was a blur of late nights, alcohol, studying and one-nighters. In the past decade, I had two serious relationships. By serious, I mean we were more than sex. We shared meals and went to movies and spent time together for months. One lasted three months, and the other lasted seven months. With both, they wanted more than I was willing to give at the time.

But I am not that person now. Although I like to have a good time, my priorities have changed. Work and rent, food and sleep rule my life. Going out tonight was an exception. And women... as much as I love sex, women have been on the back burner for weeks.

Ella is a deviation from the straight path I have been walking. A deviation I plan to follow and get lost on.

She smirks, then glances to the side. "What's so special about me?" she whisper-asks.

I grip her chin and steer her eyes back to mine. "Not sure what it is, but I feel it here." I tap her hand still over my heart. "This odd twist in my chest. It hurts, but in a good way."

"Oh," she whispers.

"So, please... come home with me. I don't care if we crash the moment we walk inside. But I'm not ready to say goodbye. Not yet."

Her lips press to mine in a chaste kiss. "Okay, I'll go home with you." A bright smile lights up her face. "Just don't kill me in my sleep."

I laugh, then draw an X over my heart. "Promise."

What I didn't say was I want to keep her. That the need brewing inside me would never let me hurt her. Nor would I ever let anyone else hurt her. And I am a man of my word.

CHAPTER FIVE

ELLA

I wake to a palm on my breast and an erection against my ass. And for a moment, I don't know where I am. I don't move or take a breath.

The hand on my breast sweeps beneath the sheet and trails down my midline. Glides down my bare mound and dips between my folds. In and out, in and out. Then he swirls the slick digit over my clit and my breath stutters.

"So responsive."

Thomas.

He sweeps my hair off my neck, kisses between my shoulder blades, then licks up my spine. My moan in response is harsh and throaty and unladylike.

"And fucking perfect."

He wraps his free arm around my torso and pinches my nipple. I press my ass into him. Gyrate my hips and grind against his erection harder with each circuit.

"Pretty little pet. Fuck my hand. Come on my fingers." He bites the skin beneath my ear. "And maybe I'll reward you."

Reward me? Not sure what that means, but every nerve ending in my body screams to be rewarded.

"Promise?" I ask as I rock my hips harder. Fuck his fingers with aggression.

He pinches my nipple harder and I whimper. "Only if you're a good little pet and do as I say."

His teeth sink into my neck. For two breaths, I feel nothing but the sharp burn. And then the burn fades. In its place is an ache for more. More teeth. More pain. More of him.

I reach around and palm his ass. Grind harder against his thick cock. Fuck his fingers as if my life depends on it. "I'll always be your good little pet."

He twists my nipple and my walls constrict around his fingers. I come on his hand, soak my thighs and the sheets. Cry out as he continues to pump his fingers in and out. And just before I tell him I can't take anymore, just before I beg him to stop, he pulls out his fingers and sucks them off.

"You are the sweetest little pet. I could spend my life between your legs and not get enough."

What if I wanted him to spend his life between my legs?

Turning around, I shove Thomas flat on the mattress and straddle his hips. Lean down and crush my lips to his. His fingers bruise my upper thighs as I rock my hips over his length. And as much as I want to ride him, I also want him in my mouth.

I break the kiss. Bite my way down his chin, his throat, his torso. Shuffle down the bed until I hover over his pulsing cock. Fist the base with one hand while I kiss the tip.

"Goddamn, pet. You're killing me," he groans out. His stare heats me from crown to heel as he gazes down at me. "Put my cock between those pretty lips." Fingers toy with my hair before he cups my cheek. "Take what's yours."

Fuck.

I have never been this wet. Never been with someone so possessive and commanding. On the street, those characteristics would be an automatic turnoff. In the bedroom, though... I want more.

My tongue darts out and I lick his tip. Taste his saltiness in my mouth. His fingers curl and fist my hair. His moans echoing off the walls. The pleasure I give him makes me heady. Puts a wicked grin on my face before I flatten my tongue at the base of his cock, lick up his shaft and take him down my throat.

"Sweet fucking Christ," he chokes out. He yanks my hair as his back bows off the bed. "You'll unman me in no time if you keep that up."

His words only encourage me further.

But after I take him again, his hands swoop under my arms and he drags me up his body.

"Hey," I protest. "Wasn't done."

"Tell me you're clean." The tip of his cock grazes my folds.

My brow lifts. "I am." Hands on his pecs for balance, I glide up and down the surface of his cock. "Are you?"

He fists my hips. "Yes," he bites out. "And I had a vasectomy years ago." I freeze, tilt my head and study him a beat. "Don't want kids. We can talk about it later."

I shake my head. "Not necessary." My hips rock as I dip to kiss him. "I get it."

Before he responds in turn, I line him up with my entrance and sink down. He grips my hips impossibly harder. Grunts as I claw his pecs and rock up and down his length. Curses as I fuck him faster, harder. Sits up, clamps down on my nipple with his teeth and punishes my body until I climax.

Still in the haze of my orgasm, he flips me onto my belly, hikes my hips up, slaps my ass and slams back into me. He paws my ass, spreads my cheeks and growls as he fucks me relentlessly. A thumb presses my puckered hole and I groan.

"Has anyone touched you here?" His thumb circles the hole; adding more pressure every other circuit.

"No," I pant out.

"Good." Moisture slides down my crack and he uses it to lubricate the puckered entrance. A burning sensation consumes my hole and I stop breathing. Thomas bends over me and kisses my neck. "Breathe, Ella."

Although I love it when he calls me pet during sex, my name on his tongue while we are this intimate is potent. Intoxicating. An all-new brand of arousal. And I want to hear it more. Daily, and often.

With a deep breath, my body melts into his touch. "Such a good little pet." He kisses my neck, then pushes his thumb inside. "So tight." He alternates rocking his hips and pumping his thumb. "Fuck, you feel good."

Leaning back, he rests his free hand between my shoulder blades and pins me to the bed. His hips work like a well-oiled machine; his cock pounding my pussy while his thumb assaults my ass. I push back into him, silently beg him to give me more. And he rewards me by giving me his whole thumb.

Another thrust and I am in sensation overload. My nipples beg to be pinched. My clit screams to be rubbed. Every nerve ending in my body is on fire. On his next thrust forward, he hits deep and my body detonates. As it does, he continues his assault on both holes and drags out the sensation.

I fist the bedding and cry out against the cotton. "Ohgod, ohgod, ohgod."

He slips his thumb from my hole, fists my hips with a bruising grip and fucks me with abandon. And when I think my body can't take any more, he hits that spot deep inside again and another orgasm swallows me whole. Then his weight is on me, his arm banded around my middle as his release fills me.

"Never leave," he says, breath hot on my back as he squeezes me tighter.

"Can't stay here forever," I tease.

He kisses along my spine. "Lies." When he reaches my mouth, he kisses me with unparalleled tenderness. A bit awkwardly, he slips out of me and lies so we are eye to eye. "Wasn't joking when I said you're mine."

I lower my hips to the mattress and bring a hand to his cheek. "And I believe you. But we just met."

"And?"

"And we know nothing about each other." I laugh. "You may love sex with me, but what if I'm a total psycho?"

"You aren't."

I roll my eyes. "Okay, I'm not." For a moment, I lock eyes with him. Try to read what is going through his head. Unfortunately, I was never great at reading people. "Why the rush?"

"Why wait?"

"Don't you want to know me before I take over your life?"

"I know enough."

I turn onto my side and tuck my hands under my cheek. "How?"

He kisses the tip of my nose. "I'm a good judge of character. Can tell when people try to deceive me. *Hazel.*" He smirks and shakes his head. "I've always been good at it. And now it's part of my job." I arch a brow. "Attorney."

"Okay, I'll give you that."

"Will you now?" he teases. "Anyway, I shared that so you understand why I feel comfortable in my stance."

Although his explanation reassures me, I still think it is all too soon. We haven't existed around each other a full twenty-four hours yet. What if he hates my day-to-day habits? By no means am I the cleanest person, and Thomas's house, from what I have seen, is pretty damn tidy. What if, weeks from now, he decides I am some annoying girl? He doesn't like the way I squeeze the toothpaste from the tube. Gets frustrated with the way I wash the laundry. Dislikes my eating habits—the leftovers I swear to eat but never do. Then what happens? He throws me aside and moves on.

I have no clue what I want to do with my life; the complete opposite of him. He already has a degree and an adult job. Me? I toss on my blue vest and stand behind the beauty counter at the local drugstore, discussing skincare and cashing out purchases. I make minimum wage and plaster on a fake smile for the masses every day.

How will someone like Thomas—a person with his shit together—stay with a person like me? Simple. He won't.

"Ella?"

I blink away my inward spiral. "Yeah?"

"Whatever you're thinking..." He scoots closer and gives me a chaste kiss. "Please, stop."

Closing my eyes, I take a deep breath. Dig deep for the courage to speak my feelings. If Thomas wants a relationship with me, I need to be able to speak my feelings. Need to voice my fears.

"What if everything is good for weeks, then one day I do something you hate?"

"I doubt that will happen."

"But it could. Then what happens? You throw me out."

Subtly, he shakes his head. "First of all, I'd never throw you out. I'm adult enough to sit down and try to resolve issues. Second, it takes a whole hell of a lot to piss me off. If you have annoying habits—who doesn't, by the way—we'll talk and meet in the middle." He leans in and kisses my shoulder. "That's what couples do, Ella."

"Then why are you single?"

Laughter fills the room. "Maybe you should go into law." I roll my eyes. "I'm single because I never connected with someone the way we connect. I tried. Just didn't work out."

"And you think we will?"

"Without a doubt."

How can this man be so damn sure? His confidence in our future is baffling... and hot as hell. Sure, he is skilled in reading people. But that isn't the same as predicting the future. I want an ounce of his certainty. A snippet of whatever instinct tells him this—us—will work.

With a lick of my lips, I swallow all doubt and take a leap.

"Okay," I whisper.

"Okay?"

I nod. "I want to stay."

CHAPTER SIX

Thomas

Ella directs me through a quaint, single-family homes neighborhood. Navigating us toward her home. Well, her parents' home. Her home is now with me. Yes, the decision was hasty, but I have never felt so sure about anyone.

Every few seconds, I peer in her direction. Notice the way her fingers pick at the hem of her top. I consider asking if she is having second thoughts, but stop myself. We spent hours together talking before getting in the car and driving here.

Her nervousness has nothing to do with me and the move. Her fidgeting fingers and bouncing knee have to do with what awaits her when we enter her parents' home.

Lifting a hand, Ella points to a beige house with forest green trim. A minivan and pickup truck parked in the double driveway. Overall, the house looks ordinary. No plant beds or decorative pieces in the yard. No exterior remodeling to make the 1960s home more current. Just plain colors, a perfectly mowed lawn, and nothing to make others feel welcome.

My poor girl.

I park behind the minivan and we exit the car. We walk toward the front door, hands locked, in a united front. Ella doesn't say a word, but the closer we get to the front door, the tighter she grips my hand. And although I want to tell her everything will be fine, I keep my mouth shut because I know nothing about her life or her parents.

"Ready?" I ask when we step up to the door.

She turns her gaze on me and bites the corner of her lower lip. I hate how worried she is. How antsy she feels. But then she nods and reaches for the doorknob. "Yeah, I think so."

Not five feet in the house, a woman's voice belts out and covers the silence. Her tone sharper than a kitchen knife. "Ella Jean, that better be you." A woman with features similar to Ella, though aged, rounds the corner, stops feet in front of us, and props her hands on her hips. "Where the hell have you been, young lady? Staying out all night without a word." Her gaze shifts as she looks me up and down, a sneer on her lips. "And who might you be?" she asks as her eyes drop to our clasped hands.

"Mama," Ella says, her voice small and frail. "This is Thomas." She looks up and meets my eyes. "My boyfriend."

Ella and I have known each other less than twenty-four hours and I feel as if we are more than boyfriend and girlfriend. We connect on a deeper level. For now, though, I let her explain us in her own words. Her mother doesn't seem the type of woman to listen to much of what Ella says anyway.

"Boyfriend?" she asks incredulously. Then she laughs. Laughs. In front of her daughter. In front of us both. As if Ella being in a romantic relationship is impossible. "Go to your room, young lady." She points down the hall.

Ella starts to move, but I tighten my hold on her. I refuse to let her be a doormat to this woman. She may be her mother, but everyone deserves respect.

"The only way she's going to that room is if she's packing her things to leave," I state firmly.

Ella's mother steps closer. Her lip curled in permanent disgust. "Is that so?"

I will give it to this woman, she is bold and daring. Perhaps this is where Ella's fire comes from. In this situation, though, she needs to back the hell off.

"It is, seeing how Ella is legally an adult."

She rolls her eyes, steps toe-to-toe with me, and jabs a finger in the center of my chest. "Adult or not, she lives under this roof. And until her father and I have a conversation with her about the real world, she's not going anywhere."

Before I rebut the woman's argument, she grabs Ella's free hand and yanks her out of my hold. Ella falls on the floor behind her mother and doesn't move to stand. Behind this woman, Ella looks nothing like the goddess I met last night. And I hate how her parents have crushed her spirit without effort.

"Get out of my house." Her mother points to the door. "Before I call the police."

Ella peeks up from the floor, tears in her eyes. I wait until our stares connect. "I'll be back." Her chin quivers. "I promise."

"If you're smart, you won't," her mother states. "I have the law on speed dial."

My gaze shifts from Ella to her mother. I lean forward, invade her personal space, and smirk. "Yeah? I bet the law I have on speed dial is better."

With that, I spin around, open the door and exit the house. Any second, I might vomit on the lawn—my nerves and anger in overdrive. Leaving without Ella unsettles me in inexplicable ways. Her upbringing and homelife have obviously been nothing short of violent. Hopefully not physically, but definitely emotionally and mentally. If her mother behaved with such cruelty in front of a stranger, I question how she is behind closed doors.

And what about her father? Two vehicles are parked in the driveway. Where was he? Is he the subject of such abuse too? Maybe he doesn't like to get his hands dirty. Or he prefers to keep his misdeeds private.

Regardless, I will rescue Ella from this place. From this wretched life.

Ella is mine. She belongs with me. Safe. Able to stand tall. Be herself. Without subjugation.

Yes, I prefer to be in control. Ella didn't seem to mind either. But after what just happened, I need to navigate us with a fresh perspective. I need to let her harness the control.

I back out of the driveway, sending a silent message to Ella. *I'll return. Soon.* Then, I drive home and work on a plan on how to do exactly that.

Not only will I return for Ella, but I will leave with her. Because once I step foot on that property again, I refuse to leave without her. Threats and violence may be the tools Ella's mother uses to keep her in line, but she has no idea what I have in my arsenal. Or what I am capable of when pushed too far.

CHAPTER SEVEN

ELLA

A week has passed since I last saw or spoke with Thomas. Seven very long, torturous days.

When he left, he promised he would return. And I believed—believe—him. Thomas isn't the type of man to make a vow and not hold up his end of the deal. But when he said he would come back, I thought he meant in a day or two.

Maybe he changed his mind. I mean, after how Mother acted toward him, he probably thought I would become a nut job like her. Yes, I may be what some consider abnormal or freakish. But only because the people judging me live in the same circles as my parents. Peers from school were different. Every guy wanted in my pants while every girl either cheered me on or ridiculed my promiscuity.

Only once had my parents learned of my sexual deviance. I remember the exact moment my mother called me a whore for the first time. Halloween weekend of my sophomore year.

I'd asked my parents if friends could stay the night after we went out and they'd agreed. My friends and I went to a small party at Troy Benson's house—the high school quarterback. There were maybe fifteen of us total, most of them football players. One of the guys brought a couple cases of beer and weed circulated on the regular.

Knowing my parents would be up when we returned home, I didn't partake—much.

At this stage of the game, I'd been sexually active years. The number of partners I'd been with was up there for someone my age, but I was no match for some of the guys' tallies.

An hour into the party, Troy started feeling me up. Out in the open. His fingers dragged up my thigh and under the too-short plaid skirt I wore as part of my costume. He didn't ask, but I didn't tell him to stop. I loved the way guys gravitated toward me. The way they couldn't keep their hands off me. How my body was in control of their needs and urges.

In the middle of his living room, I let Troy Benson finger fuck me. I made no show to disguise what happened. If anything, I put on a show. Knowing the people present comforted me enough to be so vulnerable.

Without words, I invited others to join. And they did. After my first orgasm, other people in the room paired up. When Troy pushed my skirt up and panties down, then started eating my pussy for all to watch, a few other guys from the team joined us. Within minutes, I was stripped bare and the guys took turns pleasing my body.

Hours later, in the confines of my bedroom, my friends and I whisper-gossiped about the night's events. That is, until my mother burst into the room without knocking. Her face was so red. Her eyes practically bulging from their sockets. Before I asked if everything was okay, she backhanded my cheek.

"Whore!" she shouted loud enough for the neighbors to hear. "You disgust me, Ella Jean. This is not the daughter your father and I raised." I shrunk in her presence and she just kept going. "Out late at a boy's house. Doing unspeakable things with said boy and others." She spit at me. "Have fun with your friends tonight. Because tomorrow, you're grounded. And I'll be speaking with the school about sexual deviancy."

After that night, sex was never discussed with me among my friends. We made a pact. Created our own language of sorts. Months later, my parents finally allowed me to do more than go to school and be at home. Not that I hadn't been fucking guys in bathrooms and closets at school. But I used the guise of tutoring classmates who needed extra help with math or science. Worked every time.

Now, it feels as if I am that fifteen-year-old girl again. Hiding in her room. Trying to figure out a plan to outsmart my parents.

"Ella," my mother calls down the hall. "Dinner."

This pretty much sums up our interaction the last week. Her summoning and me falling in line.

A little longer and this will all be over. Thomas will come back.

And while I waited this past week for his return, I slowly packed my belongings. Only clothes and mementos I wanted to keep. Because no matter what, I am leaving. Even if it is out the damn window in the middle of the night.

I join my parents in the dining room. The room is as arctic as ever, and it has nothing to do with the thermostat setting. I pull out the chair I have sat in my entire life and park myself at the table. Mom sets a plate in front of me with unseasoned chicken cut into bite-sized pieces, plain white rice, overcooked canned carrots, and a slice of white bread with a light coating of butter.

This is how it has always been. Mother controls the house. Although she doesn't cut father's dinner, she portions each of our plates. *"Not too much. I won't buy new clothes because you can't control your appetite."* Father isn't a feeble man. But for some reason, he allows Mother to rule the roost however she pleases.

But I have seen his ugly side too. Been victim of his belt. Heard his malicious words and disturbing grunts as he punished me. Which is why I never provoked my father. Something told me he was capable of things much worse. Nightmare-worthy things.

Outside of this house, people look up to my father. He goes to church, donates to charity, and is a favored entrepreneur in the community. Need someone to look after your business's accounting? Daniel Walsh is the man people refer you to.

To the outside world, my father is a nice man. But I hear him in the night. Watching pornography and jerking himself off while Mother sleeps. I hear him saying dirty things to the actors on screen while he comes in a hand towel. And I hear the women on the screen as they call the men fucking them daddy.

Which is why I will never call my father anything but father.

"Eat your dinner, Ella Jean."

I pick at the food on my plate and silently beg for an extra square of butter or some damn salt and pepper. Would a little parsley kill anyone? No, no it wouldn't.

Staring at my mother, I stab a piece of chicken, bring it to my lips, and eat it. After I swallow, a new fire lights my bloodstream. And for the first time, I voice my opinion to my mother.

"Would it kill you to flavor the food? Maybe some herbs or butter or garlic. We can certainly afford such things."

Clanging fills the air as Mother drops her fork. She stares at me open-mouthed for a beat. A small sense of victory floods beneath my rib cage. Until she slaps my face. Hard.

That will leave a mark.

"How dare you speak to me with such insolence. I am your mother.

You will respect me." She slams her hand on the table. "After everything your father and I have done for you. How dare you disrespect us."

Unable to contain the slow-boil rage bubbling inside, I pop up from my chair. The wood overturns behind me and hits the wall. Heat crawls up my throat and floods my cheeks, amplifying the sting further.

"How dare I?" I ball my fingers into fists. "How dare I?" I shout, letting the fury spill out. "Yes, you are my mother. But I will never respect you. You are the most despicable, two-faced person I know. All prim and proper in front of friends and a cunt behind closed doors."

Mother shoots up from her chair and raises her hand, only this time, I am ready. I catch her hand before it makes contact with my face again. This is the moment my father chooses to stick in his two cents.

"Sally, stop. Obviously, your form of punishment doesn't work. It hasn't worked for years." Father shifts his gaze to me and nausea rolls in my gut. "Time for daddy to punish you."

Bile rises in my throat. I am going to puke.

I drop my mother's hand and step back. "Don't you fucking touch me."

"Been a long time since I took my belt to your ass. Seems time to change that." He rises from his chair and I back myself into the wall. He inches toward me, a predator out in the open, stalking prey.

My eyes drop as he reaches for his belt buckle and starts unfastening it. I don't miss the bulge beneath his zipper. Vomit hits the back of my throat. Tears sting the backs of my eyes.

No. No, no, no.

He yanks the leather from the loops of his pants with a snarly smile on his lips. Inches from my shrinking frame, vomit fills my mouth. My mother stands behind him with confusion marring her brow and something sinister in her smile.

His hand reaches forward, the leather creaking under his grip. And then the doorbell rings.

Father looks over his shoulder and directs my mother to answer the door. Alone. Redirecting his gaze to me, he assumes my mother did as she was told. Obedient, as always. But she hasn't left the room. Instead, she watches her husband with fresh eyes. Stares after him as he begins pursuit of his only daughter once more.

But he doesn't get far again. The doorbell rings, then rings again, followed by a fist banging the wood.

Red fills father's face before he spins around and storms past

DARKEST DEVOTION

Mother. "Guess if *I* need something done around here, I have to do it. Stupid bitch."

Mother stares at me for one, two, three breaths. I see the questions forming on her tongue, but know she won't speak them. Know she won't ask her daughter if her devoted and loving husband has ever *touched* her. Because that would look bad for her.

And I am glad she doesn't ask. Glad she doesn't want to know the truth. It is sad I don't know if the truth will upset her or relieve her.

Yes, my father has inflicted physical punishment. No, he hasn't sexually assaulted me. I might have killed him in his sleep by now if that were the case.

Finally, she looks away and storms after my father. On slow feet, I follow in their wake. Ready to thank whoever saved me from what would have become my worst nightmare.

I hear them before they come into view. My father and Thomas. The fact that father still has his belt in his hand doesn't look good. Nor does the sneer on his face. Not when three officers stand tall behind Thomas, ready to help me out of this situation.

Thomas looks past my parents and locks my gaze with his. "Ella, are you okay?"

Tears sting the backs of my eyes while a fist tightens around my heart. Years ago, I would have lied and said yes. Because I feared the repercussions of telling the truth, of saying I was not okay. But I am no longer that girl. No longer small. And no one has the right to knock me down. Not even my own flesh and blood.

I shake my head, slowly at first. "No." My head shakes harder. "I am not okay."

With a minor jut of his chin, Thomas signals me away. "Go get your things."

Starting for the hallway, I hear my father shout "she's not going anywhere" as I step inside my room. I hustle to the closet and shoulder the bags I packed and stowed. After slipping on shoes, I take one last look at my bedroom and take a deep breath.

This is it. This is goodbye. I look up. *Thank you.*

And then I walk out and head toward the future. Toward Thomas.

CHAPTER EIGHT

THOMAS

Three days.

Three days and Ella hasn't talked about what happened at her parents' house. And her silence has me worried.

Her father made it rather evident something was happening when I arrived with the police. Between his red cheeks, angry sneer and the belt in his hand, I feared the worst. When Ella walked off to gather her bags, he put forth his best effort to not let Ella leave. Unfortunately for him, Ella was no longer a minor, nor was she in school, and had every right to leave whenever she pleased. When the police backed me up and not him, this angered him further.

For a moment, I thought he'd start a physical altercation. Thankfully, it didn't come down to that. Not sure I would've restrained myself, even with police present.

Since that night, Ella has crawled inside herself. Much as I want her to tell me what has her so pensive, I sit in silence and wait. Wait for her mind to settle. Wait for her to come to terms with what happened. And wait for her to know she is safe with me here.

Even in sleep, her brows pinch at the middle, and deep lines mar her forehead. I itch to reach out and smooth the stress away. Instead, I sweep her brilliant-red curls from her cheek and study her soft curves.

The lines shift and smooth as she wakes. Slowly, her eyes open and lock with mine. Cheek propped on my palm, I lie on my side and stare down at her. A small smile adds a soft glow to her skin.

This moment, when her eyes open each day, is my favorite. When life has yet to consume and sway her thoughts. Everything about her in this blip of time is pure and natural and untarnished.

Her arms stretch above her head, back arches, and the sheet slides down her body to expose her bare breasts. Breasts I haven't touched in ten days. Breasts I desperately want to wrap my lips and hands around.

"Morning," I whisper before dropping my lips to hers.

"Hi." The corners of her mouth tip up in a shy smile. "How long have you been awake?"

I trace a knuckle along the line of her jaw. "Not long."

She hums and rolls onto her side, her lips at my throat, breasts pressed to my abs, arm around my waist. I close my eyes and bask in the feel of her body flush with mine. Legs tangled, fingers exploring, breaths hot and heavy.

Fuck, I want to touch her. More than this. More than lazy, soft grazes of skin for mere seconds.

But I won't. Not until she tells me what happened during our time apart. Those seven days were the longest of my life. The look on Ella's face when I arrived says it was more than seven days for her too. Something during those days changed her. Ella isn't the same woman I met. Although she is still physically soft, a piece of her has hardened.

"Thomas?"

I kiss the crown of her head. "Yeah?"

"Did I do something wrong?"

Inching back, I look down at her. Absorb the concern in her eyes. Allow guilt to consume me momentarily, knowing I have acted differently with her. "What makes you think you did?"

Her fingers skirt along my spine and spread at the base to cup my ass. "Because you haven't touched me since I've been back." Before I open my mouth to answer, her hand slides around my hip and dips between my legs. As if second nature, her fingers wrap around my cock. "But this tells me you want to." She presses her lips to the hollow of my throat. "So, why?"

"Ella..." Her name a plea and growl as she strokes my erection, slow and steady. I swallow and close my eyes briefly. "Shouldn't we talk? About what happened."

With a firmer grip, she jerks my cock with more gusto. "No." She releases my cock, pushes against my chest until I am flat on my back, then straddles my hips. "I don't want to talk, Thomas." She strokes the length of my cock with her slick pussy lips. "I want to fuck."

My hands fist her hips in a bruising grip. "We should talk. You can't let it—" I don't get to finish my thought as she glides to the tip of my cock and takes me to the hilt.

"Later," she moans out. She rocks her hips, then slams back down. Our joint moans fill the room. "Right now, I want to fuck you until neither of us can walk." Palms on my pecs, her nails claw my flesh as she glides up and down my cock with desperation. "You can either get on board or lie still and shut up. Either way, I'm fucking you."

This aggressive side of Ella turns me the fuck on... and has me concerned. But I choose to dwell on it later. Right now, my girl needs a good fucking. And her needs will always come first. Always.

We crawl out of bed, literally, and shower the sweat from our skin. After we towel off and dress minimally, I cook us French toast, bacon, eggs, and hash browns. We sit at the dining table, her in an untied robe and me in boxer briefs, and eat our meal.

I stare at her nipples as they peek out of the cotton and lick my lips. Think about her bare pussy as I dunk a piece of French toast in maple syrup. Think about how good she would taste with maple syrup. *Fuck*. At this rate, breakfast will end with her on the table as I pour a trail of syrup from her perky pink nipples to her throbbing clit.

But syrup will have to wait.

Because we need to talk.

I take our plates to the kitchen, rinse them and load them in the dishwasher. Ella comes up from behind and wraps her arms around my waist, kissing the back of my neck. I grab her hands and lift them to my lips. Attempt to soften her before I urge her to talk about a sore subject.

"Ella." I peer over my shoulder and she meets my gaze. "We really should talk."

She huffs and her frame deflates. "Why?"

I spin to face her. Pinch her chin between my thumb and finger. "Because it's not healthy to keep it bottled up." When her eyes drop, I lift her chin. "And I'd rather get it out now than have it fester and become explosive later."

Leaning forward, her arms circle my waist once more. She pulls me impossibly close and rests her cheek where my pec and shoulder meet. I snake my arms around her middle and hold her tight. Minutes pass and neither of us says a word. I grant her the time because she has avoided the subject for a reason. But it is important I know everything.

She doesn't need to hold all the pain anymore. Now that she has me, I can carry some of her burden too.

"Years ago, when I was fairly young, my father used to punish me with his belt. Over his knee. Bare on my butt." I squeeze her tighter to avoid her seeing the rage boiling my blood. "When you're little, you accept punishments. You think, *'All the kids must get the same when they're bad.'*" She takes a deep breath and leans back. "Can we sit down?"

I nod, take her hand in mine, and guide us to the couch. Before she sits, I watch as she pulls her robe closed and ties the sash tight. Too tight. The rage in me burns hotter. I hate how broaching the subject makes her shelter herself.

"The first lashing, my mother was present. She approved and wanted to see that I got what they thought I'd deserved. Naturally, after that day, I did everything possible to not get the belt again. Somehow, my father found a reason. My room wasn't clean enough. My grades were not to his standard. I didn't eat all my dinner. I didn't do my chores. The reasons were endless. Mother wasn't around for those punishments, and they felt... different." She inhales deeply. "He never sexually abused me, but it *felt* as if he wanted to."

"Jesus, Ella. Why didn't you tell anyone?"

"I wanted to. But as respected as my parents were, who would've believed me? Plus, he hadn't actually done anything. It was the word of a child against a trusted adult." She toys with the sash of her robe. "Anyway, as I got older, sex entered the equation." My eyes bulge out of the sockets. "Not with my father!" she corrects immediately. "No, with other guys from school. I lost my virginity early and learned how enjoyable sex was." She peers up at me, hesitant. "And sometimes with more than one partner at a time."

A smirk kicks up the corner of my mouth. "That's a different discussion. One I won't discount."

"Good." Then she goes on to tell me all the depraved things she learned about her father and how she avoided being alone with him often. Ella unloads years' worth of strife and anxiety. Gets mountains of hurt and worry off her chest. Unleashes the demons of her past.

And I gladly accept it all. For Ella, I will take as much as she gives. Be her support when she can't hold herself up. Be her anchor when she needs grounding. Our relationship is new and started unconventionally, but from the moment I walked up to Ella, I knew she would be more than a dirty fuck in the middle of a crowd.

Her body sags into the couch when she finishes her story. The

DARKEST DEVOTION

green rimming her hazel irises glow a hint brighter. And the tight knot in her robe sash falls away as I tug it free.

"Thank you," I say as I slip off the couch, drop to my knees and situate myself between her legs. She doesn't move, doesn't take a breath, as I spread her knees farther apart. I kiss the inside of her thigh, near her knee, and she gasps. Then I do the same on the opposite side.

"Why are you thanking me?"

My palms trace parallel trails up her thighs and under the robe, pushing the cotton aside and exposing her delicious pink pussy. I place another kiss on each of her thighs, followed by a nip. She jolts in place, but I see the evidence of how it made her feel, glistening between her folds.

"For telling me your story..." Another kiss and bite on her thighs, midway to my end goal. "For trusting me with something so personal." *Kiss, nip. Kiss, nip.* "Fuck, pet. Your trust gets me so damn hard."

"Is that all that gets you hard?" As the last word leaves her lips, she slips a hand between her thighs and strokes her pussy inches from my lips. "Because we can play truth or dare..." Two of her fingers dip inside her cunt. "All." Her slick digits slip out. "Day." Plunge back in. "Every." Back out and move up to circle her clit. "Day."

I spread her legs as far as they will go. Don't take my eyes off her fingers as they toy with her clit and fuck her cunt. Don't move to touch her or taste her. I simply sit frozen, my mouth a breath from her sweet pussy and watch my girl finger fuck herself.

Her whimpering cries fill the air as her orgasm nears. She tries to close her legs, but I pin them in place. Leave her exposed and soaked and glorious. Her fingers rub her clit faster, harder, as she edges closer. Then she dips them back in her cunt, two fingers, then three, and pumps faster, pushes deeper.

"That's a pretty little pet. Look how pretty that pussy is. So wet and pink and hungry." My eyes lock on hers. "Feed that pussy what it wants, pet. Fuck it hard. Stroke it how it feels good and show me. Come on your fingers. Do it for me."

I watch as she strokes and fucks herself. Listen as her cries grow closer and louder. Bask in the sight of her as red blotches pattern her skin and she finally lets go. Rip her hand away and eat her raw as she continues to orgasm on my face.

"Such a beautiful pet," I say as I rock back on my heels and trace her pussy with my finger. "Now, I will reward you. Fuck you on the couch like a good little pet."

CHAPTER NINE

ELLA

The first time I met Thomas's coworkers, I mentally prepared myself for judgment and criticism. Without effort, it was easy to see I was younger than Thomas. Not to mention the fact that I looked younger than my actual age. The side-glances from strangers at stores and in public places didn't go unnoticed. Anytime I spoke up, Thomas shrugged it off. Told me to ignore it. That the opinions of others didn't matter.

Although his words repeated in my head, I prepared myself for the worst with his coworkers. But the judgment never came. Neither did the occasional stare or unspoken questions in their expressions.

It was a challenge to accept that not every person was cruel, that not every person will look at you with a critical eye. As part of the healing process, I remind myself each day, not every person is Sally or Daniel Walsh.

Tonight is the annual fundraiser for Thomas's firm. Everyone is here and dressed to the nines. Hundreds of guests mingle among the firm employees, chatting over wine and hors d'oeuvres. Ready to fork over thousands of dollars to a charitable cause.

Amazing as it all is, it boggles my mind that this is my life. That I occasionally wear fancy dresses, always have the most handsome man on my arm, and talk about money as if this is Monopoly and I have a stockpile.

Someone pinch me. Or don't.

A little more than six months ago, I was just another random woman in a filthy, deserted warehouse. Abandoned by her friend. Next to some random pervert on a couch watching other people have sex. Then, Thomas stepped in front of me, offered his hand, and stole my heart.

Our relationship is still young and we are exploring so much—of ourselves, and with others. I have zero doubts about our future, but I can't wait to see where it leads us.

"You are ravishing in that dress," Thomas whispers in my ear. "Can't wait to peel it off you."

"Is that so?" I cock a brow.

"Indeed."

I scan the room, take in the crowd and gauge how much time we have before the auction begins. "What if I said you should see what's underneath now?"

Thomas clamps onto my hip and bruises the flesh beneath the silk. "Then I'd say you're a naughty little pet." He shifts his hand to mine and hauls me from the banquet hall. We scurry down the wide corridor toward the restrooms. "Wait here." Thomas disappears inside the men's room for three rapid breaths before opening the door and yanking me inside. "In there. Now."

I bolt into the stall and he follows me in. The nice thing about upscale venues... the bathroom stall walls are floor to ceiling and the stalls are more spacious.

Thomas puts the lid down on the toilet and pushes me down. He unbuttons and unzips his slacks, shoves his briefs down, and fists his cock. Swiping the tip over my lips, he pushes his way in. "Suck me like a good little pet."

Without resistance, I do as he says. I swirl my tongue around the length of his cock and suck the tip on each pass. He fists the hair at the nape of my neck, tips my head back slightly, and thrusts forward until his balls slap my chin.

"Such a good little pet." He strokes my cheek with his other hand. "Are you wet for me, pet?"

I mumble my yes around his girth and choke when he pushes harder.

"Show me. Push your dress up and show me how wet you are." Finagling my dress while sucking his cock, I shove it above my hips and expose my bare pussy. Thomas clucks his tongue. "No panties at the party." He pulls his cock from my lips. "Naughty, naughty pet."

Slipping his hands under my arms, he hauls me upright. Then he spins me around and slaps my ass. Before a yelp leaves my lips, the main door to the bathroom opens and someone steps in. Thomas hikes my dress up, leans forward, and whispers in my ear.

"Not a peep, my pet. Unless you want me to watch you with another man tonight." I shake my head. "Good pet."

Then Thomas fills my cunt with his cock. I gasp without sound. He fucks me hard and fast in the stall, and part of me wonders if he wants the other man in the room to hear us. Wonders if he wants someone else to fill me while he watches. We both get off on it—watching each other as we fuck other people. It is more about the act than anything else.

Thomas and I are solid. Bonded like no other. He is mine and I am his. No one fucks me like him. No one loves me like he does. And he would say the same in regard to me. But we love when others join us, play with us, evoke pleasure within us. It keeps the spark between us alive and electric and fresh.

The sink in the bathroom turns on and Thomas picks up his pace. His balls slap my clit and I can't stop the guttural moan that slips out. He grabs my throat to silence me, but I know it is too late. No doubt, we have been heard.

A soft knock raps our stall door, but Thomas doesn't stop.

"All good in there?" the man says, his voice rough and vaguely familiar.

Thomas cracks the door and I look over my shoulder to see Brad, one of the guys who came to the club with him six months ago. I didn't know this fact until recently, not until Thomas told him about me, about us.

"Yeah, man. So fucking good," Thomas says as he slows his rhythm and lets Brad watch. "You good?"

Brad fists his cock in his pants and licks his lips as he watches us fuck. "Not as good as you."

Thomas peeks out the door. "We alone?"

"Absolutely."

"Go in the handicap stall." Thomas pulls out of me and lowers my dress. "C'mon pet. Time to play."

We follow Brad into the new stall and lock the door. It isn't long before Thomas fucks me from behind again while I suck Brad off. The pace is slow and steady and everything I want from my life with Thomas. Being in this position, taking two men, having two men *want* me, makes me powerful. A goddess. A queen in my own right.

Brad fucks my throat until his cum warms my belly. Thomas fucks my cunt and fills my ass with his thumb until my body can't handle any more and I let go. Not only am I sated, but I feel high on life. A high no drug would provide.

Brad exits the stall and restroom first, checks the coast is clear, then Thomas and I exit. As we walk back to the party, we make tentative plans to have Brad over at the house in the near future.

When we reenter the party, no one is aware of the debauchery that just went down. Part of me wants everyone to know, wants everyone to watch. But another part of me revels in the secrecy of it all. The lewdness and raw nature of who we are. Thomas doesn't degrade or punish me for who I am. Instead, he helps me love who I am. Teaches me it is okay to have these urges. It is okay to fuck other people, as long as he approves and is present. It is okay to be my true self.

Thomas makes me whole. Allows me to embrace my sexuality. Encourages me to show him what I want and who I want. And I love that he stands right beside me each day. Never overstepping. Always supportive. He fulfills my needs and I do the same in return.

Our love may not be conventional, but it is ours. An impenetrable force.

This is why Thomas will always be mine and I will always be his. Because we truly understand who we are, as individuals and as a couple.

"I love you," I tell him as I lean back and mold myself to his front.

His arms snake around my waist and hug me impossibly close as he kisses beneath my ear. "I love you too, pet."

EPILOGUE
THOMAS

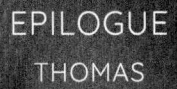

NOVEMBER 7 - TWO YEARS LATER

Took way too fucking long for this day to arrive, but today is finally here. Today, and every day going forward, Ella Walsh will be Ella Reynolds. My fucking wife. Queen. Goddess of my soul.

I didn't need a notarized piece of paper to tell the world Ella is mine. But I wanted it anyway. Wanted to connect us in every possible way. Legally seems the last way on the list.

Can't say I ever envisioned this day before Ella entered my life. My wedding day.

Before Ella, sex was just sex. Nothing substantial. A means to an end. An act to fulfill a primal need. No woman made me want more than a quick fuck. Until Ella. Before her, sex was always quick and dirty. Don't get me wrong, we have our share of fast fucks. I love quickies in bathrooms or bushes or alleys. But I have grown to love the slow and lewd moments too. Savoring each touch and stroke and moan. How I make her feel. How she makes me feel.

With Ella, everything is precise and clear. She feeds my primal urges as well as my soul. Gives life more definition. More significance. Couldn't imagine a better existence without her.

So, when she asked to have the glamorous wedding dress and big shindig, I caved without resistance.

I would have been content doing things at the courthouse; keeping things short, sweet, and to the point. But that isn't what my girl wanted. She has given me so much of herself, it is only fair I return the favor. If a gorgeous gown and saying our I dos in front of a crowd was on her wish list, then that is my gift to her.

Ella doesn't ask for much, but when she does, I never refuse her. Our wedding is far from a grand affair, but the event is big to us. Considering our form of celebration doesn't match the "typical" standard, our wedding is the most exposed we have been with people who don't know our... tastes.

That celebration is saved for later.

Four months ago, when I proposed to Ella, we celebrated for hours at home. Fucked on every surface of the living room until we were boneless. Then, I took her to our favorite place in the city. Provocateur. A small sex club hidden under the guise of a strip bar—you just had to know the right person and where to go.

We watched for hours before I told Ella to pick. Like my girl always did, she chose a couple. Although she loved dominating two men at once, every now and again, she loved the tenderness of a woman. We'd stripped bare and fucked in Provocateur until the doors locked at two in the morning. Then we invited the couple to our home and partied until sunrise.

Dominic and Chloe became quick friends with me and Ella after that night. Aside from the occasional hookup, we did things together like normal couples. Hanging out, dinner, movies, mini golf. And today, they sit in the crowd of less than fifty to celebrate our wedding.

A wedding that starts any minute.

Although she wanted the big dress and party, we kept the wedding ceremony simple. I didn't want her to worry about who would walk her down the aisle since her father was out of the equation. So, we opted for no groomsmen or bridesmaids. No flower girl or ring bearer. Just her, me, the ordained minister, and our guests.

The soft lilt of Pachelbel's "Canon in D" floats through the air and the banquet room falls silent. I clasp my hands at my waist, take a deep breath and wait for the doors to open. When they do, all air leaves my lungs.

"Fuck," I mutter as she comes into view.

I never thought it possible for Ella to steal my breath more than before. And I have never been more wrong in my life.

Crisp white lace hugs every inch of her frame from bust to knees before the skirt flows loosely and dusts the floor, a small train in her wake. Flesh-colored fabric beneath the lace alludes to exposed skin while thin spaghetti straps meet the deep V bust and accentuate Ella's full breasts. Her brilliant-red locks hang in loose waves, framing her face and dusting her breasts. A red and white bouquet of calla lilies and roses clasped in her hands.

I snap mental pictures of this moment while the photographer and our friends capture images for print. For as long as I live, I want this moment imprinted on my heart and embedded in my soul. The day Ella walks down the aisle to be my wife.

A few strides past the front row of guests and Ella stands across from me. Unable to resist, I lean forward and kiss her cheek. "You are stunning," I whisper for her ears only. When I resume my position, I note the blush pinking her complexion. "Stunning," I mouth.

Then, the minister kicks off her part of the ceremony.

ELLA

Monday through Friday, I am blessed to see Thomas in a suit. Sharp and classic and mouthwatering. Thomas, in a suit, is my kryptonite. But Thomas in *this* suit will be my undoing.

As the minister talks about finding your other half and what it means to love another person, I rake my libidinous eyes up and down Thomas.

The stylish black suit with a muted plaid pattern hugs Thomas's trim frame. Beneath the suit jacket is a charcoal-gray vest, crisp white dress shirt, and a burgundy tie; a matching handkerchief in the breast pocket of his jacket. A black belt and dress shoes pull the ensemble together.

My mouth salivates as I clamp my thighs together. One look in Thomas's mossy-green eyes, he knows exactly where my thoughts are.

"Soon," he mouths before the corner of his lips kick up.

Yes, soon. Preferably in the dressing room before the reception. Ten to fifteen minutes of Thomas taking his wife for the first time. Claiming me with a new label. Husband.

And waiting for the reception to end... that may be its own form of torture. Knowing I would be on edge, that waiting would be agony, I preemptively booked the reception for the shortest time frame possible without it appearing odd to our guests.

Thomas didn't know yet, but I had delicious plans for later.

After we exchange vows and I dos, Thomas kisses me as if no one is in the room. We break apart to cheers and applause. As the crowd exits the room and heads for a larger space several doors down for the reception, I haul Thomas into the dressing room.

"As stunning as you are in that dress, I want to tear it off you," he says as the lock clicks into place.

"Time for that later." I saunter to where he stands near the door, palming his dick. "Right now, husband" —he groans— "you need to take care of your wife."

He steps into me, brushes his knuckles along my jaw. "I will always take care of you, wife. Always." His lips meet mine in a hungry kiss. "No one is more important than you."

I peel the spaghetti straps from my shoulders and push my dress to the floor. Clad in a nude garter belt, stockings, a garter and nothing more, I squeeze his cock through the fabric and drop to my knees. Making quick work of his belt, I undo his slacks and shove them down. Followed by his briefs. His cock springs free and I lick my lips, eager to taste him.

"You want to suck me off, pet?"

Peering up at him, I lick the tip of his cock. "I want you in my throat before you fuck my cunt, husband."

He growls and cups my jaw. "Then take what you want, wife. Take what belongs to you."

And I do, until he retreats, yanks me up from my knees and spins me around. With time of the essence, he slams into me and pistons his hips. Works my body religiously until we both climax. Until our bones are jelly. He leaves a trail of kisses from beneath my ear to the edge of my shoulder as we catch our breaths.

Ever the gentleman, Thomas helps me back into my dress. Kisses me possessively one last time. Then we exit the dressing room with heated skin and glowing smiles. Enter the reception, greet our guests, and celebrate our love for each other with close friends and family.

When I walked into the underground party a little more than two years ago, I never expected to leave with my future husband. But I did.

The first night with Thomas felt fantasy-like. Yes, I was reluctant to have sex with a stranger for all to see. But then I took my first real breath after a lifetime of being suffocated. And I let my desires take over. Unbeknownst to him, Thomas fulfilled my depraved needs. Made me feel safe and whole and more myself.

Thomas not only embraces my darkest fantasies, he encourages them. There is no jealousy or misplaced trust. Since the moment we met, there has been nothing but honesty between us. Some truths were more challenging and took more strength to reveal, but every piece of our pasts is exposed. Nothing and no one will come between us or sever our bond.

Thomas Reynolds is more than my lover and husband. He is the key to my heart, the missing piece of my soul, and the king of my lechery. And I will spend the rest of forever giving him what he needs. Fulfilling our darkest impulses as his devoted wife and naughtiest pet.

ABOUT PERSEPHONE AUTUMN

Persephone Autumn lives in Florida with her wife, crazy dog, and two lover-boy cats. A proud mom with a cuckoo grandpup. An ethnic food enthusiast who has fun discovering ways to veganize her favorite non-vegan foods. If given the opportunity, she would intentionally get lost in nature.

For years, Persephone did some form of writing; mostly journaling or poetry. After pairing her poetry with images and posting them online, she began the journey of writing her first novel.

She mainly writes romance, but on occasion dips her toes in other works. Look for her poetry publications, and a psychological horror under P. Autumn.

Distorted Devotion
https://books2read.com/DistortedDevotion
Undying Devotion
https://books2read.com/UndyingDevotion
Sweet Tooth
https://books2read.com/SweetTooth

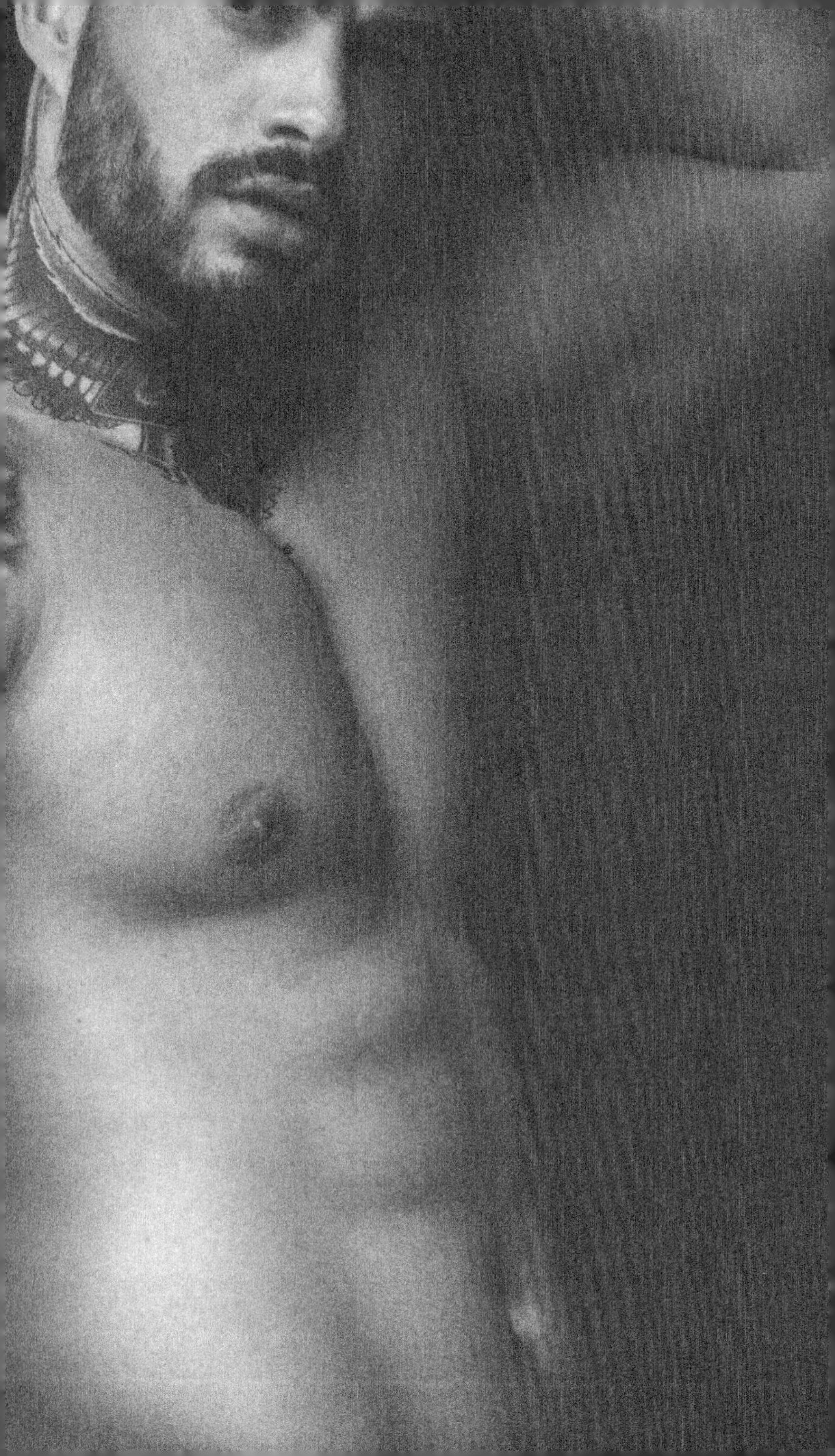

CRACKS

AN OBSIDIAN ELITE NOVELLA

BY ALLY VANCE

BLURB

Jonathan

I am an expert in blurring the delicate balance between excruciating pain and exquisite pleasure. Vincent's unwitting mistake landed him in my hellish domain, and he's going to be punished for his transgression. He will learn to see the pleasure in pain, but in order to do that, I must push him until he *Cracks*.

The question is; will he survive, or will I shatter him completely?

Vincent

Awaking in the dark, I'm trapped, alone, and helpless. I've been locked in with a monster and it doesn't take long to realize there's no escape. His touch brings pain and torture. He's threatened to make me crave him, submit to him, and embrace the pain. I'm not sure how to fight him, or how to resist what he's forcefully awakening inside of me.

Will I ever regain my freedom, or am I going to perish down here in the dark?

*To Renee, who embraces and encourages the darkness in all of my anti-heroes.
This one's for you, babe.*

PROLOGUE
JONATHAN

They say that your early childhood experiences shape the person who you're meant to become as you grow older. But what if the memories of your youth are almost completely lost to obscurity? What then? I was abandoned by my worthless parents and left in the hands of my physically abusive uncle. I have no memory of a life before pain.

I was ten when I first tasted the sweet bliss of torture and witnessed the beauty of pain before it was followed by a slow and agonizing death. I repaid the bastard in kind for everything he ever did to me. The cuts, the beatings, the cigarette burns on my skin. The problem was, he was one of the Obsidian Elite, and they don't take kindly to the murder of one of their own. After one of my uncle's maids discovered me standing barefoot in a pool of blood, next to the body of my butchered relative, I was hunted by the Charon.

Several years passed in a haze of frenzied bloodlust and death. Blood, pain, and death became my way of life. With every passing year I grew older, my soul grew colder, my heart crueller, and the emptiness inside of me took over.

For a long time I remained off their radar, undiscovered and free to kill and maim as I pleased, but it didn't last. Eventually, they found me, but when they did, they didn't kill or torture me like I expected them to; instead, they offered to train me. They honed my skills and gave me a way to harness the need inside of me, turning me into the monster I am today.

Throughout the years I spent under the tutelage of the Charon and then working for them, I often wondered if they had known the reason why I killed my uncle, if they knew about the abuse I was going through at his hands. If they *did* know, then why they didn't the Elite or the Charon step in and stop the abuse? The rich and powerful like to keep their scandals secret, and the Obsidian Elite are more secretive than most organizations. The only condition of my release from the contract binding me to them was my vow to never breathe a word about them.

Even though I'm no longer one of them, I've never stopped hunting for the perfect victim, searching for the one who can withstand the force of my desires.

My newest plaything has been here for nearly a week now, but it's not time for me to take any action, yet. A few more days, and he'll be ready for me; then he'll learn what pain really is. My cock hardens at the thought of the blood and suffering I'll extract from him. I only hope he can hold out long enough to fully sate the craving that flows through my veins.

I bring up the feed from the cameras that are angled carefully to provide maximum visual coverage of his cell. He's sleeping fitfully, tossing and turning on the cot fixed to the floor in the corner of his prison. He must know I'm coming for him, that I'm nearly ready to drag him into the hell I'm going to create for him. I'll be doing everything in my power to make him suffer.

I can't deny his attractiveness, and the thin, minimal clothing I've provided for him does nothing to shield his body from my gaze. I'm struggling to wait, but I know firsthand that denial is the best form of torture.

I want him to beg me for the pain, to crave it as much as I want to inflict it... and when he does, I'll show him what a monster *truly* looks like.

CHAPTER ONE

JONATHAN

Curiosity has driven me to stand outside the door that now separates me from the man awaiting my presence on the other side. He's resilient, I'll give him that. It's been a week since I captured and imprisoned him in these cells.

At one time, wrongdoers were brought here and abandoned to me by the Charon, the assassins of the Obsidian Elite, and under my expertise, they became nothing more than toys to be broken and erased. This is the place of the forgotten, and anyone imprisoned within these walls is on a one-way trip to the hell I have dominion over. No one questions what I do down here. It's *my* dungeon, and I'm the master of the fates of all those who enter.

There are many ways to inflict pain, and as a proud, former member of the Charon, I am practiced in them all. Pain and suffering are an art form, and I am a master wielder of the tools required to create it. On the other side of this door lies the foolish man who wandered somewhere he shouldn't, and he's about to find out exactly what I'm capable of creating.

When I pull a large set of keys from my pocket, the sound of clinking metal fills the silence of the corridor. I thumb through them, searching for the key corresponding to door sixteen. The current inhabitant of this cell is going to be promoted. He's about to become the new occupant of cell seventeen, and he'll witness firsthand what that special room conceals.

I insert the key into the lock and turn it slowly until I hear a resounding click as the pins are depressed and released. I grip the handle and twist before pushing the door open to reveal the man trapped inside.

My captive stopped shouting two days ago, but I wanted to let him stew in his own thoughts and loneliness a little longer before gracing him with my presence. He didn't beg, and that has piqued my interest in him even further. He's not like the others I've kept down here in the dark where no one else ventures. He's stronger than them, and that's going to make him so much sweeter to break beneath my will.

He's lying on the cot with his back to me, and he stirs when the heavy metal door hits the concrete wall. He sits up to look at me. Light blue eyes stare at me from a pale, narrow face framed by black hair that hangs limply just above his shoulders. He's beautiful and all mine to bend and shatter. I'm going to enjoy every moment of our time together.

"Why am I here?" he asks, and his voice is low and husky with a rough edge to it from shouting every day for almost a week.

I'm not about to enlighten him with words, so I don't answer, but my lips twist into a smile at his question because he'll know very soon exactly why he's here. I want to see the fear burning in his eyes when he learns that there'll be no escaping what I've planned down here.

Moving into the cell, I approach him slowly, enjoying the trembles of fear that wrack his body the closer I get to him. The cuffs around his wrists keep him from lashing out, and the excitement begins to build inside me at how vulnerable he is. The power and the promise of inflicting pain makes it very hard to resist doing everything I can to break him right now. But, I know the gradual cracking before I shatter him completely will bring me the most satisfaction and pleasure.

"Tell me your name," I demand, and he flinches before turning his face away from me.

Anger spikes in my blood at his refusal to answer, and I stride the last few feet toward him and fist his hair, using it to pull his head back to face me. The small gasp of pain that escapes his lips at my rough handling makes my cock twitch, and I'm eager to hear what other sounds he might make in response to my cruelty.

"Name," I order, the single word sounding more like a threat.

"Vincent," he utters quietly.

"That wasn't so hard, was it?" I whisper in his ear.

I loosen my grip, detangling my fingers from the black strands of his hair. Then dragging my eyes slowly down his body and back up, I devour every inch of him with my gaze. Over the coming days, I'll learn and memorize every sharp and smooth plane, taking my time to mark his gorgeous pale skin with my touch.

Unchaining the cuffs from the bed, I wrap my fingers around Vincent's upper arm and haul him to his feet. He doesn't fight or try to flee; he just stands on unsteady legs, swaying slightly on the spot. Heaving out a sigh, I pull him toward the door.

Before we start, he needs a shower. The only blemishes allowed on his skin will be the ones I put there myself. So far, since I entered his cell, Vincent has been docile, but I know that as soon as we cross the threshold of his prison the struggling will start. As we leave his cell, though, to my complete surprise, he doesn't glance down the corridor or even look up from the floor to search for a way out.

"Come on," I say, tightening my hold and guiding him toward the shower room.

Just as my fingers close around the handle to the room, Vincent wrenches his arm away and darts down the corridor. The sound of his bare feet slapping against the cold concrete is muffled by the heavy clomp of my boots as I turn and give chase.

"Get back here!" I thunder as I speed after him, even though I know he won't be able to escape.

There's a thrill in the pursuit and in the knowledge that his fleeting hope of freedom will be swiftly ripped away the moment he discovers there's no way out. When Vincent encounters the locked door, his howl of frustration bounces off the stone walls, and I smile at the sound.

"Let me the fuck out of here," he growls when I approach, and I tilt my head in faux sympathy.

"No," I reply simply, inching closer until I'm invading his space, trapping him between my body and the secured door, leaving only a hair's breadth between us.

He swings his bound hands at me, and anticipating the move, I grab the chain hanging between the cuffs and stop him before he can land the blow. Using the chain, I lift his arms and pin them above his head. Then using my few extra inches of height, I close the gap between us until I'm pressing right up against him once again.

"You are going to do everything I say, or the more you resist, the harder you'll be punished. Test me, Vincent, because I'm going to enjoy every second of your pain," I hiss, grinding my semi-hard cock against him before loosening my grasp and lowering his arms.

"Fuck you," he bites out as I step away.

I laugh, "Don't worry, I intend to."

CHAPTER TWO

JONATHAN

I drag him back down the corridor to the shower and shove him inside. He stumbles and nearly loses his footing but manages to catch himself before he hits the floor.

"Strip," I order him. "I want you cleaned up before I can begin."

"And if I don't?" he retorts.

I take a step closer, smiling menacingly when he shrinks away the smallest fraction. "You *will* shower, even if I have to clean you myself."

Vincent closes his mouth, his lips thinning with barely restrained anger as he proceeds to unbutton his jeans. The handcuffs hamper his progress, and he struggles to maneuver as he works to remove them. I don't offer to help, and he grunts and mutters under his breath, mumbling incomprehensible curses and insults at me; but that's okay, I'll be sure to pay him back for every single one in due course.

When he goes to take off his fitted black t-shirt, he throws me a filthy look and raises his cuffed wrists before biting out, "I can't exactly remove this shirt with my fucking wrists fastened together. Fuck, just let me out. I don't even understand why you're doing this to me. I've done nothing to deserve this."

I don't answer immediately. Instead, I walk slowly toward him, and as I do, I take note of his minuscule reactions. I'm not sure whether it's from cold or from fear, but I observe the nervous breaths and shivers that shake his entire frame.

"Oh, Vincent. You will know soon enough why I'm doing this. I'm going to make you suffer, and before I'm even close to being finished with you, I'll have you begging me...for more, and I'll be only too happy to oblige."

"You're delusional. I would never ask for this, and you still haven't answered my question," he snaps.

Drawing a small pocket knife, I flick the blade open, and Vincent flinches perceptibly. *My cock is so fucking hard.* I want to cut his pretty skin and watch him bleed for me. I want to bruise, slice, and mark him until there's no doubt about who he belongs to.

As soon as Vincent crossed the threshold of my property, where I hold all the power, he became mine to do with as I please.

"You're correct, I didn't answer," I respond, grabbing the bottom of his t-shirt and slicing through the material, being sure to nick his skin with the sharp tip of the blade.

He lets out a sharp gasp. "You cut me! Watch what you're doing with that thing!"

Within moments, his t-shirt is lying on the floor in unrecognizable tattered, black strips of fabric, and Vincent is standing before me, handcuffed and wearing nothing but a pair of plain black boxers and displaying a small bloody mark where I cut him.

"Everything off," I whisper softly, trailing the flat side of my knife up his thigh and teasing the edge of his boxers.

His icy glare is cold, and his jaw clenches, but he complies. When he's left with nothing but skin and handcuffs, I slowly drink in his bare form. He's pale, and the dark mop of hair framing his face and tickling the tops of his shoulders is a stark contrast, making him look almost ghostly, like his touch could bring death...*though I'm sure it won't.*

Vincent is not heavily built, but his arms are toned, and the muscles on his body are subtly defined. He drops his hands to cover his cock, attempting to preserve what little modesty he can grasp while standing butt naked in a shower built in a dungeon of my own design. He's being foolish, but I'll let him have this single moment of feigned dignity... *because it'll be his last.*

I press a button on the wall behind him and step back toward the doorway. Water starts to spray from the shower head fitted to the wall, and I twist the thermostat to a suitable temperature and set the timer next to it for three minutes.

"Clean yourself. You have three minutes before the heat turns off, and it'll feel like you're showering in an ice storm," I tell him, hitting the start button on the timer.

Vincent stands there as if in a daze, and I let out a heavy sigh.

I glance at the timer and shrug. "Two minutes, thirty."

He darts over to the shower, and as he stands under the streaming water, I see the heat start to relax him. Watching the droplets running over his skin, I adjust my cock, which is starting to press uncomfortably against the teeth of my jeans' zipper. Vincent is beautiful, and even unstimulated, his cock looks fucking tempting.

Vincent's hair is plastered to his face and neck, and if possible, it looks even darker. My mouth is watering at the sight of him on full display, so vulnerable to my gaze, as he attempts to clean himself with his wrists still in restraints. He brushes the hair from his face with long, narrow fingers, using the water to slick it back over his head. He's hurrying now—and for good reason.

Out of the corner of my eye, I see the timer ticking steadily, swiftly creeping down to zero. When it beeps, I smile. The grin lifts my lips into what I know is a twisted smirk.

"Times up, Vincent," I say, reaching out to the thermostat and viciously twisting the dial from hot to cold.

The yelp that escapes him, the moment the shower loses all heat, bounces off the tiled walls and floor of the room, and he leaps out from beneath the now frigid water, shivering and dripping wet.

"Bastard!" he shouts, throwing himself at me, but I'm ready to catch him, and spinning us both around, I pin him against the wall with my body while my palms are pressed flat against the tiles on either side of his head. I don't give a fuck that he's getting my clothes wet; I'm already having fun.

"You have no fucking idea, Vincent. But you will," I growl in his ear while grinding my stiff, aching cock against his bare ass before biting down hard on the curve where his neck meets his shoulder.

CHAPTER THREE

VINCENT

Pain radiates through me when my captor's teeth close over my flesh, and I can't stop the yell that comes bursting from my chest. I'm uncomfortably aware of the vulnerable position I'm in: naked, cuffed, and trapped between the wall and the man behind me who's caging me in. My stomach twists with unease when I feel his solid erection pressed firmly against my ass.

Suddenly, it becomes all too clear what he's planning for me, and I'm in no damn state to stop him taking whatever he wants. No one knows I'm here, and it's more than likely that no one will come looking for me, not even my brother—not if his bitch of a girlfriend has anything to do with it. I'm all alone in this damn world, and there's nothing to stop my captor from making me disappear completely.

A curious stroll after my tire blew out has turned into a living nightmare, and I have no way of escaping. Nausea bubbles in my stomach when he grunts and grinds himself against me. His dick seems to stiffen more, and even through his clothing, I can feel just how hard he is.

"Stop!" I gasp, the fear and adrenaline making my heart race.

The sharp pressure on my neck eases, and I let out an involuntary gasp when he runs his tongue over the sensitive area he's been biting. He chuckles in my ear, and I flinch away, but there's nowhere to move to except closer to the wall. I shiver when the cold tiles connect with more of my exposed, wet skin, and he crowds me even more.

I slam my head back, and connect with something solid. He grunts in pain but doesn't relinquish his hold or shift his position.

"You're practically begging for me to punish you, Vincent," he whispers, and I can hear the husky rasp to his voice. His next words are punctuated by another sharp bite to the other side of my neck. "I can't wait to paint your skin red."

"Let me out of here," I repeat, but the words sound weak, even to my own ears, as the helplessness of my predicament continues to sink into my body, like the chill of the bricks I'm being tightly pressed against.

My wrists are aching from the unnatural angle they are being forced into between my body and the wall. My captor digs cold fingers into my right hip and gently strokes the skin there with rough fingertips, but the soft touch is a devil's caress. Suddenly, the heavy presence at my back vanishes as he moves away, and I slide slowly down to the freezing floor, awkwardly hugging my knees as I try to regain some of the warmth that has been stolen from my body.

"Get up," he orders, but I don't move, the shivers from the cold still wracking my frame.

A hand wraps around my upper arm, and his fingers bite into my skin as he squeezes and hauls me to my feet.

Standing on unsteady legs, I glare at him before pulling my arm from his grip. "Don't touch me."

He laughs, and I back away from him toward the shower that's still running. As the water hits the floor, it bounces up, and I feel the icy droplets landing on my skin. There's nowhere to run to. I'm trapped down here with a fucking psycho, and the chances of me escaping, intact, are looking slim to none.

I don't know exactly what he intends to do with me, but something tells me it's not going to be pleasant, and I'd be a fool to think otherwise. I'm locked in a fucking dungeon at the mercy of a madman. He closes in on me again, and I inch even closer to the shower, being careful not to step under the water. When he lunges at me, I slip and lose my balance, and even though he catches me, I still end up submerged.

"Fuuuuuck!" I scream when the icy water coats my skin, and I thrash about, trying to shift away from it.

"No. You're going to learn that disobedience will have painful consequences," he growls, holding me in place.

Minutes pass, and the chill settles deep inside me. It feels like I'm being stabbed all over my body with shards of ice, and my teeth are chattering so hard my jaw is aching.

"You want me to stop?" he snarls, and I nod frantically, unable to form any words.

He pulls me out, and shivering uncontrollably, I take shuddering, painful breaths.

"Lesson learned. If you behave, you'll discover just how accommodating I can be. Pain doesn't always have to be a bad thing, Vincent," he soothes, running a hand down my wet cheek and along my jaw, and I almost lean into the warmth emanating from him.

I'm so fucking cold and my skin feels raw. I'm shaking too much to fight him, and he easily drags me from the room, my wet feet scraping over the floor as he hurries me faster than I can currently move unaided.

"W-where are you taking me?" I stammer, quivering as he hauls me back into the corridor.

He doesn't answer, but the look he throws over his shoulder toward me sends a new wave of fear flooding through me. Wherever he's taking me, I just hope it's warm and I can dry off. My sluggish brain can't fathom anything worse than what he's already put me through.

CHAPTER FOUR

JONATHAN

With one hand holding onto Vincent, I draw out my keys with the other. The metal jingles as I thumb through them, searching for the correct one while keeping a firm grip on my shivering captive. His lips have a blue tinge to them, his hair is plastered to his face and neck, and his pale skin is peppered with goosebumps. I'll have to do something to help him get warm.

Letting out a heavy sigh, I insert the key into the door of cell seventeen. The click when the lock disengages sends a burst of anticipation rushing through me. My body is hot, my cock is hard, and I'm aching for the man I have in my grasp. In my head, I can still hear his pained scream from the ice cold shower he's just endured, and it excites me.

I've so much planned for Vincent, and I'm eager to begin the next step. I know how to warm him up, and the thought makes my cock throb. Pushing the door open, I relish the low gasp that escapes from Vincent's pretty mouth, and without further ado, I drag him into the cell with me and kick the door closed behind us. The bang when it hits the frame makes Vincent jump.

Too easy. Fear is part of the game I'm about to play with my newest toy. Fear can cause almost as much suffering as physical pain, but the sight of pain being inflicted gets me harder than anything else I've ever experienced. Being the one to create it, though, it makes me fucking euphoric; it's the highest form of pleasure I can get without actually fucking.

I turn to look at him and frown when I see how much he's shivering. Water still coats his skin in droplets that glisten in the low light of the room. Vincent is...extremely tempting. I want to hurt him, make him scream, and most of all I want to fuck him into oblivion.

Backing him up against the closed door, I pin him with my body once again, and with a hand shackling his wrists, I press them up against the solid sheet of metal behind him. I can feel how cold he is, and leaning closer, the heat from my body sinks into him as I lick some of the water from his neck, making sure to apply extra pressure to the mark I left with my teeth.

Vincent whimpers, and I groan against his skin. His naked body and helpless state is almost too tempting to resist, especially with my close proximity to him.

"Why?" he whispers, and I tilt my head back to look down at him.

"Because I can and I want to," I answer, smiling when I see he's not trembling so violently now.

"That's not an answer," he snipes, and I shake my head.

"Doesn't fucking matter. You're here and you're not going anywhere," I inform him.

Then lowering his hands, I use the restraints to pull him toward the far end of the room where one of my favorite pieces of equipment is fixed to the wall... a wooden St. Andrews' Cross.

"Please," he begs, and my cock twitches.

"Keep begging, Vincent. It gets me so fucking hard, and trust me, you'll be doing plenty of it before I'm done. Whether it's pleading for mercy or for more, it will make little difference." I taunt.

"You're insane," he mutters dejectedly.

I turn him, so he's facing the cross, and press his body against the wood. Then I lift his arms again using the chain binding the cuffs together. He attempts to pull away, but I dig my nails into the sensitive skin of his wrists and snarl at him, "Maybe that's true. In that case, I wouldn't try anything stupid if I were you."

I use the loop attached to the thick leather cuff around his left wrist to secure it in place to the top corner of the cross before I unclasp his right cuff from the chain. I'm prepared for the swinging punch, and catching his fist easily before he can connect with my face, I wrench his arm back into an unnatural angle until he's groaning in pain.

Vincent is a fighter; he's fucking perfect. I almost don't want him to submit to me, but I'm greedy, so I'm going to break him and push him until he craves what only I can give him.

"The more you fight, the more it'll hurt, and the more likely you are to get fucked. I promise it'll hurt, and I'll enjoy every single minute of your pain. There's no one around to hear you scream, Vincent," I chuckle, barely able to contain my excitement.

He stops struggling and throws a filthy look at me from over his shoulder. He winces when I apply additional pressure to his arm before moving to clip his other wrist into place on the right side of the cross. His ankles are next. I run a teasing hand up his left leg, smirking when he shivers.

His firm, tight ass is close to my face, and his balls are hanging low; it takes all of my self restraint not to move my hand higher. *Soon*, I promise myself. I will fuck Vincent, but not until I've played with him some more. When he's finally restrained, I take a few steps back to admire the tempting sight of him: spread-eagled, exposed, helpless, and ready for me to begin.

I readjust my aching cock in my pants, which is just as eager for him as I am. When I'm sure I'm in control of myself again, I move up behind him and run my hand down his back, scratching and digging my nails into his skin. His face is turned to one side, his eyes are tightly closed, and he's biting down on his plump bottom lip.

"Open your eyes, Vincent," I order him, and when his eyelids flicker open, ice-blue eyes meet mine.

He watches me closely and silently, not letting go of his lip. I move toward the black leather case sitting on a nearby table and open the lid, smiling down at the objects inside. Reaching in, I pull out a small, sharp blade, and the wary apprehension shining in Vincent's eyes quickly morphs into terror.

"No! Don't kill me! Fuck!" he curses, finding his voice.

I scoff, "If I wanted you dead, I would have slit your throat while you were sleeping and left you to bleed out in the cell. What I have in mind for you with this blade is much more fun."

I approach him. When I'm close enough that he'll be able to feel my breath, I push his head against the wood of the cross with my hand on the back of his neck and trail the knife slowly down his back, lightly enough not to break the skin.

"Do you feel that, Vincent?" I whisper, my voice low and husky.

My balls are heavy and my cock is so hard it's almost painful. He doesn't answer, and I repeat the action with the blade, applying enough pressure to draw a faint line of blood to the surface of his flawless skin. He doesn't make a sound, but the hiss of breath escaping from between his clenched teeth is all the answer I need.

By the time I'm done, his skin will be painted with blood, and when it heals, he'll be forever marked visibly as *mine*.

CHAPTER FIVE

VINCENT

The sting of the knife being dragged down my back burns, and when my body involuntarily tautens, it feels like a trail of fire across my skin.

"Don't tense!" he barks, but I can't relax.

"Hurts," I hiss, and he laughs.

"This is nothing. I've barely even touched you. You'll learn to love it. Breathe through the pain, and it'll take you to new heights of pleasure," he says, moving closer until our faces are inches apart.

I watch as his lips lift into a smirk, and I feel the cold bite of the blade kissing the top of my arm. I grit my teeth against the groan of pain I'm unable to stifle. His hot breath blows against my neck, and I shiver at the sensation and heat on my exposed skin. Tensing again, I strain against the leather cuffs binding me to the cross. The metal loops rattle against the clasps that are locking me in place.

I can't move, and the sadistic fuck behind me is still chuckling quietly.

"Fuck!" I shout when he slices my arm again, more deeply this time, and my breaths escape in ragged pants as I attempt to breathe through the agony.

"If I didn't love the sounds you make so much, I'd gag you," he taunts, slowly etching a line down my back with his blade.

My jaw is beginning to ache from clenching my teeth so tightly, and my muscles are screaming from holding such a rigid position. He continues to cut shallow slices all over my body, and I can feel my vision beginning to blur as the sensations start to blend together. Blackness encroaches on me, threatening to drag me under. I refuse to surrender, but I can do nothing to stop him while I'm bound to this infernal contraption.

"You're already learning to hold your tongue," he praises, and I close my eyes to shut him out because I can't cover my ears. "Embrace the pain, Vincent."

His own breaths are sharp, and when he finally stops his bladed torture, I let out a heavy, shuddering sigh of relief.

"We aren't finished, yet. I'm far from done with you," he says, moving up behind me again, and I can feel the hard evidence of his excitement pressed firmly against my ass.

Cringing, I growl with renewed frustration at my own helplessness and struggle even more to pull free from the restraints. It feels like my wrists are about to snap, and I let out a yell when pain erupts from my ass and radiates outward. I stop, and whipping my head around as far as I can, I glare at my captor who's wearing a smirk, has a visible hard-on, and is clutching a paddle in his hand.

"I'm sorry. Did that hurt?" he asks in a tone full of false innocence, but his eyes are glittering with dark glee.

"You know it bloody well did," I grit out, my breath whistling between my teeth.

"Hmm, that was just a warning," he says, and I feel the air move as he swings the paddle again and lands another solid blow to my already smarting asscheek with a noise like a gunshot.

I howl, and the sound mixes with his low groan, which is then swiftly followed by his laughter. He continues the onslaught, this time on the other buttock until my entire ass feels like it's about to burst into flames. A sharp *thwack* just below one of the cheeks forces an ear-splitting yell from my throat, and ripples of pain shoot through me, radiating outward. I blink away the agony that mists over my eyes, and when he repeats the action on the other side, blackness finally swallows me whole.

When I open my eyes again, I'm still secured to the cross. I slowly force my limp body to straighten, wincing at the ache in my wrists and back and the acute stinging in my ass.

"You did better than I expected, but there's still so much more to come," my captor says, his voice washing over me like a bucket of ice water, and I turn my head to meet his gaze. He's lounging in a black leather chair with his legs outstretched and crossed at the ankles, and the paddle is resting across his lap.

"How long was I out?" I rasp, my voice rough from shouting.

"No more than a few minutes," he responds with a shrug before standing and moving slowly toward me.

"Let me go," I plead, but he shakes his head with a smile.

"Why would I? The fun is just beginning," he responds, trailing his fingers down my back and brushing over the damaged skin.

I flinch at the contact, and averting my gaze, I close my eyes and attempt to block out the sensations. I can't stop the pained groan that escapes me, though, when his hand reaches my sore ass and massages the aching flesh there.

Lightly slapping his palm against the sensitive area, I whimper as he growls, "Red looks fucking good on your pale skin, Vincent."

"Fuck you, asshole," I bite out, breathing heavily against the sting as his hand connects with the other cheek.

"Mmmm, not yet," he says with amusement in his tone, and I freeze when he teases a finger against the crack of my ass, and venturing downward with his hand, he taps the tight ring of muscle there, physically taunting me with his threat.

"Well, you won't be the one fucking me, but you are going to take my cock... here. I'll soon have you on your knees begging me to stretch out this tight, little hole," he informs me, removing his finger, but his words sound more like a dark promise than a threat.

"I hope you enjoy disappointment," I snap.

"Keep telling yourself that, but I know I'm right. Soon enough, you'll be swallowing those words along with my cock. Then I'm going to fuck you so hard you won't know whether you're screaming in pain or in pleasure," he retorts, and I shake my head furiously at his foolish assertion.

CHAPTER SIX

JONATHAN

Vincent can deny me all he likes, but it won't make a lick of difference to the final outcome. He's here, and he won't be going anywhere else. My playthings don't get to choose how they're toyed with and used, and I'm sure Vincent is going to enjoy it far more than he realizes. I don't mind educating him. There's fun to be had in the lessons I'm all too willing to impart to him through the careful application of pain and discipline.

I take a step back and lightly tap his bare ass with the flat of the paddle, and he winces. I'm in control and fully aware of my own strength, and that was a fraction of what I'm capable of inflicting. I don't want to kill him by pushing him too far this early in our little game, but I'm not going to entirely hold back either. He needs to learn and learn fast, or he won't be able to withstand what's coming.

Dropping the paddle to the floor, it lands on the concrete with a slap of leather, and I chuckle at the nervous flinch that escapes Vincent. Once again, I admire the color of his tender skin that's now a pleasant shade of dark pink, and I squeeze my aching cock through the black denim of my jeans and stifle my responding groan. He looks fucking delicious, and I want to bite those toned cheeks of his ass until he screams.

Unable to resist tormenting him, I land a sharp spank on one asscheek and then the other, relishing the yelp that leaves his mouth and the sound of my palm against his flesh. The noises he makes are hard to resist when I roughly squeeze each buttock. His groans fill the room, and I bite my lip, my breaths coming faster and harder as I fight the urge to see what else I can do to make him respond.

Restraint. I must exercise restraint before I lose all control and simply claim every inch of Vincent's body and mind. Don't get me wrong, I will have it all, eventually, but I need to take my time and ensure I remain both calm and collected.

I swallow slowly and trail my fingers up his exposed back. Tracing over the shallow cuts, I smudge his blood with my fingers, creating red smears over his body. With a smile he can't see, I paint a letter J on his skin, staking my claim with his blood.

That's more than enough for now, I muse, placing my stained finger into my mouth and tasting the metallic tang on my tongue. Walking over to the small chest standing in the corner of the room, I rummage through it for a blanket before making my way back over to Vincent, who is standing as relaxed as he can manage in his bonds.

Bending down, I place the blanket on the floor next to the cross and unfasten the cuffs around Vincent's ankles and gently rub the reddened skin of each one. Looking up, I clench my eyes closed at the vision in front of me, and unable to find the will to resist, I lean forward and run my nose up the crack of his ass,

"What the fuck are you doing!" he exclaims, tensing, but I ease his asscheeks apart and lap at his exposed ring of muscle with my tongue.

Vincent's resulting shudder and incoherent mumble as I prod him with the tip of my tongue encourages me to continue, and soon he's almost welcoming me to take him. His responsiveness brings a smile to my lips and leaves me aching even more to claim him fully with my cock. I want to tear through him, split him open, and fill his ass with my cum.

Rising to my full height, I nip at his shoulder before breathing in his ear. "You can't tell me you didn't enjoy that a little bit."

"You're wrong," he bites out, turning his head until his furious eyes meet mine.

"You can't deny it, Vincent. Your hard cock betrays you," I say with amusement, my fingers brushing against his hip as I reach around to palm his rigid length.

I watch him as he pinches his eyes shut. Shame tinges his face a shade of pink as I squeeze his cock, and pumping my hand a few times, I swirl one of my fingers through the precum at the tip.

"Stimulation has an involuntary effect on my body, but it doesn't mean I'm enjoying it," he says between gritted teeth, and I can hear the faint breathiness in his words as I move my hand faster.

"Really? Then why did your cock twitch and thicken when I beat your ass pink with the paddle?" I ask, but he doesn't answer me.

A moan falls from his lips, and I can tell he's getting close to coming, so I start to slow my pace, leisurely moving my hand that's fisted around his cock. I watch his face closely, admiring his delicately handsome features screwed up with pleasure and the way he's biting his bottom lip hard between his teeth. His breaths are ragged...*he's so close now.*

Just as he's about to tumble over the precipice, I stop and remove my hand from his cock. Vincent's strangled cry of frustration and dismay at my denying him his release is pure music to my ears.

"I'll be back very soon, Vincent," I tell him, satisfaction bleeding from my tone, and I quietly hum nonchalantly as I pick up the blanket and cover him with it.

"Don't leave me like this. You fucking bastard, don't leave me here!" he yells, but I don't answer.

My own cock is swollen and aching, and I need to take care of the painful erection tenting my jeans, especially before I do something stupid like plunging my length deep into Vincent's unprepared ass. It's not the right time for that. I haven't had nearly enough fun with him yet. This is simply the beginning.

CHAPTER SEVEN

JONATHAN

I won't be leaving Vincent secured to the cross for long, but I need to take care of my raging hard-on or I won't be able to think straight long enough to keep control. I've a feeling he's going to be the most perfect toy I've ever kept here. None of the others awoke such a hunger in me, and none ever responded to my vicious touch the way he has.

Wandering over to the cot in the far corner of the room, I lie down and free my aching cock. I groan as the cool air washes over my heated skin, and I fist my hand around the rigid length. My gaze sweeps across the room to where Vincent is standing, his wrists still pinned in place as he struggles on the cross. *He can't see me unless he turns his head, but I can see him.*

When his movements send the blanket covering him to the floor, my eyes travel over his body, drinking in the sight of his bare flesh and lingering on the marks now marring his perfect, pale skin. My hand moves faster, harder, and my breaths are getting harsher and heavier the closer I get to coming.

A groan flies from my parted lips, and Vincent twists his head, eyes searching for the source of the noise. I pin him with my gaze, and I catch a fleeting glimpse of the longing that briefly passes over his features. I grin wickedly at him and slow my pace for a moment, savoring the tortured expression on his face before he turns away from me once more.

I'm so fucking close now. Precum is leaking from the tip of my cock, my balls are tight and heavy, drawing up closer to my body, and I can feel the familiar tingle beginning at the base of my spine.

Pleasure rips through me, and I come hard with Vincent's name on my tongue, but I manage not to shout it out loud. White hot ribbons of cum spurt from my cock, coating my hand and stomach where my t-shirt has ridden up. I shudder and let out a low moan. Closing my eyes, I slowly squeeze my length and continue jerking off until I'm spent and my balls feel completely empty.

My heart is thudding in my chest, and the aftershocks of the intense orgasm are still rippling through my body. Vincent makes a noise, and I open my eyes to look at him. He's squirming where he stands, wiggling his ass from side to side and moving his hips forward and backward. I bolt upright when I realize he's trying to create enough friction between the wood of the cross and his still-hard cock in order to come.

I stride across the room until I'm standing behind him, and I'm almost tempted to let the impudent little shit find completion, if only to use it as a reason to punish him later for defying me. I didn't expect him to get creative in order to chase the orgasm I denied him, and I'm almost impressed. Vincent is so absorbed with chasing his impending release he doesn't hear me come up behind him.

Licking my lips with anticipation, I tuck my slowly hardening cock back into my jeans and prepare my next move. He's close, so close it won't be too long before he shoots his load all over the wall behind the cross he's currently rubbing himself against in a slow, methodical way. I wince because it can't be all that pleasant a sensation. He must be really desperate to relieve the ache, and I can't bring myself to look away.

My lips tilt upward into a wicked grin, and I flex my fingers, watching Vincent closely, waiting for the right moment to strike. Just as he's about to tumble over the precipice, I swing my arm and land a harsh spank on his ass. His subsequent yell of pain is swiftly followed by a guttural growl, and he comes—hard. For a split-second, I'm mesmerized by the look of rapture mixed with pain on his features before my eyes drop to where his cock is jetting streams of cum all over the wall and floor.

Vincent drops his head, and his knees shake as his body attempts to slacken in the restraints. He's panting hard, and a thin sheen of sweat is glistening all over his skin. Taking advantage of his weakened and endorphin-riddled state, I reach up and unlock the cuffs binding his wrists to the cross. He slumps against me, and it's impossible not to react to his nakedness and proximity to me.

I half carry, half drag him across the room to the metal-framed cot I was lying on moments before and lay him down. His eyes meet mine briefly before he closes them and looks away, unwilling to face me. Anger bubbles in my gut, but I refuse to let it rise to the surface as I restrain him to the bed with his arms by his sides rather than raising them above his head this time. His ankles, I bind to the bars at the bottom.

I throw the blanket back over him, and he opens his eyes and looks at me quizzically.

"No sense in having you die of dehydration and hypothermia," I state, and reach for the bottle of water on the nearby table and unscrew the cap.

His tongue darts out to wet his lips, and I let out a breath as desire sends blood rushing to my groin.

"Please," he whispers, raising his head. I hold the bottle to his lips and tip it gently.

His Adam's apple bobs as he gulps down the water, and I fight back the groan as visions of how he'll look swallowing my cock enter my mind.

"Thanks," he rasps, and I let out a small laugh.

"You won't be thanking me tomorrow, Vincent," I smirk, "You came without my permission. Sleep well."

Standing up, I march across the room and open the door.

"Don't leave me here! Let me out!" he calls, just as I'm about to leave.

I pivot slowly on the spot until he's within my line of sight and then lift my hand to the small switch on the wall just inside the door.

"See you tomorrow," I say. Flicking the lights off, then exiting the room, I slam the door shut behind me.

Vincent's muffled shouts filter through the metal, and a smile spreads across my face as I make my way to my own room, ready to relieve more of my tension and get some much-needed sleep. I need to regain my energy so I can carry out what I have planned for Vincent over the coming days.

CHAPTER EIGHT

JONATHAN

Walking out of cell seventeen and away from Vincent was the sensible thing to do. If I tell myself enough times, I may start to believe it, but the simple fact is, my cock disagrees, and to be quite honest, so do I. However, it wouldn't do to lose all my control and unleash my inner beast on Vincent. Not yet, anyway. I need to build up to that moment. I need to pace myself and make sure I don't lose my head or I may find myself buried balls deep inside Vincent's ass sooner than I planned.

Fuck. I swear, it seems like no matter how many times I jerk off to all my filthiest fantasies of Vincent I'll never be satisfied...not until I finally have him beneath me. My conscience niggles at me, questioning why I'm doing this, but as always, I stifle it. He wandered somewhere he shouldn't, and he must pay the price for his mistake. Nothing else matters other than the fact that he's here with me now, and I'm going to enjoy extracting every ounce of pain I can from him, rejoicing in his screams and reveling in his moans.

I hurry up the corridor to the secure door Vincent tried and failed to escape through earlier. Extracting my keys, I unlock the door and exit the basement where I keep the dungeon cells. Making my way up the stairs, I enter the main body of the house. The quiet is unnerving but also refreshing. I never have visitors... unless you count the unwitting trespassers I snatch up for my own amusement. So far, no one has suspected me after they've vanished into thin air. Believe me, I've checked, and I'm not stupid enough to leave any evidence that could be traced back to me.

Not all of them have had the *pleasure* of visiting the seventeenth cell. Some of them I've killed immediately, and others have held little interest for me beyond seeing how much pain they could endure before they died. However, there have been those I've had a little more fun with. The St. Andrews' Cross was already stashed away in the basement when I moved into the house. I cleaned it up, thoroughly refurbished it, and then installed it in my special room. I must say, it's ideal for when I'm in the mood to create sweet agony for my victims.

It's been too long since I had someone as promising as Vincent. He's different from the others. He's got a spark of something that speaks to my inner monster, the one that craves the pain of others. Unlike my previous toys, Vincent seems to be enjoying it even though he's trying hard not to. I felt how hard he was against my palm. I wander through the house, reflecting on the way he felt and reacted to my touch and the perfect vision he made, spread out on the cross and vulnerable to my every sadistic whim.

I make my way to the living room, and reclining on the large couch that leans against one wall, I pull out my phone. Using the buttons on the touchpad, I bring up the feed to the cameras I have installed throughout the dungeon and the house, which stream directly to my phone, and I enlarge the one that's directed at my latest toy. He's still lying exactly as I left him, not that he has much choice in the matter. Even through the lens of the camera, I feel myself drawn to Vincent in the same way I was when I first laid eyes on him:

My phone vibrates in my pocket, and I take it out. No one calls me, and no one ever sends a message. I'm dead to everyone now. I left the Charon so long ago. Truthfully, they seemed pleased to see the back of me. I let out a sigh when I see the alert. It's the alarm announcing an intruder, probably another stray cat or fox, but I jerk upright when I see it's neither of those creatures. It's a man, and he's young, attractive, and most importantly...alone. It's been quiet around here for a long time now. I don't welcome guests into my home, not in the traditional sense at least, but it looks like I'm about to have some company.

My lips twist up into a smile, causing my muscles to ache from the rarely used expression...but I'm ready to meet this handsome stranger. Wait, handsome? I frown as my eyes follow the man who's stumbling through the overgrown weeds and brambles that litter the rarely used path leading to my front door. The driveway is clear, but to outsiders, this place appears abandoned, and that's just how I like it. I pay the bills online, and other than the rare trip into town for groceries, I keep to myself. No one suspects my true motives and none of the locals have a goddamn clue what lies hidden beneath this house. If any of them did stumble upon the truth, then they wouldn't live long enough to tell anyone else, anyway.

There's a crack in the window at the front entrance to the house, and as the stranger draws closer, I grab up the dart gun I keep by the door for such occasions as this. Bullets are too messy and would draw unwanted attention, I prefer to knock trespassers out with a tranquilizer dart and then draw out their punishment somewhere more private.

"Foolish, boy," I mutter as I prime my gun, the dart loaded and ready to send this stranger into a slumber. "It's time to sleep," I mumble, as I take aim and gently squeeze the trigger.

CHAPTER NINE

VINCENT

My arms and legs ache, the strain in my shoulders from having my wrists bound to the bed frame is starting to become a persistent throb. Blood coats my skin with fresh red trails from the cuts on my back, and some of the dried bloodstains are starting to dry and crack. But, despite all of this, I'm fighting down the intense desire to beg him to continue in his torture.

The pain is intense and like nothing I've ever experienced before. It's awoken something that's always been lurking inside me, and all my private, inner thoughts and cravings have come flooding to the surface of my mind.

I know that if I were to encourage him to act upon the desires that plague me, I'd never be the same again. The bastard was right when he said I'd soon be begging for more, but I don't intend to give him that satisfaction. Let's face it, the chances of me ever getting out of here alive are pretty much nil. Given this psycho's alarming interest in torturing me, though, I'm not sure a quick death will be a likely option either. You can't torture someone once they're dead.

I know everything about this is wrong, and the knowledge of just how twisted, fucked up, and beyond saving I am, guts me. In this place, there'll be no salvation unless I choose to stop fighting and embrace the torture he's inflicting on my weary body and mind. I can tell he wants me to bow down and accept I'm never going to escape from this place, but his words say one thing, and his actions suggest another. I'm left drowning in confusion over what he really wants. In one breath he's telling me how much he wants to hurt me, but in between the bouts of pain he's unleashing on me, he's also bringing me pleasure.

He's left me alone. Why? I'm aching, confused, and struggling to keep my eyes open. I've never been more afraid in my life, but I've also never been more aware of myself and my body. I don't want to acknowledge the thoughts whirling through my mind like a dervish and attempting to claw their way to the surface. I want to keep them buried, hidden where they will never see the light of day.

I suppose the cruel fact is, just like me, they're trapped within a dark prison there's no escaping from.

"Help!" I shout, my voice scratchy from dehydration and overuse.

I know there's little point in begging and pleading to be set free, but it makes me feel more in control and less like I'm simply lying back and accepting my new fate. Hours pass, dragging slowly by, and I begin drifting into a daze. I'm neither awake, nor am I asleep, but a semi-lucid mix between the two. *How long has it been since he imprisoned me in this place? How many days? Weeks?* I've no real sense of time. Before today, I only had infrequent contact with my captor when he brought me food and water.

Casting my fuzzy mind back, I attempt to recall the last thing I remember before waking up here. I was heading to see my younger brother, Xander, at his girlfriend's parents' house. He's recently moved in with Kim and her family, and he's just started college. I've never liked Kim, and she feels exactly the same way about me. She's controlling, manipulative, and spiteful with her words. Since he started dating her, he hasn't been the same. He's always known about my disdain for her, I've never made it a secret, but he chose her over his own family.

My stubborn little brother refused to even see me because he knew I would insist on him coming home. He was offered a partial scholarship in one of the best colleges in our state, but he turned it down to be with her. I knew she'd gotten her hooks in him, and no matter what I did or said he just couldn't see it.

His girlfriend...or rather fiancée, as the little witch so gleefully informed me when I arrived on their doorstep, told me to get lost and not to bother them again or she'd have me arrested. I wasn't going to give up on Xander that easily, and Kim was deluded if she thought I would walk away from him without a fight.

Needless to say, I ignored what I considered an empty threat and returned to see him the next day. It was another failed visit, where my brother allegedly refused to see me. Driving back home on a long, deserted road, I got a flat outside a seemingly abandoned house.

CRACKS

Curiosity led me to halt the tire change and take a look. The overgrown and desolate land surrounding the large, brick building was a disappointment. I remember deciding to head back to my car, to finish swapping out the tire, and the rest is nothing but a blur.

———

I've been drifting in and out of consciousness, but the sound of a door opening rouses me from my restless daze. I haven't been able to sleep due to my discomfort and also because my mind refuses to settle. My survival instinct has been keeping me alert while I've been running through all the events that led me here, to this mysterious chamber of torture.

My voice is little more than a croak as I call out to my captor, "Please. What do you want from me?"

My question is met with silence, and when the room illuminates, I blink against the harshness of the light burning my eyes as they rush to adjust to the brightness. I attempt to clear my throat, but the dry ache makes this impossible.

"Can I at least have some more water?" I rasp, my eyes fixating on the bottle sitting on a table next to me.

The man approaches me, and I'm reluctantly struck by his features. I've been desperately trying to block myself from thinking of how handsome he looks. Tall, with dark hair that hangs loose and messily, contrasting with the well groomed scruff coating his jaw. I'm sure I shouldn't be wondering how it would feel against my skin.

Would the fine hairs rub softly, and would the thicker ones leave faint scratches? Why am I fantasizing about this man?! He's evil, and a villain in my true life horror story. He's locked me in this damn basement and treated me like a slave he can hurt for his pleasure. I shake my head to clear it of the lust-filled fantasy that's temporarily blinded my senses. I need to get out of here before I lose my mind entirely and allow myself to become a victim to my captor's warped desires. More importantly, I must never let him know how much his agonizing touch truly affects me.

CHAPTER TEN

JONATHAN

I barely get any sleep; instead, I spend the night tossing and turning, my thoughts entirely consumed with my weary prisoner who's bound like a gift in my dungeon. I eventually manage to drift off into a light doze at around 3am, and when I eventually awaken four hours later, I feel as though I haven't slept at all. With a yawn, I sluggishly get up to begin my day.

After grabbing a quick breakfast, I prepare something for Vincent who must be getting hungry, and probably thirsty too. *I have something he could drink,* I think with a smirk. Shaking my head, I attempt to stifle the train of thought that makes my cock stir, and I grab him a bottle of water. As I head toward the heavy, sealed door that leads downstairs, I grab my keys and tap in the security code. The lock disengages with a quiet beep, and I push the door open.

The air gets colder the farther I descend, and I shiver slightly. Sometimes the temperature difference hits me hard, and other times, I welcome the chill. There's no heating down here even though I've fitted in a plumbing system so my guests have the use of facilities in their cells and for the shower, of course.

I hum absentmindedly as I walk along the corridor, each step bringing me closer to Vincent. With a jingle of metal, I insert the key into the lock and enter the room, flicking the light on as I venture inside. Carefully securing it behind me, I approach Vincent, who is curled up awkwardly on the cot. Standing beside him, I smile at the peaceful expression on his sleeping face.

"Good morning, Vincent," I say calmly, watching as he opens his eyes and stares blearily up at me. My lips twitch sadistically, and I tack on, "Sleep well?"

"Fuck you," he mumbles sleepily, trying to stretch and wincing when his movements tug on the restraints, applying pressure to his joints.

"Tut, tut. Is that any way to thank me for bringing you breakfast? I hope you didn't forget the punishment you're due after your little indiscretion yesterday, because I haven't."

"Sorry," he says with a yawn, and I blink at him in surprise. *I wasn't expecting an apology.* Sighing, I bend over and loosen his restraints, freeing him. "Thanks," he adds, groaning as he stretches out his arms and legs, before slowly getting to his feet with the blanket around his shoulders.

"Where are you planning to go, Vincent?" I probe lightly.

"Bathroom," he grunts sarcastically. I frown at his tone and then nod, pointing in the direction of the small bathroom attached to the room.

He walks stiffly toward it, wincing when the cold floor connects with his feet and his aching muscles start to respond to his movements. While I await his return, I lie on the bed and inhale deeply, absorbing his scent and also the lingering warmth from his body. Before I can stop myself, my eyes drift closed.

Hands on my body, stroking my skin and teasing my slowly hardening cock. I moan, jerking my hips toward the touch, eager for more. I'm on edge, wanting and needing the hands to press harder, to take my cock and bring me the sweet release of pleasure.

I open my eyes and fight to remain still when I see Vincent crouched next to me, his hand buried deep in my pockets. He's searching for the keys. I narrow my eyes into slits and let him continue while I quietly plan my next move. His hand brushes against my cock, and it takes all of my will not to lose my shit. When his fingers close around the keys, I jolt upright and stop him with my hand around his slender throat.

"What the fuck do you think you're doing?" I snarl, relishing the way his eyes widen with fear and his face drains of all color, making him look more like a specter than a man. Vincent attempts to withdraw his hand, but I catch his wrist. "If you're going to lay your hands on me, you'd better do it properly."

The breath escapes his lungs with a whoosh, and I abandon all sense and drag him onto the cot, twisting until he's pinned on his back beneath me. My weight holds him captive, and the feel of his naked body is too damn tempting. "Hmm, I think I've decided how I'm going to punish you, now. Take out my cock."

"What?" he gasps, and when I teasingly roll my hips, rubbing the denim of my pants against his dick, a badly concealed moan escapes his lips.

"You heard what I said. You can beg for forgiveness with your lips wrapped around my cock, and maybe I'll consider rewarding you for good behavior."

He begins to shake, but when he eventually lifts his hands they're steady. My lips twist as he reaches for the zipper. With his hands so close to me, and his hardening cock against my body, I know I'll be able to break him. When he attempts to wriggle free, I grab his wrists and slam them down against the bed.

"Bad boy, Vincent. I'm beginning to think you want to be punished…"

CHAPTER ELEVEN

VINCENT

Do I want to be punished? My mind feels foggy, and my body is reacting to his proximity and the friction against my dick. It's difficult not to respond. My captor is all sharp edges and darkness, but there's something about him that also draws me in. I shake my head, fighting it. I don't want this, I don't want to be here, and I certainly don't want *him*.

I don't answer. He huffs, and lifts himself off of me. Relieved, I slowly twist onto my side to try and get up, but a hand on my back, shoving me down, stops me in my tracks. A stinging touch of a sharp blade on my skin makes me, gasp, and I attempt to push him away.

"Stay still, you wouldn't want me to make a mistake. One wrong move and all you'll be is a pool of blood and a corpse."

I grit my teeth as another sting comes before warm breath hits my bare back and I shiver; nothing could have prepared me for the feel of his mouth on my skin, tracing the fresh cuts with his tongue. Then he ventures lower, and I freeze, tensing every muscle in my body when he licks along the seam of my ass. He finally withdraws from me, and I breathe out a sigh of relief at the thought the torture might be over.

I realize I'm wrong when another nick makes me wince. My teeth are beginning to feel like they'll crack from the pressure I'm exerting on them in my bid to stay still and quiet. A hiss spits through my teeth when he cuts me again, this time on my ass. It felt deeper this time, and I'm beginning to wonder whether my flesh will resemble ground beef by the time my ordeal is over. One cut follows another, and I'm beginning to lose control over myself. Humiliating whimpers are hovering in my throat, and when he cuts me yet again, I yell out at the pain and at him.

"Keep screaming, Vincent. Your pain makes me so hard," he taunts as he continues to carve lines all over my skin.

"No," I manage to grit out.

"You need this as much as I do. Admit it, and I promise I'll stop."

His assurance sounds empty of sincerity, and as intent as he seems on causing me pain, I can only doubt the truth of his words. I don't answer.

"Have it your way, then," he says in a nonchalant tone.

Tears spring from my eyes as he begins to ravage my skin with the blade, and I can no longer hold back the sounds of physical anguish breaking out of my chest.

"Music to my ears," he groans, slicing into my back so forcefully that black spots are beginning to coat my vision. My body is soaked in tears, sweat...and blood.

CHAPTER TWELVE

JONATHAN

When Vincent goes limp, I finally pause in my assault on his flesh. My breaths are coming out in heavy pants, and I'm hard as a fucking rock. I stand up and back away from the cot. Coming to a stop a few feet away, I stare down at Vincent, admiring my handiwork. The skin on his back is a beautiful patchwork of red lines, smeared with blood. My eyes track down his bare skin to his ass, and I smirk when I see the deep 'J' embedded in his skin.

I could've taken him, then and there, but for some reason, I held back. I'm not exactly sure what's come over me; something about him calls to me. His blood sings in his veins, begging to be released, and glistens enticingly on the surface of his skin, and yet I have a deep ache inside me that wants to claim him... but it's not his life I want to claim, it's *him*. Shaking my head, I settle down on one of the plush leather chairs in the room and wait for him to awaken.

I've imprisoned so many people down here, before, during, and since the time I worked for the Charon, men and women, alike. Yet, I've never, not once, felt toward any of them the way I do for Vincent. *What is it about him that appeals to me so much? Is it his delicate beauty, his inner strength, or is it simply his innocence?* I simply can't put my finger on it, but if there's one thing I'm certain of, it's that I'm not going to let him walk out the door and away from me.

With a heavy sigh, I lean my head against the backrest of the chair and rub my hand over my face. I mustn't let him see any weakness. The men and women of the Charon are taught to be strong, and even though I'm no longer one of them, the training sessions still resonate within me.

The art of torture and the exchange of pain for information has always appealed to me, and in the time I spent with the Charon they gave me purpose, but when there were no more informants that needed to be *persuaded* to talk, and they decided my methods were too brutal, they let me go. It didn't stop me from continuing to search for a way to prolong the high brought on by unleashing my sadistic tendencies.

In an attempt to stifle my pleasurable reminiscences, I focus my attention on Vincent. He's so pale that anyone not watching closely might believe he was dead, but the steady rise and fall of his back and chest with each breath only proves how strong he is. Maybe he'll be tough enough to withstand everything I can give him: the pain, the pleasure, and the promise of what's to come.

When I eventually come to realize he won't be regaining consciousness any time soon, I wearily get to my feet and walk to the bathroom. Once inside, I grab a cloth and soak it beneath the faucet before wringing it out and venturing back into the room. Vincent hasn't moved from his position on the bed, and I smile, knowing that everything is going exactly how I planned.

I stride back over to him and carefully sit on the edge of the cot. Fresh blood still glistens on his pale skin while some patches have darkened until they're almost dark claret in color. With the cloth in my hand, I gently wipe away the bloody smears and clean his wounds. As soon as the damp cloth touches the broken skin, he mumbles in his sleep and flinches at my touch. I am cruel, and the marks on his skin are clear proof of that.

Sometimes, I know I take my actions too far, but nothing gives me the same level of joy or satisfaction as harming another human being. After discarding the now bloodied cloth, I sit back down and trace the patterns I've carved on his skin. The majority of his wounds have stopped bleeding, but a few still leave a trail of red smears across his back where my fingertip passes.

Vincent stirs and then rolls onto his back. As his face scrunches up with pain, I feel myself beginning to crack. *He's so fucking irresistible.* The cool and distant façade I've tried to retain drops, and I immediately lunge at him, straddling his body as I pin him on his back with my hand around his throat. I don't know why he's bringing out such a visceral response from me, and not just a physical one. I'm falling off the edge and into the unknown, and he's the cause.

"You are so damn tempting, Vincent. Especially now you have my initial carved into your ass. That letter is mine, and so are you. I'm going to own every fucking bit of you: your pain, your tears, and your body. All of you belongs to me, and you're going to feel me everywhere...whether you like it or not."

His eyes widen at my declaration of ownership, and when his eyebrows pinch together in a frown, I brace myself for his refusal, his denial, and his pleas to be set free.

"You carved your initial into my ass?" he yells, causing his throat to vibrate against my palm while his voice echoes around the room.

I reach around and underneath him with my free hand, smirking as I lift his hips and squeeze the cheek I branded with my blade. His wince as I dig my nails into his flesh and press against my mark is like an aphrodisiac to me, and my cock stiffens in response.

"Yes, I fucking did," I growl.

Massaging the tender area with my hand, I slip my fingers into the crack of his ass and wiggle them around until I find what I'm looking for. Without hesitation, I push a finger inside him. Vincent tenses, and I slide it in deeper, stretching his tight ring of muscle while he tries to clench around my intrusion to stop me. His efforts are fruitless, and all it does is pull my digit in farther. Ignoring his pained whimper, I drop my mouth to his shoulder and bite down. His response is addictive. His groans and whimpers only serve as fuel for my burning desire. *I need more.*

Adjusting my hand, I slip another finger inside, moaning at how tight he is and wondering how delicious he will feel when it's my cock being squeezed inside his hole.

"It hurts," he manages to gasp out, and I tighten my grip around his throat more firmly as I force a third finger in, stretching him even wider.

"You need to start learning to savor it. I'm going to split you wide open and show you the true meaning of pain, and how pleasurable it can be," I tell him through panted breaths as I withdraw my fingers to the first joint before thrusting them back in until my knuckles are flush with his asshole. Carefully, I angle my hand so I'm rubbing against his prostate, and his whimpers become garbled moans against my hand still at his throat.

"I thought you'd like that," I growl, increasing the speed and depth of my thrusts until he's shaking beneath me. His body is responding to me, and I feel his cock stiffening against my pelvis and digging into me.

Loosening my grip on his throat, I move down his slim torso until my face is level with the hard length jutting out from between his hips. I open my mouth and swallow his cock deep until it hits the back of my throat and then I slowly pull back, dragging my teeth lightly along the shaft until the tip is pressing against my tongue.

"Fuck!"

I chuckle darkly and remove my fingers from his ass, wiping them clean on the sheets. I let his cock flop out of my mouth and dip my head lower. I force his legs apart and move between them. Lifting his hips to gain better access, I lean forward and run my tongue down from just behind his balls to his asshole. The gasp and way he shivers at my wicked teasing makes me grin, I repeat the action and he lets out a shaky laugh.

I tease the tight ring with my tongue, and Vincent shudders again. Probing the puckered hole, I feel the saliva pooling in my mouth. Vincent's low moans surround me, encouraging me as I devour him before teasing him more when I move my mouth down to his balls. I drag my tongue slowly back up, applying pressure to his taint. His loud groan motivating me to continue, I replace my tongue with my thumb, and continue to massage that spot with it while I drive him wild with my mouth on his asshole.

As Vincent relaxes, somewhat, under my ministrations, his muscles loosen even more, and I'm able to fuck him deeper with my tongue until my lips are pressed right up against his ass. I eat him out like a man starving for his next meal. Drawing my head back slowly, I swirl my tongue around the sensitive skin, and when I slowly push it inside him again, I relish the way Vincent quivers beneath me as I alternate between speeds, driving in and out of him.

I keep sliding my tongue from his depths, just so I can plunge back in, fucking him with it like I'll soon be doing with my cock. Vincent clenches involuntarily, and it feels like his ass is trying to suck me inside of him. I groan against his skin, imagining how it's going to feel when it's my cock his ass is accepting instead of just my tongue.

"Fuck," he groans, his words drawn out over a long sigh as I pull away.

"With pleasure," I respond, leaning back so I'm looking down at him.

Vincent's eyes are wide with confusion, and the irises have been swallowed by his pupils. I'm not sure whether he's turned on, afraid, or a tantalizing mixture of the two. One of my hands is still cupping his thigh, and I use the other to unzip my pants. Having foregone wearing underwear this morning, I'm able to free my rock hard cock from my pants with ease.

"Wait," he pleads.

I tilt my head while raising my eyebrow at him.

"No."

CHAPTER THIRTEEN

VINCENT

My plea falls on deaf ears as my abuser positions himself between my legs with his dick against my ass. My lower back is raised up off the bed while his hand is firmly gripping the underside of my thigh to keep me in place. I grab at his hands, trying to pry them free, but he slaps me away as he pushes the tip of his dick into my ass.

"It hurts," I bite out through gritted teeth as I once again try to push him off me and wriggle away from him.

"Keep fighting me and you'll only prolong the pain," he chuckles, catching my wrists with his hands and pinning them at my sides.

He lurches forward, and I cry out as he sinks in another inch. My captor's face is pinched tight with concentration and pleasure, and I find myself briefly captivated before he forces himself the rest of the way in and the pain snaps me back to reality. My vision turns white, and my ears are ringing with the sound of my own scream of agony. I'm gasping out rapid breaths as I try desperately to get enough oxygen into my lungs and manage the pain.

"Breathe," his voice says softly; it sounds far away even though he's right above me, close enough so I can feel his breath on my face.

I'm vaguely aware of him releasing one of my wrists, and a surge of heat shoots straight to my dick as he dips his hand between us. Wrapping his hand around my length, he begins to stroke it in a smooth but firm rhythm. I feel as though I'm having an out-of-body experience right now. My mind can't process the fact that my asshole has just been tunneled into by my merciless captor.

"Fuck, Vincent. You're so fucking tight," he groans as he begins to move inside me while keeping up the motion of his hand.

I fist the blanket beneath me until my knuckles feel like they're going to crack. I'm overwhelmed with the myriad of sensations sweeping over my body: the acute stinging in my ass, the burn as my back rubs against the blanket, and the zings of pleasure in my dick. I can barely function enough to form coherent speech between my whimpers and the sound of my captor's grunts as he slowly fucks me with his dick and his hand.

His thrusts increase in tempo, and when he adjusts his position slightly the pain becomes a dull ache as he hits deeper inside me and tingles begin to spread through my body. It's a sensation I'm extremely familiar with, and shame heats my cheeks at the realization he's managing to forcefully coax such a visceral response from me, and in a twisted, fucked up way, I'm enjoying the way it feels...the way *he* feels inside me.

My captor's movements become jerky, and the rhythm of his thrusts are lost as he begins to fuck me like a wild animal, chasing his impending release. His face is contorted with pleasure, but his eyes are fixed on me as he continues to work my dick with his hand. My balls tighten, and my body shudders as cum shoots out the tip and coats his hand and shirt with the sticky mess. I go lax and limp beneath him, shivering as the orgasm ravages my body with as much fervor as the man fucking me.

"Vincent," he growls, low and husky with arousal as he stills, and with his eyes closed, he twitches and shakes as he finds his own release inside my ass.

The sensation of his cum spurting into my body is alien and unfamiliar, and I briefly wonder if he realizes this is my first time with a man. I've always been curious, but I never expected it to be like this: down in a dungeon and being taken against my will in such a brutal fashion. My cheeks heat even more when I consider the fact that, once the pain had begun to subside, I actually enjoyed the experience. But, that's something I will never vocalize...especially not to him.

Once he's done, he slowly pulls out and tucks himself away. Glancing down at the sticky mess on his clothing, he shrugs and removes his shirt with a smirk pointed directly at me.

"You enjoyed that," he says, and I realize his words aren't posed as a question.

I remain silent, unable and unwilling to even attempt to form a response. Humiliation runs through me, fast and unhindered, like my

CRACKS

blood, and I don't know how to even start processing what just happened or consider the implications of what we just did.

He shakes his head, and standing, he looks down at me, still frozen in place on the bed. "I'm going to get cleaned up. You made a mess of me," he states, his mouth quirking up at one side in a knowing smile.

"Wait," I manage to say quietly, and he raises his eyebrow expectantly. "I don't even know your name."

Surprise colors his expression, and he tilts his head thoughtfully to one side, running a hand through his messy hair. "Jonathan," he says, glancing toward my ass. "I'm imprinted on you forever."

"Jonathan—'J'," I reply.

I go to move but wince in pain and decide against it for now. I'm exhausted. So much has happened, and I don't know how long I've been here, or what he truly wants from me, but I know deep down in my heart there will be no way out of this for me. Not now that he's staked his claim and marked me as his, both outside and in.

A part of me wonders if anyone has noticed my absence yet, and if they have; are they looking for me? The closeness I once shared with my brother has been all but destroyed by his fiancée, who has blinded him to everything but her. The little witch has probably convinced him that I was too much of a pussy to return to her parents' house after she threatened me, and with her controlling nature, she's no doubt forbidden him to contact me. Even if he has contacted me, I'll never know. Jonathan has taken my cell phone, exchanging one type of cell for another kind altogether.

I don't know how to feel about all of this. In the time I've been here, *Jonathan* has robbed me of my dignity, used me in his macabre games of blood and torture, but today is the first time he's ever given me something back, as twisted as it may seem. His recent actions have contradicted everything I've come to learn about him; the way he works, and the almost methodical manner to his madness. It seems I really know nothing about him at all.

EPILOGUE
JONATHAN

Several months have passed since I snatched Vincent and imprisoned him within my dungeon. It's been at least three months since I marked his body and claimed him as my own. I still don't fully understand the change that's come over me. The unfeeling, former assassin for the Charon is fading away, only to be replaced by something softer.

I still fight to tame the sadistic beast that rears its head whenever we're in the same room, and I'm no less cruel when the mood takes me, but Vincent accepts my cruelty, just as he accepts the rare moments of mercy I give him. I'm feeling more than I ever expected. The hollow place inside of me that was carved out by the Charon is slowly filling with a warmth that still feels alien to me.

I've begun to care, and while I still keep Vincent locked safely away where he can't escape, for now, he has more freedom than I've ever granted any of the previous inhabitants of my dungeon. I know he wants to come out, to see the sun and feel its warmth on his skin, but I'm afraid...I fear that one day he'll walk out into the sunlight and never turn back to embrace the darkness I offer him.

I'm losing control of myself, of my feelings, and over Vincent. He's fighting back harder now, giving as good as he gets, even though he still submits beautifully beneath my will. During brief flashes of curiosity, I want to give *him* all the power for once, if only to see what he'll do with it.

Will he hurt me as I've hurt him?

Will he take everything from me like I've taken from him?

Will he mark my flesh with my favorite blades, making me the one who bleeds?

Will he make me feel everything I've held back for so long, and finally set me free?

I brought him here for my pleasure. I've tortured him, pushed him to the brink, and I've done everything in my power to make him shatter... but in the end, I'm the one left with the fissure in my soul—I'm the one who has cracked, and it's all because of him.

ABOUT ALLY VANCE

Ally is an International Bestselling Author who writes in the Dark Romance & Horror genres. Ally lives in Kent, in the United Kingdom with her husband, stepson, and their two mad cats, Kian and Declan.

Find Ally
Visit Ally's Website
Visit Ally's Reader Group

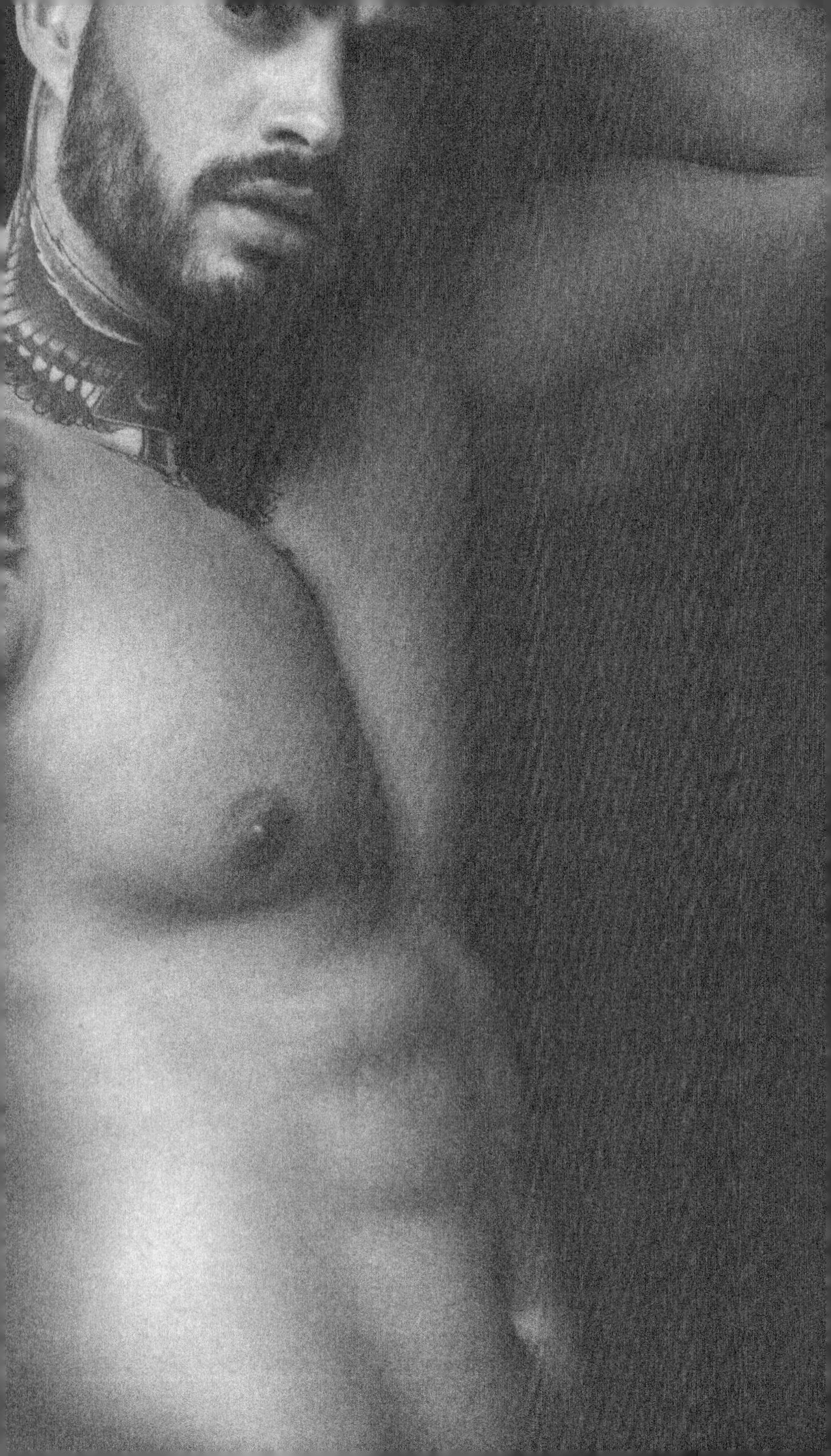

PAINTED IN THE SHADOWS

BY NICHOLE GREENE

CHAPTER ONE

LEIF

Eleven years ago

It only took twelve seconds. Twelve seconds for the little girl whose presence I was unaware of to walk out onto the aft deck of the yacht I just triggered an explosion on. Twelve seconds of horror as I watched the vessel explode in a ball of violent flames against the black sky and obsidian water.

Even from five hundred yards away, I could see her tiny body fly through the air like a living rag doll. I didn't stop to think of the consequences as I tore my leather jacket off and dove into the calm, dark waters of the bay. I just knew I had to get to her, to save her. Not to prevent me from my sure future burning in the depths of hell, but to save her from the torment of a cold, watery death she didn't deserve.

By the time I got to the burning wreckage, I couldn't see her, even with the flames casting an orange glow over the glossy surface of the sea. Dragging a lung full of acrid, smoky air into my lungs, I dove beneath the surface. The salty water stung my eyes, but I knew she was down there. I swam down about fifteen feet and turned in a circle, finding nothing but sinking debris.

After a few powerful kicks, I breached the surface and took another deep breath. This time I swam further from the boat, the water was so dark I could barely see. Just as I was about to give up on this spot, I spotted a flash of ivory in the water. I dove further down, pushing all my limits as I saw her lifeless form slowly sinking.

I grabbed the sleeve of her white nightgown and tugged her up with me. My heart felt like it was going to beat out of my chest as I looked into her unseeing honey-colored eyes. In my mind, I started begging a God who had long since forgotten about me to save her. I bartered with fate. I swore to spend my life protecting this innocent girl if only she would draw another breath.

By the time I pulled us both onto the dingy I was using to set off the explosion, my muscles were straining, and exhaustion was closing in quick on the heels of the endorphin high that strengthened me. She was limp and lifeless as I started CPR, or at least as close to CPR as I knew. I take lives, not save them. It took several minutes, but then, miraculously, she coughed. Water and spittle flew from her cool, blue lips, and her eyes fluttered but stayed closed. Her nightgown was soaked, so I tucked my jacket around her body to keep her warm.

Scanning the horizon, I could see coast guard boats speeding toward us. I knew I had to get out of the dingy and away from the scene. I pressed my fingers to her neck, just to make sure there was a pulse, surprised when one of her cold hands wrapped around mine. She turned her head and looked at me through glazed eyes.

"Help is almost here," I told her softly.

She nodded and then closed her eyes again. I threw the detonator and my gun overboard, erasing my only connection to the explosion. With one final look at her, I dove back into the ocean, hoping I could make it to shore before being seen.

CHAPTER TWO

OCTAVIA

Present day

A bright flash of lightening illuminates the loft I'm working in right before a crack of deep thunder makes the glass panes of the windows rattle. I'm glad I'm not on my houseboat during this thunderstorm. Most of the time living on a boat doesn't affect me, but thunderstorms on boat bring me back to the worst night of my life.

My parents were killed in an explosion on their yacht when I was eleven. I was pulled from the water by someone, a man presumably. He left me on a dingy covered in a leather jacket to be found by the coast guard. He never came forward, and while my parents' bodies were recovered, no one else ever was.

Most people think he was caught in a current while trying to help and ended up drowning. When I was younger, I used to have flashes of vibrant blue eyes and flowing blond hair in my dreams. I imagined him as a mermaid, pulling me from the wreckage and saving me before diving back into the dark waters of the Pacific.

Now that I'm an adult, I realize that he probably is dead. He probably gave his life so that I could live. Sometimes I think I hear his voice, telling me help is coming. I try to shake those memories off as a way for my brain to romanticize the trauma of that night and everything that followed.

I went to live with my uncle, his wife, and her son from a previous marriage. At first Scott and Cecilia doted on me and took care of me like I was their own. Within a few months though, they both began brushing me off and ignoring me. That's when nightmares began and my step-cousin, David, started coming into my room.

He would lay beside me, sometimes he'd hug me until I fell asleep again, but when I woke up, he was always gone. The touching turned to groping which turned into rape. I tried to tell my uncle, but he claimed I had to proof and that it didn't matter anyway.

I started sneaking out of the house at night, which was made extra hard by the fact that my uncle had taken over my dad's business and needed to employ on-site security. I found one camera on the perimeter of the property that didn't work and climbed the fence in that section.

I hid an old bike in a copse of trees at the end of the road from the estate and would ride that into Devil's Pointe. The town is your typical northern California beach town with a lot of artists and free spirits. That's where my love of art came from. I used to spend hours of my days walking around beautiful exhibits and art studios until a woman named Sheila offered me an apprenticeship.

She had long, curly, silver hair and weathered, brown skin. Her eyes were a changeable hazel, and she always smelled of the palo santo she burned every day. She taught me the history of art and allowed me to experiment with the different methods and mediums. I never explicitly told her what was happening at home, but she figured it out because one day a futon showed up in the tiny space she let me use. Soon after that there was a mini-fridge and microwave. Then the bathroom was renovated to include a tiny shower stall. She saved my life, and I've made sure to tell her that every Sunday night when I call her.

Another flash of lightning streaks across the sky, illuminating the majestic skyline of Seattle across the deep gray clouds. I jump at the proximity of the thunder, the floors vibrating with nature's fury. As juvenile as it sounds, storms still scare me. The violence and volume making me feel like a little girl all over again.

I set my palette and paintbrush down on the table beside me before turning back to the almost finished canvas in front of me. Most of my work is monochromatic, swirls of color that don't have meaning to anyone but in my mind are visual treatises on a specific emotion. The one before me is a riot of blues symbolizing the peace that only comes when you accept regret.

The longer I stare at it, the more I realize that something is missing. I pull my phone out and FaceTime Sheila, directing the camera at the canvas. Her face fills the screen as she answers with a smile. As soon as she sees my painting, she slides her glasses on and narrows her eyes as she looks it over.

"I love it. The top right corner could use some blending though."

I flip the camera while smiling. "I think I'll leave that glob of black, just for the sake of chaos."

"You would," she says with a laugh. "How are you doing, Tavi?"

"I'm okay." I sigh as I glance out the window; rain is falling in sheets now. "Riding out a storm here in my studio."

Concern deepens the lines around her eyes. She knows how storms stir me up. She knows everything.

"Listen Tavi, I think you should spend the night at your loft. There's been talk around town about your uncle bringing you home for a wedding. Do you know anything about this?"

"No," I answer as I try to remember the last time I spoke to Scott. He didn't mention anything about a wedding. I sure as fuck won't be going to David's wedding if that's who it is for. "I didn't even speak to Scott when I graduated a few weeks ago."

"Okay," she says with a feigned smile. "Just stay at the loft tonight, okay? For my peace of mind?"

"Of course." The loyalty I feel to this woman wouldn't let me do it any other way. Her shop bell rings in the background, and she smiles and greets her student. "I'll let you go so you can start your class."

"Give me a call tomorrow. We didn't get a good conversation in tonight."

I laugh. "We talked for an hour two nights ago."

"Yes, and that means there's forty-eight hours to catch up on," she says with a teasing lilt to her voice. "I love you, be safe."

"Love you, too. Pulling the murphy bed out as we speak." I flip the camera again to show the bed coming down from the wall. "Talk soon."

"Bye, Tavi."

I set my phone down when the screen goes black and pick up a stick of incense to light. The room smells of paint and turpentine. It'll be easier to sleep with it masked. I strip off my clothes and run through a few yoga stretches to ease the aches from painting all day. I should probably shower and eat, but I'm so tired from painting all day that I can't bring myself to do either.

I slide in between the cool sheets and instantly fall asleep. The sleep isn't deep and restful though. It's full of darkness and water, explosions and death. I toss and turn as the storm continues to rage outside the industrial windows of the old loft.

One of the reasons I rented this place was because of the incredible natural light and views from the corner windows. I didn't think about how exposed it would feel in storms. At one point, I'm jarred awake by the creak of the door, but I know I locked it behind me when I came in.

I fumble around for my phone, trying to see what time it is. Rain still pounds on the window, but it's just a steady drumming, not torrents like it was earlier. I gasp when the light from the bathroom floods the open space of the studio and a man's shadowed silhouette stands over my bed.

Before I can even scramble to the other side of the bed, his warm hand wraps around my wrist, holding me tightly.

"Don't be scared," he says in a gruff voice. "I'm here to help you. Sheila sent me."

"No, she didn't." I tug my arm free and slide to the other side of the bed, nearly forgetting to take the sheet with me when I stand up. "I just talked to her tonight, and she said nothing about sending a strange man to break into my studio while I was sleeping."

"We didn't know the timeline would be so quick." He holds up his hand, showing me the set of keys I gave Sheila for when she visits. "I'm here to take you to my cabin for safety before your uncle's men get here."

"What?" Nothing about this makes sense. I sidestep toward the dresser where I keep ratty paint clothes. "Why would he be sending people to get me?"

"Because you're supposed to marry David in eight days."

Nausea swirls in my gut at the thought.

"That's insane." My mind finally catches up to my eyes as I look at the stranger in front of me. He's tall, like really tall, at least a foot taller than my average height. His hair is pulled back into small knot on the back of his head, but it's blond and shaved on the sides. His eyes are a pale blue. He is menacingly beautiful, how I'd imagine a Viking warrior to look.

I shake the thoughts of how attractive he is out of my mind because the man is obviously confused at best, a full out psychopath at worst. I grab a hoodie, keeping him in my line of sight the entire time.

"Do you mind turning around?" I ask sarcastically.

"Yeah, I'm not going to risk you running while my back is turned." He pulls out his phone and tosses it on the bed. "Your uncle's men are just finishing up at your houseboat. They'll be here in minutes to haul you back to Devil's Bay and into the arms of your betrothed."

I snatch the phone off my bed, and my heart sinks as I see the interior of my cozy home torn apart. What in the actual fuck is going on?

Why would Scott be trying to force me into marrying David of all people?

"Better hurry. Clock is ticking."

"What's your name?" I ask as I grab my hoodie and pull it on over the sheet. "How do you know Sheila?"

"Name's Leif." He doesn't avert his eyes as I grab a pair of yoga pants and pull them on. "I know Sheila the same way you do."

It's not really an answer, but I suppose I don't have time to get his life story. "I'm not just going to get in a car and let you drive off with me. You could be serial killer for all I know."

He reaches behind his back and points a gun at me. "You will go with me. Now. Or I can leave you here and let your uncle and his pervert stepson find you. You looking to relive all those nights of abuse he put you through?"

How does he know about that? Everything about this feels wrong, but I definitely can't risk staying here and ending up being dragged back to California. Just the thought of David getting his hands on me makes bile rise in the back of my throat. I look around the room, there's not much here for me to worry about taking with me. I keep it as impersonal as possible. A blank space makes it easier for my mind to wander.

"There's no time to take anything with us." Leif must be a mind reader.

CHAPTER THREE

LEIF

Tears fill her big, brown eyes as she glances at the stacks of finished canvases we put in a locked storage closet. Barely contained rage bubbles inside my chest as one lone tear rolls down her pink cheeks. I swear if one of those idiots manages to get the lock open and destroys any of her work, I will tear them limb from limb.

It wouldn't be the first time I killed for her, and I doubt it would be the last. From the moment I pulled her tiny, lifeless body from the water, I've followed her from shadows. Threatening, beating, or killing anyone who hurts her. She is completely unaware of the trail of blood that follows her everywhere.

As we go out into the hallway, I tuck her slim body behind my hulking frame. Instead of using the elevator or interior stairs, I take her up to the roof where we'll go down the fire escape. I'm not risking an encounter where we end up penned in.

I lean down and whisper in her ear as I guide her where I want her to go. It's been years since I was this close to her. I can't help but notice how silky her hair is when it brushes my cheek. She has a smudge of blue paint on her neck, and even though I know it's dried, I want to rub my thumb over it.

Fucking focus.

I curse myself for letting her proximity distract me. We exit onto the roof, and I lead her over to the rusted fire escape. The metal groans and clangs under my weight. She's quiet as a mouse though, something for me to remember when we get to the cabin.

Luckily Sheila played her role perfectly as a stand-in mother. I couldn't have asked for a better person to watch over Octavia while I was away on jobs. They might even have ended up finding each other without my meddling all those years ago.

Octavia stops above the ladder at the last flight of stairs and looks over at me. Her eyes are huge and haunted but so full of life my blood sings with the need to protect and ruin her. I grab the ladder and lower it down. There's about a six-foot drop from the last rung, so I go first. When I land on the ground, I look around the alley and motion for her to join me. She moves delicately down the rungs and dangles until the bottom when I reach up and grab her waist, using my body to gently guide her down to the pavement.

The rain is relentless as we hurry through the alley to where I parked my truck. The smell of rotting Thai food from a restaurant fills my nostrils. I look over at her; she's almost at a jog to keep up with my long strides, but we can't move at her pace. Her uncle's men are smart, I would know as I once was one of them. I would have followed that man into the pits of hell right until I realized he ordered me to not only kill his brother and sister-in-law, but also his niece in a desperate attempt to take control of the family business and the millions of dollars his brother was sitting on.

I was only twenty when I placed those explosives on that yacht. Over the years, my anger and disgust have done nothing but grow for Scott Simmons. I almost blew it when Sheila told me what she thought was happening to Octavia inside her family home on a nightly basis. Someday I will kill David Peterson. It will be slow and deliberate and horrifically painful.

I unlock the doors to my truck and slide behind the wheel while Octavia slides into the passenger seat. She peels off her hoodie and tosses it in the backseat. I fight every urge inside me to look at the skimpy white tank top she's wearing. I watched her sleep for a few minutes before I woke her up. I know how her nipple piercings poke out enticingly against the thin material. It's a good thing I have somewhat decent self-control and was able to stop myself from running my thumb over them while she slept.

She's quiet as take the highway north out of Seattle. The rain provides enough ambient noise to not need music, which is just as well because Octavia has terrible taste. I don't want to sit in the truck listening to sad girl music for hours. We're exiting onto Highway Two in Monroe when her stomach rumbles.

I look over at her with an arched brow. "Are you hungry?"

"No, that's the sound of a perfectly satisfied stomach," she says with a little too much sass for someone in her position.

"You could try being grateful," I say as I pull into a gas station parking lot. "Come on, let's get you fed." I toss her discarded hoodie in her lap as she unbuckles.

She tries to shake her hand free when I grab it as we enter. I just squeeze her harder and lift the back of her hand to my lips. She scowls as I wink at her, playing up our interaction for the cashier.

Octavia is, for the most part, a predictable woman. She's kind and empathetic, rarely does anything extreme or out of pocket. But she does have moments when she gives no fucks and acts completely out of character. I love watching those moments, but I don't need to deal with one when I'm so close to finally having her. Doubly so when I'm trying to get her to safety.

I'm not sure when my obsession with her transformed from a need to protect her as an innocent girl caught in the nasty web her uncle was spinning to just plain need and desire. Regardless of when and how it happened, it's fucked up. If I had any morals, I would step back after I see that she's safely removed from her family. But I don't, and I won't be letting her go, ever.

She sets a bag of peanut butter M&Ms on the counter beside a can of Cherry Coke. I add my jerky and water while the cashier rings us up. I catch her looking quizzically down at our hands. I didn't realize I was running my thumb back and forth over her knuckles.

I drop her hand immediately. I might know everything there is to know about her from the way she stumbles around first thing in the morning to how her back arches off the bed as she makes herself come, but she knows nothing about me. I obviously don't want her to figure out I've been stalking her for half her life.

We get back in the car and head east toward the mountains. Each town we pass gets progressively smaller until we we're winding through the forest under the shadow of Mt. Index. Octavia rolls down her window and takes a deep breath, closing her eyes.

"I love the way it smells out here." She sniffs the cool air blowing in. "I wish I could paint this smell. The damp earth and wet granite would be a blend of blacks and browns. The pungent pine would green with hints of brown shaded in. The river would be swirls of emerald and blue with gray and white mixed in chaotically. The sharp zing of ozone from the storm would be navy and steel with slashes of angry white."

Her eyes are still closed, so I take the opportunity to study her profile. She's the artist, but I'm the obsessed. I could paint the curves of her body with my eyes closed at this point. Her pale features, almost fairy-like, stand out in contrast to darkness surrounding her in the cab of my truck. From her pointed chin, over her plump lips, her slightly up-turned nose and delicate brow, she is angelic perfection. I'm going to ruin her light with my darkness, and I can't bring myself to feel one bit of guilt.

"I don't trust you." She opens her eyes and meets mine.

"Good. You shouldn't trust me."

"Something about you feels familiar though," her voice trails off as she takes her turn to study my profile.

My heart rate increases as she levels her keen observation skills at me. I know from news articles she didn't remember what I looked like when I saved her, but that doesn't mean something couldn't trigger her memory out of nowhere. Trauma is a bitch like that. My stomach churns with a feeling so unfamiliar to me I have trouble identifying it.

I don't want to lock her up in my cabin, but I am prepared to do so out of necessity. I have everything I need to subdue her if she tries to escape, zip ties, rope, handcuffs, and gags. My cock swells at the idea of her tied to bed.

I clear my throat before speaking. "Must have seen me once or twice at Sheila's place."

She makes a non-committal noise before murmuring, "Maybe."

She goes back to looking out the window as the trees rush past us. She's thinking so hard I can practically feel the wheels turning in her mind. I tap my thumb against the steering wheel, irritated that the one place I can't reach is where she's currently losing herself.

CHAPTER FOUR

OCTAVIA

The first light of dawn is creeping over the sky when Leif pulls up to a cute little A-frame cabin deep in the Snoqualmie National Forest. We walk through a non-descript door into a tiny mudroom. He toes off his boots, and I follow suit, shivering at the cold tile beneath my feet. I follow him into an open space with a pitched walls meeting twenty feet above.

A small kitchen space lines the wall to my left and wood stove stands open and empty to my right. The entire front of the cabin is glass, and a sliding door opens to a wooden porch with a small hot tub. The cabin is sparsely furnished, but that doesn't diminish is magical charm. I look over my shoulder at the hulking man leaning against a pilar that supports the loft above.

"This is beautiful." I look up, noticing two symmetrical skylights in the roof. "It's yours?"

"Yep, had it for a couple years now." He points upward. "The bedroom and bathroom are up in the loft."

I move to the spiral staircase and start up them with Leif following right behind me. I'm surprised by how roomy it feels when I reach the top. A large bed faces the wall of windows with two floating shelves on either side. A small lamp sits on one and a few books fill the space on the other side. A low dresser is against one wall, and a door opens to what I assume is the bathroom.

Leif moves to the dresser and tosses a pair of athletic shorts and a white t-shirt on the bed. "You can wear those to sleep in until we get you some other clothes." He starts down the stairs. "I'm going to lock up before we catch a few hours of sleep."

"Okay," I reply as I grab the clothes and walk into the bathroom. Another skylight lets soft dawn light into the space before I flip on the light over the sink. It's surprisingly large. The all-glass shower is in the center of the room where the ceiling is tallest. A toilet is to one side and the sink and vanity are on the other. A rack hangs from the door with several towels. I decide to take a quick shower before I go to sleep. It's been a long night, and I'm still gross from being sweaty while painting.

After my shower I squeeze a bit of his toothpaste onto my finger and brush my teeth that way. It's not the best, but he didn't have a spare anywhere. After combing the knots in my hair out and braiding the wet strands, I walk out to find Leif sitting shirtless on the side of the bed. The wide expanse of his chest is covered in tattoos and cut muscles.

He looks up at me and smirks as he catches me checking him out. He stands slowly, his eyes roving over me in his clothes. Desire darkens his eyes. I'm not innocent or naive, I know the effect my unique features have on men, and I've been known to use them to get what I want. It's good to know he is affected. It'll make him easier to manipulate if necessary.

"I'm going to clean up, feel free to crawl in bed and go to sleep," he says as he walks past me into the bathroom.

I had every intention of doing just that, so I pull the corner of the comforter down and could cry tears of joy at the flannel sheets tucked beneath. I smell the wood stove burning, but the cabin still has that deep chill of having been vacant for a while. I slide beneath the covers and fall asleep within moments.

I wake up to sun streaming in through the windows above me and the warmth of a body curled around me from behind. I shift to look over my shoulder, and as my hips move, I feel the unmistakable poke of an erection against my ass. I go still as Leif mumbles something in his sleep and grips my hip, grinding his cock against me.

I wait until he settles back into a deeper sleep and roll away from him. I cry out when his arm goes with mine as I move, realizing that he handcuffed us together while I was sleeping.

"What in the actual fuck," I yell as I slap him in the chest with my other hand.

He wakes up slowly and rolls to his back as he blinks the sleep out of his eyes. He grins when I lift my arm and shake it to get his attention. I make the mistake of moving my eyes from his, noticing how his apparently massive dick has tented the sheets over him. A dimple appears as he smiles even bigger noticing where my eyes traveled.

"If you want to hop on and take it for joy ride, I wouldn't say no." His voice is gravelly from sleep.

The sound I make isn't quite as disgusted as I hoped, being part tortured laugh. "You handcuffed us together," I accuse.

"I did." He reaches over and pulls a key out of the drawer. Instead of politely asking me to move closer he yanks me across the bed, forcing me to tumble partly across him.

"You're an asshole," I say as he unlocks the cuffs.

"Glad you picked up on that." He rubs my wrist where cuff was. "Did you know you snore?"

"Fuck off." I snatch my wrist away and rub the tender flesh myself. "I do not."

"You do. Sounded like a toy tank engine chugging all night."

My lips part as I search for some witty come back, but all I can think about is how blue his eyes are in the light of the sun.

"Better close those pretty lips before I fill them up." The air between us charges with a foreign electricity. "And if you don't stop looking at me like that, I'm going to flip you over and fuck you with the intensity you are eye fucking me with."

I scramble back from him. I'd like to think he was messing with me, but the dark glint in those cerulean eyes makes me think he might be just as dangerous as the men I'm running from. I look over his shoulder at the clock, startled to see it is nearly four in the afternoon. I can't remember the last time I slept eight hours let alone almost twelve.

He stands up, not bothering to hide or adjust himself as his cock juts out proudly. Even as I make certain not to look directly at him, it's so massive I can't but notice out of the corner of my eye. He chuckles as he closes the bathroom door behind him.

I don't want to think about what he's doing in the shower, so I go downstairs in search of coffee. I find everything I need in short order, there's no cabinets in his kitchen, only open pine shelves. I grab a pot and start boiling water while I get the French press ready.

I glance around the cabin, looking for keys, just in case I need to get away.

I'm debating whether to make him a cup when I hear his heavy steps coming down the stairs. I look over my shoulder and take him in all his glory. His hair is pulled back again, but he is wearing a pair of wire rimmed glasses which don't make a dent in the dangerous air that emanates from him. He's wearing a pair of jeans and a tight black t-shirt.

"You want some coffee?" I ask, turning back to what I'm doing.

"Yeah, I'll take some." He stands behind me and puts the ceramic mugs I grabbed back and pulls out two travel mugs instead. "I'm going to take you into town to get some clothes and other necessities. I need some food, too."

"Oh," I say as I turn to face him, "okay. I have to work tomorrow though, so you can just take me back home instead."

He scratches the blond stubble on his chin as he looks down at me. "You're not going home, and you definitely won't be going back to work."

"What?" I try to take a step back but bump into the counter.

"Your uncle has half his men in Seattle looking for you. We're staying here until I throw him off your trail. Even then, it'll still be too dangerous for you to go back to the houseboat and loft."

"I can't just leave my life behind. My belongings and paintings are there." It's absurd to think I could just walk away. That houseboat is one of the only things I bought with my inheritance.

"It's just stuff. Your paintings are safe in the closet. I can have an associate pick them up when things settle down."

"An associate? Who are you? What do you even do?"

"Yes. Leif Black. I'm an assassin." He answers each question directly with matter-of-fact delivery.

For a second, fear and skepticism battle within me. But then I laugh and roll my eyes. "You might look intimidating but come on, an assassin? Yeah right, and I'm Wonder Woman."

He gives me a dark look with a slight nod. "Believe what you want then Diana, but you have two minutes to go change into the clothes I laid out for you, or I can handcuff you to the bed while I go buy you clothes."

I think about challenging him, but something about the way he's looking at me makes me think he isn't playing around. He really will lock me up. There are times he seems really in tune with my thoughts, like he can tell what I'm thinking or something. It's bizarre, but my intuition says to trust him, at least for now.

"Fine." I hold my hands up in surrender. "You win. I'll go change and be right down."

"Smart choice. I'll finish the coffee."

I hustle up to the bedroom and find a pair of joggers and a Seahawks hoodie laying on the bed. The pants have to be cinched tight and rolled to stay up. I do another finger toothbrushing and pull my hair back in a ponytail.

CHAPTER FIVE

LEIF

Octavia comes down the stairs in my clothes, and fuck if I don't rethink buying her some of her own clothes. She looks absurdly cute all but swimming in my hoodie and pants. All I can think about is how much I want to tear them all off and bend her over the closest available surface.

"Are you okay?" she asks with an attitude.

"Never better." I hand her a mug and turn on my heel to go out to the truck.

My control is already slipping. Years of her being just out of reach as my obsession morphed from protection to possession. Now all I can think about are the sighs and murmurs she makes while she sleeps and how perfectly we fit together.

I should tell her who I am. She deserves to know that the man with her life in his hands is the same man who almost took it years ago. But I won't tell her. Now that she's here, in my presence, my bed, my clothes, I can't let her go. I will never let her go.

I wait until she's buckled up before turning on the ignition and backing out onto the dirt road. She looks everywhere, taking in the afternoon light slanting through the trees. A sexy moan escapes her lips after she takes her first sip of coffee.

"This is perfect." She takes another sip. "It's like you knew exactly how I take it."

If she only knew. I know everything from how she takes her coffee to the brand of art supplies she uses. Fuck, I even know what brand of tampons she prefers and what day her cycle starts.

"Do you ever talk?" She looks over at me with those big brown eyes as she rests her temple against the headrest. "Like an actual conversation instead of just barking orders and shooting cocky smirks at women."

I give her one of those said smirks and look back at the road in front of me.

She scoffs, annoyance dripping in her voice. "Why do you even care what happens to me anyway? Who are you?"

"I told you who I was and what I do." I cut a glance at her, but she's not looking at me. "I used to work for your uncle."

That has her head snapping back to me. Her eyes narrow as she looks at me. She scoots just the tiniest fraction away from me.

My fingers tighten around the steering wheel at her reaction. "I don't anymore and haven't in over ten years. He's a terrible person. I'm just trying to keep you from falling into his web."

The muscles of her face relax just enough for me ease my own tense grip. "I don't want to go back to Devil's Bay. Nothing but nightmares there for me." She catches her bottom lip between her teeth, a haunted look darkening her eyes. "Except for Sheila."

"What do you know about your inheritance?" I ask quietly.

"Not much." She shrugs and looks back out the window. "I know that I won't get it all because I'm not taking over the business or getting married." A moment goes by while she thinks. "That's probably why Scott wants me to get married, so I don't lose all the money. I've only used what I do already have of it to buy the houseboat and my studio and to pay for art school."

I barely hold back the sarcastic comment on my tongue. Her naïveté has never been more apparent. He wants her to marry David because control of the money and assets will bypass her and go to her husband. It's archaic, and while her dad wasn't a total piece of shit like her uncle, he was still a dirty businessman with a hefty dose of misogyny.

I'm no angel either, but even I know that passing daughters around like chess pieces and selling them into loveless and likely abusive marriages is disgusting. I've worked through all the possible ways to save her from her fate and the best, and only guarantee of her safety is for me to marry her.

Sheila is on her way up to help me convince Octavia. She doesn't agree with my plan but has no way to stop me. According to the terms of the will, she has to be married for two years for all the money to be released. She's sitting on fifteen million, and I doubt she's even aware of how much she's worth to the money hungry vultures in her life.

"Do you know anything about it?" she asks, pulling me out of my thoughts.

"About as much as you." Lie. "I was in the area when your parents passed and heard off-hand comments about it and you." Truth.

I let the conversation die. The less we talk, the less the risk of me slipping up runs. I hand her my phone with instructions to find something to stream through Spotify. It's not my main phone, so I give her the passcode, a bonus of building trust with her.

She makes remarks here and there about the distinction between the western side of the pass and the eastern, how crazy the change in vegetation is. She's lived in Seattle for four years but hasn't ever travelled north or into the Cascades. Her face lights up at the sight of Leavenworth; with its charming Bavarian architecture, it looks like it belongs in the Alps instead of central Washington.

I was fully prepared to spend a few hours picking out clothes in any of the little boutiques, but she surprises me by asking to hit up a big chain instead. We have to drive a little further, but she's quiet and the scenery is nice.

I'm shocked when it takes her all of twenty minutes to fill the cart with all the essentials she needs. She pushed the red cart and navigated the store like it wasn't the first time she'd been there. We left, and she asked to stop at an art supply store she saw from the highway. I agreed even though I have an entire cabinet full of everything she regularly uses.

After an hour spent wandering the aisles of the paints, canvases, and brushes, we get back into the truck and head back toward the cabin. I suggest stopping for dinner in Leavenworth at one of pubs we drove past earlier.

They seat us on patio with lights strung overhead and large potted plants breaking up all the space between tables. The entire feel is romantic and private. Looking across the glass mosaic table at her, it almost feels like it could be a date. She bought a sundress and wore it out of the store. It's lavender and compliments the milky expanse of her skin perfectly.

She must be feeling the chill of the mountain air because her nipples are poking through the thin cotton. It's a test of will power not to reach across and pinch them, other patrons be damned. The way that I want the woman sitting across from me is unnatural. She blushes when she notices where my gaze is resting, and I give her a slow smile as the flushed skin creeps down her slim neck and across her chest.

I know my intensity can be a lot to handle, but while her reaction is shy, she also parts her lips as she holds my gaze. Her tongue slides across them as she returns my appreciative look with one of her own. I know she's not a virgin, but she's also not very experienced with grown men. She's had one boyfriend, who barely escaped with his life after he broke things off with her and moved to the other side of the country. She's been on a few dates. Two of which ended with the losers encased in concrete at the bottom of Puget Sound.

"So," she takes a sip of wine, "Leif Black. Let's get to know each other."

I set my water down and nod. "Ask me anything."

"When's your birthday?"

"December third."

"Oh." She pulls a face somewhere between appalled and acceptance. "It all makes sense now."

"What does?" I smirk at her, already aware of her love of astrology and true crime.

"You are a Sagittarius." She leans forward conspiratorially. "And an assassin."

"Yes," I confirm.

"Sagittarius is a mutable sign. Most serial killers are mutable signs. Ted Bundy was the most prolific Sagittarius serial killer."

"Know what the difference is between me and Ted Bundy?"

"What?" She still hasn't leaned away from me, and I can smell the wine on her breath.

"I kill for the money, not the thrill."

"I'm not sure that's any better." Her eyes fall to my lips as I move closer.

"Guess it's a good thing I don't give a fuck," I whisper into her ear as my lips graze her jaw. Her skin is so fucking smooth against my lips. Goosebumps race over her arm as I lose my composure for a second and flick her earlobe with my tongue.

CHAPTER SIX

OCTAVIA

Thank God the server interrupted us with the check before I climbed over the table and fucked him right there on the patio. I don't know what it is, but something about him draws me in. I know he's not safe, but he makes me feel protected in some insane way. Nothing about this makes sense.

I keep trying to talk myself out of trusting him. He's an assassin. He must be at least ten years older than me. He kills people without remorse. I will not fall for him.

But then I remember that Shelia trusts him. He saved me from my uncle. He's hot as fuck. Maybe it wouldn't hurt to live dangerously for once. Just a taste of how wild life could be. I'm sure he has no plans to ever settle down. How would that even work for him?

I have these warring thoughts the entire time we drive back over the pass. By the time we're pulling off the highway, I have gone round after round of internal debate with myself. I am keeping myself far away from him. I'll tell him I'm sleeping on the floor tonight.

As set as I am on my plan, a hot ache has been building between my thighs since I felt his lips on my skin. I'm questioning everything I thought I knew about myself as I confront the desire I have for a self-admitted killer. I squeeze my thighs together to relieve some of the need that's come out of nowhere.

There were times over the past four years that I wondered if my experiences as an adolescent had shaped me into an asexual being. I enjoy the companionship of a boyfriend, but I've never been driven by sexual urges or desires. I feel completely out of my element here in the most intriguing and exciting way possible.

I'm not innocent or naive, I can tell that Leif wants me. When we drive under lights on the highway, I can see the bold outline of his heavy cock. He's partially hard the entire ride.

"If you don't stop looking down at my cock, it's going to end up buried in the back of your throat while I drive us home." His voice is deep and throaty with need.

"That sounds dangerous."

His blue eyes cut to me. "I am dangerous."

I cut eye contact with him and look out the window. He reaches in the back seat and tosses a coat in my lap before rolling his window down. The chilly mountain air fills the cab and cools the mounting tension between us.

By the time we pull up to the cabin, I'm ready to fuck just about anything. I tell Leif I'm going to take a shower, because I'm afraid if I stay near him, I'll jump him, rational thoughts be damned. I pull the dress over my head and step into the shower.

As soon as I have the water heated to the right temperature, I set my leg on the tile bench. I don't tease myself with light strokes along my thigh like I do when I lay alone in my bed. I'm so turned on I can feel my heartbeat in my pussy.

I immediately zero in on my clit, circling my fingertip around and around. I brace against the glass wall of the shower with one hand and slide my fingers deep inside myself. I'm so embarrassingly wet that I can hear the sloppy sounds of my desire over the rush of the shower water as I pump my fingers in and out.

I can feel the explosive orgasm building deep inside me. My foot slips as I hit the edge of my climax, knocking bottles over in a loud crash. Before I can even react, Leif is charging through the door. Our eyes meet as I gasp through the first wave of my orgasm, my fingers still buried inside me.

"Stop." His command comes out as a growl, and he closes the distance between us. He wrenches the shower door open and steps in fully clothed. "That orgasm belongs to me."

I hold my arm up to stop him. "Get out."

He drops to his knees and pushes my thigh open further, completely exposing me to him. He looks up at me once, ravenous hunger rolling off him in waves as he leans in and runs his nose along my slit, inhaling my scent my in the most primal and raw way I've ever experienced. And then he's spearing me with his tongue and pinching my overly sensitive bundle of nerves. I have to brace myself against the corner of shower as wave after wave of molten pleasure roll through me. My body feels lit from within as he paints his masterpiece over the canvas of my body.

He moans into me as I latch onto his hair and pull him closer. I don't ever want him to stop. Any thought I ever had about my sexuality is smashed to pieces as devours me like a meal he's been craving for years. I come again with his name falling over and over from my lips. He licks and finger fucks me through the final tremors of my orgasm.

He grips my hips, his t-shirt stuck to his heaving chest as if it is painted over his chiseled muscles as he stares at my pussy in wonder. He grips my hips as he stands back to his full height, towering over me. Our eyes lock, and for the first time, I see an emotion in his other than smug confidence. He's as shaken as I am.

He turns and leaves the shower, soaking clothes dripping a trail after him. I blink once, twice, trying to figure out what just happened. Did I really just have the most transformative sexual encounter of my life only to have him walk away without saying a word? Tears sting my eyes, but I refuse to let them fall.

If it weren't for the way my body is still trembling from him, I would wonder if that even happened at all. Did I do something wrong? Was I too loud? Too quiet? An endless string of questions play on a loop through my anxious mind as I finish showering.

By the time I'm dried off and dressed, I've had time to let the anger build. How dare he? Who does that? A fucking psychopath, that's who. I vow to never let him touch me again. I can't believe I let him make me question myself like that. Well, fuck him, at least I got an orgasm out of it.

I step over the puddle of clothes in the bedroom and walk down the stairs. I don't see him anywhere, but my eyes do catch on the art supplies we picked up earlier. It's dark outside, but there's lights strung up around the patio. I could start sketching out the idea I had while we were driving and then start painting it tomorrow.

I pull out one of the canvases and a package of charcoal pencils. The cool breeze skims my bare legs sending goosebumps up and down their pale length. The planks of the deck are slightly damp when I sit, but they're smooth so at least I don't have to worry about splinters. I close my eyes and think about the way the light cut through the trees earlier, the contrast of the trunks and branches against the milky light.

Half an hour later, the entire canvas has been covered in light lines, a tentative map of the beauty it will hold by this time tomorrow. I roll my neck and shoulders and stretch my legs out. I walk to the banister of the deck and lean against it as I take in the space beyond the cabin.

The view is stunning. A sapphire ribbon of rushing water glints under the moonlight through the trees. The scent of the forest coming alive after a long winter and cool spring fills the air. It's crazy how focused I am while I'm creating a new piece of art. How did I miss this natural beauty?

This location is idyllic for an artist. I love the life of the city, but there's something to be said for peace and fresh air of the mountains. When I close my eyes and listen, all I hear is the hoot of an owl and the rush of the river over the rocks and boulders.

"Time for bed." Leif's deep voice startles me out of my mediative state.

When I turn around, I see he's picked up my canvas and pencils. "I think I'll sleep out here." I turn my back on him to look back into the valley. "And I don't need some asshole telling me when it's time to go to bed."

Cold metal closes around my wrist before I even noticed he moved behind me. "No. You won't sleep out here." He leans forward, his lips brushing behind my ear as he whispers. "And yes, you do need this asshole telling you what time to go to sleep. Otherwise you'll—" He stops mid-sentence.

"I'll what?" I ask venomously as I spin to look him in the eyes.

His eyes bounce back and forth between mine for a moment. "Otherwise, you'll catch a cold. A cold front is coming through tonight."

"That's not what you were going to say. Not to mention incredibly hypocritical considering you aren't even wearing a shirt."

Instead of answering, he pulls me along behind him back into the cozy heat of the cabin. I follow along behind him like a child as he's handcuffed us together again. I lift our joined arms with a shake.

"Is this really necessary? I don't particularly like you, but I'd pick you over David any day of the week. I'm not a flight risk."

He scoffs and keeps locking up the cabin.

"I cannot believe you have the audacity to be acting like I did something wrong," I say incredulously. "Especially with that stunt you pulled in the shower."

"What stunt? Showing you what an orgasm should feel like? Making you cum until you saw stars? Eating your pussy like it was seven-course meal?" He looks over at me with stormy eyes. "You were seconds away from begging for a ride on my cock."

"Please. I've had better sex than that in the bathroom stall of a dive bar."

He raises an eyebrow and smirks at me, somehow seeing directly through the lie. He starts ascending the stairs, still dragging me along behind him.

"We're going to brush our teeth and go to bed."

"Okay, Daddy," I say, my voice dripping in sarcasm.

At the top of the stairs, I'm yanked against his hard body and backed against the dresser. His hips press against mine, his substantial erection digging into my stomach. With the hand that isn't cuffed to me, he wraps his fingers around my neck and squeezes.

"You better be ready for the fucking consequences of that sass." His midnight blue eyes hold mine until I look away. I think I'm off the hook until he spins me around and bends me over the dresser. "Count."

"What?" I yelp as he pushes my pants down my hips and spanks me. Searing heat explodes across my ass as his hand makes contact with my skin.

"Count."

"Are you insane?" I cry out again the stinging pain of his open palm spreads over my ass.

He leans over my back and brushes his lips over my ear. "This is the last time I tell you. Count." His voice is deep and commanding.

"One." I try to move away at the last minute, but his hip pins me in place as his hand comes down. This one doesn't hurt like the others, in fact if feels surprisingly good as the heat from the impact has traveled to my core.

"Two." Instead of crying out, a combination whimper and moan falls from my lips.

"Good girl." He rubs his hand over the curve of my ass, his fingertips grazing my slit. "One more."

"Three." Why do I like this? My face burns with confused shame over what just happened, what I let happen, as he pulls my pants back up gently. I follow him in a daze into the bathroom.

My pulse races as we stand side by side at the sink brushing our teeth. A new unfamiliar need has been unlocked inside me. I know it's dangerous, but there's an impulse to understand what that was. Why I liked it. It was humiliating and degrading.

I look at our reflections in the mirror. We are complete opposites in every way. He is tall with blonde hair and blue eyes, wide shoulders tapering down to a narrow waist and covered in muscles that put

Michelangelo's sculptures to shame. But inside him lives a darkness, I can see it clinging to him to like a shadow.

Then there's me, pale skin with dark hair and deep brown eyes, petite in stature as well as feature. My mom used to call me Tinkerbell because I was so small, like a fairy. The fleeting thought causes the unending grief to show across my face for a fraction of a second. I meet his eyes in the mirror and find him watching me. A tightness shows in eyes as he picks up on my sudden mood change.

Instead of offering comfort, he takes my toothbrush from me, sets it down beside his, and pulls me back out into the bedroom. He drops his sweatpants to floor, confidently standing in nothing but a pair of black boxer briefs low on his hips and waits for me to get in bed.

I hate myself a bit for it, but as I push my own sweats down my legs, I can't help but give his cock, half hard, an appreciative look. I barely hold off the impulse to stroke my hand over the bulge he's doing nothing to hide.

CHAPTER SEVEN

LEIF

All the blood in my body goes racing south as soon as I watch her crawl in my bed in nothing but a white t-shirt and light purple cotton panties. They sit low on her hips and cover everything except the bottom half of her perfect little ass cheeks, still red from my hand.

I lay down beside her, our thighs and shoulders touching, and reach over to shut off the lamp with my free hand. Feeling the heat of her body against me is a special kind of torture. I don't have morals on a good day, and this temptation is making me fucking feral.

She's feeling the same way, I can tell by the restless way she moves beside me. After ten minutes of listening to her squirm and sigh, I reach over and pull her on top of me.

"Slide down my cock if you need something between your legs," I say as I grind my dick against her hot pussy.

She tries to move off me, but I grip her waist with both hands, anchoring her right over me. "Let me go," she says as she wiggles against my hold. "I don't understand what's going on here."

Her hips rock forward, causing her core to run the length of my cock. She gasps as if she is surprised. All I can think about is how I hope she sounds like that when I thrust inside her the first time.

"Keep moving like that, and I'll be buried inside you before you even have time to realize what's happening."

"You think I'd let you fuck me?" Her eyes glitter with challenge in the moonlight.

"You think I'd ask permission?" I challenge her right back as I move my thumb down, dipping it under the edge of her panties. "I take what

I want." I ghost my thumb lower, over her smooth skin to the top of her slit.

Her hips shift just ever so slightly toward my finger, seeking contact. "You wouldn't take me without knowing that's what I wanted."

"Think again." I move quick, sliding my thumb down to her clit and circling the tiny nub with ruthless intensity. "I'll take whatever I want, when I want it, and you'll fucking love every second."

Her lips part as her head falls back. She moves against my hand, lifting enough for me to easily change the angle of my hand. She is dripping for me already as I slide two fingers back inside the heaven between her thighs.

I can feel the blood pumping angrily through my body, making my cock throb for her. I know I won't be able to last long once I'm buried inside her, and she's going to come apart multiple times before that. I lift her and drag her up my body until her knees are beside my head and her pussy is above me, a damp patch of cotton all that separates me from her.

"What are you doing?" She tries to scoot back but I hold her in place.

"I'm going back for seconds. One round of devouring this juicy cunt wasn't enough." I tear her panties at the side seam. "And you are going to sit on my face. You're not going to hover. You're not going to worry about suffocating me. You're going to ride my face like it's your favorite fucking ride, and when you cum, you will scream my name."

I don't give her time to think, I pull her down over me and immediately start licking and sucking her lips and clit. I reach up and work my fingers inside her pussy. This is how I've always wanted her, surrounding me, consuming her as she does me.

I hear her moan as I hook my fingers toward her front wall while my tongue and lips continue their assault against her sensitive nub. Another whimpered groan from her, and soon she's grinding against my face. She grabs the headboard for support as she loses herself in the pleasure I'm bringing her.

I feel the beginning of her orgasm as her pussy pulses around my fingers, and she trembles through the onslaught of ruthless pleasure. I can feel her cum coating my face and stubble, running down my neck, and I've never been happier to be such a mess.

She lifts her hips, her belly and chest heaving with deep breaths. It takes me by surprise when she shifts back down my body. Her lips take mine, and she explores my mouth like she can't get enough of her taste on my tongue. She nibbles my lips and smiles against me I take over the kiss, my free hand threading through her hair and pulling her back, so I can attack her neck with my lips. She fights my hold and fastens her mouth to mine, and I can feel her desperation in the kiss.

When we finally come up for air, she wastes no time pulling my cock out. She moves like she's going to take me in her mouth, so I grab a fistful of her hair and pull her head back to look in her eyes.

"Someday I'm going to love choking you on my cock, but today is not that day." I line my cock up with her, dragging the tip through her soaked folds. I slam inside her, and fuck if I don't see stars. "Fuck," I hold her there without moving, "you are so tight and wet and goddamn perfect."

Her fingers dig into my abs as she clenches around me. I can see the battle in her eyes between desire and common sense, but if she thinks she has a choice in this she's dead wrong. She and I are inevitable.

I sit up with a growl, pushing her shirt over her tits. The sliver barbells of her piercings catch the light and feel cool against my tongue as I take one into my mouth. I circle the other while I move beneath her, fucking her from below. I switch breasts and move my free hand back down to her clit. I have to feel her come fucking undone over my cock.

I watch as our bodies move perfectly in sync with each other's and know that she was always meant for me. I'm fascinated by the stretch of her around me and obsessed with the sounds filling the room. Eleven years of watching her, four years of desiring her, and now she's mine. We'll both die before she belongs to another.

He eyes dart to my lips as he takes a second to answer. "I can't actually tell you why, but I just know I can."

I give him a slow nod. I get it. I feel like I've known him forever, too. We must just have one of those connections from a past life that make you familiar to each other in this one.

"So, is that a yes?" He gives a boyish grin. "You going to be my wife willingly, or am I am going to have to force you?"

"Do I actually have a choice?"

"No."

"Then I guess you have your answer."

―――

"How do I look?" I ask turning around in a circle in Sheila's hotel room in the simple white slip dress she brought for me.

"Breathtakingly gorgeous." A glassy film covers her eyes as she looks at me with same type of warmth and love a mother would give. "Let's do something with your hair."

I sit down on the edge of the bed and feel her brush out my hair. Since I went to bed with it wet last night, it flows down my back in unruly dark waves. I feel her twist most of it into a low bun and start artfully arranging the remaining pieces with bobby pins. I can't help but think about my mom as she works to get me ready. My thoughts always wander to my parents at times of importance in my life.

"Am I doing the right thing?" I ask while I pull at a thread on the scratchy comforter beneath me.

"I think you're making the best decision out of a handful of shitty choices."

"Can I trust Leif? Truly trust him to tie my life to his even if it's only for a short time?"

"You can absolutely trust Leif with your safety." Her answer is worded a little too carefully for my liking.

"That's not what I asked."

"It's the best I can tell you."

"How do you know him, anyway?" Every time I ask him about Sheila, he gives me vague answers and shuts down.

"He helped me out of a sticky situation years ago. Before I ever met you, actually. Without Leif, I'd have never met you and grown to love you as my own. I owe Leif so much." Shadows fall over her eyes as they meet mine in the mirror. "But guard your heart. Heartbreak and pain will inevitably follow when you take his hand and pledge to be his wife."

I brush off her ominous tone. "We're not in love. This is just a sham until I get out from under Scott."

She exhales heavily and kisses my forehead. "I hope you're right."

A hard knock sounds at the door. "That must be Leif."

Sheila moves toward the door and looks over her shoulder at me, "You ready?"

I glance at myself in the mirror. My dark waves are swept back from my face in a loose style with a few face framing tendrils left out. They soften the sharp lines of my jaw and chin and along with the soft makeup I applied lend a dreamy vibe to my look. I look like someone who's planned all along to get married. I nod at her with a soft smile as nerves dance in my stomach.

I'm not ready for the man who walks through that door. Although this wedding is a sham, I am breathless at the sight of Leif in a suit. Head to toe, he is masculine perfection. A black, perfectly cut suit hugs his muscular frame, quietly hinting at the perfection that lies beneath. He's forgone a tie, the top few buttons of his white shirt open to expose an expanse of tan skin.

"You look hauntingly beautiful." It isn't until I notice his Adam's apple bob that I realize he's looking at me just as intensely. A flush spreads from my cheeks, down my neck, and across my chest. His chest rumbles before he commands Sheila to give us a moment of privacy.

He doesn't wait for the door to close before dragging me against his body and claiming my lips like a starving man. He wraps his hand around my neck and tilts my head back. His tongue slides against mine possessively, as though I've always belonged to him. I gasp as he runs the back of his fingers over my pebbled nipples, the juxtaposition with his fierce hold on my neck has heat racing through me to my core.

All too soon, he ends the kiss but rests his forehead against mine. "It's time to go."

"Aren't you going to ask me if I'm sure?" I ask as he steps away and straightens his jacket.

He looks at me with clear eyes and a serious expression. "No."

CHAPTER NINE

LEIF

The Justice of the Peace is saying something I should be paying attention to, but all I can do is look at the woman currently vowing to join her life with mine. There a million things I have done wrong when it comes to Octavia. I can't bring myself to regret one single decision.

From the second I saw her on that boat to the words 'I do' that she just spoke, our lives were always meant to thread together. She is mine. I am eternally hers. There will be no one else for either of us.

I look down into her warm chocolate-colored eyes and pledge my life and loyalty to her. She's nervous; I can count her heartbeats as her pulse throbs away in her neck. She doesn't want to admit it, but she's on the edge of falling for me. I want to push her all the way down into the bottom of this well I've been stuck alone in for years. Where it's just us, drowning with each other, in each other.

Sheila and Ace, my associate, politely clap while I give Octavia a chaste kiss. If Sheila knew how fast and far things have progressed with her Tavi, I'd be getting a heated earful. She might feel indebted to me, a feeling I have no trouble exploiting, but she loves Octavia fiercely. At the end of the day, Sheila knows exactly who I am, and she doesn't trust me.

As she shouldn't.

Octavia slides her delicate, pure hand into mine as we walk out of the room and past a line of other couples waiting to marry. I organized a lunch for the four of us at a French restaurant that overlooks Lake Washington. Ace guides Sheila over to his car while I help Octavia into the truck.

"Is Ace the associate you were talking about the other day?" she asks as soon as I get in the car.

"Yes. He'll stay with you while I'm gone." I battle the urge to touch her. "It'll only be one night."

"One night is all you need to take a life?" she asks with distaste.

"Seconds is all it takes." I'm not surprised that she has a low opinion of my chosen occupation, but it doesn't sit well all the same.

"Have you ever thought about doing something different?"

"No." I look over at her. "I'm good at killing."

"Do you ever feel guilty?"

"Once." Her.

"How many people have you killed?"

I don't answer. I'm not sure how she'll respond.

"Dozens?" she guesses.

I shake my head.

"Seventy-five?"

I shake my head again.

"Hundreds?" Her voice is barely above a whisper, and I hear her audibly swallow when I nod my head. "Out of hundreds you've only felt guilty once?"

"Yes." Irritation seeps into my voice at this line of questioning. We shouldn't be discussing how many people I've killed on our wedding day. "How many men have you drawn nude?" I ask, trying to change the subject.

"Hundreds, probably." She thinks about it for a second. "Yeah, starting back in high school when I'd sneak into Sheila's studio during classes or her private sessions. Plus, art school." Then she cuts me a sharp look. "Although drawing, painting, and sculpting the nude body is nowhere near the same as taking lives. I don't know where you are you going with this line of thought."

Honestly, neither do I, but now I have a whole list of names to add to my kill list. The jealousy surging through my veins is hot and caustic. "If you have a problem with my profession, you are more than welcome to go back to your family. I'm sure they'd love to have you under their thumb again."

"Would you actually hand me over to them?" Her face is stricken as she whispers the question. All her fight instantly drained.

A better man would feel guilty. I'm simply not a better man. "Yes." A bald-faced lie. I would die before seeing them get their hands on her.

She nods and looks out the window.

"You'll use me a model from now on," I blurt out, forgetting that she is under the impression this is temporary.

"You'll do for the time being."

I'll do for the time being. Anger, frustration, and need battle within me. I want to slam the truck in park and show her much further beyond 'you'll do for the time being' I am, but I have to keep myself in check. At least until tonight, when I'm going to make her pay for that comment in denied orgasms.

She giggles softly and then louder when I turn my head and scowl at her. She lifts her hands in surrender. "You asked and then went all possessive caveman on me." She leans over when I pull into the restaurant parking lot. "I'm an artist. I appreciate the human form on all bodies, but it doesn't mean I look at and want them sexually."

"You better not." I drag her across the center console, almost into my lap. "I don't share."

"That's a bold statement for a fake husband."

I hold my left hand up between us. "There's nothing fake about that gold band on my finger."

The surety that has been feeding her sass for the past half hour drains from her face as she looks between my face and the ring and back again. "I almost believe you." She leans back and opens her door, gracefully exiting the tension of the truck.

Ace and Sheila meet us at the door. The girls pair off, talking quietly as they follow the host to our private table on the patio. I paid to have the entire deck to ourselves to celebrate, including a bottle of vintage Dom Perignon.

"So," Octavia says after finishing off a glass of champagne, "Ace. Are you a hitman as well?"

Ace nearly spits out his whiskey as he sends me a nervous look. "Uh," he wipes his mouth with a napkin, "no. I'm more of a fixer than a killer."

"Tavi." Sheila shakes her head slightly. "Not here."

"Why? No one's out here but us." She gestures around with her hand. "A fixer, huh? I thought that was only for the mafia."

"Almost every powerful person has fixer," he answers.

"How did you two meet?" She looks back and forth between Ace and me.

"That's a story for another day." I stand from the table and lean down to kiss Sheila's cheek and squeeze Ace's shoulder. "Time to go home."

Octavia's goodbyes last longer as she lingers in Sheila's arms.

When they break apart, both of them are misty eyed. Ace shakes her hand and tells her he'll see her soon. I let my hand drift from her waist over the curve of her ass as I lead her back out to the truck.

She doesn't know it yet, but we're not going back to the cabin tonight. I have something entirely different planned for her.

CHAPTER TEN

OCTAVIA

"Where are we?" I look up at the contemporary glass and wood home surrounded by a tall privacy fence.

"Home," Leif answers.

"You live here?" I look over at him, unable to hide my surprise. I know how expensive this part of the city is. My houseboat is not too far from here. I look back up at the structure. "It's gorgeous."

"It is." When I look over at him, he's not looking at his house, and by the way he's looking at me, I doubt he's talking about it either. "And I don't live here. We do."

I catch my lip between my teeth, fighting the smile that always seems to be determined to appear under his attention. I keep trying to remind myself that he's a killer. That this is temporary. He's just doing me a favor.

"Let's show you around," he says as he turns off the truck.

I'm shocked when I walk around the truck and see my car sitting in the garage. "When did yo— how did you get my car here?"

"Ace." He opens the door into the house and motions for me to enter first. "He salvaged what he could from your loft and houseboat. Unfortunately, your uncle's men tore both places apart. A lot of your belongings were too ruined to save."

I nod as the news sinks in. At the end of the day, I'm not deeply attached to material things, aside from some of my art and mementos from my parents, most of which I keep in a safe deposit box along with the leather coat of the man who saved me. I used to sleep with it at night but stopped that when David started coming into my room. I didn't want him to ruin it.

"Are you okay?" Leif leans down, getting eye level with me. His blue eyes are just a shade lighter than usual and wonder if it's the comfort of being home.

"Yeah, just overwhelmed." I look around the open space; a modern kitchen with sleek European cabinetry is at one corner, along with a large dining area. The main focus, though, is the wall of windows overlooking a terraced backyard with an incredible view of the lake. In fact, I think I could probably see my dock with a pair of binoculars. The entire main level is impeccably decorated. "Being an assassin must pay well."

"Yeah." He nods as he looks around. "I make a killing."

I pause mid-step and slowly turn around to find the tiniest of smiles lifting his lips. "That's some exceptionally dark humor, husband."

His amused gaze turns predatory. "Let me show you upstairs, wife."

He scoops me in his arms and moves to the stairs, taking them two at a time. At the landing, there's a long hall to the left and a door to the right, which is where we go. He walks into the dark room and tosses me onto the bed.

"I thought I was getting the tour." I smirk as I prop myself up on my elbows. A voice in the back of my head screams for me to stop. But I've had just enough champagne to tell that voice to fuck off.

"You'll get all the tours." He pulls his jacket off and tosses it a chair in the corner. "Starting with a tour of your husband's body."

I stand up from the bed and grab his hands as they start working his buttons. "Let me." I look up into his eyes, smiling when he nods and moves his hands into my hair to start pulling pins out.

I take my time with each button, trying to memorize the texture of his skin and where his light dusting of chest hair begins and ends. As each button falls open, I press an open mouth kiss to smooth flesh beneath. When I reach the final button and work his belt free, I drop to my knees.

My hair is loose around my shoulders as I kneel at his feet, removing his shoes and then socks. I run my hands up the smooth material of his pants stretched over his muscle. I drag my nails along his thick length before opening his pants and pulling them, along with his boxer briefs, down over his powerful thighs. His cock juts out proudly, tempting me with small bead of moisture at the tip.

I look up at him as I wrap my hand around his base and flick my tongue over his tip. A deep guttural rumble sounds from his chest as I use my tongue to trace the throbbing vein along the underside. I want to paint him like this. All his muscles engaged and his cock achingly hard for me. I could do him more justice than a photo ever could with all his raw, masculine beauty.

Instead of taking his cock like I know he wants, I suck one of his balls into my mouth. The soft skin of his cock brushes against my cheek. I release him with a pop and take his shaft between my lips and down as far as I can into my throat.

"Oh, fuuuck," he groans as his hand threads through my hair, pulling at the root as I begin sucking him. "You're not stopping until you swallow every drop."

I make a moan of agreement, the vibration causing him pulse inside me. I want to feel him lose himself in me. I want to make him feel, for a moment, how he makes me feel. I bob my head quicker and hollow my checks around him. Every twitch and moan spurring me on until his grip on my hair turns painful as he holds me still.

He thrusts all the way in and down my throat, causing me to gag. He pulls back a bit and runs his fingers over my cheek, brushing a tear away. "Look at those tears shed for me." He lifts his finger to his lips and licks them. "Everything about you is delicious. I need you to relax your jaw."

I do it and feel him slide slowly to the back of my throat.

"That's it. Good girl." He pushes further making me gag again. "You can take me all the way down. I know you can." He pushes forward slowly until my nose is buried against him. "Hold on, kitten."

He increases his speed and power, fucking my mouth ruthlessly. I'm crying from need, from pain, from confusion. Why does everything he does feel so good? Even using my mouth as a hole to fuck has me dripping with need.

My nails dig into the back of his thighs as hot ropes of cum shoot down the back of my throat. I swallow around his cock, making him gasp in pleasure and push back further into my throat. When I look up, his head is thrown back as all his muscles ripple and tense from the pleasure of my mouth.

"Such a good fucking girl." He wipes a bit of cum from the corner of my lip and puts it back in my mouth. "Don't waste a drop."

I sit back on my heels, dragging deep breaths in as I ache for his touch, or even my own, to relieve the tension radiating through me. He reaches down and lifts me to standing. My knees are weak and wobbly, so I hold onto him for support.

"Turn around," he commands.

I do so slowly. His hands skim over my arms and ghost down my chest, pinching my nipples and making my piercings feel like absolute torture. I drop my head back on his chest and his lips take mine. The kiss is annihilation of every lie I've told myself. He wants me. Really wants me. In a way that no man ever has and that is a heady feeling.

He lowers his hands from my breasts and down over my stomach, to my hips where he starts to pull the material up, gathering it in his hands. He pulls the dress over my head, leaving me in my white heels and white lace thong.

"Bend over the bed and open your legs."

I lay my chest down on the soft blanket and widen my stance. I'm glad the room is dark for the middle of the afternoon because he can see everything. He kneels behind me and moves the lace over my slit to the side. His fingers part my wet flesh seconds before his tongue licks a path from my clit all the way to my pussy.

Unlike the last time he did this, his pace is unhurried and lazy. Enough pressure and rhythm to make me want to grind against his face but not enough to have me screaming in pleasure. He adds his fingers but only teases the places inside me that trigger my release. After what feels like hours of torment and one of my legs falling asleep, I beg. I beg for him to make me cum in any way he wants.

He growls and tosses me on the bed. His lips take mine again, my desire mixing with his own addictive taste. I wrap my legs around his hips wanting so desperately to feel him slide home deep inside me. He finally takes the hint and thrusts inside me in one hard movement.

I'm breathless for a minute, my pussy stretched so far around him my mind goes blank. He feels so incredible inside me. Like I was made to fuck and be fucked by him. My toes curl as his thrusts increase in both speed and power.

He pumps inside me until I start to feel my walls pulse around him. An outraged cry leaves me as he pulls out right before my orgasm hits. I was so close to the edge that my pussy might as well be screaming.

"What are you doing?" I whine.

He looks down at me, his eyes just as hungry as mine. "You'll never look at another naked man."

I almost laugh. "Is that what this is about? Proving some claim over me?"

"Yes. You are mine. I am yours. If you need inspiration or a model, I'll stand for you for as long as you need. No. Other. Men."

"Leif." I pull him down to me. "You're all I want."

He slams back into me before the words are even all the way out of my mouth. He fucks me with a relentless passion. Our bodies glide across each other, and the way he slams into me fills the room with sound of skin slapping and our panted moans against each other's lips.

He grips one of my thighs and tosses it over his shoulder. His fingers circle my clit while he pounds into me. "Come for me, kitten. Milk my cock with that tight pussy until we're both seeing stars. Such a good fucking girl." Each word is punctuated by a thrust.

I come at the last word. Why hearing him praise me like that sets me off, I'll never know. But if he wanted to call me a good girl every day, I would welcome it. I feel him cum, he twitches inside me as he fills me with his release. When the final spasm ends, he drops on top of me. His chest heaving and sweaty.

"You are fucking incredible, Mrs. Black."

"As are you, Mr. Black.

A dull ache wakes me hours later. A short-lived moment of unfamiliarity at my surroundings pulls me fully from my lingering slumber. In the muted gray light of a rainy Seattle day I realize I'm in Leif's bed. The spot beside me is cool and empty when I run my hand over it.

I stand and walk into the bathroom, flipping the lights on to look at myself in the mirror. My eyes catch on my neck where a blue and purple hickey angrily decorates my neck. He was a beast last night. At one point I felt as though I was going to faint from the intensity of the orgasms he was giving me. I didn't know things could feel so good that they would end up hurting like that.

An origami swan sits on the marble counter, my name scrawled over its neck. I pick it up, admiring the neat folds and skill it would have taken to fold. Inside is a note from Leif telling me to make myself at home but not to leave the property under any circumstances. He tells me that Ace is already there in his place and that he's been given permission to restrain me if necessary.

I roll my eyes at the threat. Clearly the ring on my finger doesn't mean I'm any less a captive than I always have been. Instead of going off in search of Ace I decide to poke around upstairs. I know the rooms are probably just guest bedrooms but you never know, I might find something to put us on an even playing field.

The first door I try is locked. That's irritating.

The second door is an impersonal guest room.

The third door is a home gym. I consider working for a second but then quickly change my mind. I don't need to workout, I need to paint or draw. Maybe even read. A key falls from the door jam when I close the door behind me.

I bend to pick it up and realize it's one of the generic keys for interior locks. I'm shocked that he would use something so easy to break into but maybe his ego is that big. I go back to the locked door and wiggle the key in the knob until I feel the lock disengage. A bolt of satisfaction slams through me as I swing the door open.

It's his office and far from what I expected. As I walk around his desk I notice my phone sitting on a stack of papers. I quickly grab it and power it on, setting it back down as I look around. Most of the paperwork looks to be about legal matters, inheritances, and the like. Boring stuff with nothing that gives me the insight I really want.

As I'm rifling through his drawers my phone begins to vibrate with all the messages I've missed over the past few days. I see my uncle's name pop up on the screen and morbid curiosity has me unlocking the phone and opening his message.

Scott: I know Leif Black has you. You better hope to God you didn't go with him willingly.

Scott: He's not who you think he is. Every word from him is a lie.

I snort derisively. As if anything my uncle has to say could change my mind. The one photo on Leif's desk catches my eye as I put the phone back down. I pick up the frame as all the blood rushes from my head. A young Leif stands arm in arm with a young Ace, both holding wads of money and arrogant smirks. What has the blood ringing in my ears is the fact that Leif is wearing the most familiar leather jacket. Supple black with a tear along the collar of the left side. The leather jacket I was wrapped in when the Coast Guard found me belonged to Leif.

I drop the frame onto the desk just as Ace appears in the office doorway. His eyes tighten as he sees the look on my face and the photo

I just dropped. He tips his head back and looks up at the ceiling, pained.

"Fuck." He sounds resigned as he pulls his phone out.

ABOUT NICHOLE GREENE

When Nichole isn't busy raising her four kids she can be found in a coffee shop writing the stories that keep her up at night. She's addicted to tea, dark chocolate, maps, and losing herself to literary worlds. She loves a woke alpha-hole and feisty heroine.

Links:
Amazon Author Page
IG: @nicholegreene.author
Facebook Page

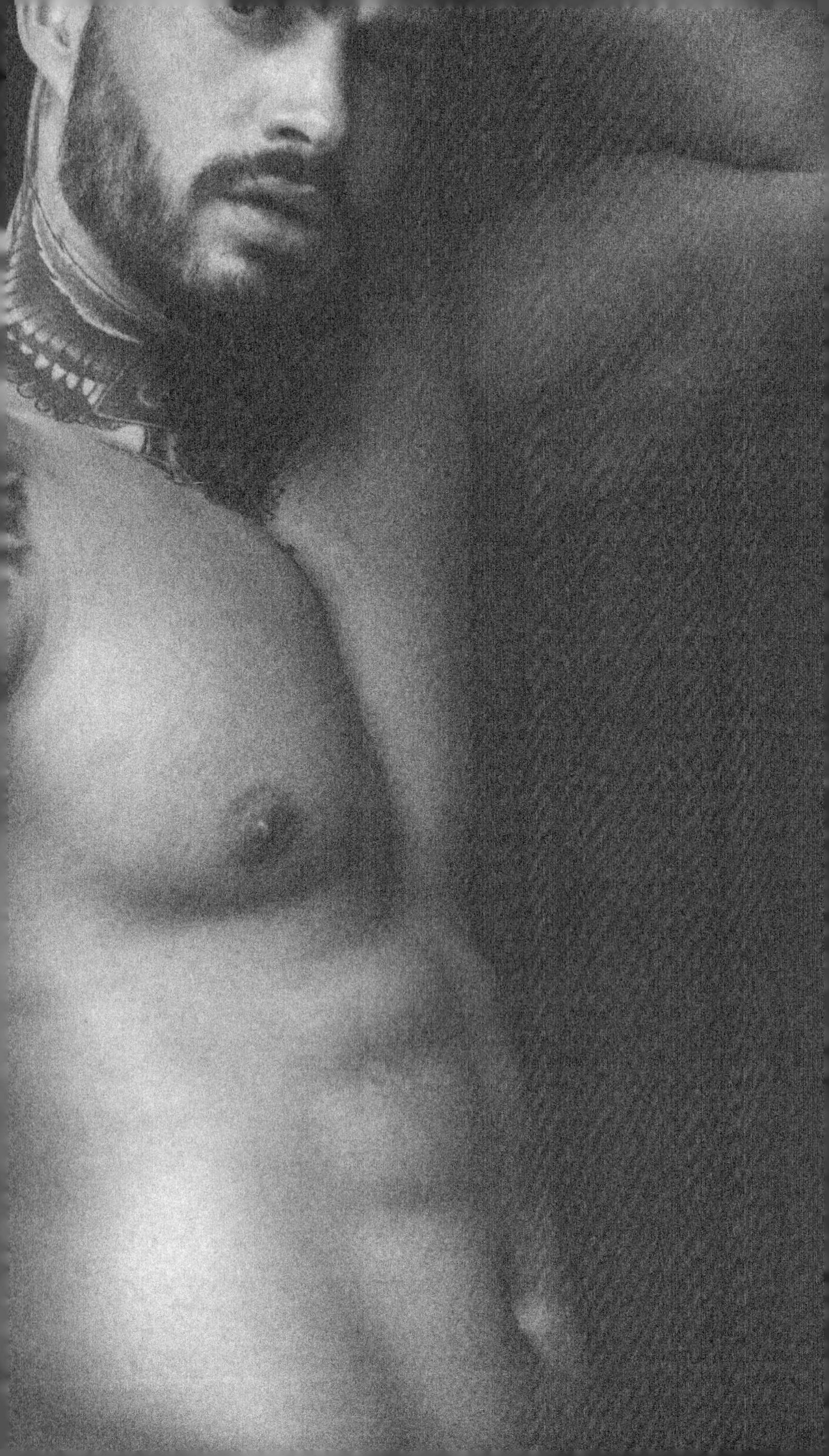

THE INVITATION

PREQUEL TO THE GAME SERIES

BY LP LOVELL &
STEVIE J. COLE

CHAPTER ONE

TOBIAS

The lights of the Manhattan Bridge twinkled through the floor to ceiling window of Lithium—the most extravagant members-only club in the city. Crystal chandeliers dripped from the ceilings, Baccarat glasses filled with only the most expensive Champagne adorned the tabletops, and the only place where the views of the skyline could be beat was from my penthouse. It's a club people fought and fucked to get their way into. One people would kill to set foot in...

The head of Tritan Bank sat at the table by the opened patio door, the attention of every man in a suit locked on him. They laughed and smiled, all while imagining they could take the knife on the table and slice his jugular open. And why? Because he had more than them. He was wealthier, more respected, more fucking arrogant. No one here wanted to be inferior.

I lifted my glass to my lips, wondering how much one of them would pay to have him killed. Because every one of them would pay something. They'd outbid each other just for show. Money was, after all, a disease of the rich. One I was dangerously intrigued with. One I would make a very fun game out of once I had my partner.

"Mr. Benton?"

I glanced up at the pretty blond stopped in front of me. "Yes?"

"We're ready for you."

Smiling, I polished off my drink, then followed the petite girl through the crowded lounge to the elevator at the side of the room. When I stepped inside, she passed me a keycard. "Welcome to The Selection," she said just before the doors closed.

I watched each floor light up. Once it reached the last number, it kept going to a secret floor high above the rest of the club. Excitement darted through me when it finally stopped, and the elevator slowly opened into the center of a circular room. A blue icon flashed on the wall directly in front of me. When I placed my keycard in front of it, the walls retracted, revealing a series of windows.

An overhead speaker crackled to life. "A number will appear to the side of each cubicle. To choose an item, scan your card across the numeral."

One through twenty-five flashed to life around the room moments before the shutters covering the windows lifted. Behind each pane of glass stood a naked girl. A beautiful, willing, naked girl. These were not slaves. Oh, no. They were trained. Elite commodities worth every last penny men paid to have them for an evening. I didn't want her for sex. I wanted her for a game. I wanted her to use as a test.

I made my way past each window, inspecting, fantasizing. When I reached number fifteen, I stopped. Auburn red hair and long, lean legs. Smiling, she fiddled with the diamond pendant around her neck, then turned around to show me her perfect ass. Much to my pleasant surprise, she bent over, showing me her tight asshole and pink pussy. If she'd do this for ten-thousand dollars, what would she do for a million? Maybe two? That was the problem with having an endless supply of money at my disposal—I could ruin people all too easily.

When I swiped my card over her number, the shutters lowered with a creak of hinges.

"You've chosen number fifteen. You may pick up your receipt at the bar. Enjoy your purchase."

Oh, I would. And I only hoped I would enjoy Preston Lucas half as much...

CHAPTER TWO

TOBIAS

SIX MONTHS LATER

I sat in my car with the engine cut. The only light came from the video footage playing across my phone screen. It was a video I had watched endlessly over the last few days. One I could barely get enough of.

A scream came through the speakers just as the shaky footage of Leah—the beautiful redhead I'd purchased months ago—running through the thick woods came to a full stop. Preston's angelically ruthless face came into view. The moonlight made his blond hair appear silver. If this were a movie, the director would get accolades of praise for the way the lighting caught in his blue irises, almost setting aflame the darkness that lurked within.

My cock hardened as she screamed louder, begging him to let her go. And one thing I had learned about Preston Lucas from his browser history, those screams made his dick hard, too. He was a deviant through and through, and that was one reason I had chosen him. What I couldn't have fathomed all those months ago was just how nefarious he truly was. And I delighted in it.

Everything about the situation from her gasps for breath to the possessed look in Preston's eyes as his hands closed around her neck made me desperate to fuck him. "Stop fighting, Leah," his gruff voice broke through the desperate pleas for her life. "You know if you pass out, I'll only come harder..." And then he came and hard, at the precise moment she left this earth. I smiled as the realization she was actually dead set in on his face. He wasn't half as terrified as a normal person would be. And it was what the camera I paid Leah to keep hidden on her at all times caught afterward that beckoned the darkest of my demons to the surface. I'd spent hours watching this video over and over, stroking myself and coming to the grunt he released when he climaxed. And it was how perfect it felt when we came together that told me Preston Lucas was everything I'd been looking for. It was that feeling of dark euphoria that allowed him to possess my thoughts and plague my dreams.

Dirt covered the lens, and I cut off the video, smiling as I thought of all the fun I was about to have with him. I readjusted myself before I grabbed the shovel and plastic tarp from the passenger side, then climbed out of the car.

It was time to go dig up the redhead I'd paid so much for and make sure she had a proper burial, and I had a proper partner...

CHAPTER THREE

PRESTON

I dropped my towel on the bench of the steam filled shower room, then stepped beneath the spray just as the last guy left. The heat eased the tension in my exhausted muscles as I closed my eyes and let my body relax beneath the warm water. I needed this moment of reprieve away from prying eyes.

Moments later, another shower head cut on, putting an end to my solitude. I opened my eyes just as Tobias Benton stepped beneath the stream of water. I couldn't help the momentary once over I gave his ass before I faced the shower wall again. While Tobias's honed and sculpted muscles were enough to shame a Roman gladiator, it wasn't just his looks that made him hard to ignore. It was everything about him. From the way he held his shoulders to the way he looked down his nose at everyone around him, screaming of wealth and power. The Bentons had more money than God, thanks to Mr Benton developing surveillance technology that every government in the world wanted a part of, and Tobias was an heir to that seemingly endless fortune. More than anything, though, what drew me to Tobias was the way he watched me. I'd never spoken to him, but whenever I was around him, it seemed his dark gaze always waited for me.

Sure enough, when I glanced over my shoulder again, his dangerous stare snagged mine. With a smirk, he placed his back to the tile wall. Water cascaded over his defined chest and abs, and I tried to force myself to look away, but I couldn't. I was like a mouse in a trap, watching as he trailed his hand down his stomach to his hard cock. There was something animalistic and raw to the way he fisted himself, something that made my dick twitch and beg for every sordid thing he could give.

Steam billowed in the space between us in the empty shower room. Tension cloyed the air, promising to suffocate me as I watched Tobias's fist pump with more purpose. My balls grew heavy and tightened. I'd only ever fucked girls, but this—this was erotic as fuck. It was alluring and taboo, something I told myself I shouldn't want, but given the way my dick hardened, my body definitely wanted something from him— And he knew it.

I fought not to touch myself, but when Tobias dropped his head back on a low groan, I lost that battle. I fisted myself, stroking a thumb over the bead of pre-cum on my tip as I watched ribbons of come spurt out of Tobias's cock and splatter the shower floor.

As soon as he was done, he turned the water off. He hadn't soaped up; he hadn't washed his hair. It was as though the only reason he'd set foot in the shower was to give me a show. And I liked that thought. His gaze dropped to my hard cock as he wrapped a towel around his waist. Then he raked his teeth over his bottom lip before he rounded the lockers.

I may have never publicly dated men, but that didn't mean I wasn't into them. I'd kept those desires hidden only because my self-righteous, church on Sunday father would disapprove. He was a good man, so long as everything in his life fit into a perfect box. I did not. And while I didn't care for his approval, he funded the college fees my scholarship didn't. But... Tobias Benton made forbidden seem so intoxicating...

One of the football players entered the locker room, and I turned back to the wall, hiding the erection Tobias had instigated as I finished my shower, then dressed. Thoughts of Tobias still danced in my head as I stepped into the hallway, but every inch of that lust vanished when I spotted Sarah Brown standing by the bulletin board outside the locker rooms. She'd been hassling me every day for the last week. Every day since Leah had gone missing. *Had I seen her? Heard from her? Did we have a fight?* It was too much. I'd helped them look for her, steering clear of the woods I'd fucked her in. I'd cooperated with the police and lied when I answered all their questions.

When I got closer, I saw what she was tacking to the board—a missing person's poster for Leah. My pulse ticked up, forcing beads of sweat across the back of my neck.

Sarah placed the last pin on the piece of paper, then stepped back. The second she spun around and saw me, her face crumpled.

Sympathy shined from her. She was Leah's best friend, and I was Leah's "loving" boyfriend, only I wasn't a person capable of love. Emotions did not register in my mind. Darkness did, though. It had always called to me, dancing along the periphery of the golden life my surgeon parents had mapped out for me. Captain of the football team, top of the class, prom king—and it all just felt like an act. Like I was pulling the strings on a puppet, never feeling, never truly present.

I took one look at the poster and slipped into one of the many masks of emotions I had become so good at wearing. Tears blurred my vision. A sob worked up my throat, and I ducked away before Sarah could utter a word to me, leaving her feeling even more sorry for me than before because I played the part of the devoted boyfriend so well.

If the police ever gave me a lie detector test, I'm not sure I would pass. I imagined them asking me questions about her death and I feared the memory of that night would be enough to show my guilt because I had never felt so utterly ablaze as I did that night in the woods with her. Her running from me and pretending she didn't want me to fuck her was only meant to be role play. Leah loved when I wrapped my hands around her neck and choked her as much as I did. We regularly toed the line where she would lose consciousness and I would imagine her taking her last breath. That night I came so hard at the thought of her actually dying, that I got carried away, not realizing she was, in fact, dead until it was too late.

My dick hardened again at the memory. I was long past feeling any kind of shame over my dark desires. I'd accepted the monster I was.

Leah dying, Tobias coming in the shower earlier... it was the perfect culmination. One that had me working over my dick until I came over my bare stomach.

CHAPTER FOUR

TOBIAS

They say hard work pays off, and I was beginning to see that, although I wouldn't call the work I did necessarily hard. Smart, not hard... New York City has eleven coroners, and all I had to do was find the one enduring financial woe—a gambler, a divorced father of four who owed not one, but two women alimony—and hand him over a measly two-hundred thousand dollars. And now dear Leah sits in his office, her murderer to be named by me when I saw fit. Two-hundred grand, and the man would forge evidence. He would let me play god... I smiled at the thought. So it seemed there really was no stopping a man with the means to barter and bargain for someone's soul.

I parked my car outside the quad, dusting lint from my shirt as I stepped out into the warm afternoon sunlight. A group of Leah's sorority sisters stood outside the dorms in a sunset vigil, handing out flyers. Too bad Preston killed her. She truly was good at playing a part. She'd thrown herself into the role of college student with every bit of gusto I could have imagined—rushing for Lambda Lambda Lambda, attending such trivial things as football games. Worth every penny I'd paid her to date Preston and give into his depraved kinks. A twinge of regret rose within me knowing I could no longer enjoy watching her and Preston fuck, but alas, to all good things there must come an end.

I maneuvered through the group of sniffling girls, taking the flyer one of them shoved against my chest. Chuckling to myself, I balled the paper and chucked it into a trashcan on my way through the dormitory doors.

The RA glanced up from her book, her cheeks reddening when her gaze landed on me. I was well aware I had a reputation most girls wanted to be a part of. I'd fucked my way through many of the girls at the University, but none of them came close to satisfying me.

"Who's the lucky girl?" she said, when I grabbed the pen to sign in.

"Not a girl..." I smirked before walking off, leaving my signature beside Preston Lucas's name on the clipboard.

Leah's missing person flyer decorated every bulletin board in the hallway. I guessed this was how people made themselves feel better about not doing anything to really help. Simply shoving four thumbtacks into a black and white print off lightened their souls enough to let them sleep. Consciences were funny, weak things. Things I wanted no part of.

I climbed the stairs to the third floor, then made my way to the end of the hall to room 303. I knew Preston was behind that door, but he hadn't a clue I was so close. I liked that. I pressed my ear to his door, listening to the heavy pants coming from the other side. The slap of skin on skin bled through the wood, followed by a deep grunt. The question was, who was he beating off to the thought of—me or the lovely Leah?

My bet was me. I had, after all, given him a show earlier.

If only he knew I'd come into the showers to rinse the dirt from Leah's grave off, I bet he wouldn't have been able to wait until he'd gotten home to beat one out. Because he was sick—just as sick as I.

I pulled the invitation addressed to Preston from my pocket, then slid it underneath his door. "I'll see you soon, my dear sweet Preston," I whispered. And with that promise, I left and went to get everything prepared.

The next evening, I stood at my penthouse window, staring out over the sprawling, twinkling city of Manhattan as I waited for my guest. Was there the possibility that Preston would decline my invitation? Statistically speaking, of course there was. But would he? No.

He was too curious, and I was too rich. Even someone who hated me would show up—I knew. I had tested it last year. Money had power over politics, friendships, and even egos... Who a man knew was so much more important than who he hated.

The buzzer from the concierge desk sounded. "Mr Lucas is on his way up."

"Very good."

CHAPTER FIVE

PRESTON

Warm night air wrapped around me as I took in the skyscraper reaching into the night sky like a glittering beacon of wealth. I glanced back at the invitation in my hand. The one that someone had slid underneath my dorm room door the night before.

You are cordially invited
The home of Tobias Benton
57th Street NYC, NY 10019
Friday the 20th of March
7:00 pm

So, here I was, outside the doors to a marble lobby, with his invitation in my hand. I didn't even know what I was coming to. A party? A dinner? If it were a party, surely I'd see some other students entering the building, but the only people gathered around were businessmen...

I stepped into the ritzy lobby, hoping this was an invitation of the private kind, that maybe Tobias wanted to expand on his show in the shower.

With one look in my direction, the concierge made a beeline to me —like he'd been waiting on me. "Mr Lucas? Right this way..." He led me away from the main elevator and toward one at the side of the room. Smiling, he waved a badge in front of a panel and motioned me inside the mirrored box. Before I could protest, the doors closed, and I was on my way up. If I had any reservations, any desire to turn around, they were now irrelevant.

Moments later, the doors opened to a glamorous penthouse—one without music or people loitering in the entrance.

Just me then.

A smile pulled at my lips as I exited, taking in the sparkling chandelier hanging in the foyer. I came from what most people would consider a wealthy family, but this, I thought as my attention went past the leather sofas to the floor-to-ceiling window at the far side of the room, this was money. Millions upon millions of dollars.

I rounded the corner and stopped when my gaze landed on the dark and alluring Tobias Benton, dressed in a suit with a glass of Champagne in his hand. The expansive New York City skyline served as his backdrop, a flashing neon sign denoting his wealth and status.

"It was nice of you to come, Preston." He smirked before he took a sip of his drink.

He seemed so civilized but based on the memory of him in the shower yesterday, one thing was for sure, he was far from civilized. "Well, you did invite me." I held up the invitation.

"That I did..."

Tension thickened the air between us as I waited to see what Tobias would do. After all, he was the aggressor here, the one who welcomed me into his domain. But all he did was stare at me from across the room. "Why *am* I here, exactly?"

"Why do you think?"

I fought the smile that tried to make its way onto my lips. "Based on your performance in the gym showers? I can take a guess, but I don't like to presume."

"And so, you accepted because you're willing?" Tobias pushed away from the window, placing his glass on the coffee table before he circled me like prey. "Are you curious about how my fist would feel around your hardening cock?" He trailed his fingers over my shoulder, and my dick twitched at the thought.

"I'm always curious, Tobias."

He stopped moving, and I turned to take in the sculpted planes of his face, to drink in the heat of his breath tinged with the scent of Champagne. This was unchartered ground for me, and not unwelcomed. But Tobias Benton was nothing, if not intimidating.

"Good." He grabbed my belt and yanked my hips to his. "I was thinking of what it would be like to take your virginal ass when I came."

My mind teetered along the edge of curiosity's cliff. I'd always dominated women, and I had always assumed if I ever fucked a guy, I'd be the one doing the fucking... Yet the thought of being dominated by *this* man excited me. "You assume I'd let you have my ass?"

"Yes."

He was right. I would let him.

"There is something dark and sordid about you that calls to every depraved whim I have," he said, sliding my belt through the buckle. "And I know when I eventually fuck you, I'll come in your ass with the hardest orgasm I'll ever experience."

My attention dropped to his lips. I craved violence and savagery, and I imagined Tobias would be brutal.

Without warning, he cupped my dick through my pants. "Despite how willing as it seems you are and how much I'd enjoy taking you right here, we're going to be late if we don't leave."

And with that, he took my hand and led me to the elevator.

CHAPTER SIX

TOBIAS

It was nearing midnight by the time the chauffer parked behind the government building. The lot was empty aside from the Honda of the attendant I'd paid off to be indisposed during our visit.

"We won't be long." I told the driver as I stepped into the warm evening air and motioned Preston out.

He straightened, lifting a brow as he glanced at the building. "Not quite what I had in mind when I took you up on that invitation."

"I hope you enjoy surprises." I fought the sadistic smile threatening my lips as I headed toward the back entrance. I couldn't wait to see Preston's reaction. Would it be one of shock or anger—I hoped not remorse, because that would be a rapid end to this test. There was no room for guilt in this game.

The lock clicked when I swiped the government badge the guard provided me over the scanner, and the door swung open into a sterile-looking hallway. Preston frowned as I motioned him inside. If only I could be privy to the thoughts swirling through his head.

"It's just down this way," I said, leading him through the maze of hallways. And he followed, without question, until I stopped outside the coroner's office.

He took a step back, his gaze locked on the sign above the doorway. "Look, I'm open minded, but if you're into dead bodies... "I'm out."

"Oh, I see. You're only into them *as* they die, then?" I said, opening the door and flipping the light switch.

"What?"

The warming flicker of the fluorescent lights danced over his pretty face. I delighted at the way the color drained from his cheeks as he stood clinging to the doorframe. "I think you know what I'm talking about, dear, sweet Preston." Smiling, I proceeded to the row of stainless-steel cabinets, grabbed the handle to number three, and pulled it open with a clank of the rollers.

Leah's dirt-covered, decaying body lay perfectly still on the metal table, and Preston's horror-filled gaze was right on it. He rushed to the sink at the side of the room and threw up. As much as part of me wanted to view it as weakness, maybe it was a bit much to stomach.

"What's the matter, Preston? Not so fond of her now?" I crossed the room and latched onto his shoulders, then spun him around to face her body. "Look at what you did."

"What the fuck?" he whispered, closing his eyes as he swiped a hand over his mouth. "You... She's dead."

And what a good little sociopathic actor Preston was. He almost sounded shocked. "Preston," I tsked. "Don't take me for a fool. I know you killed her. I know how hard you came as she drew her last breath." I trailed a finger over Leah's cold, rigid arm. "And you haven't quite found a release that good since, have you?"

There was a moment—a fleeting moment where he looked uncertain, but he quickly masked it with a heavy frown. "I don't know what you're talking about. Leah's been missing for a week." His gaze drifted to her corpse, but his steadfast expression never wavered. "I wasn't aware she'd been... found."

He would deny it as long as I would let him—most people would. But my patience was wearing thin and my dick ached for his lips around it. "Stop fighting, Leah," I repeated the words he said to her that night as I stepped toward him. "You know if you pass out, I'll only come harder... and then you did. You came hard in her dying pussy and then you buried her in the woods."

His jaw ticced as his gaze drifted from me to Leah then back. Oh, he was upset. Not filled with remorse or shock. Upset that his secret had been unearthed, and that pleased me so. "When did they find her?" he asked.

"*They* didn't..."

"What the fuck?"

"You didn't bury her very deep..."

"You?" He shook his head, the realization that I was the one who found her setting in. "How did you—"

"The technicalities don't really matter, do they? Not now, when you have the title murderer looming over your pretty head." I smiled at him.

"What do you want?"

"You."

His brow furrowed. "I don't understand."

There wasn't much to understand. I wanted him, bound and tied to me. "I want to own you, Preston." I closed the space between us and grabbed his hair, yanking his head back before I placed my lips at his throat. "And now, I do."

He shoved me away. "I don't want any part of whatever the fuck this is. I never... I didn't mean to do it."

Maybe he didn't, but the fact of the matter was, he enjoyed it. There was no undoing that. "It's too late for that, I'm afraid," I said.

"What are you going to do, Tobias? Tell the police that I killed her? That you dug up her rotting body, just to what? Blackmail me into fucking you?" He shook his head as he paced away from me. "That right there—" he pointed at Leah—"is fucked up."

And wasn't that the pot calling the kettle black? I stalked toward him and grabbed him by the nape of the neck. "What's more fucked up, Preston? That I dug her up, or that you killed her and buried her?" His gaze dropped from my eyes to my lips. He was mine, and whether or not this depraved little shit wanted to admit it, he wanted to be. "Or that you still want to fuck me?" No matter what words followed, I knew I had him.

"I came when you invited me," he said. "I was obviously willing to fuck you. So, why are you doing this?"

"Because it's more fun." I brushed a hand over his crotch, noting the semi hard-on underneath the material. "Because this way, I have complete control over you. You fuck up, and I fuck up your life." The moment I released him, he staggered back a few steps.

"So, you're blackmailing me. Fine." Hate burned in his eyes as he glared at me. "For how long?"

"Six months." I could have said forever, but I liked the idea of false freedom. I wanted to make him believe he could eventually walk away from me. But what I knew was that it takes about sixty-six days to form a habit. Six months was plenty to make sure Preston never wanted to leave my side again. It was more than ample time to let him see exactly how much fun money mixed with darkness could be. "A small price to pay considering the alternative," I said as I waved a hand toward Leah's body.

His jaw tensed, and I took the silence which followed as an agreement.

Smiling, I went for my belt. "Good. Now suck my cock."

CHAPTER SEVEN

PRESTON

He pulled his hard cock out of his slacks. I took in the map work of veins, hating that, despite everything he was doing, part of me wanted him to taint me until darkness and shadows were the only thing left. He'd dug up a body just to get me here, and in some fucked up way, it made me want him more. In some monumentally screwed up corner of my mind, this whole thing flattered me. And I hated it.

"Put it in your mouth, Preston."

Like Tobias had snapped shackles in place, I dropped to my knees on a glare.

"Don't act like you don't want to do this..." He brushed his cock against my mouth, smearing precum over my lips before he grabbed my hair and forced his dick between my lips.

A musky, masculine taste washed over my tongue, and while my mind rebelled, my body craved his brand of retribution. Leah's cold body was just a few feet away, a glaring reminder of exactly why I was doing this. I froze, squeezing my eyes shut as I tried to force myself to submit to his whims.

"Surely those pretty lips of yours can do better than that." He stared down at me like a malevolent god before he thrust forward with such force his dick hit the back of my throat. I choked and fought to push back, but he held me in place. "Take it all down, like a good boy, Preston."

I scraped my teeth over his shaft in warning. But instead of retreating from the threat, he groaned, and the sound went straight to my dick. I secretly wanted this—wanted him—and I hated it. I swallowed him back, gripping his balls and squeezing hard enough that it should have hurt, but he only fucked my mouth harder.

"Yes. Just like that, Preston."

Fuck. My dick hardened. I wanted to stroke it and come to the sound of Tobias losing it.

What started as a position of weakness suddenly felt powerful, and in that moment, *I* owned *him*.

The harder Tobias thrusted between my lips, the deeper I sucked him, until his come hit the back of my throat on a groan. And I fucking swallowed it. The moment felt binding, as though our awful agreement was now sealed and bound.

Tobias Benton now owned me, and there was nothing I could do about it.

The dimly lit sidewalks empty of any passerbys when Tobias's driver dropped us off in front of his apartment building.

I silently followed him inside the lobby, around the corner, and into the elevator. As soon as those doors slid closed, his presence felt stifling, like it sucked every ounce of oxygen from the confined space.

I watched him from the corner of my eye as the elevator passed floor after floor, taking in his perfect face, his body in that tailored suit. His stillness was unsettling, like a predator lying in wait. And oh, he was certainly that. I hadn't even seen him coming before he sunk his teeth into my throat.

He'd brought me back here to stay in his penthouse with him. For what, though, I wasn't sure. "Why do you want me to stay here?" I asked.

His gaze cut over to me just as the elevator came to a stop. "Because I like power..." The doors opened.

Power. And he'd taken so much of that from me. Right now, I could do nothing but submit to his every whim, and I despised him for it.

He shrugged out of his jacket as he stepped into the foyer. "It's time for bed," he said, like taking a man to a morgue and blackmailing him was a normal, everyday occurrence.

He disappeared down the hallway and I remained in the foyer, glancing wistfully back at the elevator. What would happen if I just left?

"Preston?" Tobias's voice echoed down the hallway.

I gave one more glance at the elevator, then sighed as I took a step forward, crossing the foyer and heading down the hall. Tobias waited in the doorway of what I assumed was his master bedroom. He ducked inside when I was a few feet away, and I followed. I had no choice in the matter.

Light from the city below poured in through the floor to ceiling windows, casting an electronic haze over the massive bed in the middle of the ridiculously oversized room. Wealth dripped from every fixture, every furnishing. It was another world, one far above mine—one far above most peoples. It was a world most would do nearly anything for, and suddenly I felt like Hansel, salivating over the lovely gingerbread house which promised to indulge every greedy desire I could ever have. And Tobias was surely the villainous creature who lurked inside, waiting to devour me. I knew that as I watched him strip out of his suit, piece by piece, and carefully lay each item over the back of a nearby chair. I took in each perfect line of his body as he stepped out of his boxers and stood naked in the residual glow from the city far below.

He patted the bed as he climbed into it naked. He wanted me to sleep with him? Yeah, that wasn't happening.

I hooked a thumb toward the door. "I'll just, take the couch." As hot as I found him, I did not want to share a bed with him. One, he was blackmailing me. Two, I didn't trust myself not to let him fuck me, only to hate myself for the weak display of submission.

"You'll sleep in here." His stare hardened. "With me."

Of course. Tobias got what he wanted, because he'd destroy me if I didn't bow to his whims. I think I'd rather suck his dick than this though. This felt too intimate.

I stripped down to my boxers, then crawled onto the soft, expensive-feeling sheets that smelled of cardamon and pine. That smell embodied Tobias, and I had to stop myself from sucking it deep into my lungs.

"Sweet dreams, my depraved little monster." He kissed my forehead before reclining onto his back.

Again, the intimacy of the act was unsettling, disturbing even, but the weight of his eyes, combined with how far he was evidently willing to go to have me, made my dick hard.

The room plunged into darkness when he switched off the lamp. I lay in the dark, fully expecting his hand to stroke over my cock; for him to fuck me—why the hell else would he want me in his bed—but he made no move to breach the distance between us. While I was part relieved, the ache in my dick begged him to slide his hand over my stomach. I was desperate to feel his perfectly manicured fingers wrapped around my cock. Fuck.

I laid tense beside him. My dick twitched at every slight move he made while my mind ran a hundred miles an hour. I hated I was this hard for him. Hated that I was literally his prisoner; like some kind of pet sleeping in his bed.

Tobias's breaths evened out in sleep, and my erratic pulse pounded along with my cock. I couldn't trust him. He'd hold that body over me and fuck me over the first chance he got. And I sure as hell knew whatever he was going to ask in exchange for his silence, it would be a lot worse than a blow job. The thought of sneaking into the kitchen and grabbing a knife to slit his throat with surfaced but was quickly snuffed out. Despite the situation with Leah, I wasn't a killer. Not to mention, the risk with a man like Tobias was too high, and one accidental body was plenty enough problem to deal with. I couldn't stay here, but what was I to do? Disappear? It would look suspicious, but if they couldn't find me...

I eased the covers away, carefully slipping from the bed to gather my clothes. Thoughts swirled through my head as I crept into the hall and quietly dressed. What was I supposed to do? If I left, God only knew how Tobias's psychotic ass would react, but if I could just manage to disappear... Sure, it would look suspicious, but if the authorities never found me, I'd be free.

I glanced over my shoulder when I reached the elevator. The penthouse remained eerily silent as I pressed the call button. My pulse climbed, adrenaline firing through me as the moments passed. Moments where the motor to the elevator never whirred to life. I jabbed my finger against the button a few more times, clamping down the sense of hysteria rising within me when I realized it wasn't working. This was the only way out of this apartment. I was trapped.

"Trying to run away?"

The deep bass of Tobias's voice startled me, and I spun around to find him looming in the dark hallway. Naked, his semi-hard dick pointing at me. The blood flow shifted to my cock at the sight of him.

"Maybe." I clenched my jaw. "Seems I'm trapped though."

"Regardless of whether or not you could get on that elevator, you're trapped."

My gaze dropped to the floor on a nod, defeat weighing on my shoulders. There was no way out of this bar acceptance. His footsteps retreated, and I resigned myself to following him back to his room and into his bed.

We lay in silence, and soon enough, Tobias had drifted back to sleep. But I was still very much awake, with the remnants of adrenaline refusing to fizzle out. I stared at the high ceiling, listening to Tobias's heavy breaths, and all I could think about was how much heavier they'd be when he finally fucked me. I could almost feel the phantom heat on the back of my neck. *Fuck.* I couldn't help but to grip my cock, stroking over the length as I imagined Tobias taking me. Within seconds, heat drowned my body as I got close to that edge. Tossing the covers off, I fought to remain silent as I came on my stomach with a low grunt. Shallow breaths slipped past my lips as I tried to regain my breath. My body relaxed into the soft mattress just as Tobias rolled onto his side and swiped a finger through the pool of come. Wide awake. "We'll make such the perfect pair," he said, before sucking the taste of me from his skin. Fuck, I wanted to lick my come from his lips. And that was problematic. He was blackmailing me, controlling me, basically keeping me captive in his bed, and yet here I was, jerking off right next to him. Worse, when he sucked my come off his fingers like that, there was very little I wouldn't do to have him fuck me. He was a poison I would willingly die to consume.

CHAPTER EIGHT

PRESTON

The next afternoon, we sat in some fancy ass, Michelin star restaurant for lunch. It was the kind of place my father took his work colleagues to impress them, only to go home and bitch about the exorbitant prices and tiny portion sizes.

Silence filled the meal just as it had filled this morning. The total lack of conversation was unnerving, and I downed my wine as Tobias cut into his steak.

"So we have a dilemma," he finally said, dabbing a napkin to the corner of his mouth.

"More than the obvious?" Ergo, the dead body hanging over my head like a swinging axe wielded by none other than Tobias.

"You'll be a suspect..."

I glared at him. I knew it was only a matter of time before the police asked more questions. Time I had until he interfered. "Well, if someone hadn't handed them a fucking body..."

"Likewise, if someone hadn't killed her..." One of his perfectly sculpted brows arched. The man infuriated me.

"If you'd just left her where she was, I wouldn't be a damn suspect. She'd just be a runaway."

He shot a disapproving frown at me before taking the last bite of his rare steak. "Somebody must take the blame. Her family deserves closure, Preston."

Fuck, how did he mange to paint me like the asshole when he was blackmailing me? I did kill her, but still... Not like it was deliberate. I hated the muted pinch of guilt that attempted to break through the fog of indifference surrounding me. "Don't pretend you give a shit about her family, Tobias."

He grinned over the rim of his wineglass, like there was some secret I wasn't privy to. "I thought you liked her mother. The first time you met her at the Hot and Hot Fish Club, you told her she was lovely. Was that a lie, Preston?"

"How the hell do you know this shit?" I said through gritted teeth.

"I know so many things about you." A sinister smile settled on his lips as he reached across the table to clasp my hand in his. "So many, *many* things."

I was usually pretty unshakeable, but Tobias and his all-knowing abilities were starting to freak me out.

His attention drifted from me to the waitress as she placed the check on the table. Without looking at it, he passed a stack of crisp bills to her. "Keep the change." He watched her closely as she crossed the restaurant, and the moment she was out of earshot, his gaze snapped back to me. "Now onto more important matters. Who do you want to take the blame?"

Take the blame... That seemed counter-intuitive. Surely my blame was his entire point here? I pinched the bridge of my nose. "Let me just get this straight. You deliberately exposed her body so you could threaten and leverage me. And now you want me to pin it on someone, when you could have just left her in the ground to begin with."

"Chad Davis, Brendon Walters, or Christian McClure?" He'd listed off students. People I barely knew. "Who do you want to go to jail for her murder?"

God, he was diabolical. "You want me to pick a fall guy?" This made zero sense to me, but then, Tobias wasn't exactly sane.

He circled his finger over the rim of his wineglass. The muted hum mixed with the tinker of cutlery around us. "Unless, of course, your conscience tells you to turn yourself in..."

I had no conscience, not really.

"None of them are nice people, Preston." He chuckled. "But I don't think it would matter if they were..."

Was anyone really nice? Out of the three guys Tobias listed, the only one who even flickered within the bleak, gray sea of my peers was Chad Davis. He'd tried out for my captain position on the football team. He also hit on Leah a time or two while we were exclusive, and the rumor circulating campus was that he date raped a freshman last year. In some righteous corner of my mind, that made this feel like justice—not that I could judge him, but there was something distasteful and cowardly about fucking an unconscious girl. "Chad Davis," I said, then took another sip of wine.

"Very well, then. Now if you'll excuse me." Tobias pushed to his feet, smoothing a hand over his suit jacket before he crossed the restaurant.

Was he going to handle the situation right now? And how—how would he pin Leah's murder on Chad when my DNA was all over her body? Maybe Tobias was fucking with my head. Round and round my thoughts went until they no longer made sense, and the longer I sat alone at the table, the more an edge of paranoia slowly crept in.

I grew suspicious of the server who moved past our table, the damn wine he picked up from our table and poured into my glass—even though we'd both been drinking it throughout lunch. Tobias had reduced my life to a waiting game, one which depended on what move he intended to make next.

By the time Tobias came back to the table, my nerves were on edge.

"I apologize it took so long," he said, taking a seat beside me instead of across from me where he'd been for the duration of lunch.

I lifted my wine, studying him from the corner of my eye. Waiting...

"Unbutton your pants." One of his dark brows lifted, daring me to deny him. And maybe I would have if he didn't hold the power to destroy me in the palm of his hand. Or maybe I wouldn't have, because when his hand landed on my thigh, my dick hardened at the prospect of whatever he had planned. Tobias might have been a crazy asshole, but my cock sure as hell didn't care.

I pulled the tablecloth over my lap and unfastened my pants, telling myself it was because I had no choice. Pretending the entire situation didn't send dark excitement skittering through my veins.

Tobias leaned in by my ear. "Take out your cock." His warm breath teased my neck, and I fought back a groan before doing as told.

"Good boy." His hand inched closer to my hard cock, so close I could feel the heat of his skin. I waited in anticipation as he lifted his glass to his lips with his free hand and took a sip. I wanted his touch more than my next breath. His gaze met mine, hard and dark and full of sordid promises I knew only he could fill. "Chad Davis did a terrible thing, didn't he, Preston?"

Fuck, he was such a psycho. Why was it so hot? My jaw clenched as his fingers edged closer. "Terrible," I whispered.

"He murdered your loving girlfriend, raped her with no regard you had made love to her hours before. The DNA evidence will make that apparent."

The fact that he had the power to pull these kinds of strings at the drop of a hat... My dick twitched.

"You'll have to play the part of a grieving lover." Then he fisted me, his grip firm, commanding. Tobias Benton was my torment and salvation, and I hated him as much as I craved him. "You may even have to kill him, Preston."

"I'm not above killing." I could barely form coherent speech due to the pent up want finally being released.

"I know..." he said, twisting his way up my shaft. "Your dark harbinger is one thing I find undeniably irresistible about you."

He went harder, faster, edging me with a hint of pain until his fist pounded the underside of the table and caused the dishes to rattle. The strength of his fingers, his voice, the risk of getting caught... It all sent me hurtling toward the edge of climax faster than I ever had before. My balls tightened as pleasure tore up my spine in a heated blaze. I bit the inside of my cheek and swallowed back the groan my body wanted to release as I came hard all over Tobias's fist.

"How very satisfying," he said as he lifted his hand from beneath the table and licked my sticky come from his fingers like it was a decadent dessert. Fuck, he made it hard not to want him.

The dark, sordid fantasies that only ever lingered in the shadows of my mind were now very much in the light. I wanted Tobias Benton to possess me, and given our situation, that was foolish.

Later that evening, Tobias dropped me off at my dorm with the promise that he'd be in touch.

The black town car rolled away, leaving me on the curb in a state of confusion. Last night, he all but held me captive, and now he was leaving me here. Just like that?

A sense of foreboding crept through me. The police now had that body, had my DNA all over her. Was I really that naïve to trust a maniac to cover up a murder for me? What reason would he have to go to such lengths? Regardless, it was a ticking bomb waiting to blow up in my face, and Tobias Benton held the detonator. So far, the only thing I'd done to stop him from pressing it... suck his dick.

I went into the dorm, ignoring the posters of Leah tacked to every bulletin board on my way to my room. The moment I closed the door behind me, I grabbed the bottle of bourbon from my dresser drawer and chugged it. I drank until my vision crossed and I collapsed back on my bed.

This was beyond fucked up and I was beyond fucked.

The next morning, I woke with a start to someone pounding on my door. I groggily glanced at my phone, groaning when I realized it was only nine in the morning. Another series of knocks rattled the door.

"I'm coming," I said as I slipped into a pair of track pants. I yanked the door open and the dorm's RA quickly stepped to the side, revealing two police officers. Shit. I fought to keep my racing heart under control and schooled my features into a frown—The sight of police at someone's door would concern anyone, right? Not just murderers.

"Mr Lucas, we need you to come down to the station and answer some questions about Leah Andrews."

I knew this would come at some point. I was her boyfriend, the last person to be seen with her, and undoubtedly, a suspect.

"Of course. Anything I can do to help find her..."

When they told me they'd found a body, I would paint myself as the grieving boyfriend, heartbroken at the death of my only love. And hope like hell that Tobias actually kept his word and pinned this on someone. Either way, my fate was firmly in his psychotic hands.

CHAPTER NINE

TOBIAS

Right on time, at half past noon, the elevator doors to my penthouse slid open to reveal a fairly shaken Preston. I must say, seeing him rattled sent a slight blip of joy through me.

He glared at me as he crossed the room and headed toward the window. I'm sure these little mind games of mine were wearing on him. I meant them to. Destabilization was key in manipulation—making the person feel as though they had no control and I had all of it, which I did. I always would when it came to Preston, until he gave in that is. Then I'd share the power—almost equally.

"Did you have a good morning?"

"You fucking know I didn't."

"How would I know, Preston?"

"Because you know everything, Tobias. You orchestrate every damn thing." He dragged a hand through his golden hair, his agitation clear.

"Do I?" I smirked.

"Fuck!" He punched the glass. "Are you going to fuck me over?"

Tsking, I gave a dismissive glance at the bloody knuckle prints left on my otherwise pristine window. "Such a temper..."

"They just took a DNA sample, Tobias. My DNA is all over her." He paced in front of the glass.

And it had him so frazzled. If only he knew what I did—that it didn't matter because I had DNA from each of the three men I'd told him to choose between planted all over her body. It didn't matter who he chose. Every one of those men were horrible creatures—ones I had painstakingly found, ensuring the only alibi they had wasn't trustworthy. If he only knew the invisible strings I've pulled. And one day he will... When he finally lets go, when he's ready to embrace his true potential and is truly willing to tap into the most savage and brutal parts of humanity. "Of course it is," I said, stepping forward to cup his jaw.

And oh, how conflicted he looked. He must hate me—he should, but in this moment, the only salvation he had was the very monster who created him. "Do you feel remorse for what you've done?"

His jaw ticced beneath my palm. "Honestly? No. But you already knew that, didn't you?"

"I did. And I'm so proud of you." I leaned in and pressed a kiss to his lips. All the possibilities of what and who we would be danced through my mind like tiny skeletons. "And you are right. I know everything about you."

Seconds passed, and I couldn't quite make out whether it was annoyance or flattery darkening his eyes. "And you want someone to play with you—someone without morals. Without remorse."

"Precisely."

"You didn't have to blackmail me for that, Tobias. You only had to ask."

What he didn't understand—I couldn't simply ask. I had to be certain his demons would play well with mine. I had to witness, for myself, that his depraved whims weren't merely a form of entertainment, but a bone-deep calling. Something that coursed through his veins like a life force. "Am I blackmailing you though?"

His face reddened, and he held up his hand, his fingers centimeters apart. "I'm this close to being arrested, Tobias. So yeah..."

"And you think her body wouldn't have been discovered eventually?" I swept a tendril of hair behind his ears. "I told you earlier, you didn't bury her deep enough."

"So, you did me a favor." He huffed a humorless laugh at the statement.

"I did us a favor."

"By digging her up and handing them a body?"

Annoyance lanced through me. It was crystal-fucking-clear what I'd done for him, but he was so blinded by his cloud of narcissism he couldn't see past anything besides himself. "Do you not understand it's my need for you that's driven every damn thing I've done? I couldn't leave her there to be found and have them take you away." I brushed my thumb over his bottom lip. "Don't be so messy next time."

His brows furrowed and he stared at me for long seconds. "You... care for me."

Care was a word equated with emotions. And I could only care for him in the most selfish of ways, the way an art collector cares for an extravagant piece of art which brings them joy. "I've always wanted to own you, Preston," I said, stroking his cheek as my gaze dropped to his perfect mouth. "And now I do." Then I slammed my lips over his in a brutal kiss. One he returned. Violence and hate-tinged passion filled each thrust of our tongues. And that one kiss sealed Preston's fate forever. I knew it. He knew it.

"You make me hate you..." He palmed me through my pants, making the ache in my balls grow nearly unbearable. "And want you. It's fucking maddening."

The buzzer from the concierge desk sounded, and I cursed myself for always needing to plan everything. There was nothing more that I wanted to do at that very moment than strip Preston out of his clothes and spread his ass cheeks before I sank my cock into him, fast and hard, but I would have to wait just a bit longer. After all, anticipation was the best type of foreplay.

The buzzer sounded again, letting me know I'd passed the time I'd given the concierge, and I tore away from his kiss, adjusting my dick in my slacks. "I can give you so many things, Preston. Such unimaginable, dark things. The question is, are you game?"

"Like I said, all you have to do is ask." A small smile played at his lips. "Yes."

And now the tides had shifted, dark and stormy and oh so promising. It was time to play our first game.

CHAPTER TEN

PRESTON

Everything had changed. Want and need now tainted what had at first, seemed like a heinous act. It wasn't blackmail, but ownership dressed in a shiny bow of protection. I still didn't like the power Tobias held over me, but the lengths he had gone to just to have me shackled and bound to him spoke volumes. So much so, I didn't even want to escape my chains. I wanted his possession.

A knowing smirk danced over his lips, as though he knew he finally had me right where he'd always wanted me.

He backed away from me, telling me to sit as he left the room. A few moments later, he came back with a handful of dossier-type files in his hand, which he spread out on the coffee table.

"Pick who you want to play the game with," he said, taking a seat on the couch beside me.

I opened the top folder and glanced over the content before shuffling to the next. Each one had a picture of a woman pinned to the top and underneath it, details about her life. Her job. Her family status. Her financials. I flipped through each one, finally stopping on a redhead. I recognized her. I'd noticed her downstairs in the lobby before I came up, along with—I opened a few more folders—that blonde and the pretty Asian girl.

I'd already learned not to question Tobias's eccentricities. He'd obviously brought them here for this game. And now I had to pick from a list of beautiful women. So of course, I went back to the redhead. It was morose, twisted as fuck, but I had a definite type when it came to women. "Her." I stabbed a finger over the page of Lacey Daniels, a twenty-year-old art major.

Tobias grinned. "Very good choice. She's in a very vulnerable position." He took the folder, skimming the contents. "Lost both her parents. Mountains of debt. About to be kicked out of the university because she's defaulted on her loans."

"Are you looking to fuck her or save her, Tobias?"

"Both—if she wins, that is." He pulled a paper from the back of the folder, handing it to me with a grin.

A contract. He had drafted a fucking legally binding contract.

THIS AGREEMENT, made on this __ day of _____, 20__, by and between Lacey Daniels (participant) and Tobias Benton (host) and Preston Lucas (host), (collectively "The Parties") shall set forth all matters relating to and concerning the agreement.

WHEREAS the parties agree that all activities are voluntary in nature; and

WHEREAS the parties agree that no physical harm that could intentionally result in death shall occur; and

WHEREAS, upon the completion of the agreement, LACEY DAVIS will receive the lump sum of one hundred thousand dollars, contingent upon the aforementioned rules and stipulations outlined in section1, rules

SECTION 1

NONDISCLOSURE

The participant agrees that they shall keep all knowledge of this agreement and occurrences that happen within the agreement strictly confidential. The participant may not speak of or mention anything to do with the host. The participant shall not make disparaging remarks about the host in person or on online accounts over which the participant has access or control.

ENFORCEMENT OF AGREEMENT

All provisions of this Agreement shall be enforceable in a Court of law.
IN WITNESS WHEREOF, the parties hereto have set their hands and seals the day and year set forth in the Notary Seal.

WITNESS

_____

_____(SEAL)
LACEY DANIELS
WITNESS

_____

_____(SEAL)
TOBIAS BENTON
WITNESS

WITNESS

_____

_____(SEAL)
PRESTON LUCAS
WITNESS

"You drafted a contract for her?" I glanced over it again with a grin. "With an NDA."

"Of course. The legalities of such things are of the utmost importance, Preston."

But I was pretty sure no laws covered the depravity he wanted to enact.

He collected the rest of the files from the table and carried them back to his room before calling down to the front desk to request Lacey's presence. A few minutes later, the ping of the elevator echoed through the penthouse.

The redhead stepped off, hesitant with each unsteady stride her long, slender legs made.

"Don't be shy, Lacey. We won't bite." Tobias's dark gaze flickered to mine, full of sadistic anticipation.

She took a heavy breath, and my attention snapped back to her. I took in the way her short skirt played at the top of her toned thighs, the way the tight top exposed everything she offered. So it seemed she had dressed to sell her body and pay those debts off, and oh, how I wanted to make her scream for every penny.

"So nice of you to come," Tobias said, his deep voice so charming and debonair. I could see her easily falling into his web—much as I had—with each step she took towards him, but the difference was, it wasn't his charm that dragged me in. It was his darkness. I doubted Lacey saw the darkness. She seemed sweet and innocent, completely unaware such things existed.

Tobias's attention fixed solely on her as she moved toward him, and a volatile spark of jealousy ignited within me.

"Sweet Lacey, I told you I had a proposition for you. The question I need you to answer is, what would you be willing to do for one hundred thousand dollars?" Tobias's gaze drifted to me on a deep-seated smirk. "Or rather, what wouldn't you do?"

"That's… a lot of money," she said. "Is this a joke?"

"Not at all." Tobias stepped forward, contract in hand, as he skimmed a finger over her bare shoulder. "Would you fuck us?"

Blush stained her cheeks as she glanced between us. "Yes."

Of course she would. What woman wouldn't want to be trapped between Tobias and me, regardless of the money?

"Would you fulfill our deepest, darkest desires?" He fisted her hair and yanked her head back until her back created a perfect bow, and I bit back a groan. "Would you scream for us?"

My dick hardened at the thought of watching him fuck her face until she gagged and cried; until mascara streaked her face and spit covered her chin.

I moved behind her and met Tobias's dark gaze over her shoulder. "All those debts could disappear, Lacey." When I swept hair away from her neck, I couldn't help but imagine how pretty her skin would look covered in bruises. "The alternative seems… bleak."

"Think of everything you could do," Tobias countered, passing the contract to her along with a pen. "And all you have to do is sign."

I ran my fingers through the silky strands of Lacey's red hair while breathing against her neck. It was just a shade darker than Leah's. Close enough that I could almost imagine it was Leah.

Anticipation and need built as I watched her shaky hand scrawl a signature over Tobias's contract. The moment she lifted the pen, I snatched the papers from her grasp and placed them against her back, then signed my name.

When Tobias finally added his signature, it felt final and binding. It felt like freedom.

I gripped Lacey's chin and jerked her head to the side, brushing my lips to the corner of her mouth. "Such a pretty little whore."

Tobias grabbed both our chins, kissing me then her—then us both. "Come. Let us play."

The car rolled to a stop. I stared through the window at the dark woods beyond. Woods I recognized all too well even in the moonlight. Coincidence? Nothing with Tobias was ever coincidence.

He silently got out of the car, pulling Lacey with him as I exited from the other side, inhaling the scent of earth and pine. Anticipation buzzed through me as I rounded the back of the vehicle. The red glow of the taillights played over Tobias's face when his attention drifted to me, and I couldn't help but acknowledge how much he resembled a demon waiting and ready to steal Lacey's soul.

He swept a hand over her cheek. "One hundred thousand dollars, little one. And all you have to do is endure the next few hours." His gaze moved to mine moments before he stepped forward and grabbed my belt, yanking it open. The heat of his hand wrapped around my shaft when he pulled my dick out.

"He has such a perfect cock, Lacey..." His dark eyes held mine, whispering, promising. "Get on your knees and suck it."

I wasn't sure what I wanted more, his hand or her mouth, but it was she who stepped forward and sank to her knees. Moonlight danced over her face as she wrapped hesitant fingers around my dick, then her warm mouth encircled me. *Fuck.*

"Does it feel good, Preston?"

"So fucking good." My teeth scraped my bottom lip. "I want to fuck her face until she chokes on me, Tobias."

"Then shove your fucking cock down her throat." He stepped behind her and fisted my hair. "Make her gag." Then his lips were on mine, demanding repayment for the gift of her hot, wet mouth. His violent kiss contradicted Lacey's soft licks, and I wanted more.

The taint of his aggression bled through me until I thrusted into her mouth. With Tobias behind her like a wall, she had nowhere to go. Nothing to do but take my dick.

She gagged and wretched as she fought, raking her nails over my thighs.

"Harder," Tobias commanded, and within minutes, I teetered on the edge of climax.

Right when I was about to shoot my load down her throat, Tobias grabbed the back of her neck and pulled her upright. "That's enough, little one."

My balls ached with the need to come, and I tightened my fists, glaring at Tobias for cutting me off. "I wasn't finished..."

"I know."

Lacey swiped at her mascara-stained cheeks when Tobias placed his lips by her ear. "He's a murderer, Lacey. How does that make you feel?"

She looked me up and down as though she couldn't believe it. Maybe it should have flattered me—I evidently didn't see the creature I truly was. "I... Is this part of the game, Mr. Benton?" she whispered. She was one step off calling him sir, and from the pleased look on his face, that did things to him.

"It's the truth, isn't it, Preston?" He flashed a devious smile.

I held his gaze, wondering where the hell he was going with this. "Yes."

"And so, my dear, sweet, Lacey..." He kissed her cheek, his eyes still locked on me. "What you're going to do, is recreate the night he fell into the pits of hell."

He wanted me to kill her? Despite the obvious, I wasn't actually a killer.

"I don't want to die. Please..."

"Oh, no. You won't, little one. He will." He pulled a knife from his suit pocket and forced it into her hand. "Consider it a due form of justice."

What the fuck? My attention went from the knife in her hand to Tobias. Was this just part of his game or something more sinister? It was Lacey who was meant to be the player here, but what if I was too? Wasn't I always playing by Tobias's rules, anyway?

When he pulled a hidden gun from the waist of his pants, I froze. "Run." He cocked it. "Both of you." There was nothing on his face, zero emotion, and I had no doubt he was more than capable of pulling that trigger.

When neither of us moved, he rammed the barrel against Lacey's temple. Within her terrified expression, I could see the realization settling over her. She hadn't sold herself for sex. She'd sold her soul to a demon.

"I suggest you run, Preston. Or she can't chase you. And then pity —you'll both be dead."

A mixture of fear and excitement wormed through my chest at the thought of her fighting. Not that I wanted to kill her, but I delighted in the thought of her thinking she was the hunter when she would soon become the hunted.

Tobias fired the gun in the air. She may not be able to kill me, but he could. Twigs snapped beneath our feet as we wove between tall pines.

I got a few yards in front of her, then shifted behind a tree and hid within the shadows as I waited for her to get closer. She slowed beside the trunk and I stepped out, a smirk on my face. "Are you really going to stab me, Lacey? Are you a murderer?"

Moonlight washed over her, highlighting her mascara-stained cheeks. "I didn't sign up for this." The knife trembled in her hand. "I don't want him to kill me, but I don't want to kill you."

"Then don't."

Tears fell down her cheeks. Her attention went from me to the knife. "Are you really a murderer?"

"Yes." There was something liberating about voicing it without hesitation. "The question is, Lacey, are you?"

She took an unsteady step back. I fully expected her to turn tail and run, but then another gunshot sounded not too far away. I saw the moment she made a choice between her life or mine, and she chose herself. She shrieked before launching at me like a cornered animal. Only I wasn't cornering her, Tobias was.

As one of my hands went to her throat, the other reached for her wrist, but not fast enough. She drove the blade toward my chest. I sucked in a breath, braced for the sting of metal slicing through skin, but there was nothing. No ripping or tearing, no blinding burn. Just the soft thud of the hilt touching my chest. When I glanced down, there was no blood. She screamed, then stabbed me again—only she didn't. I watched the blade retract into the handle. It was prop. Oh, Tobias. A smile pulled at my lips as I dug my fingers into her soft throat. "You tried to kill me, Lacey."

She fought against me when I slammed her onto the ground, then fell on top of her. "Please." Her nails clawed at my hand. "I didn't—He said..."

"Shh." I squeezed her throat until she had no choice but to shut the fuck up. I brushed my mouth against her parted lips as she gasped for breath.

Twigs snapped behind me and I tensed, instinctively knowing Tobias had found us.

"The contract specifically stated no physical harm that could *intentionally* result in death would occur." He tsked. "Now look at you."

I glanced over my shoulder as he stepped into a pool of silvery moonlight shining through the tree limbs. "So shooting her would be a breach of your precious contract?" Lucky her. Lacey choked beneath me, reminding me of her fleeting oxygen levels.

"I don't know. Would it?" He took another step forward. "I gave her a fake knife. My gun has blanks, but your hands..." A deep chuckle broke through the silent night. "Your hands are very much taking her life away, second by second. Just like Leah..."

I narrowed my eyes. "This one tried to kill me with your fake knife. Leah was an accident."

Tobias stepped forward, crouching beside me. "Is this accidental?" He swept a hand over my hard dick, and my violence became tinged with lust.

I gritted my teeth, annoyed at the entire situation. "Would you like me to release her, Tobias?"

"Oh, no." He pushed to his feet, then stripped out of his jacket. "I wouldn't."

With each piece of clothing Tobias took off, my grip loosened. Enough for Lacey to catch a breath. Even though she tried to stab me, I needed her to witness Tobias in all his perfection. I needed her to want him, despite knowing he would kill her. I wanted her to be oh so weak for him, just as I was.

Finally, Tobias stepped out of his boxers, the moonlight highlighting the length of his hard dick. A hard dick I wanted to drag my tongue over.

Lacey whimpered beneath me, trying to get away. Like she didn't crave him. She did. She wanted us both.

"I thought you wanted that money, sweetheart." I chuckled at her fake fear. "You didn't think you'd only have to spread your legs, did you?" I glanced at Tobias, then back at her. "That you'd get paid to fuck someone as beautiful as him."

Tobias moved closer as I stroked a hand over his muscular thigh. "You see, he's twisted and depraved." And that made me long to fuck him. "A devil luring you to your own demise."

He took my hands and moved them away from her throat before he straddled her face. "Suck me, Lacey. Please me." He forced his cock between her lips as she struggled and gagged. "Swallow it back." He was like a dark god who refused to be denied until she took him back and gagged. My focus should have been on that—on her choking on his

THE INVITATION

cock. But it wasn't. It was on the firm muscles of his ass as he bent in front of me, and I couldn't stop myself from spreading his cheeks to take in the sight of his tight hole.

"Do you want to lick it, Preston?" he groaned as he thrust into Lacey's mouth again.

Fuck, yes, I did.

Leaning forward, I swiped my tongue over the length of his crack before pressing it into his ass. He groaned and bucked. I tightened my hold on him, reveling in his reactions. He may say he wanted to fuck me, but I had no doubt, given the right opportunity, I could have Tobias squirming and writhing on my cock. And fuck, how I wanted that.

He groaned when I sank my tongue deeper inside his channel.

"See how wet she is for us, Preston," he said, his voice strained, body tight and on the edge.

I reached down and stroked my fingers over Lacey's pussy, smiling when I found her wet despite her fear. Laughing, I bent down and bit his firm ass cheek.

"She's wet for us, Tobias. She wants us as much as she fears us."

On a groan, he pushed to his feet, then spun around and leaned down to kiss me. "Stand up, Lacey."

She scrambled to her feet on shaky legs. Twigs and leaves clung to her hair, and I found a primitive satisfaction in it.

Tobias stroked a finger over her chest, tugging the top of her short dress down to reveal her breast. "You're going to let him take your sweet pussy while I take your tight ass."

The prospect of her taking both our dicks sent blood straight to mine.

Lacey's attention snapped to me when I undid my pants. "Come here." I crooked a finger at her, and she approached me as a fawn would a lion, trembling and doe eyed. She seemed scared, but curious. Unwilling yet willing. The lines all so wonderfully blurred.

I unzipped her dress, letting it fall to the ground before I dragged her panties down her long legs. She was stunning. All milky skin and sleek curves.

Tobias pressed in beside me, rolling a condom over my dick, but all I could focus on was the girl in front of me and the promise of the warm pussy I was about to be sheathed in.

Gripping Lacey's waist, I lifted her until her thighs wrapped around my hips and I sunk inside her wet heat. Her nails dug into my shoulders on a moan as I filled her. She wanted this, and maybe that made her a little sick, too. As sick as me for wanting Tobias. Perhaps he just had an eye for those of us with dark desires. Maybe he wanted to corrupt her as entirely as he'd already corrupted me.

Lacey tensed when Tobias spat, and then stepped up behind her. "Have you ever taken it in the ass, Lacey?"

She rode my dick a little harder as she nodded, and a grin pulled at my lips. "Of course she has, Tobias," I said. "Depraved little creature."

He reached around her and placed his hands on my hips, then thrusted forward. I felt his dick crowd against mine through that thin wall, and we all groaned. "She's a good, dirty little whore," I panted, and her warm, tight pussy tightened around me.

"Choke her again, Preston," Tobias said, his voice strained as he slammed into her again.

My fingers wound around Lacey's throat, and a sense of déjà vu washed over me. This same place, those same fingers, but on a different throat. My dick twitched as I reveled in the memory of Leah's gasping breaths, of how hard I came while she clawed at my hand and drew blood. I didn't want to kill Leah, and I didn't particularly want to kill Lacey now, but as she whimpered and writhed and clawed like we were offering her the best gift by stuffing her to the brim with cock, my balls tightened in anticipation.

"Come for me, Preston." Tobias's hands moved from my hips to my throat, pressing Lacey's bare breasts harder against my chest. He squeezed. The pressure of his fingers pressing into my neck, fight for control coaxed a groan from me. Then he squeezed harder. "Come in her pussy."

The thrill of it all caused my grip on Lacey's throat to tighten. But instead of panicking, Lacey fucking came. Her pussy clamped around me coupled with Tobias's firm grip on my neck, sent me hurtling over the edge. I came, twitching and grunting as the orgasm ripped through me like a wildfire. Tobias's hold on me tightened until black spots dotted my vision. Tobias growled out my name like a curse, then pulled out of Lacey's ass. He ripped the condom off as he moved to the side and shot his warm come over us both. And fuck I wanted to be cursed by him, poisoned and tainted entirely.

CHAPTER ELEVEN

PRESTON

"Chad Davis, Brendon Walters, and Christian McClure have been arrested in connection with the brutal murder of Leah Andrews, a sophomore at the local university."

The news report cut off when Tobias opened the driver's side door to his Mercedes. He'd done it, followed through on everything he promised. I was free of my burden... as long as I wasn't free of him. And though, at that very moment, I didn't want to be, I had no doubt if ever there came a time when I did, this would all come back to haunt me.

I stared through the window at the cemetery. Rows upon rows of tombstones dotted the hillside, the city skyline a distant mirage behind the sea of people dressed in black.

Tobias stopped by my door to open it. The warm wind wrapped around me as I placed my foot on the uneven ground. Was it morbid as fuck that I was coming to the funeral of a girl I killed? Absolutely. But it would be suspicious if I didn't attend. As far as the world knew, I was the heartbroken, grieving boyfriend of a murdered girl.

"I'm so sorry for your loss, Preston." Tobias pressed a kiss to my temple, and I fought a smile. He was such a twisted fucker. I had to come, of course, but the fact he'd insisted on coming with me for "emotional support". He truly was warped.

We stepped behind the group gathered at Leah's graveside, and my gaze almost immediately met her mother's. An uncomfortable feeling stirred in my chest when I took in the woman's tear-stained face. I didn't really have the capacity for true guilt, but I also didn't want to witness the pain I'd caused. Maybe it was denial. Maybe it was indifference.

"Death is such a cruel part of life, isn't it?" Tobias asked.

I turned my attention away from the consequences of my former dark fantasies, to my new one—Tobias. "Tragic," I said.

After the funeral, I was taken back to the dorms, but instead of dropping me at the front of the building, the driver pulled to the side of the lot, cut the engine, then got out.

Tobias watched through the window as the chauffer walked to the median in the middle of the lot and lit a cigarette. Seemingly satisfied with that, he turned to face me and took my hand in his. "I want to give you a choice."

Choice. The word wasn't synonymous with Tobias Benton. "Okay..."

"Go back to your mundane life..." He waved his free hand toward the dorms. "Or stay with me and enjoy everything. Money. Women. Games..." His lips pulled into a devious smirk, one that promised wonderfully dark things.

I'd ask him what the catch was, whether he'd turn up new evidence to get me arrested, but none of it mattered. And maybe I didn't want to know. Because I knew I'd choose him regardless of blackmail, or how devious he was. He wanted me enough to dig up a body for me, to frame three strangers for murder. And I wanted him, wanted the shiny yet tainted future he painted for us, his obsession and possession.

"Tobias." My hand landed on his firm thigh. "Why would I ever want to go back?"

Cupping my jaw, his narrowed eyes searched mine. "What I've shown you is only the beginning, my dear, sweet Preston. We'll build an empire together; become monsters no one will ever believe to be anything but gods."

Ah, Tobias and his god complex. He was right though; we were monsters. And we belonged together. I knew it. I felt it in every fiber of my being.

"This is your last chance to tell me no, Preston."

"You almost sound like you want me to run from you, Tobias." I lifted a brow. "Would you chase me?"

He smirked. "You think I already haven't?"

"I suppose you have." I laughed, my gaze sweeping over his body in that dark suit. He really looked like a god. "So, are we going home or fucking in the car?"

Apparently, Tobias was above fucking in a parking lot because he signaled the driver, and then we drove away from the university campus that suddenly seemed so inconsequential.

The moment we stepped inside the penthouse, Tobias shoved me against the wall in a brutal and unforgiving kiss. He fumbled for my fly, swearing against my lips before he finally lowered the zipper. I craved him like an addict longing for their next hit, knowing he was the only thing that could bring this twisted form of bliss.

He shoved my pants down and didn't even go for my dick, instead he spun me around and forced me over the foyer table. The motion sent the flower vase crashing to the floor. "I'm going to shove my cock in this tight hole of yours." His finger circled my asshole, and I tensed in anticipation.

I never thought I would want to be fucked in the ass, but as his thighs pressed to the back of mine and his hard dick rubbed against my crack through his pants, I wanted him to possess me in the most primal ways. My dick ached with the promise of having him inside me. "Yes."

He spat and warm moisture landed on my ass before he pressed a finger into me. A heavy groan fell from my lips at his intrusion. It felt foreign, yet so right, so good.

"If you beg me to stop, I won't." He went deeper, twisting his fingers in my asshole.

My palm slammed over the table. "Fuck, Tobias." I expected no mercy from him, and I wanted none. He shifted behind me, unfastening his slacks. My body tensed when his warm cock slipped between my crack, stroking back and forth. "I'm going to ruin you," he said, fisting my hair and yanking until my back bowed. He spit again, massaging saliva over my hole. "This ass is mine."

The head of his dick nudged my entrance, and when I tensed, he pulled harder on my hair. "Are you going to take it all in like a man?"

I pressed back against him, and he slammed inside me. I gripped the sides of the table as a stinging pain ripped through me.

"Fuck," he whispered, pulling out before pushing right back in. "Your ass feels so good."

Pain mixed with a sense of satisfaction that I was taking him, pleasing him. I wanted Tobias Benton to fall apart, to be as addicted to me as I was to him. And I would make sure he was.

"Tell me how it feels, Preston." He pounded into me without mercy, to the point I couldn't speak. I couldn't tell him how good it felt, how utterly possessed I was. "That's right, sweet Preston..." A loud clap echoed around the room when Tobias smacked my ass cheek. "Milk my cock with your ass."

He was so filthy. I rocked back against him, craving the sensation of him filling me while reveling in the desperate ache that gripped my cock. My balls tightened to the point of pain. I wanted to grab my dick and stroke over it like a madman, but before I could, Tobias wrapped a hand around my throat. He dragged me to my feet, placing my back against his front as he continued to fuck me without mercy. "You're mine now." He squeezed my throat until I couldn't pull in a decent breath. "Aren't you?"

"Yes," I said in a ragged breath, my mind lost in a haze of lust and testosterone. "Yours."

His pace quickened. "Come with me, Preston."

Fuck me. It was a sensory overload that had liquid fire ripping through my veins. It was frantic and raw and savage.

"Fuck." Tobias's teeth sank into my shoulder on a groan as he buried himself hard in my ass.

On his next deep thrust, pleasure ripped down my spine. Heat tore through me as my ass clamped down on his cock. I groaned his name as my dick erupted without even being touched, shooting a sticky film all over the table in front of me. Tobias coaxed spurt after spurt of endless come from my cock as he held himself inside me, grunting and swearing in my ear.

We both collapsed forward over the table. My legs were too weak for me to give a shit that I was lying in the mess of my own come.

After a few heavy breaths, Tobias kissed the back of my neck and pulled out. His come trickled between my ass cheeks, his filthy promises ringing in my ears. "Welcome home, Preston."

CHAPTER TWELVE

TOBIAS

Morning light danced over Preston's toned ass as he clenched around my cock. I delighted at the way he fisted the bedsheets as he backed up to meet each of my hard thrusts. But what I delighted in even more is when we came together in a chorus of deep groans.

It had been a week of fucking him, owning him, sharing my deepest, darkest fantasies with him. And while I thoroughly enjoyed this, what I knew I would enjoy even more was the intimacy we would find within the dark dances we would soon enough orchestrate.

I pressed a kiss to the back of Preston's neck before I withdrew from his ass and collapsed onto the soft bed beside him, swiping my fingers through the puddle of cooling come he left on the sheets.

He rolled onto his back, breathless and spent.

"Are you ready to pick a new player?" I asked, licking his come from my hand before I placed a come-covered fingertip to his lips.

"Yes." Preston's blue eyes brimming with anticipation as he sucked my finger into his mouth, then released it with a pop. "As much as I like your dick, I miss having a pussy wrapped around my cock."

"I want to try something a little different with the next game." Lacey's contract had been vague enough that it should have scared her, it should have made her think twice, but still, she signed her name. And while that night had been well worth the money I awarded her, I knew Preston and I could do so much more. So much better. After all, one-hundred thousand dollars was hardly anything, really.

"Care to share with the class?" he said.

"What if we made rules?"

"What kind of rules?" His lips quirked. "Will they only be allowed to call you master?"

Oh, playful Preston. "They can ask no questions. I want their complete submission. And there will be no safe words."

A flicker of a smile shaped Preston's lips as he adjusted himself on the pillow. "Even for a hundred grand, I can't see many girls agreeing to that, Tobias. Only the truly desperate."

"Maybe that's who I want—the truly desperate. After all, money isn't a luxury for most, Preston. It's a necessity. And everyone barters something for it, be it their time or their innocence or their sanity. And I'm offering to pay someone far more than they'll ever make in the real world." Like Leah. She'd been more than willing to do whatever I asked her for that money. And I'd basically owned her for six months before Preston's dark harbinger took her away. If I only asked seven days of someone... I had a feeling there was very little they wouldn't do.

"A sacrificial lamb."

"Oh no, not a sacrifice, Preston. A player in a game we control." Sunlight streamed in through the window, dancing across Preston's beautiful face. It was a face anyone would believe to be honest, the perfect mask for the sadistic creature underneath. "Do you have any idea what someone would do for a million dollars?" Because I did. That was the exact amount I had paid Leah, but I couldn't confess that to Preston. He had no idea she was a part of his life I had played puppet master to.

"You'd pay a million dollars just to fuck and play with someone?" A slow smile worked over his lips. I could see the dark cogs of his mind turning. He saw the possibilities. I knew he did.

"Only if they played the game and won..."

"So if we make it impossible to win..." His teeth raked his lip as a flicker of depravity ignited in his eyes.

"Exactly. There would be no limits to what you and I could do." I gripped his dick, then scooted down the bed to straddle his thighs. "Especially if we found a woman as dark and depraved as us. Think of the possibilities." I leaned over and sucked the head of his cock into my mouth.

Groaning, his hands went to my hair. I thought of everything we would do, of all the spiderwebs we would weave, all the souls we would trap. Of all the moral compasses we would shatter... "We could have them do awful things." I swallowed him back again until he hit the back of my throat. "Questionable things."

"That's a tame way of putting it." He laughed, then groaned.

"We could blur the lines of morality until they no longer knew right from wrong." I licked over his tip, gently raking my teeth over his swollen head before taking him all the way back again. "You could come in a tight pussy while I come in your ass." I slipped two fingers into his hole, massaging the bulge of his prostrate until a string of grunts and groans traveled up his throat. "Because this ass is mine, Preston. No one else's."

His hold on my hair tightened as he guided me up and down his shaft. "Fuck. Tobias."

A warm, salty explosion coated my tongue, and I swallowed it down with a satiated groan. "There is nothing to stop us, Preston. Nothing." I leaned over him and pressed a kiss to his lips, letting him sample how sweet he tasted on my tongue. "All we have to do is find an unfortunate girl whose body and soul we want to own."

Because if the rich would do things for money, there would be no limit to what the unfortunate would do.

And now for the beginning...

If you want to see how Preston and Tobias's game evolved over time,
click here to check out
The Game: A Dark Taboo Romance.
Free on Kindle Unlimited.

Printed in Great Britain
by Amazon